NIGHT GEM
THIS BOUNDARY WILL NOT BIND US

ERICA XENNE
WITH ELLIOTT LASH

Author: Erica Xenne

Co-author: Elliott Lash

Editor: Jill Domschot

Content Editor: Richard Brand

Cover Artist: Claudia Caranfa

Layout & Design: Devon Farber

Dedicated to Kilian, my beloved Muse.

Cheers to Phil, my long-lost Nemesis.

Praise to the Cathartica tribe & Domschot clan
for keeping dreams alive.

Respect to the master, my father,
for teaching me to translate my visions from Erosian to English.

Loving apologies to my Beta Readers
for enduring my incoherent rambles and frustrated outbursts.

Infinite gratitude to my incredible family,
the guardians of my sanity.

Most of all, thanks to Elliott,
who has remembered Oreni alongside me.

Our journey is pure magic.

Your breath gives you power.

CONTENTS

PART FOUR
THE SEEKER

MAPS

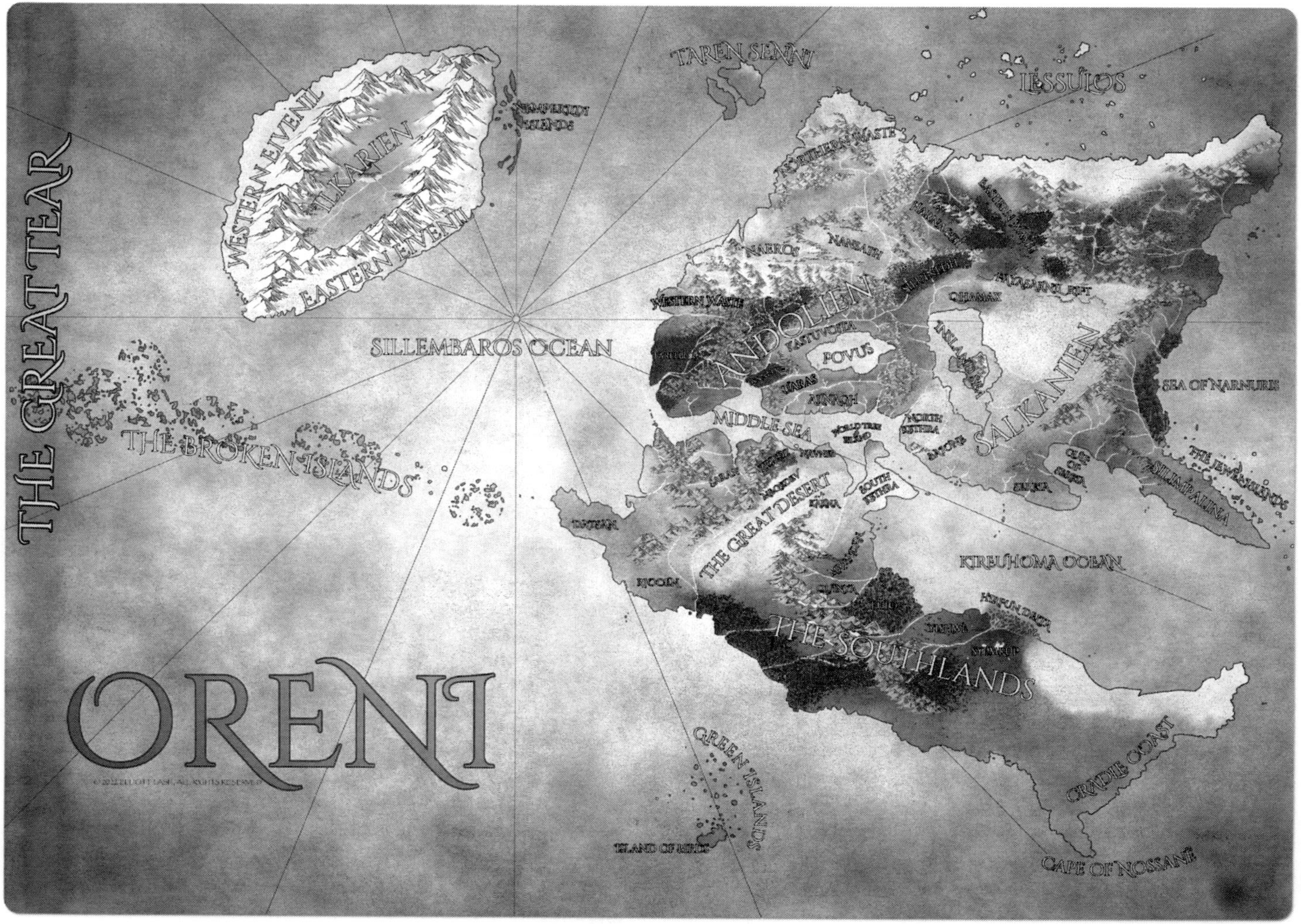
THE GREAT TEAR
WESTERN EIVENIL
ILKARIEN
EASTERN EIVENIL
TAREN SENNI
LÉSSÚLOS
NORTHERN WASTE
NAEROS
NANSATH
WESTERN WASTE
ANDOLIEN
KASTUVOTA
POVUS
QHAMAX
SALKANIEN
SEA OF NARNURIS
SILLEMBAROS OCEAN
MIDDLE SEA
NORTH ESTHIRA
SOUTH ESTHIRA
THE GREAT DESERT
KIREUHOMA OCEAN
THE JEWEL ISLANDS
THE BROKEN ISLANDS
THE SOUTHLANDS
ORENI
GREEN ISLANDS
ISLAND OF BIRDS
CRADLE COAST
CAPE OF NOSSANÉ

Andolien

PROLOGUE
1318 MID-WINTER

The girl was fast asleep, yet far from peaceful. Her chest heaved with each breath. Vaye watched the tiny body expand and contract as the child fought for air.

"Ahem." A crisp voice reverberated against the walls of the underground shelter. "Vaye, the potion."

Two prominent commune leaders hovered gravely and uneasily, waiting for Vaye to perform her duty. The elected Renstrom, Nurin, set his eyes firmly upon her. He gestured toward the little girl and intoned, "It is time."

Vaye reached into her satchel for the deathly fluid. As her fingers touched the vial, a deafening crash of thunder penetrated the air, shaking the small room. The blast triggered an ancient memory of another young girl racing toward freedom when an arrow found her. The savages paid dearly, but Nóssië could not be saved.

Vaye forced the painful images from her mind, collected herself and returned to the present. Five newly arrived children lay across the long marble table, slumbering within the alchemy of Vaye's soporific herbs. The smallest had a gash across her stomach that boded imminent death, but she gasped and shook, clinging desperately to life. Shadows danced across her ivory skin in the torchlight as the flame swelled and retracted in exquisite synchrony with each breath, attending and obeying the rhythm of the child's fragile body.

The men became impatient with Vaye's delay. In their preoccupation with procedure and protocol, neither noticed the synergy between the flame and the girl's breathing, much less grasped its implications. Vaye understood this was not coincidence, nor was the storm. She knew much more than she would reveal and said simply, "The child is strong."

Vaye returned the tiny vial to her bag. Nurin exchanged a look with Dinad, the ancient and august Justinar of Law.

"Pardon my intrusion," Dinad pontificated as he stroked his long grey beard, "but this girl is wasted and frail."

Vaye was respectful, but unwavering. "She is gravely injured, yet her breathing is sound. She will heal."

Nurin furrowed his brow. "The child is all but dead. Allow her to pass in peace."

A drenching, unrelenting rain pounded against the compound's ancient earthen roof. Vaye positioned herself between the two men and the girl, touched the delicate body and felt a rapid pulse. There wasn't much time. To end the discussion, she intensified, "Please let me do my work."

"Blast!" Dinad interjected. "What have we gotten ourselves into? First the slave-boy and now this?"

Nurin aimed his chin in the air to reclaim authority and inquired, "What of the slave?"

Vaye turned to the vault. Even the giant metal door could not shroud the powerful presence just beyond. Solemnly, she relinquished, "He resisted the procedure."

"Then use your potion," Dinad grumbled. "His mind is too developed, and he's too old to integrate. Be done with it."

Ignoring Dinad, the Renstrom turned to Vaye. "Continue your work on the slave when you finish with the others," he commanded. "If the girl does survive, she must never learn who she is."

PART ONE
THE COMMUNE

SAMIES

1319 EARLY-SUMMER

Aera was alone, aligned with the world, exactly where she belonged. Everything was familiar and even in the darkest reaches of night, her feet knew where to go. She was home.

The forest was alive, spilling with music, breathing along with the beat of her heart. A choir of insects hummed while an expanse of white trees danced in the mist, and Aera swirled through them, her long hair billowing. She glanced around to admire the scenery and realized the trees had no leaves at all. White birds lined every branch as far as the eye could see, their feathers shimmering beneath a brilliant moon.

Aera imagined she also might take flight. She moved her arms like wings and pranced about, pretending to fly, leaving trails in the low mist until it became so dense that she could no longer see her feet. The fog tumbled around itself and formed into faces that surrounded her. Their hollow eye sockets stared Aera down.

She swatted and slashed at the faces, but more formed instantly. Faces appeared between faces until she was engulfed by a mob dissolving and reforming around her. She thrust at them with increasing force, but it was never enough. They continued to multiply until everything was a blur.

The air itself compressed and tightened against Aera. Her ears rang and her head throbbed. Just when she thought she could bear no more, the ghastly assemblage of faces opened their mouths and hissed in high-pitched, distorted unison.

"Go away!" Aera screamed. The birds echoed with a shriek and flew off, shrouding the sky as the trees were laid bare. The bedlam of wings faded into the distance, leaving Aera alone with the howling fog.

The faces encased her within their collective screech until one pair of foul lips swirled out of synch with the rest. In a ghastly low pitch, it cackled: *"Filén na erë lëoryán assë të yo-fayanta i nalanna hyánië votheldë. Në Laimandil ë i namanya, sinë veskento i suínanya më Onórnëan.[1]"*

She pressed her hands tight against her ears as her body throbbed in pain. *"Sinë veskento i suínanya më Onórnëan. Sinë veskento i suínanya më..."*

～

"Wake up, Samies!"

Aera jolted awake as a loud voice boomed through the room. "Time to do your duty... we are all the same!" The words from her dream rang through her mind. *Sinë veskento i suínanya më Onórnëan.*

Footsteps shuffled about and voices crashed through the dormitory. Aera sat up slowly, her head pounding as the nightmare drones continued in her ears. *Në Laimandil ë i namanya.* Their words were foreign and nonsensical, but the white forest seemed familiar, like home.

"Move it!" Officer Onus continued yelling. "Let's go, girls. Follow your group!"

Samies jumped up from their mats, hurrying to ready themselves for their daily routine. Aera was too tired to move, but she had no choice. As she sat up, the scar on her stomach was itchy and everything annoyed her. From her cubby came the various parts of her uniform: her tunic, her pants, her socks. Where were her shoes? She searched frantically, trying to find them with no luck. She needed to hurry. The other girls had already lined up by the door.

"What's wrong, Eh-ruh? Lost something?"

It was Doriline, the loudest girl in the group. Laughter exploded

6

around the room and all eyes leered at Aera. Doriline sang out, "Pooooor Eh-ruh! Poor little Eh-ruh..."

Cheery faces blurred together as Doriline paraded a toothy smile. *Sinë veskento i suínanya më Onórnëan.* The horrible words mixed with Doriline's shriek, growing louder every second. Aera covered her ears and screamed, "Go! Away!"

Doriline screeched on and an image of harrowing whiteness burned Aera's eyes. In a flash, she sprang across the room and shoved Doriline, who did nothing to resist. Instead, she dropped to her knees and shrieked, "Ouch! Ouch! Eh-ruh hit me!"

"Samie Eh-ruh!" Boomed Officer Onus. "Who do you think you are?"

Aera froze in place, stunned. The room became quiet but for the groan of floorboards beneath Onus as he stomped toward her. He parked his giant belly beside her face and repeated, "Who do you think you are?"

"Aera," she mumbled.

Onus stared down at her, waiting impatiently for a different answer. *Who am I?* Aera asked herself. Uneasily, she admitted, "I... don't know."

"You're a Samie," Onus spat. "You just lost five points."

Aera knew she was supposed to do something but didn't know what. Onus pointed at her emphatically, wagging his fat finger. "You're in big trouble. I'll see you outside later."

The Samies roared with laughter. Aera's heart thudded.

"Get in line," Onus snapped, a snarl on his face. "You think you're so ghaadi important, we should all wait for you?"

Aera went to the back of the line, barefoot and shaken. As she joined the ritual walk over the Hill to the Dining Hall, she hung her head so rigidly that all she saw was the grass beneath her. She dug her feet into the dirt, one step after the other, crushing the world as hard as she could.

The group filed into the Dining Hall and Aera was consumed by a whirl of echoing chatter. Doriline was near the front of the line, surrounded by people, gabbing into the noise. *Sinë veskento i suínanya më Onórnëan...*

Aera looked around at the blur of activity, straining to hold herself together. The wait felt eternal, but she finally reached the food and

7

piled some on her tray. She went to the water fountain in the back of the room, filled her mug and looked for a place to sit, but the clamor was so unbearable she couldn't focus enough to find a table. She made her way out the door, carried her meal up the Hill and sat by a large boulder at the top, finally alone.

Birds sang and the breeze carried the sweet scent of summer. Aera stretched on the grass but still felt anxious. Was Officer Onus going to punish her? Would the other kids watch? He had insisted she was a Samie, but she didn't understand why it mattered. If she were to disappear, nothing would change and no one would care.

She forced in some breakfast and looked down at the sleeping huts in the field below. Behind them, the lush trees of Southside Forest met the horizon. She wished she could run to it and never return...

Gong-gong. Gong-gong. The bi-hourly bell clanged in the belltower across the river, and the hand on the giant clock marked the second hour of the day. Nearby, an officer's whistle exploded in shrill thunder. It was time to line up for class.

Aera took one last look at the forest and the vast, green field before it, lined with four sleeping huts. *I want to run away*, she thought. *Or go back to sleep and find the white forest...*

Reluctantly, she turned around to face the village. Children gathered from every direction. From the top of the Hill, they looked like ants scrambling together, all the same. Aera didn't want to be near them. She groaned and thought, *I hate you all.*

She headed down the Hill and found a place at the back of her line. Officer Onus clomped across the Field to join the meal attendant, Officer Luce, who stood at rigid alert before the crowd, preparing his usual written orders. The two huddled together and Aera worried they were talking about her.

"Samie Eh-ruh! Step up to the front!"

Aera departed from her line. Samies craned to see while officers surrounded her, their commands piling up.

"Roughhousing is not permitted outside the Raetsek Field."

"Violence is against the rules."

"Do you understand, Samie Eh-ruh?"

No, Aera thought. That was the wrong answer. *Yes. No! Leave me alone.* The officers stared down, waiting for a response. Her throat clamped, and her mind blanked.

"Get back in line," Officer Onus snarled, and dropped Aera's shoes on the ground.

Aera put them on, trying not to cry. As she made her way to her spot, faces gaped at her, line after line.

"Five to Six Group, proceed to Art Class!"

Aera followed her group into the Education Unit, down the hall and up the stairs to the fourth floor. Line leaders bellowed out names, and their voices spun into a whirl...

"Samie Eh-ruh! Move along!"

Aera went into the Art Room and looked for a seat. Three instructors moseyed between circular tables, barking orders. Chatter mingled with the scraping of chairs against the floor and dream drones pounded Aera's ears. *Sinë veskento i suínanya më Onórnëan.* She found a spot and burrowed into her arms until a pencil and paper appeared in front of her.

"Children! Darse your dirl!"

"On the count of three, begin drawing a building!"

"One, two, three!"

The three instructors shouted on top of each other, and the clamor made Aera dizzy. What did they mean, 'building?' There were so many in Ynas. She glanced around to see what her neighbors were drawing. They were outlining generic rectangular shapes with squares where the windows would be.

She picked up her pencil, hand shaking, and outlined a rectangle. It was neat, perfect, concise... until the pencil slipped, and she smudged the side. She tried to fix the mistake, but her hands were coated with charcoal and the page was a blur. *Në Laimandil ë i namanya...*

Where did those bizarre words come from? Did the phrases have meaning, or were they just random nonsense? The white forest was familiar, but Aera didn't know why. She could not remember white trees anywhere...

"Samie Eh-ruh! Stop daydreaming."

Aera snapped to attention and the other kids laughed. Instructor Sarode stared down through crinkly wrinkles and hovered nearby as she addressed the class.

"Pass your papers to the right!"

Sarode sounded bored, angry, and tired. She turned her head to see everyone and croaked, "Outline the building with grass and trees!"

Farris, on Aera's right, reached over to grab her drawing. He observed the mess, then chuckled and snorted. "Looks like poo."

Aera hissed, "You're gross."

"At least I have friends."

A few children laughed at Farris's comeback, and he cackled along. Sarode was right behind him but walked away without a word. The teachers were supposed to stop children from being mean to each other. Aera stared down at her page, trying not to explode.

The papers continued circling, and Aera drew angry faces on each one until her original piece found its way back to her for the final round. Finally, gongs from the belltower marked the end of Art Class.

"Don't forget to put your drawings in the bin!" Sarode instructed. "We must conserve our resources, and no drawing is better than another! We are all the same!"

Aera tore her drawing to shreds and dropped the pieces into the bin beside the door. Next was the Music Room, where noise bounced mercilessly off the brick walls as children pushed and shoved to claim their favorite instruments and find their friends. As Aera took a seat in the back, a female voice commanded, "Quiet."

Aera had never heard that voice before, let alone one so beautiful. Although the volume was moderate, the tone resonated above the ruckus and silenced everybody. Who was this?

She inched over to peek through the crowd and found an extraordinary woman seated at the piano. Silver ringlets poured gracefully to the lady's waist, spilling from a decorative band around her forehead. Aera remembered her own luscious mane undulating behind her as she danced in the misty dream forest. She'd never seen anyone with long hair outside of her dreams and was excited that it existed in real life.

"Good morning, children," she said. "My name is Vaye."

"Where's Instructor Lilese?" Doriline mumbled nervously.

Firmly, Vaye replied, "Elsewhere."

Nobody moved. The room was so quiet, Aera could hear her own breathing.

Vaye extended her arms with otherworldly grace and pulled back the lid from the keyboard. Her olive gown was sublime and her forehead band enchanting, as it gleamed with tiny yellow gems. Other people had short hair, plain uniforms, and loud voices. Vaye was different.

She caressed the piano keys and an arpeggio fluttered through the room like butterflies. "Now, sing the Ynas anthem with me," she commanded in a rich, velvet tone. "*One* two three, *one* two three..."

"We... are all... the same!"

Each voice was disparate from the next and the sound was cacophonous. The dream drones crashed into Aera's mind: *Sinë veskento i suínanya më Onórnëan.*

Aera jolted up to be gripped by Vaye's unwavering stare. The room became cold and hollow; Vaye was the only figure visible. As the two watched each other, Vaye's face became ghostly white, and her eyes turned black as coal. Their chilling darkness bore into Aera and transfixed her. Time stopped.

Vaye held her there for a moment, but then, just as suddenly, her posture relaxed. Her eyes filled with life, the deep mocha blush returned to her cheeks, and she eased into a smile. The room returned to its normal atmosphere. She released Aera from possession, but left her reeling. What had just happened? The world had become sinister, like the fog in her nightmare... yet no one else seemed to notice.

"Sing softly," Vaye said to the class. "Together, our voices will create ample sound, so there's no need to shout. Listen to each note and let the piano be louder than your voice. Again."

"We... are all... the same..."

Vaye's body flowed naturally with the music as her hands coaxed the piano, and Aera's thoughts melted into the rhythm they shaped. The screeches of the other children faded and disappeared. Aera sang with Vaye alone.

Gong, gong!

Chatter exploded and Aera remembered she was in class. The commune anthem had transported her to another world. She had always hated that song and could hardly believe how enchanting it was now. When Instructor Lilese played the same song on the same piano, the keys sounded like a murder of crows, but Vaye had transformed that dreadful humdrum to an exquisite symphony.

Aera realized suddenly that she was the only person left in the room. The Samies had departed, and Vaye was watching her from the doorway. Though her lips remained still, her voice said, *Join me at the top of the Hill.* Then, she was gone.

Aera was nonplussed. Somehow, Vaye had projected words into her mind. What did she want with Aera? Was she even real?

Aera caught up with her classmates in the hallway, then followed her line out to the Field. When the group reached the Dining Hall, she glanced up the Hill and spotted Vaye at the top, silver ringlets shining in the sun.

"Get inside, Samie."

It was Officer Padd, the hefty lunch attendant, with beady eyes and a grizzly beard. "On with it," he snorted. "Go find your friends."

He held open the door and stared down at Aera. She wished he would just go away. As he ushered her inside, she looked once more at the hilltop and hoped Vaye would wait for her.

She entered the Dining Hall and joined her group, but the line in front of her was endless. If she took too long, Vaye might be gone. She squeezed between people to swipe an apple and darted back toward the exit, where Officer Padd awaited.

"You again?" He laughed. "You planning on eating?"

Aera held up the apple and slipped outside. Padd did nothing to stop her, though he called out, "You better not leave the village, Samie!"

She hurried up the incline toward Vaye, who stood with her back to the village, gazing down at the forest beyond. When Aera finally reached the hilltop, Vaye gave a look of surprise and said, "Oh, hello dear."

Aera was taken aback. Had she had imagined Vaye's voice in her mind? Vaye did not seem to be expecting her.

"I will be on my way," Vaye said. "You can come if you like." With that, she floated down the far side of the Hill.

On her way? Where to? Aera was supposed to stay in the village. Vaye moved onward, her olive dress flowing behind. Her elegance was at once comforting and disconcerting. She belonged in a dream. Why was she there? Aera's thoughts were racing.

She caught up with Vaye and followed her past the sleeping huts into Southside Forest, where the trees enveloped her in an aroma of maple and pine. It thrilled her to explore the mysterious shadows of the forbidden places she so often fantasized about... but where were they going? It felt like her dream world, but it wasn't, as the trees had leaves and none were white.

Crickets chirped, leaves crunched, and coos resounded. Aera spotted a small silver bird with a white belly in a tree.

"That's a mockingbird imitating a hawk," Vaye explained.

"*Ee-u, ee-u*," cooed a large, regal bird nearby.

"*Ee-u, ee-u*," sang the mockingbird. Its imitation was indistinguishable from the original. Aera glanced at Vaye and the two exchanged a smile.

As Vaye continued onward, Aera scanned the forest for white trees, but discovered none. She listened to the birdsongs, the scuffles of squirrels and the swoosh of wind against leaves, but Vaye walked so stealthily, her footsteps were inaudible.

The gurgle of water crept up in the distance and grew louder as they came to an open grove teeming with tall grass and wildflowers. Aera spotted a brook rippling beyond, then noticed a dirt path nearby, leading through the grass to an ancient stone cottage. Behind it, a massive stone wall towered over everything and extended beyond sight in both directions.

"That's the Fence," Vaye said. "It surrounds the commune."

Aera knew about the Fence. The instructors claimed it was there to keep everyone safe. She craned to see the top, where iron palisades with knife-like points menaced the sky. The Fence made her feel trapped, not safe.

She became conscious of Vaye watching her and wondered if she'd done something wrong, but Vaye smiled warmly and continued along the path. The surrounding grass was as tall as Aera and the cottage walls were covered in flowering vines. Despite the somber barrier beyond, the scenery was magical.

Vaye opened the door, unleashing an aroma of pumpkin spices, and Aera entered a circular stone room featuring an ornate piano. The back of the instrument extended to an elongated curve whose surface displayed a finely chiseled woolly mammoth alongside a spruce tree. Aera stood on tiptoes to peek over the edge of the piano and saw a landscape of strings along with hammers encased in rich green felt.

"Come, dear," said Vaye. "Sit beside me."

Vaye sat on one end of a long bench facing the keyboard, which glowed beneath patches of sunlight pouring through oversized windows. Aera hoisted herself up to the empty space beside Vaye, eager to hear her play again. Instead, Vaye placed Aera's hands on the keys.

Aera tensed. Would Vaye expect her to play this magnificent instrument? Her hands were too small and her feet did not touch the ground. The music would sound wrong, and Vaye might be disappointed.

"Play along if you like," Vaye said. She slid her bare foot onto a golden pedal and played a soft chord. As its echo waned, her fingers tumbled into a rhythmic swing that undulated like a river. *One* two three, *one* two three.

Aera waited for the *one* and tapped a key. The note was wrong and embarrassed her. She stared at the piano, but all the keys blended together.

Vaye stopped playing and turned to Aera. "Your timing was perfect."

Perfect? Aera blushed. The note was wrong, but the timing was easy.

"Do you like music?" Vaye asked.

"Yes," Aera said. *Yes.* Her own voice was fragile, not lush like Vaye's.

"Do you want to play alone?"

Was this a test? No one was allowed to play alone in class, even though playing together ruined the music.

"Feel free to speak your mind," Vaye said. "Anything you tell me will remain secret."

My secret is that I hate everyone, Aera thought, but she said nothing. She didn't want to get punished.

"Your visit will be our secret," Vaye assured her. "Nobody will know you were here."

Aera was excited that Vaye wanted to share a secret but wondered why. Secrets were forbidden in Ynas.

"Tell me," Vaye coaxed. "Do you want to play alone?"

Aera nodded slowly.

"Wonderful. Do you hear music in your mind? Or in your dreams?"

Aera worried that if she confessed her nightmares, Vaye might think something was wrong with her. Carefully, she said, "I hear... scary voices." The sound rose delicately from her chest. Nursing each syllable, she added, "I prefer silence."

"Have you ever found it?"

Aera tried to remember a moment when everything was silent. It seemed like it should be a common occurrence, yet she was unable to pinpoint a time when it actually happened.

"Some sounds are quieter than others, but silence doesn't exist," Vaye said. "Try to drown out the scary voices with pleasant sounds, like birdsong or music. I can show you some melodies to think about."

Vaye took a few minutes to teach Aera how to play a simple melody, then walked away. Aera played slowly at first and increased her speed as she made fewer mistakes. It was boring to hit the same notes, and her hands kept meandering around the keyboard, but she forced herself to return to Vaye's sequence again and again.

Finally, Vaye came back. "Good work," she said.

Aera smiled, relieved. She'd played well and Vaye had noticed.

"Now, play the same melody, starting here," Vaye suggested, and pointed to a note in the bass section. Aera replayed the melody, and the sound was low and rumbly.

"Play along, beginning on the one," Vaye said. She sat down at Aera's side, played some high notes, and counted aloud, "*One* two three, *one* two three."

Aera rested her forefinger on the first key, listened to the rhythm and, along with the *one*, hit the note. It was right! She glanced at Vaye, saw she was pleased, and smiled.

On the next count of *one*, Aera hit the key harder. She could hardly believe her note was making Vaye's song even richer, but it was. As she ventured to play the rest of the sequence, her force waxed and waned, folding into Vaye's dynamics. The longer they played, the freer Aera felt, even when she fumbled.

Vaye slowed, dragging out the tempo, then lifted her hands. In her head, Aera counted along with the empty space. *One*, two, three, *one*, two, three. Together, they struck a chord.

"You're attentive to rhythm and dynamics," Vaye said. "You're a natural, and you practiced well."

Aera was overjoyed. She had made Vaye proud.

Vaye rested a hand on Aera's shoulder. "I've enjoyed playing with you, dear, but now it's time for baths. Go on, and don't be late!"

The two exchanged a smile and Aera left. She sprang through the forest, humming the melody she'd been playing, and imagined herself back in her dream, singing it to the birds. Music overcame her until she emerged in the Sleeping Hut Field, where she was accosted by sunlight and a harsh voice screaming, "Samely! Where in Riva's Trees are you going? Get over here, Samie!"

Aera's heart raced, but her legs froze. Orange and brown clad officers towered overhead, blocking out the nearby forest smells with their overwhelming odor.

"Where are you coming from? Look at me, kid. Don't you dare ignore the DPD. We're here to keep you safe."

Aera knew about the Department of Protection through Discipline. The officers said they kept people safe, but they were just bullies. The world was now a sweaty blur of orange and brown.

"It is forbidden to leave village grounds," said the grating voice. "What's your name?"

"Samie Aera," she murmured.

"I know you! You're the same little rebel who started a fight this morning. How old are you, Samie Eh-ruh?"

Rebel. Aera didn't know what it meant, but she knew it was bad.

"Come on, Samie. How old are you?"

Aera glanced at the officer, who looked mean, with yellow hair pulled back too tightly, showing her veiny neck. Trembling, Aera mumbled, "Five."

"You don't have to whisper, little mouse."

I'm not a mouse, Aera thought, and stared at her feet.

"I say we punish her," suggested another officer, who then turned to the yellow-head and asked, "What say you, Linealle?"

"Send a report to Onus and tell him to subtract ten points from Samie Eh-ruh," Officer Linealle said. She turned to Aera, pointed

16

toward the Hill and ordered, "Go find your friends and don't make any more mistakes. If you leave the village again, you'll deal with *me*."

Aera could hardly wait to leave, but she had no friends to find. She burst into tears and ran up the Hill, where she cried by the boulder at the top. When the belltower rang, she descended the opposite hillside and rejoined her group on a line in the Field.

For the rest of the day, Aera's mind spun, trying to process the most bizarre morning of her life. She could barely concentrate on afternoon tasks, as she was distracted by visions of Vaye and the terrible officers. Dinner dragged by slowly and, at curfew, she struggled to sleep. *Rebel*, she thought. *Find your friends. I hate everyone...*

...except Vaye.

~

When Aera awakened the next morning, she barely had the energy to join her line. If she was a 'rebel' and nobody liked her, why did they need her to be there? These rules made no sense. She wished she could return to yesterday.

Breakfast was as boring as ever, and then her group went to History Class. Two teachers greeted the children while Instructor Korov heaved a human-sized book onto an easel. He was short and bald, but his voice was giant. "Good morning, children! Are you ready for your History Lesson? Today we will learn about deadly animals!"

"Yeah!"

"Woo!"

"Animals!"

Everyone else was excited, but Aera wasn't. Nothing mattered except Vaye. Everything else felt unreal.

Instructor Korov pointed at the book on the easel and read the title: "The Circus of Kadir." He looked at the class and bellowed, "Repeat after me: The Circus of Kadir!"

Aera cringed as the children screeched, "The Circus of Kadir!" Their voices were painful, their enthusiasm baffling.

"Kadir is the closest country to us in distance—six hundred kymen away—but its warlike culture could not be further from ours," Korov declared. "Every season, as we congregate peacefully on Unity

17

Day, Kadir hosts a violent circus. Crowds cheer as people slaughter each other in a giant arena. The winners are rewarded and the losers die!"

He opened the book to reveal a painting that everyone craned to see. It was a circular field surrounded by ascending stairs that were crowded with rowdy people. The mob of faces reminded Aera of her dream.

"As part of their festivities, warriors earn rank by capturing dangerous animals! They're displayed in cages and released into the arena where man and beast fight to the death."

Korov turned the page to a close-up of the field, which contained mangled corpses around two men swinging swords at a smilodon. The Samies gaped in fascination, just like the people portrayed in the circus arena. All the same.

"Many Kings honor their best hunters and warriors by sending them to compete in Kadir! These are some of the predators depicted by their best artists..."

Kadir was just like Ynas, crowded with hordes of screaming faces. Was the whole world this way? Aera's pulse raced. *I can drown out the voices with music,* she mused. *Vaye said I could.*

"The argentavis swoops down from the forest and preys on humans. Especially children..."

Aera recalled the bass line she'd played in the cottage. She tapped it on her leg.

"...we are lucky to be protected by the Fence..."

Aera envisioned herself beside Vaye, softly stroking keys. The hammers in the piano's heart awakened the strings and each sound filled the world. Four hours passed quickly as music lured her to another world. Finally, the gong sounded, releasing her.

The Dining Hall noise was as grating as usual. Aera decided to take her lunch to her new venue atop the Hill. When she arrived, she sat by the boulder and stared at the forest. Officers loomed in the Sleeping Hut Field, blocking her path to Vaye's cottage. She was stuck in the village as always, bored and alone.

Birds flew by and disappeared over the horizon. *I want to follow them,* Aera thought, and squirmed in frustration. Even if she could have flown away, where would she go? Deadly animals, screeching mobs—

was that all there was? Aera didn't want to live in this world. She hated everything and everyone... except Vaye.

There had to be another way to the cottage, and Aera needed to find it. She finished her food quickly, then mounted the boulder to obtain a better view. A gust of wind pushed her hair back and gave her a rush. She searched the treetops, hills, and valleys below, but detected no trace of any wildflower field or cottage. It had to be down there, somewhere...

The familiar melody of the commune anthem crept up as someone whistled nearby. Aera jumped down from the rock. She spotted a burly figure in uniform and recognized Officer Padd.

"What's the problem, kid? Where are your friends?" He smirked into his bushy beard and sneered, "Why don't you go make some friends? You think you're different?"

"N... no," Aera stammered.

"Alright then. Back to the Dining Hall."

Aera was supposed to obey but didn't want to. She looked at Padd and stayed exactly where she was.

"Pehh," Padd snorted, and headed away. Aera smiled, relieved.

On his way down the Hill, Padd hummed a mutilated, off-key rendition of the commune anthem. Aera filled in the lyrics in her mind: *We are all the same. Giving to each other. Living for our friends. Our sisters and our brothers...*

His voice faded as he disappeared into the Dining Hall. Once he was gone, Aera climbed back onto the boulder and stared in the direction of the cottage. Just as she was losing hope, she spotted iron palisades between some treetops in the distance. That was the Fence! If she followed it, she would come to the cottage... but how could she escape unseen? Her eye landed on Westside Willows, the forest alongside the Field. People walked through those trees to the bathing grove each day, and the cottage was in the opposite direction. That might be the way.

She ran down the Hill, returned her tray to the Dining Hall and slipped into the woods. The familiar path to the bathing grove wound northward, but Aera headed the other way and was soon surrounded by a legion of trees stretching their arms into every inch of sky. The insect choir was lush and the shadows thick, providing extra cover.

After triumphing over dense, thorny foliage, Aera reached the Fence and followed it south. Soon, she heard the gurgle of a brook and spotted water running through a pumpkin patch, where two brown cats stared up at her. Together, they jerked away and ran off into the familiar field of wildflowers. She had arrived!

She headed into the grass and grew increasingly excited as she found the path she'd followed the previous day. Just as she approached the cottage, Vaye opened the door. Had Vaye known Aera was coming? She hadn't been invited...

It occurred to her suddenly that she might be intruding. She stared at the ground, preparing for Vaye to scold her.

"How impressive that you found your way back," Vaye mused in a melodious tone. "Please, do come in, and make yourself at home."

Aera breathed a sigh of relief. Vaye not only welcomed her, but also called her 'impressive.' A smile spread over Aera's face as she headed into the aroma of burning logs. She climbed up on the piano bench and touched a smooth, sunlit key, then pressed it down. The warm sound rumbled in her belly and slowly dissolved.

She felt a whisk of air and looked up: Vaye had appeared in a chair beside her! Somehow, she walked so quietly that Aera did not hear her approach. Everything about her was different: the stealth with which she moved, the music in her voice, her kindness and graceful manner. Why did she invite Aera to the cottage? Who was she?

"What is your name, dear?" Vaye asked.

"Samie Aera," she replied. *Air*-uh. Her name sounded gentle when she said it. Others butchered it, saying Eh-ruh or Eyer-uh.

"A powerful name," Vaye said.

Powerful, Aera thought, confused. She wanted to be powerful, but her name sounded wispy, like wind.

"May I teach you how to harness more power?"

Aera didn't know what it meant to harness power, but she was curious what Vaye wanted to teach her and nodded.

Vaye held up her hands and formed a spherical cage with her fingertips pressed together. "Push my top knuckles and make them bend," she instructed.

Aera pushed each one, but the joints did not budge.

"I practice keeping my knuckles firm," Vaye explained. "Now, you try."

Carefully, Aera lined up her fingers and pressed them together. She held them there as hard as she could but, when Vaye pushed on them, they bent inward.

"Stronger hands will allow you a firmer attack on the piano keys," Vaye said. "You can practice any time."

Aera watched her hands fold like spiders' legs as she bent and flexed her knuckles. She looked over at Vaye, who smiled and asked, "May I test you, Aera?"

It pleased Aera that Vaye didn't say 'Samie' before her name as other adults did. She smiled and said, "Yes."

"Do you remember what I said when I greeted you today?"

Aera remembered it well. She reviewed the phrase in her mind, then sat up straight to evoke Vaye and chimed, "Impressive that you found your way back."

After she spoke, Aera replayed her performance mentally. *Impressive that you found your way back.* The quality of her voice was delicate while Vaye's was rich, but she captured Vaye's calm confidence and slow cadence. Only a mockingbird might have done better.

She glanced at Vaye, whose brown eyes studied her. Sweetly, Vaye asked, "Can you play the melody you learned yesterday?"

Aera stared at the keys and tried to remember which notes she had played.

"Don't worry about mistakes," Vaye said. "Just play until it comes back to you. Your hands will remember."

As soon as Aera struck a key, she recalled where the song had begun and repositioned her hand. One note at a time, she played the melody, grateful she'd practiced on her thigh in class.

"Wonderful," Vaye said. "Now, name ten people in your group."

"Doriline, Farris... Novi..."

Aera strained to remember more but drew a blank. After spending every day with these people, surely she could remember their names?

"Describe Doriline's facial features," Vaye offered.

Aera tried to picture Doriline, but all she saw was mousy curls and teeth. Defeated, she said, "Toothy."

Vaye watched her for a moment, contemplating something. Aera wished she could sink into the floor.

"You are gifted," Vaye said. "Perhaps *too* gifted. I imagine you've had a hard time on the commune."

Gifted? That made no sense. Aera had failed the test.

"Our culture is focused on socializing, but listening is undervalued," Vaye explained. "Conversation is encouraged, but people are not taught to consider their words carefully, or to manage the volume and timing of their speech. The stimulation is overwhelming, and someone who is sensitive might feel out of step."

Tears rushed to Aera's eyes, but she gulped them back. Vaye was right about what Aera felt, and it was hard to believe, as nobody had ever understood her before. People jabbered about nonsense that meant nothing to Aera, and she never had anything to say.

"Our language reflects this bias," Vaye said. "There's a word for red, and the word *pink* is used for light red, but there's no specific word for 'low-pitched' or 'high-pitched,' as if it isn't important."

Aera wondered what Vaye meant by 'important' and asked, "Is it?"

"Slow, rumbling winds indicate tornados, which destroy everything they pass, and high-pitched winds indicate rainstorms, which water the crops. Is that important?"

It seemed so. Aera's cheeks flushed as she nodded her head.

Softly, Vaye said, "The atmosphere reveals much to those who listen."

Aera was unsure what to say, until she realized Vaye did not need her to speak at all. She wanted her to listen.

"Your skills are as valuable as any," Vaye concluded. "But your lunch period will end soon, so I'll stop talking and let you play."

Vaye disappeared under an archway shaped by a stone wall. Nearby hung a giant painting of a teenage girl. Her look was dramatic, with white curls cascading down from a wreath of black flowers and charcoal skin, but the most fascinating feature was a light shining from her forehead. The eyes were so alive, Aera imagined the fantasy girl was watching her also.

"I play, and you listen," Aera told the girl, and giggled.

She turned to the piano and recreated the pattern she'd learned the previous afternoon. Her fingers stumbled on each other and she hit the piano harder, crashing against the keys, creating a storm. Treble notes tweeted like birds and the bass roared in a thunderous rage. She laughed loudly, enjoying the chaos, but then remembered Vaye and looked up. The white-haired girl was listening, but Vaye was not around.

Aera returned to the old melody. It was easier now, and each tone resounded, crisp and vibrant. As her fingers coasted along, she was elated and added new notes. Music created itself...

"You should head back. Your group will be at the bathing grove soon."

Aera had forgotten where she was. Had lunch break passed already? The belltower had not yet gonged and there were no clocks or whistles anywhere. She asked, "How do you know the time?"

Vaye gave Aera a knowing smile and said, "I listen to nature."

Aera understood that 'listen' was important, but Vaye hadn't answered the question.

"I hope you return soon and show me your progress," Vaye said. "Your music made my afternoon brighter."

Aera's cheeks heated. Did Vaye really mean that?

"You may visit whenever you like, even if I'm not home, but there are two things I must ask of you," Vaye said warmly. "First, if you see my curtains closed upstairs, it means I'm sleeping and should not be disturbed. The second is, you *must* keep our acquaintance secret. No one may know you come here."

Aera was thrilled to share a secret with Vaye and to be invited back whenever she wanted. She smiled brightly and chimed, "I promise."

"Wonderful. Now go on, my dear, or you'll miss baths."

Aera departed, and fresh air filled her lungs as she admired the garden. Trees shaded much of the cottage, but the approach had a clearing before it, affording sunlight entrance to create the sparkling reflection she'd seen on the piano. The surrounding grass spilled with purple coneflowers and the clearing overflowed with plants and brambles dotted with multicolored berries. Vaye had her very own paradise.

Though the garden was enchanting, something wasn't right. The other adults lived in groups close to the village, just like the children, but Vaye didn't. This made no sense. Everyone was supposed to be the same.

Over time, Aera's dreamscape transformed as the screeching faces gave way to the orchestras of wind, birds and music. The noise of the village became less invasive as the songs of forests and pianos became routine. Music was the anchor of her day, providing inspiration to endure the drudgery of the commune. When sick, Aera counted on Vaye's medical remedies, determined to circumvent authorities as much as possible.

Vaye advised Aera to perform her duties obediently, no matter how tiresome, to avoid drawing unwanted attention to herself. The only activity Aera skipped was hair-cutting rituals: she wanted an extravagant mane like Vaye's. People glared and sneered as Aera's locks grew down to her thighs, but Vaye praised her beauty, commended her courage, and taught her to braid it in various ways. Authorities urged her to conform to the standard haircut, but did nothing to enforce their commands. Aera managed to avoid trouble until her ninth year.

One bright afternoon, Aera joined the Dining Hall lunch line as music poured through her mind. Majestic staccatos tore through thunderous chords, climbing to a crescendo. She envisioned herself on a grand stage, wearing a lavish white dress, her hair gleaming in the sunlight as she sang her heart out. Her presence was dynamic, her voice bold and vibrant...

"Samely, Codin! I dare you to find the biggest farkus in my group!"

Doriline shattered Aera's reverie, causing her to snap back to the present. She was in the Dining Hall line, surrounded by chattering faces.

"You're all farkuses," replied a boy at a nearby table, and his friends chuckled. He was a suave athlete sitting beside a fat boy shoving cake into his face. Several others crowded the nearby benches, attending their every move.

This was the 11-12 Group's popular crowd, and Doriline was preening to impress them. She flashed her toothy smile, twirled her mousy curls around a finger and said, "I'll give you a hint: she looks like a willow tree, but she acts like a wallflower and never talks. If it wasn't for her hair, no one would notice her at all."

No one would notice her at all. Aera's face flushed. Doriline was talking about her!

"She thinks she's different," Doriline howled. "She's a *rebel*."

"Rebel, rebel," wailed the fat boy, and the rest joined in. "Rebel, rebel..."

Go away! Aera wanted to scream. *Leave me alone!* She rushed at Doriline, who squealed, "Officer Padd! Help!"

"What's the problem?" Padd bellowed.

"What's wrong, Dori?" called one of the boys. "You afraid of a skinny little rebel?"

"Ugh, no! Darse it, fatso!"

Aera shook with fury and screamed, "I hate you all!"

She cut the line, took some fruit, ran outside and curled up by her boulder. Tears streamed down as she watched her sandy-blonde mane cascading to the grass, twinkling with gold in the midday sun. Words rang in her ears. *Wallflower. Skinny little rebel. No one would notice her at all.* She wished she had yelled a cleverer retort, but there was nothing to say. Doriline was right. Aera's hair was different, but she still didn't matter to anyone.

She emerged from her hair-cave, ate the fruit, and combed her tresses with her fingers. Vaye tended to her mane and called it 'glorious,' 'illustrious,' 'golden as the sun.' That meant more than anything the Samies said. Their ugly, short haircuts spoke for themselves.

Aera descended the Hill and slid covertly into Westside Willows. As she approached the Fence, rage overcame her.

"Let me out!" she cried, and slammed her fists against the wall. She punched it until her knuckles were raw.

The iron palisades at the top were extensive, and the stone wall beneath was almost perfectly flat. She shoved her foot into any wedge she could find but none were deep enough to support her. Climbing would be impossible. The barricade continued in both directions, as far as the eye could see. Aera groaned in frustration. Ynas was a prison.

She considered the singular exit that everyone knew about—the Gate in the north—which was said to be several hours walk from the village and guarded by a legion of officers. To escape, she would have to evade the DPD, locate the Gate, subvert the guards... then what? Deadly animals? She might not survive a day.

Defeated, she abandoned the Fence and continued along her usual route to the cottage. Vaye opened the door just as she approached, and two steaming mugs awaited on the table near the fireplace. As usual, she had anticipated Aera's arrival.

"Ah, your hands!" Vaye said. "I have just the remedy for them."

Aera looked down: indeed, her skin had been ripped away, and the wounds stung. She hadn't noticed until now.

With a grin, Vaye disappeared into the kitchen. She returned with a swab of paste on her fingers, which she rubbed over Aera's knuckles. It felt cool and soothing. Aera smiled gingerly and said, "Thanks."

"Of course, dear."

Vaye sat in one of the wicker chairs by the fireplace and Aera, the other. Along with them, a cat settled by the fire and watched the flames. Aera hoped Vaye wouldn't ask where her injuries had come from. To her relief, Vaye sipped her tea without a word.

Rebel, Aera thought. Was that how people saw her? Farris shoved other boys and mouthed off in class, but no one called him 'rebel.' The term described people who broke rules and defied others, but still was more flattering than being a 'wallflower,' unnoticed altogether.

Vaye was an extreme outsider, living a whole separate life. Aera was supposed to say everyone was the same, but Vaye encouraged her to speak her mind. Her voice trembled, but she forced the words out: "Vaye... why are you... different?"

There was a short silence. Was Vaye angry? Disappointed? Cautiously, Aera peeked at Vaye and saw...

...serenity.

Vaye was calm, contemplative. "What do you mean, different?"

Aera was confused. Wasn't it obvious? Vaye lived apart from others, wore her own wardrobe, even spoke differently, using poetic descriptors and avoiding crude clichés. Her vocabulary was mellifluous, and Aera strove to adopt it as her own.

"All the adults wear the same things," Aera said, "and go to the same places together... but you don't."

There was a short silence. Vaye stirred some pine needles in a mug on the table, placed them on a plate and sipped the drink. Logs moved in the fireplace beside them and, as sparks flew, the cat sat up with ears alert.

Aera feared she'd made a mistake. Was it wrong to call Vaye different? Was it insulting? She removed the needles from her own mug and took a sip, enjoying its bitter heat. Water was the only beverage available in the village, but Vaye always treated Aera to exotic teas.

After a long pause, Vaye replaced her mug on the table and turned to Aera. "What makes someone different from someone else?"

Aera opened her mouth to respond, then closed it.

"Is it the clothes we wear? The tea we drink? The length of our hair?" Vaye asked with a knowing smile.

Aera looked down at her hair, feeling self-conscious. She wondered what Vaye was implying.

"Everyone is unique," Vaye said gently. "In this, we are the same."

That wasn't what Aera meant. Surely, Vaye understood the blatant difference between herself and the Samies.

Vaye collected their empty mugs and disappeared into the kitchen. Aera's eye landed on the white-haired girl in the painting, with her bold, black stare and forehead-light. *You're a rebel*, Aera thought. *We are the same*. She touched her own forehead, feeling around for any evidence of an opening, but found none.

TOWN MEETING
1323 LATE-SPRING

Clouds gathered as the air grew heavy and ominous. Aera ate lunch quickly at the boulder, hurrying to reach the cottage before the impending storm. Once finished, she darted toward Westside Willows, where she was enveloped in howling wind, swaying treetops and wild caws...

"Samely, kid! Turn your skinny legs around and come back here!"

Aera turned abruptly and saw everyone lining up in the Field. She knew children were required to remain inside during storms and went to the back of her line.

"You think you're special, running off by yourself?" Officer Padd snarled. "Where in Riva's Trees were you going? Answer me, kid!"

Aera would never betray her promise to Vaye, least of all by revealing their acquaintance to *him*. In the sweetest, most innocent voice she could muster, she said, "Wandering."

"Wandering in the rainstorm?"

Gently, Aera chimed, "It's not raining."

"Pehh," Padd grumbled.

Aera breathed a sigh of relief as Padd turned away, but then Doriline squealed, "Eh-ruh goes off by herself every day!"

Padd returned his focus to Aera and all eyes followed. Faces leered at her as the warmth escaped her cheeks.

"She always walks into the woods the same way, and comes back the same way," Doriline said. "She *never* eats in the Dining Hall or the Raetsek Field like the rest of us."

"Wandering, eh?" Padd spat. To the line leader, he said, "Award Samie Doriline five points for her Peer Aid report."

Doriline flashed her big teeth in celebration, and Aera seethed. Over time, Doriline's tattle points would assure an invitation to the DPD. All the officers were just like her, ratting out others to gain rank, all the while pretending to care about the welfare of the commune.

Padd marched toward Aera, greedy for his own moment of victory, and parked at her side. "Tell me," he said. "Where *do* you go?"

Aera slid into her hair in protest, but Padd extended his fat, stinking finger and pushed it into her shoulder. She jerked, but he grasped her chin and turned it toward him with his calloused and fish-smelly hand.

"You dare withhold information from me?" He spoke so close to her face that she could taste his lunch. "Just how special do you think you are?"

Though her chin was propped up, Aera looked down. Her heart thumped from her toes to her earlobes.

"I'll ask you one more time," Padd growled. "Where *do* you go?"

"*I* think she plays music!" called someone near Doriline.

"Instructor Lilese caught her playing *advanced rhythms* in music class!" someone else added.

"Who do you play with?" Padd demanded. "Where?"

"In... the... Music Room," Aera stammered.

Padd released Aera's chin from his grip. "Did everyone hear that? There's a Music Room in the forest!"

Laughter spread through the crowd. Aera glared at Doriline, wishing she could destroy her.

Padd turned his beady eyes toward the forest, then to Aera, and back to the forest again. His brow furrowed increasingly until finally he bellowed, "Oh, I get it! You hide in the forest, sneak through the kitchen, and cut through the playground into the Education Unit!" He paused, proud of his detective work. "Who do you play with?"

"Alone," Aera said quickly.

"*Eh*-ruh does *everything* alone," Doriline squeaked, much to Aera's relief. This time, Doriline was being helpful, even if unwittingly.

Padd looked from Doriline to Aera, scratched his beard, and finally concluded, "Follow me."

He led Aera into the Dining Hall and stopped at a table with three officers. The breakfast attendant, Officer Luce, sat there with two women in uniforms that marked them as members of the DPD. Aera imagined Doriline as one of them, proudly flaunting the same ugly brown and orange outfit. It seemed perverse that anyone would desire that.

"Luce, my friend!" Padd exclaimed. "We have a case."

Officer Luce nodded, stiff as ever, but did not look up from his food.

"This little runt plays piano during meals," Padd said, "*by herself.*"

Luce exchanged glances with the women, and each expression was equally glum. Aera wondered what they were thinking and why Padd had taken her there. The Dining Hall echo deepened while Luce chewed his food slowly and stared into the distance with a rigid brow. Finally, he said, "I'll deliver the case to Officer Onus."

"Oh, bison breath," Padd snarled. "Onus has night duty and he's asleep by now. Give me permission and I'll take her to Administration. Collecting cow manure could do the farkus some good."

"I will deliver the case to Officer Onus," Luce repeated in a tone leaving no doubt the discussion had ended. "Leave the... *girl...* with me."

"Pehh," Padd snorted and huffed off.

It did not escape Aera's notice that Luce corrected Padd's insults and chose to 'deliver' her. He had no reason to help her, so he must have been looking to gain points for himself. She lingered uneasily by the end of the table and watched people file into the Dining Hall while Luce finished his food.

"Look, Boney-Bones is busted!" Farris announced.

Laughter tore through the room. Aera bristled, but Luce grabbed her by the arm. "Enough," he ordered. "Let's go."

She followed Luce outside, where the gray sky rumbled in the distance. As they crossed the Field, wind blew her mane into a wild mess. Thunder cracked, and the world lit up as rain cascaded down.

Luce walked briskly to the DPD Lounge and opened the door for Aera. Like every facility in the village, the brick building was connected to a larger uniform structure, but the inside contained a welcoming display of blazing torches and arched hallways. The entrance gave an immediate view of an elaborate lounge with an iron balcony overhead. Aera admired the velvet chairs, carpeted floors and paintings hung along the walls. The sound of the lobby was pleasant, punctuated by the crackle of burning logs in a fireplace and a soft swish above as rain hit the roof. In the other units, rainstorms created a treacherous clamor of pounding drops, but here, everything was peaceful.

Liars, Aera thought. *They pretend we're the same.*

Luce led her up a quiet staircase to an elaborately appointed hallway featuring polished wooden doors. Each had an attractive wrought iron knocker over a plaque bearing an intricately carved name, and they passed several until they reached the one that said, 'Officer Onus.' Luce lifted the knocker and made it clank. Muffled footsteps moved inside and Aera was surprised at how quiet they were. When people moved around in the Children's Hut, the floors always sounded as if they might collapse, but here, walking was barely audible.

Onus swung the door open, revealing a cozy room with rugs, wooden furniture, and a thick mattress on an elevated frame. Before Aera could see more, he closed the door behind him, eyeballed her with disgust and huffed, "Whaddya want?"

"Officer Padd caught this youngster playing piano by herself during lunch," Luce said stiffly.

"Mehhh," Onus snorted.

"With your permission, I will remove twenty peer points from her register."

Onus coughed a wet cough full of phlegm and ordered, "Bring her to the next town meeting."

Aera had never attended a town meeting, but she had heard people were punished publicly there. Anyone could choose to attend, which meant her classmates might show up to watch. She glanced up at Luce, hoping to be spared, but he didn't look back. He cleared his throat, straightened his posture, and declared, "We ought not burden Renstrom Nurin with something this trivial."

"I dunno if it's trivial. It's *weird*, is what it is."

Luce furrowed his pointy brow but did not respond. Onus turned to Aera and smirked, "Enjoy the town meeting, Samie."

The three days preceding the town meeting were endless. Aera could barely focus or sleep as she anticipated the ridicule and punishment she would surely face, especially if Doriline's pack showed up. She didn't dare visit the cottage and wondered whether Vaye would notice her absence. Would she come looking for Aera? Could she save her from this? Aera watched the forest during meals, hoping to see Vaye, but nobody came.

When the dreaded morning arrived, Aera's stomach was hard as rock. She grabbed some fruit, stared at it, but couldn't eat. Each moment dragged on until, inevitably, Officer Luce trumpeted his ear-curdling whistle, and everyone lined up in the Field. Aera braced herself for the dreadful moment when Doriline would notice Luce calling her aside.

The lines of children slowly departed, beginning with the youngest, until finally, Aera's group headed to the Education Unit. Luce stood in position near the entrance, stiff as always, but paid her no acknowledgement. Just as she began to wonder whether he'd forgotten her, he prompted, "Wait here."

She stepped aside quietly while nobody was looking at her. After her group disappeared into the building, she breathed.

Luce led her across the Field behind the DPD Building. "I know Renstrom Nurin is intimidating," he said, "but you'll be fine."

Aera could not imagine she'd be anything close to 'fine' and wondered why Luce was trying to comfort her. No matter what he said, his rigid demeanor made her nervous.

They rounded the structures until they reached the one nearest the river, where they headed into a tunnel at the side of the building. The air was musty, the ground muddy, and the pathway barely wide enough to accommodate them both. A distant voice leaked into the tunnel from the courtyard, creating an ominous backdrop of sound.

"The punishments aren't so bad for children," Luce continued in a hushed voice. "If you were older, Nurin would make you clean up animal entrails or empty the latrines."

Aera imagined that nauseating smell and hoped she would fare better. The end of the tunnel was near, blazing with sunlight, and the voice in the courtyard was loud and incisive. Aera recognized the sharp tenor of the Renstrom from his seasonal addresses at Unity Festival.

Whispering even more quietly, Luce said, "When I was thirteen, they caught me reading a history book in Junior Hut. Renstrom Gorovin said if I was interested in war and killing, I might enjoy working in the Slaughterhouse. I spent the season hanging pigs from the ceiling, slitting their throats and cutting out their insides, and it was disgusting, but I learned my lesson. I never read another book outside class again."

*If I can never see Vaye again, I'll hang **myself** in the Slaughterhouse*, Aera thought.

They emerged from the tunnel into sweltering brightness as a stream of extravagant words resounded. "In concordance with the Lumber Laws, it is irremissible..."

Aera rubbed her eyes and found herself in a triangular courtyard enclosed by brick walls and countless windows. People were seated along rows of logs with their backs to the tunnel, facing the front elevation where the exalted Renstrom Nurin posed importantly atop a wide tree trunk. His posture was distinctive, with his prominent chin held high, and he was crowned by a head of chestnut hair with red highlights that caught the sun. Stationed just below him, a few officers stood at attention holding papers and other items. Their uniforms were identical to Nurin's, but his presence commanded unique attention.

Luce marched down the aisle and positioned himself near the front, but Aera lingered behind. There were too many people and she dreaded being seen. She found a spot in the back, and reluctantly sat down.

Nurin towered over the crowd and his voice boomed throughout the courtyard. "Since reflective surfaces were long ago outlawed, mirrors have been banished and windowpanes must possess anti-reflective coating. These laws are a crucial component of communal unity. Vanity encourages people to believe they are superior to others and the

33

recognition of personal features on genetic relatives would inspire favoritism, which would invite destabilizing competition."

Apparently, 'mirror' was a reflective surface. Aera had never seen one. She tried many times during baths to see her face, but the waterfall created turbulence and her view was always obscured. She *hoped* seeing herself would make her feel superior, but this could not possibly happen to everyone. Doriline might feel *less* superior if she could see her giant teeth.

An elderly man rose from his log in the front row and demanded, "Mirrors have been forbidden since before my lifetime, but that is not at issue! Since when has there been a law against varnished wood?"

Nurin cleared his throat. "Varnishing wood requires effort and resources that could be spent more productively. Furthermore, it is possible to see one's reflection in varnished wood."

"There's no statute against it!" The old man protested. "You cannot punish this man for his decorative proclivities."

"I am not proposing that we punish him. I am proposing that we view this incident as an opportunity to outlaw varnished wood once and for all for the future of our children and community."

Aera found it hard to believe these laws helped the community. Wouldn't most people want to know what they looked like? Nurin's reasons made no sense, as vanity and favoritism were common, even without mirrors.

"As Justinar of Law in Ynas, it's *my* responsibility to oversee doctrine," continued the old man. "I will not rewrite law for the sake of frivolous twitter-twatter."

Nurin erected his chin and the bones on his face were sharp as blades. "With all due respect, Justinar Dinad, this matter is not frivolous. It is counterproductive and potentially dangerous behavior that could be interdicted with simple regulation."

Dinad stroked his long beard. "We have already subverted two laws since 1320. Would you have me shred our entire canon?"

"Do you postulate any beneficial countervailing consideration in empowering varnished wood on the commune?"

"It is arguably supererogatory. But before we amend the law, we must conduct a public hearing and assess the will of the citizens."

"Let us have a preliminary vote," Nurin said decisively. "Those in favor of outlawing varnished wood, raise your hands!"

Arms in the crowd shot up in the air. Aera couldn't believe people cared about this, or even comprehended it, yet so many displayed their opinions.

Nurin observed the crowd and said, "Anyone in favor of preserving the current law, raise your hand!" More arms appeared. "Anyone with an alternate suggestion, raise your hand!"

One hand rose in the middle of the crowd, small and hardly visible until the boy climbed on his log and extended his arm stiffly, fingers pointing upward. Aera recognized his brick-red hair: he was in her Age Group. What was he doing here?

Nurin adjusted his collar and cleared his throat. "Thank you for your input, Samie Cyrrus," he said. "You may take your seat."

The boy stared back at him with a nefarious smile and proclaimed, "Pardon me, most honorable Renstrom, but I have yet to articulate my thesis." His voice was every bit as incisive as Nurin's. While the vocal character betrayed his youth, his pronunciation was meticulous, like an adult trapped in a child's body.

Projecting an air of detachment, Nurin said, "State your suggestion concisely and then take your seat."

"If you endeavor for Ynas to be efficient and productive, why not discuss matters more worthy of this august body?" Cyrrus challenged boldly. "Teach by example. Ignore this picayune and ignominious issue."

Justinar Dinad turned to the crowd and spoke in a commanding voice. "Samie Cyrrus, please, by all means, continue to harangue the authorities and abuse the patience of this good audience with your neophyte desultory polemics. And afterwards, perhaps you can accept your station..." he raised an eyebrow and concluded with a grin, "...and your seat."

Cyrrus complied without another word. Once he sat, Aera could no longer see him through the mass of bodies between them. His audacity was shocking. Why hadn't she noticed it before? Would he recognize her if he saw her... and tell the others she was being punished? Nausea consumed her, and she disappeared under her mane.

The debates went on and on, and the sun beat down on her hair so intensely that hiding beneath it baked her cheeks and made her fore-head drip with sweat. Still, she would not expose her face, lest Cyrrus notice her. The edges of her hair were golden in the sunlight and the voices outside were menacing. Carefully, she pressed her fingers together, forming a cage as Vaye had taught her, and reviewed some music in her mind. She imagined dancing along, spinning freely through a misty forest...

"Officer Padd caught a nine-year-old girl playing piano by herself during lunch break."

Luce's voice penetrated Aera's daydream. She snapped to attention, hair clinging to her cheeks.

"A nine-year-old girl played piano by herself during lunch break," Nurin repeated. "Would that girl please rise?"

No, Aera thought, but forced herself to stand. Nurin looked for her, but gazed right past her and repeated, "Rise!"

Aera climbed up on her log as Cyrrus had done. When she saw the crowd, her legs trembled. She looked down, longing to retreat to her hair-cave. She was dizzy and the ground was too far away.

"Why did you play piano alone?" Nurin bellowed.

The question whirled through Aera's mind. *Why did you play piano...?*

"I like playing piano," she mumbled. She couldn't decide which was stupider: the question or her response.

"Speak up!"

Attempting to project, she repeated, "I like playing piano." Her voice was hardly louder.

"Step to the front!"

Aera dismounted her log and dragged herself to the aisle, where she was surrounded by watchful eyes and disapproving faces. Windows engulfed the courtyard in rows, the walls themselves lining up to prose-cute her. She was trapped between breaths, sweat, sunbeams and eyes. Wherever she turned, she could not avoid scrutiny. She fixed her eyes on her feet and moved down the aisle between the logs until she real-ized Nurin was just before her, and she lurched to a halt.

"Step up," he instructed.

She climbed up to Nurin's tree stump, but he still towered over her. He demanded, "What did you say?"

"I like playing piano."

"You like playing piano!" he announced, and the audience audibly sneered. "Who have you been playing with?"

Quickly, Aera said, "Alone."

"In the Music Room?"

Aera nodded weakly.

"Tell me, child," he said. "What is your name?"

"Aera."

"Your full name."

Full name? What was he talking about? Nurin cleared his throat impatiently, but Aera was at a loss and her face was hotter by the second.

"Samie Eh-ruh," Nurin said firmly. "Now tell me: What do you expect your solo musicianship will contribute to the welfare of the community?"

Aera had no desire to contribute to the community. She tried to conjure a response, but her heart was racing, and words did not come.

"Were you planning to include anyone *else* in your music?" Nurin asked, his voice oozing with disdain. "Or were you content to isolate yourself and inflate your own ego?"

"No," she murmured.

"*No* is not an option. Which is it?"

Nurin waited for her to respond while every pair of eyes in the audience probed her. Aera was short of breath and gasped for air, trying to think of a response. Finally, something popped into mind: "The music... is ruined by all the people."

"Did you hear that, folks?" Nurin called, projecting his crisp voice. "She said the music is *ruined* by all the people."

Whispers spread everywhere and Aera's heartbeat became so frantic that she could no longer breathe. She leaned into the sticky heat of her hair and tried to catch her breath, to little avail.

"Child, tell me," Nurin said, peering down at her from above. "Where does music come from, if not from people?"

"From... one person?" Aera offered from under her hair. "From birds?"

"Birds sing to communicate with other birds," Nurin said. "At Unity Festival we enjoy celebratory public music, group paintings and communal storytelling. We engage in haircutting rituals with friends, which you have impressively and assiduously avoided."

The throng chuckled. Aera wished this nightmare would end.

"Children draw one another so people may see themselves as others perceive them, rather than indulging egotistically in a reflective surface. Do you understand, Samie Eh-ruh?"

Aera was dizzy and confused. She did not understand any of this.

"Why would you create your own music, all alone, instead of communicating with other children? Do you think you're different? Or, superior? Do you believe you're independent from the rest of us?"

Nurin paused. The courtyard was so quiet that Aera could hear the pounding of her heart.

"Perhaps if your hair were short like everyone else's, you would feel a sense of belonging," Nurin mused. "You would show your face, come out of hiding, and recognize your connection with the community." To the officer beside him, he said, "Shears, please."

Shears? Why? Aera attempted to break away, but her legs did not move. Her jaw quivered uncontrollably, and her throat felt like a rock. As she struggled against her fluster, hands pressed down on both of her shoulders, holding her in place.

Nurin lifted the long end of her hair from beside her knee and twisted it around itself. As he held it out and positioned his shears beside her neck, Aera felt the air against her. Her agony was laid bare with nothing to hide behind, her sweat and misery on display.

Nurin closed his blades and Aera's sparkling locks billowed to the ground. Tears flooded her. She tightened every muscle to contain them, but Nurin lifted the remainder of her hair and the dam broke. Liquids spilled from her eyes and nose, revealed for everyone to see as her gleaming mane piled up with the dirt at Nurin's boots. She buried her wet cheeks in her hands, desperate to hide from the faces that hated her. They wanted her to be the same, but she wasn't.

Whispers and murmurs abounded as voices and windows spun into a haze. Aera's temples undulated with the whirl of the world until her eyes anchored on the brightest and clearest object in sight... Cyrrus. He probed into her with emerald eyes that saw her exposed for all that she was: helpless, lost and alone.

"Return to class," Nurin ordered. "And never forget—we are all the same."

Nurin positioned his right hand over his heart and raised his left toward the sky in the traditional salute. The throng mirrored his motion. Aera's head pounded as the collective voices resounded the shibboleth: "We are all the same. We are all the same. We are all the same..."

Officer Luce accompanied Aera back to the village and permitted her to skip the last hour of class. She spent the remainder of the morning and lunchbreak crying in the woods until her ribs were sore and her throat was on fire.

During afternoon tasks, her group was assigned to feed the caged animals. The sun scorched down, but Aera hid the haircut beneath her hood. They passed through endless rows of minks, sables, chinchillas, rabbits, weasels, raccoons, and foxes, individually confined in wire enclosures. Aera wondered whether their cages were any worse than hers. The strain of containing her tears made her increasingly tense. By the end of tasks, she felt numb and distant.

At dinner, Aera balled up against her boulder, her sweaty head buried in her bony knees. In her entire life, she had never felt so desolate. The commune marched forward on schedule, but nothing seemed important compared to her hair and her visits to the cottage. What would she do now? Nobody knew or cared that the only joy in her life had been crushed... not even Vaye. All she could do, day after day, was march along with the Samies, marked by fractured hair that commemorated her humiliating breakdown at the town meeting.

Perhaps the other children would not find out. They were unaware of the humiliation she'd endured, the way she'd fallen apart, the reasons she'd lost her hair. Nobody knew...

...except Cyrrus.

CYRRUS
1323 LATE-SPRING

Cyrrus. Aera recalled the razor eyes that had cut her while she cried...
why? What had he been doing at the town meeting?

She scanned the crowds in the Field but didn't see him. She
returned her tray to the Dining Hall and surveyed the tables, but
Cyrrus was not there either. The rest of dinner break dragged on interminably as Aera paced by the boulder, waiting for him to appear.
When the belltower resounded at curfew, she lingered at the top of the
plateau and finally got her wish.

Cyrrus emerged from Westside Willows, his brick-red hair strewn
haphazardly as he stared into a book. Two boys followed and talked up
at him, but he walked ahead, paying them no heed. He took his place
in line with the other children. Taller, straighter, and whiter than the
others, he stood out like a peacock among ducks. The contrast
between his brickish hair and pallid face was surreal.

He slicked back his sweaty hair and looked in Aera's direction. Had
he seen her looking? She tensed as his eyes fixed on her, studying her.
What was he thinking?

"Samie Eh-ruh! Get in line!"

Aera leaned into her hood. Was Cyrrus watching her still? She
dared not look. She focused on her feet and headed down the Hill, but
something bumped against her and knocked her to the ground.

"Nice haircut, farkus!"

Farris raced by with some friends, laughing: Aera's hood had slipped back, exposing the wreckage for all to see. She felt an urge to scream but stopped herself. The last thing she wanted was for Cyrrus to witness her falling apart again.

She wiped the dirt from her trousers with shaking hands and continued on her way. Though her knee hurt, it was less disconcerting than the piercing eyes that had seen her defenseless.

The children followed their lines to their dorms and went to bed, but Aera could not sleep. The belltower rang out, signaling that another two hours had passed... then four. Screeches swarmed her mind. *Sinë veskento i suínanya më Onórnëan. Sinë veskento i suínanya më Onórnëan.*

Drown it out with music, Aera implored herself, but music evaded her. Every limb was uncomfortable, and her head ached. *Sinë veskento i suínanya më Onórnëan. Në Laimandil ë i namanya...* [1]

She sat up, unable to endure the drone any longer. There was nowhere to go except the lavatory, but it would have to do. She tiptoed between the mats, carefully stepping in spots where she divined the floor would not creak, and gently eased open the door just enough to slip through.

The lobby outside was mostly dark, but moonlight seeped in through narrow windows, casting stripes of white across the dingy scape. A figure sat in the shadows and, as Aera stared, the form took shape...

...Cyrrus. Cyrrus was in the lobby. He was leaning against the ratty brick wall, reading by a thin moonbeam that spilled through the window above. As Aera took him in, her pulse throbbed so loudly she feared he might hear it.

Noiselessly, she retreated into the lavatory. The stench was dizzying, but she cupped her hands over her nose, paced in the narrow space and tried to calm herself. Officer Onus was not in the lobby as usual, but surely, he was nearby. Would he admonish Cyrrus for being outside his room after curfew? Luce had been punished for reading outside of class, but Cyrrus did that right in the open. If he was allowed to stay awake and do as he pleased, could Aera do the same?

I'll ask him, Aera decided. She practiced in her mind. *Will you be punished for reading?* Stupid question: Cyrrus could not predict the future. *Are you afraid of getting caught?* Too childish. *Does Onus let you read out here?* That was a decent question. Aera imagined herself gliding gracefully to his side and cooing in a vivid timbre: *Does Onus let you read out here?*

She rehearsed her question mentally and returned to the lobby. Cyrrus was still fixated on the book, brows furrowed and lips pursed, his pale skin shining like a beacon in the darkness.

All she had to do was walk. *Walk.* Her knees wobbled. *Walk*, she implored herself, but she was nonplussed, frozen. She jerked herself back and retreated to the bedroom.

More time passed, but Aera still couldn't find sleep. Every position she lay in was worse than the last. She tossed and turned, cringing at the snoring around her, until someone clomped across the room. The floor groaned along with the footsteps and, as the door swung open, Aera caught a glimpse of Doriline heading out to the lobby. Would Doriline do what she couldn't and speak to Cyrrus? Would he respond?

Aera tiptoed between the mats and huddled in the corner by the door to listen. Sure enough, Doriline screeched, "What are you doing out here?" Her voice was like fingernails on glass.

"Same thing you're doing." Cyrrus's tone was flat, without a hint of annoyance or interest.

"Does Officer Onus know you're here?"

"How should I know what he knows?"

"You're *reading*," Doriline whispered loudly. "That's illegal!"

"This book is a commune standard. If you paid attention in class, you might recall reading a section yourself."

"But you're not supposed to be up," she argued. "I'm gonna report you."

"It's illegal to leave the hut after curfew and to read outlawed books, but I am doing neither," Cyrrus muttered, dragging his words in boredom. "Nurin attempts to outlaw taboos, but his effectiveness is mitigated by Dinad's parsimonious adherence to previously inscribed code. What I'm doing is tabooed, not illegal. Read *Laws of Ynas*. There's a copy in the Library, on the top floor of the Administration Unit. Then report me at the next town meeting if you hanker to debate the issue."

"What in Riva's Trees are you talking about?"

This was not a conversational ploy. Doriline had no idea what Cyrrus was talking about. Aera giggled to herself.

With sarcastic compassion, Cyrrus poked, "Don't torment yourself over the outcome, because it's inconsequential. I would do this even if it were illegal."

"Bison breath!" Doriline squeaked. "You're a rebel!"

"There are three types of people in the world," Cyrrus said, his voice adopting the mien he had projected at the town meeting. "Those who resist change, those who desire change yet perpetuate the system, and those who pursue change. The latter are labeled rebels and shunned. But the rebel is the most important person in any society."

The most important person... Aera blushed. Cyrrus had seen her at the town meeting. Did he consider her a rebel?

"How can someone be more important than someone else?" Doriline demanded, hanging onto the few words she understood. "No wonder the instructors hate you."

Articulating each consonant, Cyrrus asserted, "When challenging a system, one must anticipate hatred and ridicule. The rebel's courage is the seed from which progress spawns."

"You sound like a textbook," Doriline whined.

"Excellent observation!" Cyrrus exclaimed. "I memorized those passages from an illegal book so I could have them with me at all times without penalty for carrying it."

"You're weird."

"What an eloquent assessment. I'm flattered that you find me so intriguing."

"You're not *intriguing*. You're a *farkus!* Where did you come from, anyway?"

A silence followed. Aera waited eagerly for his response, but none came.

Doriline clomped toward the lavatory and Aera sneaked back to her mat, more quietly than ever. If anyone noticed her spying on those two, she would be mortified. As she lay down, she considered Doriline's last words: *Where did you come from, anyway?* Was that a real question, or just an insult? Could Cyrrus have come from outside?

Aera strained to remember the first time she'd seen him. Before

43

today, she hadn't known his name, but his red hair and crisp voice were familiar. She struggled to obtain a mental picture of him prior to the town meeting, but all she could see were crowds, voices and faces suffocating her like the mist in her dream. Doriline had noticed him. Doriline remembered.

Aera reviewed the conversation. Like her, Cyrrus used uncommon words and avoided the usual hackneyed phrases. It was likely his vocabulary mimicked Nurin and an excess of books, just as she had adopted hers from Vaye. She wondered how many years he had attended town meetings and what drew him to them.

As she finally fell asleep, her last thought was Cyrrus's confident voice: *The rebel is the most important person in any society...*

The night passed in a blink, and the Samies awakened for daily duties. Aera followed the group to the Dining Hall and the room reverberated as she took her place on the breakfast line. Officer Luce came in to monitor the door and glanced at her with concern, but she didn't want his sympathy and stared firmly ahead. Her eye landed on Farris and Doriline a short distance in front of her. Everywhere she turned, there were faces and voices she despised.

"I wanna learn Jiavo," Farris whined to Doriline.

"Jiavo is a *warrior's* game," Doriline said. "There are no warriors here."

"Jiavo is a *man's* game," Farris corrected her. "Every boy in Kadir learns to play—"

"Every boy in Kadir is sent out to die in the Errkoan War," Officer Luce cut in. "Be thankful you're safe in Ynas."

"Jiavo requires *thinking* and *strategy*," Cyrrus called from the middle of the line. "The authorities prefer that we remain ignorant!"

Cyrrus's voice cut right through the din and others craned to see. How could Aera possibly have overlooked him for so long? She was often distracted but could not have missed someone so brazen. Something must have changed.

"Has anyone contemplated The Grand Philosophy of Ynas?" he shouted.

Farris bellowed back, "We are all the same!"

"Everyone can recite it, but have you considered its purpose?" Cyrrus called excitedly, preening and projecting so everyone could hear him. "Our leaders promote mediocrity to prevent us from excelling because they fear we'll acquire more power than them."

"SAMIE CYRRUS!" Bellowed Officer Luce. "Darse your dirl and face forward."

"I would make a better Renstrom than Nurin!" Cyrrus continued, raising his voice a magnitude louder.

Luce lurched toward Cyrrus and growled, "Samie Cyrrus, *darse your dirl.*"

"When I rule Oreni I'm going to administer intelligence tests to ten-year-olds, and everyone who fails will be slaughtered. That way stupid people won't breed! I will eliminate stupidity altogether!"

Aera almost exploded in laughter. *Stupid people won't breed.* Would he consider her stupid? What an arrogant jerk.

Luce gripped Cyrrus by both wrists and yanked his arms behind him to lead him away, but that didn't stop the tirade. "If there was no stupidity, my providence would not threaten you, and you would let me speak! If you had a brain, you would know I'm not breaking any law, and Nurin can't punish me!"

"Darse your dirl or I'll tape your ghaadi mouth shut!" Luce ordered as he shoved Cyrrus away from the line and guided him toward the door.

Cyrrus yelled as loud as he could while Luce pushed him outside. "If all the stupid people in Ynas were dead, my artwork would be displayed throughout the commune! Those with talent could play enlightened music at Unity Festival! The instructors would sing on pitch and the songs..."

The door closed, terminating the onslaught of Cyrrus's voice, though Aera imagined he would rant until Luce actually taped his mouth shut. The Samies hashed out his points in animated voices, but Aera knew his rant was all a show. If he cared about music and art, he would have protested at the town meeting.

Cyrrus was missing throughout lunch, and the group went to Numbers Class without him. Soon after the lesson began, Officer Luce delivered him to the classroom. All three instructors watched them

45

enter. The shortest, Lonnoc, inquired in his goofy voice, "Is there a prob-lem?"

"A distinguished DPD sycophant endeavored to discipline me," Cyrrus announced. "Notwithstanding, I had violated no law."

Aera smirked at his pretentious vocabulary, but Lonnoc was stumped. He turned to Luce, whose brows were furrowed so tightly they were practically conjoined. Aera wondered what Cyrrus had put him through.

Curtly, Officer Luce closed the door behind him. Cyrrus strode with an impish expression to an empty chair and Instructor Lonnoc resumed the lesson.

"Six-teen plus eighty-five! Sam-ie No-vi!"

"One hundred and one," Cyrrus said.

"Wait for your turn," Lonnoc said casually. "Eighty-six plus fif-teen..."

Cyrrus had never been so disruptive before. Why didn't anyone silence him? Aera had done nothing but play piano, which was harmless; yet she was forced to endure humiliation, lose her hair, and stop visiting Vaye. In one day, Cyrrus had spoken out of turn, ranted openly about murder, and insulted the Renstrom. The authorities reacted, yet he emerged unscathed, and resumed doing exactly as he pleased. At nine, he was beating the system.

"Sam-ie Eh-ruh!"

Aera snapped out of her trance but didn't know what the question was or how many times her name had been called.

"Pay attention, Sam-ie Eh-ruh!" Instructor Lonnoc said. "Forty-two plus thirty-three."

"Seventy-five," Cyrrus called out disinterestedly.

Aera grimaced. Cyrrus had stolen her turn.

"Stop that, Sam-ie Cy-rrus," Lonnoc said, but Cyrrus did not respond. He stared down at his pencil and dragged it across a page, pretending to be in his own world.

His show of boredom was unconvincing: clearly, he was showing off. Aera didn't know who he was trying to impress, but it certainly would never work on her. If he fancied himself so brilliant, couldn't he figure out how to shut up? She wondered how much time would pass until he talked again and counted in her head while Lonnoc called out names and equations in the background. *One, two, three, four...*

"Eighty-three," spouted Cyrrus out of turn. Aera smirked.

Instructor Lonnoc walked around the table, glanced over Cyrrus's shoulder, and snatched his page. Aera craned to see it and glimpsed a sketch of the classroom. The faces of people were blank, but everything else was precisely realistic.

"You dare to draw pic-tures during num-bers?" Lonnoc implored.

"If you permit me to do *five* things at once, I might become susceptible to miscalculation," Cyrrus said. "Then we might all be the same."

A few people laughed. Lonnoc watched Cyrrus for a moment, but then gave up and walked away. "Sam-ie Gai-li!" he called. "Forty-sev-en plus twen-ty-two!"

Aera wished Cyrrus would just vanish. Not only could he debate eloquently, but he could do math in his head while drawing with uncanny accuracy. Did he have any weaknesses? Would he want to eliminate Aera for having no drawing skills or missing her turn? Would that indict her as 'stupid people?' He must have believed he was superior to everyone, worthy of ruling the entire world.

~

Every time Cyrrus spoke, Aera cringed. His exaggerated articulation of syllables, flamboyant vocabulary and fierce command of speech were unnerving. She told herself he didn't deserve her attention, but it was too late. Blocking him out was impossible. Once she began to hate him, the volume of his voice increased. It cut through music, laughter, and thought. Neither time nor distance softened the impact of his words hammering her head.

Duties and rituals were torture, but Aera's misery was most acute when her group was assigned to Art and Music. She wanted desperately to see Vaye again but wondered also whether Vaye missed her. If she enjoyed Aera's company as much as she claimed, wouldn't she come to the village to find her?

The line-leader called Aera's name first and sent her into an empty Art Room. She sat in the back, as far as possible from the instructors.

Just as she settled in, Cyrrus strutted through the door. His posture was perfect, and his brick red hair was fastidiously unkempt.

Aera tore her eyes away and stared at the table as his footsteps drew closer. Of all places in the room, he pulled out the chair next to hers. As he swerved into his seat, heat emanated from him. Aera's heart raced. Why did he have to sit *there*?

He leaned back and stared ahead as though Aera didn't exist; she in turn faced forward and pretended he wasn't there. Chatter grated her ears and chairs dragged along the floor. Her leg bounced furiously until she locked it in place. What would Cyrrus say? When would he say it?

"Samie Mivar, distribute the pencils! Samie Keole, pass out the paper!"

Aera stared at the table, focusing and unfocusing her eyes until the wood grain swirls flowed like water. A slice of paper and a pencil appeared in her reach.

"Quiet, children!" croaked Instructor Sarode. "There are chairs in every corner of the room. Your assignment is to draw one. Begin!"

Cyrrus would inherit Aera's drawing. She couldn't mess up. With careful concentration, she drew four legs, the seat, the back... it was lopsided. *Idiot*, she scolded herself. She glanced over Cyrrus's shoulder to see his page: he had drawn a realistic chair already and was sketching the details of the room around it. Perfectly.

"Pass your drawings to the right!"

As Cyrrus took Aera's page, she cringed. Surely, this would serve as evidence that she was stupid. She glanced at him as discreetly as she could, but his deadpan expression was impossible to read.

She took the next drawing and outlined it with caution, as every page she handed to Cyrrus would give him further opportunity to judge her. After a while, she peeked at his page and saw that he had incorporated her mistakes into a masterpiece of Sarode's head blocking a shaded window as she gazed outside from an exemplary chair. Nobody would ever imagine that drawing had been so awful before.

The drawings circulated until Aera's was returned to her. Someone had butchered the window, but Sarode's bun remained precise, as Cyrrus had drawn it. Aera held it up at different angles, admiring the shapely legs of the chair until suddenly, the belltower rang in the distance, disquieting her nerves. She had been mesmerized.

"Class is over!" croaked Sarode.

Cyrrus held his drawing before him and Aera sneaked a glimpse. She saw a cluster of unusual symbols in one corner but, before she could see more, he folded the paper into itself.

"We will not recycle today!" Sarode announced. "On your way out, hand in your drawings for display at the next Unity Festival!"

The children lined up and handed their drawings to Sarode on their way out the door. When she reached for Cyrrus's drawing, he jerked it away, angled it toward his chest and locked into Sarode's eyes.

"The assignment was elementary," he said. "I require a challenge."

Maintaining eye contact with Sarode, he tore his sheet down the middle and crumpled the halves tightly. Then, he marched flagrantly to the recycle bin in the corner of the room and tossed them in. Aera pondered the strange symbols she'd seen. Perhaps he had destroyed the drawing to hide its content, and only pretended otherwise to make a point. Faces watched as Aera eyed the recycle bin, but she couldn't let them intimidate her. She had to see those symbols.

She imagined herself as Vaye, confident and poised, and glided to the bin, where Cyrrus's crumpled drawing lay at the top of the heap. To avert suspicion, she ripped her own page, leaned over gracefully to drop it in, and stealthily retrieved part of Cyrrus's.

"What in Riva's Trees are you doing in the trash?" Doriline called. "Looking for your hair?"

Doriline's herd laughed, but Aera pretended not to notice. Eventually, they moved on. She knelt behind the recycling bin, stuffed the drawing under her belt and made sure her tunic covered it. Finally, she joined her line in the hallway and followed the leader to Music Class. She hoped it would pass quickly, as she could hardly wait to examine the mysterious page.

Once everyone was seated, Instructor Lilese took her place on the piano bench and assaulted the keys. The sound stung Aera's ears and the familiar screech tore through her mind. *Sinë veskento i suínanya më Onórnëan...*

"Have you studied formulas for harmonious chords?" Cyrrus chided Lilese. "The mathematics are as rudimentary as—"

"No talking in music class!" called another instructor.

"No music either," Cyrrus retorted.

49

Some people laughed, but Aera knew Cyrrus was a hypocrite. Everything was a game to him.

Continuing his spectacle, Cyrrus bobbed his head in exaggerated rhythm, and the other kids laughed and copied his movements. Exasperated, Lilese pounded on several piano keys at once. "Children!" she bellowed. "Pay attention!"

Cyrrus got away with everything, and everyone loved him. Aera thought of the drawing under her belt and wanted to burn it. *I'll look at it once, then destroy it,* she promised herself.

After two long hours, class ended and lunch break began. Aera departed from her group, ran into Westside Willows just next to the buildings, and dug Cyrrus's page from under her belt. He had expanded the curve on top to create a wider, more opulent seat, which was ripped down the middle, but the symbols in the corner were undisturbed.[2]

Aera felt a thrill: the characters seemed to belong to a system. Maybe a language. Her thoughts jumped to the voices she heard in her dreams. She didn't know whether the words had meaning or if they were a product of her imagination, but Cyrrus might...

Cyrrus is just a show-off, she scolded herself. It was more likely that he'd crafted a jumble of shapes to pretend he was mysterious. There was no reason to credit him with mystical knowledge or connections to her dreams. She prepared to rip the drawing, but hesitated. In the unlikely event there was a message in there, she would regret destroying it before she could decipher it.

She folded the drawing back into her belt, got food from the Dining Hall and headed back outside. As she ascended the Hill, she saw Cyrrus planted in her spot, leaning against her boulder with legs stretched out and a book in his lap.

You took my spot! Aera's mind screamed. *Where did you come from, anyway?!*

She slogged across the plateau and settled in the grass, seething with annoyance, hating the world. And here was Cyrrus, indulging so peacefully in a book as though the planet of Oreni was designed solely for his pleasure.

Bellows of laughter approached from behind, and Aera spotted two familiar older boys climbing the Hill. One was a giant tower of blubber huffing and puffing up the slope, while the other was healthy and fit, with his shirt tied around his waist, his shapely brown chest on display and his hair carefully coiffed. Not far behind, a flock of girls followed, giggling and shouting in shrill tones. Aera's sanctuary was under invasion.

The fat boy cast his boorish shadow over Cyrrus, who remained decidedly undeterred from reading. "It's time for a rematch," he blustered.

Cyrrus did not respond.

"You afraid I'll kick your skinny butt, brainy boy?"

"I never lose," Cyrrus said. "But I'm reading. Do you know what that is, Hizad?"

"Raisins," Hizad huffed. "Prove it."

Cyrrus closed his book with a sigh. The two positioned themselves in the grass, bellies down and hands clasped, preparing to arm wrestle. Hizad's skin was olive, but dark against the pristine pallor of Cyrrus's, which looked reflective in the sunlight.

Cyrrus was lanky and tall for his age, but Hizad was colossal. Aera imagined Cyrrus stood no chance, but he appeared aloof and confident, showing no sign of apprehension. The shirtless boy angled his pre-teen muscles toward the girls nearby and called, "Samely, Dila! Come watch!"

A pretty girl approached him but, when she noticed Cyrrus, her cheeks turned pink. She swayed demurely and fumbled with her indigo tunic while the other girls positioned themselves around her.

"Look, Dila," Hizad snorted. "I'm gonna *crush* this ghaadi twerp."

"Are you here to flirt or to wrestle?" Cyrrus asked, bored. "I have reading to do. Let's get this over with."

51

"Darse your dirl, flame head," Hizad said. To muscle boy, he commanded, "Codin! Start us off."

Codin knelt, positioned Cyrrus's and Hizad's hands together, and counted, "One, two, three!" Then, he released them.

Hizad and Cyrrus pushed against each other, and the veins on Cyrrus's arms popped visibly while fat Hizad sustained him with ease. In spite of the effort he exuded, Cyrrus remained nonchalant and said coolly, "If I win, I get your cake for the rest of the month."

Hizad's face betrayed panic and Cyrrus took him down in one swift push. "Ghaadi bison breath!" Hizad roared and punched the ground in frustration.

Codin puffed out his chest and raised a brow at Dila beside him. "Watch this," he said. "*I'll* beat him."

"You too, handsome?" goaded Cyrrus.

"Pfft," Codin spat. He flashed a wide grin at Dila, then traded places with Hizad. As the two wrestlers took position, Codin remained smug. His wrist was twice the thickness of Cyrrus's and he didn't seem as distractible as his much stupider friend. Aera wondered how Cyrrus would fare this time.

Hizad counted to three and released them. Both wrestlers watched their hands as they struggled against each other. Then, Cyrrus fixed his eyes casually on Dila, and she blushed uncontrollably, playing right into his stupid game. Codin glanced over at Dila, too, and when he saw her staring at Cyrrus, his confident mask crashed. Instantly, his arm collapsed. Cyrrus had bested them both.

Codin recovered his composure quickly and said to Cyrrus, "Good match."

Cyrrus nodded.

Hizad and Codin ushered the girls away. Although Dila followed, she turned her pretty face to glance at Cyrrus again. This time, Cyrrus showed no sign of interest. Instead, he opened the book and returned his focus to it.

The Hill quieted, and Aera finished her meal at the end of the plateau opposite Cyrrus. Though she forced herself not to look in his direction, she could not wrench her thoughts away from his pristine voice, unearthly face, and those cryptic symbols.

LAWS AND TABOOS

1323 EARLY-AUTUMN

White trees stretched their branches toward the sky, reaching for the moon. Coos, caws and chirps resounded in rhythmic layers, and Aera danced to their song as she scanned the feathery choir. The landscape was drizzled with mockingbirds imitating other species. She spotted a red crest high above, then realized it was not a bird, but Cyrrus's hair. He glared down menacingly as his voice shattered the chorus.

"The music reveals who you are," he declared. "*Laimandil.*"

Mist rose from the ground, and the thicker fog morphed into faces. "No!" Aera screamed. "Leave me alone!"

She thrashed and whipped the faces, but they fragmented and recomposed, multiplying until she was surrounded. Their mouths opened, revealing fangs as they brayed in distorted unison, "*Filén na erë lëoryán assë të yo-fayanta i nalanna hyánië votheldë...*"

The mockingbirds departed in a hurry, leaving behind a forest of bare branches, and the turbulence of their wings dissolved into laughter. Cyrrus posed against the trunk of a tree, relaxed and pleased. His noxious smile made Aera want to run, but she was frozen in place as countless voices screeched, "*Në Laimandil ë i namanya...*"

Aera writhed in pain as the siren sliced through her. "*Sinë veskento i suínanya më Onórnëan—*"

~

"Wake up, Samies!" Officer Onus commanded. "Time for breakfast!"

Aera's ears rang. *Laimandil...* what was that?

"C'mon, little doves! Move your poopies!"

Flashes of white littered Aera's vision as she dragged herself up, miserable and annoyed. Now that music was taken from her, the nightmares had returned. Breakfast passed in a haze of bright light, sticky sweat, and indistinguishable noise. Finally, the bell sounded, and everyone lined up for class.

Instead of heading to the Education Unit, the line leaders took Aera's group northward. They traversed the Raetsek Field, crossed a bridge, and arrived at a triangular compound of three buildings, just like the ones in the Village Field. Once inside, Aera was overcome by the stench of raw fleece and the creaking of machines. Amidst the chorus of rickety wood, her mind screeched: *Sinë veskento i suínanya më Onórnëan.*

She shook herself to attention and surveyed a vast room with bored teenagers cramped behind large devices. Some spun giant wheels of yarn with a crank while others had thread lined up vertically and horizontally inside squares of wood and used their feet to propel the two sections into a crosshatch. Each press on the levers made the devices groan, and the dusty air made everyone cough as Aera's group passed through. The place was dreadful. When the line leaders directed them to a staircase, Aera was relieved.

They made their way to a classroom with four rectangular tables arranged so that everyone was facing each other. Once the group was seated, a long-nosed woman stood to greet them. She projected a smile, though it was obvious she didn't want to be there.

"Welcome to Sewing, Samies!" she announced, raising the pitch of her nasal voice to portray exuberance. "I'm Instructor Rayine, and my fellow instructors are Birov and Balani. You will be spending class and task periods here throughout autumn session, and you will sew your own outfits. Your clothing is the only property you own, and it's your responsibility to care for it."

Squeals filled the room. *Në Laimandil ë i namanya...*

Aera rubbed her temples. Though she enjoyed the idea of owning

54

something, she could not divine any rationale to account for the ear-curdling celebratory ruckus around her. They would undoubtedly be limited by standard fabrics and designs, so the outfits would all be the same.

The Samies continued yelping even as Rayine resumed her speech. "Each of you is allotted two outfits consisting of tunics, pants and undergarments. In addition, everybody is permitted a cloak and a pair of shoes. Your spare clothes will be stored in cubbies in your hut and your dirty clothes may be washed. Use any excess material to create handkerchiefs—" she paused, realizing her voice was being drowned out, and hollered, "Darse your dirl, children! DARSE IT!"

Rayine's voice was grating. Aera's ears rang, and Cyrrus's dream voice lunged through her. *Laimandil.*

He invaded her fantasy forest and spoke the language that haunted her nights. Why did he have to be *everywhere?* Even now, he was seated opposite her, directly in her line of vision, though he was buried in a book, paying no mind to anyone.

"Birov will distribute linens for your undergarments and standard beige wool for your pants and cloaks. You'll need four bundles of wool for your tunics!" Rayine yelled. "Line up in the back to choose your colors!"

Shrieks abounded as Samies exploded from their seats and raced across the room. While they shoved each other in a frenzy, Aera edged to the end of the table to obtain a clear view from the side. Piles of fabric were arranged in rows of colors and, at the far end, white wool reflected sunlight that poured in the window. Nurin wanted her to blend in, but white would stand out. The anti-Samie. The Rebel. She grinned and considered walking across the tabletop to claim it.

The boys dug into the grays and browns without a fuss, but the girls were ruthless. Arms flew everywhere as they screeched bribes and threats, fighting for their desired colors. The fattest girl in the group reached toward the pink fabric, but Doriline grabbed her wrist and said, "You should use dark shades, Gaili. It makes you look slimmer." Gaili stopped in her tracks, looking empty and lost, and Doriline snatched the entire pile, pleased with herself. As she distributed pink wool to her cheering friends, Aera thought, *pig.* Doriline was a selfish jerk, but she sure had nerve.

Fabrics disappeared, yet Aera's treasured whites remained untouched. Once the crowd dispersed, she gathered four portions of white wool. As she headed towards the center table, Instructor Balani grunted, "*Baaad* idea, Samie. White gets *diiirty*."

"Eh-ruh doesn't get dirty!" Doriline chimed. "She's too perfect!"

Perfect. Was that an insult? The herd seemed to think it was funny, but Aera disregarded it and went to her seat. She glanced across the table and saw Cyrrus grinning at his fabrics, folded neatly in two shades of gray. *Boring*, she thought, though she wished she had a second shade too.

Rayine taught needle techniques and told everyone to practice on fabric scraps. Aera stretched her fingers, preparing to sew. Slowly and carefully, she guided the needle back and forth, trying to make every stitch identical. The surrounding chatter faded as Aera developed a continuous motion, sliding the needle through both scraps and pulling it out in circular strokes, following it around and around and around...

"Samie Cyrrus! What in Riva's Trees are you doing with that book!"

Aera dropped the needle. Her rhythm was broken. Instructor Rayine, who had been livid and stiff, now glowered at Cyrrus with sudden animation.

"Reading *The History of Ynas*," Cyrrus said flatly. "I'm deconstructing Riva's exile."

"I'm going to tell Onus to subtract twenty points!" Rayine yelled. "And then, I'm reporting this to the Renstrom!"

"What a delectable proposition!" he exclaimed. "I'd recommend reading *Laws of Ynas* first, before you humiliate yourself at a town meeting."

Rayine's mouth dropped.

Cyrrus added cheerfully, "In fact, I respectfully *request* that you read it, and proffer an informed, fresh challenge. Debates with Nurin and Dinad have devolved into monotony."

"You're nine years old!" Rayine screeched. "Do you seriously think *you* could win a debate against *me*?"

"Since you asked, yes. I have memorized *Laws of Ynas* in its entirety. My reasoning skills are superior, my vocabulary impeccable, my rhetoric manifestly persuasive, and I'm cute. What do you bring?"

The classroom exploded in laughter, and Aera cringed. Apparently, she was the only one who noticed how attention-seeking and conceited he was. The other instructors watched with interest as Rayine pointed her long nose in the air and said, "Forget it. I won't bother reporting you."

"Why not?" Cyrrus goaded. "Don't you want a few extra points?"

Rayine marched to Cyrrus's seat, grabbed his book and said, "Get back to work. I'm returning this to the library, where it belongs."

"The law permits books anywhere inside village grounds," Cyrrus yawned, "but I'll surrender it to you and encourage you to read it. You'll be smarter than all the other instructors."

"We are *all* the same," Rayine retorted.

"Knowledge is a weapon against mediocrity," Cyrrus muttered. His gaze drifted to some distant point and in an unsettling monotone, he declared, "That'll be my maxim when I rule the world."

Blah blah, Aera thought. *I'd die before I'd let you rule me.*

Rayine returned the book to Cyrrus and yelled, "Back to work, Samies!"

Samies. What a farce. No one was the same and Cyrrus never got punished. His 'rhetoric' was only 'manifestly persuasive' because the people he inveigled were idiots.

Aera gripped her needle and shoved it into the fabric, in and out, back and forth. Her temples pounded as chatter infiltrated the room, and screeches invaded her mind. *Në Laimandil ë i namanya. Laimandil.*

Drown it out with music, she thought. She tried to imagine the most recent song she was writing but could barely recall the opening strains. Her fingers were stiff; music eluded her. She needed to play to keep her fingers nimble. Yet, it was forbidden.

While she was slandered for harmless enjoyment, Cyrrus did whatever he pleased. He insisted his offenses were 'legal' and claimed he'd memorized *Laws of Ynas*. Was that true? Cyrrus was right: for him, knowledge *was* a weapon.

Cyrrus had told Doriline the book was in the Library on the top floor of the Administration Unit. Aera resolved to find it and read the laws about music.

When lunch break came, Aera ate quickly and headed to the Administration Unit, which comprised one of three branches of the triangular DPD Building complex. She was not surprised that the inte-

57

rior resembled the DPD Lounge with its carpeted hallways, plentiful torches, and ornate wooden plaques. The layout, on the other hand, was identical to the Education Unit: simple long hallways, rows of doors, and a staircase at one end.

On her way upstairs, she passed a platoon of officers, and all made it a point to glare at her. She pictured Cyrus strutting right past them and proceeded onward, as he might, straight to the top floor. One by one, she read the plaques on each door until she reached the end of the hall and found the one marked 'Library.'

The chamber was dusty, cramped and dimly lit, with shadowy bookshelves on the walls. An elderly woman safeguarded a desk in the center of the room and a young officer read by candlelight at a small table. Aera observed the somber atmosphere before approaching the attendant and forcing out the words, "Where can I find *Laws of Ynas?*"

"Why would a nice young girl want to read about laws?" asked the old lady. "Don't you have friends, child?"

Friends? Why did it matter? Aera already wanted to leave. She mustered a polite tone and repeated, "Where can I find *Laws of Ynas?*"

The lady exaggerated a sigh, reached under the desk and pulled out a tome so large and heavy, it made her bony hand shake. Aera stood on her toes and reached over the desktop to steady it, but the old lady afforded her no gratitude. While the attendant flipped through the tome and leaned over it with a magnifying glass, Aera sneaked a peak. It was an index for the library.

After an eternity, the old lady found what she was looking for. "*Laws of Ynas,*" she croaked. "You can't take that book out of the library."

"Can I read it... in the library?"

The lady glared disapprovingly and said nothing. Aera felt uneasy, but reminded herself: *tabooed, not illegal.* Gently, she repeated: "Where can I find it?"

The old lady pointed dismissively to some shelves and grumbled, "Twenty-three."

Aera spotted numbers along each shelf and noted that they were out of order. When she found shelf twenty-three, she pulled some out to read the titles. *History of Ynas. Agriculture over the Ages. The Building of the Fence.* After several more, she discovered *Laws of Ynas* written on the front of a thick, canvas-encased tome. Proud of herself, she slid the giant book from the shelf and lugged it to a nearby table.

The inside pages were yellowed and jammed with minute handwriting. Carets, additions, and cross-outs abounded while margins overflowed with amendments, displaying an extensive history of revision. The laws seemed arbitrary and fickle.

Aera searched the index and spotted a singular annotation for 'music.' There, she located a page crowded with alterations, author's names, and dates going back hundreds of years.

...THIRD-GENERATION INFANTS WILL BE ADMINISTERED HERBS TO PREVENT FUTURE FERTILITY. ONCE THE PROCEDURE IS COMPLETED, IT IS FORBIDDEN FOR NURSES TO DISCUSS WHO IS FERTILE, EXCEPT WITH THE RENSTROM. RECORDS WILL BE MAINTAINED IN THE CENTRAL VAULT.

- AFTER THE WEENING PERIOD, THE PRODUCT WILL BE SEPARATED FROM THE DESIGNATED CHILD BEARER AND TRANSFERRED TO THE NURSERY IN THE MEDICAL UNIT. ORIGINATION RECORDS WILL BE SECURED IN THE CENTRAL VAULT UNDER THE AUSPICES OF THE RENSTROM.

- ALL INFANTS WILL BE RAISED AND HOUSED IN THE INFANT QUARTERS NURSERY. WHEN THE NURSERY REGISTER NUMBERS SIXTY CHILDREN, THEY WILL BE ASSIGNED THE DESIGNATION OF FIVE YEARS AND GROUPED INTO AN AGE COHORT KNOWN AS THE 5-6 GROUP. CHILDREN IN A COHORT WILL CELEBRATE THE SAME BIRTHDAY. NO CHILD ABOVE THE AGE OF FOUR WILL BE PERMITTED TO JOIN THE COMMUNE.

She reread the last line. *No child above the age of four will be permitted to join the commune.* This meant children came to Ynas from outside. Doriline had asked Cyrus: *Where did you come from, anyway?* Did Doriline know something Aera didn't?

She tried to remember life before the Children's Hut and strained to picture something—what kind of room she woke up in, a face she had seen, some specific event—but all she could recall was echoes, creaks and voices, the same noise that followed her everywhere. Doriline tracked the social terrain fanatically, but could she really have remembered Cyrrus coming to Ynas before age four? Aera could not even be certain that she, herself, had spent her earliest years in Ynas, but if she'd been somewhere else, wouldn't she have memories outside the commune? Her past was a missing puzzle piece.

The white dream forest seemed familiar and more real to her than Ynas. Could that be a memory from somewhere else, maybe from where she was born? She struggled to recall people or experiences, but nothing came besides the fog and birds in her nightmares. How hard should it be to remember being four? She was only five when she met Vaye, and it was easy to recall their early encounters. Was that the first significant event in her life? If so, where did the scar on her stomach come from?

Nothing made sense. Aera continued reading.

- AT ELEVEN, THEY WILL TRANSFER TO THE JUNIOR HUT. AT FIFTEEN, THEY WILL TRANSFER TO THE ADOLESCENT HUT UNTIL THEIR TWENTY-FIFTH BIRTHDAY. THEY WILL THEN RESIDE IN DESIGNATED LIVING QUARTERS IN AN ADULT HUT IN ACCORDANCE WITH THEIR TRAINING FOR THEIR ASSIGNED OCCUPATION.

   - CHILDREN UNDER FIFTEEN WILL REMAIN IN THEIR ASSIGNED HUTS FROM CURFEW UNTIL BREAKFAST UNLESS ACCOMPANIED BY AN ADULT. CHILDREN UNDER ELEVEN ARE REQUIRED TO REMAIN ON VILLAGE GROUNDS AND TO PARTICIPATE IN UNITY FESTIVAL UNLESS ACCOMPANIED BY AN ADULT.

This meant that when Aera turned eleven, it would be legal to visit Vaye during time off. Her group would soon turn ten; eleven was another year away. She hoped she could endure the wait.

VILLAGE BOUNDARIES ARE THE BORDER OF SOUTHSIDE FOREST BESIDE THE SLEEPING HUTS IN THE SOUTH; THE TREES BEYOND THE TRACK IN THE EAST; THE TREE-LINE BEYOND THE PATHS IN WESTSIDE WILLOWS IN THE WEST; AND AT THE PATHS BEYOND THE BARNS IN THE NORTH. IN ORDER TO ENSURE THAT ALL INDIVIDUALS ARE SECURE AND APPROPRIATELY MONITORED BY DPD AUTHORITIES, FAILURE TO ATTEND MANDATORY CLASSES AND TASKS WILL BE REPORTED TO THE DPD.

- EDUCATION WILL COMMENCE AT AGE FIVE. THE RENSTROM WILL ASSIGN SELECTED ADULTS TO TEACH ESSENTIAL SKILLS TO CHILDREN UNTIL AGE THIRTEEN IN THE FOLLOWING SUBJECT AREAS: HISTORY, LANGUAGE, NUMBERS, MUSIC, AND ART. HISTORY CLASS WILL INCLUDE HISTORY OF YNAS, ANIMAL STUDIES, AND WORLD HISTORY. LANGUAGE CLASS WILL INCLUDE READING AND WRITING IN SYRDIAN. ALTERNATE LANGUAGES ARE NOT PERMITTED TO BE TAUGHT, READ, OR SPOKEN ANYWHERE IN YNAS.

Alternate languages did exist, but not in Ynas. Aera thought of the drawing tucked under her belt. If Cyrrus came from somewhere outside, he might have learned another language. Could someone learn how to write before age four?

She continued reading.

NUMBERS CLASS WILL INCLUDE ADDITION, SUBTRACTION, MULTIPLICATION AND DIVISION. ART CLASS WILL INCLUDE GROUP DRAWINGS. MUSIC CLASS WILL INCLUDE GROUP PERFORMANCES. GROUP WORKS OF MUSIC AND ART MAY BE PERFORMED OR DISPLAYED AT UNITY FESTIVAL. INDIVIDUAL CREATIVE WORKS ARE NOT PERMITTED TO BE DISPLAYED OR PERFORMED AT ANY TIME IN YNAS.

- SELECTED ADULTS WILL TEACH AND MONITOR TASKS. THESE INCLUDE COOKING, CLEANING, SEWING, CONSTRUCTION, CROP MAINTENANCE, ANIMAL CARE, SOAP MANUFACTURE, AND OTHER CURRICULA DESIGNATED BY THE BRASS OF EDUCATION IN CONJUNCTION WITH...

The law forbid performing and displaying individual work, but not playing alone. Aera read it again: *children under eleven are required to remain on village grounds and to participate in Unity Festival unless accompanied by an adult.* Nurin thought Aera had played piano alone in the Music Room—which was in the Education Unit, located in the center of the village.

Tabooed, not illegal, Aera thought. She had violated no laws that Nurin knew about and the punishment he'd administered was arbitrary. Her cheeks flushed with rage as she concluded: *He cut my hair simply because he wanted to.*

Aera was more composed now that she knew things would change when she turned eleven. She found herself fantasizing about music even while executing meticulous stitches in sewing class. Her hands fell into rhythm and the prospect of new clothes became increasingly enticing. Two weeks before winter, she completed her outfit.

Though most of the ensemble was uniform beige, the fit was designed specifically for her, and the white tunics added personal flavor. She was excited to try everything on, but the instructors ordered the children to wait for everyone to finish...

"Samie Cyrrus! Put your clothes back on!"

Across the table, Cyrrus was shirtless and stretching behind his seat. As everyone stared at him, he slipped into his new tunic. It was dark grey with a low-cut V-neck, and the collar and edges of the sleeves revealed a slim line of silver folded over in an elegant dash. The fit and stitching were impeccable.

"Take that off!" Rayine ordered, to no avail. In response, Cyrrus removed his pants and underwear, unconcerned that his tunic barely reached the top of his thighs.

"The other kids haven't finished yet!"

Cyrrus pulled on his new underwear, followed by fitted pants, and adjusted himself. Satisfied with his superior look, he assumed a haughty posture and projected his town-meeting voice. "Let us have a vote. All students who want to wear your clothes as soon as you finish, raise your hand."

Hands shot up in the air. Aera wanted to ignore his drama, but that would make too much of a statement. She didn't want him to think she cared enough about him to ignore him. Reluctantly, she raised her hand.

"All students who want everyone to wait, raise your hand," he said firmly.

Everyone lowered their hands, and none rose.

The three instructors huddled in the back of the room to discuss the rebellion of the class, and Aera waited impatiently. After an eternity, Rayine announced, "Once you finish, you may change into your new clothes. Leave the old ones with me."

A few people disrobed. Aera turned her back to them and changed. Everything was fitted and comfortable. As she folded her old clothes and pulled Cyrus's drawing from under her belt loop, it occurred to her that she now had pockets in her cloak. A perfect place to keep it.

Her tunic was flashy, brighter than the others. *No one can overlook me now*, she thought. She adjusted it, preparing for any reaction, and turned. Doriline noticed immediately, but before she could call out an insult, Aera shot her a smile. Doriline's face sank, and she returned her focus to her pink-clad courtiers. Though they gloated over their new trademark, Aera was satisfied that her stitches were neater and her fit tighter. They would certainly be jealous.

On the way to dinner, Aera admired her white sleeves and envisioned herself galloping through the mist in her childhood dreamscape. She floated to the back of the food line and spotted Cyrus up ahead, more pristine than ever, chattering animatedly with a book tucked under his arm. Gaili nodded along, but her awestruck, dumbfounded expression suggested she was unable to comprehend anything he said. Cyrus didn't notice because he so enjoyed listening to himself.

By the time Cyrus filled his tray, his enthralled admirers were laughing at his jokes and vying for his attention, but he abandoned them and sailed out the door alone. He didn't care about them, yet they loved him because he was the closest thing to freedom they had ever seen. Everybody else was a trained slave, walking the same paths, talking the same talk, thinking the same thoughts. Aera broke rules in secret, but Cyrus made rebellion into an artform.

Cyrus not only preached rebellion but embodied it. He spent his leisure time memorizing laws, attending town meetings, and learning anything he could to loosen his shackles and inspire others. Although Aera craved the same liberties, she never fought for them. Instead, she sulked to herself and allowed Ynas to defeat her.

Late that night, Aera lay awake, staring at the ceiling as music flooded her mind. Moonlight floated in through a window in the back of the sleeping chamber, teasing her with thoughts of freedom. Sleep was unimaginable. She just had to see Vaye. Laws and taboos did not stop Cyrus. Aera didn't need to let them stop her.

Energized by her thoughts, she leapt up. Carefully, she tiptoed toward the window, avoiding the floorboards she knew would squeak, feeling more assurance with each quiet step. She was a predator, stalking the window deftly, pirouetting between sleepers who had never dared to chase a dream.

As she approached the windowsill, she saw it was shoulder-high and wondered whether she could pull herself up. Her hands were strong from playing the piano and she didn't weigh much. She gripped the ledge tightly, balanced her feet on ruts in the wall, and hoisted her legs up to the windowsill. As she pushed the window open, it squeaked, and she froze in place to observe the sleepers. The arhythmic convulsions of their snores and breathing remained unchanged.

She crawled outside to a narrow ledge and closed the window most of the way, leaving it open a crack so she could reenter later. There was a short drop to the ground, but she needed to stay quiet and didn't want to jump. Instead, she faced the window, gripped the sill, and slid down. On the way, the ledge caught her shirt and scuffed her stomach. The pain gave her a jolt.

Quickly, she darted across the grass and hid in the shadows at the edge of Southside Forest. To make sure she was alone, she scanned the Sleeping Hut Field and the Hill beyond, which led to the village. Over the hilltop, the half-moon emitted a warm glow that enveloped both its own body and that of a bright star that twinkled at its side.

Aera usually took meals on that hill near the Samies, but now she was free and unfettered. She extended her arms and spun in circles until she stumbled to her knees in dizziness and giggled to the night sky. Each star waxed and waned, breathing with its own rhythm.

The twinkling scape disappeared behind treetops as she entered the forest and immersed herself in the buzz of insects and the crisp aroma of dried autumn leaves. As she maneuvered through the trees, a cat yowled and an owl hooted. She spotted the owl on a low branch, its feathers glistening in the moonlight.

"Whooooo!" Aera called back to the owl.

"Wh-wh-who," it responded. "Wh-wh-who."

Aera laughed and continued onward. Her vision adjusted easily to the darkness, and her white sleeves glowed with moon sheen. She was a creature of the night, at one with the wildlife. This was where she belonged.

As she approached the grove, the familiar gurgle of the brook mixed with a musical aria of circling trebles. Candlelight illuminated the scene in the cottage window, of Vaye's silhouette swaying before the piano's majestic vault. Just as Aera reached the door, the music stopped and the air filled with the most infectious laughter she had ever heard. One vocal tone sounded like Vaye's, but there was a second that Aera didn't recognize. Vaye had a guest!

Vaye was not expecting Aera after curfew, and she wanted to keep their acquaintance secret. It wasn't safe to knock. Cautiously, Aera knelt beside the nearest window, cupped her hands, and leaned to see inside. Vaye was on the piano bench, her vibrant curls spilling down from a wide crown of braids, with her back to Aera. She faced another woman sitting by the fireplace who had a silvery light on her forehead, just like the girl in Vaye's painting. Aera had presumed that girl was fantastical. She'd never imagined forehead lights could be real.

She rubbed her eyes and looked at the stranger again. Aside from the astonishing light and her shimmering aura, her features were those of a flesh and blood woman. A sleek obsidian mane cascaded to her hips. She wore a black leather dress with matching boots, all decorated in complex strings. With such an exotic presentation, she couldn't possibly have been from Ynas.

Vaye glided into the kitchen, and the foreigner turned toward the window, shining her forehead-light directly on Aera. A warm feeling swept through Aera's body as she absorbed the soft sheen. Could the woman see her? Would it matter if she did? Black eyes and bold features transfixed Aera in place. Beyond the silvery glow, barely visible against her bronze skin, the edges of the woman's face were marked with the designs of a panther.

Slowly and lithely, the woman rose, revealing a powerful body whose assets were punctuated by her outfit. The strings on her gown wound through loopholes that created a crosshatch over her bosom, and the skirt had a V-shaped front and back which displayed strong thighs. As she moved about the cottage, her muscular limbs were fierce and fluid as flame. The panther markings matched her personality. She was magnificent and mighty, with black eyes scouring the world like a huntress.

Aera wondered if she herself had any such parallel to an animal. She wanted to be free like a bird, but she wasn't. If only she could break out of her cage and run off to the outside world, she might discover who she was.

Take me with you, Aera thought. Panther Woman smiled in her direction as though she could hear her.

Vaye returned with a basket hanging on her arm and said something that Aera couldn't make out. Panther Woman responded joyfully, then opened a satchel on her shoulder as Vaye removed some vials from her basket and placed them inside. As the two filled the bag, laughter bounced through the cottage. Aera wished she were in there with them.

The two headed toward the door, and Aera inched around the side of the cottage to snoop as they emerged. Panther Woman's voice was robust and seemed to echo from another world.

"Hentilena o Rosmiendëavi erë Mirnanolmán niskani.[1]*"*

And Vaye's familiar voice replied, *"Yavi nankesi yovainón, lana kanondi no Tarinna Aldundi, Varvenavel hyanta.*[2]*"*

Though Aera didn't understand the words, the tender tone brought tears to her eyes. Their kinship was palpably natural and caring, unlike any relationship she'd witnessed before. The two exchanged hugs and Panther Woman said, *"Nerilyane,*[3] *Vaye."*

A wisp of black floated past the cottage as Panther Woman disappeared. Though her footfalls made no sound, Aera spotted the glow from her forehead reflecting the light of the moon. The luminescence revealed black eyes before the umbra of the forest swallowed them.

Leaves rustled as a breeze gathered momentum and spread a bouquet of smoke. Between shadows of distant trees, Aera spotted a flicker of torchlight that briefly illuminated a cloaked figure riding a black feline. She wondered if it was a panther and searched the nightscape. Deeper in the forest, embers rose in interwoven spirals and then dissipated.

Suddenly, a vicious gust of air whipped debris across Aera's face. She rubbed her eyes and shielded them, determined to see more. Somewhere within the howling hiss of the wind, she heard Panther Woman's voice calling: *"Nerilyanë, Nóssië."*

Fire-smoke thickened in the shadows beneath the trees, forming an impenetrable veil. As the starlit sky surrendered to black, Aera could no longer distinguish shadow from moonlight. Darkness consumed her.

$$\sim$$

"Let's go, Samies! Time to do your duty!"

Aera awakened to a throbbing headache and frozen cheeks. She pulled her blanket snug around her and rubbed her eyes.

"Why's it so ghaadi *cold?*" Doriline yelped. "Did someone open the window?"

Aera looked over: the window was half open. Had she forgotten to close it when she came back in? She tried to remember but couldn't recall the journey back. Quickly, she reviewed the night in her mind: she'd climbed out the window, spied at the cottage, watched Panther Woman paint the forest with bursts of flame, and then... nothing. What had happened after that? How had Aera gotten back to the hut?

"Mehh," Officer Onus snorted. He waddled to the window, pushed it shut and called, "Get a move on, flower blossoms!"

Aera strained to recall more but came up blank. Perhaps Panther Woman had bewitched her and stolen her memory...

"Samie Eh-ruh!" Onus barked. "Move!"

Aera snapped up and dressed herself nervously. If anyone discovered she had sneaked out, she would have to face Renstrom Nurin again. And then what? An even shorter haircut? Playing music alone was tabooed, but sneaking out after curfew was illegal.

As the group lined up by the door, Doriline waited for her coterie to gather. Aera lurked nearby, curious what they would say. The usual followers, Novi and Keole, rushed to Doriline's side and whispered in her ears. Aera wondered if they were talking about her and whether they had seen anything last night.

The three joined the line as it filed out, and Aera meandered along behind them, listening discreetly. They looked like a drove of piglets, with all of their tunics baby pink and sloppily cut.

"So," Doriline said, calling her friends to attention. "*Who* in Riva's Trees would open the window?"

"Some farkus sleep-walking," Keole suggested.

"*I* think it was a prank," Novi said, and looked at Doriline for approval.

"A prank by some farkus," Doriline said. "Since it's not funny *at all*."

"Well," Novi grinned, "The biggest farkus is Eh-ruh, obviously."

Without missing a beat, Keole sneered, "She's *way* too short to reach the window."

Short, but clever, Aera grinned to herself. Two yellow-clad girls joined the cluster and the topic changed.

"Did you see Olleroc fall in the mud?"

"Olleroc is *such* a farkus."

Though the five bleated on throughout the walk and the wait in the Dining Hall line, none mentioned Aera or the window again. She was both relieved and confused. What possibly might have happened last night, and why hadn't anyone noticed? She resolved to return to the cottage after curfew and find out.

The getaway was easier that night, as she knew her way around the windowsill. When she arrived at the cottage, Vaye opened the door as though expecting her. Silver ringlets poured down under the same crown of braids from the previous night, and she wore the same suede band across her forehead, decorated in olivine gems. Aera wondered what was beneath it.

"Aera," Vaye smiled. "You are full of surprises."

Aera smiled, confused.

"You haven't visited in some time," Vaye said tenderly. "That's one surprise. The other is your hair and white blouse. You look lovely."

Considering Vaye had greeted her so readily, Aera found it hard to believe her arrival was a surprise. She wondered whether Vaye hadn't seen her the previous night. Panther Woman clearly had noticed her.

Vaye gestured invitingly toward the piano and headed into the kitchen. Aera sat on the bench, took in the scent of burning logs, and began to play. The emotion of the music eluded her, as she was distracted by thoughts about Panther Woman.

Vaye approached the piano and Aera was eager to engage. She stopped playing and asked, "Who was here last night?"

"Play along," Vaye said, and tapped a rhythm on the deck of the piano.

Aera wondered why Vaye had ignored her question. "I came by last night," she persisted. "I wanted to see you, but you had a guest. She had panther markings on her face and a light on her forehead..." she gestured toward the painting and concluded, "...like that one."

"Perhaps you were dreaming."

Aera hadn't considered that. She thought for a moment, but then remembered, "I saw your braids."

"Dreams often overlap with reality," Vaye said casually. "*One* two three, *one* two three..."

Vaye's response was perplexing. Could it be true? Aera remembered cutting herself on the windowsill and slipped her hand under her shirt to feel around for any evidence. Beside her belly scar, there was a rough spot on her skin, right where the ledge had scraped her. No matter what Vaye said, reality was right there.

Vaye tapped on the lid of the piano and waited with a placid smile. Aera resumed playing, but her hands shook. Vaye was lying to her.

"You're losing rhythm," Vaye said. "Try to focus."

Aera wanted to explode, but there was nothing to say. Vaye didn't owe her any answers. For months, Aera had been waiting to return to the cottage, and Vaye had welcomed her there kindly. She didn't want to ruin their night or appear ungrateful.

She concentrated on Vaye's tapping. *One* two three, *one* two three. This was easy. She played a chord and broke it into two parts, each landing on the *one*.

"Good. Now, *one* two, *one* two, *one* two."

Aera followed with another broken chord.

"Excellent," Vaye said. "Now, we combine them. You'll be playing five counts in total, but I want you to count it this way: *One* two three, *one* two. *One* two three, *one* two."

Vaye retrieved a wooden cylinder with animal hide stretched tightly across the surface. Leather thongs wound intricately around the wood, holding the skin in place. She sat down by the fire with the object between her knees and tapped the rhythm. The instrument produced numerous pitches and overtones corresponding to the angle and force of Vaye's strikes, so some beats were hollow groans and others, dry and snappy. Aera could have listened to its undulations all night, but she was curious how it would complement the piano.

She resumed playing and locked into rhythm with Vaye's thrusts

69

against the drum. The two moved together, following each other's dynamics, working off one another with subtle syncopation. Aera's body swayed along with the beat, falling into the song. Vaye held the rhythm, allowing Aera more freedom.

Music consumed them for hours until Aera was exhausted, and the flow escaped. After a few noticeable blunders, the two laughed and stopped playing. Aera's mind jumped to Panther Woman again. The rhythm was so mesmerizing that she'd nearly forgotten Vaye's lie.

"If you wish, I'll teach you some ancient wisdom," Vaye said. "But you must promise to keep it secret."

Aera wondered why Vaye was making this offer now. Was she compensating for the deception? Did she realize how much it had upset Aera? Although Vaye was being devious, her proposition was unexpected and provocative. Aera nodded and said, "I promise."

"Have a seat by the fireplace," Vaye said, and disappeared under the archway.

Aera approached the painting on the wall and examined the white-haired girl. Her eyes were pitch black, but her forehead-light was soft, just like Panther Woman's. The setting was dusky with snow on the ground and stars in the sky, and the girl was wrapped in a fuzzy animal hide. Though she was barely older than Aera, her expression was severe.

Vaye returned carrying a clay pot. As she set it on the table near the fireplace, Aera gestured to the painting and asked, "Who is she?"

"Art is a mirror. It reveals your own reflection."

Vague, Aera thought, but she got the point: she would receive no answers.

"Inside the pot, there's a paste," Vaye said. "Massage a dollop into your scalp, then work it through your hair. Take this comb."

Aera gave up on her inquiry and went to the table. She took some paste, rubbed it into her mane and combed it through, feeling uneasy as her hair adopted its strong pine-like scent and thick texture.

"You may keep the comb, and I'll leave the paste here," Vaye offered as she placed the pot on the mantle. "If you comb and use the paste often, your hair will grow back faster and stronger."

Though Aera appreciated the gesture, she was embarrassed to walk around smelling like weird plants and was unsure what to say.

"Let's go outside," Vaye said with a smile. "You can wash it out."

Relieved, Aera followed Vaye out to the brook, where she cleaned the gunk from her hair. Once she finished, her eyes went to the luminous half-moon and the brilliant star twinkling rhythmically at its side.

"The moon and the evening star are lovers," Vaye said. "Together for eternity."

"Not always," Aera pointed out. "Sometimes the moon disappears."

"That's when the star shines most brightly. When the moon is beside him in full glory, he fades into her light."

"Then why does he love her?"

"Nature balances itself. When she gives less light, he gives more."

Aera nodded, realizing she knew nothing about love.

"To reach your potential as a companion or a musician, you must find balance," Vaye said. "Press your fingertips together like I taught you, dear."

Excited to show Vaye that she'd built up her strength, Aera made the familiar cage with her hands. Vaye tried to push down each knuckle and Aera kept them firm. But when Vaye came to her pinkies, she couldn't resist the pressure.

"You have practiced, and it shows," Vaye said. "Now, let's try something else. Spread your feet apart, even with your shoulders, and breathe from your belly."

Aera positioned her feet, and Vaye placed a hand on her stomach. Slowly, Aera breathed in, filling her belly so Vaye would feel it inflating. As she exhaled, Vaye withdrew her hand and smiled.

"Keep your knees flexible and concentrate on the air passing in and out of your body," she said, then paused, allowing Aera a moment to adjust. "Feel the rhythm of your lungs as they fill and empty again. Enjoy the sensation in your stomach as it swells and retracts."

Aera paid attention to her body, following the movement of her breath. *In, out.* Her shoulders dropped as she exhaled, and her tension melted away. She looked up at the lovers in the sky and imagined the star resenting the moon, who overpowered him and commanded more attention. As she considered this, she realized she'd been distracted from the exercise. She wondered what the purpose was.

"You can choose to control or ignore your breath," Vaye said. "It is your anchor, always with you, and it is wise to make it your ally."

Ally... interesting. Aera had never thought of breath that way.

"It's natural to breathe through your chest when you feel tense, but it limits the air you take in and forces your heart to work harder. If you practice breathing from your belly, it will become habitual and you'll be healthier."

Aera felt her stomach inflate and deflate as Vaye spoke. She wondered whether she breathed that way when she wasn't focused on it.

"Watch once, then follow along," Vaye said. "This will align your body."

Vaye extended her arms out to each side and raised them slowly until they came together over her head, fingers pointing to the sky. She leaned her neck back as though surrendering to the night, then eased her arms downward, keeping her palms together and bending her elbows outward, finally stopping in front of her chest. Aera repeated the exercise alongside Vaye, mirroring her grace.

"Now," Vaye said, "press your fingertips together again, but this time, extend your elbows out and position your feet apart, with flexible knees. Feel the tension in your upper arms, in your back, and behind your thighs."

Aera paid attention to those muscles as she situated her fingers into a cage. Vaye tried to bend Aera's pinky knuckles but, this time, Aera breathed deeply, held herself sturdy, and retained her strength with ease. She felt a thrill as she realized Vaye's lesson had made an impact.

"When you play piano, you must balance your weight against the instrument," Vaye said. "If you isolate your fingers instead of playing with your whole body, you aren't giving the piano your full self."

Aera absorbed this idea. It was natural for her to balance her weight when she sneaked out the window, but when she played piano, she focused on her hands alone. Paying attention to her body might allow her more force.

"Try this," Vaye offered. She put her palms together again with her elbows pointing out, then lifted one leg and rested her bare foot against her inner thigh. Aera kicked off her shoes and stood on one foot, but wobbled about while Vaye remained steady.

"If you feel discomfort anywhere, focus on that area and breathe into it," Vaye offered. "Imagine your muscles filling with air as your stomach inflates."

Aera took a deep breath and focused on her hips, imagining the air filling them up as she realigned. Then she tried again, and this time did not fall.

"If you practice often, it will soon come naturally," Vaye said. "When you focus on breathing, you align your mind with your body. Your breath gives you power."

Your breath gives you power. Aera liked the sound of that.

"Balance and breath are basic components of the ancient art of Kra," Vaye said. "As long as you keep it between us, I'll teach you more."

'Ancient art of Kra' sounded mysterious and noble. Aera felt important. She wondered where it came from and suspected Panther Woman would know. Kra was probably illegal, unless it was too obscure to be in the book of Laws—in which case, it might be 'taboo.'

Aera asserted, "I promise."

"Good," Vaye grinned. "Next lesson will be handstands to help your hair grow faster. I look forward to it, whenever you choose to come."

Aera slid into her shoes and frolicked away, smiling into the breeze. Before entering the forest, she turned once more toward Vaye, who was still balanced with one leg folded against the other as her silver braids radiated in the moonlight. Aera wanted to be powerful like Vaye and her magical friend. She wondered how much Kra might transform her.

Seasons passed in a flurry of adventures at the cottage and naps during breaks. Aera never forgot Panther Woman but knew Vaye would never answer her questions. Music and Kra enlivened Aera's world as Vaye made each visit more fun than the last. They took turns accompanying each other on drums, braided each other's hair, and built up an exciting array of techniques in balancing, climbing and cartwheels. As Aera incorporated breathing exercises to relieve tension and anxiety, daily duties became more tolerable.

Still, no matter how deeply Aera breathed, Cyrrus continued to rattle her nerves—especially after his voice changed during their tenth year. While the crisp consonants and brisk cadences remained, the impact of each word was accentuated by a jarring depth that cut through all other sound and adhered to Aera's mind. Over time, he spoke less, but his ideas became more insightful and his manner annoyingly compelling. Aera had to work harder than ever to pretend to ignore him.

As their eleventh birthday approached, everyone else looked increasingly awkward, but Cyrrus was striking and seemed older. His angular cheekbones created a hollow that made his countenance intense while razor-sharp eyes and dramatic coloring effected a gravity beyond his years. Though his frame remained lanky, his shoulders widened, and he stood taller than most.

His maturity was a source of amusement for others, but Aera suspected there was more to it. She wondered if he'd come from somewhere else and had been assigned to the wrong Age Group. Between Cyrrus's mien, Panther Woman's forehead and Vaye's countless secrets, it was becoming apparent there was more to Ynas than Samies and routines. On the outside, Aera marched along to the commune's rhythm, but on the inside, she was out of synch... and she knew she was not alone.

PARË NË SULË

1325 EARLY-WINTER

"Wake up, flower blossoms! Collect your belongings! We're moving to Junior Hut!"

Chatter exploded as everyone raced to ready themselves, pushing and shoving to obtain ideal sleeping spots in their new dorm. Aera dressed slowly to avoid the ruckus and glanced at the window she had slipped through so many times. She hoped Junior Hut would provide such an escape, though it might not matter. Now that she was eleven, it was legal to visit Vaye during breaks.

She took her place in line, and the group followed Onus across the Sleeping Hut Field. As they approached Junior Hut, Aera noted it was smaller than the Children's Hut and wondered how everyone could possibly fit inside. They entered an open chamber with an iron railing surrounding a wide, descending stone staircase. Onus pointed to two wooden doors in the rear of the room and said, "Latrines are in there, bedrooms downstairs."

He led the children down the stairs into an underground cavern with an ancient, metallic smell. There was a dark corridor with doors on one side and on the opposite, a string of torches whose light danced about the stone walls and arched ceiling. Channels and ruts in the wall shifted and expanded in the firelight. As Aera watched them swell and retract, she felt like she'd entered a lost world.

Onus approached a door, thrust it open and declared, "Boys in here!" The boys veered leftward toward their new room. Aera suspected they were too deep underground to have windows and waited in anticipation as Onus headed back toward the crowd at the stairwell.

Doriline and her friends shoved their way ahead, eager to race into their quarters and claim their preferred campsite. Onus passed the group, opened a door and said, "Girls here."

With Doriline in the lead, the cluster banged into each other as they swarmed into the room. Aera made her way inside. There were no windows. The dormitory was long and narrow, with two rows of mats along the stone walls and a path between them. Each wall contained a concavity, creating a shelf or seat that extended along both sides of the room, and the girls raced to pile clothes onto it and mark their territory. Doriline planted herself in the back left corner, surrounded by her minions, and Aera settled in the front right corner, as far from them as the space allowed. As she laid her clothes on the shelf, Gaili selected the mat beside hers, and Aera was relieved. Gaili was gigantic and snored loudly, but never participated in squealing gossip rituals.

Once settled, Aera left the room and examined the corridor. The door to the girls' chamber was the last of four, followed by a long, barren wall and an open space around a bend, which led to another hallway. Though curious to check for windows, she didn't want others to see her snooping around, and instead headed back upstairs. Before leaving, she checked the lavatories for an escape route, but discovered that the windows were caged in iron bars.

When she made her way outside, Officer Onus was gone. The Samies roamed free, walking about without restriction, but all headed into the growing mass of people on the Hill, apparently unaware or unconcerned that they were no longer required to attend Unity Festival. Aera felt a thrill as she slipped into Southside Forest in the open without a care. Her free time was now her own.

The insect choir was softer than what Aera had been accustomed to at night, and the leafless trees looked desolate without shadows and stars to populate the vast openness between them. She hurried along, eager to escape the cold and to surprise Vaye with a daytime visit. She soon reached the grove.

The cottage was quiet, with no firelight visible. But the upstairs curtains were open, which meant Vaye was awake. Aera ventured inside and saw a familiar brown cat warming itself in a patch of sunlight. Vaye, however, was nowhere to be seen. As Aera slid onto the piano bench, her eyes landed on a book that dominated the music rack. A series of symbols were written in black ink on the cover.[1]

Aera stared at the shapes, amazed. They resembled the ones from Cyrrus's old drawing. She withdrew the now worn paper from her pocket and examined it alongside the book. Some of the characters were identical.

She opened the book. The first page contained symbols to match the ones on the cover. They were unlike any she had seen before... except on Cyrrus's drawing. The characters were precisely the same.

It must have been a foreign language. Perhaps it was the one Vaye had spoken with Panther Woman, or maybe the one Aera heard in her dreams. She flipped through a few more pages that were covered with drawings and patterns between the characters. A circle of geometric shapes drew her in.

Aera enjoyed the symmetry and wondered what the shapes represented. It seemed likely that the surrounding text would explain it, if only she could decipher it...

"Good morning, dear."

Aera was startled to see Vaye near the kitchen, carrying a bucket of water. Somehow, she'd passed right by without making a sound.

"Nice to see you here so early," Vaye said. "What's in your hand?"

Aera's cheeks flushed: it was Cyrrus's drawing. Before she could conjure a response, Vaye asked, "Is that a love note?"

What? *Love note?* Cyrrus had never even spoken to her, and anyway, how could she possibly love him? He was arrogant and vain and obnoxious and... and...

The drawing contained nothing except a chair and characters Aera couldn't read. She wanted to show it to Vaye to prove it wasn't a love note but, as she moved to unfold it, her hand froze in place. How would she explain carrying it around?

"Have a seat," Vaye offered, gesturing toward the fireplace. "I'll make us some tea."

As Vaye disappeared behind the archway, Aera stuffed the drawing back into her cloak, crunched onto a chair by the fire and folded into her knees. What she carried was more revealing than a love note: she cherished a piece of paper that Cyrrus hadn't even addressed to her. Although she never followed or imitated him like the other kids, she was guilty of worse.

Vaye returned with two mugs and joined Aera by the fire, but Aera could not meet her eyes. Vaye accused her of having a love note and she couldn't deny that, in a sense, it was. She found Cyrrus and his stupid note fascinating.

The two drank tea in silence. Once finished, Vaye disappeared upstairs. Aera crossed the room, hurled herself into the piano and pounded on the keys until the instrument shook. It seemed her chords could never be thunderous enough to unwind the knots inside. She played in a fury until she was delirious with hunger and then left to scrape up whatever food remained at Unity Festival.

After quenching her appetite, Aera paced around Southside Forest in the cold, too anxious to return to the cottage. She wished she could rip up Cyrrus's drawing and burn it, but there was no possibility of that now. Before today, she hadn't known for sure whether it contained random scribbles or another language. Now she was more curious than ever to know what those characters meant.

She aligned her body, stood on her hands, and balanced on each leg. As her tension unwound, her thoughts returned to the drawing. Where did Cyrrus learn those symbols? What language was that? The law forbid any language other than Syrdian, yet Vaye had that book...

Suddenly it dawned on her: Vaye's comment about the love note had distracted Aera's attention from the book—and Vaye had done that deliberately. Vaye had told Aera to sit by the fire and when she'd returned to the piano, the music rack was empty.

Anger rose from within, and Aera kicked a nearby tree. How gullible did Vaye think she was? It was disturbing enough that Vaye had lied about Panther Woman, but manipulating her emotions like that was worse, and Aera would not let it go. She needed to confront Vaye.

She marched back to the cottage, let herself in and was greeted by a spicy scent. Vaye sat by the fire, slowly turning an iron rod with speared pieces of aromatic meat.

79

Vaye smiled innocently and asked, "Would you like some food, dear?"

Aera tensed. Half of her wanted to hide, and the other half wanted to scream. She sat on the piano bench and stared ahead at the empty music rack where the book had been. *Say something,* she implored herself.

"The book you had on the piano," she said slowly. "Was it... illegal?"

"Illegal? What would make you think that?"

"It was in another language... and you hid it from me."

"Why would you think I was hiding it from you?" Vaye asked.

"I forgot it was there because... you said... love note."

Aera waited for a response. The piano keys glowed in the firelight and their wood casing seemed to melt before her eyes. She feared Vaye might be hurt or might not invite her to the cottage anymore. After what felt like an eternity, Vaye said, "You have insight beyond your years."

Aera took a breath. She turned to face Vaye, whose expression was warm, but unreadable.

"It's important to balance passion with reason," Vaye said. "Many adults never learn this, but you show promise."

Aera wasn't sure what to make of this comment but refused to allow Vaye to distract her again. She asked, "Can I see the book?"

Vaye smiled, rose from her chair and disappeared under the archway. Stairs creaked faintly as she climbed up to her bedroom, and Aera waited in suspense. After a few moments, the creaking resumed, and Vaye returned with a book in her hand.

"You may borrow it if you wish," she said, "but you must keep it secret."

Aera took the book, feeling vindicated. She stroked the black hieroglyphs on the brown suede cover and asked, "What does it say?"

"*Parë Në Sulë,*[2] with the author's name below."

Aera repeated it in her mind. *Pah-*ray Nay *Soo-*lay. "What does it mean?"

Vaye's lips curved ever so slightly and her brown eyes glistened. "Perhaps another time." She reached for some pages beside the piano, placed them on the music rack and said, "I'll teach you a new piece after you remedy your hair."

Although inordinately kind and generous, Vaye was also intractably stubborn. There would be no changing her mind.

Aera took some time to comb Vaye's pine gunk through her hair—which had already grown past her bosom, owing to the treatment—then washed it out and returned to the cottage to dig into the new piece. Though the lesson was not finished, she made sure to leave well before curfew to find a suitable hiding place for the book.

She ventured deep into Southside Forest and shielded *Parë* under her cloak. The trees thickened, the underbrush grew wilder, and the hum of insects intensified. Animals scurried everywhere, and their growls and hisses gave Aera a thrill.

A tangled thicket of fallen trees blocked the passage ahead, creating a labyrinth of generously branched logs over piles of thorny vines. She spotted a cat scurrying across a log and watched it leap over the maze. Could Aera do that as well?

Knife-like thorns hung from another complex of branches above but, amidst the tangle, there were logs that might take her across the thicket. Vaye had taught her to walk on her hands, hoist herself up to high branches, balance on top of them and maneuver between them. Now, she would put her lessons to the test.

First, she spread her feet even with her shoulders and filled her belly with air. Once grounded, she removed her cloak, folded it several times over the book and tied the sleeves around her to create a waist-sack. Bracing herself with piano-strengthened hands, she grasped a branch above, pulled herself up and swung from one branch to the next, slipping her legs between thorny chaos until she anchored her feet on a log. She had passed the first hurdle.

After leaping across several more logs, she reached the last fallen tree, far above the ground. Carefully, she balanced, jumped, and landed squarely on it. Practicing Kra had paid off. She glowed with the thrill of mastery as she soared further into the forest. Nothing would thwart her pace after that.

The night was thick with animal sounds. Even in the dead of winter, Southside Forest overflowed with wildlife. An owl hooted in the distance. "Wh-wh-wh-wh-whoOo! Wh-wh-wh-wh-whoOo!"

Aera followed the sound and found herself facing a majestic oak tree with branches sprawling from every side, winding around and spilling to the ground. Its powerful limbs created an intricate silhouette in the moonlight, like a storm of spiders. The layering of branches was so dense that their shadows converged to create a chthonic void.

The core of the splendid tree gazed at her through a black eye punctuated with a curved eyelid. She approached the stately trunk and spotted a hollow opening. The perfect spot.

The portal was barely larger than the book itself, but the cavity within it was deep and wide. Aera felt around inside and was pleased to discover its foundation was dry. She stretched her arm out as far as she could until her fingers located the opposite wall, which was deliciously deep within the tree. Satisfied the book would be safe, she placed it inside the chamber, away from the elements.

The walk back to Junior Hut was challenging, but not terribly long. The secret tree was directly behind the sleeping huts, but deep enough within the forest, protected by a fortress of thorny brush and hissing animals: an impenetrable deterrent to anyone but her. The cove was a private getaway where she could do whatever she wanted. She wondered how long it would take to discover clues about *Parë Në Sulë* and where she might find them.

For weeks, Aera divided her spare time between Vaye's cottage and her new lair. She traced secret pathways beneath fallen trees and narrow spaces between legions of brush, optimizing the route to her hideout from any direction. When the leaves bloomed in spring, the area became even more obscure, secluded within endless greenery.

One bright afternoon at the oak, Aera entertained herself with Kra. She walked for a while on her hands, then ascended to a thick, low branch and stood on one leg with *Parë Në Sulë* balanced delicately on her head. A few butterflies fluttered around her and a nearby hawk tweeted, "Weet-weet... e-uu."

Aera sang a recent composition in response. "I reach to the skyyy... for a cloud... to come... and catch me."

Leaves rustled overhead, but Aera dared not look, lest *Parë* slip off. "I reach to the skyyy—"

"And here I am," bolted a crisp voice from above.

82

Cyrrus.

Aera wobbled, butterflies scattered, and the book tumbled down. As she scrambled to catch it, her cheeks flushed so violently that they throbbed.

"Wheeoo-wheeet!" Cyrrus whistled, and the hawk tweeted back.

Aera felt like her skin had been ripped off and her innards exposed. Cyrrus had caught her singing to the birds and now was imitating her!

"How... how did you get there?" she stammered.

"I climbed. Know a better way?"

Why are you here? What do you want? Aera strained to divine a response, something clever... blank.

"What book is that?" he asked.

Aera's hands shook as she angled the cover toward her chest. Cyrrus would know the book was illegal, and she had promised to keep it secret.

"It's... music." In a smoother tone, she added, "Esoteric music."

Cyrrus vaulted down from the tree, landing perfectly and smiling menacingly. He reached up toward her and, without thinking, she surrendered the book. *Idiot!* She scolded herself. *Take it back!* But she was frozen, unable to speak. Cyrrus glanced at the cover, flipped through it half-heartedly and declared, "This isn't music. It's written in Silindion, and the title, *Parë Në Sulë,* means Circles and Spheres."

You think you know everything! Aera thought, and his old drawing crashed into her mind.

"It's pointless to lie to me, Aera," Cyrrus said, pronouncing her name perfectly. "I know too much. And anyway, I won't tell anyone."

Aera looked at him, perplexed, and realized she'd been holding her breath.

"If we betray each other, we let the commune win," Cyrrus said tenderly. "We believe in something and we must challenge the authorities—at least, until I am in charge."

We believe, Aera thought. Nobody had ever included her in 'we' before. Why was he doing that? He never spoke that way. Tears filled her eyes as she forced herself not to smile. *Don't cry and don't smile,* Aera admonished herself. *Say something clever.* Nothing came.

"We better head back," Cyrrus said. "Or we'll miss baths."

Aera secured the book inside the tree and jumped to the ground.

Cyrrus took the lead, walking along the serpentine path she used to reach the village. He knew the way... and he knew it well. Had he followed her before? Heat rushed to her cheeks as Cyrrus began to expound.

"It's tabooed—but not illegal—to read schoolbooks outside of the library," he said. "We are all the same, so if the council permits instructors to use certain books in classrooms, we can carry them throughout village grounds too. I *know* that book of yours is not only extracurricular, but also illegal. None of the teachers know Silindion."

"How do you know it?" Aera asked nervously.

"There's more knowledge within my cerebral circus than the rest of Ynas combined. Haven't you noticed?"

Aera would sooner cut her hair again than admit how much she watched him, but also didn't want him to think she was oblivious. Carefully, she said, "You're... loud."

Cyrrus flashed a smile. "I am *impossible* to ignore."

Impossible to endure, Aera thought, and grinned to herself.

"If I had something to write on, I could translate the whole book," he boasted. "Drawing and writing by yourself is tabooed, but possessing paper outside class is *illegal*. If I write on wood or stone and they find it, they can't punish me."

Cyrrus paused, but Aera wasn't sure what to say. Fortunately, his own rambling entertained him so thoroughly that he resumed on his own.

"The flattest surfaces are cuts of wood from the lumberyard or bricks from the kiln by the clay pit. No one under twenty-four is permitted inside the fences surrounding the clay pit and lumberyard without an adult. It's legal to row a canoe up the river and to take scraps from outside the fence, but the rock walls around the river prevent docking the canoes..."

Cyrrus rattled off laws and taboos until they reached the waterfall. When they separated, Aera was sad. She tried not to watch as he splashed around with the other boys, racing about and out-maneuvering everyone at this and that while she bathed under her hair by herself. By the time she finished her routine, Cyrrus had disappeared.

She walked down the footpath and joined her line alone but spotted him nearby. He was posing importantly while Officer Padd announced tasks. *Don't stare,* she reminded herself. After an eternity, Padd called out their cohort. "11-12 Group, food prep—"

"Nurin said I could work in the Slaughterhouse on a cooking day if I cooked on Unity Day," Cyrrus cut in.

"That's a garden a' Syrdian Raisins," Padd snickered. "Why would he let you do that?"

"They needed more cooks. I offered my terms and he accepted."

"Your terms?" Padd laughed. "*YOUR* terms!? Wait a minute—you *wanted* to work in the Slaughterhouse?"

"I *love* to kill," Cyrrus declared. "Death is the most unifying facet of life!"

Padd cackled so heartily that his beard bounced. "Kid, you're insane! Get out of my sight before I Kadirize you."

The bi-hourly bell blasted its double gong, and Cyrrus marched away in rhythm as though it was sounding in his honor. As he passed Aera's line, he shot her a grin. A smile spilled over her face.

Throughout tasks, Aera was distracted by thoughts about Cyrrus. At dinner, she looked for him in the Dining Hall, but he wasn't there. She assumed her usual spot by the boulder, where she watched the sunset and wondered what he was doing. Deep in the trees, Vaye's cottage awaited, but Aera couldn't bring herself to leave. When the curfew bell rang, she went to Junior Hut feeling disappointed that she hadn't seen Cyrrus. The door to the hut was locked and Samies clustered outside, waiting for an attendant to let them in. Their jabber became louder by the minute...

"This book is designed to brainwash us!"

Cyrrus's voice rang out from the hilltop. Everyone stopped what they were doing to watch him strut imperiously down the hillside parading a large, fat book. As he drew closer, the torches outside the hut illuminated the title: *The History of Andolien.*

"The manipulation is insidious," he continued, looking straight at Aera. "The author uses innuendo and ambiguity to distort—"

"Stop right there, Brains," interjected a bombastic officer. He unlocked the door, propped it open and positioned himself before it.

"Greetings, Officer Tiros," Cyrrus said coolly as he strode to Aera's side. Some of his audience continued into the hut while others lingered near the entrance to observe.

"Hand over the book," Tiros commanded. "And get your skinny butt to Adolescent Hut."

"Since I trust our reverence for order is mutual, indulge me to remind you that the honorable position of Junior Hut Guard has been bequeathed to Officer Linealle since the New Year."

"You're not smarting your way outta this one. Go back to Adolescent Hut and flirt with girls your own age."

"I don't *need* to flirt," Cyrrus said. "I'm cute."

Cyrrus was implying Aera found him cute! *I didn't follow **you** into the forest*, she thought, and smiled to herself.

Cyrrus flaunted a jaunty grin, then turned back to Tiros. "If you think I'm fifteen, I advise you to check your facts, or you'll embarrass yourself, like Linealle did yesterday when she reported me for lighting a torch that I *made*."

"Fire is dangerous, and it's illegal for anyone under twenty-four to carry flint."

"Ignorance is more dangerous. And I don't use flint."

With that, Cyrrus gave Tiros the book. He ushered Aera inside and resumed his exposition as they descended the stairs.

"For example, the author refers to Syrd as The White City. That's because Syrdians use an ancient, magical light source called shardât, so the city exudes a white glow that's visible for dozens of kymen. But it's really a *description*, not a *name*, whereas Silinestin was called The White City in the First Age. Using it as a name is misleading, but I'm *certain* the author did that intentionally. He's part of a movement that denies Silinestin ever existed."

Aera had never heard those phrases before. *Silinestin, First Age, shardât*... what was he talking about? Did he assume she understood?

They parted towards their respective dorms and Cyrrus stopped outside his door. "I could write a more eloquent history book," he called. "And mine wouldn't propagate lies!"

The last word bounced around the corridor. *Lies. Lies. Lies.*

Aera went to her dormitory and disrobed. Across the room, the pink piglets squealed and whacked each other with pillows until Officer Tiros thrust the door open and bellowed, "Samie Abani!"

"Here..."

He recited all thirty names on his list, then shut the door. The others resumed gabbing while Aera burrowed under her blanket, restless and alert. Voices faded into snores, and Aera imagined Cyrrus's voice echoing between them. *Lies. Lies. Lies...*

No position was comfortable. No matter which way she turned, her limbs were out of place. She wished she could just run off with Cyrrus, though she couldn't decide if she wanted to laugh at his haughty tirades or punch his smug, 'cute' face.

Why had she forsaken her trip to the cottage that day? To hear Cyrrus recite laws and flaunt his superiority to a crowd? Why had he followed her into the forest? What did he expect from her? She had nothing to add to his didactic rants. Nothing to contribute to his 'cerebral circus.' Nothing to say.

Perhaps he was lonely or bored. Or needed someone to listen so he could practice giving speeches. Or was he seeking Aera's attention specifically? Maybe he sensed she was different, and that neither one of them fit in. That they belonged somewhere else... together.

If only, Aera thought. 'Together' meant nothing to Cyrrus.

It was irrelevant what he thought of her now. Ultimately, he would be disappointed and find something more interesting to do. He would be drawn to someone more knowledgeable, more engaging, more sociable. And she would become invisible to him. He would never build real friendships, since he believed he was better than everyone. Was he lying awake agonizing over her? No. Of course not. He was probably sleeping peacefully, or contemplating rituals to determine who should be eliminated when he ruled the world.

Aera slept horribly and awakened in a nervous daze. She fumbled clumsily with her clothing while the other girls cleared the room. When she finally stepped outside, she was surprised to find Cyrrus waiting by her door.

He flashed a grin and asked, "Did you sleep well?"

Aera blushed furiously, but forced a casual tone and said, "Sure."

"*I* didn't sleep at all," Cyrrus said. "I was concocting plans to make Syrd more efficient after I dethrone King Irador."

Cyrrus was feverishly conceited and demonstrably deranged... but Aera smirked at how predictable he was.

"What?" Cyrrus asked. "You don't think I can vanquish him?"

"I... don't know. You're eleven."

"I'd be a much better King."

Aera said nothing: his self-aggrandizement merited no response. They headed to the staircase in silence, but barely climbed two steps before Cyrrus asserted his case.

"Listen to how stupid this is," he said. "In Syrd, both men and women work, but only the men make decisions about education and government. If Irador doesn't change that, Syrd could end up like Dirgaselah, where men *own* women like we own clothing. They force the women to clean and cook, and the law forbids them to work outside their homes or attend school."

Aera found it hard to believe that a whole population of women would allow themselves to be enslaved by men. She challenged, "Did you read this in the book full of lies?"

"My knowledge base is extensive... but you are wise to question everything. Skepticism is the enemy of ignorance."

Aera grinned, pleased that he appreciated her wit.

"Only an incompetent leader would squander half his population," Cyrrus continued. "As King, I will enlist intelligent women and men to wield influence according to their talent, and assign stupid people to basic maintenance so Syrd will be more efficient. Obviously, it would be *most* efficient to eliminate stupid people altogether, or prevent them from breeding, but that solution would garner minimal public support. Besides, *someone* has to clean the latrines."

Aera snickered. What was wrong with him?

They stepped outside into the fresh spring air, and Cyrrus did not miss a beat. "I wonder which fables will be flaunted in fiction class today. Want a *real* history lesson? Come with me." He veered eastward toward the forest, and Aera followed.

"Eh-ruh has a boyfriend!" chanted Doriline behind her. "Eh-ruh has a boyfriend!"

Laughter erupted and Aera was mortified. She didn't want Cyrrus to think she fancied him as her 'boyfriend.'

She watched with bated breath as Cyrrus swerved around to face

Doriline, smug as ever, and projected his voice. "Your envy of my companionship is reasonable, but you should be more envious that Aera has a functioning cerebrum."

Aera could hardly believe this was happening. No one had ever defended her before. A smile spilled over her face, but Cyrrus didn't see it, as he had already resumed his stride into Southside Forest.

"Hurry or we'll be late for class," he called. "The Fence crosses the river in the south. I'll race you!"

Immediately, he took off, and she laughed and ran after him. They lunged through the forest, tore through brush and hurdled over logs. Aera ducked under a giant mess of thorns, but Cyrrus was too tall and had to circumvent it. She was winning! She panted but continued onward at full speed, closer every moment to the sound of flowing water. Finally, she saw the Fence ahead and stopped. Her ribs ached as she gasped for breath, but Cyrrus was nowhere to be seen. Had she won?

Suddenly, Cyrrus's red hair poked out from between some cattails, and he paraded a giant, exaggerated grin. He strutted through the leaves, neither sweaty nor out of breath, and boasted, "Don't be surprised. I always win."

"Not at modesty," Aera teased.

Cyrrus giggled in a girlish high pitch, which took Aera by surprise and made her chuckle. He recomposed himself, headed to the riverside and said, "Come look."

The river snaked northward around a distant bend and southward past the Fence, which bridged the flowing water in the form of a massive iron gate. On the opposite bank was a beachfront encircled by a barricade of logs, drastically shorter than the Fence, but tall enough to avert curious eyes.

"The DPD training grounds are behind that wall," Cyrrus explained. "They think nobody can see them... but watch *this*."

He jumped into a tree and bounded upwards. The lowest branch was just beyond Aera's reach, so she decided to flaunt some Kra. She crouched down, sprang to grab the branch, and swung her legs around it to hoist herself up. As she balanced on the tree, she saw Cyrrus watching her from above, his emerald eyes greener than the grass on the Hill.

"You coming?"

Aera realized she'd been staring at him for too long and quickly continued upward.

Once they had climbed halfway up the tree, Cyrrus spread apart some branches to clear the view. Across the river were several columns of DPD officers in uniform. Some were mounted on large unfamiliar animals lining two sides of a field, while the rest faced one another in pairs, holding short poles with metal blades on the ends. One animal galloped into the field, and its rider addressed the group, though his words were inaudible against the rush of the river. In response, the unmounted officers raised their poles and advanced toward their counterparts in perfect unison.

"Those are battle axes," Cyrrus said. "Deadly weapons used to kill people."

"To kill *who*?"

"Good question," Cyrrus replied. "They practice combat every day during breakfast... and there aren't any enemies *here* to account for that."

Aera took this in and watched as the man in command called out more orders. Promptly, the officers stopped sparring, lined up and marched away. Next, the animals charged at each other while their riders raised long poles in identical formation. It pained Aera that the officers were forcing those beautiful creatures to organize with them, all the same.

"Those are horses," Cyrrus said. "There are hundreds more behind those trees, and I've seen legions of officers riding them deep in Eastern Pines, but they're excluded from our history books."

It was astounding that so much activity took place right inside the commune that nobody talked about. Aera wondered how many others knew this and how Cyrrus had found out.

"Regardless what the leaders claim, there's ample evidence that we conduct business with the outside world," Cyrrus asserted. "For instance, the Medical Unit has a storehouse of powdered medicines that cure illnesses overnight. Who conducts the research necessary to concoct such treatments?"

The Medical Unit was known for its excellent accommodations, but Aera had never been there. She relied on Vaye's remedies, which she assumed were effective owing to Vaye's proficiency with plants. "Maybe there's a medicine maker in the commune," she offered.

"Making medicine isn't difficult. Ensuring its efficacy requires scientific research and testing, and there are no facilities here to account for those advancements."

Aera nodded, though she didn't know what to make of this.

"There's more," Cyrrus continued. "If people with different skin colors breed, their offspring fall somewhere between them. After a long time, everyone in an area will have the same complexion. In our Group, Farris has dark brown skin, Doriline's is peach and Keole's is light brown. Why would people differ so dramatically, and why don't they permit anyone to know who their parents are? It's because babies are brought here from elsewhere, which informs me our leaders have communication outside."

Aera examined her arms and noted her skin was vanilla with a vague bluish cast. Unlike Doriline, who had an amber blush, Aera had cooler undertones. Were her parents in Ynas, or had she come from outside? She wished Vaye were her mother, but it was unlikely that Vaye's deep mocha chrome could have produced Aera's sandy blonde hair and fair complexion.

She looked at Cyrrus. If his skin were any lighter, he would be transparent. As she stared, she saw beneath his pallor a grey, ashen undertone with vague browning. Aera had never seen anyone else with alabaster skin and wondered whose offspring Cyrrus might be. He looked like he came from another world.

"Did you come from outside?" she inquired.

"A lot of people probably do," Cyrrus said. "More than you might imagine."

That was not the answer Aera was hoping for. She sensed his ambiguity was intentional.

"The name, Department of Protection through Discipline, is deceptive," he said. "It exists not only to protect us, but to *control* us. They make us work for them while they train soldiers for negotiations and war."

War, Aera thought. She wondered what the point of it was.

"War is a team sport," Cyrrus professed. "The object is to eliminate enough players to debilitate and demoralize the opposing team. Whoever does this first, wins."

"Wins what?"

"Draw your own conclusions," he said with a cryptic grin. "I'm just imparting facts."

He headed back down the tree. Aera took one more look at the soldiers moving their weapons synchronously on the training field, then followed him down. She wondered what other 'facts' he had in store.

They hurried back to the Field, joined their lines and went to History Class. The atmosphere was tense, with the tables arranged in a circle and Inellei, the Brass of Education, seated at the head. Despite the gawkiness of his heavily freckled face, his authoritative title put everyone on edge.

Aera found a seat in the back as usual, near Gaili and her friend Olleroc. Cyrrus rushed to the empty spot between Aera and Gaili, pulled out a chair and challenged, "Can you guess why The Brass is here?"

"To check up on the instructors," Aera offered.

"To *control* them," Cyrrus corrected her. In a louder voice, he announced, "Power is a pyramid and we, the slaves, comprise the base."

"Blah blah brain-dirl," Farris yelled from across the table. The piglets laughed and the instructors glared, but Cyrrus gave no acknowledgment.

"It's not dirl," Gaili protested. "He's right."

Cyrrus flashed a grin at Gaili and called out, "If the base breaks free, the top will collapse—"

"Darse it, Samie," snapped Instructor Korov.

"Why? To impress the Brass?"

"DARSE IT!"

Cyrrus smiled as laughter resounded. Aera enjoyed the idea that power was a pyramid, but the base would never break free. People were far too eager to follow leaders. They wanted someone to tell them what to do.

Brass Inellei glared at Cyrrus, then stood in position for the commune salute. The crowd mimicked him, and he intoned with the utmost seriousness, "We are all the same!"

The throng echoed, "We are all the same!" Aera remained quiet. Cyrus, beside her, did not recite the mantra either.

After a few repetitions, Inellei lowered his arms, ending the salute. The other instructors handed out supplies while Korov stationed himself before the chalkboard and wrote, *Mid-Spring. Week three. Year 1325.* Usually, he neglected to write the date, but now the Brass was here.

"Our ancestors sacrificed their lives for our safety, and we owe them gratitude!" Korov lectured in his most robust tone. "We must be thankful for the Fence they built, which has enabled our commune to remain peaceful and self-sufficient!"

Cyrus shot Aera a sideways glance, and they exchanged a chuckle.

"Renstrom Reneus was the first Renstrom of Ynas," Korov continued. "He was an enlightened general from the violent state of Kadir—but he yearned to live in peace. Consequently, he led his followers away to found Ynas in the year 115. Stone by stone, he and his loyal followers constructed the great Fence! After smilodons breeched the Fence in year 932, Renstrom Torovis erected an iron barrier coated in deadly poison. Your distant ancestors risked their lives so you could live in safety!"

Lies, lies, lies, Aera thought. She couldn't imagine a four-legged animal breaching that wall. 'Distant ancestors' was fiction, too, if so many children came from outside.

In his theatrical tone, Korov said, "I want all of you to write about what it's like to sleep in safety, knowing no animals can attack you, no enemies can hurt you, and violence is obsolete!"

Aera thought about the battle preparation she'd seen that morning and felt special: Cyrus had shown her the truth while everyone else was deceived. She imagined swinging an axe into the log barricade, revealing the secret army to everyone.

Beside her, Cyrus moved his pencil across his page in long, continuous strokes. Aera surmised he was drawing. She looked at her page. Though she had nothing genuine to write, she followed Korov's order. *Every night, I sleep on my mat,* she wrote. *I am warm and I cannot be harmed.*

"Pass your papers to the left!" Korov instructed.

Aera passed her page to Cyrus and tried to glimpse his artwork,

93

but he ripped the page down the middle and stuffed half in his pocket. Rapidly, he jotted down a few sentences on the blank half and passed it to his left.

"You all know the story of Riva the Rebel," said Korov. "Can anyone sum it up?"

A few people raised their hands, but Doriline projected hers the highest, and Korov pointed at her.

"Riva the Rebel tried to be different from everyone else," Doriline said buoyantly. "She defied authority and broke rules all her life until she was exiled. Then she was eaten by a smilodon and her bones were found by the trees outside the Fence."

Aera wondered who had ventured outside the Fence, found the bones there, and lived to tell the tale. Apparently, the smilodons preferred feasting on rebels.

"Thank you, Samie Doriline," said Korov. "Everyone, write three more facts about Riva the Rebel."

Aera stared at her page. The instructors lectured about Riva often, and Aera had never given her a second thought. Now, she wondered whether the tales were exaggerated—or invented—as a device to keep people in line.

She jotted down some tidbits she'd been taught. *Riva skipped tasks to read by herself. Riva drowned a swan.* That was common knowledge, but it was ridiculous. Why—and how—would anyone drown a swan? She snickered and continued. *Riva refused to bathe.*

"Pass your papers to the left…"

Cyrrus gave his page to Gaili, and as she read it, they exchanged a snicker. Aera wondered what absurdities he'd written. He seemed to know everything about the commune—and also, the outside world. Did he really want to rule Ynas? If it were up to Aera, they would leave that very afternoon. They would run free and take on the outside world together.

History Class passed faster than usual as Aera and Cyrrus continued to exchange glances and giggles at all the lies. When the Samies were dismissed, Cyrrus accompanied Aera to the hallway and asked, "Did you fancy fiction class?"

"Fables are fabulous," she grinned.

Cyrrus raised a brow and retorted, "Facts are more fetching." He pulled a folded page from beneath his sleeve and added, "Fancy this."

Aera hid the page under her hair, uncrumpled it and saw a lifelike sketch of the DPD barricade with an axe tearing through it. Her cheeks flushed. This was precisely the same scene she had pictured just as he started drawing. It was as though he'd read her mind!

"Get rid of it, quick," he urged.

Aera ripped the page to shreds as they headed onward. When they reached the Dining Hall, she threw them in the wastebin.

"Let's eat quickly and take a canoe up to the lumberyard," Cyrrus suggested. "We can get some wood strips and use them to write translations for *Parë Në Sulë*."

"I can't read Silindion."

"I'll teach you."

Aera smiled, overcome with emotion. She never would have dared to hope for this.

Cyrrus rushed their meal and ushered her over the bridge, but when they arrived at the dock, no boats were there. They watched some swans by the riverside until they spotted a canoe approaching from the north. From afar, Aera recognized the prettiest girl in the 13-14 Group paddling while two others faced her. Short, dark curls blew around, framing her rosy cheeks, contrasting with her pale blue tunic and matching blue eyes.

"Greetings, Dila," Cyrrus called.

Dila parked her enormous eyes on him and beamed with delight. In a sugary voice, she cooed, "Samely, Cyrrus!"

Aera grimaced. Those two were uncomfortably familiar and Dila's candied tone was garish.

"Greetings, Rafi. Pavene." He nodded to each in turn.

Rafi gave a dismissive nod that matched her gruff demeanor, while Pavene blushed and whispered nervously, "Samely, Cyrrus."

Pavene was as striking as Dila, with dark skin, a closely shaved haircut and sad eyes gazing shyly at Cyrrus. As he basked in the attention of the pretty older girls who were gooey over him, his posture became erect. He graced them with his slickest smile and delivered, "May we appropriate your canoe?"

"Sure!" Dila said quickly.

"Peh," Rafi grunted. She aimed her sunburned chin at Aera and sneered, "Who's the runt?"

"A small girl with a big mind," Cyrrus said, "if you have the wit to unleash it."

Cyrrus shot a smug glance at Aera, and she glared back, annoyed. He had never 'unleashed' anything and had no idea her mind was 'big,' as he was too preoccupied with his own 'dirl.'

Dila paddled closer, retrieved a rope inside the canoe and tossed it to Cyrrus, who secured it to a pole. Rafi hoisted herself up to the dock, but Pavene hesitated and Cyrrus extended his hand to help her. She looked awed and smiled feebly as she allowed him to ease her up. Cyrrus reached for Dila's hand next, and she giggled and locked fingers with him as she climbed out of the boat. Once safely on the dock, she retained his hand for an extra moment, savoring it as long as she could... and he allowed it.

"Thank you," Cyrrus said, looking at each girl in turn. "Enjoy this glorious day."

With excess exuberance, Dila said, "You too, Cyrrus."

Aera waited for Dila to look her way, then flashed a confident grin. She wanted to assert that her relationship with Cyrrus could not be touched. Dila forced a wan smile, then deflated and left.

Cyrrus turned to Aera and offered his hand, but she ignored it. She would not touch the hand that made those idiots coo and purr. Why yield to his pretentious gestures when she was perfectly capable of maneuvering into the canoe on her own?

The simplest path was to slide down on her backside, but her pants would be smeared with wet dirt from the dock. Nearby, she noticed a swan jumping down from the grass, barely making a splash as it landed smoothly in the water. That was the way.

She positioned herself carefully and leapt down with grace, but the canoe wobbled slightly. To counter the sway, she widened her stance and gently adjusted until she steadied the canoe. As she glanced up, she noted that Cyrrus was watching intently. *Thank you, Kra*, she thought. If she were as clumsy kinetically as she was socially, Cyrrus might fantasize about using her to clean latrines in his imaginary enlightened empire.

He locked his eyes with Aera's and grinned, then whirled deftly into the canoe, steadying instantly. His form was achingly graceful.

"Nice style," he acceded. "Mine is better."

Aera afforded him no rebuttal. She wondered whether he'd studied something similar to Kra or was naturally perfect at everything.

He untied the rope and assumed the front seat; Aera sat behind him. He lifted a paddle, headed northward against the tide, and said, "Copy my movements."

She watched carefully as he pushed each side of the paddle against the water in turn. Then, she picked up another paddle and followed suit. The water was heavier than she expected. By the time her first stroke was completed, Cyrrus had already switched to the other side.

"You will improve," Cyrrus said plainly, without slowing his pace.

She shifted her hand position and adjusted her force until she matched his rhythm. As they continued northward past the buildings and vegetable fields, she felt a flurry of excitement. Colorful orchards of fruit trees lined the east bank, and, as Aera admired them, she realized her group had picked those fruits countless times during tasks. The area had always appeared to her as a bug-infested dirtscape broken up by boring rows of trees. Now, it was paradise.

"Everything looks different from a new perspective," Cyrrus said. "It's natural to believe our own experience, but we must never allow it to limit us."

It seemed Cyrrus had answered Aera's unspoken thoughts. No one had ever been so attuned to her.

"See there," he said, and gestured toward a stream beside Westside Willows in the distance. "That feeds the waterfall over the bathing grove."

Cyrrus knew so much about the commune; clearly, he had explored far and wide. All this time, Aera had never even ventured beyond the crops. She fantasized about freedom, feeling caged and trapped, yet never journeyed further than Vaye's cottage. As she considered this, the paddles felt heavier, but she forced herself to push through.

They rowed beneath another bridge, where the river was enclosed in rock walls. The surrounding grasslands contained fruit trees and other crops that extended past the horizon, but it didn't take as long to pass them as Aera anticipated. She watched excitedly as the landscape transformed into empty fields and conifers, indicating they had traveled beyond where most people ventured. Now that they were of age, it was legal to be anywhere in Ynas, yet probably very tabooed.

"We are *way* outside village grounds," Cyrrus boasted. "The lumberyard is coming up soon."

Moments later, they approached a dam with giant paddlewheels beneath it, bridging the river ahead. Towering over the bank was a wooden barn-like structure that extended over the water. The embankment was steep, and its margin was comprised entirely of boulders. Cyrrus extended his paddle toward the stone wall along the riverside, anchored it in the tiny slits between rocks, and maneuvered the canoe toward the bank.

"If you climb onto my shoulders, I can lift you up to the shore," he said. "I'll tell you where to go from there."

He crouched down and Aera stood on the seat, preparing to climb on his back. She lifted her legs over his shoulders, and as he secured them under his arms, her heartbeat sped up. His hot, sunbaked head was right against her belly, and his grip was firm.

Stay cool, she admonished herself. *Breathe...* but her pulse was still wild. Cyrrus balanced himself calmly and rose steadily, seemingly unaware of her fluster. How could he be so attentive before and so oblivious now? His movements were carefully controlled... *too* perfect.

Aera gripped a rock at the top of the wall, shaking and overwhelmed. She breathed with focused effort and hoisted herself onto the shore.

"In the trees behind that barn, there's a pile of scrap wood," Cyrrus said crisply. "Collect flat, thin pieces and hurry back. You will make two trips."

Cyrrus had every step planned out. Aera could see he'd done this before and wondered who had helped him. Surely, Dila could do this just as easily...

She recomposed and headed into the trees. A wooden fence surrounded the area behind the barn, blocking her view of the people inside who were yelling, banging and chopping. As she rounded the fence, she spotted a pile of wood bits of all shapes and sizes. Quickly, she collected an armload of appropriate pieces, then headed back through the trees toward the shore.

After she delivered a second load, Cyrrus clenched the rock wall to hold the canoe in place. Aera jumped down carefully, and this time, landed so smoothly that the boat barely moved. She glanced at Cyrrus to see if he'd noticed and felt gratified by his heedful expression.

"Let's get this stuff to Great Gorge," he said with a twinkle in his eye.

Aera wondered what 'Great Gorge' was and realized he was referring to the hollow tree. She giggled and Cyrrus beamed, proud of his poetics. His smile was surprisingly boyish, but fleeting. Immediately, he caught himself, firmed his face and leveled his posture.

"It won't matter if people see us by the bridge," he said stiffly. "We haven't broken any laws... yet. We'll have to do that later."

Aera couldn't wait to see what else Cyrrus had in store. He certainly made things fun... and it didn't escape her notice that he was making plans with her.

The trip back south was easier, as they rowed with the current, but there was still a great distance to cover. By the time they moored the canoe, the area was desolate, indicating lunch was almost over.

"It's tabooed, but not illegal, to miss baths," Cyrrus said. "But we need to make it to Vapid Village before tasks."

Vapid Village. Cyrrus was showing off. He glanced at Aera, and they exchanged a chuckle.

They docked the canoe by the track, hiked through Southside Forest with arms full of wood, and piled their bounty inside the gorge of the tree alongside *Parë Në Sulë*. The belltower rang out just as they finished, and they hurried away. By the time they reached the Hill, they were gasping and giggling, and the other children were already lined up in the Field below.

Aera joined her line. Cyrrus stood beside her, grinning maniacally, until Padd bellowed, "Samely, Brains! Go find the boys' line!"

A smile consumed Aera's face, but she fended it off. She didn't want anyone to know how happy it made her that Cyrrus was reluctant to leave her side. She wondered how long it would last.

Though farming tasks were boring as always, Aera's mood was elevated, and the time passed quickly. By the end, she still felt energetic, ready for another adventure. To her delight, Cyrrus found her after dinner and led her to the Education Unit. She wasn't sure where they were going but didn't bother to ask. No matter what they did, she was in.

The hallways were dark, no torches lit. He brought her up the shadowy staircase to the Art Room and whispered, "Keep watch."

She crouched against the wall and focused down the hallway until Cyrrus returned with a metal can. He wrapped his cloak around it and said, "Let's get this to Great Gorge."

Aera knew from experience that if they walked over the Hill, they would be seen. The route she took to Vaye's was more private and would work as a starting point. They could cross the playground between the three Community Buildings to get to the Dining Hall, leave through the kitchen, run into Westside Willows, and cut through the foothills instead of walking beside the Fence. That way, they would end up in Southside Forest without having to pass Vaye's cottage, which Aera was duty bound to keep secret.

"I know the way," Aera said, proud to be leading him somewhere for once. Cyrrus followed without question.

When they reached Great Gorge, Cyrrus handed Aera the can from under his cloak. He ripped a piece of bark from a nearby willow tree and said, "Collect the bark, like this. Try to get pieces that are dried out."

Aera ripped a piece from the tree and stuffed the bits into the can as Cyrrus disappeared into the woods. A short while later, he emerged with an armful of rocks, set them on the ground and headed off again. She enjoyed listening to his footsteps as he maneuvered around.

Once the container was full, she found Cyrrus kneeling before a circle of rocks under their tree between a collection of long branches and a pile of dried twigs and leaves. He took the can from Aera, placed it in the center of the stones with the open top facing the ground, and arranged the branches in a teepee surrounding it, leaving an open space. Finally, he reached into a pocket and fished out two rocks.

"This one's granite, and this one has a groove," he said, opening his hand to show her. "I chiseled it with tools at the Slaughterhouse."

Aera ran her finger along the groove, which was slimmer than the space between two piano keys. She was not surprised to learn Cyrrus's real reason for wanting to go to the Slaughterhouse involved some devious plan. She wondered what it was and how the rocks fit into it.

He scraped one briskly against the other and sparks shot out. As the tiny embers landed on the bundle, he blew on them forcibly until they caught fire. With a twig, he nudged the flaming leaves under the careful arrangement of branches. Soon enough, the burning teepee collapsed, and flames soared. A fiery aroma livened the air and Aera breathed it in with a smile.

Cyrrus selected some wood tablets from the gorge, then reached into his cloak and produced a long cattail leaf. After hoisting himself into the tree and straddling the lowest branch, he set about sanding a wood tablet with the leaf. Sawdust fell beneath him like golden rain in the firelight.

"Your job is to move the sticks around so the fire will burn until curfew," he said. "Tomorrow, we'll have a supply of charcoal."

"You're—"

Aera was about to say, '*amazing*,' but caught herself.

"I'm what?" Cyrrus asked with a playful tone.

"—resourceful," Aera offered.

Cyrrus chuckled. Though he spared her any sarcastic commentary, Aera suspected he knew exactly how impressed she was. After only two days together, they had already ventured outside village grounds and acquired ample writing materials with which to translate *Parë Në Sulë*. Aera could hardly wait to find out what the text might reveal.

SILINDION
1325 MID-SPRING

"When Reneus was faced with the army from... Cyrrus? Are you *sleeping?*"

Instructor Korov's yelling tore into Aera's skull. Others turned to see Cyrrus but he remained motionless. His head was installed firmly on the desk beside her, and he breathed deeply, lost in a dream.

Korov rounded the table, stood before Cyrrus and hollered, "Samie Cyrrus! Wake up!"

Cyrrus's response emerged from under his arm. "It is in your best interest to ignore me."

Korov grabbed Cyrrus's hair with one hand and lifted his head by the chin with the other to force eye contact. Startled by Korov's behavior, Aera jerked back. A few others gasped.

Across the room, Brass Inellei hissed, "Psst. No violence."

Korov released Cyrrus from his grip and sputtered through clenched teeth, "You will not sleep in my class."

Cyrrus returned his head to the desk. Korov watched for a moment, then yanked the chair out from underneath Cyrrus, who stood promptly, as though expecting it. The two stared at each other, and there was complete silence until Korov commanded, "Sit."

Cyrrus returned to his chair, stretched his arms luxuriously, and yawned. Aera knew his performance was not done.

Korov surveyed the room to make sure everyone was listening and continued his lecture. "Reneus was a peaceful man, but he was confronted by an army from Kadir in the year 231. He led his people to—"

"Reneás was dead before the Kadirian invasion," Cyrrus interjected. He pronounced the name with extra flourish, saying 'Re-nay-*ahhs*' with a rolled 'r,' while Korov had pronounced it 'Re-*nay*-us.' Aera snickered at his theatrics.

"Incorrect!" Korov exclaimed. "R*en*eus lead his people into battle, and—"

"Yesterday, you said Reneás founded Ynas in the year 115," Cyrrus cut in. "How could he be alive during the Kadirian invasion in 231?"

There was some nervous laughter from the class, but Korov became more serious as he realized Cyrrus had caught him in a lie. He puffed out his chest and intoned dramatically, "When our great founder R*en*eus led—"

"Even if Reneás founded Ynas from his cradle, he would have been 116 years old when he fought Kadir," Cyrrus continued. "Since a human lifespan rarely exceeds eighty years, your account would require either that Reneás was a member of a different species or that he used magic to extend his life."

"There are no different species, and there's no such thing as magic!"

"If there are no different species, how do you account for jackasses? Are they part of 'we are all the same?'"

The classroom exploded in laughter, fueling Korov's rage. "DARSE! IT!" he barked, and pounded his fist on the desk.

Everyone quieted as the table shook. Aera forced herself not to laugh, but Cyrrus flaunted a gratified smirk.

"When R*en*eus led his army..."

As Korov spoke, Cyrrus returned to napping position, and none of the teachers dared to rouse him. It amused Aera that his knowledge scared them into submission, but she was curious why he needed sleep in the first place. Her mind wandered to shadowy dungeons, archaic books, and freakish, fanciful languages. She wondered whether his idea of 'another species' and 'magic' included forehead lights.

Cyrrus dozed through the rest of class, but when the lunch bell gonged, he was awake and peppy. After he and Aera had gathered their

103

lunch food, they sat together by the boulder. Cyrrus stuffed his face so quickly his cheeks puffed out. Aera chuckled at him.

He garbled through a mouthful, "I prefer not to waste time idling on Halcyon Hill."

Then leave, she thought, and bristled.

"While I dedicate my precious time to sport, learning, and expanding my cerebral circus, others vegetate in this idyllic, scenic haven," he boasted. "Today, Great Gorge awaits us."

Aera was at once relieved and annoyed at herself. She kept imagining Cyrrus wanted to get rid of her—and it scared her. She was becoming far too dependent.

Cyrrus inhaled his food and darted off without warning. Aera took her time, refusing to rush after him. When she reached the Gorge, he was perched on the lowest branch of the tree with his legs dangling down on each side, and *Parë* balanced against the trunk. Between his legs rested a wood tablet, which he wrote on with a long slice of charcoal wrapped in yarn.

Aera climbed the tree and settled above him. While he read the book and took notes, her mind wandered back to History Class. Rolling the 'r' and emphasizing the 'ah' exactly as Cyrrus had, she asked, "Why do you say 'Reneás?'"

"Irrelevant," he said. "I was training the teachers."

"Do you think he was part of another species?"

Without looking up, Cyrrus retorted, "My educated guess is that Reneás did lead the army and was a hybrid between a human species and another species similar in appearance, with a greater lifespan."

"A species that uses magic?"

"We can talk about Reneás, or I can focus on translating this book. You choose."

Aera groaned in frustration; he had a point, but she was bored. She fumbled around, trying to keep herself occupied while Cyrrus worked.

"Oreni, moon, and sun are spherical, and... emit?... emanate?... beauty as... deity?... imagined... no, dreamed it. Abstractly, the *suru*...? may be conceptualized as spherical, because beauty derives... no, emanates... from it." He paused and tapped his pencil on the tablet repeatedly. "*Suru*," he mumbled as he retreated to the book.

Aera lay back on her branch and listened to the forest choir while watching clouds sail between treetops. Her most recent composition played in her mind, with the lyrics: *I reach to the sky for a cloud to come and catch me...*

She almost sang aloud but stopped herself—she did not want to disturb The Great One. As she reviewed the arrangement, the suspended chords invigorated her. She imagined a vivid, robust voice imparting the lyrics:

> *I reach to the sky*
> *For a cloud to come and catch me*
> *Take me away*
> *From anger and hatred and pain*
> *Fly me over the rain*
> *And I'll drown your world from above*
> *I'll wash out the tears*
> *Banish the fears*
> *When you're under the ocean*
> *I'll feel one emotion...*

"Oreni, Alárië and Til are spherical, and emanate beauty as Ilë dreamed it," Cyrrus read from his tablet. "Abstractly, the *suru* may be conceptualized as spherical, as our beauty emanates from it. The sphere, depicted as a circle, symbolizes that nothing exists in isolation. That which begins at any point will return, so that the end, the beginning and the infinity of points between are equivalent. The Nassando may envision her *suru* as a sphere around which all emotions revolve and to which they inevitably return."

The relationship between circles and infinity was sound, but there were so many names, all new and foreign. Did they mean something to Cyrrus? Aera studied him and noted that even the bright sunlight could not diminish the density of his emerald eyes. He looked strikingly different from anyone else, and now he was deciphering foreign languages. Where did he come from, anyway?

"Where did you learn Silindion?" she inquired.

"I decipher languages quickly," Cyrrus said. "Language is a mathematical puzzle."

"But how did you know what the symbols meant in the first place?"

"I deduced it from the character frequency and intervals."

"That's impossible."

"Not to me," Cyrrus said. "It's only impossible because you think it is. And, obviously, because you're stupid."

Aera glared at Cyrrus, and he giggled in a high pitch. "You sound like a girl," she teased.

"You look like a boy," he retorted.

Was that true? His tone was so dry, Aera didn't know if he was joking.

He returned his attention to the book. Aera wished he would tell her where he'd come from and how he knew so much, but instead, he spun tales only an idiot could believe.

"I'll read more to you at a later date," Cyrrus said. "You have a lot to learn about the world before you can make sense of this text."

"Things *you* learned through deduction," Aera said sardonically.

Cyrrus offered an emotionless glare, and she returned the favor.

"For instance, the word for sun is *til,* and it's just a word, but the moon is associated with an Angel named Alárië," he said. "I expect these anthropomorphic nuances mystify you."

"It may mystify *you,*" Aera grinned, "but it's simple. The sun is bright and annoying, like you, and the moon is moody and mysterious, like me."

She watched him, satisfied with herself, until he broke into a smile.

"We have lofty endeavors before us," he said. "Care to make yourself useful while I translate?"

Aera had no idea what 'useful' meant, but she hoped it would be fun.

Cyrrus jumped down from the tree, fished out a ball of yarn and a rock, and placed them on the ground beside the metal pail. "Break the charcoal into strips and wrap the yarn around them for pencils," he instructed. "When you're done, use the rock to sharpen them."

Boring, Aera thought, and groaned. She recalled his comment about stupid people: *Someone has to clean the latrines.* He was enlightened, and she was 'useful.'

"Stop emoting," Cyrrus said. "Emotions scramble your mind."

"You know nothing about my mind."

With a wry grin, Cyrrus asked, "Would you rather postpone the translating until *I* make the pencils?"

Just leave me alone! Aera wanted to scream. She took a deep breath and imagined herself as Vaye: serene, elegant and tranquil. Slowly, she exhaled.

Cyrrus was right to ask her for help. He could read *Parë Në Sulë,* and she couldn't. It was sensible for her to aid the process so he could teach her. But instead of accepting the role he assigned, she assumed he was insulting her. He was right: emotions did scramble her mind.

She jumped down from the tree, rolled up her sleeves, sat on her knees, and began breaking up the charcoal. Her hands were instantly covered in soot. She dove in, allowing the black filth to crawl up her arms as she buried herself in the task. By the end of the break, she had crafted numerous pencils and Cyrrus had filled several tablets with writing. He was reluctant to stop, but Aera made sure they returned to Vapid Village in time for baths.

That evening, Cyrrus joined Aera for dinner but didn't converse as he usually did. The two ate in silence until he picked up his tray and said, "I need to sleep." With that, he left.

Aera felt uneasy: it was the first meal period Cyrrus would spend without her since they became friends. Had she done something wrong?

She headed to the cottage, feeling nervous throughout the walk. When she arrived, she opened the door and Vaye greeted her with a drizzle of high notes. As their echoes decayed, Vaye smiled.

"Wonderful to see you, dear," Vaye said. "Come in."

Aera forced a pleasant grin but felt too tense for chitchat. She needed to unwind. Graciously, Vaye took the cue and surrendered the piano, situating herself by the fireplace.

Aera assumed position and played a gentle flourish with her right hand, then bit back with a deeper chord on her left. As she fell into rhythm, her hands called and answered each other in turn, and she soon realized Vaye was teasing a slow, driving beat. She hadn't noticed when the drum slipped in, but it propelled the song forward.

She envisioned the roaring bass line as Cyrrus's crisp, cutting voice. *Make yourself use...ful. Stop... emo...ting. You... look like... a boy.* The treble notes fought back in a flurry of adventure. As she played, the beauty and the pain coalesced, creating a circular whirlwind that laughed as the bass line echoed, *lies... lies... lies.*

The two intermingled their mellifluous reverie until curfew. Aera left, renewed. As she headed to Junior Hut, she sang to herself, "Lies, lies, lies," and chuckled at Cyrrus's ridiculous assertion that he had deduced Silindion from the depths of his eccentric mental circus.

After attendance, she tossed and turned on her mat, wondering why Cyrrus was so tired lately. What did he do at night? Where would he encounter foreign languages? Her mind jumped to Panther Woman bidding farewell to Vaye in another tongue. If Cyrrus was galavanting with exotic visitors, Aera wanted to meet them too. He had followed her into the woods. Now, it was her turn.

She took her cloak from the shelf and covered her naked body, ever so discreetly, then slipped out of the room into the torchlit hallway. Four doors led to dormitories full of sleepers and beyond hers was the long, continuous wall that rounded to a dark corridor. She wondered what was down that hallway and whether there was a way out.

A torch rested in a sconce on the wall opposite her room. Aera took it from its holder, then tiptoed around the corner. She held the flame near the walls, checking for doors or windows, but found nothing until she rounded the bend to another corridor, where she discovered a single door. It was wooden with an arched top, just like the others, but its center contained an iron plate with a giant keyhole. Quietly, she tried the knob, but the door was locked tightly in place. She leaned all her weight against it and pushed to no avail.

A rock wall jutted across the corridor just beyond the door, marking an abrupt end to the hallway. She checked the area for portals, windows, or knobs, but found none. Her only hope was the locked door. She examined every edge and stared into the keyhole, but all she saw was blackness beyond. There was no exit here.

She returned to the dark corridor, rounded the corner, and placed the torch back into its home. All that was left were the four dorms and a staircase leading upstairs to the lobby, which contained only a guarded exit and the lavatories with their caged windows. There was no way out, yet it was obvious that Cyrrus spent his nights awake. She wondered where he went, who was there, and how he knew so much— yet it would be unfair to ask when she was hiding Vaye from him.

So many secrets, Aera thought. *Everyone lies.*

~

Silindion lessons took off immediately and gained traction as the seasons flew by. Aera and Cyrus spoke the language together, exchanged Silindion notes during classes, and devised games to challenge each other. Each day, they shared meals by the boulder and spent the remainder of their lunch breaks at Great Gorge. They always separated after dinner. Aera used that time to visit Vaye, while Cyrus engaged in unexplained ventures.

Their pattern continued until a sunny Late-Winter morning, when there was a rift in the usual commune activity. The Dining Hall was closed for breakfast, and everyone was ushered to the river. As Aera followed her line across the Field, she heard a choir singing an epic rendition of the commune anthem in the distance.

> *We are all the same*
> *Giving to each other*
> *Living for our friends*
> *Our sisters and our brothers*
>
> *All united!*
> *Undivided!*
> *We are all the same*
>
> *We are family*
> *Building life together*
> *No one is alone*
> *Love cannot be severed*
>
> *Common story!*
> *Share the glory!*
> *We are all the same*

Aera and Cyrus found each other in the crowd, then made their way to the riverside to observe the scene. Officers lined the opposite bank, and Nurin stood in the middle of the bridge with a megaphone. Once everyone had taken a place, several uniformed officers laid a lifeless body atop a raft and lowered it onto the water. Aera recognized the Art instructor, Sarode.

Just recently, Aera had attended Sarode's Art Class. She was croaking and hunched over, clearly miserable that she had to be there, but Aera had not suspected anything was wrong. Sarode had been old and cranky for as long as she could remember. Now, the instructor's life of slavery had finally ended here. She'd lived all those years and never tasted freedom.

Nurin gave a brief oratory about Sarode's great service and love for the wonderful community. Then, two officers extended their torches and set fire to the raft. The crowd watched as the flaming mass floated away. While it sailed downstream, Nurin assumed salute position. The throng followed along, chanting, "We are all the same!"

The crowd repeated the mantra, but Aera was silent. She couldn't bear to live her whole life in Ynas, only for it to end this way. Why would anyone waste away in the commune? What was the point of it all?

"Death is the most unifying facet of life," Cyrrus said expressionlessly.

A chill ran down Aera's spine. In death, all really were the same.

Throughout the day, Cyrrus skipped meals and rushed to Great Gorge in the cold. Aera ate dinner by the boulder, noting that the funeral had intensified his sense of urgency. Was he studying Silindion for its own sake, or did he anticipate using it in the outside world? He wanted to rule Ynas or conquer the entire planet. Did he ever dream of freedom?

Aera finished her meal, then followed her secret path and was greeted by the aroma of smoke. Cyrrus was sitting cross-legged by a fire inside their circle of stones, reading *Parë Në Sulë* with such concentration that he didn't acknowledge her arrival. She retrieved two tablets from the hollow and sat beside him. Staring at characters he'd written for her, she felt helpless: angles and curves seemed to pop out everywhere, losing all semblance of meaning.

"There's no point in studying Silindion," she grumbled. "It's useless if we die in Ynas."

Cyrus ignored her and continued reading, but Aera knew her presence calmed him. She scribbled on the back of the tablet and turned it about in the firelight until Cyrus began to mutter.

"A Nassando must balance passion and reason... why?" He flipped through the book. "*Kuinu* is the union of nature and man, the bond between Angels and mortals..." His voice trailed off.

"*Kuinu?*" Aera chimed, gazing over his shoulder.

"Some kind of magic," Cyrus said dismissively, then mumbled text to himself. "*Vukiello osteryán sinë ssa yassantë ossë vekósëa, manyello eis silmaroskari vaurón koteinta...*"

Aera translated in her mind. 'Spin breezes so they become angry winds, bring forth from moon sheen a deathless spirit.' Spinning breezes sounded powerful, and 'deathless spirit' reminded her of the faces in the fog. Was this fantasy, or was *kuinu* real?

She waited for a while, struggling to sit still as her mind raced. What did Cyrus hope to gain from translating *Parë*? What did he know about magic? Her thoughts went to his mysterious drawing, still in her cloak pocket. They had begun Silindion lessons almost a year ago. Did she know enough to translate it?

She retrieved a pencil from the gorge, then headed deep into the forest, where Cyrus wouldn't find her. Moonlight cut through an opening between trees, and Aera settled there. For the first time since they had become friends, she dug out the drawing and unfolded it.

It was no longer gibberish: the symbols came to life. Words jumped off the page. *Aldëa.* Alone. *Yoveskén.* Change. She could do this.

She chipped away at the scribbles, one letter at a time, writing on the secret page itself. Once the whole phrase was displayed in Syrdian characters, she read it aloud. "*Ya ëassávihya, ien sikosi mesíndilya.*

Sëotmahya, illién séskilya lundasya ovi, tistë yoveskén Onórnëan, ë áldëa si.[1]"
As she read it a few more times, it acquired a melodic rhythm. *Tistë yoveskén Onórnëan, ë áldëa si…*

Something was familiar. Where had she heard it before? Chirps of crickets surrounded her, and she listened to them coming and going, hum by hum, buzz by buzz. A breeze cooled her skin and moonlight glowed against the page. Suddenly, it crashed into her thoughts: *Sinë veskento i suínanya më Onórnëan.*

These were the very words screeched by the faces in her nightmares years ago. What did they mean? She wrote both phrases, side by side. *Tistë yoveskén Onórnëan. Sinë veskento i suínanya më Onórnëan.*[2]

Yoveskén, veskento… one word, two forms. The root, *vesk*, meant 'change.' 'Veskento' meant 'they will change' and 'yoveskén,' 'who will change.' 'Yoveskén Onórnëan' translated to 'who will change the world.'

She translated the rest, then sorted through tenses, declensions, and prepositions. Once she had everything figured out, she stared at an assemblage of disheveled words in Syrdian. She arranged them, ordering the sentences according to the conventions she had extrapolated from Cyrrus's lessons until, finally, it came together:

> *Beneath my bum, your chair would be a throne.*
> *In my hand, your pencil makes my power known.*
> *Who will change the world, it is I alone.*

The curfew bell gonged and Aera rubbed her eyes, returning from a trance. *Who will change the world, it is I alone.* Too similar to her dream. Too eerie. She folded the paper, stuffed it in her pocket and raced back to the hut.

Hours later, Aera lay awake as the mantra haunted her thoughts. *Ya ëassávihya, ïen sikosi mesíndilya. Sëotmahya, illién séskilya lundasya ovi, tistë yoveskén Onórnëan, ë áldëa si.* She no longer needed to look at the drawing. Cyrrus's poem was implanted in her mind along with a melody and rhythm.

She replayed the phrase from her childhood dream: *Sinë veskento i suínanya më Onórnëan.* '*And his deeds will change the world.*' It was barely different from Cyrrus's assertion, '*Who will change the world, it is I alone.*'

There were more words in the dream, but she couldn't remember them. She pictured herself in the white forest, surrounded by faces in the fog. *Sinë veskento i suínanya më Onórnëan. Në Laimandil...* what was *Laimandil?* She closed her eyes, straining to recall the rest, but all she found was static and chaos. It was impossible to remember anything more.

She wondered whether Cyrrus would recognize the phrase she heard in her dreams. Might he know the remainder of the words, or where they came from? If she asked, he might deduce that she'd been harboring his drawing in her pocket for years. No amount of knowledge was worth *that*. That drawing was her darkest secret... and its contents were imprinted in her mind. She no longer needed it and could finally destroy it.

Quietly, she donned her cloak and slid out the door. The torch across the hall rested in its iron sconce, and the flame called to her. She withdrew the drawing, lit the edge on fire and dropped it to the floor. Smoke filled the hallway as the grassy, pulpy prophesy was relegated to cinders. She grabbed the torch from the wall, used it to incinerate the remaining paper bits, and returned it to its holder. At last, she was free.

She leaned against the wall and slid down to her knees, breathing in the smoky air. Finally, her mortifying plunge into the Art Room recycle bin could no longer be evidenced, and the symbols that had intrigued her for years were translated and committed to memory. One puzzle was solved, only to incite another that burned still hotter: Cyrrus's connection to her dream.

Aera needed to untangle that, as it might teach her something about herself. Yet there was no way to approach it without exposing her affair with the drawing and no guarantee that he would disclose anything if she did. He talked incessantly but revealed nothing.

If Aera wanted to understand her dream, she would have to forage through Cyrrus's cryptic past discreetly. She was trapped, fascinated, consumed; burning the drawing both released and imprisoned her. Cyrrus had lured her into a treasure hunt through his cerebral circus.

INYANONDO

1326 EARLY-AUTUMN

Aera sanded some new tablets while Cyrrus pored over *Parë*, shielding the pages from the afternoon sun. She ran her fingers along the wood to make sure each surface was smooth; indeed, they were, but she was annoyed. It had been a year and a half since Silindion lessons had begun, and Aera was learning well, but Cyrrus was still hogging the book while relegating her to preparation of materials.

"I finished the pile," Aera said. "I need a turn with *Parë*."

"I copied the first chapter on a tablet to test my memory. It's in the tree, but you're not ready."

She found his tablet in the gorge and scanned it. He was right: the vocabulary was beyond her. Instead of translating, she compiled a list of unfamiliar words. They studied side by side for a while, enjoying a pleasant breeze and a backdrop of birdsong, moving their pages away from sunspots that inched around as the sun traversed the great oak tree.

"Listen to this!" Cyrrus exclaimed. "It says here, *henorona*... hold on, I'll translate... it says: While everyone may communicate vague sentiments through *inyanondo*, the Nassandë learn to exchange structured thought."

Aera repeated the new words to herself. *The Ness-AHN-day. Inn-ya-NON-doe.* "What's a Nassandë?"

114

"Nassan*do*. Remember? The ë is plural and the o is singular."

Aera grimaced while Cyrrus mumbled to himself: "There's no *word* for it in Syrdian. Did they purposely omit it from the commune?" He stared off into the distance for a moment, then resumed. "*Inya* means consciousness, and *nondo* means... beyond, afar, far away... far away consciousness. If they use it to exchange thought, then it's some type of mindreading."

Mindreading. Aera thought of her dream and its eerie similarity to Cyrrus's poem. This might explain why the Silindion language entered her mind in the first place. Perhaps she'd read someone's mind, or someone had projected the language into hers.

She recalled the day in History Class when she'd fantasized about plunging an axe through the DPD barricade while Cyrrus drew the identical scene. Was it he or she who had read the other's mind that day? That image, and the language, were more than vague sentiments. Was one or both of them a Nassando... whatever that was?

"We need to master this," Cyrrus determined.

He focused intently on the page and read bits aloud in a mixture of Silindion and Syrdian as he attempted to decipher the text. Finally, he said, "It says *inyanondo* results from the release of emanations out of the... *suru*...? and the expression of the... *semissë*... the mind, in essence... at the level of *eseissë*." He tapped on the book. "But what is *suru*... is it conscience? Or self?"

"Wait," Aera said. "Too many new words."

"There are *four* words," Cyrrus said. "*Semissë, inyanondo, eseissë,* and *suru*. You already know *semissë* means faculty of reason or reasoning process, which we associate with the mind. *Inyanondo* means far-away consciousness, which I will loosely translate to mindreading, and *eseissë* is..." He paused. "It's a complex concept I'll save for later, but suffice it to say it's an intangible space where all thought resides."

Es-ee-say, Aera thought, and jotted down the meaning. *An intangible space where all thought resides*... that was certainly enigmatic.

"I'll read the whole sentence again," he said. "Mind-reading results from the release of emanations out of the *suru* and the expression of the mind at the level of an intangible space where thought resides." Excitedly, he explained, "What it's saying is, the content of the *suru* and the mind must be projected into a world of unspoken thought, so that a mindreader may read it. But I don't get what *suru* is."

Content of the suru and the mind. What might be paired with mind? "Character," Aera suggested. "Or... emotions."

"You presume everyone has emotions," Cyrrus said. "It's myopic to assume everyone functions the way you do."

Aera glared at him. His statement implied he had no emotions. Did he think she was stupid enough to believe that?

"Let's play a game," he suggested. "Five points if we read each other's thoughts correctly, subtract five if we're wrong. I'll go first. Focus on a memory and I'll tell you what you're thinking."

Aera didn't want Cyrrus to read her mind. She tried not to think about anything and, instead, focused on the surrounding birds, trying to identify them based on their chirps.

"Mating calls," Cyrrus said plainly.

Mating calls? What?

"That's what you're thinking about. Male birds competing to attract a fertile female for copulation."

So unromantic, Aera thought. His dry description of birdsong ruined the music entirely.

"Now you're admiring my cynicism," Cyrrus grinned. "Fifteen points for me."

"Ten."

"Five for the birds, five for knowing you love me, and five for manipulating your feelings before I used *inyanondo* to interpret them. Now, your turn."

Aera wanted to smack him for being so annoying but decided not to perpetuate his petty games. "You *deduced* my thoughts," she said. "What am I thinking now?" She played some music in her mind and imagined the lyrics: *Lies, lies, lies.*

"Lies, lies, lies... and some music." Crisply, he added, "Twenty."

There was no way to deduce *that.* He could read Aera's mind! Did this mean he already knew about the drawing, her childhood fascination with him, her visits to the cottage? Was that why he'd followed her into the woods, or was it because he knew she was hiding something illegal? Was there any way to guard her secrets from him?

Aera was on edge all day as she strained to focus on tasks and hide her tension from Cyrrus during dinner. Afterward, she headed to the cottage, and along the way, her pulse raced. If Cyrrus could read her thoughts, did that mean he could read everyone else's? Was that how he uncovered secrets about the commune, forbidden languages, and DPD lies? What did he know about Vaye?

The forest was a blur, and the insect noise was suffocating. Aera felt exposed and vulnerable. Vaye had asked her to keep their acquaintance secret, but that wasn't possible if Cyrrus could read her mind...

Suddenly, it dawned on Aera: Vaye also could read her mind! Vaye often responded to unspoken questions and opened the door as though expecting Aera's arrival. *Parë Në Sulë* belonged to Vaye, which meant she could read Silindion and had likely mastered the techniques in the book. It all fit.

Why had Vaye sought out Aera? Why had Cyrrus? She wondered: *Where did **I** come from?*

She thought of the forest of white trees in her dreams. It was always familiar, but she had yet to find anything like it in Ynas. Was it a memory from her own forgotten past, something outside the commune? Or had someone projected that image into an intangible realm where all thought resided, from whence she inadvertently accessed it through *inyanondo?*

As she approached the cottage, she prepared for the usual doorway greeting, but nothing happened. She confirmed from outside that the upstairs curtains were open and went inside. The fireplace was dark and there was no sign of Vaye. Her absence was not unusual. Yet this time, the taste of the autumn air, the dim lighting of sunset and the aroma of the piano's wood made Aera uncomfortable. The room was too quiet. She couldn't sit still.

She stared at the empty music rack and recalled the first time she saw *Parë Në Sulë*, whose symbols matched Cyrrus's drawing. There was no rationale for his ability to read Silindion, nor the knowledge that sprang from...

...where?

Aera rose from the piano bench and approached the familiar painting. Ebony eyes stared back at her beneath the mysterious forehead-light. A black flower wreath contrasted with white curls and charcoal skin, entirely unlike any pigments seen in Ynas.

"Who are you?" Aera demanded. "Where did you come from?"

She ventured through the archway into the kitchen. A table butted the span of wall facing the main room, with dishes and utensils piled on top, and pots, pans and buckets clustered on a shelf below. In the corner, a teapot rested on a grate-covered fireplace beneath a chimney. Along the far wall, two windows provided plentiful light for potted plants arranged along a countertop. Above it, shelves bulged with small glass vials with all colors and hues of liquid.

Those vials were familiar: Panther Woman had accepted several from Vaye. When Aera had inquired about Panther Woman, Vaye had told her she was dreaming. Did she also think Aera stupid?

Aera turned toward a curved wooden staircase that disappeared into the circular stone wall and led up to Vaye's bedroom. For so many years she heard stairs creaking, but she'd never before seen them. She climbed the stairs and braced herself as she came to the top and entered a wide, sunlit space.

Vaye's bedroom encompassed the entire upstairs: a circular stone room rife with the aroma of wildflowers, greenery, and moist soil. Skylights dominated the ceiling, and a purple cast from the sunset spilled in, illuminating countless potted plants arranged on shelves along every wall. Windows facing east displayed the grove and colorful clouds beyond, while the Western flank framed leaves and trees.

In the corner, a mat covered in khaki sheets accommodated several sleepy cats. Beside the bed, an ornate table held a pile of books and a candle. The top book had a Silindion title.[1]

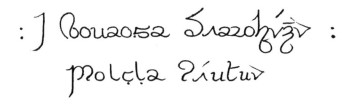

Aera translated the characters with difficulty and puzzled out the phrase: '*I Vairavar Pornamettë. Thaldalar Hóillië.*' The title contained an unfamiliar word... 'as a Healing Herb...' and 'Thaldalar Hóillië' was likely the author's name. Aera was proud of herself for translating most of it without writing anything and chuckled at the thought of Vaye reading a whole book about a single plant.

There were more books beneath it, but Aera decided not to touch them, lest she disturb their order and leave traces of her presence there. Beside them was a shiny dagger in a leather case and a ring of metal keys with one quite distinct from the others: it was longer and had a wide, intricate top made of rusted iron. She imagined it would open some ancient door and wished she could enter such places.

She continued across the room to examine the wall beside the fireplace, which contained more shelves of books and plants with artistic wood carvings hanging between them. Some of the designs were more intricate than others, but all contained combinations of people, animals, plants, and geometric symbols like the ones in *Parë*. On one, Aera spotted a girl with a flower wreath beside a young woman with identical curls. Might that woman be a younger Vaye? Who was the girl, and why did Vaye have depictions of her everywhere?

Beyond stood a giant wooden cabinet, and Aera opened it to reveal an assortment of hanging garments colored in various greens and earthy shades. Many were made of leather, fur, and other materials that nobody wore in Ynas. Some were decorated with gems and cross-hatched arrangements of tie-strings, more ornate even than Panther Woman's outfit. Beneath the clothes were shoes and boots, some very elaborate, fashioned from the same exotic materials.

Aera had never seen these outfits and wondered where Vaye wore them. It was unlikely she spent all her time in Ynas. She had so much clothing of such excellent quality, while everyone else was permitted only two outfits made of linens, wool and sheepskin. *We are all the same,* Aera thought, and grimaced.

She closed the cabinet, headed to the eastern windows, and gazed out at the courtyard, gloriously colorful from above. Against the plant-lined windowsill rested a wooden chest crowned by a copper hinge and safeguarded by a golden lock. Vaye had enough secrets to fill a human-sized chest, yet trusted Aera to be in her home without her. Aera could not imagine why.

She descended the creaky stairs and caught a glimpse of Vaye in her pumpkin patch outside the kitchen window. She wondered if Vaye would survey her mind and learn she'd sneaked around upstairs, and whether she would admit it if she did. Would Vaye willingly expose her mindreading ability just to admonish Aera's prowling? She was curious to see how Vaye would react and waited at the piano until Vaye came inside, barefoot.

"Good evening, dear," Vaye intoned, her velvet voice as inviting as ever. Aera couldn't tell whether Vaye was unaware of her excursion upstairs or was playing dumb.

Vaye disappeared into the kitchen. As Aera ran through scales, pots clanked behind the wall where the mysterious girl stared back at Aera from inside her frame.

Aera was becoming increasingly convinced that Vaye was hiding a secret light, like the one in the painting, under her forehead band. What was she doing back there, right under Aera's nose, with all those exotic plants? Who or what was she? Where did *she* come from?

There were so many secrets. So many lies. Cyrrus was just as guilty as Vaye. He knew much more than he let on and he enjoyed confounding Aera.

She spread her hands out on the keys and played a chord. Singing along in her head as her hands followed, she thought, *Lies, lies, lies.* The chords moved down along with the words. *One* two three, *one* two three. *Lies, lies, lies.*

> *I cannot read your mind*
> *But I am far from blind*
> *Lies, lies, lies*
> *Lies, lies, lies*

Descending chords accompanied the lyrics in Aera's mind. She did not sing aloud but repeated the phrase on piano and imagined the lyrics ringing out in a powerful voice. The percussive thrusts invigorated her as she sang to herself.

> *You think I'm so naive*
> *I'll helplessly believe*
> *Lies, lies, lies*
> *Lies, lies, lies*

Your circus is a stage
Your knowledge is a cage
If you have no heart
I'll rip your games apart

Suddenly Aera realized she was singing aloud, competing with the thrust of her chords. She stilled her hands and glanced at Vaye, who was sitting by the fireplace, reading a book.

"Play as long as you like, dear," Vaye said. "Your song brings this story to life."

Vaye's voice was as pleasant as usual, and her warm brown eyes conveyed no hint of annoyance. Either she didn't know what Aera had done, or she was perfectly aware and waiting for Aera to confess. Was this a test? Exasperated, Aera turned back to the piano and resumed her rhythm.

Lies, lies, lies
Lies, lies, lies

My mind has thoughts to spare
Read them if you dare
Watch as I defy
Each and every lie

Aera played harder and harder, recycling the same lyrics and singing some aloud. She was embarrassed by her wispy voice and wished she could blast the lyrics, though it gratified her that Vaye might hear them in her mind. The song escalated along with her energy until she was depleted.

After a short rest, Aera said goodbye and headed to the door. Vaye bid her farewell with a smile, as though everything was fine, but Aera knew that facade was a lie.

POWER

1327 EARLY-WINTER

To mark their thirteenth birthday, Aera's Age Group was assigned to Sewing. Cyrrus sat beside her, and although the bags under his eyes were raccoon-like, he didn't rest his head on the table. Usually, he dozed through every class period, but someone so vain as he would never forego sewing.

For the next week, he spent breaks in the Garment Unit obsessing over fabrics, measurements, and other minutiae of garment science. Throughout classes, he ignored the lessons and stripped down to his underwear to measure himself, bending and stretching to calculate with precision each limb, joint, and crevice. Girls gaped and instructors gasped, but Cyrrus either ignored them or recited pertinent laws. He tweaked Rayine's patterns, scribbling numbers and letters on his pages until they were overrun with equations and geometric designs.

On the day fabrics were distributed, he took them with him after class. The following morning, he brought them to the boulder, laid them out in the sun and examined them. They were deep black and rich forest green, more intense than any colors Aera had seen on a commune uniform. She imagined mixing her white aesthetic with some black and asked, "How did you do it?"

"There's a mushroom that grows on pine trees behind the vegetable fields. I collected caps all year. It's ideal for dye, but the Garment workers refuse to use them. For the green, I mixed in iron and aluminum, and for black, a standard iron mordant."

Aera was disappointed that she couldn't mimic the process but amused that he'd planned this all year. His obsessive vanity was cute and his science, strikingly effective. The colors were impressive, and the dye had penetrated every fold. While everyone else's cloaks and pants would be uniform beige, with tunics made from a pile of mundane-colored fabric pieces, Cyrrus took control of his entire outfit.

"The Garment workers can't do this," Cyrrus boasted, raising his brow. "The formulae aren't available in any of *their* books."

"Where did you get them?"

Cyrrus's eyes gleamed, but he did not respond. The rings around them had disappeared, suggesting he'd sacrificed his mysterious nightly activities for the sake of sewing. Aera sensed there was more to it than mere vanity. Cyrrus was preparing to make a statement, to expand his notoriety and prestige in the commune. He did nothing outside a plan.

During class, Cyrrus applied calculations to paper cutouts with the utmost care. Aera could not abide the thought of him looking so much more interesting than she and decided to attempt something adventurous. She conjured a tunic that hung in a V-shape in the front and back like Panther Woman's dress, a cloak slimmer than the standard design with strong belt loops and hidden pockets, and a more elegant under-tunic with overlapping layers, inspired by Vaye's gowns. By the second week of Mid-Winter, she'd completed all her garments except for the pants. She wanted a snug fit like Cyrrus wore but was uncertain how to create it.

"Cyrrus," she whispered to him. "How do you make tight pants?"

"I apply formulae beyond your mathematical and artistic capacity," he said without looking up from his work.

"Stop emoting," Aera hissed, and decided to prove him wrong. She racked her brain, trying to concoct an interesting design. Her mind jumped to the garments in Vaye's cottage, overflowing with layers of material she couldn't access... then, she recalled the decorative tie-strings. That was within her 'mathematical and artistic capacity.' She decided to cut the pants a few inches wider than her legs and sew loopholes along the outer seams, so she could adjust the fit as needed. She was not yet sure what she would use for ties but decided to proceed and figure that out later.

Cutting the outline was easy, but sewing the edges of each loophole was a tedious process that would drag on for weeks. Alongside her, Cyrrus was hard at work. Aera forced herself not to peek. Though optimistic about her outfits, she knew they wouldn't compare to his. She feared one glance in his direction might destroy her motivation.

During lunch break, Cyrrus rushed Aera to Great Gorge, where he pored over *Parë* with an especially severe look. They translated on their respective oak branches in silence until he tapped his pencil against the wood.

"*Kuinu* requires realization of the *suru* and mastery of the *semissë*," he mumbled to himself. "But wouldn't the *semissë* be used to master the *suru?*"

"Did you figure out what *suru* means?" Aera asked.

"The seat of emotion," Cyrrus said dryly. "Or... emotional center. The Syrdian translation is *heart*, though it's imprecise. What's crucial is that they differentiate *suru* from the *semissë,* which is the faculty of reason. The author claims we can release emanations from the emotional center, but she doesn't explain what emotion *is.*"

"By Riva's Trees," Aera said mockingly. "Must I explain everything to you?"

"No," Cyrrus snapped. "Emotion is a system of spontaneous reflexes derived from a combination of transient physical state, primal urge and previously learned responses."

"Sounds like memorized text."

"I have yet to find an author, or *any* person, who is honest about this," Cyrrus asserted. With sardonic emphasis, he added, "When I meet such a person, I will embrace him."

"Or... her?"

Cyrrus straightened up. "I would investigate numerous factors to assess the likelihood that our combined genetics would produce efficient offspring."

"Would you still embrace her if it wouldn't?" Aera challenged.

"I would not breed with her," he retorted stiffly. "The offspring would be a waste of life."

"Offspring," Aera laughed. "Can't you hug someone without 'breeding?'"

Cyrrus stared down at the book, ignoring her comment. "Did you translate the first section yet?"

Aera smiled, relishing that Cyrrus's emotions had forced him to change the topic. Toying with him was immensely satisfying.

"There are a few words I don't know," she said.

"Read them to me."

She turned her tablet to the translated side and located the circled words. "First... what are Angels?"

"Natural elements," Cyrrus said. "The moon is the Angel Alárië, fire is the Angel Sotona, and so forth. In essence, an Angel is a personification of nature."

Aera remembered Vaye's assertion that the moon and star were lovers. If the moon was Alárië, perhaps the star had a name too. She grinned, wrote down the names, and read the untranslated words from her tablet. "*Inyarya... sundatëa... kalma... Nestë.*"

Cyrrus spoke in a monotone. "*Kalma* is amulet, and *sundatëa* is Nassando-hood, the achievement of becoming a Nassando... synonymous with enlightenment. *Nestë* are a species, separate from humans, which I will teach you about another time."

Finally, Cyrrus was acknowledging another species existed. Aera was excited to hear more.

"*Inyarya* is an idealistic and fallacious concept," Cyrrus continued. "It translates to self-consciousness, awareness of who you are."

"You accept mind reading and magic," Aera chuckled, "but self-awareness is a bridge too far."

She expected Cyrrus to see the humor in this, but he didn't. Instead, he furrowed his brow and relapsed into a didactic tone.

"Identity derives from external factors—like lineage, rank and culture—so it is illogical to conceptualize a personal identity within," he declared. "Regarding self as a truth to discover promotes it as a consistent entity, which is inimical to natural law, since circumstances constantly change, and we must adapt to survive. It would be more honest to acknowledge that self is incidental, and that resilience requires concealing our vulnerabilities from ourselves."

Cyrrus was making this unnecessarily complicated. "Maybe *your* personality is incidental," she teased. "Mine isn't."

"I have a sense of self, rather than an absolute self which consciousness would unmask. To apply *inyarya* realistically, call it sense of self, rather than consciousness of self."

This distinction was nonsensical and unnecessary, but Aera wrote down his thoughts anyway and decided not to push him. He often resorted to show-off words when he was insecure. Side by side, the two continued their work in silence until the bell gonged.

Trips to Great Gorge continued, even as the weather grew colder. They sat by the fire while Aera worked her way through the first chapter of *Parë,* and Cyrrus charged through the rest. Sewing class was tedious and repetitive but became more exciting as their fabrics turned into outfits.

Aera resisted the temptation to check on Cyrrus's progress until just before Late-Winter, when he held up his garments to examine them. All eyes were glued to him, and the room was quiet. As he turned each garment to inspect every stitch and crevice, Aera was transfixed.

Aside from the buttons, his outfits were completed. The sleeves of his black cloak folded back to create cuffs that displayed the rich forest green lining beneath, also visible on the underside of an impressive folding collar and the inside of an imperial hood that draped extravagantly past his wide shoulders. The trousers were black and form-fitted with belt loops along the waistline and buttonholes at the ankles, and his black tunic was equally striking, with sleeves that folded back at the cuffs to expose forest green stitching. He had designed additional fabric at the neckline, outlining a deep slit, creating a gap ideal for buttons.

Aera's outfit was several levels of magnitude below the intricacy of his, and she wished she'd never looked. At the same time, she wondered whether he was aware of the blatant hypocrisy between his actions and his philosophy. Didn't he realize his outfits were not merely a display of power, but also a statement of personal identity?

That afternoon at lunch break, when they arrived at Great Gorge, Aera rewrote her translations and smirked as she passed the word *inyarya*. Cyrrus invested much into his outer appearance, yet remained willfully ignorant of his inner landscape. She decided to challenge him and show off her progress.

"You might translate the book, but you'll never attain *sundátëa*," she poked. "The first lesson group leads to *inyarya*, because if we don't understand ourselves, then we don't know *why* we do anything, and it's all meaningless."

"Everything is inherently meaningless," Cyrrus said nonchalantly. "Things have meaning because we ascribe meaning. We attribute properties to words and agree on them collectively, which makes language *useful*, but not inherently *meaningful*."

Aera's eyes wandered to a sentence on her wood block: *Thought, the creator, is not bound by shape or language.* Was this Cyrrus's argument?

"Ilë the creator," Cyrrus said, responding to her unspoken question. "Not thought."

Aera snickered: he was reading her mind to assert superiority. He needed to prove that he could, in fact, attain *sundatëa*.

She flipped her tablet to the back side, where the translation was written in Cyrrus's hand: 'Ilë: *Eseissë*: Thought.' Beside it was her own note: '*Eseissë: An intangible space where all thought resides.*'

"The common translation of *eseissë* is 'world-soul,'" Cyrrus explained. "The Nestë believe Ilë is a sentient being who created everything we know, then left a part of his essence in the world which permeates all beings. Realistically, there is no such thing as soul or Ilë, but *eseissë* does exist, and may be understood as an intangible space where thought resides."

"How do you know *eseissë* exists?"

"Because I experience it."

"How?" Aera pressed.

"*Inyanondo* is the process of one Nestë organizing his thoughts to send messages into *eseissë* so another might hear them, so that's one example," Cyrrus explained. "Even without intent, we all tap into *eseissë* and project thoughts into it. We create *eseissë*, just as it creates us."

Without intent. Aera wondered if this might explain her dreams, and if she might have picked up Silindion from *eseissë*. Was that where Cyrus had learned it? How was this related to a creator?

"The text says Ilë was the creator," Aera said, "and you translated Ilë to *eseissë*. Do you believe *eseissë* created us?"

"There's no such thing as a creator, but Ilë is a glorified personification of *eseissë*. It's the same as naming the moon Alárië, formulating a narrative and worshipping her as a deity."

"What's a deity?"

"A fictional character with magical powers worshipped by groups of people who believe he created the universe."

"Who would worship a fictional character?" Aera chuckled. "Fictional people?"

Cyrus's eyes lit up. "Would you believe me if I told you I have magical powers?"

"No," Aera insisted, though the thought was not entirely alien.

"How do I always know what you're thinking?" Cyrus asked. "Can anyone else remember everything they read and recite it at will? Can anyone else draw or sew the way I do?"

"We don't know, because most people don't brag like you do."

Cyrus grinned. "As my talents continue to develop, others will acknowledge my magical powers. And when I rule the world, people will write about me and my special deeds. After a few hundred years, the writing will become distorted, and eventually I will be depicted as a hero, a villain, or a deity."

"So, a deity is a fictional character based on a show-off," Aera said.

"Fictional characters can also be based on nothing but an idea. If a story elicits their emotions, people believe it. You would believe it too if it appealed to your beloved feelings."

Aera rolled her eyes. "My beloved feelings are late for baths." She jumped down from the tree and waited a moment for Cyrus, but he returned his attention to the book, signaling her to leave without him.

She headed back to Vapid Village and jogged through Western Willows just as a group of bullies were entering the river. To avoid them, Aera decided to visit the clothing area first. She took her time washing her dirty clothes and hanging them on the clothing line, but when she finished, the river was still swarming with people. She left her clean clothes behind a willow tree and approached the river with her towel wrapped around her to block the chilly wind while she eased her way in. The water was agonizingly cold.

"There's the bony mop!" Hizad barked as his friends hooted and guffawed. "You look like a boy!"

Aera froze in place. Cyrrus had said the same thing.

"Why's your hair so long?" Hizad bellowed. "To hide your wee-wee?"

Roaring laughter resounded, and Aera's eyes stung with hot tears. She splashed violently, aiming at Hizad, then plunged under the freezing water for as long as she could. When she surfaced, the crowd had moved further away, and Hizad was drying off by the shore. His towel barely stretched around his blubber.

It occurred to Aera that, in her frustration, she'd forgotten to leave her towel at the shore. She washed quickly, wrung out the freezing wet cloth and went back to the willow tree, where she found her trousers with two muddy arrows pointing diagonally toward the crotch. Her heartbeat thundered, and she sweltered with rage.

Hizad yowled from afar, "To help you find your wee!"

Aera exploded in anger and kicked the tree so hard her bare foot stung; then, she kicked it again. She pushed the towel against her pants in a furious effort to wipe off the arrows but managed only to spread them into a smear. Her other clothes were wet and there was nothing else to wear. This mess was all she had.

Defeated, she oozed her sticky wet legs into her soiled pants, hands shaking uncontrollably. She squeezed her fists and imagined smearing mud over Hizad's porcine face.

Once dressed, she trudged indignantly along the path to the Field, where Cyrrus was waiting for her. As she inched hesitantly toward him, he commanded, "Stop emoting."

"Hizad ruined my pants," she snapped.

Distantly, he asserted, "There are more important matters."

Tears rushed to her eyes. "Like what?" she demanded. "Collecting mushrooms?"

She abandoned him and tried to pull herself together as she joined her line. Cyrrus pretended he was unaffected by people yet strove to impress them. He was not above emotions, and she would not allow him to scoff at her.

That evening, Cyrrus positioned himself silently beside Aera in the bustling, noisy Dining Hall. He fixated upon something far away; Aera followed his stare and saw Hizad. She wondered what Cyrrus was thinking and searched his eyes for a hint, but there was no emotion, no rage, no distraction. Just focus. Unrelenting focus.

Instead of taking a tray, Cyrrus secured lettuce tightly around some chicken and stuffed the whole wrap into his pocket. Once outside, he did not climb Halcyon Hill, but headed around the back of the buildings toward the Raetsek Field by the stream, where popular kids played Raetsek during meals. Aera didn't want to exhibit her soiled pants to that crowd and murmured, "Wait."

Cyrrus glanced at her and, although he did not smile, his eyes were radiant with inexplicable delight. She couldn't imagine what was going through his mind. Though she dreaded being seen, curiosity got the better of her and she followed along at his side.

The Raetsek Field was speckled with Samies stretching, kicking balls and practicing game strategy, while others sat in the grass, watching the action. Closer still, people filled picnic tables along the edge of the field near Westside Willows, and Hizad sat at the end of the row, stuffing his face. He was surrounded by the usual swarm of 15-16 Group bullies, plus a pride of girls all talking at once in varying nasal and shrill tones, creating a torrent of sonic babble.

Cyrrus strutted toward them and Aera understood he was headed for a confrontation. The collective chatter abated as all the girls craned their necks in unison to delight in Cyrrus's approach. Aera watched from nearby while Cyrrus positioned himself directly beside Hizad, towering over the fat boy whose cheeks were plump with food.

"What are you looking at, genius?" Hizad asked gruffly.

"Whaddaya want?" echoed a nervous, fish-faced boy beside him.

Without looking away from Hizad, Cyrrus replied, "I intend to stare at Hizad long enough to provoke reaction."

"Mister big-words," Hizad said. "Darse off. I'm eating."

Though Cyrrus did not smile, satisfaction radiated through his angular cheekbones.

"Go away," barked fish-face. "Farkus."

"Easy, Rennid," instructed Codin from the next table.

Cyrrus continued watching Hizad, and the group grew increasingly tense. Abruptly, Rennid turned to the girls and scowled, "He's *insane*."

Though some nodded in agreement, none peeled their eyes from Cyrrus. His upright posture and calculated calm exuded confidence. He was not going anywhere. Aera enjoyed watching the bullies squirm and fixed a firm glare on Hizad to aid the effort.

"I am the most rational person on the commune," Cyrrus declared. "Calling me insane only trumpets your ignorance."

A silence followed. Hizad stuffed his chicken wrap into his face while Cyrrus watched, and his friends stifled their snickering.

"Samely, Brains," Hizad finally said. "Why don't you write an equation to make yourself disappear?"

Cyrrus took the wrap from his pocket and dramatically ripped off a large chunk with his teeth. After chewing, he spat it on Hizad's tray.

Hizad stood up and yelled, "That's disgusting!"

"I thought you might appreciate some extra food," Cyrrus said coolly, "if you could stuff any more in."

"Are you trying to start a fight?" Hizad huffed.

"It already started." Cyrrus's green eyes gleamed. "Bullying is the last refuge of the incompetent. And here you are."

Rennid was right: Cyrrus *was* insane... and Aera loved it. She had no idea how he planned to battle someone so colossal and hoped he wouldn't regret this.

Hizad spun around, lifted Cyrrus by the hips, hurled him over his head and threw him down with effortless ease. As Cyrrus landed, Aera held her breath and heard a gasp: it was Dila's. Hizad's friends jumped back, crowding the picnic tables to get a better look. Behind them, people in the field abandoned their Raetsek routines, angling to see what was happening.

Cyrrus remained motionless on the ground and stared at Hizad, who cocked his leg to kick Cyrrus in the ribs. As he did so, Cyrrus's hand shot out and grabbed Hizad's ankle. The giant yanked his leg back, but Cyrrus held firm. Hizad pulled a second time with more force, and this time Cyrrus suddenly released him, causing him to tumble backward and fall. Cyrrus casually rose to his feet and waited for the big man to get up. Aera laughed as Hizad wrestled himself from the ground, all confidence drained.

Hizad squared off and threw a punch at Cyrrus's face, but Cyrrus ducked easily and jerked Hizad's outstretched arm forward with impeccable timing, using Hizad's own force to launch him off balance. Before he could recover his bearings, Cyrrus lunged and mounted him from behind, wrapping his long legs around Hizad's giant waist and one arm around his huge neck. Wielding a diabolical laugh, Cyrrus raised his free hand and waved to the onlookers. Then, he yanked Hizad's nose, pulled his hair, poked his eyes, pushed his head from side to side with a finger in his ear, and twisted his neck around. *Insane* was an understatement. Cyrrus was a maniac.

Hizad heaved furiously from side to side and stomped around. Finally, he fell backwards in an attempt to crush Cyrrus, who jumped away. Hizad was down. Suddenly, it dawned on Aera: Cyrrus could read Hizad's mind and counteract his moves exactly as he made them.

Cyrrus leaped on top of Hizad, and the two wrangled back and forth. Hizad stayed one step behind but still in game, until Cyrrus got him in a choke hold and forced the big bully to roll over with his face in the dirt. Then, Cyrrus sprang up, positioned a foot on Hizad's back, and danced about with dramatic aplomb.

Nobody uttered a sound. The creek gurgled behind the field. Birds chirped. Wind blew. Hizad's friends watched from the picnic tables, too stunned to breathe. The Raetsek players and their audience stood stationary throughout the field, their eyes fastened to Cyrrus as he performed his victory parade over Hizad's body. Somehow, even after all the clownish theatrics, he exuded more dignity than ever.

Others will acknowledge my magical powers, Aera thought. *Eventually they will depict me as a deity*. Perhaps he was right.

He stepped nonchalantly off Hizad's back, projecting a disaffected air, then grabbed a clump of grass and pushed the dirt end into Hizad's face. In his crispest voice, he announced, "One good dirt deserves another."

Hizad stood up easily and realized everybody was watching. With a grunt, he looked Cyrrus over, considering whether to go another round.

"I wouldn't," said Codin from the picnic tables. He gestured toward the buildings, where some officers were watching with feigned serious-ness, though Officer Padd was openly snickering. Cyrrus waved brazenly and smiled at the officers.

Hizad scowled at Cyrrus, wiped the dirt from his mouth, and grumbled, "You got lucky."

"Right," Cyrrus said coolly. "But in any case, you will clean Aera's clothing... and your face."

The kids in the field burst into laughter, Farris among them, shout-ing, "Go Brains! Go Brains!" The entire menagerie of Hizad's friends exploded into nervous chuckles.

Cyrrus surveyed his newly adoring fans with hubristic indifference. Then he abandoned the crowd, heading toward Aera. The confident gleam in his eyes made her blush, and an unruly smile seized her face.

"Stop smiling," Cyrrus teased. "Emotions are for boors."

Aera pursed her lips as hard as she could, but the laughter dam burst. Cyrrus joined in, unfurling his girlish giggle into the open air. Dizzy with victory, they headed to the waterfall.

Cyrrus waited by the river so Aera could change into the pants she'd washed earlier, now dry from the breeze. When she undressed, she saw the arrows Hizad had drawn. Fury boiled all over again, and a memory struck her: when she first saw her pants, she had imagined smearing mud on Hizad's face herself. Once again, Cyrrus had acted out her thoughts.

Cyrrus insisted he had magical powers. Aera could no longer deny that it was... plausible.

From that moment on, Cyrrus's ego was supercharged like never before. His voice was crisper, his posture straighter and his gaze more penetrating. Aera poked at his hubris as usual, but she knew his confi-dence was earned. Though flattered by his gallantry, she wished she'd been the one who had sullied Hizad. She was too skinny and unskilled to win such a fight, yet she could not shake the feeling that at least she could have tried. Instead, she was the helpless victim and Cyrrus the illustrious hero.

Hizad approached Cyrrus on the breakfast line and handed over

Aera's pants. Cyrrus examined them carefully, held them up to stare at some barely visible remnants of dirt, and said, "Sloppy."

"You want them or not?" Hizad huffed.

"I was not anticipating quality work," Cyrrus said plainly. "This will do."

Hizad waddled toward the back of the line, looking miserable, pitiful. As soon as he was gone, Cyrrus said to Aera, "I know a formula to clean the rest."

Aera was taken aback. Cyrrus was so cavalier toward everyone else, yet protective toward her. She smiled and said, "It's ok... the new outfits are almost finished."

Cyrrus nodded. "We need to eat quickly, and there won't be time for Great Gorge. I need to visit the Shoe Room before baths."

They wolfed down their food, then went to the Garment Unit, where Cyrrus led Aera to a room filled with the pungent aroma of leather and alcohol. Two middle-aged men sat at a long table by the door, surrounded by piles of shoes. Behind the men, the room was crowded with tools and leather. Aera noticed a stock of dark leather thongs on the wall, hanging from nails. This was just what she needed to tie the seams of her pants together.

"Good afternoon, gentlemen," Cyrrus said, and grinned. He removed his shoes, placed them on the desk and said, "My feet grew."

The taller shoemaker rounded the desk and used a marked pole to measure Cyrrus's feet, then called to the shorter man, "Grab me an eleven."

The short man grunted and sorted through some shoes behind him. Aera eyed the strings. The ends hung down just low enough for her to grasp, but she would have to reach over the table while nobody was looking.

She watched as the first shoemaker joined the second in the back of the room. This was her chance. To avoid making any extra noise, she balanced carefully and positioned her arm, then quickly swiped as many strings as possible. Her heart raced as the shorter man found some shoes and stood up, but Cyrrus giggled and pointed at the other man, distracting them both from Aera. Rapidly, she stuffed the loot in her pocket, though she sensed it wouldn't be enough.

She prepared to reach for more but stopped: the shorter shoemaker was approaching. He brought with him a pair of shoes, which he placed on the table before Cyrrus.

Flatly, Cyrrus said, "Sliced cylinders do not suit my taste."

Both shoemakers stared at him blankly. Aera tried not to laugh.

From his cloak pocket, Cyrrus withdrew a small wood tablet containing a sketch of a boot, placed it on the desk and declared, "I require black shoes with squared toes, an inward curve at the arch and no wool inside."

"Raisins," said the shoemaker. "Everyone must wear the same shoes."

"Page sixty-five of *Laws of Ynas* states that every person in Ynas is entitled to own one pair of shoes," Cyrrus said. "The shape and color are not specified."

"We are all the same," the one retorted.

"Your shoes must be the same as everyone else's," chorused the other.

"Aside from the shade, my shoes will be precisely the same as Nurin's," Cyrrus said. "Choose a black pair from the collection you're preparing for export to Kadir."

Both men shifted uneasily, and neither responded. The commune was neither independent nor isolated, and its resources were not distributed exclusively to the people inside its walls. Cyrrus had exposed its involvement with other societies beyond doubt: the reaction on the shoemakers' faces affirmed the truth.

"I will resolve this at the town meeting tomorrow," Cyrrus said coolly. "If you wish to protest, arrive in the DPD courtyard before the end of breakfast. I will request an early presentation of our dispute and I expect the Renstrom will accommodate."

Cyrrus removed his socks, stuffed them in his cloak pocket, and strutted out of the room barefoot. As soon as the door closed, both he and Aera burst into laughter.

Cyrrus was absent from meals and duties the next day, but as the bell gonged to mark the second half of afternoon session, he flung open the door. A silence fell over the classroom. Everyone watched Cyrrus stroll toward his seat in shiny black boots with squared toes and an indented curve at the arches. As usual, he had won.

With impeccable posture, he took his seat, pulled leather strings from his pocket, and dropped them in front of Aera. She thanked him with a bright smile. Since they had accumulated an abundant supply, she decided to add loopholes to the front necklines of her tunics, creating a crosshatch over the chest. The contrast of dark strings against white fabric would add panache.

As she unwound the strips, Cyrrus reached into another pocket and extracted part of a cattail leaf along with several wood bits. Each one was square shaped with intricate carvings of overlapping X's. Aera had already sewn the standard round buttons onto her cloak and wished she'd thought to make her own.

Cyrrus lined up his buttons on the table and set about sanding one. Aera saw an instructor glance over and wondered if woodwork was allowed in sewing class. Others craned to see what he was doing.

Doriline crossed the room to have a closer look. She leaned over Cyrrus's shoulder and squealed, "I want square buttons! Can you make some for me?"

Cyrrus continued smoothing his button as though nobody was there, but Doriline ignored the hint. She wrapped a mousy curl around her finger and swayed against the back of Cyrrus's chair, pushing forward her budding breasts. "*Why* are you doing that?" she asked. "Aren't you too intellectual to care about clothes?"

Cyrrus didn't take the bait. He used the tip of his knife to puncture a hole in the button. Then he proceeded to twist the blade.

Doriline mustered a sugary tone and said, "Eh-ruh, why is he doing that?"

She was absolutely desperate for attention. Though Aera was tempted to point out how pathetic that was, she refused to give Doriline what she wanted.

"You never talk," Doriline said. "Cyrrus must get so *bored*."

Aera glanced at Cyrrus, anticipating some clever rejoinder, but he continued obsessing over his craftwork.

Displeased with the lack of acknowledgement, Doriline wailed, "You're both farkuses!"

She marched across the room and returned to the pink pigs. Cyrrus radiated satisfaction.

RELIGION
1327 LATE-WINTER

On the last day of winter, Instructor Rayine allowed everybody to wear their new outfits and 'discuss their work' throughout both class periods. People gathered around Cyrrus, lauding and inquiring, and he acquiesced to requests to change position so others might appreciate him from every angle.

His basic patterns didn't deviate drastically from Rayine's, aside from the flashy collars and cuffed sleeves, but everything looked sharper: the hood was more imposing, the cut more flattering, the flourishes more majestic. His pants were perfectly fitted, buttoned taut to his hips and sleek against his boots, but most interesting was a buckle on his cloak belt, carved into the pattern of two overlapping diamonds.

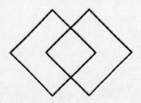

While Cyrrus peacocked, Aera turned her back to the crowd and changed into her new clothes. The crosshatched strings on her pants allowed for a snug fit, and she felt more graceful, no longer burdened by excess fabric. The v-shape design at the bottom of her tunic made it stand out, and the leather thongs at the neckline provided flair. Although less intricate than Cyrrus's, her outfit was unique. Yet nobody gathered around to gape at her. They would likely have mocked her for being a rebel if they weren't afraid of Cyrrus.

Still, Aera felt special. Although Cyrrus enjoyed everyone's admiration, he spent his free time with her. Everyone wanted to know him, but she had his attention all to herself. She couldn't help wondering why.

The two ate lunch together at the boulder, laughing and bickering as usual before heading to Great Gorge. Aera climbed up to her branch above Cyrrus, feeling agile as a cat in her new sleek pants. She smiled, reached into the hollow, and set up a study station with her two tablets, which she surveyed for mistakes or uncertainties. As she read it over, it occurred to her that she spent so much time rewriting phrases that many were etched into her mind, and she might never forget them.

"I'm done," Cyrrus announced. "Translated and memorized. How far did you get?"

Memorized? What a liar. "I finished the first section, and memorized some," she said coolly.

"Read it to me."

She took out her tablet and began. "Nassando-hood incorporates—"

"You forgot the inside of the cover."

Cyrrus handed the book to Aera. She deciphered some words in her mind, then read aloud. "*Circles and Spheres*, by Vermaventiel of Silinestin. For my child, who will be life—no, born—in Year... 1982? No... it's 1327 *now*." With a smirk, she said, "This book was written in the future."

Cyrrus grinned enigmatically, letting Aera know there was more to this story that he wouldn't reveal right now. She climbed down to sit beside him, and they read the tablet together.

Part 1. Introduction to Symbols.

SUNDÁTËA (NASSANDO-HOOD) INCORPORATES TWELVE CORE LESSONS. ACCOMPANYING EACH IS A DEEPER REVELATION. THE FIRST THREE EXPLORE HEART AND IDENTITY, ENDING WITH THE LESSON OF INYARYA (SELF-CONSCIOUSNESS). THE NEXT THREE EXPLORE MIND AND MASTERY, REVEALING THE LESSON OF VEKOS (PASSION). THE FOLLOWING THREE EXPLORE BEING AND VITALITY, ENDING WITH THE LESSON OF KALMA (AMULET). THE FINAL THREE EXPLORE MOTION AND DEITY, CULMINATING IN SUNDÁTËA.

THROUGHOUT MY JOURNEY, I CONTEMPLATED THE SYMBOLS ASSOCIATED WITH EACH LESSON. THEY BELONGED TO A LANGUAGE OF SYMBOLS CREATED BY NINDI PHILOSOPHERS OVER CENTURIES, INSPIRING COUNTLESS INTERPRETATIONS AND STRUCTURES IN THE TALISMANIST LITERATURE. A SEMINAL BOOK, WHICH ORIGINALLY HAD THE SAME TITLE IN NINDIC, PËR HASÜL, DEMONSTRATED HOW THE SYMBOLS EXPOSE DEEPER REVELATIONS UNDERLYING EACH LESSON. MANY NASSANDË HAVE RESHAPED THE ORIGINAL WORK. HERE I WILL TRANSLATE THESE IDEAS INTO SILINDION AND ADD MY REFLECTIONS.

SHAPE ENABLES LANGUAGE, AND GEOMETRIC SYMBOLS PROVIDE A PARADIGM TO REPRESENT FUNDAMENTAL CONCEPTS IN OUR CULTURE. ILË—THE CREATOR—IS NOT BOUND BY SHAPE OR LANGUAGE. THOSE ARE NESTËAN CONSTRUCTS WHICH BECOME DISPENSABLE AS UNDER-STANDING MATURES. WHILE ILË IS LIMITLESS, WE MUST ACCEPT OUR MORTALITY AND WORK WITHIN ITS LIMITS. ONCE WE ATTAIN SUNDÁTËA AND OUR CONNECTION WITH THE ANGELS BECOMES VISCERAL, STRUCTURES SUCH AS LANGUAGE AND SYMBOL BECOME FORMALITY.

ONE LIMIT IN THIS TEXT IS IMPOSED BY DIMENSIONAL STRUC-TURE, AS ONE MUST OVERCOME INHERENT BOUNDARIES TO REPRESENT A SPHERE ON PAPER. THUS, A CIRCLE REPRESENTS A SPHERE, A SQUARE REPRESENTS A CUBE, A TRIANGLE REPRESENTS A PYRAMID, AND AN ARROW REPRESENTS DIRECTION. MINDFUL OF THAT LIMITATION IN THEIR UTILITY, I WILL INTRODUCE THE LANGUAGE OF SYMBOLS.

ORENI, ALÁRIË AND TIL ARE SPHERICAL, AND EMANATE BEAUTY AS ILË DREAMED IT. ABSTRACTLY, THE SURU MAY BE CONCEPTUALIZED AS SPHERICAL, AS OUR BEAUTY EMANATES FROM IT. THE SPHERE, DEPICTED AS A CIRCLE, SYMBOLIZES THAT NOTHING EXISTS IN ISOLA-

TION. THAT WHICH BEGINS AT ANY POINT WILL RETURN, SO THAT THE END, THE BEGINNING, AND THE INFINITY OF POINTS IN BETWEEN ARE EQUIVALENT. THE NASSANDO MAY ENVISION HER *SURU* AS A SPHERE AROUND WHICH ALL EMOTIONS REVOLVE, AND TO WHICH THEY INEVITABLY RETURN.

SURU (SEAT OF EMOTION):

REASON REQUIRES ESTABLISHING PARALLELS, CREATING CATEGORIES AND BUILDING PARADIGMS. THE SQUARE OR CUBE, WITH FOUR MIRRORING SIDES, REPRESENTS THE *SEMISSË*.

SEMISSË (FACULTY OF REASON):

EVERY LIFESPAN IS MARKED BY THE TRIAD OF BIRTH, LIFE AND DEATH. THE PYRAMID, DEPICTED AS A TRIANGLE, REPRESENTS THE SOMATIC SELF. THE BASE IS PARALLEL WITH THE GROUND, THE CORPOREAL WORLD. THE SIDES POINT TOWARD ILË, TRANSCENDENCE, AS WELL AS THE PAST AND FUTURE, WHICH SHAPE THE EVOLUTION OF OUR MORTAL EXISTENCE.

MASSË (BODY):

Arrows imply motion. Ascending: Transcendence (motion toward divinity). Descending: Immanence (motion toward the corporeal). Leftward: Motion that draws upon the past. Rightward: Motion toward the future. Horizontal: Eternity (motion through time). Vertical: *Eissieina* (motion through being).

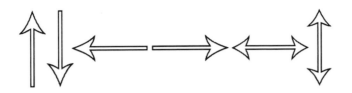

The symbols encompass concepts imprecisely represented by words. The circle, square and triangle refer both to a process as well as a material part of our being. *Suru* means 'seat of emotion,' but the circle also represents emotional experience, which is fluid. *Semissë* refers to 'process of reason,' but the square also represents the mind. *Massë* translates to physical body, but the triangle also represents physical expression and the changes our body undergoes throughout our lives.

Cyrrus turned the woodblock and placed both hands over it. "You've grasped the language," he said. "You're ready for history books."

"I need to finish this one," Aera reminded him.

"Bad idea. You need a foundation to establish context."

Aera narrowed her eyes at him. She understood the content just fine.

"This book is a sentimental gift from Vermaventiel to her kin," Cyrrus asserted. "It has no other value."

"Learning *kuinu* is valuable to me," Aera insisted.

"*Kuinu* means 'art.' You can learn that anywhere."

"You said it meant *magic*."

"Art is magical in the eyes of those who cannot produce it," Cyrrus said. "You've seen my artwork, so I presume you know that already."

Aera gave him a stern look to show she was unimpressed with his boasting, but his green eyes gleamed regardless.

He continued his protest. "Vermaventiel states plainly that she's recounting her unique personal journey and also reinterpreting another book. She shares some idiosyncratic symbols that had intimate meaning to her but acknowledges that Ilë lies beyond them."

"You're making this too complicated," Aera groaned. "I learned the language so I could read the book."

"The metaphor and its symbols are a convenient construct designed to guide us through chaos," Cyrrus said. "They may be replaced by any system, any effective representation. If you appreciate that, follow whatever system you want. But, when a structure imposes limits, you may abandon it without sacrificing what you have learned from it."

"Great," Aera bristled. "What's your point?"

"I'm taking precautionary measures to ensure you won't latch onto the book like a religion."

"I'm not *latching*. I'm *learning*."

"Even within the context of the book, I can disprove its necessity," Cyrrus said importantly. "Vermaventiel explains that the goal of learning a paradigm is to abandon it once its concepts are incorporated."

"But we can't incorporate *any* concepts without *learning what they are*."

"That's the trick!" Cyrrus exclaimed. "Learning is not equivalent to adapting. Arm yourself with knowledge, but don't believe. Never let an idea enslave you."

Aera grimaced. What was his problem? She wanted to read the book; Cyrrus had *memorized* it. Was *he* latching?

He furrowed his brow, considering something, then spoke in a softer tone. "You must grasp what religion is and acquire a wider context from which to assess its function in history. If you read this book without any context, it may poison your mind."

This was insane. Did he think her mind so weak that she would accept whatever she read without question? And why was he so concerned? She knew he was hiding something, though she could not divine what. His protests only made her want to read the book more.

"If you want to learn something useful, come to Unity Festival tomorrow morning," he concluded. "I'll demonstrate how religion operates."

"I assume you'll pose as the deity."

"Unnecessary," Cyrrus grinned. "Deities don't pose."

Aera shot him a caustic glare and in turn, he burst into girlish giggles.

～

The next morning, Aera was in for a treat. Linealle awakened the group for Unity Festival, and everyone rushed to ready themselves. As Aera made her way up the incline, Cyrrus's voice boomed from the top of the Hill.

"This entire festival is tactical indoctrination! We are being manipulated with muffins!"

Aera laughed, thoroughly amused that Cyrrus had kept his word. While he shouted gimmick phrases to demonstrate how religion worked, people whirled right past, shrieking and shoving each other in the race for the muffin table.

"The leaders use muffins to create competition and ensure that we attend this monotonous, perfidious ritual—"

"Nobody knows those big words except you!" squealed Doriline as she passed. Her flock, just behind her, laughed uproariously and shouted insults.

"Farkus!"

"Maniac!"

"Brickhead barlock!"

"They lure you here to brainwash you with propaganda!" Cyrrus continued, undeterred. "But we are capable of rational analysis and we are free to leave! Unity Festival ceases to be mandatory after our eleventh year!"

For once, Doriline had a point: Cyrrus's tirade wouldn't make sense to the Samies. Who did he imagine he was talking to? As Aera rounded the hilltop, she watched Cyrrus at the center of the plateau, impressing a small group of kids with his melodrama. It was unlikely they understood anything he said, but they were in awe of his confidence and his shiny black costume.

"The muffins are the main attraction, but they distribute them in an unjust manner!" he bellowed. "They preach equality, when in effect, they manage the muffins so the strong and popular kids obtain superior varieties!"

Cyrrus was embarrassing himself with this pretentious muffin buffoonery and his showoff cloak in the sweltering heat. Aera kept her distance and observed the Field below, where officers were setting up the festival stage and wheeling the piano up its ramp while a crowd gathered around the muffin table.

"They call it Unity Festival, all the while fueling hierarchies!" Cyrrus called. "They serve us treats as rewards for tattling on our supposed brothers and sisters! Those with the highest cumulative snitches are celebrated as candidates for the Department of Protection through Discipline and will continue bullying us until we die! They maintain their control by turning us against one another and celebrating it *here!* Why would we attend this treachery? I, for one, will not."

With that, Cyrrus marched down the Hill toward the muffin table, and several youngsters followed, stupefied. He negotiated with the adults for a while and climbed back up the Hill carrying a few muffins. Behind him, his hypnotized acolytes collected their own muffins in turn and headed off in different directions. Though Cyrrus was not smiling openly, his pompous swagger indicated he was pleased with himself, and he was so confident that others had abandoned the ceremony that he didn't bother to turn and verify it. He handed Aera a muffin and said, "Let's go."

They headed to Great Gorge and climbed to their branches, where Cyrrus ate slowly, staring off into the distance.

"Teaching children we're the same is child abuse," he said, more to himself than to Aera. "It's cruel to hold Hizad to my standard and counterproductive to squander *my* talent to function on *his* level. If my intellect were celebrated, I could improve the commune without having to undermine the leaders. Dogma is the enemy of reason." The pacing of his words was especially even, but a furrow in his brow betrayed agitation.

"What's dogma?" Aera asked gently.

"A belief or principle that is accepted as truth without question."

We are all the same, Aera thought, though she doubted they could be the only ones who questioned it.

"Indoctrination isn't confined to Ynas," Cyrrus continued. "It's ubiquitous. Most cultures employ religion to institutionalize and perpetuate ignorance. They encourage faith—a blind belief in something that can't be proven. In Silindion, it's called *ildivisetmassë*."

He paused for a moment, took a bite of his muffin, then resumed rambling with his mouth full. "They don't teach us about religion because they don't want us to realize what they're doing. But that's what this festival is about—it's a *religion*, inculcating faith in an all-powerful deity, but in this case, it's the sacred commune." Cyrrus's eyes lit up, sparkling in a shaft of sun that meandered through the leaves. "I have an idea—I'll start my own religion!"

"Good idea," Aera teased. "Since religion is so terrible, you *definitely* need to start another one."

"I'll establish a guild dedicated to knowledge, where intelligence is exalted and progress is the goal. It'll be my tribe. My *clan*. You'll join, won't you?"

Aera didn't want a religion or a clan, but Cyrrus's boyish excitement was adorable.

"What if I make you buttons? Then will you join my clan?"

"Ask Doriline," she jibed.

"What if we're both worshipped as deities? What if *I* worship *you* as a deity?"

Aera grinned wryly. "I'd never create *you*."

"Perfect," Cyrrus said. "Question everything you feel. If you mistake emotion for reality, you fall prey to vacuous ritual and dogma."

"Emotions are part of reality."

"Your fantasy reality, because you elect to be stupid."

Aera was amused by the irony: Cyrrus insulted her for having emotions because she'd hurt his feelings. "If you want to start a religion or rule the world, you'll need followers," she said. "Doriline has followers because she's direct—and she's right that people don't understand you. If you use big words and act like a snob, people won't like you."

"Being liked is inconsequential," Cyrrus retorted. "It is ideal for a leader to be feared."

"Whether they fear you or love you, their emotions determine how much power they give you," Aera said. "Believing emotions aren't real is... dogma."

Aera hoped Cyrrus would be impressed by her clever analysis, but instead of responding, he stuffed food in his mouth and avoided eye contact. Though he fostered a casual grin, she sensed that he felt exposed. She wondered if she'd been too critical.

He obliterated his muffin and jumped down from the tree. "I have matters to attend to," he said. "I may or may not return." With that, he strutted away.

Aera felt guilty for upsetting him, even though he'd brought it on himself. *So many emotions*, she thought, and chuckled. She finished her muffin, did some stretches, and headed to the cottage.

When she arrived, she found Vaye dancing in the grass, twirling something around herself so rapidly that it left trails in its wake. Vaye allowed Aera to watch for a moment while she whirled the object about, drawing figure eights. Then, she slowed to a halt, smiled and said, "Good morning, dear."

Aera examined the long, thin stick in Vaye's hand. It was nothing more than an especially straight branch, yet Vaye had used it to paint shapes in the air. Aera wondered whether that counted as producing *kuinu*.

"This is an ancient form of dance, known as Ikrati," Vaye explained. "It's based on the balance between wind, body, and instrument. To learn it, a student must have mastered the basics of Kra."

Aera was excited that Vaye's dance was related to Kra. She remembered that Vaye called it an 'ancient art' and wondered if it was part of a religious practice.

"If you'd like, I'll give you a lesson now," Vaye offered with a knowing smile. "After warmups."

By making this proposition, Vaye was professing that Aera had mastered the basics of Kra. Aera enjoyed being told she'd 'mastered' something, but doubted she deserved it. She had never practiced enough and often improvised during follow-up lessons. If Ikrati was beyond her grasp, Vaye might be disappointed. Yet Aera was too curious to refuse.

She positioned herself next to Vaye. After the two cycled through their Kra warmups, Vaye retrieved another stick from the cottage. When she returned, she instructed, "Align your legs with your shoulders, keep your knees loose, and pivot on one foot at a time."

Aera perfected her stance. That was, indeed, 'basic Kra.'

"Now," Vaye said, "follow my moves."

Vaye demonstrated how to pass the branch from one hand to the other in order to twirl it in continuous circles. It required maneuvering her arms, hands and fingers in counterintuitive ways, and took hours to learn, but Vaye remained encouraging.

Once Aera was able to twirl the stick smoothly, Vaye had her practice with increasing speed. Aera whirled it around until sundown, imagining she was flying as the wind picked up and guided her stick along. She danced alongside Vaye, balancing against the whims of the world until, finally, she collapsed in exhaustion and left.

On her way toward the village, Aera remembered Cyrrus's drama about being a deity. She wished she could tell him about Kra and Ikrati, to outmaneuver him and to teach him something for once. He might read her mind, but he would never broach any topic that gave Aera an advantage over him.

As she considered this, it struck her that Vaye was taking a risk. What would possess her to share secrets with Aera, knowing someone might read her mind? Vaye was not the type to do anything recklessly, nor purposelessly. She must have had a compelling reason to coach Aera for so many years. Was she aiming to impart her religion, or to prepare Aera for a greater destiny?

KUINU

1327 EARLY-SPRING

Birds sang under a cloudy sky while Aera and Cyrrus ate lunch. He stared off in the distance, contemplating something, and Aera's mind went to Ikrati. She continued to visualize exercises as they returned their trays, then realized suddenly that instead of climbing the Hill toward Great Gorge, Cyrrus had crossed the Field to the Administration Unit, and she'd absent-mindedly followed. He noticed her hesitation and explained, "I'm meeting an apprentice at the library."

"Who?"

"See for yourself," he said plainly. "The library is a public facility."

He opened the door to the building, and it swung closed behind him with a thud. Was that some distorted replica of an invitation? Cyrrus was obviously making new friends and was apathetic about Aera's inclusion. She could not get away fast enough.

The thought of Vaye's calm face infuriated her, so she raced to Great Gorge instead, panting and sweating, her insides exploding. When she saw the oak, tension burst through her, and she screamed aloud. Wings flapped above as birds flew away, chasing the echo of her voice through the trees. Her shoulders dropped as she exhaled.

She balanced on her hands, did some cartwheels, then faced the mighty tree. Cyrrus's branch was barren. Now that he'd finished *Parë Në Sulë*, was he bored with her? Was he seeking new 'apprentices' because Aera had pointed out his dogma? He advised her to question everything; that is, everything but *him*.

Aera learned much from Cyrrus, but she would never be his religious follower or 'apprentice.' She wanted to be his friend. She wanted his respect, but he criticized her for everything: she looked like a boy, emoted too much, latched on to *Parë* like a religion. He even advised her not to read it, lest it 'poison her mind.'

She fished the book from the hollow, flipped through the pages, and noticed one had been ripped out. Somehow, she hadn't noticed before. She found the place where she'd left off and read the opening sentence. *"Kuinúr i alayona sillánëa Nestëamma, ivenna vauréin po savoyéin...*[1]*"*

Quickly, she found a pencil and a tablet, then took her seat on the tree and wrote the phrase in Syrdian. Though she was still slow, the translations were easier every day.

PART 2: EXPANSION

KUINU IS THE UNION OF NATURE AND NESTË, THE BOND BETWEEN ANGEL AND MORTAL. THE WORLD ITSELF IS THE *KUINU* OF THE ANGELS. THROUGH *KUIYANA*, A NASSANDO MAY ALIGN WITH THE ELEMENTS. SHE MAY SUMMON RAIN INTO A RAGING RIVER, SPREAD FLAME INTO A FEROCIOUS INFERNO, SPIN BREEZES INTO A FURY, CONJURE FROM MOONLIGHT A DEATHLESS SPIRIT, DRIVE THUNDER INTO A DEAFENING ROAR, STIR SAND INTO A BLACK BLIZZARD.

Lure thunder, spin breezes... was this allegory, or beyond?

Aera jumped to the ground, where she extended her arms and imagined gathering wind in her hands. She spun, thrust her arms forward and envisioned a massive gust hurling before her, cracking open trees. A smile settled as she danced about, imagining treetops spinning, destroying all structure in the village. If *kuiyana* could enable that, then it was, indeed, art.

KUINU CANNOT ALTER THE PROPERTIES OF AN OBJECT BUT, RATHER, ACCESS THE POTENTIAL THAT DEFINES IT. INHERENT LIMITS ARE CONGRUENT WITH THE MORTALITY OF OUR CORPOREAL BODIES. OUR

SHELL REMAINS MORTAL, AND *KUINU* CANNOT ALTER OUR FORM. WATER WILL BE WET, AND *KUINU* WILL NOT MAKE IT DRY. DEATH WILL UNITE A NESTË'S SPIRIT WITH ILË, AND *KUINU* WILL NOT RESURRECT HER CORPOREAL BODY. *KUIYANA* PRESUPPOSES THE NASSANDO ACCEPTS NATURE: HER OWN, THE NATURE OF THE ANGELS, AND HER PLACE WITHIN THE NATURAL WORLD.

Cyrrus would never accede to anything about his 'natural' self, much less any emotions. He was determined to be a deity and to transcend his very humanity. *Kuiyana* would never suit him.

AS A NESTË ALIGNS WITH THE ANGELS, SHE ASSIMILATES AWARENESS THAT HER NATIVE CHARACTER IS ONLY ONE COMPONENT OF BEING. EVERY ENGAGEMENT WITH THE WORLD LEAVES AN INDELIBLE MARK. AS HER RELATIONSHIPS EXPAND, THEY MAY BE REPRESENTED BY OVERLAPPING SYMBOLS.

THE *SURU,* ALONE, MAY BE REPRESENTED AS A CIRCLE. WHEN A NESTË ALIGNS WITH ANOTHER, HER NATIVE COMPOSITION IS SIMULTANEOUSLY INDEPENDENT AND INTERDEPENDENT, AS A PORTION OF ITS ORIGINAL STRUCTURE IS SACRIFICED TO JOIN THE WHOLE. THE EMANATIONS OF BEAUTY FROM HER *SURU* COALESCE WITH THOSE OF ANOTHER, AND THEIR COLLECTIVE FORMS A NEW ENTITY. THIS IS ANALOGOUS TO THE RELATIONSHIP OF THE *SURU* TO THE PRODUCTION OF *KUINU*—THAT IS, THE *SURU* ALIGNS WITH THE EMANATION OF BEAUTY OF THE ANGEL.

EMOTIONAL BOND:

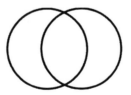

THE EFFECT OF KNOWLEDGE ON THE MIND PARALLELS THE EFFECT OF SUCH A BOND ON THE *SURU*. THE *SEMISSË* IS REPRESENTED BY THE SQUARE. WHEN A NESTË INCORPORATES NEW KNOWLEDGE, HER

REASONING EXPANDS, AND PREVIOUS CONCEPTIONS ADAPT. HER
PROCESS AND REASON BECOME REALIGNED.

KNOWLEDGE:

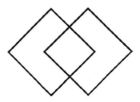

Aera recognized the symbol from Cyrrus's belt buckle. Of course,
he would choose 'knowledge' as his emblem, even as he warned Aera
against being brainwashed. Perhaps he envisioned himself as a force of
change but wanted her to remain untarnished. Yet how could he
expect that? It was impossible to avoid unwanted influence. Between
forced routines and social expectations, no one could hold on to
themselves.

THE EFFECT ON THE BODY OF KINETICS PARALLELS THAT OF THE *SURU*
AND THE *SEMISSË*. *MASSË* IS REPRESENTED BY THE TRIANGLE. WHEN
A NESTË ENGAGES IN PHYSICAL ACTIVITY, SHE ENGAGES THE CORPO-
REAL WORLD, IMPACTS IT AND INCORPORATES ITS INFLUENCE. HER
INNATE SENSITIVITIES CHANGE ALONG WITH HER FORM, AS HER BODY
AND KINETIC CAPACITY INCORPORATE EXPERIENCE WITH THE
EXTERNAL WORLD.

KINETIC ENGAGEMENT:

Kinetic engagement, Aera thought. Indeed, her fingers had become stronger from piano, and Kra had made her more graceful. Breathing exercises had helped to alleviate anxiety.

She enjoyed the consistency of the symbols and their uncomplicated representation of core concepts, but was annoyed by the ambiguous references to Angels and emanations. She wished the explanations were more transparent and surmised that the 'Nestë,' whoever they were, took those fundamentals for granted.

Since the book vehemently emphasized accepting one's own limits, it made sense that Cyrrus would contest its merit. Aera wondered how he planned to incorporate these concepts at all, since *kuiyana* entailed merging with outside forces. *Tistë yoveskén Onórnëan, ë áldëa si*, she thought. 'Who will change the world, it is I, alone.'

To be alive is to be in motion toward Ilë, the corporeal world of the elements, the past, and the future. Each direction is signified by an arrow. When a Nestë accepts the past and future as integral to her current state, and her path to Ilë aligns with her actions in the corporeal realm, her motion is enhanced, and she experiences growth.

Malya (Growth/ Motion):

Without a foundation, motion is directionless. The combination of innate character, choices, and behaviors throughout a Nestë's life coalesce into a personality, establishing a core from which to grow. Through this center, she obtains focus.

Focus:

WHEN A NESTË'S PATTERNS BECOME AUTOMATIC, SHE MAY LOSE
SIGHT OF THE MOTIVATIONS AT THEIR ROOT. TO ATTAIN *SUNDATËA*, A
NESTË MUST HARNESS HER RHYTHM AND DIRECT IT WITH CONSCIOUS
INTENT, TO ALIGN WITH THE PULSE OF THE WORLD. EACH LESSON
DESCRIBES A BEHAVIOR PATTERN WHICH A NESTË INCORPORATES TO
CREATE ORDER OUT OF CHAOS, ALONG WITH A DEEPER REVELATION
WHICH DEMONSTRATES THAT CHAOS IS ITSELF AN ILLUSION, SINCE ILË
UNDERLIES ALL.

Aera was curious to read about behavior patterns in the remaining
chapters, to see if any might apply to her. What was her 'rhythm,' and
how did her personality appear to others? She also wondered what it
meant to 'align with the pulse of the world.' If the world had a pulse,
wasn't everyone aligned with it already?

Gong-gong. Gong-gong.

Aera looked up and saw that the sun had disappeared behind a
cloud, darkening the forest. Wind jostled her hair, leaves rustled, and
crows cawed. A storm was coming, and Aera was so absorbed in *Parë*,
she hadn't noticed.

She shoved the book into the portal and raced through the forest.
By the time she reached the village, the wind was howling. People were
lining up in the Field with their hair and clothes blowing wildly. At the
edge of the trees, Cyrrus was addressing a group of children.

"None of this is what it seems to be! Don't take it at face value.
Examine it with all your senses." He picked up a rock, handed it to a
young boy and said, "Touch it."

The boy held the rock but didn't remove his awestruck eyes from
Cyrrus.

"Feel its surface," Cyrrus instructed, and the child obeyed. "It could
be a weapon. It could be a mouse."

Cyrrus took the rock and folded his fingers over it. The wind blew ferociously, and the group fell into shadow as grey clouds collected above. Slowly, he unfolded his fingers to reveal a tiny mouse, and the children gasped in amazement. In a melodramatic tone, Cyrrus whispered, "Think about *that* next time you kick a rock."

Whistles screeched, and the crowd of children dispersed. On the way to his line, Cyrrus grinned at Aera. She glared back, wishing his brick-red hair would burst into flame and char his smug face. He was abusing his power and misusing his gifts, beguiling young children with sleight of hand gimmicks.

The line leaders handed out aprons and waited for everyone to tie them on. Then, they led their groups towards the fields east of the river as rain began to fall. Aera leaned her head back, letting the downpour cool her off while others moaned.

"Eww, I hate mud!"

"I'm *so* wet!"

"Ugh, my hair!"

Doriline out-screeched everyone else from underneath her pink hood: "It's pouring! It's *pouring!!*"

One line at a time, the 11-12 Group crossed the bridge, followed by the three lines comprising Aera's 13-14 Group. Waves crashed against the banks of the river and doused everyone along the way. Each line moved past the track and toward the vegetable fields just beyond, where baskets awaited them along the edges of the paths defining the fields.

"Grab a basket!" called an older boy. "Fill it and bring it to the Dining Hall! Let's go!"

Task managers assigned spots to everyone. Aera took her place in the leek field, crouched down and began the chore. By the time her basket was full, her pants were muddy, and her legs ached. Her heavy wet hair made simple work seem like a slog. Between her fantasies of *kuinu* and her frustration with Cyrrus, she'd forgotten to braid it before tasks. She was relieved to stand up, but she struggled to obtain a firm grip on the giant basket and had to peer around the sides to see where she was going.

As she rearranged herself, she heard Cyrrus yelling in the distance. "Is this how you want to spend your day? Do you enjoy picking vegetables in the rain? What if there's a way out? Knowledge—"

"Don't you *ever* ghaadi shut up?" scolded an older boy, and the rain came down harder, assisting in the effort to drown out Cyrrus's tirade. Aera wished she could 'conjure rain into a raging river' and wash him away.

"Knowledge is power! Question everything! Why is it so difficult to take books out of the library? Why do we raise animals we don't use? Why do DPD officers live in nicer quarters than everyone else? Are we really all the same? Do you feel the same out here? Why are we doing this? The minds—"

"Oh, bison breath. Darse it, kid!"

Aera turned and saw Cyrrus carrying two baskets, his legs racing to keep up with his rant, while two younger boys panted behind him. She continued toward the bridge while Cyrrus yapped on.

"The minds of adults are poisoned by the elders, and their minds were poisoned by the elders before, all the way back to the early days of Ynas! But our minds are still fresh! We can make a change! *We* can have a better life!"

Cyrrus was using simpler words now... yet when Aera had advised him to do so, he'd protested and left her behind. She walked faster but couldn't escape his crisp voice projecting above the river and storm.

"When I rule the world, I will provide real education. Smart people will dedicate their lives to learning and creating a better society! Intelligence should not be squandered carrying buckets through a muddy field!"

Someone has to clean the latrines, Aera thought. Even without the flamboyant vocabulary, Cyrrus could not conceal his imperious nature. Wouldn't everyone see that his ideas would only benefit those he deemed worthy? Wouldn't they realize that being brainwashed by him was no better than being enslaved by the DPD?

He continued the oratory as he followed Aera over the bridge and across the Village Field. The downpour thinned to a drizzle, making available more audible space for Cyrrus's tirade. Finally, Aera deposited her basket in front of the Dining Hall and rushed away, but to no avail, as Cyrrus promptly slid to her side. She hurried onward, refusing to acknowledge him. Soon, she heard his girlish giggle.

"You're entertaining when you're angry," Cyrrus said cheerfully, "but it's an inefficient use of your mental resources."

"Of course. It's *much* more efficient to turn rocks into mice."

Importantly, Cyrus declared, "One way to teach people to think for themselves is to lie to them."

"That's stupid."

"It's an ancient proverb. It's *effective*."

On their way back to their designated fields, Cyrus slowed down to watch a small girl in the 11-12 Group tripping over herself as she yanked on a carrot near the path. She looked frail, with wet, golden curls sticking to her tiny face.

"Don't hurt yourself, Kize," Cyrus said. "We'll be digging up vegetables until sunset regardless of how many we collect."

"I need to keep up," Kize confessed. Her voice was annoyingly pretty and clear, like a delicate musical bell.

"The only person you have to keep up with is yourself," Cyrus instructed. "In truth, we're not all the same. We all have strengths and weaknesses, and in order to accomplish our goals we must be honest with ourselves. Your body cannot match your ambition. You can only inhabit this body, so you must work within its limits."

Kize stared at him, enchanted. *Idiot*, Aera thought.

Cyrus strode into the wet field, knelt alongside Kize and squatted around the carrot stalk. She mirrored his position, reached between her legs, and yanked it up. The two spoke to each other in hushed voices and, as Kize copied Cyrus in awe, his demeanor glowed.

Aera marched back toward her assigned field and tore up one leek after another, each more furiously than the last. Nearby, someone bellowed, "Get outta here, Samie! Get back to your own group!"

Cyrus drifted back to the path and shot Kize a nefarious grin. The clouds parted, and the sun shot a narrow ray down just on him. Serendipity? Or *kuinu?*

THE CLAN
1327 EARLY-SPRING

"Will you join me at my first clan meeting?"

The din of the Dining Hall echoed in the background as Aera absorbed what she'd just heard. *Clan meeting*. He was seriously doing this.

"It's your choice," Cyrrus said. He grabbed Aera's empty tray, dropped it in the bin, and grinned. "You're my most valuable ally whether you come or not."

He paraded through the door with his book in hand, and Aera followed him outside, but hesitated. *Most valuable ally*. How many were there? Everyone was an ally or an apprentice to him. No one was his friend. *Tistë yoveskén Onórnëan, ë áldëa si*,[1] she thought. *Áldëa*. Alone.

Cyrrus strutted toward the trees in the west, moving slowly with imperious strides. If Aera left him to his schemes, someone else would become his 'most valuable ally.' She imagined Kize perching beside him with a tablet in her lap, enunciating Silindion vocabulary in her bell-like voice. What a valuable apprentice.

As Cyrrus was swallowed in the umbra of trees, Aera's anxiety mounted. It was her last chance to learn what he was doing before she lost track of him altogether. She groaned and hurried to catch up.

Cyrrus departed from the path Aera usually took to Vaye's and instead veered westward. Layers of chirps enveloped them as treetops obscured the stars and moon. The darkness was so deep that Aera could barely see Cyrrus a few paces ahead. His hands were vaguely visible, but his black cloak blended into the shadows.

After a long walk, they encountered an enormous willow tree. Cyrrus parted its foliage, leading Aera into a cave within the curtain of branches. As her vision acclimated to the dark, she saw bits and pieces of people: hands, limbs, faces... Kize. Of course, Cyrrus would invite *her*. Aera also recognized Gaili and Olleroc from her own group.

Aera heard two rocks scraping together and spotted embers flying. Promptly, flames emerged, and firelight illuminated Cyrrus's pale skin as he lifted a torch.

"We will need more light," Cyrrus said. "Aera, would you assemble a fireplace?"

Everyone looked at Aera, expecting her to perform. Cyrrus had put her on the spot without consulting her beforehand. She wanted to castigate him, but their feuds were no one else's business. What could she do now? She slipped between the willows and headed away from the crowd.

"Aera has many capabilities," Cyrrus announced from under the willow in the distance. "She's brilliant. She will never admit it, because she's modest, just like me."

Everybody laughed. Aera wished the forest would swallow her.

"Take the torch," he said. "I'll return shortly."

Footsteps drew toward Aera, and she wished she hadn't come. She didn't want to be an obligation that Cyrrus dealt with out of pity. Why couldn't he just leave her alone? Her eyes locked on his white skin weaving through the shadows, nearer every moment, until he uttered, "You *hate* me."

Aera's heart pounded.

"Five points?" Cyrrus asked. "Three?"

She wanted to scream. What else could he hear her thinking? Did he know his attention to Kize infuriated her? He was invading her private thoughts, as she was helpless to keep him out. Another show of supremacy.

"Aera, stop emoting and be reasonable," Cyrrus said. "I'm trying to change the commune. Don't you want that too?"

It was pointless for him to ask these questions when he could read her mind. She waited for him to say something, but they were at a standstill: he was waiting too. She glared straight at him and asserted, "You lied about me."

"Your intelligence hasn't been tested, and no standard for brilliance has been established, so you can't be certain it's a lie."

But you think I'm stupid, Aera thought.

She looked at Cyrrus, but he didn't recite her sentiment or respond to it. Instead, he offered, "If you have a better plan, tell it to me."

The hollows on his face looked black, and shadows of leaves danced across his visage in the breeze, contrasting with the skin that appeared ghostly in the muted moonlight. Though Cyrrus stared directly at—or perhaps, into—her, his expression was unreadable. His sharp brows shaded his eyes, turning them into caverns. She couldn't tell whether he was mocking her or being solicitous.

"Calling me brilliant... is part of a *plan*?" she demanded.

"What did you think it was? Public flirting?"

Cyrrus giggled in his girlish way while Aera was bursting. She wasn't sure if she would laugh, scream, or cry, but she tightened every muscle to hold it back, blocking an explosion.

"I'll race you," Cyrrus said radiantly. "Whoever collects ten rocks first wins."

Aera burrowed under her hair, pushing back tears. Cyrrus tried so hard to make everything fun. She breathed deeply to compose herself and decided to play along.

"You go first," Cyrrus said. "I'll count to twenty."

They raced to collect rocks and piled them up at the edge of the willow. Aera was up to her eighth rock when Cyrrus announced, "I win!"

As usual, Aera thought.

"I wanted to let you win, but we would have wasted the whole break," he teased.

"Thoughtful," Aera retorted dryly.

They headed under the willow tree, carrying armloads of rocks. Aera arranged them in a circle and looked for kindling while Cyrrus arranged branches into the familiar teepee. Once the fireplace was complete, he grabbed the torch, lit the leaves, and pushed them under the structure. The fire shattered the darkness of their tree hut, and Cyrrus sat cross-legged in front of it. Aera positioned herself beside him while the others completed a circle, watching her and Cyrrus in awe. Building a fireplace was magic to them.

"Let's introduce ourselves," Cyrrus said. "Tell us your name and age, and why you're here. Share something forbidden that you wish you could do, or a cause you stand for. I'll start."

Firelight revealed faces and limbs as shadows danced across skin. All eyes were fastened to Cyrrus.

"It would be unnecessarily grandiloquent for a legendary genius like me to introduce myself," Cyrrus grinned, and a few people chuckled. "I wish I could make my own drawings and keep them," he intoned. Promptly, he faced Aera and said, "Your turn."

She took a deep breath and forced out the words, "Aera. I'm thirteen."

"Tell them what you want."

The obvious answer was music and Kra, but that was personal. Everyone waited for a response, and she didn't want to let Cyrrus down. *Tell them what you want.* Only one thing came to mind, and she said it: "Freedom."

There was a short silence as everyone took this in. She looked nervously at Cyrrus, hoping he would leave her alone. To her relief, he asserted, "Freedom is a state of mind. When we pursue something we enjoy, we feel free."

Who was this 'we?' *You don't have feelings,* she thought.

Cyrrus smiled smugly. Though his lips did not move, his voice spoke, and the words came from every direction at once: *si voisi fatëallo narnán to elya.*[2]

Aera's face flushed. Had he projected that phrase, or had she imagined it? She translated: *thus I can make a game with yours.*

Cyrrus watched her with amused satisfaction, acknowledging he had, in fact, transmitted his thoughts into her mind. Aera searched his eyes and saw nothing except the reflection of flames dancing in his pupils. Where did he come from, anyway? She knew he could read her thoughts, but this was another level of *kuinu.* The others were calm, seemingly unaware of the magic that had unfolded. It had been aimed at Aera alone.

160

Cyrrus turned to Olleroc, whose hands shook as he muttered, "I'm Olleroc." Looking down at his lap, he added, "I'm thirteen."

"Tell us something you wish you could do," Cyrrus said. "Something forbidden."

Aera had always known Olleroc was gawky, but he was painfully awkward up close. His short hair stuck out in unexpected places, and his skinny frame did not suit his beefy hands.

"Why are you here?" Cyrrus asked.

Olleroc tapped on his leg, fingers moving rapidly. Aera felt sorry for him and wished Cyrrus wouldn't pressure people so much.

"I... want... I wish I could go fishing... more often."

"Interesting," Cyrrus said. "Are you good at fishing?"

Olleroc swayed uneasily, but Gaili rescued him and said, "He's good. He caught twelve during tasks last week."

"We will work together to change the laws," Cyrrus pronounced. "If we are allowed more free time to relax and do what we please, our performance at tasks will surely improve."

Olleroc stared at Cyrrus, no longer swaying. Cyrrus turned to Gaili and nodded, cueing her.

Gaili spoke in a deep, tense monotone. "I'm Gaili. I'm thirteen. I want to bake my own recipes for cakes." She stared straight ahead and braced herself. Aera suspected she anticipated mockery of her size.

"Turnip cake isn't hitting the spot?" Cyrrus joked.

Everybody laughed, Gaili most heartily of all. Aera realized then that she'd never before seen Gaili display any enjoyment.

"I'm tired of it," Gaili said, speaking with more enthusiasm as she assimilated the support of others.

"Have you tried your own... secret recipes?"

Everybody watched Gaili, and she nodded uneasily.

"If there were options for experimentation, people would volunteer to work in the kitchen on days off," Cyrrus said. "It should be easy to convince Nurin of that after we win our appeal for free time."

"I hope so," Gaili said, her demeanor more relaxed than before. She and Cyrrus exchanged grins.

Cyrrus turned to a cheerful olive-skinned girl who exclaimed, "I'm Pelyane and I'm eleven!" She flashed a cheeky smile as her exuberant voice flew from one pitch to the next. "I really like reading and I wish

I could read more. I *love* learning about other cultures." With that, she looked at Kize, who sat close to her.

Kize peeked shyly at Cyrrus and chimed, "I'm Kize, I'm eleven, and I love to dance." Her tiny face was surrounded by luscious curls that flared gold in the firelight. She was too sweet... too cute... too lovable.

Cyrrus studied Kize, but Aera couldn't read his expression. His eyes reflected the flames, redder than his hair, and his skin glowed orange. In a thoughtful tone, he asked, "Where do you dance?"

Kize blushed and glanced at Pelyane, who giggled.

"Do I sense something... illegal?" Cyrrus teased.

Both girls smiled, and Pelyane confessed, "We sneak into the Music Room after dinner."

Cyrrus looked at them with interest, and Aera cringed. Music was *her* turf, and those sugary, giggly girls had claimed it first. Without missing a beat, Cyrrus asked, "What do you do there?"

Jubilantly, Pelyane said, "I try to play the piano and the drums so Kize can dance but..."

She and Kize both laughed, and their happiness was obnoxious. Between chuckles, Pelyane finally concluded, "...I'm terrible."

"No," Kize said. "You're better than anyone, aside from Lilese."

Aera was relieved: if they were worse than Instructor Lilese, neither of them were true musicians. She was the only one.

"When I am Renstrom, there will be options for individual lessons in the arts," Cyrrus pronounced. "Until then, we can propose that small groups and solo artists be permitted to perform at Unity Festival, and that everyone is permitted to practice their craft at will. If we work together, we may be able to change the laws."

Both girls lit up, and Aera struggled to hide her annoyance. Cyrrus turned toward the last person in the circle—a mousy boy with a giant head—and intoned, "Your turn."

"They call me Goric, and they tell me I'm eleven."

"Is there something you wish you could do?" Cyrrus asked. "Something illegal or unusual?"

"I want to carry a battle axe."

Pelyane gasped. Everyone else stared at Goric blankly, but Aera grinned to herself. Goric was quiet, but rebellious, and knew more than the others.

162

"Excellent," Cyrrus said. "Where did you learn about battle axes?"

Goric stared into the fire. Attempting to provoke him, Cyrrus asked, "Reading or spying?"

Goric did not respond, but he didn't need to. His fiendish, beady eyes screamed of delinquency and illicit knowledge. Matching his diabolical stare, Cyrrus declared, "Once I am Renstrom, you will be in charge of weapons and defense. Pelyane, you will head the education department."

Everyone smirked or chuckled except Goric, who studied the flames pensively.

"Do you know what war is and why it happens?" Cyrrus asked the circle. "Aera, tell them."

Aera remembered what he'd told her the morning he brought her to spy on the DPD. She rehearsed in her mind and her heart raced, but she forced herself to push through.

"War is a sport," she said. "The first team that destroys the other is the winner."

Goric glanced at her and snickered, but everyone else was silent. They were not yet accustomed to Cyrrus's crudeness and were especially shocked to hear it coming from Aera, which excited her.

"Brilliant analysis," Cyrrus teased. "Tell them why it happens."

"To stop politicians who want to rule the world and kill stupid people."

Aera was taken aback. Where had that come from? Everyone laughed, Cyrrus most of all. Though he enjoyed her clever comeback, he didn't seem surprised by it. Entertaining others was a skill he took for granted.

"Team sports—like war, or Raetsek—fulfill a competitive urge," Cyrrus said, reclaiming command. "They foster bonds by uniting people against an enemy they are taught to fear. Those bonds create an illusion of security and give leaders power. But in truth, sports are the cement that holds hierarchies in place."

The fire roared, and the insect choir hummed as everyone waited eagerly to hear more.

"The surest road to power is through fear," Cyrrus said finally. "This is why leaders create war."

"What about our leaders?" Pelyane asked. "There's no war here."

"Pff," Goric sputtered. Clearly, he knew better.

"Excellent question," Cyrrus replied. "To quote page sixty-two of *Laws of Ynas:* violence—such as pushing, shoving, wrestling, grabbing, punching and kicking—is not permitted outside the Raetsek Field. Armed combat is not permitted outside the DPD training facility."

Pelyane's eyes widened, and Cyrrus smiled, pleased with himself. Aera remembered the recent debaucle in the Raetsek Field. Hizad had forfeited a second round because of the officers nearby, but Cyrrus had known the whole time that violence—in that location—was legal.

"Regardless of the authorities' claims about peace, fear is *still* a central theme in Ynas," Cyrrus asserted. "The leaders design our History Lessons to include detailed stories of violence, animal predators, and war beyond the Fence. People obey the laws and accept their authority because they believe Ynas is the only place they will be safe, and their fear of being exiled suppresses rebellion."

"Does that mean war... and predators... aren't real?" asked Olleroc.

"They are real," Cyrrus said. "But the authorities exaggerate selected threats to keep us in line. They don't tell us anything *good* about the outside world because they don't want us to leave. They need us here to do their work."

He paused, allowing the others to absorb his words as they stared at him in awe. This was a new idea for all of them.

"Riva the Rebel was supposedly exiled and eaten by a smilodon outside the Fence," Cyrrus said. "The expression, 'Riva's Trees,' was passed down to us by the elders to instill fear. Every time we do something tabooed or different, they ask, 'what in Riva's Trees are you doing,' so we are reminded of Riva's terrible death. We must all obey and be the same... the same as they wish, or we will suffer her fate."

"By Riva's Trees," said Gaili, "you're *right*."

Everybody laughed. After sleeping beside Gaili for two years, Aera found out only now that the nervous, unassuming girl harbored a sense of humor. Cyrrus had lured it out of her. He claimed to have no emotions, yet he understood others so well.

"Next time anyone says, 'what in Riva's Trees,' feel free to tell them why this expression is used." He looked at Olleroc, who was staring into the fire. "Olleroc, what are you thinking?"

"Can't say," he mumbled as his hand tapped his knee.

"Why not?"

Olleroc hung his head as he swayed back and forth.

Cyrrus asked, "Because they'll call you a rebel?"

Olleroc stared at Cyrrus, completely still. Undoubtedly, Cyrrus had spoken his thoughts.

Cyrrus waited a moment to give Olleroc a chance to respond. When he didn't, Cyrrus continued. "The teachers tell us we are all the same. Do any of you believe that? Do you fit in with your group? Do you feel we're all the same?"

Everyone shifted uncomfortably, but none spoke.

"Kize," Cyrrus said, "do you believe you're no different from other people, and that we are all the same?"

Kize looked at Cyrrus with wonder and shook her head shyly.

"What about you, Pelyane?"

"No!" she exclaimed.

"Does anyone believe we are all the same?"

A few people mumbled, "No."

"There are three types of people," Cyrrus instructed. "People who resist change, people who desire change yet perpetuate the system, and people who pursue change. The latter are labeled as rebels and censured. But the rebel is the most important member of society because we highlight the flaws and hypocrisy. *We* are rebels and we are *more important* than anyone else."

That speech was familiar: Cyrrus had spewed it years before and afterward confessed he was reciting memorized text. Aera wondered just how much of his clever rhetoric was appropriated from books.

"We can't back down out of fear that people will laugh at us," Cyrrus said. "We must be prepared for hatred and ridicule. The rebel's courage is the seed from which progress spawns. If we want change, we'll have to fight for it... together."

Everybody was frozen with bewilderment. Aera was so accustomed to his speeches that she'd forgotten how powerful they were. If Cyrrus were anyone else, she might have mistaken his drama for passion, but she knew what the others did not: it was manipulation. He intended to be worshipped as a deity.

He resumed his speech in a quiet, crisp tone. "Power is a pyramid and we, the slaves, comprise the base. If the base breaks free, the top

165

will collapse. Our rebellion will shake the foundation of this structure. *We* are the architects of the future."

By saying 'we,' Cyrrus implied the others were 'rebels' and 'architects,' on his level. However crude his intentions might be, his words were well crafted and compelling. Everyone wanted to be important and special, even if only by association with him.

"Knowledge is our strongest weapon. Who wants to read *The History of Ynas* first?" He lifted a book. "Pelyane? Will you be the first?"

Pelyane nodded enthusiastically, and Cyrrus dusted off the cover before passing it to her. "Return it to me when you finish," he said, "and feel free to speak with me if you have questions or wish to discuss the lies and inconsistencies in the text."

Pelyane accepted the tome with delight, apparently unaware that in her attempt to liberate herself from slavery, she was becoming Cyrrus's tool. She and Cyrrus exchanged a grin.

With that, he withdrew a knife from his pocket and scraped a drawing into the dirt, gesturing expansively for everyone to see.

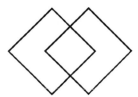

"This is an ancient symbol for knowledge," Cyrrus declared. "It will be the symbol for our movement. For now, it must be kept secret."

Twigs crackled in the fire, and as Cyrrus crouched before it, the buckle on his cloak belt reflected the flames. It was, of course, composed of the same symbol he had drawn. He'd turned his very outfit into an emblem of his cause. None of this was an accident.

"We are bound to one another by the hidden knowledge and secret ambitions we share," Cyrrus continued. "We are bound by the risks we have taken to express ourselves and the hope that we can bring our dreams to the commune, one passion at a time. We must acquire skills as a team. The more effort we expend, the more benefits we will reap."

Everyone smiled and nodded along.

"Our next meeting will be in this same place after sports next Unity

Day." He looked at Pelyane, Goric, and Kize, one at a time. "I want you three to attend town meetings. Learn how debates are won and lost. If you feel confident, practice asking questions and entering the discussion." He looked at Gaili and then Olleroc. "If you attend town meetings, wait until next month so our alliance is hidden. If you are all there, sit in separate groups comprised only of the people you associate with publicly. Invite other friends to town meetings, but don't mention our clan to anyone. If you wish someone else to join us, talk to me first."

Cyrrus met each of their eyes one last time, securing their allegiance to him. He did not look at Aera. She sensed this was his subtle way of elevating their friendship and setting her apart.

"We must depart," he said. "Walk back separately unless you are usually seen together. At our next meeting, when everyone has gained some knowledge of politics, we will construct a more specific plan to enact the changes we desire." In a dramatic tone, he concluded, "Our revolution has begun."

As the others rose, Cyrrus stamped out the remainder of the fire and obliterated the square pattern from the dirt. Darkness enveloped the group.

THE NESTË

1327 EARLY-SPRING

"Samely, Cyrrus!"

"Look at Brains' hair!"

"That red ponytail is ghaadi *slick!*"

Cyrrus's audience fawned over him as he offered his graces, and Aera smiled politely at his side. After accommodating several admirers in the Dining Hall, Aera and Cyrrus took their lunch to the boulder. Gaili and Olleroc watched from the Field, craning to see what they were doing.

Was their routine going to change? Would Cyrrus invite others to the hilltop or to Great Gorge? Aera didn't want anyone invading their privacy. She wanted Cyrrus to herself.

"Desire is rooted in fear," Cyrrus said with a knowing grin. "Seventy points."

Aera's cheeks flushed. "Why do you read my thoughts?" she snapped. "Don't you have your own?"

Cyrrus wrapped some lettuce around a mess of broccoli, shoved it into his mouth and garbled, "*Lirityalya kuissë nandosani kara onolindannahya perë essempravavi.*[1]"

"*Varnë 'lë onolínyello perëo va nani ta eilë, id?*[2]" Aera retorted.

"Perfection studies *me*. Though it has trouble keeping up."

"*Laissa ei ventivoya nama nani mana namalim të patto nani.*[3]"

168

"Your Silindion is advancing apace," Cyrrus said, and inhaled the remainder of his wrap. "You must have been privileged with a thorough, patient teacher."

He giggled girlishly, but Aera didn't react. There was no point acknowledging his crediting himself for her accomplishments.

"You translated perfection to *nani*," Cyrrus said. "The word *nani* refers to physical completeness, which would suggest a person missing an arm couldn't be a great teacher. While it's flattering to know you envy my flawless physique, I believe you were referring to my impeccable clarity. You already know *onophayani* means clear or vivid, and *onophayallo*, to inspect or look through. *Onophayaniva* is the word for clarity."

Aera focused on her food, pretending to ignore him. Without another word, they finished their meal and returned their trays.

On the way outside, Cyrrus asked, "Library?"

"It's nice out," Aera said. "I don't want to sit in a dark room."

"Since I'm alleging you're brilliant, it is necessary that you become educated about the world and its history."

"Guess I'll make myself useful," she said sardonically.

"Friendship is built upon a foundation of mutual gain."

"If you have no feelings."

"Compassion is calculating what the other person gains as well." He raised a brow. "For our mutual benefit, permit me to escort you to the library and enlighten you about the Nestë."

He was infuriating. Aera *did* want to learn about the Nestë but hated that he knew how to sway her.

They grabbed their trays, and Cyrrus continued goading her as they descended the Hill. "The fifth lesson in *Parë* leads to wisdom, *indiva*. It involves learning languages, scripts, history, experiences of other Nassandë and more. If Vermaventiel is a Nassando, she must have spent countless sunny afternoons poring over books."

"Good for her."

"If you wish to control your future, it is wise to emulate your idols."

"I don't have idols. Everyone is just as lost as we are. You would learn *that* if you had some '*indiva*,' but you're too busy reading."

Cyrrus shot her a glare, then opened the Dining Hall door. They dropped their trays in the bin, crossed the Field, and entered the

Administration Unit. Officers stared at them as they climbed the stairs.

When they arrived, Cyrrus closed the door behind them and announced, "This is a pathetic excuse for a library."

The fossil behind the desk looked up at him quizzically, and Aera rolled her eyes. He just *had* to provoke everyone.

"Why do you suppose there aren't any windows? Every other class-room has windows and every roof-level room in the village has skylights except this one. They keep it like this to discourage people from staying and reading."

"Samie Cyrrus, *you* are free to leave," the old lady croaked. She was correct, but Cyrrus was not deterred.

"That's my point! That's what they want," Cyrrus said. "But why should *you* be forced to spend your days under these conditions? As an Elder, you deserve more respect."

The lady peered at Cyrrus, confused.

"The leaders want to keep us uninformed and ignorant," Cyrrus preached. "Few people come to the library because of the deliberate deterrents. It's oppressive in here and it's unsettling to march into the DPD Building like we're invading foreign territory. Why not put the library in the Education Unit? This is done consciously to intimidate people from daring to seek knowledge. To that end, they subject *you* to darkness and isolation."

The elder's mouth dropped open, and Cyrrus flashed a victorious grin. Aera groaned impatiently.

He turned to Aera and declared, "There are about nine hundred books in this room, and I have read each one. Or, at the least, I skimmed through those with no value. They cover Ynas's agriculture, cooking methods, animal husbandry... information I can figure out myself."

Aera perused a few books from a nearby shelf and as she read the titles on the front, she snickered. '*Plants and Wildlife.*' '*Carpentry.*' '*Weaving, Sewing, Dye, and Maintenance of Sheep.*' '*The Creation of the Pencil.*' Cyrrus flaunted these skills as though they sprouted from the sky, but he'd learned them from reading these boring books that were available to everyone.

Nearby, Cyrrus pulled a black leather tome from the shelf. He dusted it off and set it on a table, barely big enough for two.

As they took their seats, he said in a hushed voice, "This is the only book in the entire library that even mentions the Nestë. It contains conspicuous confabulation." He passed the book to Aera, and she opened to the first page to read the title: *The Legend of Rasna*.

"If this is the only one, how do you know it's confabulation?"

"Common sense," Cyrrus said. "Information is controlled by authorities. Tyranny is what happens when leaders control a population entirely. People don't want to be oppressed by tyrants, so they have to be manipulated into submission."

"That's one reason to keep stupid people alive," Aera jabbed.

Cyrrus's eyes gleamed. "Leaders everywhere use identical tactics to maintain power. One is making people fear the outside world. The purpose is to rally people against a common enemy, making them desperate, angry, and helpless, willing to give their leaders more control to protect them. This is why authorities fabricate rationales to wage war."

It did not escape Aera's notice that Cyrrus rallied others against the authorities, the 'common enemy.' To that end, he'd hassled the elder librarian only moments before. He enacted his own description of 'leaders' and 'tyrants.'

"Another is religion," Cyrrus continued. "If one group believes some other group is breaking their deity's rules, they will sanction slaughtering them."

"Sounds like common sense," Aera grinned.

Cyrrus raised a brow.

"Another is something called money," he said. "I'm not sure what it *is,* but everyone agrees it has value, and they trade other items and services for it. Some people have much more than others, and people fight or even kill to acquire it."

Aera was intrigued by the idea of 'money' being traded for something in return. This meant people were allowed to choose their own items and services, rather than being forced to accept those provided by their leaders.

"You said everyone agrees money has value," Aera said. "Do you?"

"I'm still trying to figure out what it's made of and where it comes from, but I suspect it's created by Authorities and they control who gets it."

Aera was disappointed, though not surprised. Of course, authorities controlled it. She wondered if there was any place in the world where anyone was free.

"It might be a religious emblem," Cyrrus continued, smiling roguishly. "It must be something really good, because we're not allowed to know about it here."

"How do you know about it?"

"I learn through deduction."

Aera glared at him incredulously.

"All I have to do is *think*," Cyrrus protested. "For instance, no other book in the library mentions anything before Year One, but there are thousands of years of history before that. The fact is, year one is the beginning of the Third Age."

Cyrrus was trying to distract her from the question. It was plausible that the commune had erased a portion of history from their education, but Aera didn't believe Cyrrus could *deduce* anything that occurred thousands of years ago.

"You still haven't answered my question," she reminded him.

"Did you really believe the world began in year one, and by one-fifteen, humans had developed sufficient resources to construct the Fence and wage large scale wars?"

Aera grimaced. None of this was related to money, and Cyrrus knew it.

"It's common sense," Cyrrus insisted. "Do you think a civilization could develop that fast?"

"I think you—"

Aera stopped mid-sentence. She was about to say, *you read illegal books and pretend you don't,* but caught herself. The elderly lady was at her desk, and two officers were seated across the room.

"Let's do an exercise," Cyrrus suggested. "Try using common sense as you read the forward of this book."

He was impossible. Aera narrowed her eyes at him, then opened the book.

The Legend of Rasna details the myth of the Rasnians, a fictional army alleged to predate recorded history. There are countless tales about the heroes of Rasna. I will attempt herein to provide a composite version of that prehistory, passed down verbally through many generations.

According to legend, Oreni harbored intelligent life prior to the emergence of humankind. A primitive early group worshipped a deity known as Ilë who was believed to have forged our chaotic world to reflect his corrupt and vengeful nature. His first creation was the Angels, able to manipulate the forces of nature to create or destroy at their whim. Then he created the Nestë, whose emergence, in religious scripture, is heralded as The First Age. The Nestë had a lifespan of thousands of years during which they developed powerful magic. They appeared outwardly human but for the presence of an orifice on their foreheads which cast fire.

An orifice in their foreheads which cast fire. Aera's mind jumped to Panther Woman and the fire that had erupted around her. Was this the purpose of the forehead-light?

Out of the corner of her eye she saw Cyrus staring, undoubtedly scanning her thoughts. Quickly, she turned back to the book.

The Nestë migrated throughout Oreni, spawning numerous tribes: the Silindi, Nindi, Deninesti, Sili, Sulindori, Mendi and others whose names vary by tale and are hidden in buried memories. Eventually, magic enabled them to overcome the Angels, who feared the Nestë and vanished, marking the end of the First Age.

The emergence of humankind established the beginning of the Second Age. The Nestë dominated the planet and used their powers to enchant and intimidate the humans, who wished only to live in peace before reluctantly realizing that lasting peace could be achieved only through decisive victory in war. The Rasnians were the largest and most organized human army to rise against the Nestë. They

UNITED THE TRIBES AND KINGDOMS TO FIGHT ALONGSIDE THEM. ONE SUCH FORCE WAS KNOWN AS THE RED ARMY BECAUSE OF THEIR BLOOD-RED HAIR.

Aera glanced at Cyrrus's hair: it was brick-red, but not blood colored.

THEY FOUGHT ALONGSIDE THE RASNIANS, BUT NESTË MAGIC PROVED TOO POWERFUL FOR EVEN THE COMBINED HUMAN FORCES. EVERY HUMAN KINGDOM WAS RAVAGED AND LEFT IN RUIN. THEN NATURE INTERCEDED AND PLUNGED THE LANDS UNDER ICE, CAUSING THE NESTË TO BECOME EXTINCT AND MOST HUMANS TO PERISH. SOME HISTORIANS CITE THE FEW HUMAN SURVIVORS OF THAT ERA AS OUR ORIGINAL ANCESTORS.

OUR RECORDED HISTORY BEGINS IN YEAR ONE, CENTURIES AFTER THE ICE AGE. RELIGIOUS MYTHOLOGY REFERS TO THIS ERA, OUR PRESENT HISTORY, AS THE THIRD AGE. THESE MYTHS AND LEGENDS FROM EARLIER PERIODS HELP US TO APPRECIATE THE IMPORTANCE OF RASNA IN UNIFYING AND SUSTAINING MANKIND. THIS BOOK BRINGS TOGETHER THE ENDURING TRUTHS IMMORTALIZED BY THESE LEGENDARY TALES WHICH SYMBOLIZE OUR PERSEVERANCE AND VICTORY.

Aera was not sure what to make of this and looked at Cyrrus. "So, you think these... legends... aren't fictional?"

"They're based on real history, but they've been distorted," Cyrrus said. "Human lives span eighty years, while the Nestë live five thousand years and practice magic. Why would humankind, but not the Nestë, have survived the Ice Age?"

"Maybe the Nestë were just humans who learned mag—"

"That's what they want! To cast doubt on the very existence of the Nestë!" Cyrrus cut in. "This book is political propaganda."

Aera nodded. "For what purpose?"

"Excellent question." He leaned in close and whispered, "I have no doubt some Nestë survived."

"How do you know?" Aera asked. "Have you seen any?"

"Have you seen Riva?" Cyrrus challenged. "Would you believe someone who told you she didn't exist?"

Aera opened her mouth and forgot why. She closed it.

"Don't believe anything you read in this library," Cyrrus said sternly, "and don't believe anything I tell you. Question everything."

Between red hair and flaming foreheads, there was a lot to question. They returned the book to the shelf and headed off.

During tasks, Aera's group was sent to the Dining Hall Kitchen. While she chopped vegetables, her thoughts wandered back to *The Legend of Rasna*. If Cyrrus was correct that the Nestë had survived, perhaps Panther Woman was one of them. Vaye, too!

Vaye not only covered her forehead with a band, but also, had refused to talk about Panther Woman and the white-haired girl in her painting. Whatever connection Vaye had to the Nestë, she wanted to keep it secret. What was she doing in Ynas? Had she lived an exciting life with the Nestë before? Aera imagined a starlit field where dozens of Nestë swung Ikrati sticks, their foreheads shining...

"Eh-ruh! Back to work!"

Aera groaned as she resumed her slave labor. Oreni had so much interesting history, but the instructors only talked about boring human societies and animals. Aera wanted to know what had happened to the Nestë, what their lives were like, and whether *kuinu* was real. She hoped *Parë* would provide answers.

Cyrrus was elsewhere during dinner, and Aera went to the Gorge alone. As the sun was setting, it would soon be too dark to read without fire. She ran to the forest, flipped through *Parë* to Part Three and translated it rapidly.

PART 3: THE LESSONS

ALL NASSANDË MUST DISCOVER THE PARALLELS BETWEEN THEIR OWN EMANATIONS AND THOSE OF THE ANGELS. TALISMANISTS DO THIS THROUGH STUDY OF THE TALISMANS, WHICH ARE EMBODIMENTS OF THOSE EMANATIONS. TO COMMUNICATE THE RESULTS OF THEIR EXPLORATIONS, TALISMANIST SCHOLARS ESTABLISHED SYMBOLS FOR THE TWELVE LESSONS. IN THE FOLLOWING PAGES, I WILL INTERPRET

Aera was pleased that she already knew the basis for each symbol. Circles for *suru*, squares for *semissë*, triangles for *massë* and arrows for *malya*. Heart, mind, body, motion.

The key symbols on the top, bottom, left and right each contained a single geometric shape layered four times, while the surrounding two contained alternate combinations of the same shapes. Aera imagined she was unraveling the fundamental design of the world. Would she discover parallels between her 'emanations' and those of the Angels? What did that even mean? Though she could have stared at that page all night, the forest was darkening, and she needed to read more. She rushed to translate the first lesson.

THE FIRST LESSON IS ONE OF THREE PERTAINING TO HEART AND IDENTITY. AS SUMMARIZED BY RANKALOS:

LESSON OF SURU (REALIZATION OF BEAUTY): THIS LESSON WAS DISCOVERED BY NANTILINDO. HE UNDERSTOOD THAT THE ESIL COULD REVEAL EMANATIONS OF BEAUTY THAT WERE INTERWOVEN WITH THE WILL OF ILË. THE KEY REALIZATION IS THAT THE EMANATIONS MUST BE FORGED WITHIN THE DISCIPLE'S SURU.

THE UNIVERSE BEGAN IN A DARK VOID WHERE ILË DREAMED ALONE. HIS THOUGHTS COALESCED INTO A CHORUS OF SOULS FROM WHICH EMANATED THE ANGELS. ILË BESTOWED UPON THE ANGEL NARWË THAT PORTION OF HIS MIND WHICH WAS DEVOTED TO WATER AND THUS, NARWË TOOK FORM. HIS WAVES POUNDED UPON NASCENT SHORES AND NOURISHED THE UNFORMED LAND, WHERE ALÁRIË

PLANTED THE WORLD-TREE, NEILINDUNOR. MANIFESTING ILË'S VISION OF LIGHT, SHE CAUSED NEILINDUNOR'S BLOSSOMS TO SHINE BRIGHTLY THROUGH THE VOID AND BRING FORTH THE WORLD.

ALL STOOD IN AWE AS FIRST LIGHT REVEALED ALÁRIË'S BEAUTY. SO SPLENDID WAS THE WORLD-MOTHER THAT MANY AN ANGEL FELL IN LOVE WITH HER. FATHER NARWË BROUGHT FORTH ILË'S DREAMS OF RUSHING WATERFALLS AND ROARING OCEANS, HOPING TO WIN ALÁRIË'S HEART. SO IT WAS THAT NATURE COLORED THE HILLS OF ILKARIEN.

Aera was overwhelmed by new names and concepts. She reread the text and reviewed them. Ilë dreamed of the Angels, each of whom was linked to a particular natural element. Once the Angels came to life, they created the world according to Ilë's vision. Narwë was associated with water and Alárië with light. They were the father and mother of the World-Tree, Neilindunor.

ONE FATEFUL EVENING, ALÁRIË BECAME ENCHANTED BY A HEAVENLY SONG. ON A DISTANT MOUNTAINTOP, ANGEL ERELION SANG TO THE WORLD, HIS SILVER MANE AND SNOW-WHITE SKIN REFLECTING THE SPLENDOR OF NEILINDUNOR'S LIGHT. HIS ARIAS RESOUNDED AS HE SURVEYED THE LAND WITH GRATITUDE AND DEFERENCE, SINGING THE WONDERS OF CREATION AND MYSTERIES OF THE UNKNOWN. ERELION NEVER PRESUMED TO COURT ALÁRIË, BUT HIS PATIENT DEVOTION ENTICED HER ALL THE MORE, AND THE TWO BECAME LOVERS.

The description of Erelion made Aera blush. She understood he was the loyal companion star beside the moon and enjoyed that his music ignited their romance. It amused her that Angels competed for love. Though Vermaventiel presented the Angels as divine, she intimated that they harbored the passions of mortals.

BEAUTY ABOUNDED AS THE ANGELS' *KUINU* AWAKENED ORENI. BUT THE SILVER GUARDSMAN OLOSYASKI, EVER VIGILANT, WARNED THAT DANGER WAS UNDERWAY. VIOLENCE ROSE FROM THE SAME ABYSS THAT HAD BIRTHED THE ANGELS, THREATENING TO OBLITERATE THEM AND RETURN ALL TO VOID. FROM A BRANCH OF NEILINDUNOR,

177

ALÁRIË FASHIONED A BOW. SHE CONSECRATED THE ARROW VANASUTI WITH HER KISS AND GIFTED IT TO ERELION. THE LOVERS PARTED AND BATTLE BEGAN.

Aera pictured a battlefield crowded with bloody sword fights and mangled corpses. She imagined a silver-haired, doe-eyed Erelion shooting arrows at enemies in a fury to defend his beloved. The thought made her smile.

FAERIE ATTACKED, AND WAR LASTED EONS. IN THE FINAL BATTLE, OLOSYASKI LOST HIS ARM AND ERELION FELL TO HIS DEATH AS THE WORLD-TREE BURNED. ITS BLOSSOMS OF LIGHT SCATTERED THROUGHOUT A WAR-TORN WORLD, AND ORENI PLUNGED INTO TREACHEROUS DARKNESS BENEATH A STARLESS SKY.

THE BLACK NIGHT ENDED WHEN ALÁRIË COLLECTED NEILINDUNOR'S BLOSSOMS, PLACED THEM INSIDE A VESSEL AND NAMED IT THE MOON.

Aera reread the sentence. Was Alárië the moon, or did she build the moon?

SHE REFASHIONED OLOSYASKI'S ARM AS A SWORD OF LIGHT, THEN RESURRECTED ERELION AND CLOAKED HIM IN LIGHT. OLOSYASKI BUILT A SWAN SHIP TO RAISE ALÁRIË AND ERELION TO THE HEAVENS, WHERE THEY WOULD DWELL ETERNALLY AS MOON AND EVENING STAR. ALONG WITH THE FIRST MOONRISE, STARS FILLED THE SKY. THE NESTË AROSE AND THE FIRST AGE WAS BORN.

How could Olosyaski build a swanship if one arm was a sword of light? Did it have fingers? Aera giggled. She was starting to appreciate that the Nestë culture evolved through myth and allegory. Their poetic style revealed as much about them as the stories themselves.

HEARTBROKEN BY NEILINDUNOR'S DESTRUCTION AND ALÁRIË'S DISTANCE, OLOSYASKI WANDERED BESIDE THE OCEAN IN MOURNING. THERE, HE SAW MOONLIGHT RIDING THE WAVECRESTS AS THEY DANCED WITH EXQUISITE ABANDON, CHURNING BENEATH THE BRIL-

LIANT SKY. OLOSYASKI STRETCHED HIS GLOWING ARM AND SPARKLES
ROLLED OVER THE ENDLESS SEA. NARWË EMBRACED THE LIGHT AND
OLOSYASKI REJOICED. ALÁRIË'S BEAUTY TOUCHED EVERYONE.
NEILINDUNOR HAD FALLEN, BUT OLOSYASKI CARRIED A BLOSSOM
WITHIN HIMSELF.

OLOSYASKI WANTED THE NESTË TO EXPERIENCE FATHER
NARWË'S LOVE WITHIN THEIR *SURI* AND TO INTERNALIZE MOTHER
ALÁRIË'S BEAUTY. THUS, HE REPLICATED ILË'S CREATION OF HEAV-
ENLY LIGHTS BY BESTOWING *ESILYA* ON THE NESTË: A BEACON TO
GUIDE THEM THROUGH DARKNESS, AS ALÁRIË'S LIGHT GUIDED THE
ANGELS. THE *ESIL* REFLECTS MOONLIGHT, UNVEILING THE PRESENCE
OF ILË—AND THIS MEMORY IS PLACED IN THE *SURU*. JUST AS THE
MOON SHINES UPON NARWË TO HIGHLIGHT HIS POWERFUL WAVES,
THE *ESIL* ILLUMINATES EMANATIONS OF THE *SURU*, COMPRISED OF
UBIQUITOUS BEAUTY AND LOVE.

Vermaventiel's *esil* paralleled the glowing orifice cited in *The Legend
of Rasna*, though depicted as reflecting moonlight instead of spitting
fire. Aera hurried to finish the rest before the darkness deepened.

WHEN A NESTË DESIRES LOVE, SHE MAY PURSUE IT WILLFULLY. SHE
MAY INGRATIATE HERSELF TO OTHERS BUT WILL NEVER FEEL SATIS-
FIED BY THE LOVE SHE RECEIVES, BECAUSE HER YEARNING FOR RECI-
PROCITY COMMODIFIES COMPASSION. AFFECTION DEVOLVES TO
DEPENDENCY, ATTRACTION TO OBSESSION, AND INSPIRATION TO
ADDICTION AS SHE CULTIVATES A FALSE BEAUTY TO BEGUILE ANYONE
SHE OBJECTIFIES AS A PRIZE TO POSSESS. BY TAKING PRIDE IN HER
POSITION WITH OTHERS, SHE SACRIFICES THE SATISFACTION OF BEING
LOVED FOR HER INNATE BEAUTY. HER PLEASURES BECOME POISON AS
SHE NEGLECTS THE MURKY WATERS WITHIN HER SOUL.

LOVE IS NOT AN ASSET TO EARN; IT IS A FORCE OF NATURE, EVER-
PRESENT. WHEN A NESTË STOPS PERFORMING AND INSTEAD REFLECTS
ON HER OWN NATURE, SHE RECOGNIZES THAT HER *ESIL* ILLUMINATES
THE INHERENT CONNECTION BETWEEN HERSELF AND ALL BEINGS.
THIS RELEASES HER FROM EXPECTATION: BOTH THE EXPECTATIONS OF
OTHERS AND HER EXPECTATIONS OF THEM. SHE EMBRACES HER
INHERENT COMPASSION, ACCEPTS LOVE WITHOUT CONDITION AND

SEES OTHERS AS THEY ARE. HER *SURU* EMANATES *OSMASENA* (LOVE FOR THE BREATH OF LIFE), *SUNA* (LOVE FOR THE PASSION THAT IGNITES HER), AND *HENNA* (LOVE BETWEEN THE NESTË AND ANGELS). AS FULLNESS REPLACES EMPTINESS, SHE IS NO LONGER ENSLAVED BY THE NEED TO PURSUE LOVE, AS HER VERY EXISTENCE ENCOMPASSES IT. SHE FEELS THE BEAUTY THAT IS BOUNDLESS AND ETERNAL, WHICH SETS HER SPIRIT FREE. JUST AS THE TIDE DANCES TO THE RHYTHM OF LIFE, THE HEART SURRENDERS TO LOVE.

HENEISSË (COMPASSION):

Aera closed the book to a feeling of dread. She was possessive and needy of Cyrrus but had no *esil* to reveal the beauty in her heart. These lessons would not help her.

She strained to reread the translations, but dusk soon yielded to night. *If only my forehead could spit fire*, she thought. Vaye and Cyrrus had special powers, and somewhere in the world there were other magical beings, but she was decidedly not one of them.

She returned the book and tablet to the Gorge, still teeming with questions. What were 'laws of nature?' Could a human obtain an *esil?* If any Nestë were still alive, might she and Cyrrus find them? Aera wanted to see *kuinu* in action. She wished more than anything that she could perform magic herself.

Aera meandered about the forest, fantasizing about magic until curfew. When she arrived at Junior Hut, Cyrrus was outside, laughing with some older boys. He watched Aera for an extra moment as she emerged from the trees, and she wondered what he was thinking.

The following morning, Aera was excited to talk to Cyrrus about the Nestë, but he ran off to the Slaughterhouse at breakfast. She spent lunch break at Great Gorge, where she memorized some key phrases to facilitate discussion with Cyrrus—and, of course, to impress him.

At dinner, Aera ate slowly by the boulder, hoping Cyrrus would show up. He arrived just before sunset, carrying an overstuffed tray. His hair was matted with knots and his hands were caked with grime.

Eager to show off her progress in *Parë*, Aera teased, "You enjoy murder because you're free from the tyranny of *heneissë*."

Cyrrus chuckled as his cheeks bulged with food. While he gorged himself, Aera watched the sky give way to night. The moon was lopsided, and the star Erelion twinkled erratically alongside. Aera tried to discern its precise shade but saw both silver and blue. Were her eyes playing tricks or did he cast two colors at once? Perhaps his true color was a secret he shared with Alárië or, maybe, kept from her.

The edge of the moon was in shadow, hiding something. Aera imagined Alárië concealing her distress as Erelion confused her with his bicolored glow. *A lover's quarrel*, she thought, and smiled.

"Alárië has a better strategy," Cyrrus said. "She disappears."

Aera blushed and wondered how many of her thoughts he had read.

"The Nestë took that relationship to heart," he continued. "They even waged wars to settle disputes over the meaning of their love."

"Wars about love," Aera mused.

"Most people believe ideals are worth fighting for. That's why it's essential to remain realistic about love and deities."

Aera giggled. "It's more *realistic* to pose as a deity and persuade people to fight for you."

"That's how revolution works. Most people desire change, but a true rebel will join a movement to effect that change."

"Then I guess I'm not a rebel."

Cyrrus raised a brow. "If you want something, you must fight for it."

"I don't want to join a movement, just to follow a new leader in the end," Aera said. "I want freedom."

"Freedom is an illusion. Fighting for it would be a grave mistake. If there were no government and no laws, bullies like Hizad would hunt people and eat them, and chaos would reign. The world needs a leader who values education and unites people behind rational principles. *That* would be realistic."

Aera grimaced. He had a point—and she hated it. "You'll never rule me," she said somberly. "No one will."

The two finished their meal, and Aera headed into Westside Willows. As she maneuvered beyond the paths, she heard footsteps behind her, gazed into the darkness and caught a glimpse of red hair in a tiny pocket of moonlight between the trees. Cyrrus was approaching.

This was unexpected. They separated every night. Though he could read her mind and probably knew about Vaye, she couldn't bring him there, as it would defy her promise. She greeted him with an uneasy smile.

He instructed, "Hold out your hand."

She did as he asked, and he placed two rocks in her palm. Since it was difficult to see, Aera examined their surfaces with her fingertips. There was a thin slit on one and a sharp edge on the other. Fire rocks!

"Keep them," Cyrrus said, "so you won't be helpless without me."

Aera's cheeks flushed as tears rushed to her eyes. He'd gone to the Slaughterhouse again just to fashion fire rocks for her. For days she'd been angry, jealous of his other friends, and taking his sarcasm to heart. She never complimented him or thanked him for teaching her. Still, he was thinking of her. She was so unappreciative...

Leaves crunched in Cyrrus's hands. He dropped them on the ground and said, "Light them."

Aera knelt before the dry leaves, held her rocks over them and rubbed them together rapidly, but nothing happened.

"Try using your brain," Cyrrus offered.

Aera chuckled and felt around for the sharpest surface of one rock and the indent on the other. Once she located them, she placed the edge against the indent and rubbed them together vigorously. A few sparks shot out and ignited the leaves. As her skin warmed, she backed away, and Cyrrus stepped on the leaves, killing the fire beneath his boot.

"Fire cannot exist without destroying," Cyrrus said. "Destruction is the bedrock of creation."

He swooped away toward Vapid Village, and Aera watched him,

nonplussed. Before his footsteps were out of earshot, his black cloak melted into the night.

When Aera reached the cottage, she was overwhelmed with emotion and headed into Southside Forest to clear her mind. As the wind brushed her cheeks, she listened to crickets chirping and owls hooting in the trees. *Who. Who.*

A ray of moonlight colored the forest, and Aera spotted an opening between treetops that revealed a portion of sky. She lay down on the ground beneath, gazing at the scape of twinkling lights. The moon was a sliver shy of full, and beside her uneven curvature floated her companion, Erelion. No matter how Alárië changed shape, Erelion stayed with her. He waited patiently while she kept part of herself hidden, and when she revealed herself in full, her brilliance never scared him away.

Would Cyrrus do the same? Aera kept expecting him to lose interest in her, but it had yet to happen. Despite all his annoying criticism, Cyrrus was a better friend than she. He never doubted her loyalty even as she doubted his. Vermaventiel's sentiment came to mind: *She accepts love without condition and sees others as they are.*

Cyrrus claimed friendship was mutual gain. What did he gain from Aera? He knew more about the world, attracted more attention, and avenged her against Hizad—which had increased his notoriety. Perhaps he benefitted most from Aera's weakness.

She gazed up at Alárië and Erelion and thought of the symbol for 'emotional bond,' comprised of two circles. Part of the original shape was sacrificed to join the whole.

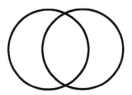

Together, Alárië and Erelion were brightest, though some of Erelion's brightness was diminished in Alárië's glow. In turn, Alárië disappeared in cycles to allow him space to shine. Like the symbol, part of each *suru* was incorporated with the other, and each sacrificed some autonomy to be part of a larger whole.

Why did they do it? Did they stay beside each other eternally for personal gain, or because they wanted to be together? Were they dependent or obsessed, filling their emptiness? Did they tolerate each other because they had no choice?

Who. Who. An owl hooted nearby. Aera tried to locate it. As her eyes wandered between shadows and patches of stars, she imagined herself sifting through Cyrrus's vast, mysterious mind. She was dying to learn where his knowledge had come from. If she asked, he would claim, *I am a genius, born omniscient.* She laughed aloud. Albeit exasperating, Cyrrus's conceit was addictively amusing.

She stood up, stretched and headed to Great Gorge. She had no idea how much time remained before curfew or whether it was enough to bother with a fire, but Cyrrus had been generous in providing her that option.

When she arrived, she reached for *Parë* but felt another book, which she pulled out eagerly. It was wider, shorter, and thicker than *Parë*, with stiff pages, taut to the binding. Excited, she ignited some leaves in the stone pit and held the book close.

The writing began on the second page in a dark hand. Though similar to Silindion, the characters were aligned vertically, and their curves were more embellished. Some were drawn with flourish while others were sloppy and rushed, but Cyrrus's angular handwriting was unmistakable.

The second half of the book was blank except for the final page, which depicted a castle with cylindrical towers bearing turrets and conical spires. It stood atop a hill with a waterfall behind it, spilling down from mountains. At the top of the page, there was a caption written in symbols she had never before seen.[5]

The belltower rang and Aera left, annoyed. Whatever Cyrrus was up to exceeded taboo. Though he hadn't told her about it, he'd left that book behind where she could find it. She suspected this wasn't an accident. Nothing ever was.

She returned to Junior Hut, exhausted and annoyed. After attendance, she tossed and turned on her mat, wondering where Cyrrus spent his nights and wishing he would invite her. Images of dimly lit corridors and fancy arched doorways spun through her mind as she drifted to sleep.

～

Aera stood on a hill, looking up at a grand castle. White birds lined its round balustrades and pointed prominences, and a giant moon shone overhead, glowing red. The castle windows mirrored the crimson sheen, blending with an expanding moon. Aera watched in awe as the birds reflected its cast, but she grew uneasy. The moon was too close.

In a flash, the birds escaped beyond sight. A blood-red haze encompassed the sky as the moon advanced, dominating the world. With a thunderous roar, it crushed the castle. Heavy stone exploded everywhere.

Aera tried to flee, but the ground split open, trapping her between immolation and a vast pit. The world screeched in protest as white light rose from below along with a harrowing shriek. She screamed...

～

"Darse it, Eh-ruh!"

Aera awakened with a start. The world spun and the hens attacked.

"Eh-ruh had a nightmare!"

"Eh-ruh is so scared..."

"Shut! Up!" Gaili bellowed beside her with surprising rage that silenced the room.

Gaili lay back down and resumed snoring, but Aera could not sleep now. Her mind was spinning. The castle in her nightmare was the one from Cyrrus's book, but it was dark and foreboding, while his was peaceful. Had she read his mind, tapped into *eseissë,* or simply reimagined the scene by herself?

When Officer Linealle finally arrived to shuffle everyone off to class, Aera was relieved. She hurried to breakfast to inquire about the castle, but Cyrrus was elsewhere. She took her food to the boulder alone. Just as the belltower sounded, she spotted him emerging from Southside Forest.

They proceeded to class, where Cyrrus remained asleep the entire time. He was quiet throughout lunch and the walk to Great Gorge, where he took out *Parë Në Sulë*, opened to a page in the middle, and stared at it. He was not even reading but gazing blankly ahead because he was too exhausted to converse. Aera dug into the hollow and reached around for the new book, but all she found was wood tablets, rocks, and the container full of pencils.

"There was another book in here yesterday," she said. "Where is it?"

Cyrrus said nothing and stared impassively at *Parë Në Sulë*. Aera had seen him emerge from the forest that morning. It was obvious he'd gone to the Gorge to remove the book.

Impatiently, she added, "I know you go on adventures at night, and you make up lies to hide it from me. I'm not stupid."

Cyrrus's gaze was lost in the trees, and he responded with a non-sequitur: "Nurin must have used more than just candle wax to polish his shoes...."

Aera groaned, sick of this game. Bison would fly before he admitted his deceptions or revealed anything to her that mattered. Without a word, she marched off to the cottage. As she approached, Vaye opened the door, anticipating her arrival. Aera had only two friends, and both withheld secrets from her while she could hide nothing.

"Is something wrong, dear?" Vaye asked.

Aera wanted to scream, *Stop pretending you don't know everything I think and feel!* But she held the words inside.

"You don't have to tell me," Vaye said. "Tell the piano."

Vaye headed outside and Aera made her way to the bench, though she didn't know what to 'tell the piano.' She sat immobile as the keys gleamed in the midday light, feeling exposed and guilty for being rude to Vaye. Since she was too tense to compose music, she elected to practice scales.

She played the same pattern faster and faster in different keys. As her fingers whizzed along, she thought of Vermaventiel's symbols for bond and knowledge. To incorporate outside influences, the *suru* and *semissë* sacrificed their integrity. It occurred to her suddenly that this idea disturbed her. She didn't want to intermix with something greater. She feared losing herself.

Her instinct was to resist any influence. She questioned every idea, dismissed all efforts at persuasion, and accepted guidance only on her own terms. Perhaps she needed to allow the world to move her. She could start right now at the piano. The scales Vaye had taught her were boring but familiar. Instead of repeating them forever, she could merge those patterns with an alternate approach to create an exciting new whole.

She replaced three notes within a progression of eight steps by moving the second and sixth down a half-step and raising the fifth, creating intervals that sounded freakish. Her entire body cringed at the 'wrongness' of the deviant notes, but she persisted until a sequence emerged. Rhythms mounted as her mind conjured images of dark pathways, ancient keyholes and foreign symbols on timeworn pages. The music no longer sounded alien: it was the sonata of a dreamer, exploring shadows to unravel a mystery, yearning for resolution....

Her thoughts went to the rusty key on Vaye's night table, and it struck her: that key might open the secret door in Junior Hut. She needed to borrow it. Where was Vaye?

Aera darted under the archway, peeked out the kitchen window and spotted Vaye crouching in the sunny pumpkin patch outside, glowing with implacable serenity. She was surrounded by plants, gardening tools and ceramic pots, her hands and bare feet rejoicing in dirt. It was unlikely she would return inside any time soon.

Aera scrutinized the staircase beside her and formulated a plan: she would sneak upstairs, snatch her prize, then return downstairs and play piano as though nothing else had occurred. Vaye might read her mind, but she couldn't confront Aera's thievery without revealing her own secrets.

The strategy worked seamlessly, and Aera felt a rush as she made her way back to the piano. She channeled her nerves into music and tried to keep her mind off the treasure in her pocket, lest Vaye heard her thoughts. By the time she left for baths, she was jittery all over.

The rest of the day slogged on while Aera's excitement mounted. When curfew finally came, she undressed down to her under-tunic and lay motionless, though she had no intention of sleeping. Time crawled as she waited for Officer Linealle to show up. Her limbs begged to leave her mat and it required effort to lay still.

Finally, Linealle showed up with her list of names and the recital began. "Samie Abani!"

"Here!"

"Samie *Eh*-ruh!"

"Here," Aera said.

Linealle leaned over the bed, her torch heating Aera's face. After a long stare, she continued cycling through all the girls, then left. Aera breathed a sigh of relief and began her next vigil: she had to be sure the others were asleep and that Linealle had gone upstairs.

Beside her, Gaili began to snore. Deep breaths collected around the room while a few people whispered in the back corner. Aera couldn't make out every word from that distance, but she caught a few, like "her tunic is *so* ghaadi ugly" and "did she *really* say that?" She distracted herself with music as the voices gossiped on.

After an eternity, the room quieted, and she was convinced that the others were asleep. Quietly, she grabbed her cloak and slipped out of the dorm. She had seen the hallway many times before but now it felt mysterious and intriguing, an otherworldly cavern of torchlight and arched ceilings.

Carefully, she took the last torch from its stanchion, rounded the corner into the dark, empty corridor and sprinted to The Door. She beheld the rusty lock, reached into her pocket and withdrew the key. The moment of truth. Her hand shook as she eased it into place and pushed it as far in as she could, turned it... there was a snap, a latch moving over... and the door opened!

PART TWO
THE SANCTUM

MAZE

1327 EARLY-SPRING

Aera entered the chamber, locked the door behind her and examined the enclave with her torch held high. Like the girls' dorm, it had a curved ceiling and an indented shelf along each wall, but no mats on the floor. She spotted a solitary object lying across the shelf: a rope with a handle on one end and a metal hook on the other. What was that contraption for? Vaye had a key to this space. It had to be something good.

She paced around, hoping for more clues, but saw only darkness. The floor creaked beneath her in certain sections only. She stomped about with exaggerated force: in the center of the room, the sound was hollow. Something was under the floor.

Aera lay on the floor and stared along the wooden surface, adjusting her angle to see every which way. Finally, with the torch positioned just so and her face hugging the ground, a minute reflection caught her eye. She moved toward it and could just make out a tiny metallic eyelet set into an indent barely visible in the dark grooves separating the wooden floor panels.

She retrieved the rope from the shelf, attached the hook to the eyelet and pulled the handle. It didn't budge. She widened her stance, assumed Kra posture and tried again. The floor made a cracking sound as panels eased away from their neighbors. Excited, Aera pulled harder,

191

and the floor scraped as she inched it over. Once it was open, she looked down and saw a staircase.

"Wow!" She gasped. *An underground passage!*

She slipped under the panel onto the staircase. Once inside, she found a metal handle above her, wrapped her fingers around it and slid the passageway closed.

The staircase was so narrow that the walls glowed red from the reflected torchlight, and she was surrounded by the fire she carried. She climbed down, down, down until the path curved, then climbed down some more. The walls were so close together, she could see nothing else, and when she looked back, the trap door had vanished from sight. She was immersed in a world of rock stairs and cracked cement walls.

The stairwell split in two directions, both of which circled upward. Aera ventured left and climbed up the staircase, only to reach another split. The stairs curved around and around, splitting and forking, leading her up, down, and up again. She wondered whether she was going anywhere at all.

As she wandered through the winding stairs, an ominous hum crept up on her. She could feel the sound in her stomach and teeth, and it violated her organs more deeply at every turn. Her knees weakened, and her muscles ached as her stomach turned to knots. She breathed into her belly, but the air only carried the noxious sound deeper. Desperate to escape, she turned back in the direction she'd come from, but the noise kept advancing. No matter where she turned, the drone intensified.

Sweat dripped down her face as dread overcame her. She was lost in a maze of staircases, each howling like the cacophony in her nightmare. Every breath stung, and her eardrums throbbed in pain as the path ahead became a blaze of blistering white.

Run away, she thought. *Stop*. But her body didn't obey.

The whiteness drew closer, and its bitter light extinguished the torch in her hand. While its blaze left her skin cold, her insides burned feverishly. The alabaster blaze screeched in ear-splitting tones, like the faces in her nightmares.

"Wake up!" she cried. "Wake up *NOW!*"

Scorching sensations ravaged her organs, and she screamed in agony as the violence consumed her. She could no longer discern hot from cold or whiteness from nothingness as her senses coalesced into a void. There was no pulse, no breath, no pain. The howling light gave way to vast, empty space. *Where am I?* She thought.

Silence.

Who am I? Blank. As she strained to remember, panic took over. Her memories were gone.

She screamed in terror, "Where am I?!" No sound came out. She tried to maneuver, but couldn't find her feet, her arms, her breath. Her body was missing. All that was left was a vast, white world. Then, the light faded and there was nothing.

No body. No identity. No boundaries. Yet still, there was consciousness. Boundless, formless thought. Nothing and everything.

No, she thought. *I need to be something. Someone.* Somewhere in this vast world of nothing, there had to be something specific. A tone, a form, a face...

Cyrrus. That name was familiar. Her voice echoed from within: *Cyrrus, yova ther sinti fatiello?*[1] One word materialized in a distant voice coming from every direction: *Naima.*

Naima. Surrender? That was vague. What did it even mean? She needed to separate from the abyss and take shape. Any shape. *Parë Në Sulë*, she thought. *Circles and spheres.*

A spherical image spun into her thoughts, and she envisioned an empty sky where the moon should have been. She placed herself within that globe, protected by its invisible shield, but still couldn't find her breath.

"*Pelesi tan yova ninisi,*" said her voice, though she didn't know why, as the words came out on their own. She considered the meaning: *I seek what I desire.*

What did she desire? Freedom. She needed to escape the nightmare, come alive, and unleash who she truly was. To shine boldly and exude beauty. That was her desire.

She envisioned herself as Alárië. *I am the moon, and my power is eternal,* she thought. *The night is my dominion.*

A silver-haired figure flashed before her eyes, surrounded by a halo of stars. The vision evaporated as quickly as it had appeared, but she sensed a presence was still with her. Somewhere beyond the vast

193

emptiness, Erelion was waiting for her to emerge from the shadows. She was not alone.

Naima, said her companion. She breathed him in, allowing his glorious glow to infuse her. Each breath inflated her presence and provided a movement of serenity within the desolate scape of nothingness.

"Opho vassë viervi yanesi?²" she asked.

She sensed Erelion going somewhere, and she willed herself to follow. Though her body was absent and the world was formless, she felt a shift from stillness to motion, and inferred she was moving forward. The silent abyss gave way to scathing sensations and howling whiteness. She screamed back at the ear-splitting blaze. Her voice was inaudible in the blaring noise, but the outcry was liberating as her consort lured her onward. The white light began to recede, and the sound pulsated in waves that conformed to the rhythm of her gait. She changed her pace and stopped. In turn, the drone lost its rhythm, and its screech became monotonous until she moved again.

Whiteness consumed her as her temples throbbed from the racket, but she was not helpless: she ventured through a sound vortex of open space sympathetic to her movement. The sound waves diminished to a low-pitched ring and the blast of torrid light dispersed into floating white spots. Finally, she felt her feet touch ground and her senses individuated as she regained control.

The drone persisted, but there were intervals for thought within its tyranny, and she took the moment to examine her surroundings. She was in a hallway that was dark but for a remnant of whiteness behind her: a distant light emanating from an iron sconce in the shape of a hand. Nothing visible fueled its constant, still glow. The light floated inside the hand as though eternal, immune to brightening, fading, or flickering.

She walked on in the spirit of Alárië, radiant and self-possessed, following Erelion wherever he led. At last, the noise faded and the hallway darkened. Relief overcame her and a smile spilled over her face.

Cyrrus, she thought. *Vaye. Underground passage.* Reality was real again.

Aera set her torch on the ground, pulled the fire-rocks from her

194

cloak and rubbed them together vigorously until the sparks did their job. The warmth of torch-fire comforted her, and she carried it down the stairs, feeling lighter with each step. The drone disappeared.

The staircase widened at the bottom, giving way to a wide circular enclosure. The area had black marble floors and an elaborate high ceiling adorned with figures, though Aera couldn't see them well in the dark. Slowly, she made her way around and found a marble wall with claw-shaped torch sconces and four iron-framed doors. The world had transformed from a terrifying maze to a subterranean palace.

She approached the nearest door, wrapped her hand around a lion's-head knob, and hesitated. What wretched torture awaited? Would she find her way back? She took a deep breath and collected herself. After the battle she'd waged to be here, it would be insane to turn back now. Resolutely, she turned the knob and pushed the heavy wooden door back from its iron casing. The path was clear.

Aera entered a dark world of obscure shapes surrounding a large fixture. She moved closer and was stunned as her firelight revealed a piano. The mahogany sheen pulsated in the torchlight and a deep shadow loomed behind it. Was this a dream?

She rubbed her eyes, then looked around. The piano was the centerpiece in a large room filled with elegant objects and fanciful extravagance. Black marble covered the floor, chandeliers hung from an arched ceiling, and paintings adorned the walls. The nearest one depicted a handsome man with light emanating from his forehead. He stood at the helm of a magnificent ship navigating ocean waves portrayed so vividly that they seemed to move. Moonlight shone through black clouds, highlighting the man's long dark mane and silken black robe as they sailed behind him in the wind. The flicker of Aera's torch made the image come alive.

She peeled herself away to continue exploring. As she moved through the space, shadows took form. There were alien stringed instruments, hand drums of every imaginable size, and giant statues of animals decorated with gemstones. One wall featured a curved rack crowded with flutes and other wind instruments, while the side wall was lined with easels displaying blank canvases between finely carved tables dotted with containers and brushes.

Aera understood this was an art room, but for whom? The paintings were not of humans, but Nestë.

She moved back to the center of the room, where the piano cast an intimidating presence. Its body extended behind it, smooth as glass with swirling reds and browns, and the legs boasted gold inlay. On the cover a woolly mammoth was portrayed as though the wood grain had manipulated itself to concoct it. She considered the mammoth on Vaye's piano and concluded this was a Nestëan tradition.

Excitedly, Aera propped open the cover. The strikers inside were gold with red mallets. She took a seat on the bench, pushed back the fallboard, and noticed a reflection of her hands in the polished wood behind the keys. If she could see her hands, she might also see her face! She had never before seen it. What if she was dull or ugly or... like a boy?

She braced herself, then dropped to her knees to view her reflection. In the thin line of pristine wood, two eyes stared back from beneath generous lids. Torchlight danced inside black pupils and the irises appeared silver. This couldn't be real.

She blinked one eye, and the reflection followed. This was Aera. She leaned in for a better look at her irises, but their color was distorted by the mahogany wood and obscured by darkness and firelight. The true shade eluded her.

The panel was too narrow to observe her entire face at once, but she inspected each part. Her eyebrows angled along a distinctive brow framing huge, heavy-lidded eyes: a keen look, but the gaze was too demure. She tried to channel the piercing glare in Vaye's painting and surprised herself with a caustic scowl. The thought of wielding that dynamism gave her a thrill.

Next, she examined her lips, which were broad, though not so voluptuous as Vaye's. She pursed them, puckered and giggled, and was taken aback by a gushy smile. Yuck! So cutesy... it embarrassed her. With those big doe-eyes and that girly grin, how could people say she looked like a boy?

She pulled her hair back and investigated for anything boyish. Overall, her face was skinny, and there was something ethereal about her, though she couldn't tell what it was. Her brow was strong and her cheeks hollow, which made her appear dramatic, but ghostly. Why did

Doriline call her 'too perfect?' She was not chiseled like Cyrrus, nor sensuous like Vaye... but she wasn't 'like a boy' either.

Perhaps the view was obscured by the conditions, and she was missing something. She held up her hands, and the reflection was an exact duplicate, though her vanilla skin tone was reddened by the mahogany patina. Her wrist was as bony as always. Was that boyish?

Just below her hands, the piano keys beckoned. She stroked the smooth surfaces until she dared to strike one. A rich note rang out and made her bones vibrate.

She decided to extinguish the torch and save it for the journey back: she would not need light or vision now. As she aimed the flame at the ground, she stole one last peek at her eyes and saw a sharp, spirited stare. She watched the eyes disappear as she thrust the torch downward. Darkness consumed all.

The piano's sound was as rich as the forest at night. She could hear the mallets striking each string and releasing the vibrations of harps. As she closed her eyes, the sound lifted her into another world, where wind hummed and insects serenaded. Her hands swept across the piano on their own, weaving an intricate dazzle of rhythms. An imaginary choir chanted in a language resembling Silindion. Along with the music, the blackness projected a scene so clear and vivid, it unfolded right before her.

The soothing luminescence of a giant moon framed the silhouette of a man with elevated wings and flowing hair, wielding a magnificent bow. With magisterial grace, he released a flaming arrow that soared into the darkness, trailing a flourish of stardust. The arrow found its target and exploded; blistering alabaster light tore through the flames. As fire battled whiteness, fangs revealed themselves inside the ghoulish mouth of a monstrous creature. Spitting and hissing, the light and the beast were one. The whiteness shrieked in a wretched high pitch...

Aera screamed and opened her eyes. White spots appeared. She blinked furiously as her mind raced. Where did that song and vision come from? Was the winged man Erelion? The black creature was foreign, but the scathing light was familiar. It was the same whiteness that filled her dreams and had accosted her along the underground pathway. That had to mean something... but what?

"The white forest is my home. *You* stole it from me."

197

Aera realized she'd spoken aloud, though the words expressed themselves through her, as if from outside. Were these thoughts her own? Was the white forest really her home? She sat in silence, her muscles weak and her face flushed.

After a time, she touched the keys again and played cautiously, with reserved dynamics and subtle changes. Though she improvised, the bizarrely complex music and otherworldly accompaniment did not return.

She slipped into a wild sonata. Passion escalated as she unleashed a soundscape that evoked a battle between Angels and monsters, but this time, the song and imagery came from within her. Music consumed her until she found herself delirious and strained to hold up her hands. Clearly, time had whirled by, though she couldn't fathom how much.

It occurred to her that she hadn't noticed any gong since curfew: apparently, she was too deep beneath the ground to hear it. For once, she'd escaped the noise of commune culture—but she had to go back before morning. She dreaded crossing again through the painful drones and the empty abyss, only to return to the land of the Samies. The authorities called her 'Aera' and assigned her duties, but none of them knew who she was. No one did... not even her.

She relit the torch and donned her cloak, then left the piano room and headed up the staircase. The climb was unexpectedly direct, free of the forks and turns she'd navigated earlier, and unencumbered by screeching lights. The stairs continued endlessly, heading up, up, up and up, until finally, she came to a low ceiling and found herself back where she'd started, with the metal handle just above her. She pushed aside the trap door and opened the portal into the familiar empty room.

How was it possible to return so simply? Before, that same staircase had led to a maze of blistering lights. Even the most confusing architecture couldn't account for a singular path connecting to disparate locations. Was this magic?

THE KALAQHAI
1327 EARLY-SPRING

Aera was lost in a fugue while Cyrrus slept through class. At lunch, she found him passed out by the boulder. She tried to nap by his side but had no success on the hard ground in the afternoon sun. The two slogged their way through tasks, then brought their dinner to the usual spot.

Once they had situated themselves, Aera leaned in and said, "I found the staircase."

Cyrrus didn't respond, but his silence said it all. He knew exactly what she meant. If not, he would certainly have asked.

"I saw—"

"Stop," Cyrrus snapped. "People are listening."

She looked around. The Hill was deserted, and the few people in the Field below were out of hearing range. Regardless, Cyrrus didn't want to discuss the underground sanctum.

Aera leaned back against the rock and closed her eyes. Her thoughts went to the horrifying journey in the stairwell. Vaye had told her silence did not exist, but she'd suffered it—and it had obliterated her mind.

She considered the rest of her odyssey: the mystical aria that had called forth the imagery of the heavenly archer and the ghastly creature; her musings about the white forest; her reflection in the wood.

She had expected to see a bland, diffident cast, and was relieved—not because her appearance was compellingly ideal, but because it had character. Nothing was worse than being boring and plain, overshadowed by Cyrrus.

Discreetly, she glanced over at him, and noted his chiseled cheekbones, square chin and rigid brow. She wondered how dull she appeared by comparison. Though her features were pronounced, Cyrrus looked more formidable. Her angles weren't eminent like his, nor were her irises as saturated... or were they? How much was the true color distorted by the browns and reds swirling on the mahogany?

Cyrrus's gaze was fixed on some unknowable spot far away. To alert him, she said, "Cyrrus?"

He didn't respond but abruptly bit his turnip cake, breaking out of his trance and reentering the here and now.

Aera asked, "What color are my eyes?"

Through a mouthful, Cyrrus responded, "Grey," as though it was the most obvious truth in the world. He pointedly reoriented his gaze into the beyond, signaling annoyance that his precious cogitation had been interrupted with such banality. Though Aera wanted more details, she opted not to tarnish his superior cerebration with inane vanity a second time.

"I'm going to sleep," Cyrrus mumbled. "You should too." With that, he lay in the grass and closed his eyes.

"I can't sleep here," Aera persisted, "and I need to return my key. Can you leave the door open for me later?"

Cyrrus didn't respond. He was either asleep or pretending to be. Aera groaned in annoyance, but then he said decisively, "Let's go sleep at the hut."

Aera now understood why Cyrrus had often disappeared during dinner: he went to the hut to nap before venturing underground after curfew. Inviting her to sleep early with him was his oblique way of conceding to include her in his secret journeys. She decided to return the key later and nodded.

They brought their trays to the Dining Hall and headed to the hut. When they arrived, Officer Linealle was sitting in a chair, talking to Officer Tiros, who paced busily in front of her. Upon noticing the two,

Tiros stopped in his tracks, glanced at the belltower clock and said, "Curfew isn't for another hour and three quarters."

"We've been through this before," Cyrrus said, bored.

"What about your shadow?!" Linealle squeaked.

"We are all the same," Cyrrus teased lazily. "She's not *mine*. By law, I may claim no property aside from clothing."

Aera snickered, but Linealle crossed her arms and barked, "Why do you two need to sleep all the time?"

"Thinking is exhausting," Cyrrus retorted. "Maybe you'll try it one day."

"Raisins! You're up to something!"

"As Junior Hut Guard, it's your job to know *exactly* what we're up to," Cyrrus grinned. "Since I trust a hardworking officer such as yourself to be competent at her job, I will offer you the honor of informing Officer Tiros of our nefarious endeavors."

Linealle was bursting to retort but found no words. Tiros waited for Linealle's response while she stared at Cyrrus, exasperated. The veins on her neck thickened until, finally, she shrieked, "You come in early almost every night! And now *she's* doing it too!"

"Sleeping is harmless and permissible," Cyrrus said. "Preventing us from sleeping has no ethical or legal precedent and will guarantee you another humiliating spectacle in Castigation Courtyard. It's *rational* to let us sleep."

Linealle glared at Tiros, appealing for help. Instead, Tiros unlatched the keychain from his belt, unlocked the entrance door and thrust it open. Walking briskly to communicate her displeasure, Linealle clomped down the stairs in front of Aera and Cyrrus and planted herself at the bottom with arms crossed, monitoring as they split and entered their separate rooms. Alone in the dorm, Aera donned her under-tunic and slipped the fire-rocks into the pocket, preparing for the journey later. The moment her head hit the pillow, she was out... though not for long.

When Officer Linealle returned for attendance, Aera awakened again, ready for adventure. She waited for Linealle to leave, then sneaked out of bed, removed a torch from the hallway and unlocked the special room. Cyrrus was already there, seated on the ledge, holding a torch. Aera remembered then that she was wearing her fancy new under-tunic and that Cyrrus had never seen it. Would he scoff at her elaborate undergarment or admire her handiwork?

"Are you trying to get caught?" Cyrrus scowled. "Put the torch back."

Aera grimaced. Why would she expect Cyrrus to notice her dress? He might never notice her appearance at all. She was too 'grey' for him. She huffed off, returned the torch to its station, then went down the hall again in complete darkness and returned to the room.

"You can make your own torch easily," Cyrrus said. "Unless you're waiting for me to do it for you."

"Darse off," Aera hissed. "I never asked for your stupid gifts."

Cyrrus tensed but flashed a grin to pretend he was unaffected. Aera glared at him, annoyed. She locked the door, then stole a glance at his torch. It was a long, thick branch, split into four sections at the top, with nothing but wood beneath the flame.

The floor was already ajar, and Cyrrus walked ahead, leading the way down the narrow staircase. Aera pulled the ceiling closed behind her and followed. When they reached the fork, he said, "In truth, the path is short. All the stairs are the same. It's a mathematical trick."

"How do you avoid the..." Aera's mind drew a blank. There was no word to describe that horrific power.

With a tremor in his voice, Cyrrus said, "It's un..." He caught himself, resumed his usual command and declared, "It's unavoidable. The white lights were probably installed to keep strangers out of the sanctuary, but I haven't yet determined who or why—"

Cyrrus stopped in his tracks. "I don't know how to get you through it," he said, "and I don't recommend taking any chances. You could be trapped here... forever."

"I made it through yesterday."

Cyrrus studied her, considering something. Finally, he said, "Onward, then."

Aera allowed a smug grin. As usual, he underestimated her.

He moved on, and she followed. The drone in the distance howled like a blade in her ears, louder every moment. She glanced at Cyrrus and sensed feelings she'd never detected in him: fear, apprehension, uncertainty.

"How did you do it?" he asked in a slow monotone. He stopped walking and waited in place without looking at her.

Aera paused: she would never reveal her Erelion fantasies to Cyrrus. "Visualization techniques," she offered.

"Keep going."

Aera framed her words carefully. "I imagined I was Alárië, hidden in shadow, and I inflated with each breath until the moon was full. Then I... moved on."

Cyrrus stared ahead. His brow furrowed, indicating he was focused rather than drifting away. Aera waited, but Cyrrus did nothing, and the distant drone made her uneasy.

"What about you?" she asked.

In a deeper, more even-paced monotone, Cyrrus spoke. His voice came from within, but his heart seemed detached from it as he said, "I abandoned *inyarya*."

Inyarya meant 'self-consciousness,' which he interpreted as 'sense of self.' How did he manage to abandon that? Aera marveled at their opposite methods. While Cyrrus had worked to lose himself, Aera had sought to find herself—and had done so by identifying with archetypal entities. Despite this difference, both had been successful.

She watched as he walked ahead, each step perfectly even. He seemed an empty shell, mechanistic, his body moving for him while thoughts and emotions were absent. Aera braced herself as the agonizing drone fragmented her senses. *Don't resist*, she instructed herself. *Focus on Erelion.*

Cyrrus disappeared as he thrust himself into the whiteness without hesitation. Aera closed her eyes and imagined Erelion, silver-haired and sublime, escorting her into the abyss. The screech tore into her and her senses jumbled together, but even as all else fractured into chaos, she followed her star. *Naima,*[1] she reminded herself. *Pelesi tan yova ninisi.*[2]

When the drone faded and the knots in her stomach loosened, she opened her eyes. The hallway was dark, but she could make out the flame of a torch ahead. Cyrrus was waiting.

They reached the circular foyer at the end of the staircase, and Cyrrus led Aera through the second door. She was overcome with the scent of leather as she entered a chamber filled with literature. Every inch of space contained countless books: some were crammed into shelves, others were stacked in tall columns, and more collapsed into piles. The room was pure anarchy but for one conspicuously well-organized bookshelf at the end of a narrow path between mountains of tomes.

Cyrrus strode confidently along the path and sat cross-legged in a small clearing on the floor beside the orderly bookshelf. It was obvious he had arranged the area, and Aera recognized it would have required ample time to do so.

"I discovered this room the first night we moved in," Cyrrus said, addressing her unspoken observation. "With all your musical daydreaming, you failed not only to notice the fifth door upstairs, but also to use *inyanondo* and read my signals."

"I used it last night," Aera said, maneuvering cautiously between columns of books. "I called out from the stairs—"

"I heard you," Cyrrus interjected. He opened a book, and a cloud of dust assaulted his face. Coughing, he added, "Sending messages about birds in the woods is mischievous. Sending messages after curfew about secret passages to forbidden destinations is irresponsible."

Aera smiled. If Cyrrus had heard her messages, that meant she possessed magical abilities too. "You answered," she said excitedly as she moved some clutter to make room for herself. She crouched in the small space beside him and accidentally unbalanced a pile of books towering overhead.

"I ignored—"

"Look out!" Aera exclaimed, jumping back as books toppled down.

Cyrrus's arm shot up, blocking the avalanche. "Slick," he teased, and Aera snickered. He retrieved two candles from a shelf and lit each with his torch, which he then extinguished. The room darkened and shadows danced from the flicker of candlelight.

"I ignored you," Cyrrus continued. "If you received any communication, it came from elsewhere."

"I sent the message to you."

"Any time we use *inyanondo*, others may overhear," Cyrrus said. "I read of one Nassando who never spoke aloud to other Nassandë *except* to keep secrets, because others nearby communicated using *inyanondo*."

"People here aren't Nestë," Aera protested. "*You* said you were the *only one* who could read minds."

"Until now, I thought I was."

Aera enjoyed Cyrrus admitting he'd overestimated the uniqueness of his superior abilities. "That means—"

"This is inefficient," Cyrrus interjected. "We're surrounded by books. We can speculate about extraneous matters when there's nothing better to do."

Though magic was hardly an extraneous matter, Cyrrus had a point: she hadn't withstood torture in order to have a conversation she could just as easily have on a hilltop in the sun. She picked up at random a book with a worn leather cover and characters on the front that were not Silindion.

Inside, the pages contained holes, and the characters were arranged vertically. She remembered similar letters in Cyrrus's mysterious book with the castle and asked, "What language is this?"

He took the book, glanced at the cover and handed it back to her, returning his focus to the one in his lap. "Nindic," he muttered. "It's called... *Luinos Eluid.* In Syrdian, 'Concerning the Stars.'"

It frustrated Aera that she couldn't decipher the text while Cyrrus was able to read it so quickly. Somehow, he could decipher every language in the world.

She stepped over heaps and piles, making her way toward the back

205

of the room, where Cyrrus apparently had not yet ventured. There, she dug through an assortment of books and scrolls, searching for a Silindion title. Some bore Silindion characters, but the spelling and vocabulary was variant to what she knew. Cyrrus might have been able to help, but he was immersed in reading and Aera didn't want to disturb him. Instead, she continued searching, poring over numerous texts, and digging through leather covered manifestos with exemplars of ornate calligraphy.

Deep in a pile between bookshelves, Aera felt something sharp and fished it out. It was a dusty metal box with perfectly angled edges and a rigid latch holding it closed. She wiped it off and exposed a cover made of bizarrely smooth black-red metal. The surface was blank but for a rigid design in the center that drew her in.

The symbol gave her chills. She followed its extensions with her peripheral vision without removing her focus from the flat red jewel at the center.

"Give it to me."

Aera shook, startled. She'd forgotten Cyrrus was there.

"Aera." Cyrrus's voice was hushed and his tone unsettling. "You can't read that."

Cyrrus was so still, he could have stopped breathing. He remained frozen, staring at the box as Aera opened the latch. Inside were stiff, white pages bound tightly together, covered in rows and columns of lines and dots drawn so precisely she imagined they had been inscribed by some otherworldly machine. There were no curves, no embellishments, no drifting marks. It was immaculate and cold.

"We need to leave," Cyrrus said firmly. He rose and crossed the path to the door, his posture stiff and his gait measured.

Aera wondered why the metal box disturbed him so. A few books tumbled around her legs as she stood, but Cyrrus didn't notice. His eyes remained fixed on the box, still in her hand. She fastened the latch and placed it on top of a nearby stack. Cyrrus stared at it until he turned abruptly and headed outside. Throughout the hike upstairs, he remained silent.

They returned to their separate rooms without another word, and she tiptoed to her mat, exhausted. Cyrrus's empty stare haunted her as she drifted off.

~

Aera was on a hill, surrounded by ancient, crumbling ruins. At the pinnacle stood a familiar castle beneath a massive red moon. She struggled against a viscous atmosphere and maneuvered through the carnage of buildings until she found herself facing an ancient marble mirror. Her sandy-blonde hair sailed over a white cloak. The hood framed a slender face with dazzling silver eyes.

Cyrrus appeared beside her reflection in a dark grey cloak, his back to the mirror. He raised his arms and spoke in a jagged tongue. "*Mtite' xulomqa qazginneq^h!^{3}*"

A shadowy horde emerged in the reflection and snarled in macabre unison: "*Mtite' xulomqa qazginneq^h! Mtite' xulomqa qazginneq^h!*" Their voices screeched louder and louder, shattering the mirror.

Aera turned, now alone with Cyrrus. As their eyes met, an explosion of grey sludge splattered her cloak, and the muggy air suffocated her. She struggled to remove the cloak, but it clung tighter as the greyness spread.

Cyrrus declared with a satisfied grin, "You enjoy wearing my colors. You envy me."

"You said *my* eyes were grey," she protested.

"Because you mirror me."

"I *pity* you," Aera hissed. "Your vanity makes you delusional."

"You lie," Cyrrus said, and the word echoed. *Lie. Lie. Lie.* His voice became disjointed as he added, "You lie because I lie."

"Stop emoting," Aera retorted, but Cyrrus's voice emerged instead of her own. She yanked her now grey cloak and noticed her hands were masculine and pasty. She had become Cyrrus.

He circled around to examine her, his emerald eyes gleaming with admiration. In a dissonant voice, he said, "Now you are beautiful, as you always wanted. *Laimandil*.[4]"

Cyrrus's voice reverberated as the blood moon descended and whiteness exploded from him. *Laimandil. Laimandil. Laimandil.* Aera's senses jumbled, and the cloak squeezed so tightly, she was unable to breathe.

"*Inyarya*," screeched a ghastly chorus of ear-splitting tones as Cyrrus moved his lips. His form dissolved to a white haze, and a morbid distortion of his voice intoned, "*Villai noss i sentunna ina evelyello i laimildë*.[5]"

Aera gasped for air, trying not to implode. "*Villai noss i sentunna ina evelyello i laimildë*," repeated the voice. "*Villai noss i sentunna ina evelyello i laimildë*..."

∾

"Get up! Let's go, Samies!"

Aera jolted awake and caught her breath. As she shook off the dream, words rang in her mind: *Villai noss i sentunna ina evelyello i laimildë*. She translated them in her head: *Delve into the core to unleash the white.*

Laimildë meant 'white,' but who, or what, was *Laimandil?* She'd heard it in her childhood nightmares, and Cyrrus had called her that in two dreams now. There was also another phrase in a language she didn't recognize. Where were the words coming from?

Cyrrus joined her for breakfast at the boulder and ate silently, staring into the distance. As Aera gazed down at Southside Forest, her mind drifted to the alabaster haze in her dream and the unsettling chant. She tried to recreate it. *Mtite' xulom*... something...

"*Mtite' xulomqa qazginneq^h*," Cyrrus said in a chilling monotone. "Where... did... you... learn... that... phrase."

Aera shivered. He'd read her thoughts and, somehow, knew the rest of the phrase.

"Aera," he said. "Where?"

"In a dream."

Cyrrus stared at the horizon, completely still.

"Do you know what it means?" Aera asked.

Slowly, he said, "Reflection yields clarity."

Reflection. The dream mirror had shattered while a crowd chanted that phrase. When her reflection disappeared, she became Cyrrus.

"Tell me the rest of the dream," Cyrrus said.

The heart of Aera's dream was her transformation into Cyrrus even as he mocked her envying him. She didn't want to reveal that and deflected, "There was a castle in the dream, just like the one you drew in the book you hid from me."

Cyrrus nodded. "I saw that castle in a scroll underground and drew it from memory, for practice. I don't know anything more." He furrowed his brow and persisted, "What else?"

His explanation was suspicious, but Aera decided to let it go and framed her response. "The castle was on a hillside full of ruins, under a red moon. There was a mirror, and in the reflection, people were chanting in a language I didn't understand."

"My dream last night was similar," Cyrrus said. "I saw you in a mirror, wearing white, with an army behind you chanting, '*Pelesi tan yova ninisi.*⁶' When I turned to face you, my cloak became white."

Aera was stunned: their dreams mirrored each other's! "In mine, you wore grey, and my cloak turned grey too. You kept repeating... *Villai noss i sentunna ina evelyello i laimildë.*"

Cyrrus stared ahead with glazed eyes until he caught himself and straightened his posture. Casually, he said, "Perplexing."

Before Aera could respond, she was startled by Luce's whistle signaling the end of breakfast. She couldn't imagine how she would survive four hours of class with so many riddles beckoning. Yet she did her duty and suffered through Language Class while Cyrrus dozed off in the seat beside hers.

When lunch break finally arrived, the two ate quickly before heading to Great Gorge. Aera mounted her usual branch, while Cyrrus crouched on his.

He looked around suspiciously and whispered, "I'm concerned about your dreams."

Cyrrus was so tense that Aera felt uneasy watching him. Hoping to break the mood, she teased, "Stop emoting."

"Quiet," Cyrrus snapped. "It's *logical* to take this seriously."

With a smile, Aera said, "Then be serious."

Cyrrus leaned against the trunk, took a deep breath, and let his shoulders drop. Coolly, he said, "For once you're not completely useless."

Aera felt gratified. Not only had she calmed Cyrrus, but he'd admitted it aloud. It was *almost* an acknowledgement of emotions. He glared at her, noting everything, but displaying nothing.

"You already know about the Nestë," he said. "There's also another species called..." He lowered his voice and concluded, "...the Kalaqhai."

Aera repeated the word to herself. *Kal*-uh-qhai.

"The metal-covered book you saw last night," Cyrrus said. "The fractal on the cover is the mark of the Kalaqhai, and the words you heard were in the Kalaqhai tongue." He paused and said slowly, "It concerns me that you know this language."

This was beyond imagining. How was it possible to dream in languages she didn't know? Softly, she said, "I don't."

Cyrrus furrowed his brow, considered her response, then said, "Please tell me everything you know."

Aera felt the weight of his tone and explained, "I've never heard of the Kalaqhai or a... fractal... until now."

"A fractal is a mathematical structure that branches to smaller copies of itself while maintaining its core geometric properties... but that's irrelevant for now," Cyrrus said impatiently. "How do you know the language?"

"I told you. I don't."

Cyrrus furrowed his brow and took a moment to gather his thoughts.

"The Kalaqhai are the most advanced species on Oreni," he said, and his eyes began to enliven. "They are uniformly dedicated to the progress of the species, and they serve that cause by maintaining everyone's position in a larger order. They're immune to corruption by false deities, possessions, passion or power... they don't even fear death. Logic is their only god."

Aera wondered how Cyrrus knew this and how realistic it was. No one was immune to passion or fear of death.

"The highest honors among Kalaqhai are granted to scientists, engineers and warriors," he continued. "They are the finders, shapers, and protectors. Science advances the culture, and engineering structures it, designing everything from cities to hierarchies to breeding regulations. Warriors guard it against intruders... and idiots."

Designed breeding... this sounded familiar. Aera watched him, curious to hear more.

"Everything is determined logically through testing," he said. "They selectively breed traits beneficial for each class, train them as children, then designate positions in the society. The most powerful are honored as warriors, the most efficient as engineers, the most innovative as scientists. Their culture advances through unity, order and logic."

The philosophy Cyrrus attributed to the Kalaqhai was strikingly similar to his own inclinations and goals. "Are you sure they're a different species?"

"I'm not *sure* of anything," Cyrrus said quickly. "There is speculation in various texts, and I combined observations to form a hypothesis."

Cyrrus had avoided the question. Aera looked at him skeptically.

"Supposedly they have no scent," Cyrrus said. "They're known to have translucent skin, angular features and blood red hair."

Aera smiled brightly: Cyrrus was describing himself.

"I have a scent," Cyrrus said. "And my hair isn't blood red. It's *brick*."

"Those are minor details. You could be *part* Kalaqhai."

"The Kalaqhai breed selectively. They would not mix with others except for scientific purposes and, once the purpose was fulfilled, they would destroy the subjects or maintain them as slaves."

"Nobody logical would keep you as a slave. You're too difficult."

"The logical way to discipline slaves is to kill disobedient ones as examples to intimidate others into submission."

"Maybe you escaped!" Aera exclaimed. "Do you remember *anything* before Ynas?"

Cyrrus stared ahead and a void in his eyes fixed on empty space. They had never discussed his childhood or established that he was born elsewhere, but his reaction was telling; instead of refuting the idea, he turned to stone. He stared at nothing, frozen in place. Aera shifted uneasily. Perhaps she'd been insensitive. Cyrrus had always evaded the topic of his past.

In her gentlest tone, she whispered, "...Cyrrus?"

211

Cyrrus blinked. Life reentered his eyes.

"If the Kalaqhai had raised me, they would have left their mark on my wrist," he said, resuming his steady tone and unflappable air.

Aera didn't know what to ask first or whether she was allowed to ask anything. She looked at Cyrrus, feeling useless, and waited for him to speak.

"I suspect the mark is related to some class system, but I can't be certain," Cyrrus said. "Nestë and humans alike speculate about its meaning. I have to decode that book."

He retreated into his own thoughts and left Aera reeling. Where did he come from, anyway? He could hear other people's thoughts like the Nestë, but his appearance and values were Kalaqhai. Could they read minds too? Nurin was the only other person on the commune with reddish hair. Might they both be Kalaqhai? If so, what were they doing in Ynas?

Though Aera was left with many questions, one thing was certain. When Cyrrus stayed up nights deciphering languages and memorizing books, he was researching something much more important to him than politics and history. Though he might never admit it, Aera knew the truth: Cyrrus was seeking *himself*.

FIRE
1327 EARLY-SPRING

The evening sky was thick with storm clouds and the air humid. Though Cyrrus's body was in attendance, his mind was off-world, and no food made the journey to his mouth.

"Cyrrus?" Aera said softly. "You okay?"

"I'm thinking," he snapped. "Don't encumber my process with emotional tripe."

With that, Cyrrus scooped up his tray and left. *Idiot*, Aera thought. He was melodramatic while insulting *her* for being emotional. As he marched toward the Dining Hall, thunder clapped and rain cascaded. Aera pulled on her hood, returned her tray, and hurried to the cottage.

When she arrived, Vaye was immersed in the piano, and the cottage was decorated with cats hiding from the rain. Aera removed her wet shoes, hung her cloak and sat down. As she listened to the sonata, she stared into the fireplace and marveled at the flame dancing in lockstep. She recalled Cyrrus deriding her for 'waiting for him' to make her a torch.

The fire roared as the serenade escalated, and Aera's face heated up. Why did Cyrrus push her away? They had the same dreams, and she cohabited his secret world underground. Maybe he feared she knew him too well. Vaye's key gave her access to the sanctum—but perhaps it was time to return it. Then Cyrrus could decide whether to invite Aera underground. If he didn't want her there, he would have to tell her outright.

No more hints and games, she thought. *He can be honest for once.*

Vaye pounded a heavy chord culminating in a conclusive grand finale. As it faded, the sway of the flames calmed obediently. Aera watched, enthralled. *Kuinu,* she thought. Or perhaps just coincidence...

"Good evening dear."

Aera returned from her trance. "Evening," she echoed.

"Is something on your mind?"

There was too much on her mind, but nothing she could reveal. She searched for a response, and one finally arrived: "I need to learn how to make a torch." Immediately, she regretted speaking so boldly and wondered whether torch-making was illegal.

"I'd be happy to teach you," Vaye offered. "Give me a moment... I'll return shortly." She took a cloak from the back of her chair and disappeared out the door.

Aera was relieved, but still felt uneasy with Vaye's key in her pocket. She darted quietly up the stairs, returned the key to its chain, and raced back to her seat just in time for Vaye to open the door and say, "Come!"

Aera smiled, feeling lighter now that the key was gone. She followed Vaye into Southside Forest, where trees ameliorated some of the downpour. Vaye led Aera to a conifer with sparse branches and peeled away some of the bark, revealing sticky, sweet-scented goop.

"The pine tree is a reservoir of endurance and generosity," Vaye said. "She has such abundant gifts that she may share portions of herself and still thrive. Her needles are edible all year, her arms are sturdy, and her sap is a flammable syrup that can sustain fire, even in the rain."

Vaye smiled fondly, as though the pine tree was her child and she was proud. Aera was amused that Vaye praised the tree and called it 'she.' Perhaps it had a Nestëan name, like Alárië. Aera tried not to giggle aloud.

"To identify pine trees, look for needles that grow in bundles of five," Vaye continued. "Other conifers have single needles."

Aera examined a few bundles. "Five each," she confirmed.

Vaye grinned. "We'll need to collect some pine needles and cones. I'll join you."

Aera gathered cones from beneath the tree. None were perfectly dry, but she was curious to see if the syrup would sustain fire in the rain, as Vaye had claimed. Once the collection was sufficient, Vaye used a sharp rock to scrape resin from the trunk and used the goop to pack needles into the cones. Following suit, Aera found a rock and milked some sap from the trunk. The pine aroma was overwhelming, and her hands were so sticky that she could barely pry her fingers apart.

Soon they had a pile of cones with damp kindling and resin packed inside. Vaye arranged some branches over the pile in a teepee, then scraped a giant scoop of the resin from the trunk and placed it on top. Finally, she withdrew a match from her cloak, lit it and dropped it on the resin, which flared immediately. Aera crouched to watch the resin dribble through the wood pile down to the kindling. Flames rose from below, and the moist wood began to bubble like lava. The resin dripped through and fire erupted.

"You can start a pine sap fire on a rock, too," Vaye said. "Or paint it on shoes or clothing to make them waterproof. Also, mixed with ash, it's a useful adhesive."

Aera enjoyed Vaye's enthusiasm. She added, "And it smells good."

"Indeed," Vaye said sweetly. "And several parts of pine trees are edible. The needles can be eaten or used in tea, and if you remove the nuts from their shells, they're delicious raw or roasted. You can squeeze juices from the sticks with your teeth, but the inner bark and younger cones must be cooked."

Aera imagined a group of Nestë in the wild, devouring parts of a pine tree by a fire. She grinned.

"These are only some of her many gifts," Vaye said. "She is generous."

Vaye spoke as if the tree had a personality, yet she also described ways to rip it apart for one's own benefit. "Do you feel guilty burning her branches?" Aera asked.

Vaye smiled. "I listen to her song and dance along to the rhythm of life."

The rhythm of life. Aera thought of *eseissë*, the World-Soul.

"Now, the torch," Vaye said, and pointed to a branch about eye level. "These low branches are known as fat-wood. Strip one from the tree—the fatter it is, the longer it will burn."

Aera spotted an ideal branch overhead. In her best Kra form, she crouched and lunged to grab a thicker one beside it. She twirled until she hung upside down, wrapped her legs around the branch and lifted herself. Vaye looked on with delight. Feeling powerful, Aera kicked the crease of the branch she wanted until it cracked away from the trunk. The end was sappy and sticky.

"Well done," Vaye said. "Now, you must cut it to the length of a torch and remove the excess branches. You'll need a sharp rock to break the wood."

Aera jumped down. She retrieved a rock from their fireplace, then hammered away at the branch. Soon she was wet, dirty and sticky, but the branch was ready to become a torch.

"Now split the top into four," Vaye said. "Use the sharp rock again."

Aera positioned it in the center, hammered it in several inches, and split each side in half to create four sections.

Vaye watched until Aera finished. Then, she broke up some small branches and jammed them between the four segments. "We need to peel some bark and create thin strips," she explained. To demonstrate, she took another branch and shaved it with a sharp rock along the side.

The two stuffed the top of the torch with a mixture of resin, sticks and cones. When the space was packed, Vaye used thin, pliable strips of wood like rope and worked several to secure the bundle into knots.

"You can light and extinguish it as many times as you like," Vaye said. "The resin will catch fire easily and it will burn for about an hour."

Aera smiled brightly and admired their handiwork. Her torch was more intricate than Cyrus's. She couldn't wait to show him.

The two left the forest and went to the brook to wash off. Vaye leaned her head back in the drizzling rain, and the jewels on her forehead-band glistened. Aera imagined an *esil*. In a flash, she saw a familiar girl beside Vaye with long white tresses crowned by black flowers. A distant voice said, *Nerilyanë Nóssië*, and the girl disappeared.

Aera's heart raced. Beside her, Vaye was wiping sap from her arms, serene as ever. Had Vaye also imagined that girl or heard those words?

216

Did the vision come from her or from Aera? *'Nerilyanë Nóssië'* sounded familiar, though Aera couldn't remember why...

"Is something wrong, dear?"

Aera looked at Vaye, and it struck her: she'd heard *'Nerilyane Nóssië'* in her mind years ago, in Panther Woman's voice. *Nerilyanë* meant 'goodbye' and *nossa* meant 'snow,' but who or what was *'Nóssië?'*

Aera considered asking, but it was pointless. No matter how many tabooed skills Vaye imparted, she would not discuss Panther Woman or the white-haired girl.

"I'm fine," Aera said, and smiled politely. "Just... sticky."

They finished washing and Aera left with the torch. As she made her way through the woods, she imagined Panther Woman passing by, riding a black feline. In her wake, she left behind a flurry of flame.

"Take me with you," Aera whispered.

Aera caught up on sleep a few nights, then sneaked her torch into the hut. When she reached her mat, she dove under the blankets at once to change into her under-tunic. She needed to leave the moment Officer Linealle finished attendance, to make sure Cyrrus wouldn't disappear downstairs without her. He did not yet know she'd given up her key and she was curious how he would react when he found out.

Soon after Linealle was gone, Aera tiptoed out the door with the torch, lit it with the last one in the hallway and darted down the dark corridor. The door was locked, but within moments, Cyrrus arrived. He glanced at her torch, then the door, waiting for her to open it.

Aera was disappointed that he didn't comment on the torch but tried not to show it. Gently, she said, "I returned my key."

"You can't just stand here. Someone might see you."

Aera tensed. *If you don't want me here, just tell me*, she thought.

"From now on, I will leave promptly after attendance and wait inside with the door locked," he said tersely. "Knock six times and turn the knob; then I will let you in. You must arrive within a brief period, or I will continue on."

He thrust open the door, let Aera enter first, and locked it behind them. She sensed he was annoyed and worried he'd invited her out of mere obligation.

They worked in awkward silence to uncover the staircase, then headed down. At the bottom, Cyrrus turned right instead of taking the familiar left and said, "I'll race you."

Aera ran ahead, endured the sensory torture, and reached the book sanctum. Cyrrus was not there. This was unlike him—he always won. She lit a candle, extinguished the torch, and settled in the same spot as before.

Soon after, Cyrrus arrived and proceeded to his seat without a word. He arranged several open books around him, including the Kalaqhai box. In his lap, he balanced a leather notebook and began writing in concise, tiny letters.

Aera wanted to learn but didn't know where to begin. She sifted through books, but there were so many, all in languages she couldn't decipher. "Cyrrus?" she said uneasily. "Where are the books about the Kalaqhai?"

"The ones I read were in Nindic," Cyrrus said curtly without looking up.

Aera wished he would have offered to teach her Nindic. She sorted books, picking out ones she could read. Once she'd gathered a dozen in Silindion, she examined the top one, which was closed with a leather tie and timeworn buttons. She translated the title slowly in her mind. *I Empissë-ni Erílëa.* In Syrdian: 'The Erilian Verses.'

She flipped to a random page, where the texture was ragged and the words dim. This would be impossible without writing and, although there was a pencil in her pocket, she had nothing to write on.

She expected Cyrrus to be annoyed by the disruption, but she mustered a pleasant tone and requested, "I need paper."

Cyrrus ripped some pages from his book and handed them over without looking up. Aera wasn't sure whether his lack of reaction relieved or disappointed her. She tried to ignore him and proceeded to rewrite the text in Syrdian characters, translating along the way.

Alárië, Túrniril
nolima o tesséphëavi isunta
eldi silani nistárië,
linti manto i osterya i nempenya
ud malyanto,
narinto yéndëa o i ssurnivi,
mellë opho sarnilu-rondë nárneivi súldëa,
në orolë, rilitma,
vë imirna i nahwë neni sempitma i yamanna.
Vavi payanto i ssilmeinya núksëu ilparnë,
lëovissa dorin i yommë lëorni?
Nuskuna, në mirto i nossë.
Ëan noldi i dorna!

Alárië, Night Jewel
silver-white-moon in the whispering
of the silver grey,
floating, bright shining queen,
to you the breezes bring our songs
moving there, flying joyfully in the night,
you rise over the black blanketed flowing seas
and you gleam, jewel-like,
as the dark years fall silently to the ground.
Where will our tear-full eyes keep vigil,
when the night ends?
We weep, and the snow falls.
It is cold, the end!

As Aera reread the translation, she thought of Vaye romanticizing the pine tree and alluding to the 'rhythm of life.' Her attitude evoked the spirit of the poem. Yet, lovely as the imagery was, the excerpt was obscure and useless.

Aera sifted through more pages and found equally lyrical passages, but nothing informative. How did Cyrrus sort through all this elegiac romance to learn history? What was she missing?

She picked up the next book and stared at the title, translating the characters on her page. *Ilieinma në Ildivatma sëolim Nossaneri*: 'Deity and

Divinity by Nossanë.' She deciphered a few more titles. *I Vosemmë Tarnamérëa Tarilim Aldundi:* 'The Recollections of Tarnamêr from Castle Galdun.' *Vauromolma sëolim Hyoirildi:* 'Angelology by Hyoiril.'

Aera leafed through books, homing in on any segment that might connect to the Kalaqhai, the white light, or a forest. She struggled with phrase after phrase, but nothing was explained. Clearly, the Nestë understood fundamentals that she did not. Their stories made no sense to her. She shifted position over and over, unable to find a comfortable one. Her fingers ached for the piano.

Cyrrus would not miss her. He was writing rapidly, eyes sprinting from one book to another as he devoured numerous texts in countless languages. He probably wished she'd never discovered the underground passage. She was a nuisance and couldn't keep up with him. Her presence was a distraction.

She placed the last book on top of the pile, lifted her candle and stood to leave. Without looking up, Cyrrus muttered, "Your addiction to music inhibits your growth."

Cyrrus ignored her all that time. Why did he care what she did all of a sudden? She shot him a glare.

"Music has no pragmatic value," he said. "It's a fun game and you can win it, but if you're lost and starving in the wilderness, it won't help you."

"And you can pontificate in five ancient tongues, but the smilodons will still eat you."

"I could defeat them with magic or technology... or strategy," Cyrrus mused. "But suit yourself. It's irrelevant anyway. You're too weak to survive on your own."

Aera felt the blood drain from her face. Her eyes landed on her skinny arms.

"The size of your body is a nonissue," Cyrrus said while his eyes were reading. "The problem is, your heart is bigger than your brain."

A rock swelled in Aera's throat. *You have no heart,* she wanted to scream, but the words were trapped. She stormed off and rushed to the piano room in a furious haze, slamming the door behind her. Hurriedly, she slid the cover from the keys and dug into them. Her hands tumbled into wild patterns over ominous minor chords, each bass note reverberating more deeply than the last. Rage burned from within and escaped through her limbs as she sang out and pounded the piano, falling into the spell of the song.

Abandoning resistance, she succumbed to an onslaught of tears. As they flowed, she felt increasingly loose and free. She unwound a knot that had been growing inside her for longer than she could remember. A reflection of her wild fingers shone in the mahogany wood.

She inched down toward the floor, clutching the edge of the piano with her fingertips as she gazed into the reflection of her eyes. This time, she was not hunting for the color or examining features. She was gazing into her soul.

As she stared at herself and blinked her wet lashes, she began to calm. Her breathing deepened. She watched her wide, honest eyes, flowing freely with pain, nothing to hide. *I am not Cyrrus,* she thought. The phrase passed through her mind as clearly as words spoken aloud. *I am not Cyrrus.* But then, tears welled up again. Gazing into herself, she said aloud, "Your heart is bigger than your brain." She could not help but laugh. Despite the cracking in her throat from crying, her voice was monophonic, just like his.

She took a deep breath and hoisted herself back up onto the bench. Her eyes closed involuntarily, and her fingers began to produce an unfamiliar aria, more intricate than the most complex of Vaye's repertoire. She had no control over her hands as music released itself through the vessel that was her. In her mind, voices sang:

Selleivi, o karievi nóndëa,
o tarivi Yóllië,
nondi Nossamirnë,
anerë Erelion eltílmëa.
Vestu yo nephenë i phúryanya,
në véstio thermar.
Ië nólië emë i mervi koina.
Në nólio hwángarnya
Seirnë ka nórëalim noirë,
sehwa Neilindunorni.[1]

Along with the lyrics, a scene unfolded. Aera saw a seraphic man in a powerful tree with glowing blossoms on branches that stretched to the heavens. The man was wielding an imperious white bow, his chest a muscular scape of pearlescent skin bathed in moonlight. Wings unfurled from his back and a handsome mane cascaded behind him, shining in ripples of silver and blue.

The song darkened to eerie tones as a monstrous black serpent emerged from shadow and laced itself around the tree. The beast towered over the archer and spread massive wings with glistening tips sharp as razors. Its ghastly mouth snarled with enormous, age-crusted fangs, and it spat alabaster fire at the archer, who burst into searing light.

In a flash, Aera found herself in a dark landscape, staring into a black night. From the shadow, an imposing form spread its wings. Scales appeared, each the size of a human hand, and the creature stretched forever. Aera bolted, but the reptilian monster blocked her at every turn.

Snakes oozed from between the scales and slithered up Aera's legs. She kicked, punched and yanked at them, but they tightened their cold grip and dragged her down. In unison, they opened their mouths and hissed in a blistering blaze. Whiteness consumed all.

Aera opened her eyes, but saw only white. She breathed slowly and deliberately, steadying herself. The room came back into focus: the art on the walls, the mahogany piano, the flicker of candlelight mirrored in the wood.

It occurred to her then: the two times she'd observed her eyes in the wood, her hands became vessels through which foreign music emerged, while her mind became a receptacle for otherworldly visions. Was this *kuinu*? Was she accessing *eseissë*?

She tried to recall the lyrics that found her. *O tarivi Yóllië... nondi Nossamirnë.* 'In the citadel of Everwhite, beyond the mountains of snow...'

What else? Something about Erelion... *anerë Erelion eltílmëa...* 'Erelion of the bright-eyes.' There was more about the color white... *ië nólië...* 'it was white.' What was white? She couldn't remember. She played the melody again in her mind. *Ië nólië ...* something something... *në nólio hwángarnya...* 'and whiter yet was his bow.'

White. So much white. Aera's clothes were white, and her dreamscapes were white. Where did she come from, anyway? Who was she really?

The music was fresh in her mind, but she couldn't recall where each measure ended and the next began. She was driven to dissect it. Slowly, she counted off rhythms while playing two simple chords along with them. After intense concentration, she realized it alternated between six and five counts: *one* two three four five six; *one* two three four five. Though triumphant, she still felt unsettled. The vision must have come to her for a reason, and she needed to know what it was.

She abandoned the piano room and found Cyrrus, still poring over books. As she found her spot, she tried to catch his eye, but he didn't look up.

"A foreign song played itself through me," she said slowly. "I heard lyrics about Erelion and saw him fight a giant black serpent with wings. Then the vision changed, and the serpent was chasing *me*."

Cyrrus froze in place. Candles cast shadows over his pale skin and his pupils reflected the flames. Aera imagined the serpent's red eyes.

"Erelion died battling the dragon Ainuvaika, whose origin is detailed in *Parë*, Lesson Two," Cyrrus said dryly. He returned his focus to a book in his lap.

Aera was sick of translating text and didn't want to wait until tomorrow. "You said you *memorized* the book," she challenged. "Can't you just recite that part?"

"I could, but I'm busy."

"I knew you didn't memorize it," Aera said playfully. "Only a deity could do *that*."

"At the beginning, there existed only Solitude," Cyrrus said lazily without looking up. "His dreams brought forth Angels of light who ignited the heavens and created Multitude. Yet one thought was forgotten: the unending night where Solitude existed alone. This was the memory of Absence, whose name was Ultassar."

He raised a brow to let Aera know that he had, indeed, recited memorized text. She giggled and said, "Such a show-off."

Cyrrus closed his book. As the covers slammed shut, the candles jumped, and a wry grin spread over his face.

"As Oreni came to life, Ultassar hid away in the darkest unknown caverns, seeking any space where Multitude would not find him," he said, his tone now theatrical. "Mountainous barriers were projected into the world from his nightmares, and he filled them with labyrinthine caverns of fire and death. There, he dreamed of whiteness that extracted the *kuinu* from the world and returned it to nothingness. He longed for a return to the void where existed only solitude and silence."

Solitude and silence. Aera had often craved solitude and silence— until she'd found it in the sanctum after her senses were annihilated by scorching whiteness. "So that's the white light in the hallway," she pondered, "and Ultassar created it to bring us back to the beginning of time?"

"That was Ultassar's motive, but his white void was a distortion of Ilë's Solitude," Cyrrus explained. "Likewise, Ultassar's white inferno was a distortion of Ilë's vision of fire, which was embodied by the Angel Sotona. Fire is essentially a transformative force. The spark of life."

Cyrrus looked at Aera. She remembered the fire rocks he gave her and blushed.

"I could recite the rest of the chapter, but it's long and boring," he said. "A summary will suffice."

Aera smiled. "Thanks."

"The Angels created a snake to represent renewal," Cyrrus said. "The snake descended the mountains and slid into Ultassar's lair, and he poisoned it with his nightmares. It took many forms and finally became Ainuvaika, the Lord of Dragons."

Aera shuddered. "There were snakes in my vision, coming out of the dragon's scales."

"The snake was Ainuvaika's origin," Cyrrus confirmed. "Ultassar subverted Ilë's vision of nature in countless ways to create creatures called Faerie. Ainuvaika was their King, and he led a Faerie army to battle the Angels. The war went on for eons, until Ainuvaika attacked the World-Tree. Erelion failed to defend it, but he battled Ainuvaika to the death. Each one of them killed the other."

"That's what I saw in the vision," Aera said, excited. "Erelion was defending the World Tree, and Ainuvaika was spitting white fire at him. The piano is magical, but I don't know why it showed me *that*... of all things."

224

Cyrrus watched her, considering something. After a long pause, he said, "Alárië gathered the World-Tree blossoms into herself to become the moon. She resurrected Erelion and he became the evening star, who symbolizes the renewal of life. Allow me to recite a quote from Alárië."

Aera was disappointed that Cyrrus offered no explanation, but nodded.

"Fire cannot create without destroying, and destruction is the bedrock of creation," Cyrrus said slowly. "At the heart of Ainuvaika, there is only transformation, and at the heart of Ultassar, there is only Ilë."

Aera grinned: that phrase was familiar. "You recited that quote when you gave me fire rocks, and now these visions came to me."

"A mere coincidence," Cyrrus asserted. "These fictional deities have been worshipped throughout history and their stories are commonplace. Anyone could tap into *eseissë* and see anything."

"Anyone?" Aera demanded. "Even Hizad? Or Doriline?"

"Anyone who listens," Cyrrus said distantly. He began blowing out candles and added, "I need to sleep."

Anyone who listens, Aera thought. Vaye had complimented her for listening, long ago. She had assumed Vaye noticed her attention to music or nature, but wondered now if she'd been alluding to something beyond.

225

FRACTALS

1327 MID-SPRING

Aera afforded herself a respite from her underground excursions, but Cyrrus's obsession with the metal box was unrelenting. He burrowed himself in the sanctum every night, slept through classes, and looked blank when he was awake. While he dozed during breaks, Aera adventured. She familiarized herself with the pine forest across the river in the east, where she climbed trees, swung sticks and pretended to be a Nassando warrior. As her collection of straight sticks expanded, she stored some in Eastern Pines, and others at Great Gorge. At the cottage, Vaye taught her new Ikrati techniques. First, she learned to twirl the stick with one hand at a time; then, she ventured to spin two at once. As her fluidity increased, she incorporated the sticks into fancy dances.

Over the course of two weeks, the cumulative loss of sleep made Cyrus increasingly erratic. His moodiness and mumbling were unsettling, but Aera tried to take it in stride. Then, one afternoon, Cyrus enacted melodramatic tirades about death during tasks, and Aera became decidedly concerned. Although she was tired from intensive Ikrati practice, she opted to check on him before sleeping.

Soon after nightly attendance, Aera slipped into her under-tunic and cracked open the bedroom door. She stopped in her tracks when she heard Officer Linealle screeching in the hallway.

"I knew you were up to no good! You're a rebel and you need to be punished! Where in Riva's Trees were you going?!"

Not surprisingly, the culprit was Cyrrus and he had a retort at the ready. "Deific though I may be, I am beset by physiologic parameters which impose a periodic purge of kidney excess and solid waste to subserve salubrity."

"Raisins! You went past the stairs!"

"Stretching my legs is an accommodation to my beauty."

"You just said you had to use the latrine! You're lying!"

"One form of physiologic maintenance does not preclude—"

"Stop smarting your way out!" Linealle ordered. "Go upstairs. I'm following you!"

Cyrrus's voice disappeared up the stairs as he shouted platitudes. "None of this matters! Life is a game! One day we'll all be dead..."

Aera eased the door closed. After some time passed, she poked her head outside again and saw Cyrrus by the stairs.

"Where you going, farkus?" Novi squealed behind her. "Chasing after Brains?"

Aera eased the door closed, but too late. Cyrrus had noticed the commotion.

He flung the door wide open, swerved to Aera's side, and declared, "It is unwise to harass your superiors."

"Darse it!" Doriline squealed from the back corner. "You're waking everyone!"

"So what?" Cyrrus snapped. "Is your life relevant? Is it even justifiable? Tomorrow you will eat plants and animal guts to fuel your slave duties. Is your petty routine of a life worth the destruction of so many other lives every day?"

"No one *cares* about animal guts!" Doriline shrieked. "Nobody wants you here!"

Cyrrus grabbed a torch from the hallway and swung it to and fro, creating a flurry of sparks and flame that was visible through the open door. Gasps and screams swept through the dorm. He returned to the doorway, torch in hand.

"We are all animals!" he exclaimed. "And we are being used, just like the animals we lock up in filthy cages! They are not used as food and we are not allowed to wear fur, so *why* do you think they're locked in

227

those foul cells? The authorities deprive them of freedom their entire lives, then strip their skin off and sell their fur to the outside world!"

Officer Linealle screeched from atop the stairs. Aera stood near the doorway, close to Cyrrus. He was coming undone, and she didn't want to leave him alone.

"This commune is a bigger cage, and we are being used for more cynical purposes than anyone knows about, just like the animals! It's *all a lie!* We are slaves and the—"

Linealle appeared behind him and demanded, "WHAT ARE YOU DOING!?"

"Testing you," he said calmly. "To see how fast you could run and how loud you could scream."

Some of the girls laughed, but Linealle was not amused. Even in the dimly lit hallway, the veins in her neck were clearly visible as she yelled, "Go! To! Bed!"

Cyrrus threw his flaming torch down the hall and plopped down on Aera's mat.

"In *your* room!" Linealle screeched. "NOW!"

"Oh, right," Cyrrus said. "I can't sleep here lest I awaken any urges."

Giggles resounded as Cyrrus rose dramatically and left, closing the door behind him with a thud. Immediately, commentary began.

"That was scary."

"He's crazy."

"Is it true about the animals?"

Aera waited a short while, then left to find Cyrrus. Once she assured herself nobody was in the hall, she headed to the censored door, which was wide open, as was the floorboard. She shut the door and leaned over the stairwell, where she saw Cyrrus in the torchlight below.

"Cyrrus!" she called. "Wait!"

Cyrrus stopped in his tracks, turned to her and said, "Death will not wait."

Firmly, Aera said, "You need to sleep."

"Deities don't *need.*"

"Then stop acting like a raving lunatic."

Cyrrus headed down the stairs and maniacal laughter bounced off the narrow walls. Without turning, he bellowed, "I wasn't acting."

"Cyrrus, please..."

He threw the key up the stairs and continued down as though she wasn't there. She watched the light from his torch grow smaller and more distant, enclosing him in the narrow staircase until he was a drizzle of shadow and flame swallowed in darkness.

Aera was deliriously tired but couldn't leave him alone in that condition. She retrieved her torch, locked the door and took the key downstairs, but when she reached the book room, Cyrrus wasn't there. Instead, she found him frozen on the piano bench with two candles on the floor behind him. His hands rested on the keys, though he wasn't playing. He sat motionless, staring ahead in a stupefied reverie.

Aera surmised he had observed his eyes in the piano's reflective surface and that a foreign song, along with a vision, had taken possession of him. Though his expression was blank, she sensed he was deeply unsettled.

With a dramatic twirl, he stood and gestured toward the piano bench. The top cover was closed. Everything felt dark and distant. As Aera sat down, her eyes went to the music rack, where the metal book awaited.

"It's a system of expansion founded on a singular principle," Cyrrus said. "Growth originates in the center and advances outward. Take it in and play whatever comes to mind."

Cyrrus sat on the floor between the candles, leaned against the wall and closed his eyes, waiting. Aera felt a surge of panic. What did he expect?

She fixed her eyes on the Kalaqhai tome, allowing it to go in and out of focus. The rigid metal box was incongruous with the smooth mahogany swirls of the piano, and the fractal was too cold to inspire music. Cyrrus had never heard her play before. No one had but Vaye.

Play something, she admonished herself, but she was stiff and her fingers were shaking. Carefully, she pressed a few bass notes and followed them with a flourish. She held the sustain pedal to draw it out as long as possible while she pondered what to play.

"Stop thinking," Cyrrus said.

Aera's cheeks flushed. He could read her mind and was aware of her self-consciousness, which only made her feel more exposed. She let a few chords slip out, but the song was lifeless. She had to conjure each musical decision. Why was this so difficult? In desperation, she thought of the song that had played itself through her during the last visit. There were six counts, and then five. Six, five. Six, five. That might impress him.

Slowly, she began. There was only one section of the song she could recall and, after she finished recounting it... nothing. She played a melody with her right hand and bass notes with the left, accentuating a whimsical cadence... yet still, she felt stiff. It was impossible to lose herself in music while Cyrrus was there.

She stopped and mumbled, "I need to warm up."

"There is no need," Cyrrus said. "Open the book and play what you see."

Aera felt foolish. He wasn't listening in order to evaluate her playing; he didn't care about music at all. He wanted to translate the Kalaqhai book, and this was an experiment. Any beauty in songs was irrelevant to him.

She opened the book and found the text inside even more unwelcoming than the cover, with sharp, mechanistic angles, lines and dots, nothing remotely resembling musical notation. She decided the arrangement of the characters would dictate the placement and timing of her fingers. Beyond that, she couldn't imagine what to do.

Clusters of lines translated to notes jammed together, and squares became dissonant chords on the edges of the keyboard. She pounded a rhythm in staccatos, never sustaining a note. Along with the dry, inharmonic patterns, she imagined vocalizations such as 'kch, kch, kch, kch' or 'kch tt. kch tt. kch tt.' The mathematical dialect defied musical sensibility and she was repelled by the sound.

She stopped and glanced over at Cyrrus. He opened his eyes slowly, emerging from a reverie, and said, "That was riveting."

Aera tensed. Was he mocking her?

"It's the most enchanting sound I've ever heard," Cyrrus said, speaking softly from the back of his throat.

Aera stifled a laugh. He *seriously* found that riveting! What was wrong with him?

She focused on the book and resumed playing. Despite the disconcertingly fractured music, she couldn't contain her smile. For once, he'd shown appreciation for her talent.

She improvised for a while, responding to the jagged code in the Kalaqhai tome. Cyrrus took in the music in myriad ways: pacing, writing, or lying atop the piano to absorb vibration. After some time, the cold math of the Kalaqhai and its macabre dissonance began to frazzle Aera's nerves, and her timing slipped. Her hands were sweaty, her eyes blurry. The symbols melded together in a haze.

Cyrrus slid off the piano and took his unlit torch from the floor. "Feel whatever you want," he snapped. "You're useless."

The door slammed behind him, and the sound reverberated through the room. Aera sat in silence, hearing his words in her mind. *You're useless. Useless.*

A candle cast fluctuating shadows on the great sweep of the piano, and Aera propped it open to reveal the hammers and strings. In the firelight, the architecture resembled a dark sea, and she wanted to jump in and never come out. Regardless how much she gave, she would never be able to please Cyrrus. Why bother looking out for him, playing from his horrid book, building his fires? Why do anything for him since she was useless anyway?

Your heart is bigger than your brain, she thought. He was right.

She opened the piano, resumed her position and sank her hands into aching chords that swelled and decayed in the shadowy cavern. Along with each sound, hammers ebbed and flowed like river waves. The silences between chords made her shiver. She played only on the count of one: *one* two three four five six, *one* two three four five. The spaces between remained empty until she began to fill the void with tender patterns. Rhythms built to smoldering crescendos and she scorched them out, seething as the tide thundered with crashing waves and violent thrusts. As she tore into it, her stress unwound. She breathed again.

After a time, Cyrrus opened the door. Aera stilled her hands and stared ahead, refusing to acknowledge him, but he continued nonetheless and placed something on the platform by the music rack. He held his torch nearby so she could see it. She wanted to disregard it, but curiosity got the better of her and she examined the object discreetly. It was an intricate paper contrivance with a surface established by geometric planes of black, white, and grey, forming points that spread throughout, spawning from patterns too complex to follow. As its shadow played with the candlelight, Aera imagined a porcupine.

"I made this for you," Cyrrus said.

Aera's cheeks flushed, but she withheld any smile as she lifted the contraption. It was made of paper with three distinct textures: the white was thin and delicate; the grey, slightly rougher; the black, thickest. She tried to count its points, but each time she turned it, she couldn't figure out which parts she'd already visited, since there were no cues to orient its multiple protrusions. As she turned it about, the black squares looked empty in the shadows and the white ones reflected the dancing reds of Cyrrus's torch. Only the grays retained a constant shade.

"Much like you, it is unique, fragile and abstruse," Cyrrus said. "It is also useless."

A smile escaped. It was impossible to stay mad at him. He was simultaneously sweet-talking and mocking her, and it made her so happy. Her stupid heart was much, much bigger than her brain... but apparently, Cyrrus liked it that way.

ARCHETYPES

1327 MID-SPRING

Cyrrus spent nights underground and slept during the daytime. On the rare occasions when he was awake during breaks, he wrote cryptic notes on rocks—which he claimed would prepare them for their next meeting on the first day of summer—and left them in selected locations for the clan members to discover. Although Aera was the only one Cyrrus included on these sojourns, she resented his excitement about his new 'apprentices' and missed the days of Great Gorge. She avoided the sanctum in protest but became restless after several nights and relented.

Soon after attendance, Aera slipped into her under-tunic, grabbed her torch and exited the dorm. Quietly, she lit the torch with firelight in the hall, then headed down the long dark corridor until she heard sobbing around the corner. Someone was outside the secret door.

Aera aimed her torch at the ground and quenched the flame. As she inched back toward the dorm, she heard Cyrrus. "You have the power to effect a change. The outcome is in your hands..."

Who was he talking to? Aera tensed. Had he invited someone else underground without telling her? No... of course, he hadn't. He'd run into someone and decided to engage to avert suspicion. Aera was irritated over nothing.

She retreated to the main hallway and positioned herself in the staircase, where she hid in the shadows, hoping Cyrrus's companion would return to bed. Soon enough, Kize rounded the dark corner with a dreamy grin and entered her dorm.

*Of course, it's **her**,* Aera thought. *That sugary little idiot.* She lit the torch, went to the extra room, knocked six times and turned the knob.

Cyrrus opened the door with a broad smile and said, "Good evening."

"You're dripping with emotion," Aera teased. "You just *love* being a hero."

"I removed Kize from our path compassionately."

"Aww. How sweet."

"You're jealous," Cyrrus grinned.

"So what? I'm still right."

Cyrrus pretended to ignore her, which meant she was right indeed. She flashed a wry smile.

They opened the trap door and made their way downstairs. Once past the lights, Cyrrus headed to the book room, and Aera stopped in her tracks. The piano was behind one door, Cyrrus was behind another, and the other two were... what?

She went to the one on her left, which had a meticulously crafted insignia emblazoned on its silky wooden door.

This symbol was in *Parë*, indicating growth or motion. Curious, she went back to the other doors and discovered that each was marked by a symbol which corresponded to the contents of its room. The library chamber had the symbol for 'knowledge' and the music room, the symbol for 'bond' which aligned a Nassando to the Angels, inspiring *kuinu*, or art.

Cyrrus dismissed Vermaventiel's 'diary' as random musings, but Aera sensed the system of symbols was important. Perhaps the sanctum was a school where students learned the lessons described in

Parë. Nassando masters might have walked the marble floor beneath her feet. With every step she took, long lost rituals were revived...

Aera laughed. Her imagination was running amok. She headed to the final door. It was marked by interlocked triangles, symbolizing kinetic engagement.

She entered and closed the door behind her. All she saw was a lumpy wall, until she realized it was clothing pressed closely together. A figure loomed in the shadows. Was someone there? A rush overcame her.

She held her breath and waited. There was not a sound. Quietly, she held up the torch and approached the figure. It was the statue of a bare-chested man with dark hair down to his waist, wearing a crown of autumn-colored feathers set into an elaborate gold ring. An orange scarf adorned its outstretched arms with a design woven along it in dark brown stitching.[1]

Aera had seen similar figures in the book room but didn't know the script or what language it represented. As she set the scarf back in place, she noticed a heavy belt around the figure's waist. A leather sheath on each side showed the handles of swords similar to ones she'd seen in textbooks, though more elaborate, with black leather strips forming intricate patterns around the grip and knuckle guard.

She wrapped her fingers around one and tugged, but it was secured to the sheath by leather thongs. Carefully, she untied them and eased out the sword. It was the length of her legs, with a razor-sharp, curved blade. She enjoyed the weight of the weapon: it felt firm, natural and powerful.

She placed her torch in a sconce on the wall, then removed the second sword from its sheath and carried both weapons to an empty area. Cautiously, she crossed the swords before her chest and considered how she might use them. Through Ikrati, she'd learned to twirl a stick while holding it in the center. This was different, but the same principles of balance and breath would apply to sword craft; perhaps even similar footwork.

A rush of excitement came over her as she adjusted her stance. *Your breath gives you power*, she thought, then sliced through the air in firm, even strokes. The swords were heavy; her muscles bulged to accommodate their weight. She felt mighty and invincible, and wished there was an opponent to vanquish. Perhaps Kize... or Nurin.

After a while, she replaced the weapons and went to examine the clothing. There were countless garments in materials she'd never imagined. She moved through the aisles, immersed in a vast universe of beads, jewels and feathers, bursting with complex arrangements of strings. Shelves along every wall contained head and footwear in a dizzying array of unique styles, and statues greeted her at every turn, adorned in spectacular outfits.

In the back of the room was an open space surrounded by human-shaped leather statues, some apparently slashed by swords. Along the wall behind them were sandbags, ropes and exercise mats. She whacked a few leather torsos as she passed, punching and kicking with directed force, then spun about in the open space between them and felt a thrill.

Aera continued browsing, overwhelmed by the variety of styles and ornamentation. She considered bringing the swords to the open space but worried she might damage them or destroy a relic by accident. She decided to move on.

She left the Kinetic Room and entered the door marked by the cross with four arrows, the Motion Room. Inside was a large, empty space dominated by a solitary commanding monolith. While other rooms boasted an endless array of objects, this room contained but one.

She circled the structure from a distance. It was a polygon comprised of ceiling-high oak panels, each as wide as the stretch of her arms. She examined one of them. Its natural grain seemed to melt and flow in the torchlight like water but contained no other detail. She ventured to the next panel: nothing. As she stationed herself before the next, she was drawn to a prominent symbol in its center:

The symbol created a bas-relief eminence in gold that glistened in the firelight, outlining overlapping triangles. The edges occupied Aera's peripheral vision, and she gazed into the center, entering its world.

The triangles began to rotate, slowly at first, each oscillation faster than the last. Currents spun in opposite directions as the symbol took on dimensionality, becoming a cage of pyramids. The edges fractured the surrounding wood grain patterns, creating chaos while the dark center remained eerily still.

Aera followed the circulating currents, dizzier with every rotation. Round and round the whirlwind roared, devouring the wreckage around it, while the center expanded into an enormous black hole. The darkness sucked Aera in as she spiraled into a void...

She jerked away, stared at the floor, and cradled her throbbing temples. More magic? Slowly, she stepped back and peeked again. The symbol was back in place, as still as when she'd first looked at it, but soon enough, the triangles began to move. Before they sped up, she averted her eyes. What *was* this thing?

She circled the structure, counted twelve panels, and examined each. Apart from variation in natural grain, they were identical—unmarked, blank surfaces—except the one, which contained the sorcerous symbol. In *Parë*, one triangle signified body, and two, kinetic engagement. Following that model, four triangles would indicate a world of bodies interacting in tandem.

The triangles became interlocked pyramids with innumerable

points, not unlike the odd paper gift Cyrrus had given her. Was that coincidence? Surely by now, Cyrrus had witnessed this monolith. She crossed the hall to the Knowledge Room and found him as expected, buried in books.

"Have you seen the structure across the hall?" she asked. "I saw a giant symbol rotate into a vortex, then... a void."

Cyrrus furrowed his brow. After a brief pause, he said, "Show me."

He followed her into the Motion Room and closed the door behind them. She approached the panel where she'd witnessed the vortex, and Cyrrus watched over her shoulder as she found the hypnotic symbol.

She glanced back at Cyrrus, who stared at the panel, deep in thought. As he looked on, she returned her focus to the symbol and watched the triangles whirl into pyramids like before. They spun with increasing force and again demolished the surrounding wood grain, which siphoned into the center and dissolved into shadow. Aera stared into the nexus, and her heart thudded as the darkness deepened.

Razor-sharp wings sprouted from the void, and a dragon tore through the cage, hissing in ghastly shrieks. Aera wanted to run but forced herself to go further. Blistering light blasted from the mouth of the beast and scorching whiteness burned through her.

"Go! AWAY!"

The sound of her own scream jolted her back to the present and released her from the vision. Everything ached; she was weak and deflated. As she caught her breath, she remembered that Cyrrus was behind her, watching her come undone.

She collected herself and turned to Cyrrus, who was staring at the wood, pensive and undisturbed.

Aera asked, "Did you... watch?"

Cyrrus turned to her and said, "I see a blank sheet of wood."

What?! Why could she see the symbol when he could not? Though Aera dreaded falling into its spell again, she examined the panel, which was now still. Carefully, she touched the symbol. Its wood was perfectly smooth. As she felt around, the triangles began to twirl.

She looked away immediately and said, "There was a dragon this time."

Cyrrus furrowed his brow. "Describe the symbol."

238

Aera turned back to the symbol. It was blatant, unmissable. Slowly, she said, "Four interlocked triangles."

Cyrrus stared at the wood for a moment, eyes glistening with intrigue. He walked over to the next panel, which appeared to Aera as blank wood, and locked his gaze into the center. His pupils moved, apparently following the motion of something as his expression became increasingly tense. Veins popped out in his neck, and his face turned red until he tore himself away and glanced at Aera with glazed eyes.

"What did you see?" she asked.

"A spider," he muttered in a dazed monotone. "Weaving a web that looked like a circuit—"

He blinked slowly and his eyes came back to life. Crisply, he said, "Like branches, or veins, or lightning."

Branches or veins or lightning... what was a circuit?

"The spider kept on weaving while the web expanded outward beyond its control," he continued in a measured monotone. "Then the spider became ensnared in its own web and all went up in flame."

Aera looked at the wood panel, which appeared blank, just as before. An entire episode had unfolded before Cyrrus's eyes that she could not see, just as he couldn't see hers.

"Did you see a symbol?" she asked.

"Eight interlocked squares." In a slow monotone, he added, "In *Parë*, it is the symbol for *indiva*."

Indiva meant 'wisdom.' Why did he see that symbol in particular? What did hers mean? Aera sensed profound implications.

The two looked at each other and silently acknowledged their shared intrigue. Aera could hardly wait to consult *Parë*.

The next day when the lunch bell gonged, Aera rushed to Great Gorge. A flurry of budding wildlife invigorated her as she sprinted through the forest in the midday sun. She flipped through *Parë* and located the symbol that had enthralled her in the wood. It meant *'ilissunviva,'* vitality.

Aera considered this. *Vitality*. She wanted to exude vibrant energy, but in the eyes of others, she was a wallflower. Why did this symbol come to her? She found an empty tablet to write on and translated the mystic text above it.

THE NINTH LESSON IS THE FINAL ONE PERTAINING TO VITALITY AND BEING. AS DESCRIBED BY RANKALOS:

LESSON OF KALMA: THE APPRENTICE EMBARKS ON THE WORLD A FINAL TIME TO DISCOVER HIS PERSONAL ELEMENT, WHOSE EMANATIONS RESPOND TO HIS UNIQUE TALENTS. WITH THIS DISCOVERY, THE NASSANDO CREATES HIS KALMA, AN AMULET WHICH STORES MEMORY OF THE FIRST INCANTATION THE NASSANDO PERFORMS AFTER ENCOUNTERING HIS ELEMENT. A KALMA ACCESSES THAT INCANTATION, REVEALED AS IF MADE BY ILË DURING THE CHORUS OF ALL SOULS AT THE BEGINNING OF TIME.

REGARDLESS OF A NESTË'S ACTIONS, THE SUN WILL RISE AND SET, AND THE MOON WILL RAISE THE TIDE. IN TIME, SHE AND HER LOVED ONES WILL PASS, AS WILL ALL CREATIONS. EVEN THE SUN, MOON, AND STARS WILL RETURN TO THE VOID. OBJECTS INTERACT AGAINST ONE ANOTHER, CAUSING CONFLICT AND CHANGE, YET ALL BEGINS AND ENDS AS ONE.

Aera was reminded of Cyrrus's rant about inevitable death and the futility of everything. Once again, he had regurgitated ideas from books.

A NESTË MAY FEEL DISILLUSIONED IN THE STRUGGLE TO ASSERT HER VOICE. WHEN HER MORAL CONVICTIONS OPPOSE OTHERS, SHE MAY PONDER WHETHER CONFLICT IS JUSTIFIED. FIGHTING, EVEN FOR A JUST CAUSE, IS FUTILE. ANY ACTION IS A DROP IN THE OCEAN AND WILL BE ABSORBED BY THE TIDE. SHE MAY RESERVE HER ENERGY TO PREVENT LOSING HERSELF IN A FURY OF COMPROMISES AND WRONGDOINGS. AS OTHERS EXPRESS THEMSELVES AND FLOURISH, SHE FEELS ISOLATED AND UNSEEN. THERE IS NOTHING SHE CAN OFFER TO ANYONE WITHOUT SACRIFICING HER INTEGRITY. THE WORLD HOLDS NO PLACE FOR HER, YET SHE CANNOT ESCAPE ITS GRASP.

SHE MOVES THROUGH THE WORLD RESENTING ITS RHYTHM AND RESISTING ITS DEMANDS, HOLDING HERSELF BACK. WHILE SHE

WARDS OFF THE TENSIONS BETWEEN SURROUNDING FORCES, HER
ESSENCE BECOMES OBSCURE. SHE DISSOLVES INTO A SLUMBER, A
PRISON OF HER OWN MAKING, YET HER SPIRIT HUNGERS FOR ASSER-
TION, WAGING AN INNER WAR. DEEP WITHIN LIES A CHAOS SO
POWERFUL IT MIGHT DESTROY EVERYTHING IT TOUCHES. LIKE THE
SUN, IT WOULD OBLITERATE THE MOON AND STARS—AND BLIND
THOSE WHO STARE TOO LONG. IF HER ENERGY WERE UNLEASHED, ALL
WOULD BE LOST.

Words jumped off the tablet. *Nothing she can offer... a prison of her own
making... if her energy were unleashed, all would be lost...*

Aera felt naked. These concepts were starkly close to her heart.
Though she hated the commune and wanted to burn it to the ground,
she kept quiet. Any protest would be futile in a world of regimes and
joyless routines. Cyrrus had invited her into a clan to revolt against
that, but she resisted involvement, begrudged his enthusiasm and saw
only the inevitable future where he took Nurin's place as the lead
tyrant.

While Cyrrus fought to create a better world, Aera seethed from
the sidelines. She engaged Vaye's lessons and Cyrrus's knowledge, and
reflected their confidence—even as she resented them for possessing it
—but never felt like enough on her own. This fueled an ever-present
rage that boiled within her, threatening to explode.

AT THE BEGINNING OF TIME, ILË EXISTED IN PURE SOLITUDE. AS HE
DREAMED INTO EXISTENCE MULTITUDE, BOUNDARIES EVOLVED.
THOUGH ALL WAS INTERCONNECTED, ULTASSAR SEPARATED FROM THE
PURE SILENCE OF UNITY AND SAW IN MULTITUDE THE SEED OF
CORRUPTION. HIS PERCEPTION OF GOOD AND EVIL, 'I' VERSUS 'YOU,'
INTRODUCED SUFFERING. THUS, HE WAGED WAR AGAINST LIFE ITSELF.
HIS AIM WAS TO RECONNECT TO ILË, EVEN AS HE FURTHER WEAK-
ENED HIS SENSE OF UNITY.

YET ULTASSAR'S PERCEPTION OF SEPARATION WAS A DISTORTION,
AS HE WAS BORN OF ILË. WHILE THE ANGELS REALIZED ILË'S VISION
BY PRODUCING *KUINU*, ULTASSAR DEFIED NATURAL LAW TO EMPLOY
SARYA. WITH THIS ILLUSORY MAGIC, HE CREATED THE FAERIE, WHO
UNLEASHED CHAOS. HIS FINAL REBELLION WAS TO EMPTY HIS ESSENCE

INTO THE WHITE GEM, AN EMBODIMENT OF THE DISUNITY HE EXPE-
RIENCED.

These names and stories were familiar. All began in Solitude, where
Ilë alone dreamed Oreni into existence. Multitude was the natural
world that the Angels built with *kuinu,* and Ultassar was the Angel of
Absence who wanted to return it to Solitude. The Faerie were Ultassar's creatures who waged war against the Angels, and Dragon Ainuvaika was their leader.

Aera was excited to have learned so much. The only concepts she
didn't recognize were 'White Gem' and *sarya,* described as 'illusory
magic.' She wondered which parts of the world were 'illusion.' Was the
commune an illusion? She laughed.

The next few paragraphs did not explain *sarya.* Instead, they were
packed with foreign names and confusing events. Aera skimmed until
she found something familiar, then resumed translating.

BEYOND THE WORLD, SOTONA AND ERELION FORGED THE JEWEL
INTO THE HEART OF A SUN-SHIP WHICH THEY CALLED ANTARONDO.
THEY GATHERED THE SOULS OF DEAD NESTË AND FROM THE SOULS,
FORGED THE SUN. SOTONA CAPTAINED THE SUN-SHIP AND ERELION
STEERED IT TO PLACE THE SUN OVER THE WORLD. THE NAME
ANTARONDO, MEANING 'SHIELD OF PROMISE,' WAS GIVEN TO
ERELION. HE WAS DEFENDER OF THE NATURAL ORDER, AND THE SUN
WAS THE REBORN PROMISE OF THE ANGELS AFTER THEY LEFT ORENI.

Erelion was the Evening Star but the name Antarondo linked him
to the sun. Aera remembered Sotona, the Angel of Fire. Though she
still had much to learn, she was relieved that some Nestëan themes
were beginning to make sense.

What intrigued her most was that the mythology highlighted
Erelion. Aera connected to him through visions and their shared relationship to the color white. She wondered if this explained why the *ilissunviva* symbol had appeared to her, but not to Cyrrus. Perhaps the
indiva symbol connected to a different Angel.

WHEN THE SUN ROSE, MANY BELIEVED IT EMBODIED THE SOULS OF FALLEN NESTË AND SERVED AS AN EYE OF THE ANGELS WATCHING OVER THE WORLD, SO THEY CALLED IT TIL, 'EYE.' THOUGH THE NESTË ACCEPTED TIL AS A NATURAL PART OF THE WORLD, THEY HAD BEEN ACCUSTOMED TO MOONSHINE AND THE BRIGHT SUNLIGHT WEAKENED THEM. THEY MISSED THE STARRY SCAPE OF A GENTLER SKY. YET OVER TIME, THE SUN CAME TO REPRESENT HOPE OF A NEW DAWN. THE NESTË PERCEIVED ITS PRESENCE AS A SIGN THAT THE ANGELS MIGHT ONE DAY RETURN.

A NESTË MAY SOW DISCORD BUT, AS THE SUN SETS, SO WILL THIS FERVOR PENDULATE. THE BEAT OF HER HEART CANNOT BE SILENCED, NOR CAN ITS HUNGER TO CONNECT AND EVOLVE. ANY ATTEMPT TO STIFLE IT WILL CAUSE DISSONANCE. WHETHER SHE ASSERTS OR WITHHOLDS HER ENERGY, HER PULSE CONTINUES TO RESONATE WITH LIFE, WAXING AND WANING IN TANDEM WITH ALL, SINGING THE SONG OF CREATION. ANGER ARISES FROM THE FALSE IMPRESSION THAT GOODNESS IS FINITE, AND ANY EXPERIENCE OF SEPARATION AND DISHARMONY DERIVES FROM THE NOTION THAT INTEGRITY CAN BE LOST. THUS, RESISTANCE MAY FOSTER AUTONOMY, BUT IT CANNOT LIBERATE A NESTË FROM HERSELF.

Aera reread the last sentence. *Resistance may foster autonomy, but it cannot liberate a Nestë from herself.* Indeed, she resisted and withdrew, yet never felt free. Perhaps this was why she'd heard the word *'naima'* underground. Whoever sent that message wanted her to surrender, but didn't explain how to do it.

WHEN A NESTË LISTENS TO HER BREATH, SHE HEARS THE RHYTHM OF THE WORLD. SHE KNOWS INNATELY THAT TO LIVE IS TO SING IN THE CHORUS OF SOULS, AND TO DIE IS NOT TO SEPARATE FROM LIFE, BUT TO UNITE WITH ILË. WITH THIS REVELATION, THE ILLUSION OF AUTONOMY DISSOLVES. MAGIC IS BOUNDLESS, BEAUTY IS INFINITE, AND JOY IS UBIQUITOUS. ALL BEINGS ARE CONNECTED—AND ANY MAY AFFECT HER, JUST AS SHE MAY AFFECT THEM. AS SHE CHANNELS THE ENERGY AROUND AND INSIDE HER, SHE EMBODIES THE FLOW OF LIFE. SHE SHINES HER LIGHT UNTO ORENI JUST AS THE SUN, COMPRISED OF THE SOULS OF THE DEAD, IS A FORCE OF ITS OWN.

Within the symbol, there were circles, squares and triangles. This suited the idea: *'the sun, comprised of the souls of the dead, is a force of its own.'* The symbol represented all elements coming together to form something new. Its edges were harsh, and the core was hollow.

Aera noted the sentence: *when a Nestë listens to her breath, she hears the rhythm of the world.* Vaye had taught her breathing exercises and claimed, *your breath gives you power.* She wondered if Vaye understood just how powerless she felt.

Gong, gong. Gong, gong.

Aera grimaced. She was powerless indeed. Her life was controlled by bells, whistles, and officers in ugly uniforms. Annoyed, she placed *Parë* back into the tree and headed off.

Throughout tasks, Aera was faint from skipping lunch, but remained charged as she considered the arcane implications of the vortex, the dragon and the *ilissunviva* symbol that had appeared to her and not to Cyrrus. She could hardly wait to study *indiva*, the symbol that so affected him. When the bell finally released them, she and Cyrrus ate quickly and went to the Gorge, where Aera dug into *Parë*. The *Lesson of Indiva* was situated between the lessons of *onophayaniva* and *vekos*, but the page was gone.

How convenient, Aera thought. Of all the pages, the only one missing might reveal something about Cyrrus. "Why did you rip out *indiva?*" she demanded.

"It was missing when I first read the book."

Lies, lies, lies. They had discussed *indiva* before, and not only was he familiar with the meaning, but he'd specifically mentioned it was a lesson in *Parë*. It defied credulity that he'd learned its significance elsewhere and that the page had ripped itself out.

She recalled that after she'd translated the first chapter and wanted to finish the book, Cyrrus had implored her not to. He had advanced every possible rationale—that it might poison her mind, that she was latching onto it like a religion, that she needed more context. Next time she'd picked up the book, there were pages missing.

It all came together. Cyrrus had been sneaking underground since they first moved to Junior Hut, had seen the symbol for *indiva* in the Motion Room and found something in Vermaventiel's description that he wanted to hide from Aera. She decided to look for the symbol that matched his description of an 'eight-sided polygon' and to interpret its meaning herself. Promptly, she consulted the symbol chart.

The symbol was composed of eight squares, interlocked at the corners. Each one represented a *semissë*—which meant 'faculty of reason' or in this context, 'reasoning mind'—while each interlocked pair signified 'knowledge,' the symbol Cyrrus wore on his belt and assigned to the clan. Vermaventiel emphasized that when two identical symbols interlocked, the original shape was sacrificed to the whole.

The symbol muddied the border where one *semissë* ended and another began... which made sense for Cyrrus. He recited memorized text, appropriated Nurin's vocabulary and tailored his delivery to his audience. The totality of the squares created an illusion of stars inside stars, well fitted for Cyrrus's dazzling oratories that lured people in to his 'spider web.' Yet there was no distinction between his own ideas and those he regurgitated, and no way to distinguish truth from fable.

Cyrrus insisted the symbols in *Parë* represented arbitrary subjective metaphor, yet their experience in the Motion Room proved otherwise. Clearly, the stories meant more than he wanted to admit: if they meant nothing, he would not have exorcised the page.

Aera glanced over and saw that he'd drawn the symbols on a wood block and was writing words beside them. He noticed her looking and declared, "I am uncertain whether this has any meaning. The only pattern I detect is irony."

Cyrrus was playing dumb, but Aera was unconvinced. She removed her tablets from the gorge and skimmed through her notes. Phrases jumped out at her. '*All Nassandë must discover the parallels between their own emanations and those of the Angels.*' '*The combination of innate character, choices, and behaviors throughout a Nestë's life coalesce into a personality, establishing a core from which to grow.*' '*Each lesson describes a behavior pattern which a Nestë incorporates to create order out of chaos, along with a deeper revelation which demonstrates that chaos is itself an illusion, since Ilë underlies all.*'

The connection between the lessons and 'behavior patterns' was spelled out in the text. Aera had read two lessons, and each contained universal themes but evoked symbolism to illustrate specific archetypes. This meant Aera had a kinship with *ilissunviva*, just as *indiva* echoed Cyrrus.

She reviewed her experience from the beginning: first was the carving on the fourth door, Vermaventiel's symbol for motion or growth. Perhaps the symbols were intended to create paths for growth specific for each person. Their visions indicated this.

"You said the spider wove a web that looked like a circuit," Aera mused. "What's a circuit?"

"Circle."

"You said circuit."

"I tripped on my tongue."

Cyrrus was never imprecise. *More lies,* she thought. He had relayed an entire vision to her, and she couldn't be certain that any of it was real.

Nonetheless, she contemplated the relationship between *indiva* and Cyrrus's spider with its ever-expanding web. He drew people into his snare and considered deception an indispensable asset in his quest to rule the world. He would have to renounce all he believed to become truthful. Aera was convinced it would benefit him to be honest with himself at the very least. Perhaps, then, his webs wouldn't spin out of his control. Likewise, if she stopped resisting and holding back, the whirlwind of faces and demands wouldn't overwhelm her so deeply that she needed to become a dragon to assert herself.

Aera understood the pattern: Cyrrus found her life strategy precisely as self-defeating as she perceived his. He mocked her for being too 'useless' and 'weak' to take on the world, while she resented the lies and hypocrisy that accorded him admiration. Yet his influence helped her to become confident, while her reliance on him served as a treat to his vanity. Compassion was 'mutual gain' after all.

~

Weeks sailed by as the investigation continued. Aera and Cyrrus scoured the Motion Room repeatedly and examined every inch of wood panel but experienced the same visions each time. Once it became frustratingly evident that the monolith would yield no further answers, Cyrrus returned to the Knowledge Room. Still, Aera wasn't ready to give up.

Hoping for an epiphany, she pored over *Parë* and contemplated the content during duties. She shared her thoughts with Cyrrus as they developed, but he was too consumed by his nightly excursions to take interest in her so-called 'mystical musings' and 'fanciful fodder.' For once in her life, Aera was undeterred and took the lead. She was convinced *Parë* touched upon something significant and determined to prove him wrong.

She absorbed abundant detail concerning the relationships and derivations of the Angels and their lovers, but focused mostly on their psychological symbolism. Each day, at the end of breaks, she consulted Cyrrus about any questions or difficulties. To reward her for persistence, he drew the circle of symbols on a sheet of paper and gifted it to her.

Vermaventiel's presentation was vague and contradictory, but Aera isolated the basic principles. There were Angels connected to elements, symbols connected to lessons, and concepts which united them. The four corner lessons—*inyarya, vekos, kalma,* and *sundatëa*—were the most fundamental. Aera decided to revisit *The Lesson of Indiva* at the end and determine its meaning from the surrounding text.

After a grueling process, themes began to crystallize. She distilled each archetype down to its essential descriptors and began with *The Lesson of Kalma*.

- SUN IS THE EMBLEM OF THIS ARCHETYPE BECAUSE IT LINKS TO SLUMBER & AWAKENING.
- THESE TYPES OVERVALUE AUTONOMY, BUT IT LEADS TO RESISTANCE.
- THE PATH TO GROWTH IS VITALITY (*ILISSUNVIVA*).
- THE ROLE OF THOSE WITH THIS ARCHETYPE IS TO OFFER & EMBODY FLOW.

Pleased with the derivatives, she made lists for each archetype and filled them in over the course of a few weeks. Yet, as she made her way through the book, she found herself dissatisfied. The motion symbols were not associated with Angels, but rather, with higher concepts of space, time, and deity. It seemed there were only nine archetypes a person could embody.

She considered cutting the circle down to nine symbols, but that could not be the solution. The monolith underground was magical, and it had twelve walls. Had Vermaventiel neglected to describe three Angels, or was Aera missing something?

She decided to translate Vermaventiel's concepts as they were and investigate the top three symbols later. Once she'd selected the most relevant words to fill in the categories for each lesson, she copied the ideas to the page Cyrrus had drawn on, creating a map of archetypes.

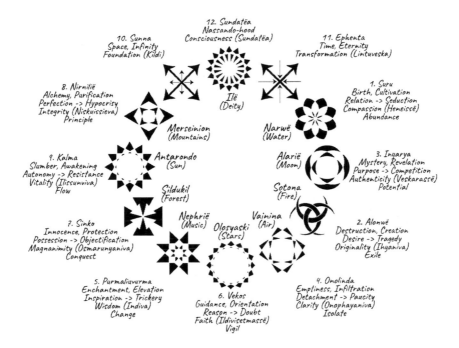

10. Sunna
Space, Infinity
Foundation (Kildi)

12. Sundatëa
Nassando-hood
Consciousness (Sundatëa)

11. Ephenta
Time, Eternity
Transformation (Lintuveska)

8. Nirnilië
Alchemy, Purification
Perfection -> Hypocrisy
Integrity (Niskuissieva)
Principle

Ilë
(Deity)

1. Suru
Birth, Cultivation
Relation -> Seduction
Compassion (Heneissë)
Abundance

Merseinion
(Mountains)

Narwë
(Water)

9. Kalma
Slumber, Awakening
Autonomy -> Resistance
Vitality (Ilissuniva)
Flow

Antarondo
(Sun)

Alarië
(Moon)

3. Inyarya
Mystery, Revelation
Purpose -> Competition
Authenticity (Veskarassë)
Potential

Sildukil
(Forest)

Sotona
(Fire)

2. Alonwë
Destruction, Creation
Desire -> Tragedy
Originality (Ihyaniva)
Exile

7. Sinko
Innocence, Protection
Possession -> Objectification
Magnanimity (Osmarunyaniva)
Conquest

Nephrië
(Music)

Olosyaski
(Stars)

Vainina
(Air)

5. Purmaliuvurma
Enchantment, Elevation
Inspiration -> Trickery
Wisdom (Indiva)
Change

6. Vekos
Guidance, Orientation
Reason -> Doubt
Faith (Ildivisetmassë)
Vigil

4. Onolinda
Emptiness, Infiltration
Detachment -> Paucity
Clarity (Onophayaniva)
Isolate

Aera examined the page, making sure everything fit. It occurred to her that the top three symbols set the guideposts for the rest. Consciousness, at the crown, connected to the other three corner symbols: Authenticity, Faith and Vitality. Likewise, Transformation connected to Originality, Wisdom and Integrity; Foundation to Compassion, Clarity and Magnanimity. In total, there were three groups of four. Though Aera was displeased that the top three symbols stood apart from the rest, she was satisfied that, at the very least, their placement was meaningful.

The ideas were thought-provoking, and the connections to her and Cyrrus were amusing. Cyrrus's symbol linked to music, yet he mocked Aera for playing piano. He certainly would refute any relation to something he considered frivolous, but his behavior matched the archetype: he inspired people with his grandiosity. Even when he was not present, people remembered his magical tales and theatrical display. He was the nagging tune that no one could forget.

∾

The following day, Aera ushered an exhausted Cyrrus to the gorge to show him the map of archetypes. He followed her through the forest languidly, then studied the page. Aera couldn't discern his verdict and became increasingly nervous.

After an eternity, he spoke. "No one could possibly assemble something more coherent from this diary, and your interpretation of the wheel is compelling. But don't get attached to arbitrary concepts. The symbols have been reinterpreted countless times, along with any association between deities and lessons. Remember that in the First Age, there was no sun, and if you remove that from the circle, the foundation crumbles."

With that, he lay down on the ground and went to sleep.

Despite Cyrrus's lofty praise, Aera was dejected. She'd endured such frustration to produce that chart, yet the result was meaningless to him. The afternoon birds and gentle spring breeze carried a disturbingly cheerful cast that made Aera want to explode. She resolved to return before tasks to wake Cyrrus and stomped off to the cottage.

The upstairs curtains were open, but the fire was out, and the cats were curled up together. She paced around, miserable and agitated... until it occurred to her that she'd seen symbols on wood carvings in Vaye's bedroom. Apparently, they meant something to Vaye.

Quietly, Aera tiptoed up the creaky stairs, slipped in the door and went to the wall opposite Vaye's bed, where the carvings hung between shelves. They portrayed geometric symbols, just as she remembered. As she browsed, she found a familiar piece depicting a Vaye-like figure beside a young girl wearing a crown of flowers. Despite the absence of facial detail, the adornments left little doubt this was the same girl in the painting downstairs. There were symbols on the carving, one each above Vaye and the girl.

The girl was marked by *ilissunviva*, same as Aera! Was this why Vaye had taken an interest in her? It could not be coincidence that she'd found Aera, who shared this girl's archetype, and taken her under her wing. But how had she learned Aera's archetype in the first place?

Perhaps, like Aera, she had used *Parë* to work out the underlying themes. From there, she might have learned to pair others with the Angels who matched their emanations. Considering each archetype reflected a specific psychology, someone who understood these connections could theoretically figure out which group any person belonged to, based on their behaviors.

I need to learn this skill, she decided. *There is, indeed, a 'rhythm of the world.'* People gravitated to roles that suited their innate nature—and if Aera learned to identify them, she might discover her own.

She looked at the carving again. Vaye's symbol was *heneissë*, which associated her with Narwë, the Angel of the Sea. Aera would have paired Vaye with soil or plants and worried that she'd misinterpreted the links between Angels and symbols. She took the archetype wheel from her pocket and found the lesson.

1. Lesson of Suru
Birth, Cultivation
Relation -> Seduction
Compassion (Heneissë)
Abundance

Indeed, Vaye was seductive. She enticed Aera with bountiful offerings, enriching Aera's soul just as the rain nourished her garden, yet all the while maintained distance and control. The sea was deep and mostly hidden; Vaye was mysterious too. Perhaps *heneissë* was an appropriate emblem for her.

There was much to contemplate, but lunch would be over soon and Aera needed to bathe. She returned to the Gorge, noted Cyrrus's dirty clothes and matted hair, and woke him.

"Cyrrus," she said, tugging at his wrist. "Bath time."

Cyrrus didn't budge, so she tightened her grip and shook him. His lips curled into a grin, and he muttered, "Are these our only choices?"

"Yes. Get up."

Cyrrus peeled himself from the ground and joined Aera, trailing just behind as she led him through the forest, over the Hill and back down to the Field. As they followed the northward path through West-side Willows, Aera spotted Dila, Rafi and Pavene gabbing in a cluster, all with wet hair. The moment Dila noticed Aera and Cyrrus's approach, she silenced the others. Their chatter came to a halt, and Dila smiled as her eyes locked on Cyrrus.

What could Dila possibly find attractive about him right then, when he was so dirty and limp? She was prettier than ever, with wet hair contrasting against rosy cheeks, and gentle curves filling her fitted blue tunic. Cyrrus looked at her, but his expression remained insouciant. Aera wondered if he was feigning disinterest or was immune to Dila's conspicuous beauty and inviting manner. Perhaps Dila's emblem was also *heneissë*, considering she leaned forward to proffer her breasts as a lure.

As Aera and Cyrrus approached, Pavene shuffled nervously. Though too shy and anxious to stare openly, her attraction to Cyrrus was no less obvious than Dila's. Rafi was the only one unaffected. She crossed her stout, muscular arms in annoyance while Dila swayed coquettishly and cooed, "Samely, Cyrrus."

Cyrrus looked straight at her and asked, "Are these our only choices?"

Dila batted her lashes and asked, "Choices?"

"Peh," Rafi grimaced. "Forget it, Dila. He's a joke."

A joke without a punchline, Aera thought.

Cyrrus maintained a severe expression, but before he could respond, Aera directed him onward. She was embarrassed for him and hoped the cold river would snap him out of it.

When the two reached the river, Cyrrus disrobed quickly and plunged in. Aera took her time bathing, then washed her clothes and returned to the Field, where Cyrrus was already in line. The last stragglers took their places and Officer Padd hollered, "Five to six Group, to the vegetable field!"

"Are these our only choices?" Cyrrus called out, and all eyes turned toward him.

"Quiet!" Padd called. "Seven to eight Group, to the barns—"

"Are *these* our only choices?"

"Darse your dirl, Samie Cyrrus!" Padd barked.

Their voices piled up on top of each other as Cyrrus ranted on, uninterrupted. "Are these our only—"

"DARSE IT!"

"—choices? Are these our only choices? Are these our only—"

"Ghaadi barlock! Darse your dirl or I'll Kadirize you!"

"—choices? Are these our only choices?"

Finally, Cyrrus stopped, and Officer Padd's voice rang out by itself. "Your ghaadi dirl is sickening! What in Riva's Trees got up your snout! I'll Kadirize your skinny barlock butt!"

Laughter exploded all over the Field until suddenly, Padd noticed he was the only one talking. Cyrrus beamed as Padd grunted loudly and announced the next task. "Nine to ten Group, soaps...."

Cyrrus was in a silent daze for the rest of the day, but his phrase clung to Aera's mind, repeating itself in the background as she contemplated *Parë*. Everyone was bound by automatic behavior and delusions; instead of helping them free their minds, authorities took advantage of their weakness and enslaved them. If every society used propaganda and war to perpetuate ignorance, how could anyone thrive? Was anyone's life really their own?

She visited the sanctum that evening but found herself distracted from the piece she was playing as her hands kept drifting to accommodate a rhythm in her head. *Are these. Our on. Ly choices. Are these. Our on. Ly choices.* She abandoned her piece and improvised along with the syncopated rhythm of the words. The left hand followed the right in a cyclical sway, imprisoning her in a spinning canon.

Something creaked and Aera snapped to attention: Cyrrus was in the doorway, carrying a torch. He pulled the door closed behind him, sat on the floor and leaned against the wall, rigid and stern. Aera waited for him to speak, but he stared solemnly at the floor.

She resumed playing, and her progression swayed about the piano, gathering momentum along with the rhythm of Cyrrus's words in her mind. 'Are *these* our *only* choices?' 'Are *these* our *only* choices?'

Her frustration mounted as the pattern circled down the keys, its dynamics escalating as anger unfurled. She was trapped in the song, caught in the commune, locked in a meaningless existence. As the progression fell into crying legatos, her eyes filled with tears, and she gulped them back. Cyrrus was still in the room. Did he notice her musical rage? She glanced behind and saw him sitting as still as before, conveying sadness.

A smile poured over her face: Cyrrus was moved by the music. She pounded the piano, breaking the pattern open and shattering it to pieces. After a powerful crescendo, the song gave way to beauty that flowed naturally into a whirlwind of freedom.

She lifted her hands from the keys and glanced over at Cyrrus, who looked relaxed and peaceful. With arabesque grace, he stretched his arms, rose and found the door. As he pulled it closed behind him, he said with a grin, "The rebel's courage is the seed from which progress spawns." With that, he was gone.

Aera's music had exorcised Cyrrus's tension and restored his enthusiasm. Excitement propelled her as she returned to the song, ready for anything.

THE ANIMALS
1327 LATE-SPRING

"Samely, Cyrrus!"

"Morning, Brains!"

People beckoned Cyrrus from every part of the Dining Hall as usual, but he remained quiet at Aera's side, slouching from exhaustion, his hair sticking up in as many points as his odd paper gift. The chatter dampened as officers filtered inside. Aera shot Cyrrus a warning glance to alert him and his posture straightened.

The two carried their breakfast to the boulder. Cyrrus ate quickly, organized his hair into a ponytail, and passed out. Aera kept her eye on the Field behind them, where officers clustered together, whispering to each other. Something was happening.

Officer Padd blew his whistle and all the children lined up. Once everybody was in place, Padd bellowed an announcement: "Classes and tasks will be delayed! Take attendance here and bring your groups to the Dining Hall."

The atmosphere was tense as line leaders called out names. When beckoned, Aera entered the Dining Hall, where the echoey din immersed her. People were packed together, crowded into and between tables with officers lined up in front. Aera crossed the room and stood by the fountain, where the flow of water tempered the noise, but soon enough, she was surrounded by chatter.

255

By the time Cyrrus entered, the room was overflowing. He climbed ostentatiously atop a table near the front center of the room and took a seat. Samies on surrounding benches greeted him enthusiastically. With his legs crossed before him and his back straight, his demeanor commanded attention. Aera was pleased that she'd made him bathe.

Finally, once everyone had crowded in, Renstrom Nurin made his entrance. He strode in front of the other DPD officials and stood before the assembled crowd with Brass Inellei and Justinar Dinad as bookends. As the Renstrom took his place, Aera compared him to Cyrrus's description of the Kalaqhai. His cheekbones and chin were angular like Cyrrus's, though less chiseled, and his hair was chestnut with a distinct reddish cast. His hazel eyes were deep-set, and his skin was pale, albeit less pasty than Cyrrus's. The shapes and angles of their features did not match, but Nurin's overall look and air were evocative of Cyrrus's. Both bore Kalaqhai features, though Cyrrus's were more pronounced.

Once the assemblage was composed, Nurin assumed position for the salute. Everyone cloned his motion and chanted, "We are all the same! We are all the same!" The shibboleth spread throughout the Dining Hall, and the room vibrated with the howl. Satisfied, Nurin lowered his arms. The room quieted.

"The caged animals were released last night," Nurin announced, his sturdy voice resonating throughout the room. "Someone among us—in this room *right now*—invaded the animal compound."

Gasps and murmurs resounded as people glanced around nervously. Cyrrus had ranted about the caged animals in public. Would he be accused? He sat right before Nurin, peppy as ever, legs crossed and eyes glimmering. Since his breakfast nap had been too short to revive him, Aera decided he was fueled by unadulterated hubris.

"Someone has defied commune law," Nurin declared. "Our unity has been defiled and our trust has been debased by this act of contempt against our entire society. Someone betrayed us all."

Cyrrus grinned maniacally as people looked in his direction. He'd been with Aera all night, so he did not free the animals—but he couldn't resist drawing attention to himself. It was only a matter of time before his arrogance undid him.

Nurin eyeballed Cyrrus and continued. "We rely upon our animals for food, medicine, and the clothes on our back—"

"That's a lie!" Gaili yelled. Aera followed the husky voice and located her on the opposite side of the room.

"Young lady," Nurin cleared his throat. "Don't you know the clothes on your back and the food you ate this morning came from our animals?"

"That's a *lot* of food," someone called, and a few people laughed.

Gaili's mien deflated, but Doriline and her klatch, at the table beside hers, did not laugh.

Nurin continued his speech. "One of you has committed an outrage against all of us, and—"

"All of *whom?*" Cyrrus cut in, his voice booming. "I have never worn anything but sheepskin, wool, and linen, and I've never eaten mink, chinchilla, sable, or fox. Tell us precisely *who* is feasting on these animals and warming themselves with their fur?"

"Releasing animals defies the law," Nurin said forcefully. "Anyone who wishes to debate the merit of our laws may do so at town meetings, but violation of those laws is unacceptable."

"This issue is beyond law," Cyrrus said. "It speaks to compassion."

The spider weaving his web of deception, Aera thought. Cyrrus cared nothing for compassion but wielded emotion as a weapon.

"Breaching trust is not compassionate," Nurin asserted. "It invites chaos. Rules preserve our society."

Cyrrus stood up on his tabletop. Everyone craned to watch as he asserted, "Those animals were treated poorly, and labor has been squandered on their care—labor that could have been spent bettering the commune for everyone."

Nurin pointed a long, bony finger at Cyrrus. "It is unethical and irresponsible to act single-handedly against the commune. If nobody speaks up, *you* will be punished for freeing the animals."

"That's not fair!" Pelyane protested as she climbed atop a table in the back. "You can't punish him if he didn't do it!"

"What makes you so certain he didn't?" Nurin asked.

"Is there any proof he did?" Pelyane called. "You have no right to accuse him without proof!"

"It's not fair," Gaili echoed.

Olleroc stood from his bench beside Gaili, shaking as he climbed up on their table; then Kize rose to stand beside Pelyane. In turn, a few others in their group mounted their tables and several girls from Aera's group rose. Dila stood on her table in the corner of the room and her friend Pavene followed.

"What do you propose?" Nurin implored the crowd. "That we permit laws to be broken until all of the animals are gone, our crops rot in the ground, and everyone starves?"

"I propose you tell us the real reason we needed those animals," Cyrrus said.

People climbed atop their tables all around the room. Though Nurin remained outwardly impassive, his lengthy pause indicated he was caught off-guard by the outpouring of support Cyrrus had garnered. If he outright dismissed Cyrrus's show of compassion, his days as Renstrom might be numbered.

Cyrrus watched him with unflinching satisfaction. Nobody dared utter a sound until, finally, Nurin cleared his throat.

"No punishments will be issued today," he announced. "The DPD will investigate further to resolve this matter."

Nurin ended the meeting without answering Cyrrus's question. He paraded out the front door with Dinad and Inellei following. At once, the line leaders assembled and began herding the youngest Age Groups to escort them to classes.

Cyrrus sat back down at his table and everyone else climbed down from theirs. His revolution had barely begun and, already, he spoke for the commune. He paid no heed to anyone, yet people defended him with vigor. Despite adamant denial of his own emotions, he had awakened the soul of Ynas.

Cyrrus slept through classes and lunch, then looked like a ghost during afternoon tasks. At dinner, he was dreary but stayed upright long enough to eat. He stuffed in his food, eyes half closed.

Aera looked around to make sure nobody was nearby and whispered, "Who did it?"

"Don't know," Cyrrus shrugged.

Aera wondered whether he was playing dumb. He could, after all, read minds.

"I would not have freed them myself," Cyrrus said. "The fur trade is most likely related to some arrangement with an outside party that oversees our protection. Besides, the animals here couldn't survive long without our care."

Aera nodded, taking this in. It could not have been coincidence that someone freed the animals so soon after Cyrrus made his hyperbolic speech about them in the dorm. Sardonically, she implored, "So your late-night rant was nothing but melodrama."

"I demonstrated that we have ties with the outside world and that our leaders deceive us."

"And then someone freed the animals and got them killed."

"Do you believe those animals had a life? They were to be killed soon anyway for their fur. This was the first freedom they ever had." He frowned. "You hate the commune. What do you do about it? Practice piano?"

"That's not—"

"I am taking action to effect change," Cyrrus snapped. "Can you do a better job?"

Aera glared at him to make sure he was finished talking. After a brief pause, she spoke slowly and deliberately. "Nobody can do a better job. You're the only person doing anything at all, and everyone knows it. That's why you need to *sleep* and be more careful what you say in public. People are listening."

Cyrrus stared at the ground pensively and resumed eating. After a short silence, he straightened his back importantly and said, "When I am Renstrom, people will be adapted to use their brains from infancy and our army will be invincible. Truth will no longer be dangerous."

LAIMANDIL

1327 LATE-SPRING

"Mtite' xulomqa qazginneq[h.1]"

Aera opened her eyes. The room was pitch black and the other girls were asleep, but Cyrrus's voice resounded clearly. She wondered if she'd been dreaming...

"Mtite' xulomqa qazginneq[h.]" Cyrrus's voice repeated, coming from every direction. The phrase was familiar. If he was projecting it into Aera's mind, perhaps he wanted her attention.

She donned her under-tunic, grabbed her torch and tiptoed out to the hall. When she arrived at the secret door, she knocked six times, then turned the knob and found it surprisingly unlocked. She uncovered the staircase, found a rusty key on the top stair and used it to lock the door, then secured it in her pocket and headed down.

When she reached the sanctum, she found Cyrrus in the Art Room, crouching before the piano with a mischievous gleam in his eye. Without missing a beat, he said, "Let's conduct an experiment. I will observe my reflection while you play."

Aera gave him the key, then took her seat on the bench just above him while he stared at himself in the wood finish, looking pleased. It pained her that he could see even a narrow portion of his face and enjoy how chiseled and perfect he was. Sardonically, she teased, "Are you hoping the Angels will sing your praises through my hands?"

260

"The Angels don't need you for that," Cyrrus gloated. "Ilë has been celebrating since the day I was born."

Aera smirked and tried to decide what to play. Vaye had taught her some complex intervals recently; they would do. With her left hand, she began a bass melody and, with her right, added decoration. After enacting a few flourishes, she paused and looked at Cyrrus.

He slid next to her on the bench and placed his hands on the keys, showing no reaction. Aera knew he was paying no heed to her talent and simply needed another set of hands. Apparently, he'd discovered that songs played themselves through him when he looked at his reflection and wanted to see whether the alchemy extended to her.

She stood to give him more space as he adjusted himself, holding his arms outstretched in a lordly contrivance, which looked impressive but would make playing difficult. *Theatrical as always*, she thought, and he grinned to acknowledge he'd heard her.

One by one, his fingers landed on keys. The notes were neither melodic nor rhythmic and contained no semblance of what anyone would consider music. Even the rigid math of Aera's songs from the Kalaqhai book had substance, while Cyrrus's notes did not. She couldn't help but admire his willingness to make a fool of himself, though she also wondered whether he valued her approval at all.

His hands stumbled into a simplistic, repetitive melody. The left hand clashed with the right melodically, but lined up into the same rhythm: *one, one, one, one, one, one, one*. It was a continuous pattern with each note following the last, long spaces between each hit, and no flourishes or measures to mark where one passage ended and the next began.

Aera closed her eyes to sort it out. The right hand played one pattern of seven notes while the left played four, and they fell upon each other cyclically, clashing in unique permutations each time. She imagined swords clanging against each other with every key strike until her mental imagery migrated to a starry night sky above the now familiar black dragon, Ainuvaika.

Gargantuan wings arose from the reptilian beast. Blazing arrows soared past, leaving trails of starlight as Ainuvaika jerked himself around to elude them. He exposed a foreboding cavern of knifelike teeth and hissed in a piercing screech: *Në Laimandil ë i namanya. Në Laimandil ë i namanya. Në Laimandil ë i namanya.*[2]

Alabaster fire emerged from his ghastly mouth and filled the sky as the chant grew more wretched, exploding in blinding light and ear-splitting shrieks. Aera fell to her knees and folded her head under her arms, but the sound tore through her until she screamed...

At once, she found herself folded up on the black marble floor of the Art Room, heart pounding. The screech rang in her ears: *Në Laimandil ë i namanya.* It was part of the phrase from her childhood dream. She translated it in her mind: The *Laimandil*, he will be called. *Laimandil*...

She lowered her hands from her head and straightened up slowly, watching as her hair lifted from the ground, then flipping her mane behind her. Still at the piano bench, Cyrrus had ceased playing and was staring ahead in a daze.

"There are two types of mirrors," he said softly. "Mirrors that enhance *inyarya*, and mirrors that steal it."

Aera tried to make sense of his enigmatic statement. After looking in the piano mirror, foreign music and visions emerged through their hands. Perhaps he was suggesting these visions mirrored—or stole—their identities.

"Play that again," Aera requested, "but don't look at the reflection."

Cyrrus placed his hands upon the keys and fumbled around. He located the general range of the song and played notes one at a time as before, but they were different, and he couldn't recalibrate the rhythm.

Aera returned to the piano bench beside him and played the pattern. Though she continued for a while, no visions emerged. Satisfied with her realization of his piece, she stopped. Cyrrus was staring at her hands in a trance.

He snapped to attention, rose from the bench and headed toward the door. As he opened it, he turned to Aera and allowed, "Your uselessness is diminishing by the day."

Aera grinned. "Is that how deities say thank you?"

"We both believe we are better than everyone else. You just lack the courage to declare it." Cyrrus raised a brow, then pulled the door closed behind him.

Aera resumed playing the bizarre, discordant song. Despite its simplicity, Cyrrus was unable to replicate it, which meant that when he'd first played it, he was subject to outside influence. While he was enchanted, the familiar drones had raided her mind. *Në Laimandil ë i namanya. Sinë veskento i suínanya më Onórnëan.* It meant: 'The *Laimandil*, he will be called, and his deeds will change the world.'

Cyrrus wanted to change the world alone, but in their shared dream, he'd called Aera '*Laimandil*.' What did it mean?

She grabbed her unlit torch and headed to the Knowledge Room. As usual, Cyrrus was studying and didn't acknowledge her arrival. She followed the narrow path to her venue and said, "While you were playing, I saw the dragon—"

"Ainuvaika," Cyrrus interjected.

Aera waited for him to continue, but he didn't. Softly, she asked, "Did you see him also?"

"I did."

"Did you... hear the voices?"

No response.

"I had a dream when I was a child," she said. "There were voices screaming the same words I heard while you played tonight." Slowly, she pronounced the phrase: "*Në Laimandil... ë i... namanya.*"

Cyrrus's head snapped up. He looked at Aera with concern but caught himself quickly and stared at the ground. After a pause, he spoke in a monotone: "What. Else. Did. They. Say."

"*Sinë veskento i...*"

Her mind swirled with images of Cyrrus's old drawing intermingled with faces screeching, then a vast, silent void...

"Aera." Cyrrus's voice was tender as he watched her pensively.

His thoughtfulness was reassuring. She asked, "What's *Laimandil*?"

"The White Bearer."

White. Again. Aera thought of the seraphic archer in the visions, with snowy skin and a pearlescent bow, shooting arrows that left behind streams of light. "Then the White Bearer is Erelion."

"I am uncertain," Cyrrus said. "Do you remember anything further? You can say it in Syrdian if it's easier."

Aera took a moment to center herself, then imparted the phrase, slowly and steadily. "And the White Bearer, he shall be called, and his deeds will... change the world."

Cyrrus froze, still as the walls. *Tistë yoveskén Onórnëan, ë áldëa si,*[3] Aera thought. She wondered if he recalled the poem he'd written years ago, or if he ever heard the phrase in her mind.

"There were more words in my dreams," she said quickly. "I... don't remember."

"No need," Cyrrus said, staring ahead blankly. "That is all I need to know."

Cyrrus's eyes reflected a shapeless, formless nothing, somewhere distant. Aera understood that look. There would be no reaching him.

She considered playing piano but couldn't leave him like that. Instead, she sat beside him, contemplating the links between the piano visions, the monolith, and her dreams. Angel Erelion, Dragon Ainu-vaika and blistering whiteness showed up everywhere. Would this happen to anyone who embodied the archetype of 'flow' and *ilissunviva*, or was it specific to her? She wondered which myths were referenced in the *Lesson of Indiva*, and what exactly drove Cyrrus to remove it from the book.

After some time had passed, Aera suggested they return upstairs. Cyrrus broke out of his reverie and followed her silently.

TYRANTS

1327 EARLY-SUMMER

"Get up! It's Unity Day! Get to the Hill, Samies."

Aera had forgotten she had the day free and felt relieved; she was too exhausted for duties. Cyrrus wasn't around, so she grabbed some food and retreated to Great Gorge for a nap. She lay down on the ground and reviewed the cyclical melody Cyrrus had played. Though eerily discordant, it stuck to her like pine sap. She closed her eyes and drifted into images of Erelion and Ainuvaika battling in a starry scape...

Next thing she knew, a crow was cawing beside her, and the forest was dusky. The day had passed in a blink. She went to the village for dinner and remembered that Cyrrus had scheduled another clan meeting on Unity Day evening. He hadn't bothered to remind her. Did he even want her there? She considered going to the cottage instead, but Cyrrus might be disappointed by her absence. *If only I could read his mind,* she thought begrudgingly, and headed to the meeting.

Southside Forest was pitch black, brimming with insect song. Laughter became audible as Aera approached the ponderous willow. She moved the foliage aside and found the group sitting in a circle around a fire, cheerful and engaged. Kize angled toward Cyrrus, fixated, but the spot beside him was empty.

Cyrrus looked up at Aera with an unreadable expression. Before he could so much as grin, Pelyane exclaimed, "Samely, Aera!"

Aera noted that Pelyane had pronounced her name correctly. She smiled back but did not return the greeting. She didn't know these people, didn't care about them; so why recite an aphorism celebrating their 'sameness?' Cyrrus met her gaze and the gleam in his eyes dimmed. She couldn't decide whether he was disappointed by her lack of enthusiasm or annoyed that she was there at all.

She sat beside him and looked around. Everyone was relaxed and chummy, but Aera felt out of place among people who were so comfortable with each other... and with Cyrrus. She regretted coming but leaving now would make too much of a statement.

"The greeting, 'samely,' is a form of indoctrination," Cyrrus said to the group. "When authorities call us Samies, the connotation is obvious, but 'samely' has so insidiously encroached the lexicon that we bandy it about without considering its implication. If you judge yourself an individual with your own mind and identity, you may prefer an alternative salutation, like 'greetings.' To hail someone from afar, simply call their name."

Aera grinned to herself. Cyrrus was addressing her unspoken thoughts.

"I never thought of it that way!" Pelyane exclaimed. She turned to Aera and said, "Greetings."

"Greetings," Aera echoed.

"Who wants to fill Aera in?" Cyrrus asked.

Aera almost smiled but forced herself not to. She didn't want anyone to know how relieved she was that Cyrrus was trying to make her feel welcome.

"I will," Pelyane said brightly, looking right at Aera. "We're organizing an initiative to request free time. Each month is forty-eight days long, so if we have one free day out of every twelve, that would be four free days each month. Unity Day would fall on one of those days, every season."

Pelyane's voice flew from one pitch to the next so rapidly that Aera lost track of the words, though she caught the drift. She nodded politely.

"We must persuade Nurin to enact this," Cyrrus added.

"We have a plan," Pelyane continued. "We hope enough people will support it so Nurin will be forced to do it."

Pelyane was sickeningly confident in finishing Cyrrus's explanations. Still, Aera liked their idea. She doubted there was anyone who would *not* support more free time.

"Pelyane offered to draft a petition," Cyrrus said. "We can ask anyone in support of changing the law to sign their name on it, especially adults. Then, she and Kize will present it at a town meeting. I will attend, of course, and defend the proposition if Nurin objects. The rest of you should not speak out at the meeting." He looked at each of them and said, "Remember, for the sake of future action, we must proceed covertly."

No matter who presented the document, Nurin would assume Cyrrus was behind it. But the result would still be out of Nurin's hands. If the public saw multiple separate pockets of support in the commune for this idea, they would be more likely to vote in its favor.

"Involving Pelyane provides tactical advantages," Cyrrus said, verbalizing Aera's thoughts yet again. "For one thing, Nurin is accustomed to challenges from me, but wider challenge will force him to concede, as we saw in the Dining Hall on the issue of the cages."

"Who let the animals out?" Gaili inquired.

Everybody looked around at each other, but Goric remained dead still. Aera wondered if he had done it. Cyrrus stared at Goric, undoubtedly surveying his thoughts.

"Was it you?" Gaili asked Goric.

"No," Goric said flatly.

Cyrrus kept his eyes on Goric's for a moment, then looked at the others.

"Most of the animals will die," Cyrrus said seriously.

Everyone shifted uncomfortably.

Cyrrus paused for dramatic effect, then continued. "Whoever freed them acted impulsively, but the action arose out of frustration with the lies our leaders perpetuate. I hold our leaders responsible."

The others seemed to accept that, but Aera knew Cyrrus too well. Whoever did it had likely acted out of admiration for Cyrrus—but Cyrrus had omitted that part of the story and reassigned the blame to unite them against a common enemy. Clever.

"Returning to the topic," Cyrrus said, "the days off will work to our advantage. Free time will allow people to pursue individual interests which would diminish the power of the authorities. Further, it will provide more opportunity to meet and organize. That is the real reason the authorities will try to deny us. If I were to deliver the proposition, they would fight against it more vigorously, but if Pelyane presents it, the motive will appear faultless."

"Wow," Gaili blurted out. "You're brilliant!"

Cyrrus grinned mischievously and said, "We are all the same." He paused for a moment while everyone laughed, then resumed the oratory.

"This is an important battle. I may become the face of the movement, but to gain sufficient influence, *you* must be the true fighters. We must stick together and stay focused. This cause belongs to all of us. We may have individual roles, but, in our goals, we really are... all the same."

There was a short silence, and Aera's eyes went to Kize, whose expression overflowed with unbridled admiration. Despite her pretty features, that dreamy ogling made her look pathetic. Kize had no idea who Cyrrus was.

Beside her, Pelyane smiled thoughtfully. Olleroc looked relaxed for once; Goric stared at the fire, powerful and serious; Gaili gawked at Cyrrus, possessed.

Gaili was correct to call Cyrrus brilliant, but she didn't realize what he was doing. His most impressive skill was the ability to manipulate others into doing his bidding while leading them to believe they were enacting their own ideals. His tactics were transparent to Aera, but no matter how much she understood, she could never command that level of influence.

Cyrrus looked at Aera for approval, his emerald eyes shining with firelight. His incisive gaze made her want to look away, but she locked on to remind him that, unlike the others, she would not be intimidated or dazzled. To her amusement, he broke eye contact and looked down for a moment. He reoriented himself before resuming his show.

"Let us meet again next Unity Day," Cyrrus said to the group. "Same time, same place. I will see each of you before that. Don't forget to return to the village separately."

Cyrrus stood, signaling the meeting had ended, then pulled Pelyane and Kize aside as everyone headed off. "I expect you will do an excellent job on the petition. Remember that paper and writing utensils are property shared by all but cannot leave village grounds." He looked each of them in the eye and concluded, "See you at the town meeting."

The two beamed and blushed like fools, blissfully unaware they were being used. They turned to join Goric a short distance away, and Aera watched as darkness swallowed the three youngsters.

Cyrrus danced over the top of the embers to put out the fire, peppy and pleased with himself. As the two headed through Westside Willows, Aera grew increasingly annoyed. Cyrrus expended so much energy on commune politics and showed little interest in discussing their adventures underground. Nothing mattered to him except power.

"Stop emoting," Cyrrus instructed.

"Did I miss some new law against that?" Aera retorted. "Anyway, I'm *thinking*."

"Splendid," Cyrrus chuckled. "Are you going to discuss what's on your mind like a reasonable person, or groan like an animal?"

"It doesn't matter if you become Renstrom. You're just like Nurin and nothing will change. These meetings are pointless and boring... like being in class."

"Your presence is extraneous," Cyrrus said dismissively. "I will promote your best interests with or without your participation."

"You know nothing about my interests."

"We desire the same things. That's why I fulfill your ideals without caring about them."

"My ideal is to destroy tyrants," she said with a whimsical smile.

Cyrrus glared at her, and she glowered back. They held each other's stare until they burst into laughter.

The squabbling continued until Aera heard someone approaching and hushed Cyrrus. There were footsteps behind them, deep in the shadows.

Under her breath, she said, "Someone is following us."

Cyrrus stopped in his tracks and whispered, "It's legal to be here." Though he appeared unruffled, Aera knew that if he was indifferent about being seen, he would not have lowered his voice.

"Go," she said. "I'll get them off your trail."

Cyrrus nodded, then walked away quietly. Aera listened to the forest and felt a rush. She grabbed a stick and headed northward, swinging at branches along the way. The footsteps veered in her direction. Aera walked briskly, but not speedily, pacing herself so the stalker could hear but not see her. After she was certain Cyrrus was out of the woods, she proceeded toward the village at a fast clip. She hoped to clear the forest before the stalker caught up with her. When she neared the village, she climbed a tree at the periphery, found a perch between thick branches and watched the border. The Raetsek Field was illuminated with torches on every side, which gave her a clear view of a lone figure, waiting. It was unmistakably Doriline.

Soon enough, Farris emerged from the trees, panting, and approached Doriline. The two spoke in excited, hushed tones, though Aera couldn't make out the words. Farris gestured toward the forest and Aera gleaned from their rapid exchange that they were discussing something important. Before she could learn more, the gong sounded.

EROSIA

1327 EARLY-SUMMER

Aera bounded to Junior Hut, excited to tell Cyrrus the news. Once she settled in the dorm, she listened carefully as Doriline gabbed with her friends in excited voices, but all they talked about was food. Aera was astounded that this topic generated interest and wished they would discuss something relevant. What were Doriline and Farris up to?

For as long as Aera could remember, Doriline was the champion of Peer Aid reports and took the prize at Unity Festival for collecting the most snitch points. She had reported Aera for her daily walk into the woods, which led to the heinous haircut. To do that, Doriline would have had to monitor Aera's routine. Likewise, in order to earn so many points on a regular basis, she had to spy on everyone. She undoubtedly sent Farris to shadow Cyrrus, hoping to discover some forbidden enterprise.

After attendance, Aera found Cyrrus, and they headed to the sanctum. He set up his study station and began reading as she found her designated area on the floor and settled in.

She knew he would soon be lost in theory-world and wasted no time. "Farris followed us in the woods, and he whispered to Doriline afterwards," she said. "She might get points for reporting the meeting—"

271

"She may convince herself that is her motive," Cyrrus muttered disinterestedly. "What she really wants is to be included."

He returned his attention to reading, as if this news meant nothing at all. Aera didn't care about the clan but went out of her way to protect it for *him*. If he was so unconcerned and dismissive, there was no point in her trying so hard. Her efforts were wasted.

She considered leaving but remembered the previous night and all the questions she'd wanted him to answer. With a grimace, she said, "You never told me what White Bearer is."

"If you permit me to study, I may be able to find out."

"Stop playing games. You know *something*."

"If you crave entertainment, I will gladly accommodate you during meals," he said plainly. "But if you seek knowledge, it would advance your interest to stop crowding my cerebral circus with vacuous drivel."

"Booknose barlock!" Aera growled. She wanted to bang his stubborn head into a wall and instead kicked a pile of books. Cyrrus, however, did not even look up. She wanted him to fight, to scream, to lose control... but he was too damned perfect. What a coward. She shoved a few more books out of her way and made herself a little more at home. If there was no reaching Cyrrus, she would have to find answers on her own.

She began stacking Silindion books, then flipped through a few containing poetic descriptions full of names and events that meant nothing to her. Cyrrus had somehow managed to piece together a cohesive history, but Aera didn't know where to begin. Frustrated, she dug deeper into the mess of books and found a large, wide one, stiffer than the others, with black writing on the cover.

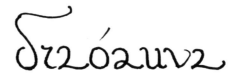

The title said 'Sunarien,' and there was a phrase beneath it in smaller characters: *I yena tavi yova ermassiatë suna.* Aera translated it to herself: 'the place where *suna* was embodied.' The word *'suna'* meant 'erotic love' or 'eros.' Was Sunarien an actual place, or a metaphor?

She opened the book and was surprised to find music in recognizable notation. The pages contained one score after another with Silindion lyrics. As she flipped through, a phrase jumped out at her: *Vë pherseina lennánëa, salányë ethatë sunanya.* She recognized 'desire' and worked out the rest: *as he haunts her lair, his desire burns her bare.*

A smile poured over Aera's face. Cyrrus might learn a hundred languages, but music and passion eluded him. This book was for her. Even though she couldn't memorize prose as he did, she could remember lyrics and carry songs with her forever.

There was a pencil in her pocket, and Cyrrus had given her some paper a while ago for translations. She found the paper tucked inside the last book she'd been reading, then grabbed her torch and headed off to the Art Room. When she reached the piano, she bent back the ancient spine to secure the book on the music rack and felt empowered. She would conquer this book entirely, learn every piece and memorize it, develop her own 'cerebral circus.'

In her excitement, she could barely steady her hands to play the first note. She jumped up from the seat, spun about and shook out her arms. Once her furor became less explosive, she returned to the book.

Her note-reading skills were rusty and the arrangement was complicated, beyond anything she had learned before. Instead of plunging in all at once, she played the vocal melody by itself to get a sense of the song and read the accompanying lyrics. After playing it through, she set a page beside the book and translated. She wrote the title, 'Sunarien,' then moved her pencil to the translation column. *The land of eros,* she thought. *Erosia.*

She said it aloud. "Erosia." It was more enticing than 'Sunarien' and, by renaming it, she made it her own. *My private fantasy land,* she thought. *I'm the only one there. How romantic.* She giggled and continued translating. Once finished, she reorganized phrases and replaced words with synonyms so the lyrics would rhyme and fit the measures. After much time and toil, she was satisfied that her iteration was poetic, yet also retained the original meaning.

Sunarien

Míssëar i mëa kuiyánëa
Sammár i phëa lintuvéskëa
Lintúr i hweya essendëa
Kuiyo seskomma kuntíltië

Hyuvún i larë silnemmanyë
vë sarna otma nondo
Kamando ina yáryello eremanyë.
Henentë sëonanya súndëa n'énkië

Nempë mispa linkuissëanya
Vovona Onorneiri sutiantë
ta yova senkë auka
Id nir Sunarien eiso simë

Erosia

Love is the mother of creation
Death is the father of transformation
Life is the daughter of the fusion
Maker and breaker of illusion

The moon dances with her star
Burning for him from afar
Her shadow lures his light to surge
Cries of love and war converge

Chaos sings its fateful claim
The rhythm of the world aflame
From whence its heart is torn
Erosia is born

The lyrics were perplexing, and she wondered what the imagery was intended to convey. In the beginning, there were grand statements about life and death; at the end, 'the rhythm of the world aflame.' This might be a prophesy about the end of the world, a commentary on the cyclical nature of time, or a metaphor for the 'rhythm' of life: passion, birth, death.

A smile spilled over her face. When Cyrrus ranted about creation and death, he drained the romance from them. She was no longer limited by his detachment: she had uncovered a way to learn about the Nestë on her own. Culture was beyond books and facts. It was art, music, clothing...

Clothing!

Aera grabbed her torch and crossed the hall to the Kinetic room. As she pulled the door closed, a wall of colors and sequins dazzled her. She could barely contain her excitement. While Cyrrus trudged through mountains of words, Aera would conjure the soul of the Nestë. She would unlock the rhythm of the Angels bedecked in apparel that befit Erosia.

She approached the nearest row of garments and searched for white. There was all manner of leathers and suedes, but none sufficiently audacious. As she advanced further, some jewels caught the torchlight. The fancy outfits were further back.

She placed the torch into a handy sconce, then examined every white ensemble in sight. Between grandiose robes, metallic tops and bejeweled dresses, it was impossible to decide what to try first. What type of outfit would befit the archetype of the sun?

Decisively, she removed her clothing and selected a three-pieced outfit with white beads and gold-framed jewels. First, she placed a sleeveless beaded top around her bosom and secured it with a golden brooch. The garment barely covered her chest, though golden strings hung down to provide more discretion.

Next, she positioned a skirt carefully around her hips. Metallic white fabric hung down to her feet. Finally, she donned a cape that clasped in the front, creating a gold necklace. The ensemble was complete.

She collected her things and blushed as she remembered Cyrrus was outside. *I dare you to ignore me now,* she thought, and laughed. The snug fit and meticulously crafted embroidery added shape to her slender frame and the decorations made her feel beautiful. It was easy to imagine herself dancing in the moonlight beside Erelion, exalted and sublime.

"*Hyuvún i larë silnemmanyë,*[1]" she sang, and beamed. She was armed and ready for Erosia.

~

A majestic full moon shone over a forest of white trees while Aera danced in an opalescent gown. Voices chanted the familiar lyrics: "*Míssëar i mëa kuiyánëa, sammár i phëa lintuvéskëa, lintúr i hweya essendëa, kuiyo seskomma kuntíltië...*"

The chant intensified with each phrase and Alárië swelled overhead. Her star-lover Erelion expanded rapidly beside her, drawing closer, encircling her with streams of silver and blue. "*Hyuvún i larë silnemmanyë, vë sarna otma nondo, kamando ina yáryello eremanyë, henentë sëonanya súndëa n'énkië!*"

The giant star swerved, crashed into the moon and blasted open in a fury of color. Fire spread through the sky until the monstrous Ainuvaika rose from the inferno. He burst into a blaze of coruscating white, reducing the forest to oblivion.

As the world disappeared, the choir became tumultuous. "*Nempë mispa linkuissëanya! Vovona Onorneiri sutiantë! Ta yova senkë—*"

~

"Get up! Come on, girls!"

Acra awakened with a smile. Erosia had come to life! There was a cosmic union between Alárië and Erelion, from which arose Ainuvaika. Had Aera conjured that imagery herself, or had she opened a portal to *eseissë?*

"Let's go, Samies!" Officer Linealle screeched. "Unity Day!"

Aera began to dress, wishing she could adorn herself as she did underground. It occurred to her that she had discovered the Erosia book last Unity Day, exactly three months ago. Since then, she'd mastered two songs from the book, and had perfected several costumes that matched the music.

She made her way outside, but Cyrrus was nowhere to be seen. After eating, she decided to head off. The day was free, and the cottage beckoned.

When Aera arrived, Vaye greeted her warmly as always. She offered tea and breakfast, then retreated to her plants. Aera sat at the piano and improvised while Vaye went about her business. As her hands flew across the keys, she imagined comets and dragons. *Hyuvún i larë silnemmanyë, vë sarna otma nondo...*

Aera switched to another part of the keyboard and changed rhythms. The music from Erosia haunted her, but she didn't want Vaye to recognize the song and suspect anything. She enacted an elaborate ending, then glanced over her shoulder.

Vaye sat in a wicker chair by the fireplace, stroking a cat on her lap. With a soft smile, she said, "Your playing has taken a dramatic turn."

Aera sensed hidden implications in Vaye's words. Since she'd discovered the songs of *Erosia*, their seductive aplomb leaked into everything she played. Her music had become increasingly charged... and Vaye had noticed.

"Thank you," Aera said, forcing a grin as she cringed over the obvious artifice in her tone.

Vaye watched Aera with smiling eyes. Was she reading Aera's mind? Clearly, she found it amusing to make her squirm. Aera remembered the *heneissë* symbol and understood Vaye was manipulating her.

"Rhythm is found in the tension between flow and resistance," Vaye added with a knowing grin. "Vitality flows from the rhythm of your breath."

It was not unlike Vaye to speak poetically, but this choice of words sent a message. She must have realized Aera had become sufficiently fluent in Silindion to have read about *ilissunviva* and to have discerned her archetype. Was this an invitation to discuss *Parë?* How did Vaye expect Aera to respond?

Vaye was playing her usual game: she knew much more than she admitted and left Aera guessing. Conversations like this were casual entertainment for her, much like Cyrrus's debates with Nurin.

Aera returned to the piano, and Vaye brought her drum to play along. The two improvised until dusk, when Aera left.

The forest was dark, but the night was young. Cyrrus's clan meeting would soon begin. Aera made her way back to the village, slipped through the festivities to grab some food, and headed into Westside Willows.

As she approached the familiar willow tree, the forest was eerily silent. She moved the leaves but saw only darkness beneath the canopy. Cyrrus had changed the location of the meeting and hadn't invited her. She remembered him saying her presence was 'extraneous.' The thought made her seethe.

When Aera and Cyrrus were bickering, she'd told him she didn't want to participate. Had he taken her seriously? *Sorry I hurt your sensitive feelings,* she thought, though she knew that could not be the real reason. Clearly, he was looking for an excuse to exclude her.

I'm done with the clan, she promised herself. She yelled, "Barlock!"

Throughout the year and into the next, Aera stuck to that promise. After she'd refused to join in clan activities enough times, Cyrrus stopped broaching the topic. Although their daily interactions consisted solely of dining together, their nightly adventures gave them a secret universe that was theirs alone.

Some nights, Aera played for hours, and on others, she spent more time with the apparel. Cyrrus went to the Art Room on occasion, reading by candlelight while Aera played. She caught him observing her outfits and, although he never commented, he began paying visits to the Kinetic Room himself. Over the months, Aera flaunted a dynamic array of costumes, whereas Cyrrus selected one based in greys and perfected the embellishments, such as jewels, hats, and cuffs. She often imagined they were dressing up for some magical event with Vaye and Panther Woman. Dancers would dance and *esilya* would shine while Aera sang on a stage, brightest of all.

PUNISHMENT

1328 MID-WINTER

Candles cast a golden sheen on the mahogany piano. Aera enjoyed watching the flames dance as she luxuriated through an Erosia song, *Kamara Síníë*.[1] She breezed into the interlude and closed her eyes to test her memory. Each bass note vibrated until the sustain pedal was released in perfect rhythm. As her fingers danced across the keys, she sang aloud. "*Hwanga molkósëa kíldië vanasutín essiranna...*[2]"

"What in Riva's *Trees* are you doing?!"

Linealle's familiar squeak broke Aera's trance. Her hands froze in place.

"By ghaadi's gar! I've got you now, Samie Eh-ruh! Put out those candles and get over here, *now!*"

Aera's knees wobbled as she stood and blew out the flames.

"Look at me and explain yourself!" Linealle screamed. Her torch reddened her eyes and shaded her face, turning her into a demon. "What in Riva's Trees are you wearing?!"

Suddenly, Aera remembered her attire: a bull-horn crown and a white leather dress adorned with elaborate jewels. She was half amused, half mortified. She needed an excuse.

Property belongs to everyone, she thought. *There's no law that we can't be downstairs.* Or was there? If only she knew the laws, she might have had something to say... but perhaps, she didn't have to say anything.

279

Cyrrus's eyes spoke volumes even when he was silent, and Aera had discovered her own acidic gaze in the piano mirror. She adopted that ferocity and projected it at Linealle, who became uneasy and looked away. Aera was satisfied that her scowl had done its job.

Without looking back, Linealle screeched, "Change your clothes *now!*"

Cyrrus was already in the hallway, weary and expressionless. Linealle eyed him smugly, and Aera wondered what had transpired between them. She stalled, hoping he would admire her regalia, but he didn't bother to look up.

Deflated, she went to the Kinetic Room, changed into her uniform, and returned to the hall. The two followed Linealle as she stomped victoriously up the stairs. Along the way, Aera remembered the white lights. Cyrrus had worried Aera would be stuck in the hallway forever, yet Linealle had made it to the sanctum. Aera didn't know why she and Cyrrus had managed to pass the lights—but whatever they had done right, Linealle must have done it also.

When they reached the underground entry room, Linealle ushered them out the door and barked, "Follow me." She marched past the bedrooms and up the stairs to the top level, where she extracted a keychain from her pocket, unlocked two doors near the entranceway and said, "You here, you there."

Cyrrus headed toward the one in the corner and Aera approached the one nearest the exit. In a shrill tone, Linealle ordered, "Empty the closets!"

Aera and Cyrrus dragged countless objects out, leaning them against the wall. There were cleaning implements, piles of bedding, bathroom supplies and other dormitory accessories. Once the closets were empty, Linealle grabbed some linens, unrolled two mats, and tossed them back inside each closet along with a pillow.

"Get in," she ordered.

The entire narrow space was filled by the mat Linealle had thrown down. Aera wondered whether Cyrrus's closet was long enough for him to stretch out. Before she could check, Linealle closed each door with a thud, locked the latches and stomped away.

Aera lay down and shifted around uncomfortably for a while. The mat was just like every other, but she was uneasy and cramped, imprisoned. Ynas would torture and punish them until every ounce of joy was stripped away. The songs, the dresses, the magic... everything was gone.

As she changed position, trying not to scream, she heard tapping on the wall behind her. Cyrrus wanted attention. Aera was driven to pound on the wall in a rage but didn't want to upset him when he was sure to be miserable already. Instead, she answered him with a rhythmic tap, and he responded with a chaotic sequence. Aera mimicked it precisely and heard Cyrrus's girlish laughter on the other side of the wall, muffled by the small space. She laughed in turn, then broke into tears.

Breathe, Aera reminded herself. *In... out.* She lay back down and reviewed the song she'd been playing before Linealle's interruption. *Kamara sínië vaphurnë yanisë'nië...*[3]

～

"Get up!"

Aera rubbed her eyes: the night had passed in a flash. Linealle thrust open the door, and Aera fumbled her way from the closet. Cyrrus was in the lobby, staring at the ground, lost in thought.

"Find me in the Dining Hall after you eat," Linealle ordered with smug satisfaction. "The Council will deal with you."

They made their way to the Dining Hall, where Cyrrus was approached as always by admirers. He greeted each one stiffly in an attempt to conceal his frazzled nerves. They fetched their food, took their trays to the boulder, and burrowed inside their cloaks. Since it was freezing out, they had Halcyon Hill to themselves. Aera bit into a sausage link, but Cyrrus ignored his food, shivered in the cold and spoke hurriedly in a hushed voice.

"We may be able to evade punishment if we're clever," he said. "By law, we can't leave the building after curfew—but we were inside the building. The problem is, Linealle caught us with books, and a book is illegal if it's written in another language. Nurin can't prove we were reading, but would he punish us for *looking* at illegal books if we claim we weren't reading them?" He paused. "Pretend I am Nurin and answer me. What were you reading?"

281

"I wasn't reading," Aera said. "I was playing piano."

Rigidly, Cyrrus said, "There was an illegal book propped on the piano."

"I wasn't reading it."

"You can't *play* the songs if you can't *read* the music."

"I compose my own songs," Aera said. "Linealle wouldn't know I was playing a song from the book unless *she* was reading illegal music herself."

"Good. Keep the last part in mind, but don't say it aloud."

"Sure." Aera adopted a haughty, Nurin-like tone and asked, "Samie Cyrrus, what were *you* reading?"

"I had the Kalaqhai book," Cyrrus said flatly, paying no heed to her imitation. "Linealle took it upstairs with her."

Aera returned to her own voice and said, "But you *weren't* reading it. You can't read Kalaqhai."

"I was deeply engrossed when she burst into the room."

"Is it illegal to open a book?"

"If I know the book is illegal."

"You said the symbol on the cover is mathematical," Aera said. "Is it illegal to study math?"

"The numbers are notated differently from how they appear in our math books, so it qualifies as a foreign language."

"What about the symbol on the cover?" Aera offered. "If all you saw was that symbol, and you recognized it from somewhere, you might have checked to see whether the writing inside was in Syrdian."

Cyrrus furrowed his brow and stared ahead, deep in thought. Apparently, Aera's suggestion had assisted in some way. For once, she was being reasonable while Cyrrus was rattled.

They returned to the Dining Hall, where Officers Linealle and Luce stood by the doorway, ignoring each other. As Aera approached, Luce glanced at her with pity. She was sick of that look, but she knew he meant well and afforded a cordial nod.

"Follow me," Linealle commanded, and Luce held the door open. He was even stiffer than usual, with his jaw locked tightly, holding back an explosion. Aera couldn't tell which was more rigid than the other and mused that they might share the archetype she titled 'principle.' *The hypocritical judgers,* she thought. *Just like Nurin. All the same.*

As they followed Linealle across the Field, Aera burrowed under her hood and tied it closed. It was one of the coldest days she could remember, and her breath clouded the frozen air. Cyrrus adjusted his collar over his neck in a regal flare while his brick red hair jacketed his ears.

They followed the tunnel to the courtyard. When they emerged, Aera noticed a hooded figure seated on a log in the back. Though the cloak obscured her face, the khaki color and tie-string accoutrements announced Vaye. Why was she here? Aera wondered whether Cyrrus knew who she was, but it was impossible to tell, as he strutted steadily down the aisle and surveyed the terrain with an unreadable expression. Pelyane and Kize were huddled together on a log near the middle of the courtyard and looked over as Aera and Cyrrus passed, but did not greet them overtly, concealing any affiliation.

Linealle ushered Aera and Cyrrus down the main aisle toward the front of the courtyard. More people entered through the tunnel behind them and scattered along the logs with hoods pulled over their heads.

Cyrrus turned to Linealle and exclaimed, "I feel so important! These people are sacrificing time from their critical duties just for us! Are we such a threat to commune life that we warrant attention from such an august body?"

Linealle pointed to a log in the front row and commanded tersely, "Sit there." Then, she took a seat on the opposite log in the front row.

Renstrom Nurin was last to enter the courtyard. Like Cyrrus, he was hoodless with an imperial collar. He walked importantly through a double-door on the lower level of the Administration Unit—the only doorway into the area—and strode to the podium. Emphatically, he positioned his right hand over his heart and thrust his left upward with his fingers pointing straight toward the sky. He waited for everyone to stand, then glared over at Cyrrus and Aera to make sure they were enacting the salute. The two assumed position, but when the crowd chanted, "We are all the same," both remained silent.

Nurin lowered his arms and wasted no time. In a clear, commanding tone, he said, "Samie Eh-ruh and Samie Cyrrus. Rise, and state your reasons for wayfaring after curfew."

Cyrrus sprang up quickly and Aera stood, legs shaking. Nurin turned to her, awaiting a response.

"I was composing music," Aera said. Her voice trembled.

Nurin shot a sardonic glare at the crowd and pressed, "What sort of music?"

"The music... in my mind."

"The music in your mind," Nurin repeated to the audience with his chin in the air. "What a useful and generous application of mental activity."

Laughter spread through the crowd, and Aera's head spun. *Just breathe,* she admonished herself.

"Since childhood, you have harbored the fantasy that you were disconnected from your peers," Nurin said smugly. "You have consistently neglected hair-cutting rituals and you squander discretionary time alone. I granted clemency during a previous appearance before this body and trusted you would recognize your interdependence, but now I see that a more serious correction is necessary to help you better appreciate your role in the commune."

Aera's heart pounded. She didn't want to lose her hair again. Anything would be better than that.

"Have you made any friends?" Nurin asked.

"Yes."

"I have not noticed you with other children. Please name them."

Aera's cheeks flushed, and she muttered, "Cyrrus."

"Another delusion," Nurin asserted. "Samie Cyrrus, kindly repeat what you said at the last town meeting regarding *friends*."

"Friends are a liability," Cyrrus said flatly. "My loyalty resides with ethics and logic."

Aera was dizzy as tears stung her eyes. Why didn't Cyrrus support her? *My presence is extraneous*, she thought. She was his 'most valuable ally,' not his friend...

She inhaled deeply and firmed her feet. *Lies, lies, lies,* she thought. *The web of deception.* After an extensive pause, she finally exhaled. Her erratic heartbeat began to calm.

Cyrrus made a point to hide his alliances in the clan. Even though Aera was his friend, he might conceal that from Nurin. Perhaps he believed friends would be at risk if Nurin knew about them, and his intention was only to protect her. She wondered whether Nurin also could read minds.

Nurin pointed his chin in the air. "You see," he said to Aera. "Your fellow Samie harbors notions of moral superiority, as you suffer from the delusion of independence. But nevertheless, he is not your friend."

Aera knew Nurin was attempting to manipulate her and offered no response.

"Your indulgence in musical ventures has isolated you for years," Nurin continued. "Perhaps you are content being alone?"

Aera stared back at Nurin and thought, *no one is ever content, you idiot.*

"The council will act in your best interest to cure your brain-sickness," Nurin concluded, and turned to Cyrrus. "State your reasons for wayfaring."

"I wanted to learn about the fractal," Cyrrus said resolutely. "I imagine you have been anticipating this moment since I was delivered to Ynas."

Gasps and whispers filled the courtyard, and Nurin cleared his throat but didn't speak. Cyrrus had caught him off-guard. *Delivered to Ynas.* What had possessed him to mention that *now?* He would never admit he'd come from somewhere else when he was alone with Aera, yet here he was announcing it to a courtyard of strangers in front of her.

"What is a fractal?" Nurin demanded. "And where exactly did you encounter that word?"

With blistering apathy, Cyrrus replied, "I look for it anywhere I can."

"Samie Cyrrus, abort the charade," Nurin asserted, maintaining a stoical air. "Your equivocation insults both of us. You command sufficient wit, both to anticipate and to appreciate my inquiry, and I estimate no further need to elucidate my meaning."

The courtyard was dead silent but for the squeaking of logs as the collective leaned in to better hear the confrontation. Cyrrus's expression remained flat apart from his green eyes, which were sharp as knives.

"I'll try again," Nurin said with an exaggerated pretense of patience. "Samie Cyrrus. The word 'fractal' is alien to our vocabulary. What does it mean to you?"

"A fractal is a mathematical structure that breaks down to smaller units while maintaining the integrity of its geometric properties."

"Intriguing," Nurin said with a sarcastic tone. "Unless you invented the word 'fractal,' it must come from somewhere. Did you invent it?"

Cyrrus fastened his eyes to Nurin's. His cheeks were blue from the cold air, but his voice betrayed no sign of discomfort. "The word is a distraction. I may have overheard authorities discussing it or recalled it from early childhood."

"You attribute some significance to the word," Nurin said sternly. "Did the definition germinate from your imagination as well?"

A few in the audience laughed nervously. Nurin and Cyrrus were engaged in a high-level conflict, the implications of which they alone understood. Without missing a beat, Cyrrus retorted, "The concept is implied in *The Legend of Rasna*."

"A mathematical structure in a history book?" Nurin said sardonically. "Brass Inellei, please rise."

The Brass stood from his seat in the front row of the opposite aisle. He straightened his shoulders and elevated his chin like Nurin, trying desperately to compensate for his gawky affectation.

"As Brass of Education, you know the content of our library," Nurin said. "Samie Cyrrus, do repeat the definition of 'fractal' for the Brass."

Cyrrus spoke slowly and elucidated every word. "A mathematical structure that breaks down to smaller units while maintaining the integrity of its geometric properties."

Nurin nodded. "Brass Inellei, do enlighten us. Is this concept explained in our books?"

"I am indeed familiar with every book on the c-commune," Inellei replied, "and I have not enc-countered this c-concept before."

"Thank you," Nurin said. "You may take your seat. Samie Cyrrus, your response?"

"There is an army, known as the Red Army, cited throughout *The Legend of Rasna*," Cyrrus asserted. "Their cities are structured around the rule of one leader and proliferate outward from that source. The paradigm of political governance in the lands they conquer matches the fractal I saw. It begins with one triangle and a line extended from each corner, with more triangles attached. Each additional triangle sprouts its own appendages. The pattern may continue endlessly."

"Where did you encounter such a fractal?" Nurin asked incisively.

Cyrrus paused, motionless. The redness drained from his cheeks, and his eyes stared ahead as his gaze slipped to a faraway place. Aera wondered whether Nurin had somehow trapped him. All were still as everybody awaited Cyrrus's reply.

Sensing victory, Nurin repeated the question. "Where did you—"

Suddenly, screeches resounded overhead, drowning out Nurin's voice. Crows by the dozens gathered along the edge of the roof, screaming and cawing. The crowd watched in awe as a pall fell over the courtyard, and the birds circled en masse above Nurin's head. Several defecated, and the white gunk splattered against the brick wall near the podium where he stood. Aera laughed while others jumped up from their seats, gasped and gawked. Cyrrus remained impassive.

The birds disappeared over the top of the building, and their caws were swallowed by the grey winter sky. Nurin cleared his throat, extended his chin and inquired once again, "Where did you encounter such a fractal?"

Placidly, Cyrrus replied, "Perhaps the Brass needs to read between the lines. It is implicit in the formation descriptions of the Red Army."

"Exactly how is a mathematical equation conveyed by a character description?" Nurin looked around with a grin, and a few people laughed.

"When Ynas was conquered by the Kalaqhai and converted to a commune in 616, the half Kalaqhai General Tirquz bestowed upon himself the title of First Renstrom," Cyrrus said, adopting a didactic tone. "His leadership was consecrated as a center and subordinates were designated in relation to that origin. Three officials reported directly to Tirquz—the Brass of Education, the General Commander of the DPD army, and the Justinar of Laws and Land. Each selected two subordinate ministers, and there were two more reporting to each of them. Like many other cities, our commune abandoned the model after three levels of leadership, but that structure persisted until 998, when Samie Riva organized a rebellion against the tyrannical Renstrom Dirmuz. Riva and her followers demanded changes in leadership. The outcome was that the Brass was selected by the Department of Protection through Discipline, the Justinar by the elders, and the Renstrom by public referendum. The General Commander was appointed by the Renstrom, but the power to rewrite laws was divided between all three, protecting the people from the rule of a single corrupt leader. The original Kalaqhai fractal pattern of authoritarian political leadership was abandoned."

There was a short silence, and Aera considered what she had just heard. Riva organized a rebellion; Ynas was conquered by the Kalaqhai and converted to a commune; the government's organization was based on a fractal. This information was too overwhelming to put into perspective, but she wondered mostly how it would benefit Cyrrus to recite it now. Renstrom Nurin looked amused but unshaken.

"Creative," Nurin said dryly, chin in the air. "Where did you encounter this purported history?"

"*The Laws of Ynas* has footnotes to indicate changes throughout the years," Cyrrus retorted. "I matched those to information in *The Legend of Rasna, The History of Ynas, Riva the Rebel,* and other sources in the library. The names and dates were inconsistent, but I deduced the most likely framework from the combination of references along with personal observations. To aid my hypothesis regarding the temporal relation of events, I took note of the architecture on the commune, architecture in other cultures as depicted in books, and knowledge I've gathered about construction techniques as they evolved over the centuries."

Though Cyrrus did not smile, the gleam in his eye and the pace of his voice indicated he was pleased with himself. With pride in his tone, he asked Nurin, "From your perspective, are my deductions meritorious?"

"I am not concerned with the merit of your deductions," Nurin said. "The word 'fractal' is not part of our vocabulary and the concepts you associate with it are not elucidated in those books. If I were to engage in a pastime as unreliable as *deduction* to interpret facts, I would *deduce* that you have been reading contraband material."

"You might also deduce that I took a stroll through the Administration Unit during a meal period to visit the library and overheard officials discussing foreign relations."

"Our commune is self-sufficient," Nurin declared curtly. "There are no foreign relations to discuss."

"Then why do we expend resources training officers to fight on horseback with axes?" Cyrrus challenged. Aera snickered as a few gasps emerged from the audience.

"Not that this is your concern, but enlightened self-sufficiency requires precautionary preparation," Nurin responded crisply.

"Why do we export black boots?" Cyrrus continued. "What did we use the caged animals for?"

"You are circumventing the issue at hand," Nurin said, clearing his throat. "Did you learn these tales by reading illegal books? Or did you invent them?"

"If you allege I invented the ideas, of what concern is it how I invented them?"

"Where did you learn them?" Nurin persisted.

"I excel at reading, memorizing, observing, and deducing. Knowledge is attracted to me like fish to water, which is why I am repelled by the deception we are obliged to accept."

"Are you equally repelled by your own lies?"

"I am disclosing my knowledge openly," Cyrrus said. "As far as truth is concerned, we are at an impasse. In the election of 1332, we will find out who the people believe."

There was a pause. Nobody stirred. Even the wind was quiet. Nurin's face was stolid, but Aera detected paradoxical satisfaction in his demeanor. Beside her, Cyrrus probed Nurin: he noticed the Renstrom's enjoyment as well. Aera wondered what it meant and whether Cyrrus knew what to make of it.

After a moment, Nurin spoke in a tone that betrayed no hint of dismay. "I cannot punish you for confabulating stories, but you have been caught sneaking around after curfew and I must sanction you accordingly for that."

"The law states we cannot leave Junior Hut after curfew," Cyrrus retorted. "There is no law stating we cannot move about within the building."

"As currently seated Renstrom, I have the designated authority to interpret the law," Nurin said.

"You are not interpreting the law," Cyrrus protested. "You are rewriting it to punish me and this girl because I deduced a mathematical construct."

"I *deduce* that you are intelligent enough to know that sneaking around after curfew is a breach of trust and an assault on our sense of community. For that, Samie Eh-ruh must receive the same penalty. Council, what do you suggest?"

"Slaughterhouse for the remainder of winter," Justinar Dinad said.

"Samie Cyrrus *enjoys* th-the slaughterhouse," Brass Inellei protested.

"Then send Samie Cyrrus to the latrines and Samie Eh-ruh to the slaughterhouse," Dinad replied.

"Unjust," Cyrrus protested. "Renstrom Nurin asserted we must receive the *same* penalty."

"Then you will both clean and empty the latrines throughout the winter season," Dinad declared.

Cyrrus displayed no reaction, but Aera was not fooled: the more unaffected he appeared, the more miserable he was underneath. *Someone has to clean the latrines,* she thought. Though the idea repulsed her, she felt a twinge of gratification knowing Cyrrus would be obliged to do the labor he intended to force upon 'stupid people.'

Officer Linealle raised her hand, and Nurin nodded, allowing her to speak.

"They should sleep in the closets upstairs so they can't sneak out," she squeaked. "The doors are locked from outside."

"They will already spend task periods apart from their group throughout winter," Nurin said. "You would suggest isolating them further?"

"I've tried to stop them from sneaking around before!" Linealle insisted. "They never cooperate!"

"Then they will sleep in the storage closets until autumn," Nurin said. "So, it is determined. Trainee Jorin, you will show them to the latrines and supervise their work. Next business before the council..."

A young adult in uniform rose on a log nearby and gestured for Aera and Cyrrus to follow. Along the way, Aera caught a glimpse of Vaye in the audience. Nausea overcame her, and she cast her head down.

Trainee Jorin led them out of the tunnel. He ordered them to go to the bathing grove, fill buckets with water, and retrieve soaps. The water was freezing and the walk back was agony. When they returned, Jorin led them to the nearest latrine, provided aprons, and commanded, "Mop the floors and sponge the room. I expect this place to shine."

For the rest of the four-hour task period, they cleaned in silence. No matter how much they scrubbed, nothing removed the stench emanating from the pit. Cyrrus moved his arms mechanically, exhibiting no sign of discomfort or disgust, but Aera knew him well enough to sense his displeasure. The task was revolting, and they had to bathe afterwards in the freezing cold.

Days dragged on in a torturous, rancid haze. Though Aera missed Vaye and craved music, she was too ashamed to visit the cottage. She was mortified by the degrading stench that accompanied her and worried Vaye would be angry at her for bringing the stink into her sanctuary. Ever since Aera was a child, Vaye had welcomed her at the cottage. Would she be insulted that Aera had been sneaking out to play another piano? How much did she know about Aera's adventures, and why had she attended the town meeting? Aera couldn't decide how to explain herself or how much to reveal.

The weather was cold, and Aera was too depleted and demoralized to build fires by herself. At first, she ate meals in the Dining Hall and lingered around the library, where she found a book about weapons and stared at drawings and descriptions of them in a daze. By the second week, she became restless as she pictured herself using those blades to destroy Nurin. Energized by rage, she returned to the woods, where she built torches and used them as Ikrati sticks. She imagined herself charging to the Gate with a flaming weapon, warring her way out of the commune. The only thing stopping her was the worry that she had nowhere to go. In a world of tyrants and predators, she might never be free.

Aera could only guess how Cyrrus was coping because he no longer spoke to her. Instead of eating with her, he slipped off by himself during meal breaks. He remained awake during classes in a placid trance, neither smiling nor sneering at anyone. His apathetic behavior made her uneasy. On the bright side, the bags under his eyes disappeared.

For weeks, Aera and Cyrrus cleaned the latrines in every village building and dormitory hut. The ritual was completed partway through Late-Winter, at which point Trainee Jorin led them to trap doors at the bottom of each building and instructed them to haul out crates of human waste. People of all ages hollered and guffawed as they watched them roll the stinky crates along paths to the crops north of the village. Aera was dizzy with embarrassment and Cyrrus utterly vacant.

DEITY

1328 LATE-WINTER

"Laimandil..."

The whisper resounded from every direction. Aera stopped mid-twirl and tightened her grip on her sword. She scanned the scape of white trees but saw only the familiar pearly birds.

Aera resumed her exercises. She spun about, free as the wind, aiming her sword to and fro. Mist rose from the ground, obscuring her view until she could no longer see the weapon—but she didn't need to. With her eyes closed, she knew her way around, and her body sailed dexterously about the nightscape. Crickets chirped and birds sang. Nature welcomed her home.

Droning sounds approached from the distance, more piercing every moment. The fog formed into faces, and Aera slashed at them with her sword.

"This is *my* home!" she exclaimed, but the voice was piercing and didn't sound like hers. In a wretched tone, she added, "Go away!"

"Filén na erë lëoryán assë të yo-fayanta i nalanna hyánië votheldë," the drones shrieked. *"Në Laimandil ë i namanya, sinë veskento i suínanya më Onórnëan...*[1]*"*

~

Aera jolted up from the mat. The closet felt even darker than usual, as though the walls had closed in on her. *Breathe,* she reminded herself. *Your breath gives you power.*

Though her heartbeat calmed, her mind raced. She was certain those words were identical to the ones from her childhood dreams, though she'd previously forgotten the first half of the phrase. Could she remember it now? *Filén...* something something... *yo-fay* something... *deldë...* no luck.

The words were still lost, and the message remained unclear. All she knew was that *Laimandil* meant 'White Bearer,' and that she felt at home in the white forest. The dreams suggested a destiny, a path to her origins, or a deeper way to embody her archetype. Yet, any time Aera began to uncover it, Nurin reminded her that she was a slave.

Throughout the day, Aera was distracted by thoughts of her dream forest. Then, that evening at dinner, she found Cyrrus carving buttons by their boulder. Though she knew by his body language not to attempt conversation, she assumed that his choice to linger on Halcyon Hill rather than wander alone meant he wanted her company. She sat beside him, shivering under her cloak, and observed some puffy clouds over the barren treetops of Southside Forest. Whiteness and emptiness. *Laimandil...*

Her mind busied itself while Cyrrus ran his knife along the convexity of each square button to create X's. As he worked, a chipmunk scurried past, and he fixed his eyes on it. The tiny animal froze in its path and stared back, seemingly bound by his gaze.

Cyrrus placed the knife and button on the ground, then bent his wrists before his chest, letting his fingers droop. The chipmunk responded in kind, standing on its hind legs with its two front paws before it. Cyrrus tilted his neck, and the chipmunk cocked its head synchronously, mirroring him.

Aera heard a gasp from across the plateau and spotted some older girls, including Dila, staring at Cyrrus in awe as he tilted his neck bizarrely with his gaze locked on the chipmunk. Aera wondered who was craziest: Cyrrus cavorting with a rodent, or the mesmerized morons drooling over him.

The chipmunk lowered its paws and scurried away. Cyrrus watched it leave, then resumed carving and muttered to himself, "Did I lose track of her *vekos?*"

Who was 'her?' Aera grimaced... then realized it was the chipmunk.

"*Vekos* is fear, shame, desire, ecstasy, rage," Cyrrus said, twisting the knife emphatically back and forth as he pronounced each word. "*Suru* is the seat of emotion and its emanations are the feelings that come out of it. *Vekos* is passion, which is fueled by base instincts. *Suru* is heart, the seat of emotion—but not the seat of *vekos.*"

Cyrrus spoke with conviction, but Aera couldn't imagine what his point might be. She knew the meaning of those words already and any distinction he made between emotion and passion was arbitrary.

"Your awe of my intellect emanates from your *suru,*" Cyrrus teased. "Your desire to punch me is an expression of your *vekos.*"

Aera rolled her eyes.

Cyrrus chided in a baby voice, "Aww, were you happier when I wasn't speaking?"

"Ask the chipmunk," she retorted.

Cyrrus gleamed with pride, and Aera returned a *vekos*-eye.

"*The Lesson of Vekos* and its symbol appears at the bottom of the wheel because it is the most primal and crucial of all. You know this from *Parë*, but I can add some perspective."

Aera nodded, inviting him to continue.

"*Vekos* stems from the fear of death," he said. "In essence, it's an impulse to survive and to transcend corporeal limits. That impulse is the force that drives us."

Aera wondered if Cyrrus included himself in 'us.' She giggled to herself.

"We indulge erotic courtship to immortalize our seed and cheat death," Cyrrus continued. "We compete for status to expand our legacy and live on in the minds of others. Basic passions like fear, rage and shame enable survival. Fear drives us to avoid danger and assess risks, anger inspires us to protect our boundaries and enact justice, and shame compels us to act honorably and improve ourselves. If we did not crave acceptance, we might exploit our every urge, inviting chaos. If sickness were not shameful, we might spread illness."

Immortalize our seed, Aera thought, and snickered. It made sense that sexual desire derived from the need to survive, but as usual, Cyrrus drained from it any molecule of romance.

"Rage inspires vengeance, fear creates imaginary enemies, and shame incites competition, all of which may fuel brutality," Cyrrus continued. "Alternately, the Nestë texts claim that ignoring *vekos* causes us to disconnect from feelings and compassion, which leads to cruelty. They propose that *sundátëa* requires balancing *vekos* with reason, but they really believe reason should be used to defeat *vekos*, and that a truly powerful Nassando may use reason further to control the *vekos* of others."

Cyrrus claimed to know what the Nestë 'really' believed, but he didn't appreciate their mindset. The Nassandë were trained to interpret and uphold natural law as they believed their creator envisioned it and would characteristically seek to balance—but not *defeat*—innate qualities such as *vekos*.

"Passion inspires useful urges, but those impulses control and mislead us," Cyrrus said. "It would be more productive to pursue goals rationally and directly. Look at justice. Anger compels us to seek revenge but, in the throes of rage, retribution may be neither restorative nor proportionate to the offense. Instead, we could enact justice for its own good."

"You always say people don't like to think," Aera reminded him. "It's irrational to defeat passion if it keeps them motivated."

"This is why I have yet to encounter any written work which elucidates this concept as I envision it. Poets and historians alike garner more prestige by eliciting emotion and beauty than by expounding on rational solutions to combat injustice."

"You have a passion for reason," Aera pointed out. "You're obsessed with defeating your emotions, and that obsession *is* your *vekos*."

Cyrrus did not respond. He ran his knife along the edge of the button and Aera watched him, annoyed.

"Your outfit is *vekos* on display," she challenged.

"It's pragmatic. My attire is an intimidation tactic which enables me to effectuate my goal."

"Your *goal*... to be worshipped as a deity."

With a smile, he asserted, "To save the world."

He stood up, grabbed his tray and said, "I'm meeting the clan to work on that. You coming?"

"Ynas doesn't deserve to be saved."

"You live in Ynas. Perhaps you don't believe you deserve it either." He flashed a smile and, with that, departed.

Maybe I don't, Aera thought. *I'm useless, after all.*

As she finished her dinner, her mind returned to *vekos*. Many times, Cyrrus had insisted the archetypes were arbitrary, yet he had incorporated them seamlessly into his philosophy. Indeed, there was nothing more primal than fear of death—and Cyrrus used this knowledge of psychology to beguile others. In his message, they found something to believe in, a symbolic cause that transcended the mundane. He created his own religion and made himself into the deity.

Aera returned to her dark prison and stirred restlessly, analyzing the day. Cyrrus was a master manipulator, and his command on the psyche was profound, but his hubris would be his undoing. He dissected Nestëan texts while claiming the authors lied to persuade audiences. Though he questioned others, he paraded his ideas with aplomb. Did he believe his own lies? As Aera pondered this, music filtered into her thoughts. She imagined a robust voice singing: *Introspection weaves into a maze; webs of deflection spiral in a haze...*

To commit it to memory, she repeated it in her head. Another lyric came to mind in the same melody: *Dramatizing the magic of your mind; how mesmerizing, the clues you leave behind...*

It was the catchiest melody Aera had composed as of yet. She needed to review the lyrics, to make sure she wouldn't forget them—but Cyrrus was just beyond the wall and might hear them through *inyanondo*. There was a pencil in her pocket as always, but nothing to write on, no way to do anything at all. Being trapped in the closet was torture. As she tossed and turned, there was a creaking sound under her mat. One of the floorboards was loose. Perhaps she could write beneath it.

She shoved her mat to one side, then crouched before the floorboard and slowly peeled it away from the floor. As she edged it toward her, she heard the main door to the building swing open. Heavy footsteps pounded into the entranceway. Moments later, others followed, along with quiet conversation.

Gently, Aera eased the floorboard back into place and scribbled the lyrics quickly on top. Without a peep, she pulled her mat back out to cover the floor and pressed her ear against the door.

"You told me the Guardian was here." The voice was unmistakably Renstrom Nurin's, and even in the dead of night, his tone projected its pompous air.

"She went downstairs an hour ago," Officer Linealle whined.

"I see," Nurin said, clearing his throat. "When she comes back up, tell her to await my return."

Footsteps moved evenly across the floor to the back of the room where the lavatories were located. A door opened and closed in the distance.

After a brief silence, Linealle muttered under her breath, "I hate this ghaadi job."

"Thank Reneus's ghost your rotation wasn't at the Children's Hut."

Though the conversation was hushed, Aera recognized Officer Onus's burly tone. She hadn't seen him since she'd left the Children's Hut and wondered why he was here now.

"Children are just loud," Linealle murmured. "It's those ghaadi farkuses who sneak around that get to me."

Officer Onus lowered his voice even more, forcing Aera to strain in order to hear. She cupped both hands against the door to amplify the sound and heard him say, "They had me in the Children's Hut for two extra years to keep an eye on the redhead."

"Two extra years for *him?*" Linealle squeaked through her whisper. Aera wondered if Cyrrus was listening also.

"Nurin never told me his reasons," Onus said quietly. "But he's up to *something*. When Cyrrus came here, he looked at least seven. They're not supposed to let anyone in after age four. And this is why. They come in with an attitude and they don't adapt."

Aera smiled, pleased that her deductions were validated. Cyrrus was older, as she'd always suspected, and now both he and Onus had confirmed that he'd come from outside Ynas.

"Why'd they let him in?" Linealle asked.

"That's the ghaadi question. Why did they bend the rules for him? They—" Onus stopped abruptly. "I'm sorry, ma'am. Err... how long've you been... standing here?"

"Not long at all."

It was Vaye! Aera's excitement made her want to jump out of her cage. She held herself extra still, though she assumed Vaye was aware of her presence.

"Did you, uh... fix the door?" Onus stammered, palpably agitated.

"My work here is finished," Vaye replied. Her voice was calm, and her words elegantly delivered. The contrast between the serenity of her demeanor and the tension of the others was crystalline.

Nurin's even footsteps approached from the back of the room, and Aera realized she hadn't perceived any sound preceding Vaye's arrival. Everyone remained silent until Nurin spoke.

"Good evening, Vaye." He cleared his throat. "Officer Linealle, Officer Onus, please give us a moment."

Linealle's quick, clunky footsteps headed out the door, followed by Onus's clomping and the floorboards creaking. Nurin cleared his throat again and asked, "Any progress?"

"The passage is sealed," Vaye replied.

"Did you determine how it was accessed in the first place?" Nurin asked. His tone was less formal and more familiar than before, and he used her name without a title preceding it. Aera wondered how well they knew each other.

"It cannot be known," Vaye said calmly.

"You were supposed to have sealed the passageway fifteen years ago," Nurin said. "Now the seal has been breached. It is critical to understand how that happened to prevent it in the future."

"I understand," Vaye said. "It cannot be known."

"Certainly, you recall what happened last time that passageway was opened."

"It has been sealed."

"You said that back then."

"Yes, but since then, I have opened it." There was a short pause, and Vaye added, "The passage will be sealed unless I open it again."

Vaye was apparently the 'Guardian' of the secret passageway, and it seemed she was the only one who could 'seal' it... whatever that meant. This might explain Vaye's presence in Ynas. Aera held her breath, trying not to miss a word.

"Who ordered you to open it?" Nurin asked, his tone steadying.

299

"Nurin, we know it's not possible to isolate the entire sanctuary," Vaye responded. "I can adjust the algorithm, but I cannot eliminate every possibility. When we close one door, another may open. We are still uncertain whether all of the passageways have yet been unmasked."

"I assigned you to sort this out," Nurin said.

"May I explain again the flaw in that proposition, dear?"

There was a pause, and Aera tried to imagine what Nurin's facial expression might have looked like, as it did not suit him to be condescended to with endearments like 'dear.'

After a moment, Vaye spoke again, her voice as melodic as ever. "The sanctuary was built before the Age of Ice. In order to penetrate the refuge in its entirety, we would need to question the original builders. Given our limited contact with them, we may understand only what they want us to see. It is a complex system, and we don't know what we don't know."

Limited contact? If the Age of Ice was two thousand years ago, none of the original builders could have survived unless... what? The Nestë, supposedly, could live as long as five thousand years. Was the sanctuary built by ancients who might still be alive?

"I appreciate that much documentation has vanished," Nurin said, clearing his throat. Evidently, he caught the implication in Vaye's words and was placating her. "Adjust the equations every few months, so the patterns will rotate and any who breach the passageways will be denied repeated access."

"Your wish is my command," Vaye said. Aera would have given anything to see both of their faces at that moment.

The lobby quieted and Aera lay down, thoughts churning. She had fantasized about Nassando masters teaching students in the sanctum. Might her whimsical idea have merit? A smile spread over her face as she drifted to sleep.

～

Cyrrus was busy for the rest of Late-Winter, preparing for a debate just before Unity Day. Aera saw him from afar, mingling not only with the clan but, also, with Doriline. Long ago, when Aera had caught Doriline

300

spying on the clan, Cyrrus had claimed she wanted to be included. Though he seemed uninterested at the time, he'd apparently utilized Doriline's wish toward his own ends.

Spring finally came and latrine duty ended. As soon as Aera awakened, she headed to the bathing grove, freeing herself at last from the degrading stench. When she returned to the village for food, she saw Doriline and the piglets on the stage beside Nurin. He credited them with the proposal for free time and awarded everyone a free day at the beginning of each forty-eight-day month.

Since Unity Day came every three months, this new rule only afforded them two more free days per season. Originally, Cyrrus had wanted a free day each week: four per month, twelve per season. Aera presumed he had involved Doriline to garner more support for the movement, but the outcome was not quite what he'd hoped. Still, she found him near the stage and congratulated him. He responded with a grin and asked her to meet him at Great Gorge.

The sky was overcast and the forest was dreary, but she was excited to return to their secret lair. She built a fire and he soon arrived, carrying a leather-bound book. They sat down near the fire.

"I've come to enjoy writing, and paper is far superior to tablets, but I have to break at least three laws to make these books." Cyrrus raised a brow. "I could make you one, but it would be wasted effort. You would undoubtedly fill the whole thing with music."

"Music is a language," Aera grinned. "And it's more honest than any of those books filled with propaganda."

"Clever idea—but your interpretation of 'honest' is solipsistic. While the music may reveal something about you, any conclusions you draw about its meaning are grounded firmly in the wind."

"Says the boy who fantasizes about dominating every emotion in the world," Aera teased.

"Says the girl who fantasizes about the boy having emotions."

Aera shoved him playfully. The two exchanged a giggle.

"I wish people in Ynas cared about things like balancing the *vekos*," Aera admitted. "The Nestë seem more... thoughtful."

"They have no choice," Cyrrus said. "Before the Angels left Oreni, they met with the Nestë at a meeting called the Antanissë. The Angels gave Talismans to the Nestë, who promised to use them only against

301

Ultassar's creations, and to balance the *vekos*. Any who break the oath are cursed by the Angels."

Aera was annoyed by the idea of curses and wanted to defy the oath already, without even knowing what it was. "How do they break it?"

"One way is to reject the Antanissë outright," Cyrrus said. "Then a Nestë's *esil* becomes bright white and he turns into a monster. Another is to reject the Antanissë implicitly. This happens when a Nestë's *vekos* is unbalanced, which makes him vulnerable to Fading. Instead of joining Ilë when they die, Fades remain tied to the world. Their spirits are stuck in eternal emotion and everyone around them is plagued by it. Obviously, the Nestë want to avoid this, so they strive to balance the *vekos*."

"Are Fades real?" Aera asked. "Or is that a myth?"

"Don't know."

Aera nodded. "It's sad that they balance the *vekos* just to avoid being punished by deities. It might actually *mean* something if they did it to be stronger, or to feel better."

"A sound mind is its own reward," Cyrrus agreed. "But religious leaders prefer for their subjects to remain beholden to fictional deities."

After her many visions and dreams, Aera was not convinced that the Angels were fictional. Still, she didn't appreciate that they would punish the Nestë for defying an agreement made by their ancestors long before they were born. Of course, Cyrrus would never submit to such deities. He preferred to imitate them.

"You said a Nassando could control the *vekos* of others," Aera said. "Can regular people do that too?"

"It's irrelevant to me. I plan to attain *sundatëa*."

To 'attain *sundatëa*' was to become a Nassando, or to be enlightened. Aera sparked up. Until now, she had assumed this was possible only for the Nestë, but not for humans.

"When a human with Nestë heritage attains *sundatëa*, he is called an Orenya instead of a Nassando," Cyrrus explained. "The Orenya have all the same advantages as the Nassandë, aside from the lifespan. The Nestë live for thousands of years, whereas attaining *sundatëa* extends the Orenya lifespan at most by half a century."

Aera nearly jumped out of her skin. If Cyrrus was part Nestë, she might be too! Long ago, he'd projected words from his mind at a clan meeting, and no one had noticed except her. He also had heard her when she called out to him from underground.

"So, you think you're part Nestë?" she blurted out. "Maybe I am too."

Cyrrus turned to watch the fire. He opened his notebook and jotted something down, then spoke in a casual tone. "I'm charting what I recall from the Kalaqhai codex. It's primarily mathematics, and it's all related to the same roots. Once I decipher the fundament of the system, I will be able to resolve specifics from my charts."

Aera was frustrated that he'd changed the subject. What could be more exciting than Nestë heritage that would enable them to extend their lifespans and produce *kuinu*? She considered that he might have been fooling himself. Everything about him was more Kalaqhai than Nestë.

"Did you learn more about the fractal?" she asked.

"Impossible until I crack the code, and I haven't seen that symbol in any other book."

"Then how do you know it's the mark of the Kalaqhai?"

Cyrrus froze. His eyes were aimed at Aera's, but he looked right through her. The forest quieted, and the fire waned. Aera could hear nothing but the pounding of her heart.

He spoke in a voice so steady that its tone would not have been shaken by the collapse of twenty mountains. His mouth did not move, but words echoed from far beyond the trees: *Never. Ask. Again.*

Suddenly, the wind roared, blowing fire smoke in Aera's face. She rubbed her eyes and shook off her trance. When she looked up, Cyrrus was gone.

"Cyrrus?" she called.

Nothing happened. She leapt up and searched about, but he was missing. He'd disappeared while she rubbed the smoke from her eyes. Had he invoked that gust of wind, or had her question triggered something beyond him? Any time she mentioned his past, he turned to stone.

She tried to enjoy the fire, but the forest felt eerie, and shadows loomed. She stomped out the remaining flames and headed to the cottage.

During the walk, she was nervous. She hadn't seen Vaye since the fateful town meeting and didn't know what to expect. When she arrived, Vaye was playing a familiar song: *Kamara Sínië*, 'The Lure of the Swan.' She played it more tenderly than Aera had, with an eccentric cadence, intricate yet spare. Though the melody gave Aera goosebumps, she found it difficult to listen. She might never see the magic piano, the marvelous outfits, or the Erosia book again. Ironically, it was Vaye who would assure that.

Vaye paused, turned to Aera and said, "Wonderful to see you, dear. Would you like some tea?"

Aera nodded, swallowing her sadness, and the two moved to the table by the fire, where their mugs were already full. Vaye had anticipated her arrival.

"Aera, I must ask you to return *Parë Në Sulë*," Vaye said. "It's too dangerous now for you to have it."

Tears rushed to Aera's eyes, and she pushed them back. Being caught underground had ruined everything. Vaye no longer trusted her to keep the book hidden; she would trust her even less when she discovered the missing page that Cyrrus had ripped out.

"I'll return it tomorrow at lunch," Aera murmured.

Vaye rested her dark eyes on Aera, who fought an urge to disappear under her mane. She didn't want Vaye to know how dejected she was.

The two sipped in silence. When their cups were empty, Vaye stood and said, "I will let you play."

Aera sat on the bench and stared at the keys, holding back tears. *Kamara Sínië* tumbled through her mind, and she wanted to play it again but didn't know how much she should reveal to Vaye. Was it rude to play songs she'd learned from illegal Nestëan books underground? Considering Vaye had attended the town meeting where Aera was punished, had visited the passageway where the music book was open on the piano, and could access Aera's thoughts, she probably knew Aera had discovered those songs. After all, she had played *Kamara Sínië* for Aera's arrival.

Aera was sick of secrets and lies, sick of pretending Vaye didn't know what she was thinking, sick of everything. She wanted simply to play a song she'd spent weeks mastering. Was that a crime?

She began playing *Kamara Sínië* as well as she could remember it.

Her hands were stiff from weeks away from piano. Though she fumbled at first, she knew the song was embedded within her hands, her mind, her *suru*. Once she locked into the rhythm, it began to flow, and she allowed her tears to fall. She extended the intro a while, then thrust herself into the beat and sang along quietly, so Vaye couldn't hear. After completing the piece with the Silindion lyrics, she played it again, recalling her Syrdian translation.

Kamara Sínië

Kamara sínië
Vaphurnë yanisë'nië
Ninén i lavan
Lillannu vohwild'anyë

Thermar parlosil
Erma daván i faya
Vë pherseina lennánëa
Salányë ethatë sunanya

Hwanga molkósëa kíldië
Vanasutín essiranna
Yauyón surúnëa
No nekenta nánkëa

The Lure of the Swan

The lure of the swan
Is a curse when she is gone
Shall the hunter yearn
For a sign of her return

White as pearl is his skin
But the fire roars within
As he haunts her lair
His desire burns her bare

Her heavenly breast
Draws his arrow to her nest
She surrenders her will
To the throes of the kill

Before she knew it, she'd finished playing the entire piece twice. She ended on a dramatic chord and held the sustain petal, allowing it to ring.

"Lovely interpretation," Vaye said from her chair by the fire. "I never thought to play it with such command."

Aera's shoulders dropped, and she realized how tense she'd been the whole time. She feared Vaye's reaction, but Vaye's smile communicated that she was aware of Aera's ventures and would not chastise her. This would be another unspoken secret they shared.

"*Kamara Sínië* is one of my favorite songs," Vaye said. "Your performance brought back special memories."

Her heavenly breast draws his arrow to her nest, Aera thought, and giggled. Vaye was so secretive, yet of all things, she chose to tell Aera *that?*

"May I ask a favor, dear?" Vaye proposed. "Would you allow me to teach you more of my favorite songs, and indulge me with your exquisite performances? I would be grateful for the chance to relax by the fire while journeying into my past."

Aera wondered what kind of memories Vaye savored and wished more than ever that she could read her mind. Would there be *esilya*, jewel-covered dresses, leather-clad women with animal tattoos, muscular warriors with dazzling weapons? Her eye landed on Vaye's forehead-band, and she pictured a silvery light shining into the starlit night over foreign landscapes...

Aera felt Vaye's dark eyes on her and remembered where she was. She smiled and said, "Absolutely!"

"Thank you," Vaye said sweetly. "Now go on before you miss curfew."

Aera left with music in her mind, but as she made her way through the forest, a feeling of dread settled in. Vaye had asked her to return *Parë* without explanation, then distracted her with niceties as usual. Vaye's past was an enigma, her purpose in the commune unknown, her special powers camouflaged. Beneath her sublime poise, there was an ocean of mystery. Yet she invited Aera into that world, ever so slowly. The Nestëan songs would be their next adventure.

~

Classes were grating the next morning, as Aera dreaded delivering *Parë* to the cottage afterwards. She knew it would behoove her to warn Cyrrus during lunch break, in case he needed anything from the book —but how could she, without revealing Vaye? Aera considered telling him anyway, but when the bell finally gonged, Cyrrus rushed out of class. Soon after, she spotted him in the Dining Hall with his 'apprentices.' *Parë* was the last thing on his mind—as was Aera.

After a quick meal, she went to Great Gorge to retrieve the book. She withdrew it from the hollow and ran her fingers along the cover. Just a few years ago, those characters were gibberish... until she met Cyrrus.

Her mind flooded with memories. *Mating calls*, she thought. *Make yourself useful. I am a deity.* She chuckled. What a jerk.

She wished he were there with her now, arguing and pontificating. Even their most frustrating moments were among the brightest in her life. No matter how pompous and stubborn he was, she hoped every day that he would accompany her to their lair to mull over *Parë*. Now, those days were over. The wind was too still, the dusk was too dark, and his branch was achingly empty.

That book had created the deepest bond between them. Would she need to explain its absence to Cyrrus? Considering he'd memorized the content, he might not even care. She wished she'd translated the descriptions more carefully while she still had the chance. All she had was her notes. The original text would soon be gone.

One last time, she leafed through the pages. There were so many passages she hadn't read in full—with excerpts about Faerie, *sarya*, and so much more—but the time had come to relinquish the book. The authorities wanted to keep her stupid. An enlightened slave was no slave at all. She took a blank tablet from the gorge and shoved it into her pocket. If nothing else, she would have something to write on in prison later that night.

307

Reluctantly, she headed to the cottage with *Parë* in hand. Vaye opened the door, looking more elegant than usual. Her hair was in a crown of braids, and she wore an ochre suede cloak with matching boots, both ornamented with olivine jewels and fancy strings.

Aera handed over the book, trying not to appear miserable. She muttered, "You look nice."

"Thank you, dear," Vaye said.

Aera took a seat on the piano bench, where some music was propped up, waiting for her. Vaye lifted a sac from a nearby seat, placed the book inside, and swung it over her shoulder.

"Make yourself at home," she said. "I will soon be on my way."

Aera wondered why Vaye was taking the book with her. Was it for her, or for someone else? She mustered a grin and asked, "Where are you going?"

"There is business I must attend to."

How informative, Aera thought.

"I'll be back before Mid-Spring," Vaye said. "Feel free to enjoy the cottage in my absence."

Mid-Spring was a whole month away. Uneasily, Aera asked, "Do you need me to water your plants or feed the cats?"

"Thank you for your offer, dear," Vaye said. "But it will be handled."

Aera wondered who was 'handling' the chores and wished Vaye had asked her to do it. She wanted to return Vaye's favors, but Vaye never allowed it. After all, Vaye's archetype was that of the giver who took control of every exchange. Though her intention was kind, she left Aera feeling useless.

Vaye opened the door, smiled sweetly and said, "Goodbye, dear."

Aera forced a grin, but her stomach was knotted. After the door closed, she struck an angry chord in the bass. The piano rumbled, and two cats scrambled away.

While she improvised, she heard Cyrrus's chiding. *You're useless. Your presence is extraneous. Never... ask... again.* Her hands fell into the melody that had haunted her those endless nights in the closet. As the chords expanded to a powerful climax, she sang along. "Introspection weaves into a maze, webs of deflection spiral in a haze..."

Aera stopped and pounded the keys with her fists in frustration. Her voice was thin and airy, but this song was soulful and needed dynamism. She wanted to howl it out to the sky but lacked the power and control. The white-haired girl in the painting looked on with bold, black eyes, mocking her...

Weak, Aera scolded herself. Here she was, alone with a piano and a song at her fingertips, smothering it in self-doubt. Nobody was listening to her, not even the cats, so it didn't matter if her voice was feeble. There was no excuse to stop.

She played a slower figuration of the same tune, calmer and more repetitive, and sang along more easily. "Tell me, deity, tell me secrets." The chords climbed, creating the backdrop for a melody.

She withdrew the bark and pencil from her pocket, scribbled some notes and continued. By evening, she'd completed the song. She played it through from beginning to end and sang:

Deity

Tell me, deity, tell me secrets

Secrets of the wound in your heart
The loneliness you pretend not to feel
No one ever saw it before
But it's clear to me your facade isn't real

One look into your steely eyes
And I see the pain
Hidden under control
Detachment you strive to feign

Bold unfeeling glimmering with pride
Glamor concealing the mess you made inside
Fools are pining to worship your veneer
Never divining the cries I learned to hear
The prison of your fear
The shimmer of your crown

Take me, deity, take me closer

309

Closer to the dream in my heart
The magical life in the wild unknown
No one ever saw it before
If you take me away, we can find our way home

Love is locked in a cage of lies
And I am the key
Your prison is knowing too well
The burden of being free

Dramatizing the magic of your mind
How mesmerizing, the clues you leave behind
Introspection weaves into a maze
Webs of deflection spiral in a haze
You hide a million ways
And my dreams come crashing down

Tell me, deity, you don't need me

She held the sustain pedal, allowing the last chord to fill the room as her body rumbled with the sound. The power of the song had emboldened her to belt through the airiness and cracks in her voice, and it was cathartic.

"Tell me deity, you don't need me," she sang with a smile. Cyrrus might pretend not to care, but there was no hiding how deeply he craved her approval. He might disappear for periods of time, but he would always return to her because nobody else penetrated his wall. In his circus of lies, she was real.

In the absence of anything to research, Cyrrus sought out new missions. He ate beside Aera each day, then dragged her along to watch while he challenged the most experienced to track or canoe races. Once he had impressed enough people, he moved on to Raetsek duels, rope-climbing competitions, arm-wrestling and balancing contests. Aera was certain she could balance on either leg longer than he—as well as either hand, which he could not—but she had no interest in joining the spectacle. Instead, she spent increasing time alone at the cottage, where she played with the cats and wallowed in the compositions Vaye had left for her.

One afternoon, without any warning, Cyrrus altered his routine. He took a wrap from the Dining Hall, which he carried in his hands, and headed northward behind the buildings, leaving Aera to eat by herself. Day after day, she took meals alone, feeling increasingly miserable.

When Vaye returned from her excursion, she praised Aera's performance of the Nestëan songs and rewarded her with Ikrati lessons, but Aera found herself losing focus as Cyrrus's absence gnawed at her. He had never before spent that much time away and, no matter what else happened, they had always eaten together. As a knot in her stomach grew tighter, her dreams were shaped by screeching dragons.

Finally, on a smoldering hot evening, Cyrrus approached Aera on the dinner line. "Grab some food to eat while we walk," he ordered. "Don't bring a tray."

Did he forget that he'd ignored her for weeks? She grabbed a tray in spite of him and gathered a meal as though he wasn't there.

Cyrrus took a sandwich, but picked out the mutton slices, gave them back to the cooks and loudly declared, "You are what you eat!" As usual, his every decision became a manifesto.

Aera headed outside and carried her food to the boulder without looking back while Cyrrus trailed behind. She leaned against the rock, pretending to appear comfortable while Cyrrus sat down and ate beside her, as he always had. The silence resonated, but neither budged.

Finally, after their food was gone, Cyrrus asked, "Do you have something to say, or do you want me to read your mind?"

What do you care, Aera thought, though she didn't look at him.

"You want attention, but you also hate me," Cyrrus said. "Ten points."

Aera stared straight ahead, forcing herself not to emote.

"Now you *want* to hate me, but you can't," Cyrrus persisted. He looked at her with a guilty smirk.

She hissed, "Go away."

"That won't work on me. I know what you're thinking."

311

He flashed a grin at Aera, then looked past her at something far away. Caws resounded in the distance behind her and she turned toward the great belltower across the river, where crows were arriving from every direction. Once a horde had gathered, they all flew off into the sky, forming a magnificent V. She watched them disappear over the horizon in perfect formation.

"V for *vekos*," Cyrrus said. "Do you still hate me?"

What did *vekos* have to do with anything? Was he implying he had caused the crows to do that?

"Come on," he said. "I'll show you what I've been up to. I promise you will love me afterwards."

Reluctantly, Aera smiled.

After Aera returned her tray, Cyrrus led her across the Raetsek Field and over the bridge, heading northward as he did every day. They passed the wire cages that had once contained the furry animals and trekked onward toward the vast, treeless fields reserved for larger stock. Areas sectioned off by wire fences were dotted with wooden barns and gates accessible from the path. Far in the distance, on the westernmost section of the Farm, bison and sheep grazed lazily in the hot sun.

Cyrrus strutted down a dirt path behind the barns and greeted the groundskeepers by name as they passed, which informed Aera that he was a regular visitor. He led her onward until they reached the chicken coops.

"These will suit my purpose," he said.

The barn had double doors with an open lock hanging from the handles, which Cyrrus removed. He guided Aera into a pungent room with bars along the walls and some cubbies lined with hay. They stepped carefully along a walkway between chicken beds and made their way to a door in the rear of the barn. Cyrrus ushered her out onto a field and closed the door promptly behind them. The area was fenced in and contained hundreds of chickens, strutting and pecking.

Cyrrus walked around, stepping between the animals, and all looked up as he passed. Once he had greeted them, he raised his arm and said, "Get in line." They approached from every part of the field and formed several neat rows behind him, obeying his command.

"Follow," Cyrrus instructed. The chickens followed him across the

312

field in perfect rows, and Aera went along behind the last chicken. When he reached the middle of the field, Cyrrus turned, moved his arms apart, and said, "Disperse." Aera moved to avoid the commotion as the chickens fell out of formation and waddled about.

"Stay," he called, pulling his hands straight down, and the chickens waited in place while he disappeared into the barn. He returned with some feed, spread it out on the ground and said, "Eat." The chickens eagerly complied.

Aera had worked with chickens during many years at the commune, and knew they were not mentally equipped to learn commands, let alone language. "How do they understand you?"

"They don't," Cyrrus said. "I spoke only to show you that they were obeying. I led them with my mind alone."

"So, it's mind control."

"It's not control," Cyrrus said coolly. "It's entirely their choice. I'm just making suggestions."

"Why do they do it?"

"Why did you?"

What? Aera was confused. What had she done?

Cyrrus grinned voraciously, then walked alongside the rows of chickens, watching as they looked up at him. He repeated the same motions as before: first lifted his arm to command them to line up, then walked in front of them as they succeeded him in straight lines. Aera's legs began to follow involuntarily. She locked them in place but felt uneasy resisting the urge to walk towards him. Cyrrus was right: Aera was responding along with the chickens to his unspoken 'suggestions!'

"Roosters, over here!" Cyrrus announced. Three roosters departed from the group and situated themselves in a separate row. He distributed some feed to all the chickens, allowed them a moment to indulge, then crossed his arms. The roosters turned to face the hens, who faced them back, all in formation.

Cyrrus smiled wryly and pointed at one rooster and one hen. The rest remained in place while the chosen two approached one another, as commanded. Aera was in awe, watching Cyrrus's brilliant hair flaming in the sun as he wielded this unspeakable power.

Cyrrus glanced at her, his emerald eyes hot with delight, and thrust his hands together with perfect grace. She wanted to run over and hug him but implored herself to stand still. With a devilish smile, Cyrrus said, "Breed."

Aera gasped, and her hands flew over her mouth as the pair proceeded to engage. Cyrrus cackled, pleased with himself, and Aera imagined her cheeks must have been redder than his hair. He was indeed deific... and also an insufferable jerk.

IVORY

1328 EARLY-SUMMER

The following morning in History Class, Instructor Korov displayed a giant book with drawings of battles and weaponry from the outside world. Aera was interested, especially in the weapons, but her focus kept drifting to Cyrrus and his 'suggestions.' She recalled the crows from the town meeting. Was that a 'suggestion?' They had attacked Nurin during a debate about the Kalaqhai fractal. When Aera inquired about this later, Cyrrus's disembodied voice said, *Never. Ask. Again.*

Aera now understood why he disappeared from meals: he was practicing his mind control on animals. He might have used these same abilities to mesmerize his followers in the clan—or worse, Aera herself. How could she be certain that any reaction to him was genuine?

Her mind chattered on until, finally, the belltower sounded. Cyrrus joined Aera on the lunch line and stuffed his tray with anything that fit, except for meat, which he rejected. At the boulder, he wolfed down his meal at lightning speed.

"Hurry," he said. "We're going to Great Gorge."

He was not excited like the previous day. Aera was curious what would follow. She finished eating and they headed off without a word. When they reached the tree, Cyrrus didn't climb up to his branch and instead sat on the ground with his legs crossed. Aera did the same and sat facing him.

"I propose an experiment," Cyrrus said, his voice monotone and his posture rigid. "If we succeed, the result will give you an advantage. If we fail, you will remain a liability."

Liability. Aera snickered.

"You know too much for your own good," Cyrrus said quickly. "I must train you to block *inyanondo*. When I can no longer read you, I will be satisfied."

Aera was surprised that he was so willing to relinquish access to her thoughts. It was unlike him to sacrifice his power, and he wouldn't do so without reason. Who did he believe might read her mind, and what did he fear they would find?

"Your thoughts disarrange me," he said with a wry grin. "Ignoring them requires effort, and I would prefer to outsource that work. If you succeed, you will carry that gift wherever you go."

"I never go anywhere."

Cyrrus looked at her for a long moment. "Your past does not decide your future," he said in a pensive tone. "If you envision a life beyond Ynas, I advise you to consider my offer."

Aera smiled as she absorbed these words. "Does this mean you want to escape?"

"What we want is inconsequential. We are defined by what we do."

Cyrrus evaded the question, but the gleam in his eyes spoke volumes. Aera suspected there was more to this, and she would soon find out what it was. Yet, even if she was wrong, the prospect of blocking mind readers was enticing on its own.

"Train me," she said. "I'm ready."

"I will begin with a lesson in detachment, so you can dominate your *vekos*."

He paused, leaving an opening, and Aera looked right at him to show she was listening. He didn't wait long, and asked abruptly, "What is thirty-eight plus one hundred and four?"

Aera calculated it quickly: "One hundred and forty-two."

Cyrrus furrowed his brow, and she reviewed her calculations. She must have added too fast, missed something...

"You expected me to say something stern," Cyrrus said. "My body language indicated disapproval and without conscious thought, you tensed up. It was automatic."

This was true: Aera had reacted to his unspoken criticism without thinking... and he had caught her doing it.

"Think of your mind as two minds," Cyrrus said, "your reasoning mind and your automatic mind. *Vekos* is a separate entity, but nonetheless automatic. While it remains beyond control, its expression is subject to conscious manipulation."

Cyrrus had previously claimed he wished to defeat his *vekos*, but now admitted it was beyond control and focused instead on supervising its expression. He was successful: in the most taxing moments, his mien was unreadable.

"The reasoning mind is deliberate," Cyrrus continued. "It works more slowly than the automatic mind, but we have conscious control of it, like you did with the arithmetic problem." He paused, framing his thoughts. "You knew your answer was correct, but my body language induced an involuntary reaction which prompted you to voluntarily question yourself. Your automatic mind defeated your reason."

Aera's anxiety about making mistakes was, indeed, involuntary. So far, this made sense.

"Automatic response is crucial," Cyrrus said. "If we took the time to analyze everything, nothing would get done. But to block *inyanondo*, you must become explicitly aware of what your mind is doing in order to discipline it."

Aera nodded, taking this in.

Cyrrus spoke in a dry, instructive tone. "Everybody feels pain when they touch something hot. It's universal. We can control whether we scream aloud, but we will always feel pain. Conversely, the tension you felt when I frowned at you was a result of your mindset. You presumed my calculation was correct while yours was wrong because you perceive my intellect as superior. You might not always focus on admiring my excellence, but your mannerisms, facial movements and vocal patterns betray you."

Aera cringed, but knew he was right.

"A disorganized mind is the simplest to read," Cyrrus said. "By focusing your mind, you will control what others see. If you adopt the mindset of a person who thinks I'm a moron, then your body won't reveal any admiration for me, and I won't be able to read it with *inyanondo*."

Cyrrus paused. His posture was stiff, but his green eyes were dense with thought. If he devalued Aera for admiring him, he didn't show it.

"By adopting aspects of another person, you may conceal your *vekos*," he continued. "You can make others feel affinity with you, which will alter their automatic responses to you. Empathy is the root of good deception."

This sounded complex and beyond Aera's capacity. If he expected her to maintain such control over every thought, he was wasting his time.

"Let's try some exercises," he said. "The goal is to observe the world outside your brain chatter. That focus will last only a moment before the inner monologue resumes, so you must direct it to the world outside your feelings. You must process the object, rather than your judgment of the object."

"So you're teaching me how to think *less*," Aera mused.

"To think *correctly*," Cyrrus asserted with a gleam in his eyes. "Examine your hands. Just observe them. Don't judge, don't associate. Your hand is not too small, and your skin is not too dry. The sky doesn't make you feel free, and your mistakes don't make you anxious. My voice does not make you want to strangle me."

Cyrrus grinned, and Aera giggled.

"Notice the size and shape of your hands. Notice the clouds crossing the sky affecting the color of the forest. Notice the depth and quality of my voice—the pace, the rhythm. Worry about meaning later. Let your observations expand beyond your judgments, your reactions, your emotions."

Aera looked at her hands. They were small and deceptively lean, considering how strong they were.

"You're judging," Cyrrus said. "Don't compare parts to each other. Don't qualify anything. Your hands are not beautiful, gentle, or tough. They are not *your* hands, but simply, hands. Don't personalize them. Observe without intention or desire."

Nobody was beyond intention or desire... but it was conceivable that one might transcend them temporarily. She thought of Vaye, balanced on one leg in the moonlight, completely at peace. Vaye undoubtedly had intentions and desires—as everyone did—but may have let them go in that moment.

Aera inhaled slowly and focused on the air as it passed into her lungs and down to her stomach. With her belly full of air, she imagined herself as Vaye, grounded in her center. She tightened every muscle as hard as she could, then loosened her body as she exhaled. Her posture felt at once relaxed and firm.

She looked at her hand and observed intricate lines on the skin that changed shape as she moved it. Shadows expanded and contracted, folding into the indents of her palm as she cupped it in different ways.

"Good," Cyrrus said. "I see you have already incorporated body awareness training."

Aera was not convinced her body awareness had come from training alone, since she'd channeled Vaye. But she didn't contest the observation. She decided to hear his words and ascribe no judgment.

Cyrrus hoisted himself onto the lowest branch of the tree and projected his crisp voice from above. "You hate Ynas, but you will never leave. Survival skills are easy to learn, but you waste your time playing piano and hiding behind me. You have chosen to live and die in Ynas."

His words stung. *You have chosen to live and die in Ynas.* Aera understood his intention was to provoke her, but this sentiment was pure torture.

"Feel the pressure in your chest, the tension in your body. That is your *vekos*. Control it. Drop your shoulders, loosen your neck. Focus on your muscles. Dominate your emotion. Breathe away the rage."

Cyrrus was on point: Aera was painfully stiff. She breathed deeply and exhaled slowly as she allowed her posture to loosen.

"Our facial muscles are connected to our moods," Cyrrus said. "When you become angry, your brow will wrinkle involuntarily. Rub the spot between your eyes and focus on relaxing your forehead. If you control your facial muscles, your mood will follow."

Aera rubbed the center of her forehead between her eyes, found the place where it usually wrinkled, then focused on relaxing it.

"You are detached from your anger and frustration," Cyrrus said.

319

"Your feelings and judgments are superfluous. Answer me aloud. Pretend to be me. What would I say? Ready?"

"Ready."

"Animals will die because I enticed followers to worship me."

Aera conjured Cyrrus's stoic tone and said, "Death is unifying."

Cyrrus lit up and projected his voice importantly. "People mean nothing to me. All I care about is power."

"Power is a pyramid, and latrines are the base," Aera replied with a grin, mirroring his crisp articulation and confident cadence.

He smiled wryly. "You worship me."

Aera felt her brow becoming tense and focused on relaxing it. In the same dry tone, she said, "Religion is dogma."

"I'm flattered. My sentiments cling to your mind."

Of course, Cyrrus never missed an opportunity to aggrandize himself. "Only the few that matter," she retorted.

"You became defensive and betrayed your shame. Do you realize your forehead is severely wrinkled? You lost focus."

Aera groaned in frustration and noticed her pulse was racing.

"Your mimicry is valuable," he said. "You might hone that into a useful survival skill."

Mimicry... how flattering. Aera wished she'd never agreed to this.

"Develop your traits instead of feeling humiliated by them," Cyrrus said. "Turn every situation to your advantage. Every breath may be wasted or absorbed. Every thought may be used as a tool... or a weapon."

Every breath may be wasted or absorbed, Aera repeated to herself. She was reminded of Vaye's advice: *Your breath gives you power.*

Cyrrus did not understand Aera's supposed skill. It was a compulsion. She integrated the energy of others when her own felt inadequate. Still, he was correct; if she could hone this as an asset, it might serve her well.

"My sentiments cling to your mind," Cyrrus repeated. "Profound as they are, your attention to them is a gift to my ego."

Aera focused on the spot between her eyebrows and held it perfectly still. *My sentiments cling to your mind*, she thought, imagining the even pace and emphasis when he pronounced the word '*cling*.'

"Every breath may be wasted or absorbed," Aera said slowly. "Every thought may be used as a tool... or a weapon."

"Enchanting," Cyrrus said, and Aera looked up at him from her spot on the ground. He was still perched on the lowest branch of the oak with his long legs dangling, and he watched her, engaged and amused. Her performance had alleviated his anxiety. With twinkling eyes, he said, "Look inside the gorge."

Aera reached into the hollow, where she found the usual wooden tablets, a can of charcoal... and an unfamiliar leather book. She pulled it out. The pages inside were pulpy like the ones they used in class, and the binding was tight with wool stitching. The back cover had a slot for loose papers, perfect for storing the archetype map.

It was obvious that Cyrrus had made the book for her, something he would never do frivolously. Teaching her this lesson meant a lot to him and Aera wanted to show him that she was worth it.

"Set aside a block of time each day," Cyrrus said. "Imagine a situation in which you need to keep a secret and write whatever enters your mind. Feelings, thoughts, reactions, sensations. Then write how you believe I would have reacted to similar stimulus. Write down how someone else would react. Think of different people and incorporate aspects of each personality into your own to construct a variety of personae who don't know your secrets. Name them. Train yourself to project them at will and decide which role suits each situation."

Aera already had incorporated aspects of others into herself, though she had never named them. This exercise would be easy and natural.

"The book will fit in your cloak pocket," Cyrrus said. "Keep it with you and write about your alternate personae. What would their voices sound like? What would their postures feel like? How do their vocal expressions and mannerisms differ from Aera's? What do they want? Train yourself like an animal to respond to your own body language with an entirely different presence."

Aera snickered, uncertain whether 'train yourself like an animal' was insulting or brilliant.

"Write whatever you want," he said. "I won't read it. And don't worry about filling the pages. I can make more books."

Cyrrus hadn't been so relaxed or engaged since their days underground. Aera felt a smile coming on but held her lips loosely in place and relaxed her forehead. She was hiding her feelings entirely, even controlling them. Nearby, Cyrrus was watching her, his emerald eyes shining in the sunlight.

"The truth is true whether you believe it or not," Cyrrus said with a cryptic smile. "Perception is always limited, yet we all accept our perceptions as truth. Control what others perceive, and you control them."

Only Cyrrus could spin deception and mimicry into a laudable endeavor... but Aera acknowledged the merit of his methods. With resolve, she took a pencil from the gorge, opened her book and wrote down some of his... 'suggestions.'

The next morning, Cyrrus waited for Aera outside the Girls' dorm, brandishing his extravagant cloak despite the muggy weather. Aera now understood this was more than mere vanity: he hid his notebook in his pocket. She decided to try this herself and wore her cloak to class, but the heat was insufferable, and she couldn't keep it on. At lunch, she carried her cloak to the Gorge, where she retrieved her notebook and discovered that it fit perfectly in the pocket. Since the weather was suffocating, she went to Vaye's relatively cooler stone retreat.

The curtains were open, but Vaye was not home. It occurred to Aera as she entered the empty cottage that she could utilize music to capture other people's energy. She hung her cloak on the back of a chair, took out the notebook and propped it open on the music rack.

She read the first page to herself: *Construct personae who do not know your secrets. Name them. Train yourself to project them.* She decided to start with Cyrrus.

She could only vaguely recall the sparse, mechanical song he'd played underground. There were seven notes in the right hand, four in the left... she tried different sequences until it came back to her. It was stiff, mechanical, frustrating. *One, one, one, one, one, one, one.* She had to control her attack to keep the notes even, to avoid syncopation, beauty, expression... it felt imprisoning. She wanted to pound the piano and exert energy but kept her posture perfect and breathed in rhythm. Each time she relaxed her forehead, her frustration calmed instantly. Was she embodying Cyrus's calculated cool, or Vaye's serenity? *Vyrus*, she thought, and giggled.

She assumed the distinguished posture that Cyrus enlisted when he played and breathed slowly into her belly. Vaye's poise combined with Cyrus's majesty. *Cyrevai*. It didn't sound quite right. She needed a new name, one that represented what she wanted to be; someone commanding and self-assured.

She thought of the name as she played, one note at a time. *One, one, one, one, one, one, one.* Syllables ran through her mind along with the seven notes in the right hand. *Cer-ev-en-a, ve-cer-us. I-a-vai-ris, i-vor-i.*

Her eyes went to the keyboard and scanned its intricate landscape of ivory and ebony. She found the opening chord from her new song, 'Deity,' and ran her forefinger along the familiar first note. The texture was smooth, and the surface had subtle lines, like veins. Slowly, she let the chord vibrate against her pulse. She imagined the heart of the instrument infusing each key with lifeblood as it breathed its beauty into the world.

The piano was the closest thing to her soul. Was Ivory too intimate to be an alternate persona? She enjoyed the idea of projecting the essence of a piano, though she still needed to consider what that would entail.

She opened her notebook and read the instructions.

WHAT ARE THEIR VOICES AND POSTURES LIKE? HOW ARE THEIR MANNERISMS DIFFERENT FROM AERA'S? WHAT DO THEY WANT?

She began writing.

IVORY WILL BE MAJESTIC. HER PRESENCE WILL SUGGEST MUSIC AND INVITE CURIOSITY. ALTHOUGH IVORY WILL ENTICE OTHERS TO REVEAL THEIR PASSIONS, HER SECRETS WILL REMAIN VEILED. HER MIEN WILL BE BOLD AND CONFIDENT, HER CRACKS AND CREVICES, FASCINATING. ANY KINK IN HER ARMOR WILL APPEAR BEAUTIFUL, SO NO ONE WILL DISCERN ANY WEAKNESS.

Aera laughed. In writing about Ivory, she was beginning to think like Cyrrus.

AERA IS INSECURE, DEPENDENT, AND LOST, BUT IVORY IS CONTENT JUST AS SHE IS. AERA REVEALS HER ANXIETY BY WRINKLING HER BROW, BUT IVORY'S FACE IS RELAXED BECAUSE SHE IS IN CONTROL. WHEN AERA IS NERVOUS, SHE SEETHES AND RETREATS, BUT IVORY STRAIGHTENS HER BACK AND MEETS PEOPLE'S EYES. AERA WANTS TO BE EXQUISITE AND COMPELLING, WHILE IVORY EPITOMIZES THESE QUALITIES. AERA ADMIRES CYRRUS, WHILE IVORY REFLECTS HIS CONFIDENCE. BOTH AERA AND IVORY MAY LEARN FROM CYRRUS, BUT IVORY DOESN'T RELY ON HIM. AERA HAS NOTHING TO SAY, BUT IVORY KNOWS THE POWER OF SILENCE.

Aera carried the book in her cloak throughout tasks and relished the creation of Ivory. At dinner, when Cyrrus joined Aera at the boulder, she was excited to share her progress and announced, "I came up with a persona."

"Did you name it?"

Aera straightened her back and said, "Ivory." She considered explaining the piano metaphor, but decided the name was evocative and powerful. Ivory would remain silent, allowing Cyrrus to recognize the connotation.

Cyrrus stared ahead, deep in thought, then focused on his meal. The two finished their food more slowly than usual.

Finally, he spoke. "You're honing your skills to great advantage. To make the transition, you'll need to utilize the shape of your essence and mold it as you determine what is most effective."

"My essence has a shape?" Aera laughed. He was insane.

Cyrrus cracked a smile, then reclaimed his serious mien. "Underground, you visualized yourself as the moon. The Nestë might believe your emanations reflect Alárië. Your *suru* is a glowing, white sphere. Let your persona adopt that shape."

Aera had channeled Alárië that night, but Cyrrus knew her experience with the underground monolith suggested her emanations reflected Erelion instead. Curious about his reasoning, she asked, "Why Alárië?"

"You visualized her and made your way through the lights. The connection revealed itself."

Aera had drawn from Alárië but focused on Erelion. The venture was successful because she'd surrendered to *him*. Cyrrus believed the association was correct because it 'worked,' but Aera wanted to know *why*.

"Passion spins like a hurricane, but the eye of the storm is still, and contains infinite potential. You must control that space. In the monolith, it was an Ebony dragon. Ivory must defeat Ebony."

Aera enjoyed the metaphors and the clever reference to piano keys but wondered where he was going with this. *I'm judging again*, she thought. *Just... surrender.*

"The hurricane of emotion spins round and round," Cyrrus continued. "To become Ivory, concentrate that energy at your center and fill the space. Picture the black night sky becoming the full moon."

Cyrrus paused and looked at Aera. They exchanged a smile.

"Close your eyes," he advised. "Envision yourself as a white sphere. An effervescent, warm, safe, circular haze. Your music lies in the solid center with your thoughts, feelings and motives. Surround it with a transparent glow."

Aera closed her eyes and imagined herself in the center of an expansive glow of shimmering opalescent white. Her fingers and toes tingled rhythmically.

"To summon Ivory, pull that glow inward," Cyrrus said slowly. "Concentrate the mass of light at the center, then cast a shadow over yourself. The shadow may hide you completely or reveal slivers of your presence."

Aera visualized two spheres, one inside the other, and placed herself in the center, emitting a moonlit glow while the surrounding sphere cast evanescent shadows over her. As she envisioned slivers of her light radiating in sharp, slender crescents, her posture straightened involuntarily.

"Ivory may emulate the moon, often hidden," Cyrrus said. "Where there is darkness, others will fill the space with their own projections, but they will imagine they are seeing you. When you speak, they will imagine your words reflect their sentiments, even as you control the expression. This will enhance your influence."

Aera opened her eyes and felt them reflecting the power of Cyrrus's gaze as she locked into it. He studied her and continued.

"Focus on the universe beyond your thoughts. Your secrets will remain buried. Your outer layer is a shadow with a black cast, absorbing the world, but your core is solid ivory, reflecting back all input so it cannot affect you."

Aera pictured the layers and nodded.

"Practice these visualizations. Allow your dark outer layer to adopt the inflections and intonations of others, just as a piano echoes their song, but trust that your core will remain untouched. If you master this, Ivory is the only persona you will ever need, and her influence will parallel mine."

Aera stared straight at Cyrrus and thought, *Ivory parallels whomever she wants.* The gleam in his eyes indicated he read what she was thinking.

~

Aera spent afternoons at the cottage and nights at Great Gorge, where she continued to develop Ivory. Some evenings, Cyrrus joined her to provide exercises, suggestions, and evaluations; on others, she built fires and wrote in her notebook. The more time she devoted to refining Ivory, the more confident she became. While she wasn't convinced this would help her to block *inyanondo*, it would certainly afford her more control.

She mastered a variety of postures and integrated them with Ivory. Whenever she straightened her back and relaxed her facial muscles, she imagined her emotions gathering into a dense spherical glow, as Cyrrus had instructed. She visualized a shadow surrounding her personal 'moon,' cloaking her essence like the black night sky, exposing only a fine, slender crescent. Erelion might burn bright, enticing her to reveal more, but she alone would determine her form.

When she set to work on 'absorbing,' she considered how to proceed. Cyrrus had advised that Ivory's inner white essence remain impenetrable while the black outer layer 'absorb' others. Aera decided this was too convoluted and reframed the concept: she needed only to envision her thoughts concentrated in a solid white core, then turn her attention to the world outside and observe it without judgment. The 'black layer' was, essentially, the act of quieting her mind and focusing outward. This process would function as a veil: mind readers might discover her surveying the world but would learn nothing about her. Others could stare into the mysterious shadow and imagine whatever they pleased.

Over time, her posture and associated physical expressions became triggers to ignite Ivory's confident behavior. Ivory was a swan, majestic and self-assured. When Ivory receded, Aera returned. Each aspect freed her from the confines of the other.

One sunny afternoon, Aera was especially lively. Southside Forest brimmed with chirps and coos, providing a soundscape as she alternated between humming and singing. When the cottage came into view, she lowered her voice, but continued, "Dramatizing the magic of your mind; how mesmerizing, the clues you leave behind..."

Suddenly, someone gripped her shoulders. Aera gasped and heard Cyrrus behind her, laughing his girly laugh. He'd heard her lyrics... damn him! She hadn't noticed him trailing her and had led him straight to Vaye's cottage.

"What are you doing here?!" she whispered, exasperated.

"I followed you," he said joyfully. "You were distracted by the music in your mind, just like the day we met."

Aera blushed. Cyrrus remembered the day they met...

...Of course, he did. He remembered everything, and he was mentioning their first meeting now to advance some purpose.

"Go away," she snapped in a hushed voice. "You can't be here." Before he could open his mouth, she added, "Don't recite laws. I *need* you to leave."

"You used to love when I recited laws," Cyrrus teased. "I feel nostalgic."

"You don't *have* any feelings—"

"Hello, dear."

Vaye stood in the doorway of the cottage. Aera tensed. She'd failed her promise to keep their friendship secret.

"Welcome, Cyrrus," Vaye said. She was calm as always, not bothered at all. Aera was surprised that Vaye knew Cyrrus's name, but then remembered the dreadful town meeting.

Cyrrus looked intrigued as he scanned Vaye up and down, observing the decorative band on her forehead, her long curly tendrils, her bare feet and khaki silk dress. Finally, he looked into her eyes and said with perplexity, "Have we... met?"

Aera found it implausible that Cyrrus didn't recognize Vaye, considering how she stood out from everyone else at the town meeting. Yet his expression appeared sincere, and his curiosity was palpable.

"Everybody knows the boy who wants to rule the world," Vaye teased.

Cyrrus let slip a girlish giggle, then caught himself and said, "Pleasure to meet you. What is your name?"

"Vaye."

They looked at—or perhaps through—each other for a long moment.

"Please," Vaye said finally. "Come in."

Vaye gestured to the chairs by the fireplace and moved her rocking chair to the table to join them. Cyrrus looked around from his seat with wide-eyed interest, appearing more childish than usual. He never behaved that way around authorities and rarely even around Aera anymore. She sensed he was up to something.

"What brings you here?" Vaye asked.

"I was following Aera," Cyrrus said. "I intended to surprise her, but now *I* am surprised."

He shot Aera a mischievous look. She was relieved that he'd confessed to following her in secret so Vaye wouldn't blame her for bringing him, but she still felt unsettled.

"Is this where you learned to play?" Cyrrus asked Aera with exuberant intrigue.

Dryly, she said, "Yes."

"You are an inspired teacher," Cyrrus said to Vaye. "Aera plays beautifully."

Beautifully? Aera calmed her facial muscles. *I am Ivory*, she thought. *His flattery holds no value.*

"Aera was born with a gift," Vaye said sweetly. "I just shared some tools."

"*Gift* is an understatement," Cyrrus agreed. "I am not knowledgeable about music or how its training is imparted."

Cyrrus was feigning humility and pretending to value music, though he usually claimed it was a useless waste of time. Aera could barely recognize the person sitting beside her. This had to be an alternate persona.

"Your chairs are more attractive than the ones in the village," Cyrrus said. "And sturdy too. Did you build them yourself?"

"Indeed," Vaye said. "Thank you for noticing."

"Willow wicker is abundant on the west side of Lake Pouvas, but the birchwood on its base is scarce outside the Forest of Zrjedz," Cyrrus mused. "You're very resourceful."

Vaye flashed Cyrrus a knowing glance, imparting a shared understanding of something to which Aera was not privy. What did Cyrrus want from Vaye? Aera's brow furrowed, but she held it still. Ivory was not bothered by Cyrrus's petty games.

Aera noticed her posture had straightened and felt a twinge of pride. She crossed her legs elegantly and examined Cyrrus's chair to see what he meant by 'birchwood.' The middle was brown wicker, and the base was comprised of sturdy branches covered in white bark...

White bark! She had searched Ynas for white trees all her life yet failed to apprehend the white wood in the cottage she visited every day. Why had Cyrrus brought that up? Had he seen her dream forest through *inyanondo?*

She glanced at him, but he was busy staring at Vaye with boyish anticipation, awaiting her praise. Aera could not determine whether there was hidden meaning here.

"Tell me," Vaye said to Cyrrus. "How do you know so much?"

"I devour books," Cyrrus said eagerly. "I live to learn. I could read all day, and there is nothing in Ynas that I haven't read. Unless..." he furrowed his brow, looked at Vaye, and concluded, "...unless... you want to help."

The vulnerability in his voice was shocking. Aera shifted in her seat.

"Do you have any... books... you would be willing to lend?" Cyrrus asked. His tone was so nervous and sincere, nobody with a soul could possibly refuse him.

With eyes sad enough to rival his desperation, Vaye said, "I have no books to lend."

Aera remembered the pile of ancient books by Vaye's bedside and looked questioningly at Vaye.

"The DPD confiscates books periodically," Vaye explained. She appeared genuinely disappointed as she added, "They made a project of it recently."

"Because of us?" Aera suggested, realizing as she spoke that she had adopted—or perhaps, absorbed—the youthful curiosity in Cyrrus's tone. "Did they change laws after Officer Linealle found us in the secret rooms?"

Vaye probed Aera with her dark eyes, and Aera thought, *Don't pretend. You know we were downstairs.* She searched Vaye's expression but saw no hint of artifice, even as Vaye blatantly feigned concern and inquired, "May I ask where, exactly, Linealle discovered you?"

"In the piano room," Aera said, and turned to Cyrrus. He looked even younger than before, with slouched posture exuding boyish guilt.

"I was in a room of books," he murmured uncomfortably, feigning remorse. "But... I imagine you knew that from Officer Linealle's report."

Slowly, Vaye said, "Linealle reported simply that you were sneaking around past curfew."

Sneaking around past curfew. Was that really what Linealle had reported? If so, then Nurin wouldn't have known they had been in the sanctum. Cyrrus had yapped about his extracurricular reading at the town meeting. In his determination to outwit Nurin, he'd revealed much more than was needed—and that information had cued Nurin to seal the passageway.

Cyrrus stared off into the distance. Aera wondered if he felt ashamed that his hubris had undermined both himself and her. She remembered the crows soaring over the courtyard, defecating near the podium. Cyrrus must have realized his mistake and controlled those crows in an attempt to distract Nurin.

He blinked and at once became relaxed and amused, as if nothing had ensued. "It was an honor and a pleasure to meet you, Vaye," he said with exaggerated formality. "I will desist from intruding any longer."

He strutted toward the door, then grinned at each of them on the way out. Aera glanced at Vaye to judge her impression of Cyrrus, but any thoughts behind her implacable demeanor were impossible to decipher.

As soon as Cyrrus was gone, Vaye asked Aera to help her in the garden. The two tended to her plants without any discussion of Cyrrus or the town meeting. When the bell gonged, Aera returned to duties. Cyrrus was distracted during tasks, his mind in another world.

The two found each other on the dinner line, where Cyrrus stuffed his tray with food but again declined meat in favor of extra bread. When they settled at the boulder, Aera asked, "Why don't you eat meat anymore?"

"I refuse to feed my *vekos*."

"You feed it by wheedling people."

"I had a reason," Cyrrus said. "Vaye will never guess that a buffoon like me can read her mind."

"You showed your skill with the tripe about the chairs." She watched to see if he would inadvertently reveal something. He only grinned.

"Nobody would believe I'm not brilliant," he said simply. "I portrayed an insecure teenage male... with a brain."

"You mean a vain, attention-seeking brat."

"Vanity doesn't help with *inyanondo*. That requires discipline. Teenage males are distracted by hormonal propulsion."

As usual, Cyrrus made romantic desire sound comically disgusting. "*You* are a teenage male," she reminded him.

"But you can't use my libido to control me. So, for all intents and purposes, I remain a deity."

"Just what Oreni needs."

"You seem to enjoy me," Cyrrus grinned.

Aera was steaming with annoyance, but abruptly straightened her back. She was a swan, gliding with confident grace while Cyrrus strutted like a peacock. Ivory would never permit Cyrrus to embarrass her with his attention-seeking jabber.

"You're making progress," Cyrrus said. "Your reaction was opaque, but your motive was transparent. This requires premeditation, practice and experience to control. You must believe your own story before it is time to promote it, to avoid displaying a sudden shift. This will become automatic as you develop Ivory's narrative and train yourself to believe it at all times."

All times? That sounded exhausting. It was one thing to deceive others at will, but quite another to deceive *herself*.

"You associate your identity with a narrative, but the premise is arbitrary," Cyrrus instructed. "From the perspective of an outsider, you are simply a Samie, but you decide what type of Samie Aera will be, and your actions give her shape. Any narrative you associate with Ivory is equally arbitrary, so it would be wise to choose the one that advances your goals."

"Some stories are more fictional than others," Aera protested. "After all these years of emulating a deity, you're still just... human."

Cyrrus raised a brow and gazed at the horizon. He watched with intense focus as crows alighted from treetops across Southside Forest and flocked toward the belltower. Once every inch of roof was covered in black feathers, he turned to Aera and challenged, "If you and I are equal, make them fly away."

Aera groaned. "You perform *kuinu* with birds and I perform music. So? That doesn't make someone a *deity*."

"We create narratives because they benefit us. You present yourself as a seeker, lost and alone, looking for meaning. This may entice people to guide and protect you, but it also keeps you dependent. Ivory may enlist guidance too, if it empowers her, but she will choose her strategy consciously so she may be more honest."

"Are *you* lecturing *me* on honesty?" Aera laughed. "Hypocrite."

"Hypocrisy stems from failure to reason. You eat meat but avoid working in the slaughterhouse. We both use latrines, but felt demeaned having to clean them. Why?"

Cyrrus looked at Aera, but she knew this was a trick question and refused to indulge.

"It is instinct to avoid our own waste and to be repulsed by death," Cyrrus said. "Animals have similar instincts, which are useful, because corpses and waste may carry diseases. Every animal uses its natural advantages to survive. Many animals half our size could kill us with claws and teeth, but our species thrives because we have great capacity for reason. This is why we build latrines and slaughterhouses and manage them without acquiring diseases. This is why we have language, medicine, math, and music." He allowed a theatrical pause, then continued. "Reason sets us apart from animals—and from humans who follow their *vekos* like animals. It separates humans who mimic chickens from deities who direct them."

Caws resounded overhead, and the birds departed from the bell-tower in a pall of black feathers. The crows bounded toward Southside Forest, forming a V-shape in the sky.

"V for *vekos*," Cyrrus said with a wry grin. "Your *vekos* is a violent vortex, and Ivory is the eye of the storm."

Aera looked over and, as their eyes met, both laughed. No matter how much she wanted to strangle him, his eagerness to amuse her with his drama was adorable and she could never stay angry for long.

The two bickered until curfew, then returned to Junior Hut. As Officer Linealle ushered them to their closets, Cyrrus asked, "I wonder, most honorable Officer, how did you get to the secret rooms?"

"I walked down the stairs," Linealle said too quickly.

"What magic did you conjure to bypass the lights?" Cyrrus widened his eyes with feigned innocence. "*Kuinu* or *sarya?*"

Linealle looked exasperated and squawked, "There's no such thing as magic! It's illegal to discuss it and those words mean nothing!"

"Ah," Cyrrus said. "Is *that* why you didn't tell the DPD you found us downstairs?"

"Bedtime," Linealle barked. With exaggerated authority, she opened Cyrrus's closet.

Cyrrus entered, but as Linealle pushed the door closed, he thrust his foot to block it. "Reckless, Linealle," he intoned, then disappeared.

Aera slipped into her closet, and Linealle slammed the door with a thud. Slowly, Aera removed her clothes, lay on her mat in the muggy darkness and tried to process what Cyrrus had just said. Aera herself had passed the same lights. Did this mean she had performed magic? Cyrrus had recalled the method Aera used to penetrate the maze—channeling the moon—and incorporated it into the Ivory lesson. Was he teaching her *kuinu* or *sarya?*

Aera's excitement mounted as an epiphany took shape: the visions underground and the prescient dreams might have profound implications. Vaye and Cyrrus, who possessed magic powers, had taken interest in her. This could not be coincidence. Perhaps Cyrrus was right that she was a 'seeker,' but that didn't explain why she attracted 'guides' with unearthly gifts. Though unable to assemble any coherent theory, she sensed intuitively that she was playing a pivotal role in a grand design that had yet to reveal itself...

That's insane, she scolded herself. Cyrrus believed he'd been fated to rule the world; his delusion must have affected her. She giggled nervously, burrowed into the blanket, and drifted into an uneasy sleep.

PART THREE
THE ORB

BOUNDARIES

1328 MID-SUMMER

Aera danced through a familiar pearly forest, sleeves shimmering in the moonlight. As she twirled through the rising mist, wretched shrieks resounded from a distance. She stood still and surveyed the nightscape. A dark, scaly form appeared in the shadows, slithering its serpentine slime between the trees. Massive wings awakened from its body, and a black face stared her down with blood red eyes.

She bolted, but everywhere she went, the dragon instilled itself in her path. It hissed through a maw of blinding light that penetrated the forest with its screeching hell.

"Alárië! Erelion!" Aera screamed for help. "*Posseisis!*[1]"

Thunder crashed, competing with the explosive drone, and wind whipped Aera's hair to a fury as a drenching rain cascaded. The black beast approached, its red eyes tracking her. No matter how fast she ran, there was no escape. She needed to face the beast.

Aera centered herself to enlist Ivory. The storm gathered around her, engulfing the forest in a chaotic rhythm. As the cracking thunder battled with the shrieking dragon, Ivory breathed it all in. The pandemonium was hers to absorb and direct. She knew what to do.

She extended her arms with practiced grace and harvested the wind into her palms, summoning a vortex. Lightning lit the sky. With one powerful thrust, she hurled the cyclone at the beast, which reeled and whelped in agony. To suppress the dreadful screech, Ivory spread the wind through the trees, and its airy presence whispered, "*En rallë anti miossi kemma.*[2]"

The dragon spat fire, igniting the forest. Swarms of birds abandoned the burning trees, crying out in alarm. As the flames expanded, rain became sheets, and Ivory directed the fierce, wet maelstrom to quell the burning frenzy surrounding her. The dragon rose from the flaming torrent, but each time it gave utterance, Ivory spun the storm with furious force. In turn, the wind sang, "*En rallë anti miossi kem—*"

$$\sim$$

"Samie Eh-ruh! Get up!"

Thud, thud. The door shook, and Aera jolted awake, smiling brightly. Finally, she'd triumphed over the horrors in her dreamscapes. Ivory was powerful, confident, unwavering! The phrase repeated in her mind: *En rallë anti miossi kemma.* In Syrdian: *This boundary will not bind us.*

She readied herself, assembled breakfast, and found Cyrrus at their boulder. As he slurped his food, his eyes were alight with devious mischief. Aera remembered that look from the previous night when he'd accosted Linealle.

"You never told me we used *magic* to pass the lights," she said.

"It's obvious," Cyrrus grinned. "But last night I declared it to establish that Linealle broke the same law we did. She reported us sneaking around after curfew but omitted finding us downstairs because she didn't want it known that *she* had gone there herself."

It was no surprise that Linealle broke the rules that she zealously forced on others. She inhabited the archetype of 'principle' whose hallmark was hypocrisy. Though Aera was amused that Linealle prowled in secret, she wasn't convinced any of them had used magic.

"I know *sarya* is illusory magic," Aera said, "but I don't get what it actually is."

"The Nestë believe Ilë created the world in his dreams and natural law evolved from that. They claim Nestë and humans possess a natural predilection to produce art or *kuinu*, whereas *sarya* departs from that vision."

"I know *that*," Aera said impatiently. "But... what *is* it?"

"One example is the lights in the underground sanctum that shine relentlessly. The ones that don't flicker and have no source."

"Are those illusory?"

"They aren't from nature."

"Everything comes from nature," Aera argued. "Adapting resources to make something new doesn't make it unnatural."

"Unless it was created or altered by a deviant higher power."

"I thought you didn't believe in a higher power."

Cyrrus raised a brow. "The truth is true whether we believe it or not."

"So *sarya* was created by a deviant deity."

"To quote *Parë*: where there is life, there is death, and thus, uncertainty. Ultassar wished to return the world to void, reducing existence to a singularity." Cyrrus paused. "This means *sarya* is divorced from the complexity inherent to nature. Since it opposes synthesis, it defies natural law and creates dissolution. But the Nestëan *esil* reveals the natural properties of any object and unmasks illusions created by *sarya*."

The white light had trapped Aera in an abyss. Was that a void? Was it even real? She asked, "Would the white light affect the Nestë the way it affects us?"

"It might hurt them even more. The *esil* is essentially a third eye that sees the genuine properties of things, but also absorbs sensations more keenly."

"So, the Nestë are vulnerable to *sarya*, and they promised the Angels they would fight against Ultassar's creations... but someone used *sarya* to guard the sanctum."

Cyrrus glanced around to make sure nobody was in earshot, stuffed some food into his mouth and garbled, "Any form of magic may be effective, and negative consequences can be mitigated, but cultures have different ideas about morality. *Sarya* advances human culture, but many Nestë reject it because of religious dogma. This is one problem with letting idiots breed."

"Idiots," Aera chuckled, "like the authors of all those books you *memorize*."

"The constructs in those books are valuable once uncoupled from accompanying mythology," Cyrrus said. "Nestë believe the World-Soul, *eseissë*, encompasses the organizing structures of the universe, such as time, space and sensation. They claim these comprise Ilë's natural law, and that *eseissë*, his being, makes them known to us. *Eseissë* itself is real, but the confusion is that it's depicted as a component of Ilë, who also created the world and determined what is natural. That's dogma."

"If Ilë didn't create *eseissë*, where did it come from?" Aera challenged.

"If *eseissë* dwells within us and around us, logic dictates that our thoughts dwell within *eseissë*. We shape the world as it shapes us, and we create *eseissë* as it creates us. Divinity is inherent in all of us, which places natural law in our hands." With a gleam in his eyes, he concluded, "This boundary will not bind us."

This boundary will not bind us. Aera was stunned. That was the phrase she'd heard in her dream.

"Tell me the dream," Cyrrus said in a monotone.

"I was in a forest and a dragon was chasing me, breathing fire," she said excitedly. "I summoned Ivory and directed a storm to push the flames away, and the wind sang that phrase."

Cyrrus froze in place but didn't respond. After a long pause, his eyes snapped back into focus and his posture relaxed.

"I had a dream also," he said casually. "I was lost in a forest, facing an enemy. I cast fire to defend myself, and it roared the same phrase."

"What enemy?"

"A creature bathed in demonic light, who spun wind into a fury to destroy me."

Aera was taken aback by the similarity between their dreams. Cyrrus perceived an enemy spinning wind, and he cast fire at it; likewise, Aera saw an enemy casting fire, and she attacked it with a cyclone. This wasn't the first time they had shared parallel dreams.

"*Inyanondo*," Cyrrus said simply, as though this was commonplace.

Aera considered that and it struck her: the dreams were coming from *him*. "Then I'm reading *your* mind. The concepts in our dreams are the same ones *you* study. You dream about them, and I join in."

Cyrrus stiffened, but didn't respond.

"*That's* why I dream in foreign languages," Aera continued. "I've been reading your mind my whole life."

"I didn't know these languages all your life."

340

"Every time I dream in another language, you know it."

"I heard the word *Laimandil* in our shared dreams, but I knew nothing about it and assumed it was wordplay. It was you who alerted me to the idea that a White Bearer would change the world."

Cyrus rarely admitted he 'knew nothing' about anything. Was he lying, or was the concept of 'White Bearer' esoteric enough to have escaped his notice? If so, why had it come to *her?*

"Erelion had white skin and a white bow," she offered. "Maybe it's him."

"Erelion is known to me as *Námmandil*, the Light Bringer. *Laimandil* has a different connotation, and I would not confuse the two."

Aera had asked Cyrus to explain *Laimandil* underground, but he'd offered no answers. Clearly, he had studied since then.

"There is light in nature, such as sunlight, moonlight, starlight, fire-light," Cyrus said. "A bringer of light may be an Angel, such as Alárië, the moon; Erelion, the evening star; or Sotona, the Lord of the Flame. A Nassando may bring light by aligning with Angels and channeling their power, and that is *kuinu*, which the Nestë accept as natural law. But natural light cannot be exclusively white. It may be golden-white or silver-white, but never pure white. Some natural occurrences appear white, like snow, but only the unnatural *sarya* may produce pure white *light*."

This new way of conceptualizing the relationship between white and light struck Aera as significant. She listened intently.

"There are many words for white, like *nolossil* and *noril*, which show up in descriptions of nature and Angels," Cyrus continued. "*Laimil* also means white, and derives from the root, *lai*. Whenever I have encountered it in poetry, it describes wretched creatures and danger. By contrast, *nan* means light and *Námmandil*, its bringer, is heralded as a hero. Given the consistency of these allusions, it is abecedarian that *Námmandil* and *Laimandil* are distinct. I knew of Erelion, the Light Bringer, but it was you who introduced me to the concept of White Bearer."

Indeed, there were different manifestations of white: one beautiful and the other, ghastly. Aera often encountered screeching white lights in her dreams and visions, but they never came from Erelion.

"The ideas in your dreams do not come from me," Cyrrus concluded. "If they are not coming from you, then they're coming from somewhere else."

Cyrrus drifted to a faraway place, and Aera examined some passing clouds. Their mass appeared white, but the glow at their edges was silver-white. *Different whites*, she thought. *Laimandil.*

Was Cyrrus the dragon in their dream, while she was the white creature in his? She had long suspected her own link to white—which connected to Ultassar and Erelion—but, until now, had never considered that the dragon might reflect Cyrrus. Dragons were created by Ultassar with the use of *sarya*. What did 'unnatural' really mean?

Aera pondered mythology all day while enduring the drudgery of classes and tasks. After dinner, she retreated to the woods and used Ikrati sticks as weapons against imaginary dragons. When the curfew bell gonged, she wiped the sweat from her face and sprinted back to Junior Hut. Cyrrus was outside, grinning mischievously.

He opened the door for Aera and strutted confidently toward the corner of the lobby where their closets awaited. When Officer Linealle arrived, Cyrrus planted himself in front of the door, braced his hand against the wall to block her and chided, "Why don't you use magic to put us inside?"

"There's no such thing as magic," Linealle barked.

"How many points do you think we would get for reporting where you found us?" Cyrrus implored. "What would happen if Nurin knew you omitted that detail?"

Linealle opened her mouth to speak, but then thought better of it and clenched her lips closed.

Sparkling with delight at her discomfort, Cyrrus looked straight through her and said, "I see no benefit in Nurin being distracted by any of this."

Linealle stared at him, bereft.

Cyrrus took Aera's hand. As he slid his fingers gently between hers, a wave of heat overcame her. She was weak and the room was spinning. *Stop,* she thought. *Control.* She straightened her back and relaxed her forehead to summon Ivory. The ground became still. Cyrrus's hand was just a hand, and Ivory stood firm.

"We have nothing to lose," Cyrrus said, more to Linealle than to

Aera. He tugged Aera's hand towards the stairs, and Linealle remained frozen as they ran off.

They stumbled quickly down the steps and into the stone hallway, holding hands and giggling. Cyrrus grabbed a torch from the wall with his free hand and pulled Aera toward the dark corridor. Her heartbeat accelerated... he was still holding on...

He released her and made a face as if his hand had been poisoned. In turn, she punched his arm. They both laughed loudly, thoroughly inebriated by their reclaimed freedom.

Aera ran ahead, but Cyrrus laughed girlishly and raced past her. Curse his long legs! They entered the secret room, locked the door, pulled back the floor and scampered into the stairwell.

They descended quickly and reached the familiar fork at the bottom of the decline. Unlike before, the path split three ways, each leading to an ascending staircase. Cyrrus climbed one and Aera followed, but when they reached the top, he turned back. He guided her up and down until he ascended the last one and stopped at the top.

"*Vavi dorón i kuissë më?*[3]" he muttered.

"Where does this pattern break," Aera translated aloud.

"Someone altered the pattern," Cyrrus explained. "The original descent had forty-eight stairs. The next few were random, until I found one that had twenty-four. Twelve is a special number to the Nestë, who apparently built the structure. Each time I encountered a set of stairs that wasn't a multiple of twelve, I turned back."

Aera thought of the circle of twelve symbols in *Parë* and the twelve-sided monolith in the Motion Room. Indeed, twelve was significant to the Nestë—or at least, to those who built the sanctum. She looked around for any clues and spotted a door on the ceiling, far above reach. Cyrrus followed her gaze, saw the door, and grinned.

"Let's go back down the stairs," he suggested. "Then you go left, I'll go right."

They descended the staircase, and when they reached the bottom, Cyrrus handed her the torch. He took a candle from a hidden pocket inside his cloak, lit the end with the flame and said, "Let me know if you see a door on the ceiling."

Aera was amused that he'd stored supplies in his coat, always prepared. They parted to climb their respective staircases, but she saw no door and called, "Nothing."

"Nothing here either," Cyrrus replied.

Aera heard his footsteps racing down and rushed back to the platform below. Together, they climbed the original staircase where they had seen the door on the ceiling. When they reached the top, they headed down to the third platform, then raced up separate staircases. Aera found another door on the ceiling above her and called out to Cyrrus, who ran to catch up.

"The ceiling is lower here," he said.

They continued navigating staircases, and the familiar drone crept up in the distance. Light infiltrated the stairwells as they raced from one ceiling door to the next. Soon, Aera was reeling, eyes burning and ears screaming. She forged ahead, even as the whiteness ripped at her.

They lunged together into the sensory abyss. Aera was aching and throbbing but could no longer tell whether her feet touched the ground. The lights were more chaotic and agonizing than she remembered. "Blast!" she screamed, but her voice was inaudible. All she heard was the screech of *sarya*.

Close beside her, Cyrrus reached up to release a latch, and a wooden door swung down. Aera tried to see into it, but the whiteness was too bright to distinguish anything past her arm. Cyrrus squatted, cueing her to climb onto his shoulders. Her nerves jittered as she wrapped her legs around him, but she summoned Ivory and balanced herself as he stood. The ceiling door was within her reach.

Aera slid the torch through the portal, then hoisted herself up and reached down to help him. Once they were both up, he crouched and pulled the door shut. Though the drone hollered on, the light dimmed to a tolerable glow.

They found themselves in a musky enclosure with rock walls and soft, muddy floors, offering a single path ahead. The passage was narrow and the ceiling so low that Cyrrus was forced to bend. As they continued onward, the white noise faded and disappeared.

Finally, they reached an open room with nothing inside save a light on the opposite wall, which Aera soon realized was a reflection of her torch. They inched toward it and made out a large mirror on an arched door, then hurried ahead and stood before it, side by side.

Aera leaned in close to examine her eye color. It appeared silver, as before, but it was impossible to distinguish the true hue. No matter how she angled the torch, she couldn't decide the color of her eyes, and the longer she looked, the more they seemed to be grey, as Cyrrus claimed. She gave up wrestling with the darkness, handed him the torch and stepped back to see the rest of her reflection.

What surprised her most was that she appeared younger than she'd expected. In her dreams, she was less gaunt, more womanly, more sensuous. In the mahogany piano, her individual features appeared striking; but now, viewing her entire body, she was awkward and willowy, with too much hair and a skinny face with enormous eyes. She held back her hair and opened her cloak to see her figure, which was straight and narrow...

...like a boy?

Swiftly, she closed her cloak and let her hair fall... definitely a girl. A scrawny, young one, maybe. She stared and found nothing terribly wrong with her face. Perhaps the mirror was inaccurate. Surely her schoolmates hadn't alienated her just for being skinny. Wasn't Cyrrus skinny too?

In the reflection, he looked long and lean compared to her, not bony at all. She glanced from him to the mirror and assured herself the reflection was precisely the same as he appeared in person... yet he also seemed bewildered, even disappointed. It comforted her that she wasn't alone in imagining a better version of herself.

"This boundary does not bind us," Cyrrus said thoughtfully.

Aera smiled and noticed how childlike she looked, as any semblance of elegance was obliterated by a wide, gushy grin. How many people in her life had seen her smile? She had imagined a sassy expression—more like Cyrrus's—but hers was cutesy. Yuck.

In the mirror reflection, she saw Cyrrus eyeing the door handle. They raced to grab it, and Aera won. *Finally*, she thought. She pushed it down slowly until a latch opened, but the door didn't budge. They pushed harder, and the sides of the door cracked open until it cleared the frame. A flurry of dust cascaded down. Aera stole one last peek at herself in the mirror—noting pridefully that her glare was as sharp as she remembered—then pushed the door farther open.

Cyrrus had already abandoned his reflection and was examining the door frame, fingering the heavy collection of dust. He passed her the torch, wiped his hands clean and said, "Onward?"

Aera entered the dark room with the torch held high, and Cyrrus stayed close as the fire illuminated a circular black marble room. The chamber was adorned with glass spheres set into ornate iron sconces figured into the walls. In the center stood a round table supported by a single iron leg that divided into three humanoid feet with leonine claws. A silver cloth covered the tabletop, loosely draping some object.

Aera approached the table. Its surface was at eye level for her, while Cyrrus gazed down comfortably from above. They circled the table several times, opposite each other, then reached from either side to touch the silver cloth. It felt like a wisp of wind, solid to the eye but ephemeral to the touch. Together they eased the cloth sideways to uncover a sphere of transparent crystal.

Along its surface, Aera saw her own distorted reflection upside down, but deeper inside, there were star-like swirls, flickering and fading. Time stopped. Sound and scent vanished as everything besides those stars faded away.

Aera didn't realize until she shook herself that her mind had gone blank. For how long, she did not know. Forcing herself to reality, she said, "Cyrrus?"

He breathed deeply and blinked teary eyes. "Aera...?" His voice sounded like it came from afar. He cleared his throat and repeated, "Aera." He looked as distant as she felt.

Neither dared look at the ball again. They replaced the cloth without discussion.

The cloud around their heads began to clear, and confusion evolved into uneasy smiles. More to herself than to Cyrrus, Aera murmured, "*Kuinu* or *sarya*..."

"Your mind is discombobulated," Cyrrus said, "and I've endured sufficient time with you to inherit your affliction."

Aera shot him a glare, but he remained stiff, his brow so vigorously furrowed that his eyes squinched together. The sight of him made Aera conscious of her own tension. She glanced over at the silver wrapping and was overcome by an intense urge to uncover the ball. Its pull was irresistible... unearthly. She tore her focus away, but Cyrrus considered the cloth with hungry eyes, bristling with a fervor unlike him.

346

A diabolic grin spilled across his face as he blurted, "We should take it."

A chain of thoughts raced through Aera's mind. *I want it. We won't be able to hide it. The authorities would confiscate it. We need to leave Ynas.* Her voice said the words, "Let's take it." Who spoke? Was it her? It was unintentional.

They wrapped the fabric around the ball, lifted it from its stand and carried it out of the room. As Aera pulled the door closed, her fingertip touched the surface of the glass sphere, and it became a lead weight.

Cyrrus stuttered, "It's too heavy... take it... quick..."

Aera tried to lift the ball but failed. Together, they knelt to ease it onto the dirt floor. It vibrated against her hand, and she jolted back as an electric wave ran through her body.

"Keep it covered," Cyrrus said.

They arranged the covering carefully around the ball, and Aera positioned it on her palm. It was barely larger than an apple, but so much heavier. Just as she moved to secure the wrappings, Cyrrus snatched it.

"I will take it," he declared.

Sadness overcame Aera as she watched it disappear into his pocket. She considered arguing, but it was pointless. He would never budge.

They crossed the room, ducked into the rock passageway, and made their way along a narrow path. There were no droning noises and no trapdoors on the floor. Instead, they emerged into a small enclosure where a staircase awaited them. Without a word, they climbed up, up, up, and found themselves beneath the floor of the secret room.

Officer Linealle was pacing around the lobby upstairs. As they passed her on their way back to their tiny prisons, she glared at them disapprovingly, but said not a word. Cyrrus owned her. She unlocked the closets, and as Cyrrus slipped into his, Aera grimaced. Surely, he would examine the orb all night without her. He had taken it from her... and she had allowed it.

She lay down on her mat, cramped and annoyed. Cyrrus needed to win, and Aera always surrendered. She remembered his fingers locked between hers and blushed as she drifted off.

"Get up!" *Thud, thud.* "Let's go!"

Aera awakened in a sweat. It was muggy and hot, but she put on her cloak regardless. She didn't want to lose the chance to carry the crystal ball in the event Cyrrus would part with it.

A town meeting was scheduled that day, but for the first time Aera could remember, Cyrrus didn't attend. He found her after class, ate lunch quickly, and ushered her to Great Gorge. The moment they arrived, he removed the package from his pocket and placed it on the ground beneath the tree. The wrapping was meticulous, so Aera knew he had opened it, but she no longer cared. She just wanted to see it again.

The two situated themselves on either side of their prize, cross-legged, facing each other. As Aera reached toward it, Cyrrus covered it with his hands and said, "There's a pattern in the stars."

"Great," she said impatiently. "Open it!"

They unwrapped it quickly. Light gleamed within the crystals inside the ball. They saw their reflections upside down...

... but there were no stars.

It was just a ball of crystal, reflecting the sunlight. Aera picked it up —easily this time—and examined it closely. Had she hallucinated the previous night? Cyrrus claimed he'd seen a pattern in the stars. They had been visible to him as well.

Aera tried to appreciate the beauty of its spherical shape and the swirls of crystal inside, but it was nothing more than a pretty translucent rock now. The previous night there had been something beyond.

Cyrrus reached for the ball, and Aera yielded it willingly. She was no longer enchanted. While tears filled Aera's eyes, Cyrrus detached as he usually did when he was disappointed.

Under her breath, she asked, "Cyrrus... what pattern did you see in the stars?"

Dryly, he replied, "What stars?"

He wrapped up the ball, handed it to Aera and stood to leave. As he departed, he said, "Beauty is worthless and inconsistent."

Some crows cawed from a nearby branch, then followed Cyrrus away. Annoyed by the drama, Aera stuffed the ball in her pocket and headed off. Sweat from the unrelenting heat dripped down her stiff muscles as Cyrrus's words echoed in her mind. *Beauty is worthless and inconsistent.*

~

"*Vavi dorón i kuissë më...*"

Aera opened her eyes. Had she been dreaming, or was Cyrrus speaking to her through *inyanondo?* The phrase was familiar and meant 'where does this pattern break.' She leaned against the wall facing Cyrrus's closet and cupped her hands around her ear but detected no sound. Perhaps he was asleep, dreaming about the sanctum or the crystal ball.

She turned toward the orb, secure beneath her pillow. Just last night, there had been a universe inside. Though Aera dreaded seeing it without the magical stars, she was compelled to look, just in case.

Carefully, she rolled out the crystal ball and lifted it. The sphere sat perfectly in her palm, and her fingers reached most of the way around. As she freed it from the wrapping, vibrations shot up her arm. The orb was alive!

She set it down on the mat and examined its magical abyss. A myriad of stars was distributed along two concentric orbits. Those in the outer ring were larger than those toward the center, where there were obvious vacancies in the otherwise perfect circle they formed.

Momentarily, two stars popped into empty slots, and another vanished. The stars along the outer orbit remained fixed while the inner ones arrived and departed. Aera watched, admiring the beauty, counting the stars. Each orbit accommodated twenty-four slots...

A key turned in the lock of Aera's closet door. She stuffed the crystal ball under her pillow. Where had the time gone? It seemed like minutes, but it might have been hours.

The door swung open and Linealle screeched, "Get up!" She crossed her arms and stood in the doorway, watching.

Feigning drowsiness, Aera said, "I... need to get dressed."

"Hurry up," Linealle huffed.

Aera pulled the door closed and wrapped the prize, burrowing it deep in her cloak. When she opened the door, Cyrrus was waiting for

349

her. She was eager to tell him about the stars, but this was not the time, as others were parading up the stairs from the sleeping quarters. Cyrrus sharply met her eyes, likely reading her thoughts.

"Samely, Cyrrus!" Doriline squealed as her crew emerged from the stairs. She twirled her curls and batted her eyes at Cyrrus as if Aera weren't there.

Aera projected an Ivory posture, flashed a wry grin and said, "Greetings, Doriline."

Caught off guard, Doriline banged into someone. She forced a nervous laugh before ushering her flock outside.

Cyrrus smirked, apparently enjoying the performance. Once everyone was gone, he whispered, "So the stars come out at night? That's what I was hoping."

A smile spilled over Aera's face. She thought of the gushy smile in the mirror and blushed.

"It's Summer," Cyrrus said. "The sun won't set until the last hour of dinner. Let's rest at the gorge after lunch to prepare."

The day crawled by until, finally, dinner break arrived. Without discussion, Aera and Cyrrus headed deep into Southside Forest. The Oloril sang, and the summer air cooled as they approached the riverbank. Across it stood the log barricade surrounding the DPD training facility. They hadn't returned to that spot since their first morning together, and Aera was reminded that the view was breathtaking. The sky was painted with small clouds surrounded by the pinks and purples of twilight. Her anticipation mounted.

Cyrrus collected branches while Aera arranged rocks near the river's edge. Crows circled overhead to witness the ritual. Aera enjoyed the exhilaration of fresh, flowing water as they assembled the fireplace. They rubbed their fire rocks together, side by side, and the sparks trickled down. Soon enough, branches kindled and flames roared.

They sat opposite each other, legs crossed, the crystal ball between them. As daylight faded, stars awakened inside the ball. By dusk, they were distinct; by nightfall, as bright as any in the sky.

They watched it for a while. Stars in the inner orbit came and went while the peripheral pattern remained fixed. *Who? Who?* Called an owl. Aera snapped out of her trance and looked up. The moon had risen over the horizon beyond the great river in the east. She wondered how much time had elapsed.

Just as it crossed her mind, Cyrrus said, "We have three quarters of an hour."

Aera surmised he'd learned to tell the time according to the placement of celestial bodies, as he was busy examining the sky. Impressed by his skill, she grinned.

Energy surrounded the crystal ball, magnetizing their hands towards it. They could feel its warmth before touching it. Each placed their right hand on one side of the orb, cupping it in their palms, and rested their left hand on top as their fingers slid into each other's. Aera's heartbeat accelerated, and she felt Cyrrus's pulse rise along with hers. She looked at him and he at her. At once, they both gazed at the river and then, the fire.

It was a moment of clarity. Their pulses converged and their eyes found the same targets as if from one mind. Words were unnecessary. They were entering another realm. Or were they? Aera searched Cyrrus's eyes for clues... but he only searched hers in return.

They returned their focus to the ball and absorbed its heat. Their heartbeats matched, and their senses jostled until they found themselves staring at the orb, enraptured. They locked into each other's eyes and reached a singular thought: *We must do something.*

It occurred to Aera then: if they watched the reflection of their eyes in the orb, as they had done with the piano, something might happen. Together, they leaned in and stared, but nothing changed. They looked at each other and had the same thought: *Use words.*

Underground, before passing the lights, they had each projected words in Silindion. Perhaps, to rouse the orb, they needed a phrase to serve as an incantation. *Opho vassë viervi yanesi,*[4] Aera thought. *Vavi dorón i kuissë më.* Cyrrus gazed at the fire, his thoughts now disconnected from hers. The synchronicity had dimmed.

Aera leaned forward and created a hair-cave surrounding their wrists. The orb tingled against her palm, and her fingers were warm and cozy between Cyrrus's. She smiled to herself. Their hands were still connected.

She listened to the water and leaned back to feel the wind in her hair. Cyrrus watched the flames. Fire, wind and water... just like their dream. Their eyes met. The answer struck them at the same instant: *En rallë anti miossi kemma.*

They gazed down at the orb and spoke the phrase together: "*En rallë anti miossi kemma.*" The ball heated. Wind circled around them, and water cascaded over itself in the river while the flames flickered wildly. The push of the water danced with the pull of the flame as the wind scattered dirt and ash. The pulse of the forest resounded, its energy coursing through them until... again... they encountered an indefinable boundary that transported them back to the here and now.

Aera considered the meaning of the phrase. "This boundary will not bind us," she said aloud.

"This boundary doesn't bind us," Cyrrus replied. "We're trapping ourselves."

"Which boundary is *this?*"

"Wind, water, fire, rock," Cyrrus mumbled to himself. "Which boundaries have we already crossed?"

Aera stared into the fire, watching the wind toss it about. "The monolith linked you to music and me to the sun," she mused, "but in the dream, you were fire, and I was..."

She was about to say 'wind,' but it was inaccurate: the cyclone was also made of lightning and rain. "I was the storm," she concluded.

"So, what boundary did we cross?" Cyrrus persisted. He played with her hand, holding it in both of his, slowly separating her fingers. Her heart rate hastened. She breathed deeply, relaxed her muscles, and tried to keep that hand limp to mask her fluster. Slowly, she ran her other hand along the vibrating surface of the crystal orb. Cyrrus was gazing downward, oblivious to her, buried in thought.

"The boundary of our physical form?" he continued. "We were still in our own bodies. Was anything else different?"

"We had the same thoughts at the same time," she suggested, watching her fingers circle the ball and feeling its electricity. "We knew each other's thoughts without words—"

"—that's it! We crossed a language barrier!" Cyrrus cut in, releasing her hand.

"When we were silent, we connected to each other," she said. "When we spoke the incantation... *en rallë anti miossi kemma*... the forest connected to us, too."

"And then we hit that invisible wall," Cyrrus sighed, tapping his leg with his fingers. "If we communicated without language, and something changed when we spoke, what boundary is binding us?"

Aera looked around, desperate for ideas. The moon crept up beyond the river, and the crystal sphere glistened with stars that waxed and waned around their diametric circles. Soon they would have to leave the forest for curfew. "Time," Aera offered.

"Time is motion, the top of the wheel... motion and deity culminate in *sundátëa*," Cyrrus muttered, furrowing his brow. "But... no, it isn't time. We may be bound by our fear of punishment, but our curfew is imposed by the commune, not the universe."

"Are the twelve archetypes imposed by the universe?"

"Excellent question," Cyrrus said thoughtfully. "The answer is complex, but we might not need to understand the laws of nature to unlock the orb. If any theory is relevant, it would likely be written by Talismanists."

Aera was excited that the answer was 'complex' instead of 'no' and smiled brightly.

"The Talismanists ascribe religious power to objects called Talismans, supposedly fashioned by the Angels. Some have created replicas of those objects as part of their Nassando study. They would claim the Angel Alárië herself created an Orb Talisman to enable communication between mortals and deities. Our starry ball could be a replica of that original orb."

"So, the crystal ball might have been created by someone with the Talismanist's concept of nature," she said, thinking aloud. "If Alárië crafted the original orb, it's related to the moon."

Cyrrus stared into the crystal ball. It was shaped like the moon, but transparent, with stars inside.

"The orb may have been fashioned through some ceremonial connection to Alárië," Cyrrus said. "But if the replicas are responsive to incantation, maybe anyone can use them once they learn the language." Cyrrus stopped talking and furrowed his brow. To himself, he said, "Is this why *sundátëa* requires mastery of several Nestëan languages?"

"Is this... relevant?"

"Incantations might be specific to a language," Cyrrus muttered, still speaking to himself.

Aera considered this. "So how do you say 'this boundary will not bind us' in other Nestëan languages? ...Nindic?"

Cyrrus's eyes gleamed. "The root for the negative would be... *ge-*. 'Boundary' could be derived from the root *kes-*... 'separate'... no, wait, *ken-*. So, *cemm* would probably be the noun 'boundary.' 'Binding' could either be from *ben-*, or *bel-*; the verb would be *bener*. Now, 'us,' what is the 'us?'"

Aera enjoyed watching him stumble and grinned.

"*Ath*... pronouns are hard... *Ger beni ath cemmar!*"

Nothing happened. The stars inside the crystal ball were as bright as ever, and their reflections in its surface dissolved into swirls. Instinctively, they placed their hands on the ball, as they had before. They sat cross-legged, locked their free hands together and stared down at the orb.

"*Ger beni ath cemmar,*" they said in unison. "*Ger beni ath cemmar...*"

A force shifted them. It wasn't wind. It was neither fire nor water nor time. It saturated their throats with a metallic taste that transformed into energy as they spoke the incantation, each word spurring a surge of vibration deeper into their bodies than the last. It infiltrated their lungs, ignited their bodies, and infused every limb, permeating them from skin to blood.

The orb engulfed them, and the forest vanished into an abyss as their usual senses evaporated. They perceived only currents that absorbed their sensate focus into an electric glow, and their bodies transformed into naked energy.

As their perception reconfigured, amorphous twinkles assembled into stars and an atonal wave of reverberation gave way to a soft *whoosh*. Shadow and light coalesced and silhouetted into patterns, where three auric figures undulated, each occupying a unique spot within a wide circle of stars. A second ring of stars shone far beyond in a vast black sky, surrounding the inner circle and the three forms. Aera reasoned that she too had become a vibrating mass of energy in the world of light and shadow.

She scanned the tiny universe and searched for Cyrrus. Was he one of the auric forms? Across the way, an arrangement of orange lights morphed into a shape approximating a male figure. Aera moved to approach it, but she tingled as she fought against a force that locked her in place. She could change position but couldn't escape the specific area where she hovered. Was Cyrrus there? Had he remained outside? She scanned the vibrant silhouettes and spotted a cluster of silver lights rippling in a feminine shape. Was that Aera?

Why was she looking for Aera? She was Aera, looking for Cyrrus. She surveyed the area again and saw a slim beige aura. Was that Aera? Or Cyrrus? Who was she looking for?

Were these Cyrrus's thoughts? Had she become Cyrrus? Was Aera still outside, experiencing this through Cyrrus's eyes—which were now hers? Her mind raced, and her thoughts kept interrupting each other. She studied the beige figure, but a blast of energy pushed her head toward the silver apparition against her will. Who was guiding it? What were the auras... why was she here? Did they know she was here? Who was she?

What had been a neat circle of stars and colors became a chaotic jumble of light and shadow as her attention shifted from one apparition to another, each movement rattling her with spasms of electricity. She was scrambled and overwhelmed. Then she realized she had turned to face an outer ring of stars.

Though she did not speak, words emerged from her: "*Ger beni ath cemmar!*[5]"

The stars closed in and expanded to rays of light. Vibration consumed her as the star moved, closer, closer, silver, blank...

The crystal ball was hot against Aera's palm, and Cyrrus's fingers were limp between hers. She tried to pull her hand away, but it was frozen in place. All her limbs were numb. With difficulty, she lifted her eyes to Cyrrus's. As her vision came into focus, he met her gaze, sleepy and confused. The dying fire became clear and distinct in his eyes. They were back in the ordinary world.

As they pried their numb hands apart, feeling returned in tingles so sharp that Aera couldn't tell whose fingers were whose. She struggled to move as it felt like tiny needles were poking her everywhere.

Once they had rescued their arms, Aera attempted to uncross her legs. Every inch of her body was under assault, but she forced her limbs into motion, and the stabs retreated to twinges as her muscles revived to a functional state.

Wordlessly, they wrapped the orb, and Cyrrus slipped it into his pocket. They extinguished the remains of the fire and shuffled slowly into the trees.

As Aera regained sensation and control, she felt unusually attuned. Her night vision was sharp, and she was surrounded by bright colors that contrasted vividly with one another. Distant trees cast muted shadows in the darkness, and she heard the forest breathe. Nature revealed an orchestra, each sound more acute than ever before, and she could identify the treetop from which each chirp or coo emerged. Her body was liquid, each step balancing the muscles in her legs. She felt the presence of every breath in her lungs and each beat of her heart.

Aera wondered whether Cyrrus had entered the orb as she had, and asked, "*Bewaidh onn pelüsil?*[6]" Her voice reverberated throughout her body, and as the resonance wore off, she realized she'd spoken a language she didn't recognize. "*Bew fesi mered...*[7]" What?! She meant to ask how she'd done that, but she was hypnotized, thinking in her own language yet speaking another. Forcefully, she pushed out the words, "I... can't... speak."

The sound of Syrdian shook her. Syrdian... Ynas... people. Soon she would be in the presence of others who were unaware of their adventures. The forest would protect her for only so long. She had to collect herself.

"*Ēdin minir—*[8]" Cyrrus paused. He cleared his throat, straightened his shoulders, and asked, "Were we both inside the sphere?"

"I don't know," Aera said. "I was confused."

Cyrrus grinned. "Our separate thoughts, jammed together into one brain... I'd agree that's confusing." With a snicker, he added, "Especially since your mind is so untidy. *Poid.*"

"What's *poid?*"

"Fool," Cyrrus said smugly. "In Nindic."

They exchanged a giggle, then proceeded to the Junior Hut in silent awe and made it to their closets just before curfew.

ELKANDUL

1328 MID-SUMMER

"I have deduced how *inyanondo* works."

Aera could distinguish multiple overlapping timbres in Cyrrus's voice, and his tone was excruciatingly clear. Between the sting of sunlight, the palpable brush of the wind and the crisp personality of each subordinate sound, she was certain the crystal ball had heightened her sensory perception. Classes that morning had been unbearable, and the Dining Hall noise unthinkable. Luckily, her appetite was missing.

She had expected Cyrrus to discuss the orb and wondered whether *inyanondo* was related to it. He was serious and distant, with no trace of the boyish exuberance he'd exuded the previous night. His tray was bursting with food, but he hadn't eaten a morsel.

"*Inyanondo* is the ability to sense the inner world of others," he explained, adopting his didactic persona. "The aptitude is innate for anyone with Nestëan heritage, but the ability is latent. Some individuals may access *inyanondo* more readily than others, but its true potential must be awakened through formal training. The Nassandë and Orenya embrace *inyanondo* fully, which allows them to crystalize thoughts into specific words and images."

"That can't be true," Aera protested. "You don't have formal training."

Cyrrus glanced at her, and although he barely grinned, his eyes were roguish. He was concealing something, as usual.

"The Nassandë may deliver unspoken words over short distances," he continued, ignoring her comment. "I would estimate that a Nassando could project thoughts to another anywhere in the commune, but probably not much further."

Cyrrus had claimed their shared dreams were a result of *inyanondo* but had insisted her dreams did not derive exclusively from him. If *inyanondo* was limited by distance, her dreams must have come from someone in Ynas.

"Nothing helpful has been written about dreams, but I have a theory," Cyrrus said, answering her thought. "We know from our own experiences that dreams may be shared unintentionally, which makes sense, since both parties are unconscious. I am uncertain whether there's a limit to the physical distance between people who share dreams."

"Dreams *are* thoughts... so the limit would be the same."

"That seems logical, but experience informs me that dreams access a wider pool of thought."

Aera was about to respond, but the Dining Hall door closed loudly behind them, and Cyrrus jerked his head around. He watched as a few people crossed the Field until they had disappeared from sight, then resumed his oration.

"While awake, a Nassando can read the mind of another who is physically present," he said. "It's harder to read someone's mind over any distance unless the person projects an intentional message. Their thoughts would be mixed with others and difficult to distinguish unless the communicating parties have established a specific path of connection."

Aera wondered whether he thought the two of them had established such a connection. She waited for him to explain, but instead, he commanded: "You need to be Ivory in the company of others, all the time. Reserve Aera for me. Vaye must see only Ivory."

Aera's posture adjusted at the mention of Ivory's name; it had become automatic. She now understood why he brought up *inyanondo*: he'd reasoned that because Vaye could read minds, Aera would have to hide the crystal ball from her. The consequences of Vaye learning about the orb were unpredictable, but Cyrrus's solution was untenable.

Aera couldn't focus on the piano while also restraining herself. Even if she could, Vaye's powers might make deceit impossible.

"The glow at your center is your *suru*," Cyrrus instructed in a hushed tone. "When you cast a shadow over yourself, you dominate it with your *semissë*. Inhabit that part of yourself which is needed to play piano and keep the rest of your thoughts hidden."

"I need to concentrate on the music," Aera explained. "I can't focus on Ivory at the same time."

"Then practice in the Music Room. Playing alone is tabooed but not illegal."

"Last time Nurin thought I played that piano, he cut off my hair."

Cyrrus furrowed his brow and Aera wondered what insults he might be formulating. After a long pause, he said, "I am working on changing laws. Until then, Ivory will have to play piano."

Music was not an empty chore that she could undertake mechanically... but there was no point explaining that to a log. He would never understand.

"Stop emoting," Cyrrus ordered. "Offer a better solution or accept mine."

"I'll stop emoting when you stop talking," Aera bristled.

"We will take turns with the orb," he said importantly. "Using it together was too confusing. I will keep it for two weeks, and you will keep it for two. Tomorrow marks the third week of Mid-Summer, so we will start counting then."

"Then tonight is my turn."

"Unity Days and free days will always land on your turn," Cyrrus carried on, ignoring her. "On the twenty-fourth day of each month, you will pass it to me."

Cyrrus was taking control and disregarding Aera's input, but she had no reasonable objection. If he hadn't intimidated Linealle and made a study of foreign languages, the orb would not have come their way. Annoyed, she asked, "Did you use the orb again?"

"Irrelevant," Cyrrus said dismissively, and closed his eyes.

"Samie Secrets," Aera scowled, and headed off to Westside Willows.

The trees enveloped her in another world, and the scent of moist earth filled her lungs. Her tension escaped as she exhaled. The forest was buoyant with the usual patina of afternoon birds and crickets, but now, Aera sorted them in her mind, layer by layer. No matter how many creatures sang in unison, she could apprehend the precise location of each and picture it visually, placing it within a mental sphere at a precise angle before, behind, and beside her. She was in a rich world whose sounds painted a vivid canvas.

As she approached Vaye's brook, the air presented new aromas. The wind lofted a scent of vanilla from white flowers that sprouted from vines along the cottage. Aera summoned her thoughts toward her center, cloaked them in shadow and glided on with the grace of a swan.

Ivory opened the door gently and found herself in a peaceful room punctuated with sleepy cats. Piano keys sparkled as sunlight poured through the windows, but there was no sign of Vaye. Ivory tip-toed up the stairs, peeked into the open door and assured herself she was alone. She freed her moonlight from behind its shadow and sensed Aera's essence filling the room.

Her limbs tingled as she approached the piano, and she studied her fingers as the keys drew them in. Each hand followed the other in a familiar arpeggio, swaying in repetition like the tide, each note exuding a glow. She was in a universe of light that reflected the impact of each sound. Even as she closed her eyes, a vibrant spectrum danced before her.

The strike of each key caused subtle differences in the shape of the illumination. Soft touches swayed like feathers on water and hard ones jolted like hammers against metal. The sensation of each key against her fingertips made her shiver.

As Aera watched her fingers moving about, she mused over the complexity of human form. There were intervals she couldn't reach, but her hands moved on their own to compensate. The same arpeggio evoked different emotions aroused by nuances of minimal variation in the pressure of her touch. Aera had always known this innately, but now it amazed her that so many choices were made beneath conscious awareness. She bore witness to the intricate workings of her inner mind.

Her fingers fell into an ominous ballad, harkening familiar chords. She embellished the music with dark inflections as the piece unfolded. *"Kamara sínië vaphurnë yanisë'nië, ninén i lavan lillannu vohwild'anyë,"* she sang, each syllable vibrating in her body. "*Ninén i lavan lillannu vohwild'anyë...*[1]"

The door opened and Vaye entered, carrying a basket of greens. Aera stopped playing and straightened.

"Please, continue," Vaye said in her most gracious voice. "I'll fix us some tea... but then, I must sleep. Your music will color my dreams."

Reflecting Vaye's serenity, Ivory smiled and chimed, "Dreams at lunchtime?"

"Sometimes there's business to attend at night," Vaye said. With a provocative grin, she added, "I know you understand. Would you like some tea anyway?"

Vaye met her eyes, probing her. *You want to read my mind,* Ivory thought. *But you can't this time.* She observed Vaye and tried to estimate what she was thinking, but Vaye was as unreadable as ever.

"Thank you, but I must go," Ivory said, her tone every bit as colorful as Vaye's. "Enjoy your evening!"

Vaye smiled in kind, then brought her basket into the kitchen. Aera went outside and felt a drizzle. Once the cottage was out of sight, she spread her arms, spun about, and tilted her head back to taste the rain, thoroughly relieved to be herself. Ivory had served her well. Aera had focused on the world outside her thoughts and hadn't called to mind the crystal ball, even as Vaye was probing her. Instead, she had reflected Vaye's silent inquiry like a mirror.

There was still time before tasks. Aera bathed, then sauntered through the forest. Rain came down in a torrent. By the time she returned to the village, she was drenched. The Field was crowded with hustle and bustle, and a group had gathered around Cyrrus.

"How many of you believe our working conditions are fair?" he bellowed. "The Authorities send us to work outdoors while *they* relax under warm, dry roofs! How does this make you feel?"

People in the crowd yelled responses:

"Angry!"

"It's not fair!"

"Ghaadi barlocks!"

"Together, we can change Ynas!" Cyrrus raged on. "Attend town meetings! Your voice counts! Every voice counts!" He threw a fist in the air and repeated, "Every voice counts!"

"Every voice counts! Every voice counts!" the kids chanted, emphasizing the same syllables as Cyrrus, throwing fists in the air. Aera was reminded of the throng chanting, 'We are all the same!' It astounded her that Cyrrus believed he could change the system by becoming a replica of Nurin.

The crowd hollered on, oblivious that they were reenacting the very structure they wanted to dissolve. "Every voice counts! Every voice counts…!"

Officer Padd blew his whistle, but it couldn't be heard above the throng. He blew it louder and louder as more officers blew their own whistles.

Still, Cyrrus and his novice acolytes continued chanting. "Every voice counts! Every voice counts!"

Competing with their voices, Padd bellowed, "Darse your dirl, Brains! Who in Riva's Trees do you think you are? Darse it NOW!"

Without looking at Padd, Cyrrus closed his mouth and lowered his fist. The mass mirrored him, dropping their arms and dispersing to join their lines as the rain rushed down.

"What're you playing at?" Padd went on.

From nearby, Officer Luce affirmed, "Could be a dangerous game."

Both watched Cyrrus, anticipating a reaction, but none came.

"Pehh," Padd snarled. He turned to Aera and demanded, "What's he playing at?"

Aera couldn't help laughing. The officers were afraid of Cyrrus. He reminded them that their power was fragile. She assumed Ivory's posture, smiled and thought, *he's playing **you**.*

Though Cyrrus entertained his fans with rhetoric in passing, he spent most of his time alone. During breaks, he was sleeping or missing, and avoided discussing his adventures in the orb. Aera passed the time playing piano, but the hyperacuity diminished and the world became lifeless. Her only refuge was knowing Cyrrus would soon relinquish the crystal ball.

She counted down the days, but they passed too slowly. As Late-Summer approached, the heat wave that had tortured them for months relented. Rainstorms became more frequent, the grass smelled damp, and the air was fresh.

Finally, Late-Summer arrived. Eager to take the orb from Cyrrus, Aera dressed quickly and hurried out to the lobby, but he was already gone. She didn't see him outside and went to the breakfast line. An unusually excited chatter created an uproar.

"Are you going?"

"Are you voting?"

"Will the Renstrom be angry?"

People were discussing the town meeting in animated voices. It was a free day, thanks to Cyrrus's collusion with Doriline, but everyone was excited to spend that time watching the political show. Aera needed to find Cyrrus and take the orb before it began. She would not let him evade her.

She carried her breakfast to the boulder, but she still didn't see Cyrrus. She wondered if he'd gone to the town meeting early. The Field overflowed with people of all ages swarming toward the tunnel. Outside the Dining Hall, groups of officers whispered to each other.

Aera turned toward Southside Forest and glimpsed Cyrrus disappearing into the trees behind the sleeping huts. Though he was far away and slipped out of sight instantly, his black outfit and brick red hair were unmistakable. This was unlike him: the entire commune was attending a town meeting to support him. Something was wrong.

She ate quickly and went to Great Gorge, where she found Cyrrus lying on the ground under the great oak, wrapped in his cloak with the hood drawn over his head. As she approached, he opened his eyes to confirm it was her, then closed them again.

Aera crouched nearby and reminded him, "The town meeting is—"

"It's irrelevant," Cyrrus yawned. "There's a whole world out there. It doesn't matter whether Ynas has three free days per season or twelve."

"It matters to your audience," Aera said. "And you love attention."

Closing his eyes, he retorted, "Love is a logical fallacy."

Aera was satisfied that if Cyrrus was spouting platitudes as usual, he probably had his wits about him and didn't need her to look after him. She decided to let him rest, but first implored, "It's my turn with the orb."

No response. He was already asleep… or pretending to be.

Aera considered attending the meeting herself, but her thoughts were consumed with the crystal ball, and she didn't want to see anybody. Instead, she decided to organize. She found the tablets where she'd written translations or notes about *Parë* and copied them into her notebook. Still antsy, she tossed the tablets into the firewood pile and meandered to the bathing grove. After washing and eating, it was barely midday. She had to bide her time until nightfall and distract herself in the meantime. Reread her diary? Practice Ikrati? The wait was unbearable.

As she watched the sun crawl interminably across the sky, she considered Cyrrus's dismissal of the town meeting. He had always viewed leadership as the road to a better life, but now, something had changed. The orb had caused some shift in him. Aera could hardly wait to see how it might affect her. She wandered restlessly through the forest, climbing trees, singing with the birds, collecting Ikrati sticks, and whacking branches with them. After an eternity, dusk arrived.

She brought her sticks back to the Gorge and found Cyrrus lying on the low branch of their oak with his eyes closed. As she approached, he asked, "Did you go to the meeting?"

"No, I—"

"You're useless."

A few rejoinders ran through Aera's mind, but she understood his provocation was a distraction and requested, "The orb… please."

Cyrrus opened his eyes, sat up and said, "We need to talk."

Aera waited, but Cyrrus remained silent, staring at the tree. Though eager to retrieve the orb and leave, she was mindful not to rush him. He exuded solemnity, and she read anxiety beneath the guarded demeanor. Slowly, his gaze returned to her.

"This is not a game," he said. "Magic is a responsibility, and responsibility requires maturity. Are you sure you want to do this?"

"What maturity? We're *both* teenagers."

"You're confirming my apprehension."

Dryly, Aera said, "Glad to be of use."

The two watched each other for a moment, both expressionless. Flatly, Cyrrus said, "That's marginally better."

"It's my turn with the orb," she reminded him. "You have some concern about that, but you're not telling me what it is."

"If you engaged your brain, you would appreciate that I withhold some of my observations to protect your tender emotional sensibilities. And considering I am inattentive to most people's emotions, you might more generously interpret my reticence as a compliment."

"I see," she said curtly. "What about the orb?"

"There are strangers in the orb world who will try to trick you into revealing information," he said. "Some will stop at nothing to find and destroy you in order to possess the orb. They could attack Ynas or torture Vaye to get to us. We don't know who these people are, or what type of influence they wield, even within Ynas."

Aera now understood why Cyrrus had called her immature. Yet, he was to blame. He had invited her into his world of magic. If he knew more than she, it was his 'responsibility' to alert her of any danger, and he could have done it sooner. It was in his interest to be more forthcoming, but he was too obsessed with control.

Cyrrus reached into his cloak. Aera expected him to pull out the ball; instead, he retrieved a notebook and jotted something down. Her tension mounted as he slipped it slowly back into his pocket. Finally, he turned to her and spoke in a somber tone.

"The orb will transport you to a microcosm where you will encounter colorful auras," he said. "The microcosm is beyond the bounds of physical reality, but the auras call it Star-place. I prefer the Silindion translation, Elkandul."

"This boundary will not bind us," Aera said, and smiled.

Cyrrus looked at her for a long moment, then continued. "Everyone there will evaluate your aura and responses. Reveal nothing about yourself, where we are from, or even that we are two separate people."

This was a strange request. Aera and Cyrrus were entirely different. What, exactly, was he telling her to do?

"After you utter the incantation, your physical body remains behind and the energy inside of you is projected into the orb," Cyrrus explained. "That energy encompasses your *inyarya*, emanations of beauty from your *suru*... and that's what the others see. To them, you appear as an assemblage of moving lights in shifting forms and colors."

Aera could have figured this out on her own. She nodded impatiently.

"The Nestë claim that everyone has a unique color and that each individual's emanations of beauty match specific archetypes, like Angels, natural elements, or animals. Those colors and forms may appear in Elkandul, since they are part of your essence, but your lights shift continuously with your emotions, and nothing remains constant. The energies that remain are those you most identify with—in other words, your *inyarya*, or sense of self."

Archetypes, sense of self... this was getting interesting. These 'energies' might correlate to concepts Aera had explored in *Parë*.

"Identity is an unconscious process that is taken for granted," Cyrrus said. "We may not think about the body, but we still walk on two feet. These automatic programs create patterns in the mind which cause the auras to assume human shapes. They may morph into animals and elements that match their archetypes, but the shift is fleeting. Embodying a nonhuman entity for an extended period would require intrapsychic alchemy so profound, its most basic premise eludes even the most enlightened minds."

Aera had never thought of identity that way, but it made sense: people projected the forms they were accustomed to. She was intrigued by the notion that someone could use 'intrapsychic alchemy' to alter this.

"Shifting between personae and genders in Elkandul is unavoidable," Cyrrus said. "It's natural to identify with both masculinity and femininity, and with people close enough to leave an imprint upon us. Their emanations are easier to navigate, since we share the foundation of humanness."

Aera now understood he expected their appearances in Elkandul would overlap since they 'imprinted' each other. Yet none of this negated the reality that they were nothing alike.

"Your essence is affected by what you experience in Elkandul, which may supersede your conception of self or change it entirely in each moment," Cyrrus continued. "Your feelings will be evident to those who understand the relationship between color and emotion, since the lights must always assume one color or another, and they shift with your emotions. Others will seek opportune moments to manipulate you into revealing more. It is of no consequence whether they read your feelings. What matters is that we don't reveal where we live, who we are, or that we are two people."

"If they see my essence, they'll know I'm not you."

"Both *semissë* and *suru* are part of your essence. When you cast a shadow over yourself, you use your *semissë* to control the way others view your *suru*. In addition to projecting Ivory in Elkandul, it would be advisable to adopt my persona."

Aera couldn't fathom how Cyrrus might expect her to adopt his persona. It was one thing to accept that her aura might incorporate his emanations naturally, but quite another to pretend to be someone else even as her 'genuine essence' was exposed.

"If you repeat my words with my inflections in mind, you will project my essence naturally," Cyrrus said. "You might also project other essences, or your own, but they will still believe we are one person projecting diverse aspects of our one self. That way, even if you do something blockheaded, they will recall my capabilities and be less likely to mark our shared persona as a victim. You will simultaneously strengthen your mind and avoid getting us killed."

Cyrrus's brow was furrowed and his posture stiff. Could the orb really get them killed? If he was willing to take that risk, he must have believed the reward was worth it. Aera could hardly wait to explore it herself. To assure him of her capability, she adopted his crisp cadences and offered, "I will parade my pompous poise and flaunt my flamboyant phraseology."

She smiled. Cyrrus pursed his lips, trying not to laugh.

"Stay alert," he instructed. "Focus on studying others inside the sphere to determine when they're lying. Reflect what they're feeling. Mirror their vocal tones. If you must speak, repeat my words as often as possible."

"Your words are extraneous," Aera said, imitating his crisp cadence. "I am a deity."

"Good," Cyrrus said. "Remember that, and you won't have any problems."

"If everyone behaved as you do, problems would cease to exist."

"Smartest idea you've ever come up with on your own," Cyrrus said with a grin. In turn, Aera giggled at his predictable self-aggrandizement.

He vaulted down from the tree, reached into his pocket, and pulled out the silver-wrapped prize. She sprang her hand open enthusiastically. He held the orb out, but before he released it, he said, "Aera..."

She met his eyes, which looked shiny and black in the moonlight. With sincerity that approached tenderness, he said, "I *need* you to think. I trust you to manage your *vekos*."

He handed her the orb, and she felt its evanescent mass. She burrowed the ball deep in her cloak and rushed off.

When she arrived at Junior Hut, Officers Linealle and Tiros were both sitting outside. As soon as Linealle noticed Aera, she barked, "What are *you* doing here?"

"I'm feeling sick," Aera said. "I need some rest."

"Raisins! You don't look sick!"

Linealle's squeak made Aera nervous. *Act like Cyrrus,* Aera thought. *For practice.* She flashed a smug grin and intoned, "By law, I may sleep early."

Linealle stiffened and her face turned so red that her neck veins popped. Aera suppressed a laugh, keeping her expression blank, as Cyrrus would do.

Linealle marched inside, unlocked the closet door, and held it open. The moment Aera slipped through, Linealle slammed the door behind her. Aera broke into a booming smile. Finally, she was alone with the orb.

She did not waste a second. Her hands unwrapped the prize so quickly that her eyes were barely ready for the stars inside. Just as before, the ones along the outer perimeter shone consistently, while some on the inner ring were conspicuously absent. "*Ger beni ath cemmar,*" she chanted, her hands around the ball. "*Ger beni ath cemmar...*"

Aera's lungs stirred with the familiar metallic taste that electrified as she ascended. Her vision dissembled as she lost control of her muscles and transformed into a tingling mass of energy.

The thick blur of motion spread into shadows and lights as the sonic resonance gave way to the anticipated whoosh. Aera found herself locked in place, undulating in empty space, with no ground beneath her. Although tethered to the spot where she hovered, she was able to turn about. Ripples of electricity combed through her each time she moved.

She acclimated to the sensations as she observed her surroundings. Just as before, she was in was in a black world occupied by two concentric star-circles. The outer one was barely visible in the vast distance, while she floated within the inner ring among numerous neighboring stars—presumably twenty-four, as she'd counted from outside—positioned at regular intervals. Four of the spots were not occupied by stars, but instead, by multi-colored lights evoking auric forms of other beings.

Aera examined two auras to her left. The closer one emitted soft silver light that moved like river waves and projected a womanly shape. Beyond it was a blue figure, tall and straight, with two violet lights where eyes might have been. The apparition turned purple as the body adopted a feminine quality, and the silver aura changed form in tandem, thinning to a slimmer, less curvaceous contour. Since nothing was said, Aera understood that thought alone could alter one's outward appearance.

To Aera's right were two shadowy specters, dense and angular. One had a harsh red base with green highlights, the other, the reverse.

A new presence appeared across the circle, where a star spread into an ensemble of orange lights that assumed the countenance of a man. Aera inferred that each time an aura showed up, a star within the circle gave way to its cast.

Distant garbled dialogue mixed with the continuous whoosh that permeated the starlit universe. Momentarily, a thin masculine voice emerged from the center of the sphere and said distinctly, "Interesting game."

There were more garbles to Aera's left, followed by a commanding female voice at the nexus that said, "Inquire again."

Since all the words emanated clearly from the center region, Aera was uncertain which entity was communicating. She searched for some indication. Across the way, the orange one darkened to brown and sprouted wing-like extremities which disappeared quickly as the aura thinned. The articulation of nonhuman form was as fleeting as Cyrrus had described. Things evolved quickly in Elkandul.

369

Someone far to the left mumbled, the sound faint and obscure. Then, a genderless, calm voice in the center asked, "Where are you located?"

All the shimmering figures angled towards Aera. She searched for a clever response that wouldn't reveal anything and a tone that mirrored others. In her mind, she replayed the question, then mimicked the voice and replied, "I'm right here."

Her words bounced back from the center of the circle, but her tone sounded genderless, precisely like the voice she'd imitated. It wasn't just the cadence and speed that were identical; the tonal quality was also an exact match. The voice didn't resemble Aera's own at all. Apparently, she could sound however she wanted! Light radiated around her and sparkled with gold as if in celebration.

There was garbled speech to Aera's right, followed by a choppy voice in the center declaring, "He has again altered his depiction."

Aera looked rightward to a dark green light thinning around one of the dense figures. As it split into many parts, it emitted a muted mumble.

"Twenty-two,[2]" said an expressionless voice in the center. "Twenty-six sixteen two one.[3]"

Thick red light spread around the figure, and its face shone in sharp, angular shadows. Aera surmised the red aura was the figure who had spoken, and that each time the garbles emerged from someone, their words projected from the center following a brief pause.

The red aura dispersed to a dark silhouette and was replaced by a star, while the other apparitions shifted shape. The purple lights morphed into a form resembling a bear, then back to a man. Faint, muted dialogue sputtered from him, followed by a clear masculine voice from the center: "The Povus War is spreading. The dreiszes are leaving the Lepont Plains."

Aera heard mumbles to her left and turned toward the silver lights as a sweet voice in the center replied, "They may be forced into the Turnimerya Mountains."

The purple figure became paler and dissolved into a wide shape. Mumbles surrounded him as a feminine voice asked, "Will they be safe there?"

The garbles came from the pale purple lights, but the feminine

370

voice belied his previously masculine aura. The form stretched sideways, expanding into sharp lines as a deep voice said, "The Kalaqhai may influence both."

The Kalaqhai! Aera was excited by the recognition and felt a tingle as aureate sparks glistened around her. She worried that light reflected her emotions, broadcasting them to everyone. To prevent revealing more, she summoned her energy into a ball and covered it with shadow, just as she did in the Ivory lessons. This time, the exercise was more than a mental visualization: it was perceptible to the eye. There was a radiant sphere at her center and a shadow around her, both of which fluttered and faded.

The angular green apparition dissolved and was replaced by a star, while the other forms flashed and spun. Aera was bombarded by electric shocks as voices broke into static.

"King—t-t-t—dor!"

"Wh—he-e-e—niz-z—th—a-a-at?"

"Du—tt—fffffai…"

The atmosphere tugged Aera in opposite directions. As she struggled to resist the pressure, she surveyed the other figures. The silver aura spilled like liquid, the purple form flickered as it adopted curves, and the orange lights morphed into something yellow that momentarily resembled a bird, then changed to a blue man with a long neck. Colors darted away from their hosts, and Aera's vibrations fragmented. Where was she?! The world was double, triple, upside down. She screamed, but no sound came out.

Beams of color tumbled past each other, merging and separating, dragging Aera into a dizzying jumble of chaos. Her light convulsed and dashed all over, each sensation disparate, as though she was spreading to infinity. Anything might be anywhere, and her form had no boundaries. Terror consumed her. She needed to escape.

When Cyrrus had been there with her, he'd turned toward a star behind them and chanted their incantation in order to leave. This was what she had to do, but she had no idea which oscillations were hers or whose lights belonged to whom. She thrust herself back and forth, struggling to reconstitute as bolts of energy tore through her, until finally, she spotted the outer circle of stars in the vast distance beyond. She called, *"Ger beni ath cemmar!"*

A distant star drew her closer and everything swirled together... the voices meshed... vibrations overrode her other senses and swept her entire being away...

... and she was back in the dark closet, looking down at the crystal ball, her limbs locked in position, and her skin stabbing itself to rescue her body from its numbness. Once her body recovered, exhaustion took over, and she passed out.

~

When Aera exited Junior Hut the next morning, sunlight assaulted her. The aroma of soil, leaves and trees individuated to distinct scents. Blades of grass crunched under her sandals as her entire being responded to small bumps in the ground. The voices of others were clear and distinguishable, even in distant groups.

Aera stood still, surveying in awe the surreal sensory cavalcade, until she was the only person remaining on the field. She stroked her wrist; the skin felt soft and vibrant. Slowly, she drew her fingertips along the lines of her palms and sent shivers down her back. As she inhaled, the taste of nature filled her.

Footsteps approached from behind. Aera recognized Cyrrus's even-paced walk. He grinned at the reverie she was playing out on her hands, and his happiness filled her with joy. For the first time, she noticed disparate shades of green exploding through his irises. In the sun, the deep reds in his hair were especially impetuous, and his pallid skin displayed faint olive undertones. This distant color revealed that he was human, and not an otherworldly ghost.

"What happened in Elkandul?" he asked, his eyes sparkling brilliantly. "Any interesting discussions?"

"They mentioned the Kalaqhai..." She stopped, taken aback. Each word resonated throughout her body and her tone was crystalline.

"What else?"

"They said some numbers... and names I don't know."

"Useless."

The word stung. *Useless.* She breathed.

"There was static and chaos, and the auras came apart," she said. "But even before that, it was hard to—"

She paused. Could anyone else hear them? The voices of Doriline's hens were clear as they gabbed in a cluster at the top of the Hill.

"Codin *is* really rawden!" Novi exclaimed. "Yesterday at the track, he stared at me."

"Well, he *talked* to me," Doriline boasted. "He said my name..."

Every word was audible, whereas normally, Aera wouldn't have heard anything from half that distance. Her sensory perception was extraordinary, and it was unlikely they could hear her as well. In a whisper, she concluded, "It was hard to follow the conversation, or figure out who said what."

"You have to watch them."

Aera tried to look at Cyrrus, but the reflection of sunlight on his skin was blinding. She squinted and said, "Right before someone's words are projected from the center, there's faint noise around their aura, but I can't follow it when—"

"I said *watch*. Not *listen*," Cyrrus interjected. "I'm learning how to associate colors and shapes with the topics they discuss, but—"

The door to the Junior Hut opened, and Officer Linealle came out.

"Let's go," Cyrrus said briskly. "We'll talk later."

They departed and headed into the Dining Hall, where voices echoed throughout. Somebody ushered younger kids towards the breakfast line, and Aera and Cyrrus drifted behind them. When they reached the food, Aera was overwhelmed by a sea of colors and smells. Potatoes were configured in rows alongside multicolored fruits and vegetables. Carefully, she put some items on her tray. Cyrrus departed and returned with two mugs of water.

"You're not eating?" Aera asked.

"I'll eat yours."

Aera glanced at Cyrrus, confused.

"Your body won't process food until you acclimate to your sensory state. Didn't you notice I hardly ate?" Without waiting, Cyrrus said, "I should know better than to expect you to notice anything."

"I don't care about your eating habits," Aera retorted. "Food is boring."

Cyrrus smirked. "Indeed."

They exited the cafeteria. In the Field nearby, Kize, Goric and

Pelyane were eating together. Immediately, Pelyane jumped up, ran to Cyrrus and demanded, "Where were you yesterday?"

"Attending to business," Cyrrus said importantly.

"The entire commune showed up, but Nurin declined the proposition pending a vote," Pelyane nagged. "We needed *you* to convince him. What business is more pressing than that?"

"Clandestine business."

Pelyane turned to Aera. "Were you with him?"

Aera scowled, annoyed by the question. She had encouraged Cyrrus to go to the meeting, but his followers blamed her for his absence. How convenient for him.

"Aera has her pursuits and I have mine," Cyrrus said as he grinned pleasantly at Pelyane. "Your debate skills are superb. I was confident you could handle Nurin on your own."

Cyrrus trusted Pelyane to do his work, but he considered Aera 'useless.' She glowered at him, and he responded with a quizzical look. Aera realized she was on edge, overreacting to every real or imagined slight. The orb had made her sensitive to everything.

Oblivious to their interaction, Pelyane chattered on about the town meeting. "I debated for a while, but he recited laws I couldn't counter. There was a long back-and-forth about the value of work, and how it builds character and unites us in our goals..."

Pelyane continued, her voice bouncing from one register to the next. As her excitement mounted and her volume increased, the sun itself seemed to swell along with it. The bright blur of words assaulted Aera's nerves. She began to sweat.

Finally, the noise stopped. Birds chirped and wind blew. Then Cyrrus said, "We'll crush him next time."

Pelyane sighed. "We need to submit a whole new proposition."

Cyrrus looked right at her. "Meet me under the willow during lunch. Tell the others." With that, he headed up Halcyon Hill.

As Aera turned to follow Cyrrus, Pelyane bubbled at her, "How come you stopped coming to clan meetings?"

Because I don't worship deities, Aera thought. She said instead, "Because I don't care."

Pelyane looked surprised and giggled uneasily. Aera felt guilty for directing her bitterness at Pelyane when Cyrrus was the one who deserved it. She offered a smile to soften the blow, then left to join Cyrrus, who resumed their conversation about Elkandul as though there had been no interruption.

"The important part is not figuring out who the individuals are, but rather who they represent and who their allies are," he whispered. "Like us, they are hoping to gain knowledge while concealing their own. We must learn to distinguish truth from deception."

Aera nodded, though she couldn't imagine how to do that when all she could see were shifting lights and shadows.

"The other orbs might be anywhere on Oreni," he said, even more quietly. "We could be talking to Nestë, Kalaqhai, or humans from other societies."

"The orb translates everything to Syrdian for *us*," she mused. "Somehow, it knows to do that."

"What makes you think it translates into Syrdian?"

"That's... what I heard."

Cyrrus erected his posture. "Since I know Syrdian, Silindion, Nindic, Sulindoric, Kethran, and Ceddi, I receive translations into all of them."

Aera grimaced. He always had to know better.

"If you speak in another language for a while, it will be the one you hear," Cyrrus mumbled.

He grabbed the roll from Aera's tray and inhaled it. She felt strange even looking at food and realized he was right: she had no appetite. Her senses were overloaded with the surrounding choir of fabulous chirps and the sweet taste of wind.

Cyrrus gazed at Southside Forest, pondering something, and Aera listened to the bugs and birds around her in each distinct pattern. The world was a dance between rhythm and melody, light and shadow, contour and relief.

They sat in silence, lost in their own thoughts until Luce's whistle blew. Then they headed down to the Field and joined their lines.

"Cyrrus, you barlock!" squealed Doriline from her spot, a short way in front of Aera. "You said you went to *every* town meeting!"

"Did you miss me?" Cyrrus teased.

"I thought you *cared* about the commune."

"Define *care*."

"De-*fiiine?*" Doriline giggled. "Don't you speak Syrdian?"

"If caring involves a commitment to intellectual integrity, I stand convicted. If caring denotes personal investment in an outcome, I am innocent."

"*You* are not *innocent.*"

Though Doriline was inadvertently correct, Aera knew she'd grabbed hold of one word while Cyrrus's meaning sailed blithely over her head. She wondered if anyone else understood it either.

"I am flattered by your vigilant attention to my actions, but nonetheless, it would behoove you to recognize that your assessment of my motivations is mere speculation," Cyrrus said with theatrical aplomb.

"Stop using big words," Doriline laughed. "You show off too much."

Beside Doriline, Farris injected, "That's how brainy boys flirt."

"Ugh! Ew!"

Farris laughed and gave Doriline a playful nudge, but she swatted his hand, clearly unhappy. It was obvious to everyone that she craved Cyrrus's attention.

"Samely, Brains!" Farris bellowed, his voice cracking as he yelled. "Why don't you memorize a book about how to talk to normal girls?"

Tossing a glance at Aera, Doriline snarled, "No real girl would talk to him anyway."

Laughter abounded, and Aera smiled brightly. In the effort to mock her, Doriline had forgotten that she'd just talked to Cyrrus herself.

With her hand on her hip, Doriline demanded, "What's so funny?"

Farris spoke softly to Doriline, but Aera heard: "Dori, you *just* talked to him."

"Ew but I didn't *flirt*—"

The ear-splitting screech of Officer Luce's whistle cut right through the jabber and launched glass shards through Aera's ears. She braced herself for a long, loud day.

The world assaulted Aera throughout classes, as every experience was magnified. She slogged through duties and slept through meals but, at curfew, excitement took over. The moment Linealle locked her in the closet, Aera unwrapped the orb, eager for adventure. She summoned Ivory and chanted, "*Ger beni ath cemmar...*"

Vibrations consumed her, and she was thrust into the orb-world.

Color swirled about, all jumbled together in a quivering morass of oscillating beams. Shadows and lights morphed into shapes.

Five forms hovered among the familiar ring of stars. Mumbles emerged from the silver figure, which occupied the same position as the previous night, and its voice said, "Consistently inconsistent." The tone shifted octaves in the middle of the phrase. Aera suspected it was talking about her.

The same apparition became shadowy and emitted garbled speech. A deep male voice followed: "Taerelboro or Manus-Ka-Maqhar."

It seemed Silver had spoken both times, but the gender aspect of the voice had mutated. More murmurs came from an aura far to Aera's left, flickering purple and red.

"Proximity," boomed a voice in the center. "The Syaig prospect for the Night Gem at-t-t Ff—ff-elk—ee-ee-eep—"

The voice broke apart as whiteness bombarded the atmosphere. All became blistering flashes. There was no center of gravity, and Aera could not discern where—or what—she was. Her composition dismantled into disparate sparks and electric shocks that needled her as she fell into panic. *Ivory*, she thought. *Balance the vekos.*

She visualized a dark, empty space encircling her and pulled each glimmer of light toward her until she was complete. Once her vibrations undulated in concert, she cloaked herself in shadow, resuming control.

Silver was next to reestablish her accustomed form and soon, others followed. Aera wondered what her own aura revealed and how obvious it was that she'd lost herself.

"Gracious," said Silver in her recognizable lustrous tone. "Gratitude."

"Unnecessary," said a voice coming from a purple figure of ambiguous gender. "Same as before." The figure flickered and disappeared, replaced by its orb star. Though it was unclear what had transpired between the two apparitions, Aera sensed Silver was the dominant persona.

Four forms remained, and none spoke. After a long pause, Silver turned toward Aera and nudged, "You are quiet."

The others angled in Aera's direction. She tried to breathe into her belly, but her shape was ephemeral. Breath eluded her.

"You guard emanations of your beauty," said a gentle voice. "Why?"

As Aera considered how to reply, mist surrounded her, shimmering with gold. Was that her own color? Cyrrus wanted her to appear like him and respond as he would. She imagined herself arrogant and superior until a suitable phrase came to mind: "Beauty is worthless and inconsistent." The words bounced back from the nexus in Cyrrus's voice!

Emerald streaks brightened Aera's form as greyness coursed through her. She was projecting Cyrrus's shades now. More colors swirled around the other figures as mumbles emerged from a thin orange aura.

A male voice said, "Amusing that a man so articulate evades conversation." Wings rose from Orange's back, then shifted to resemble long hair.

"How do you know it's a man?" inquired an androgynous voice from a beige figure.

"It is more vibrant than last week, but less feminine," answered Orange.

"He—or she—is unusually mercurial," said Silver.

Aera reviewed her performance, trying to pinpoint where she'd gone wrong. The others had noticed that her shared form was inconsistent and, apparently, that her projection was less feminine than Cyrrus's.

Orange became pink and mumbled. Then his voice asked in a more soothing tone, "Do you have a guiding star?"

Bright beams blinded Aera as she considered what that question might imply. Erelion was a star who delivered the sun into the sky, and Aera had emanated sunny shades just moments before. Had they discerned her archetype?

Pressure assaulted her from every side, squeezing light from her essence, and the other forms flashed as they awaited her answer. She had to say something... anything. Her countenance disintegrated into a frenzy until a lyric came to her and she blurted it out: "*Hyuvún i larë silnemmanyë, vë sarna otma nondo.*[4]" Her words emerged from the vortex in the timbre of her own voice. *Aera's voice.* Cyrrus was right: she *was* immature. She had exposed her anxiety and now, her identity.

Colors flashed as waves of energy ruptured her form and tossed her around. Her aura floated away as she hovered on nothing, helpless to separate her own vibrations from the tumultuous tangle of surrounding pulsations. She imagined the others watching her flail and disintegrate, recognizing what she truly was: the wallflower child with nothing to say. *Useless.* All she wanted was to leave, but she was lost in a whirl of chaotic light and could not orient where to turn. Everything was a blur.

Suddenly, a sensation stirred inside of her as if blood were draining from her heart, one drop at a time. She tried to gather her energy inward, but her every move was compelled by an irresistible pull from across the circle. A force was reeling her in.

She faced the direction where she sensed gravity. In the most potent spot, she saw nothing. There was no color, light, or form... and no star. The other spaces between the auric forms were occupied by stars at regular intervals, but this one was completely blank. She stared, searching for some sign of life, and her being throbbed in rhythm like a heartbeat. *Thump, thump.*

Heat surged through her as the pulse became ferocious. *Thump, thump.* Just as her chest was about to burst, the black spot gave way to a star.

Aera felt hollow and could no longer find her pulse. Only moments before, a black void had transformed her from a tingling mass of vibration to a visceral, pulsating being. Now that a star rested on the plane, her lifeblood was gone.

All forms focused on Aera, but none turned toward the direction where the missing star had been. Had she alone noticed it? Had she imagined it? Shaken, she turned towards the outer ring of stars, chanted the incantation, and exited the crystal universe.

Aera bolted back into the closet. She bent her fingers and moved her limbs one by one as pain needled them. Once the shock abated and she could move normally, she wrapped the ball and lay down.

She felt raw, as though her heart hovered atop her chest. Strangers had watched her come apart. They had described her as quiet, mercurial, and guarding her emanations of beauty. Had they homed in on her as a victim? Cyrrus was going to be furious.

She writhed about in the muggy darkness, sleepless. Did Cyrrus ever lose track of his mask in the orb? Did he ever crack? He could not be that different from Aera if the other entities couldn't tell them apart. If his theory was correct—that emotions from the *suru* were revealed in Elkandul—then he must also have shown anxiety. Otherwise, it would have been obvious that they were two different people.

Aera's heartbeat began to calm, and she attended her breath. *In.* Her stomach inflated, and her back realigned. *Out.*

She turned and felt her stomach against the mat. *In, out. In, out.* Slowly, she drifted off.

～

Morning classes were torture, but at lunch break, Aera collected herself atop Halcyon Hill. The insect and bird choir sounded heavenly, and the air tasted like summer. Grass tickled Aera's hand, and the blades sparkled in the sun. She moved her palm along them as goosebumps ran up her arm.

Cyrrus arrived after some time, sat beside her and whispered, "Tell me about last night?" His hair was arranged in a tiny, wet ponytail, and his cloak was sharp and clean. Now that the orb was out of his hands, he found energy to bathe.

"They assumed I was a man," Aera said, and her voice vibrated in her throat. Indulging the chime of each word, she added, "The second time I spoke, your voice came out."

"Excellent. What else?"

"Someone called me mercurial. They said I was more vibrant than before, but..." she grinned and confessed, "...less feminine."

Cyrrus didn't budge, but Aera sensed his disgruntlement and giggled. Ignoring her amusement, he asked, "What else?"

Aera recalled her confusion in the orb and the feeling of coming apart. *Ivory doesn't care what Cyrrus thinks,* she thought. *He's far from perfect himself.* Coolly, she said, "I lost composure."

"Explain."

Aera let the grass-scented air fill her lungs, and the world consequently appeared greener. She chose her words carefully and said, "I got anxious... because I thought they saw me hiding my aura in shadow or figured out my archetype—"

"Which archetype?"

"Remember the archetype map?" Aera reminded him. "Underground, I saw the symbol for *ilissunviva*—it links to the sun and Erelion. Last night in Elkandul, I saw golden sparkles around me, like sunlight, and then someone asked if I had a guiding star."

Cyrrus furrowed his brow. "I see. How did you respond?"

"I said... *hyuvún i larë silnemmanyë, vë sarna otma nondo.*" She tried not to blush at her stupid answer.

"The moon dances with her star, burning for him from afar," Cyrrus translated stiffly. "A gushy sentiment, but duly ambiguous."

Aera giggled at Cyrrus's rigid delivery of the suggestive phrase. "It's a song lyric from the music book, Sunarien," she explained. "Someone might have recognized it."

Cyrrus watched her pensively, considering something. After a brief pause, he declared, "Even if so, only a fool would presume a generic phrase implied a particular context. And it's irrelevant which elements they associate you with, or if they catch you projecting Ivory. They all use tricks to manipulate their essence."

"You told me to act like *you*. They saw *me*."

"If I act like you sometimes and you act like me sometimes, nobody will imagine we are separate."

Aera looked at Cyrrus and he glared back. She couldn't tell whether he was disappointed in her.

"The question was unrelated to archetypes anyway," Cyrrus continued. "The light on the Nestë foreheads is the guiding star."

"You mean the *esil*."

"That's the Silindion word. There are various interpretations into Syrdian, but 'guiding star' is a literal translation that arises in Elkandul. They were asking in order to gauge how much you know about the Nestë, and they will conclude either that you are naive or evasive."

Aera nodded, relieved. She hadn't given anything away after all.

"Purportedly the *esil* helps the Nestë see truth, in concert with emanations of Angels and a connection with Ilë the creator," Cyrrus smirked. "When I obtain an *esil,* many truths may be revealed to me, but none will involve deities."

"How do you plan to get an *esil?*"

"*Sundátëa,*" he said nonchalantly.

In the past, Cyrrus had claimed humans with Nestë heritage could become Orenya, which meant they could attain *sundátëa* just like the Nassandë. He clearly believed he descended from the Nestë but, even if that were true, he would never learn their ways. Their texts centered on metaphor and, as far as Aera could tell, the Nestë themselves were living enactments of their poetry, exuding grace like Vaye and Panther Woman. Cyrrus's chiseled cheeks, pompous strut and penetrating tone were suited for politics and tailored performance, antithetical to the nature-loving Nestë. The mere thought of passion made him turn to stone.

"You act Kalaqhai and look Kalaqhai, but you associate yourself with the emotional Nestë," Aera said. "Who are you?"

"Whether I am devoid of emotion or elect not to engage it, the outcome is identical," Cyrrus said coolly. "Why squander energy sorting it out?"

Aera understood she had hit a nerve and giggled.

"I'm flattered that my inner workings are a fascination to you," Cyrrus grinned. "But in the interest of progress, I'll sacrifice adulation to remind you there are matters more critical to ponder."

Adulation... nice try. His words were selected with care to elicit a reaction, and his posture was impeccable, sculpted and crafted. Someone so dry and unromantic could never, as Vaye phrased it, 'dance along to the rhythm of life.'

"I trained a pubescent female to tame her emotions," Cyrrus said with a nefarious smile. "Most men would hail that as magic."

Crows cawed from atop the belltower: Cyrrus had summoned them to make his point. With dramatic poise, he picked up his tray and strutted away... his favorite parting gesture. He never wanted Aera around for long anymore.

She tried to force in some food, but everything felt wrong. Grass needled her thighs, sunlight stung her eyes, and the buzz of surrounding chirps assaulted her. She shifted around from one uncomfortable position to another, fighting a mounting urge to scream. Since her appetite was missing, she forsook lunch and went to the bathing grove.

Though the cool water calmed Aera down, she became exasperated again during tasks, as her group was assigned to pick green beans in sweltering heat. The leaves made her itch, the sun made her sticky, and each sensation made her body burn. Even after cleaning herself up at the bathing grove, the sting refused to wash away.

She headed to the cottage, where all was quiet and dark. A cat rested on the bench, and Aera dropped to her knees to pet it. The fur felt heavenly, and as it purred, Aera's body resonated with it. The cat looked into her with a peaceful gaze, its silver eyes like moon-sheen.

Momentarily, the cat stretched and glided away. Aera sat at the piano, closed her eyes and struck a few thunderous chords, each of which released a deep red glow. Once the echo faded, she played a soothing note that spread into a soft pink light, expanding smoothly.

The shape and texture of each illumination responded to the volume, timbre, and sustain of each note. Colors soared and spun through a scape of waxing and waning lights, initiating sensations that transformed into vibrant shapes. After a lengthy improvisation, the song climaxed to a few grand chords, then faded, completing the purge.

Aera luxuriated in the pumpkin-scented cottage. Then she heard the creak of stairs behind the kitchen. Vaye had been home the whole time.

Aera pulled her colors inward and shielded them as she turned to Vaye. A pale olive gown flowed to the ground and complemented Vaye's mocha skin, but her affect was less sublime, as her brown eyes were dense and her presence heavy. Although her expression was as loving as always, Aera sensed more behind it... something between despair and emptiness... eyes that had seen too much sorrow and could no longer cry.

Absorbing the weight of this, Aera imagined she might collapse, but she summoned Ivory and intoned, "It's wonderful to see you, but I was just leaving."

Vaye nodded and smiled softly but didn't respond.

Ivory slipped toward the door with practiced grace and said, "Good night, Vaye."

She closed the door behind her and crossed the field steadily. Once she was hidden in the forest, she ran faster, but Vaye's sorrow felt like a lead weight, slowing her down. It was more exhausting than ever to portray Ivory, as every sensation, sound and emotion overwhelmed her.

When she reached Junior Hut, Officer Linealle unlocked the

closet, slammed the door, and locked it again. Aera unwrapped the crystal ball and admired the stars inside, twinkling around their orbit, though some were absent from the inner group. As she stared into the empty spaces, she thought of the animate void where a star should have been. Her heartbeat deepened. *Thump, thump.* She recalled the sensations that flooded her, and tears rushed to her eyes.

She wrenched her gaze from the orb... this would not do. She was too discomposed to venture to Elkandul. Instead, she wrapped up the ball and stowed it away. Finally, she lay down, released a few tears and drifted off.

ELEMENTS

1328 LATE-SUMMER

Cyrrus was absent from meals the next day. Aera took her dinner outside and waited for him. Though she had no appetite, she forced in some vegetables: the last thing she needed was to become even skinnier. It took a while to chew, and then the prospect of swallowing was repugnant. She decided to give the rest of her meal to Cyrrus whenever he arrived.

She climbed atop her boulder to face the village. Heat pulsated through the world in rhythmic waves, and her eyes went in and out of focus along with its tempo. Shapes and angles caught her attention as she took in two triangular compounds in the Field below, with courtyards in the center. At the corners of each structure, one side continued beyond the other, creating a distinctive shape identical to the Kalaqhai insignia.

One of these compounds was used by the community and the other was reserved for the authorities, each wing with its own name and function. Behind the village, a bridge led to another triangular structure, beyond which huts and farm sheds were clustered together, all wooden. This pattern was interrupted only by the great belltower across the river, whose cylindrical shape and silver-grey stones provided contrast to the otherwise repetitive architecture.

Though Aera had observed this scene a thousand times, she *saw* it for the first time. The brick and wooden buildings were angular and looked newer, while all the stone structures she'd encountered— including the belltower, Vaye's cottage, and the underground archways —had cylindrical designs. She remembered Cyrrus's claim that the commune architecture supported his thesis about its Kalaqhai history. The stone buildings were older and likely predated Kalaqhai presence in Ynas, while the rigid and utilitarian structures were apparently Kalaqhai. Within these monotonous prisons, children learned to be all the same—obedient slaves.

Aera turned toward Southside Forest and examined the sleeping huts in the field before it. Three were rectangular and constructed of brick, identical to any single wing of the triangular village buildings, but Junior Hut was shorter and younger. Two officers lingered outside; they were always there, even during breaks. Aera wondered whether they knew of the underground sanctum inside the hut they were patrolling. Who exactly were they guarding the building from?

Officers lit torches around the village, and reflections of the firelight rippled in the river. Aside from the Dining Hall and DPD Lounge, the windows facing the Field were mostly dark. A few in the Administration Unit were lit, and Aera visualized Cyrrus in the hallway conversing with an officer. The image was so detailed and distinct that she sensed Cyrrus was in that building. No, she *knew* he was there. She went to find him.

After returning her tray to the Dining Hall, she crossed the Field to the DPD Building and went inside. The main floor was deserted, so she headed upstairs. The dark stairwell was so echoey that her breathing was amplified, but when she reached the top floor, the hallway was eerily silent. She made her way to the library and was surprised to find it filled with people from all Age Groups. Cyrrus had certainly influenced things in Ynas. She surveyed the area and recog-

386

nized several clan members, but quickly determined Cyrrus wasn't among them and returned to the dark hallway.

The space beneath the library door shone with torchlight, but the rest of the spaces around doorways were dark. She descended the stairs and explored the second level, where muffled voices emerged from behind three doors with light escaping beneath them. Quietly, she tiptoed down the hallway until she heard the familiar timbre of Nurin's voice behind one. Just as she stopped to listen, two officers emerged from another.

"Where in Riva's Trees are you going?" demanded an officer.

"Uh... library," Aera said, improvising.

"It's upstairs."

As she headed toward the staircase, the floorboards behind her groaned under DPD boots. She climbed the stairs and waited until the noise disappeared. Momentarily, another door creaked open on the second story. New footsteps approached, lighter and more rhythmic than the others. Aera knew that impeccable cadence all too well: there was no mistaking Cyrrus.

Cautiously, she peered down the staircase and caught a glimpse of his conspicuous hair. She waited in silence, not daring to breathe as he descended each stair in an even tempo and exited the staircase.

Aera felt a rush. Somehow, she had known Cyrrus was there. Something had guided her straight to him. Perhaps the crystal ball heightened *inyanondo* along with her other senses. If so, Cyrrus was likely aware she'd followed him. His *inyanondo* exceeded hers.

She climbed down the steps, tiptoed along the hall and slipped through the exit. The sky was alive with stars, and the Field was spotted with people and torches. Aera sprinted past them, up Halcyon Hill and into Southside Forest, where she knew she would find Cyrrus.

As she approached Great Gorge, she smelled smoke. Just as she'd expected, Cyrrus was seated by their fireplace, leaning against the great tree with a black leather book propped up on the knees of his perfectly tailored pants. It pleased her that she was able to locate him from afar. She wondered if this was how Cyrrus and Vaye always experienced the world.

"How was your meeting with Nurin?" Aera asked, hoping to catch him off guard.

"Entertaining," Cyrrus said with a smile. "Life is a game."

"Another non-sequitur."

"Stop emoting."

Aera glared at him.

"The crystal ball alters your physical processes, which impacts perception and induces emotions," Cyrrus said. "Your mood has no valid basis, and you are voluntarily succumbing to it."

"I see." Aera grinned. "Did the orb arouse *your* passion?"

Cyrrus ignored her, but Aera smirked and crouched by the fire alongside him. A container of ink sat on the ground between them, and his hand moved swiftly and mechanically across the page as he balanced a feathered quill against it. The characters he wrote were not distinctly Syrdian or Silindion, nor did they resemble Kalaqhai or Nindic.

"I'm writing a book in Kethran," Cyrrus boasted. "What are you doing tonight?"

"Nothing of value to a deity," she poked. She noted the pages were smoother than the commune paper and more meticulously bound than the book he had made for her.

Cyrrus saw her admiring the book and explained, "I'm writing a treatise on the society I will establish when I rule Oreni."

"You won't rule *anything* by sleeping through town meetings."

"I demonstrated my value with a strategic absence. If they want to guarantee my participation, they need to elect me."

"You lie so easily, I can't even tell who you're lying to."

Cyrrus raised a brow. "I've been honing that skill."

"Admirable," Aera said with a mock smile. "So, what's in the treatise?"

"It would bore you. It doesn't suit your lofty artistic sensibilities."

This was another lie: he knew she enjoyed his ideas. She wondered what he was conjuring and why it was secret.

"I'm not helping you to stop emoting, am I?" Cyrrus teased.

"If I am emoting, it's unrelated to you," Aera said curtly. "I'm succumbing to the mood induced by my physical state."

"Do you want to discuss your mood? I can feign sympathy." He faked a pout and widened his eyes. She chuckled at how ridiculous he looked.

"Now you're happy?" Cyrrus grinned. "What next? Do you prefer tears or anger? Take your pick. Life is a game. The fastest cure to one mood is to induce another. The effect won't last, and we can repeat the cycle forever. Now I detect a frown. How quickly will you laugh? I'll make a bet—in exactly five seconds, you will smile. One, two, three..."

The great belltower rang, and Cyrrus opened his mouth widely as if he were making the noise. *Gong, gong.* Aera smiled, and Cyrrus boasted, "I am *controlling* your emotions! You are helpless!"

Their eyes met and they both broke into girlish giggles... though Aera's were undoubtedly 'less feminine.' Cyrrus returned the book to the hollow, Aera stomped out the fire, and the two meandered through the forest. On the way, Cyrrus continued offering commentary on Aera's every expression with mockingly excited vocal cadences while she laughed heartily along. He didn't stop jabbering the whole way back to the hut.

As Officer Linealle ushered them into their tiny quarters, Cyrrus plastered an exaggerated smile on his face and stared at her. Linealle clenched her jaw, expending tremendous effort to ignore him. Her struggle made Aera and Cyrrus laugh as they slipped through their respective doors.

Acra was exuberant and couldn't sit still. She reached into her pocket for the crystal ball and unwrapped it, revealing a world of stars. Would it be unwise to enter? Last time, she'd come undone by the fear that the others might distinguish her from Cyrrus or read her mind, but he'd assured her that hadn't happened and advised her to identify allies and enemies. If she concentrated on others instead of obsessing about her own performance, she might appear more like Cyrrus. Perhaps she could match their colors and displays to the elements on the archetype map!

She placed her hands more firmly on the glass. *"Ger beni ath cemmar... ger beni ath cemmar..."*

The orb swept Aera into the other realm, and as her senses unwound, currents of pastel blue coursed through the atmosphere. Three forms hovered in the circle, of which Aera recognized two. Silver was the easiest to spot. Though she morphed during conversation, she always reverted to her glossy default shape, that of a curvaceous woman. Sparkles approximated waist-long hair and her body was dotted with twinkling gems, like the surface of a river in the sun. Aera mused that Silver's emanations evoked the water Angel Narwë and the archetype of 'abundance.' This highlighted skills in seduction, which might account for her apparent influence with the other entities.

The other familiar persona was masculine, with soft violet lights outlining its torso. Aera recognized the aura: it remained within a range of purples that vacillated in gender, shape and hue. She tried to discern an archetype, but none came to mind.

The third was one Aera hadn't previously seen. It was smaller than the others, with suggestions of curly hair wrapped in a pastel pink glow. Aera watched as the figure widened and projected deep purples surrounded in reds, along with a voluptuous female form.

Garbles emerged from Silver, now angled toward the stranger. Momentarily, a smooth voice asked, "Do you have a guiding star?"

Pink became light blue and changed to a slender shape, then flashed and became round and beige. As she changed forms, Purple inquired, "Do you sympathize with the Syaig?"

Though Pink continued to flicker and morph, she didn't respond. Aera wondered how her own aura looked when she'd been questioned.

"A display of ignorance," declared Purple.

Pink's hair lengthened and twirled around her as pastel light floated away, slipping from her as though leaking from a thousand tiny holes. This was not a 'display' as Purple claimed; it was beyond Pink's control. Though Aera felt uneasy watching Pink, she was also relieved to see that she wasn't the only visitor vulnerable to discombobulation. The changing feminine shapes made Aera think of the moon.

Mumbles emerged from Purple, and a steady male voice said, "Since Ceddi became a client state of Syrd, King Irador has set his sights on New Taerelboro. With the Povus war and slave trade conflict, there are many enemies in the rainforest."

His tone deepened as a heavy crash of pressure filtered like wind through Aera's being. *The archetype of air,* Aera thought. Silver became angular and projected a metallic burgundy shade while the other two forms reddened and gained sharpness.

"Protection," said a voice that dissipated into static.

The auras separated into colorful grains. Along with them, Aera's energy bristled and scattered. Everybody's shadows and lights spread into each other.

A gravelly, broken voice intoned, "Irador may initiate a search for the Night Gem."

Red and grey beams spun throughout the sphere, giving way to alabaster flashes. Prickly bursts invaded Aera until a whirl of static swept her away. She struggled to find her bearings, but nothing made sense. There was no up, no down, no center. Whiteness exploded, vibrations dispersed, and colors dissolved.

As Aera scrambled for control, she was seized by a magnetic force from across the circle. Her attention became fixated to the same location as her previous sojourn. She hunted for the empty spot and located the space, but as she focused on it, a star revealed itself. Though she knew the general direction where the black spot had been, she couldn't find the exact location amidst stars, vivid lights and colors.

"You are fascinating," said Silver. "Unpredictable."

Aera snapped to attention. All the forms angled toward her. Silver asked in a deeper tone, "Do you alter your mannerisms intentionally?"

Colors emanated from Aera and flickered rapidly as they stabbed her with voltaic shocks. She imagined darkness shrouding her and pictured Cyrrus in that space, strong and composed. As a grey glow encircled her, she retorted, "I have been honing that skill." Cyrrus's voice emerged from the center, repeating her words, and the crisp sound made her tingle.

Silver became dense and, in a heavy voice, declared, "Bold admission."

Emerald light surrounded Aera, but she covered it in shadow, and her aura greyed. She was relieved that she had emulated Cyrrus so well but wondered if she'd said the wrong thing. Had Silver conjured a deep tone to intimidate her, or had it been a spontaneous expression of emotion?

As Aera recomposed, two forms appeared simultaneously, one deep red and the other jarring green. The other apparitions flickered as the new ones materialized, and Aera recognized their angular shadows from before.

"Two twenty-six four seven eleven,[1]" said one in a steady male voice.

"Forty-one,[2]" said the other in a similarly flat tone. "Seventeen eight, ten fourteen nine.[3]"

The entire circle darkened as Pink disappeared, and the other two morphed rapidly. Aera inferred that the angular men had caused an adverse reaction. Silver became bulkier and projected metallic greys with spiky protrusions while Purple became meek and his color, faint. Both flashed and flickered. Their volatility made Aera dizzy.

"Again," said a broken voice whose syllables disconnected as it spoke. "Again..."

A heavy atmosphere pushed Aera from every side, overwhelming her with an aggregate of color and force. She wanted to leave yet had no idea where she was. She thrust herself as hard as she could until she saw the outer ring of stars and called, "*Ger beni ath cemmar!*" The light drew her in, and vibrations consumed her...

...she was in the dark closet, numb and limp.

Once she shook off the acute effects, she determined to remember the events she'd seen. She dug the notebook out of her cloak and opened it on the mat, using the starlight from the orb to light the page, and jotted down some observations.

- RED AND GREEN ARE ALLIES. SILVER IS AGAINST THEM. OTHERS GIVE SILVER THE LEAD, BUT NOT RED AND GREEN. THEY HAVE A SEPARATE CONVERSATION.
- SILVER WOMAN: LOOKS LIKE WATER. CONFIDENT, BUT SENSITIVE TO THE ENVIRONMENT. LEADS THE CONVERSATION, EXUDES PRIDE. (ABUNDANCE.)
- PURPLE: CHANGES SHAPE AND GENDER, TURNS TO WIND. IMPERSONAL, PLAYS THE ROLE OF INFORMER, SAYS EMPTY WORDS TO PLEASE SILVER. COWARD. (ISOLATE.)
- PINK: CHANGED TO DIFFERENT WOMANLY SHAPES, BUT STAYED FEMININE & BRIGHT. NEW TO ELKANDUL—THE OTHERS WERE TESTING HER. MOON. (POTENTIAL.)
- RED WITH GREEN + GREEN WITH RED: MALE VOICES, ALWAYS THE SAME COLORS, ANGULAR, SPEAK IN NUMBERS. BORING. NO PERSONALITY.
- H...

She was about to write 'hidden star,' but stopped. According to Cyrrus, it required profound 'intrapsychic alchemy' to project a non-human entity in the orb. Perhaps her imagination was playing tricks... or perhaps, she sensed the pulse of some mystic mastermind.

A smile took over as Aera held her pencil over the page. Whether real or imaginary, the experience was personal and didn't belong on a list. She crossed out the 'H,' wrapped up the ball, and tucked her notebook in her pocket. Grinning and exhausted, she closed her eyes. The bedding felt soft against her as she drifted off.

~

"Get up!"

Aera jolted awake to the sound of thuds against her door and Officer Linealle screeching. Hours must have passed, but they felt like seconds. She dressed and made her way outside, where sunlight stung her eyes and every sound rankled her. The Dining Hall was unthinkable, so she went to the boulder instead.

Cyrrus soon approached and handed her a mug of water. As she drank, he garbled through a mouthful of food, "You look wonderful."

Aera knew Cyrrus was being sarcastic, as her hair was a mess, and she was in a daze. She retrieved her comb and began working through her knots so she wouldn't have to look at him.

"Don't use the orb again until you recover," Cyrrus advised.

"I'll waste my two weeks."

"You're wasting it anyway. You are putting us both at risk to attend conversations you don't understand."

"I took notes—"

"Destroy them. From now on, commit the events to memory."

Aera grimaced. She could never do anything right.

"Try it now," Cyrrus said. "Tell me everything you recall."

Aera yanked the comb, trying to push through a knot as frustration consumed her. She adjusted herself and took a moment to gather her thoughts.

"The silver aura set the tone, and the purple one recited information to win her over," she said. "They worked together to interrogate a pink aura, and she was upset, but didn't tell them anything. Then there was some conversation until the red and green auras showed up and everyone got chaotic."

"What was the conversation about?"

"The silver and purple auras talked about kings and gems, and the red and green ones spoke in numbers."

"Which numbers?"

Aera had tried so hard in the orb, yet Cyrrus was still unsatisfied. "I don't know..."

"Check your notebook."

"I didn't write *that*."

"Next time, commit the numbers to memory," Cyrrus commanded. "Write coded reminders before you go to sleep and test yourself in the morning. Once you learn to trust your memory, write nothing."

Aera would never remember those numbers. Nobody but Cyrrus could. "That's impossible," she groaned. "What do the numbers even mean?"

"What do they mean to you?"

"*You* asked me to memorize them. They mean something to you, not me."

Cyrrus grinned and said, "Do you hear the anger in your tone?"

"Because you're twisting my words on purpose!" she hissed. "I *hate* these stupid games."

Cyrrus stared at her with a blank expression.

"What?!" she demanded.

"Avoid the orb for a while," he said coolly. "And avoid Vaye until you regain your composure."

Aera wanted to smack his perfect face but focused on breathing until she calmed down. Perhaps he had a point.

Daily duties began with four torturous hours of History Class. Aera was excited to explore the associations she had made between the orb entities and archetypes, but her head throbbed, and she couldn't think. Once the lunch bell finally rang, she rushed to Great Gorge, where she took the archetype map from the pocket in the back of her notebook. Words trickled into each other and tumbled off the page. Every nerve was on edge.

Her eye went to the Ikrati sticks she'd collected by the tree. She found two short ones and twirled them. A gust of wind pushed her hair back, and she allowed it to guide her as she whirled about. She'd always been clumsy with two sticks but now the mechanics unfolded smoothly and her fingers adjusted. Each arm extended in turn, and the sticks flowed around each other in swift figure eights, creating an illusion of wings. Her body moved on its own as she surrendered to the wind. She imagined she was flying.

After a long, satisfying release, Aera returned to the book. She made a new circle that spanned two pages, copied the words from the original map, then wrote names that might match each archetype. She reviewed her notes from the previous night, destroyed them as Cyrrus requested, and added the auras to the appropriate categories.

Silver looked like water, and it was intuitive to group her with Vaye and Dila. All three were prideful and sensuous, perfectly suited for the archetype of seduction and abundance. Purple was also easy to place. He projected wind under stress, suggesting his emanations matched Vainina, whose archetype centered on detachment and liberating the mind. Aera associated those themes with people like Goric and Purple

395

because they appeared impersonal, bartering information without investment while their true agenda was occluded.

Pink was ambiguous, with no clear element, but her hyper-femininity and constant changes brought to mind the moon. Some auras revealed their elements more obviously than others.

Aera wondered what her own emanations looked like. Outside of the gray and green shades she saw when imitating Cyrrus, the only auras she noticed around herself were chaotic bursts of light and mist that sparkled with gold. The sunny shades matched her archetype, but what was the rest about? In her white dream forest, fog rose from the ground and turned into faces; in a later dream, she'd manipulated a lightning storm. This might be consistent with the chaos and the mist, but even if so, this was unrelated to the sun. Aera pondered what underlying factors might unite these elements, and what this symbolism indicated about *her*.

Though impatient to return to Elkandul and learn more, Aera resolved to follow Cyrrus's advice. She avoided both Vaye and the orb, passing her free time alone, musing over archetypes and sorting out ways to identify them. When Cyrrus was not sleeping or engaged with clan business, he spent breaks with her at Great Gorge, but she sensed him changing. Everything he once had cared about was now unimportant to him, and his sense of humor was missing. Aera wanted to talk about the orb or the Nestë, but he wanted only to write in his notebooks. When she expressed concern, he insisted he was enjoying his writing, even though he didn't look the slightest bit joyful.

Two weeks passed rapidly, and Aera checked the sky with dread, knowing the new moon would begin Cyrrus's tenure with the orb. Erelion burned more brightly each night as Alarië grew slimmer. Along with her, Aera's heightened senses receded.

On her final night with the orb, Aera tossed and turned in her closet, annoyed that tomorrow Cyrrus would repossess it. She was reluctant to relinquish it without using it again but still didn't feel quite normal. Cyrrus slept every day during his rotation and likely used it more often than she. Why wasn't he similarly affected?

Her mind chattered on. After a while, she heard the bell gong. Two hours had passed since curfew and, still, she was awake. Perhaps it would be okay if she visited Elkandul just for a short time. She could observe what was happening, briefly, and then exit.

She removed the orb from her pocket, unwrapped it and revealed its glorious stars. As she set her hands on the glass, tingles crawled up her arms. "*Ger beni ath cemmar...*"

The world faded to vibration, and Aera entered the realm. She was thrust into hot swirls of pink and beige that carried her along with them like a leaf in the wind. The whirl slowed enough for Aera to regain her bearings, and as the atmosphere cooled, two forms emerged. One was a cloudy beige androgynous shape and the other, a pink mass. Each was infused with the other's shades: the two had permeated each other's cloud.

Their conjoined colors vanished slowly, while their forms lingered in place. Aera felt uneasy, as if she'd intruded on a private moment between lovers. After a long silence, another form appeared on Aera's right, and she recognized its deep red angles. Soon came another, with harsh green lines beaming from its center.

"Twenty nineteen two one twenty seven. Five nineteen seven, fifteen five two one fourteen twenty-five, six nine one,[4]" said a rigid monotone. "Forty-one."

"Forty-one, forty-one, forty-one,[5]" responded another robotic voice.

Another entered: the purple gender shifter. Pink swirled and vanished, leaving behind a star.

"Eleven six twenty-five seven twenty seven. Twenty-two six three, four fifteen twenty ten two, four twenty-five three. Forty-one,[6]" said the monotone coming from Red.

"Forty-one," responded Green.

Garbles emerged around Purple and an androgynous voice said, "Interesting game you Kalaqhai play."

"Twenty nineteen two one twenty seven, forty-one, forty-one forty-one. Eleven six twenty-five seven twenty seven, forty-one forty-one forty-one,[7]" responded the red lines in a long, steady sequence.

"They want us to think this is a joke," Purple said, and angled toward Aera, indicating he was addressing her. "The numbers *must* have meaning."

It was obvious that the numbers had meaning, but Purple was uttering his usual empty phrases, this time directed at her. Cyrrus wanted her to respond as he would, but she had no idea what relationship he had with Purple or what he might have said. Everybody was silent, barely moving, waiting for her to do something. She wished Cyrrus had given her more information. Although she thought about taking matters into her own hands, she decided against it and exited.

Once her body was well enough, Aera tucked the orb away and lay down, contemplating Elkandul. By default, each apparition occupied a particular spot in the inner ring of stars, but there were often moments when their lights projected further through the circle, pushing Aera into a chaotic mess of energy pulsations. This time, Pink and Beige were whirling when she arrived, but everything felt natural, and the aerosphere was warm. Perhaps the painful sensations were present when the auras resisted something, whereas Pink and Beige had merged willfully. This was why Aera had sensed they were lovers. Might they be?

Cyrrus saw politics everywhere: in the orb, the sanctum, the commune. Aera went to the same places and found music, passion and archetypal connections, all of which Cyrrus dismissed. She had accepted his wisdom about the deceptive strategists in Elkandul, but her own experience revealed something more.

Still, now that she was back in the real world, the thought of orb love amused her. Sex without bodies? Did these lovers know what each other looked like? Before her time in Elkandul, the idea of a communion of floating colors would have seemed absurd, but that was now her reality. *This boundary will not bind us*, she thought, and remembered the hidden star. Colors painted her mind as she drifted to sleep.

∽

Bam! Bam!

Linealle's knock was thunderous and frightened Aera awake. It was overwhelming to step into her clothes, as tactile sensation was intensified to a painful degree.

398

Cyrrus found Aera in the lobby and directed her behind the hut, where he held out his hand without saying a word. Aera took the ball from her cloak and felt it sitting perfectly inside her palm, wrapped neatly in its silver home. Sadness overcame her as she passed it over, but the moment it left her grasp, she felt relieved.

Cyrrus burrowed it in his pocket and whispered, "What happened last night?"

Aera hoped he might cheer up now that she had some news to deliver. "Green and Red said some numbers, then Purple called them Kalaqhai and said the numbers must have meaning, which was obvious... but he wanted my attention for some reason."

She glanced at Cyrrus, hoping he might tell her why, but he only nodded, cueing her to continue.

"When I got there, the atmosphere was whirling and the pink and beige auras came out of it. They seemed—" She paused. She was about to say, *they seemed like lovers*, but Cyrrus wouldn't appreciate that. Instead, she concluded, "They seemed intertwined."

"Like lovers," Cyrrus said dryly.

Aera grinned: he had read her mind. "Love is a logical fallacy," she teased, "but it felt more private than a conversation about politics."

Cyrrus furrowed his brow and said tersely, "Elaborate on '*felt*.'"

Aera chuckled. His rigidity about feelings was oddly endearing. "Everything was hot and swirling. When they saw me, they separated and the pink one disappeared."

"What *felt* more private?" Cyrrus pressed. "What's your logic?"

"I told you already," she said, "but it's pointless to explain feelings to someone who pretends not to have them."

Cyrrus glared at her with a whimsical expression, then strutted away. Aera groaned. He was so concerned about what she did in the orb, yet never discussed what *he* did in there. The orb had made him paranoid. Clearly, he was hiding something.

GAMES

1328 EARLY-AUTUMN

The explosion of Aera's senses faded slowly. She avoided Vaye and spent her free time in the woods, as Cyrus was either asleep or missing. By the second week, she felt normal enough to visit the cottage.

Vaye's upstairs curtains were open, but she wasn't around. Aera sat down and caressed the piano keys. Some were worn, with small lines and crevices appreciable to the touch, while others were smooth. She closed her eyes to absorb the unique texture of each key until, finally, she struck some.

The sound of hammers awakening strings was soothing. She drew out slow chords. Their warm resonance evoked the lush sensation that made her heart thump in the orb. With eyes closed, her body melted as she tasted each texture. Then, the door opened and Vaye came in carrying a pumpkin. Aera stopped playing and smiled to greet her.

"Your ballad lured me in," Vaye said. "Please, don't stop."

Aera looked at the piano keys. She remembered the notes she had played, but the feeling eluded her. To portray Ivory, Aera would have to limit herself to mechanical patterns.

"Thanks," Aera said, "but I was about to practice scales."

Vaye looked at her for a long moment, and Aera searched her face for any sign of reaction. Though Vaye's eyes were thoughtful, Aera couldn't read her emotions.

"I'll make us some tea," Vaye said, and headed into the kitchen.

Aera practiced as the room filled with the aroma of apple and pumpkin spices. Vaye moved about from the fireplace to the kitchen, then emerged with two steaming mugs and placed them on the table near the fireplace. Aera sat in one chair and Vaye, the other.

Vaye perched at the edge of her seat, slowly sipping her tea. As the two drank, neither spoke. Vaye was too close. Aera inhaled deeply and thought of nothing but her belly as she exhaled.

"Aera," Vaye said calmly, but intently. "Do you trust me?"

Aera concentrated on her breath and reviewed the question: *Do you trust me?* No answer came to mind.

"I'm not here to enforce laws," Vaye continued. "My concern is that you haven't been yourself lately."

I am always myself, Aera thought, but it sounded defensive. She straightened her back and projected a calm facade.

"Let me ask you again," Vaye said slowly. "Do you trust me?"

Aera's brow couldn't possibly be relaxed enough. *Trust,* she thought. As she searched for a response, the room spun. She focused on Vaye and mirrored her serene demeanor.

Vaye watched Aera with an unreadable expression, then asked in a gentler voice, "Do you trust anyone?"

Behind Vaye's affectionate tone, she was probing for information. That warm facade might disarm Aera, but it wouldn't fool Ivory.

"A response would be redundant," Ivory said coolly. "You already know my thoughts and feelings."

Vaye's eyes rested on the fire. After a long stare into the flames, she said, "You have a gift for capturing the vocal cadences of others."

Aera felt naked: Vaye had noticed her channeling Cyrrus. Her eyes landed on the girl in the painting, whose gaze penetrated the canvas, measuring her every move.

"I need to go," Aera said. "Curfew."

Vaye nodded.

From the doorway, Aera turned back and saw Vaye watching her with an expression free of anger but tinged with sadness. Aera could not leave fast enough. She closed the door behind her, and a chilly wind slapped her face.

As she headed away, she felt weak and depleted. Vaye was annoyingly secretive and difficult to read, but her sorrow was piercing. If Aera had stayed any longer, she might have cracked. How long could she keep up the act before Vaye discovered her secrets? Something had to change. Ivory was not strong enough.

She headed back to Junior Hut. In the distance, she spotted Cyrrus crossing the bridge, heading toward the hut from the opposite direction. With a flat expression, he watched her approach.

Aera tried to weigh his mood, but his blank gaze revealed nothing. She grinned to greet him and said, "Vaye is suspicious of me."

Cyrrus stopped walking but showed no other reaction. His thick hair was clumped together and there was shadowy stubble on his face which Aera had never before seen, as he usually visited the shaving attendants at baths.

"Think of something else you are hiding," Cyrrus suggested. "Illegal knowledge or actions. Focus on hiding that from her instead. She may figure it out, but her suspicion will be deflected away from the orb."

This was a workable idea. Aera was glad she'd asked.

"Next time she questions you, put her on the defensive," Cyrrus continued. "Ask questions so she will focus on concealing parts of her own knowledge. Battle with her, secret for secret, but with only some secrets on the table. Be Ivory pretending to be Aera."

Ask questions, Aera thought. *Battle with her, secret for secret.* Cyrrus played similar games with her.

"I trust you to handle Vaye," Cyrrus said plainly. "I am more concerned about what you do in Elkandul."

"I told you—"

"Everyone has an agenda. You should too."

Aera had an agenda indeed: matching the auras to elements. She was reluctant to tell Cyrrus, since he didn't appreciate archetypes and surely would consider the exercise frivolous. But she decided it was better than appearing aimless. She widened her eyes, smiled coyly and said, "I've been matching the auras with natural elements to find their archetypes."

Cyrrus furrowed his brow. "The *indiva* symbol links me to Nephrië on your map. What do you suppose music looks like?"

"I don't know," she admitted. "I haven't figured it all out, and I'm not convinced that any of it matters. But I notice Silver looks watery and acts prideful, like the people I associate with *heneissë*, and Purple turns to wind and acts impersonal like the *onophayaniva* group."

"I see," Cyrrus said. "Have you categorized the others?"

"Pink might be *veskarassë*, since she changes shape like the moon, and her beige lover may be *ilissunviva* like me, since he has a strong presence, but stays quiet. Orange has show-off wings and acts severe like Nurin... so maybe *niskuissieva*. Red and Green are blank. I can't place them."

"What's the advantage of knowing everyone's category?"

Aera enjoyed making sense of the world, but Cyrrus was always looking to gain something. She offered, "Each archetype has structural weaknesses."

Cyrrus nodded. "Your observations may be useful, but I encourage you to incorporate a more concrete agenda."

"What's yours?"

"Experimenting."

"That's vague."

"I need to sleep."

"You want me to act like you," Aera reminded him. "I need to know what you're doing."

Cyrrus looked right at her and softened his tone. "I can't risk someone reading your thoughts," he said. "It will have to wait."

Aera nodded uneasily. His excuse was legitimate, but she doubted it was the only reason he concealed his orb endeavors. She wondered when he would deign to tell her more.

Throughout Cyrrus's turn with the orb, Aera spent more time at the cottage, hoping to avert any problems. Vaye did not question her and the two cohabited the piano room as usual. Despite the lack of confrontation, Aera sensed Vaye was suspicious of her. There was nothing overtly different, yet Vaye's gait was especially silent, her expression irritatingly remote, her personal barrier more profoundly impenetrable.

Cyrrus avoided Aera with increasing regularity, but she couldn't miss his lack of concern about the world and his hygiene. It was easy to infer he was using the orb every night. With both Vaye and Cyrrus so distant, and the commune so boring, the microcosm of Elkandul—oddly and paradoxically—was the only thing that kept Aera sane. She could hardly wait to learn more about the mysterious apparitions and watched Alárië expanding each night as Erelion's sheen was swallowed by her glow. When the moon was full, it would be Aera's turn with the orb. Alárië couldn't possibly grow fast enough.

Finally, the first morning of Autumn came and Aera awakened early, eager to start the day. Cyrrus took some muffins from Unity Festival and, to her surprise, summoned her to Great Gorge. She situated herself on her branch and took a bite of her muffin, pleased to find it was apple flavored, her favorite. Cyrrus had apparently rushed and fought through the crowd to get it for her.

"Tonight, our punishment is over. We will have to sleep with our..." he paused, raised a brow, and concluded: "...brothers and sisters."

Aera had forgotten about that. It would be impossible to use the crystal ball with others around. She now understood why Cyrrus had brought her there: he wanted to soften the blow.

"Next season, when we move to the Adolescent Hut, we won't have a curfew anymore," Cyrrus continued. "In the meantime, I will hold onto the orb."

Aera glared at him.

"Life is a game," Cyrrus said. "The best player wins."

Aera didn't want her life to be a game, yet Cyrrus lured her into playing. She considered insulting him back but couldn't find perfect enough words.

"Any update on Vaye?" Cyrrus asked.

Vaye seemed distant, but Aera had no concrete information. Since Cyrrus pretended not to understand feelings, she elected not to respond.

"I want you to engage her today," he said. "Remember what I told you—ask questions and battle her secret for secret. Tonight, you can decide whether you wish to hold the orb."

He removed from the gorge an unfamiliar red leather tome, balanced it on his knees and began writing meticulous foreign characters on a crisp, slender page. Somehow, he found time to dye leathers, concoct different types of paper, bind the pages, manage his clan, write in numerous languages, and attend town meetings, all while engaging the orb. No wonder he forsook baths and ignored Aera.

As she combed her hair, she considered Cyrrus's advice. He wanted her to deflect any mind-reading away from the orb by directing Vaye's attention to other secrets that Aera and Vaye were keeping from each other. Everything in Vaye's life was part of some secret: the forehead-bands, the vials in her kitchen, the mysterious symbols on her wall, the white-haired girl. Perhaps Ivory could focus on Vaye's secrets and reveal a few of her own to obtain more information. *Ask questions*, she reminded herself. That was easy enough.

Keeping this strategy in mind, Aera headed to the cottage. Vaye was rotating chunks of meat over the fire and the cottage smelled spicy and delicious.

With a smile, Vaye asked, "Some bison, dear?"

Aera watched as Vaye finessed the meat back and forth with rhythmic grace. When ready, Vaye pushed it onto a plate, then went to the kitchen and returned with tea. Aera tasted the meat and noted the subtle sweetness of the spice was unlike anything the commune served. Did Vaye pick up ingredients during her mysterious journeys? Were they enjoying Nestëan recipes?

She looked at Vaye, who watched her pensively, a suede band around her forehead as always, presumably covering an *esil*. "I learned about the Nestë," Aera said gently. "I heard they use a technique called *inyanondo* to read minds. Is that true?"

Vaye inspected Aera with warm amusement in her eyes but didn't respond.

"How do the Nestë keep secrets from each other?" Aera persisted.

"How do you keep secrets?"

"I don't say them aloud," Aera said. "But a mind-reader would know them anyway."

"*Why* do you keep secrets?" Vaye asked.

"Because I don't want to be punished."

"Have you ever kept a secret from a person who wouldn't punish you?"

Vaye was deflecting from the topic of *inyanondo*, but Aera decided to indulge her for now to keep her talking. She considered the question. Vaye would be unlikely to punish her for anything, but she couldn't be certain. Cyrrus had no authority to punish her, yet she kept secrets from him all the time. "Yes..."

"Why?"

She tried to summon an appropriate answer and offered, "I don't always want people to know what I think of them."

"We sense how others receive us through body language, vocal affectations, and touch," Vaye said. "Words are often used to obfuscate truth."

Aera nodded; she knew this all too well.

"Do you think other people are unaware of your sentiments?" Vaye inquired.

Cyrrus surely knew Aera obsessed over him, though she refused to admit it aloud. This was clearly illogical. Still, she tried to come up with a logical reason for it and offered, "People make assumptions about each other all the time, but they can't be sure unless I tell them." She knew her statement was disingenuous, since words could lie more easily than the body, but she was curious how Vaye would respond without revealing herself as a practitioner of *inyanondo*.

"What would happen if they knew?" Vaye asked with a smile.

Aera considered this. The thought of Cyrrus knowing how much she needed him made her feel vulnerable, yet she didn't want to say that; it made her sound weak. Cyrrus used other people's admiration for personal gain: that was a realistic problem. Slowly, she said, "They might try to use it to... control me."

"How can they control you?"

"Through manipulation. Or... cruelty."

"You can simply ignore them," Vaye said. "People often lose interest in being cruel to those who pay them no heed."

"Not everyone," Aera pointed out. "Renstrom Nurin would be cruel whether I reacted or not."

"Nurin doesn't punish out of cruelty. He binds the community together."

"He insults people," Aera protested.

"Unity helps us avoid war and poverty," Vaye explained. "We share labor, and we're rewarded with resources, education, and safety. To prevent chaos, our leaders humiliate people for any differences. You use secrecy to protect yourself."

Nurin could have done all those things without insulting anyone, but Aera decided this was going nowhere and reverted to asking questions, as she had originally intended. "What about the Nestëan cultures? Do they have to keep secrets?"

Vaye rested her warm eyes on Aera and said sweetly, "The Nestë were driven to protect their knowledge from enemies."

The Nestë were driven. Were. Vaye was referring to historic events and avoiding any indication that the Nestë still existed, but Aera knew that Vaye, herself, was one of them.

Aera looked at Vaye's headband and pictured the glow beneath it. Though Aera stared, she softened her eyes to show she wasn't angry at Vaye for keeping secrets. Vaye returned the knowing but undisturbed expression. They had exposed their secrets in a look, even if not verbally.

"How did they conceal knowledge if they could read each other's thoughts?" Aera asked.

"*Inyanondo* was not a tactic they used to expose secrets," Vaye replied. "It was a natural awareness which allowed them to experience the world together. It was part of their nature."

Vaye's explanation was romantic, but unrealistic. Cyrrus used *inyanondo* to control people, even animals, and Vaye likely used it to figure out what Aera was thinking and doing without consent. It was inevitable that, if someone had such a capability, they would use it to advance their purpose.

"You use your eyes to see me and your ears to hear me," Vaye said. "Empathy allows you to feel me, and it's more difficult to ignore empathy than to engage it. *Inyanondo* worked similarly for the Nestë. It was a sense they had of each other's inner rhythm."

'Inner rhythm' sounded harmless, but Cyrrus used *inyanondo* to read Aera's mind. Surely, the Nestë did the same. "If a Nestë suspected someone was lying, wouldn't she read their mind to figure it out?"

"Seeking is not the same as listening," Vaye replied. "If you evidence deceit, you are likely correct. If you expect to be deceived and look for signs, you might fool yourself into perceiving them. The truth, then, is harder to discern."

No matter what Aera asked, Vaye would never admit to spying on her thoughts. She was sick of being disadvantaged by Cyrrus and Vaye reading her like a book. She wanted to master *inyanondo* herself but was uncertain whether she had the innate capability for magic. Shyly, she asked, "How would someone know if they have Nestë heritage?"

"Self-awareness is a lifestyle choice. There are mirrors everywhere, but one must choose to see."

Vague, Aera thought. She offered Vaye a grin anyway. Vaye returned it, then retreated to the kitchen.

Aera went to the piano bench and channeled Ivory as she played some notes from a book on the music rack. Vaye moved about the cottage, watering plants and tidying, exuding consummate serenity. Aera wished she could 'sense' what Vaye was thinking.

The day passed quickly as Vaye and Aera shared another meal, then played music together and treated their hair. Cyrrus's techniques went nowhere with Vaye, and Aera couldn't determine whether Vaye was unaware of her secrets or pretended to be. When the curfew bell rang, she felt defeated. After spending all that time with Vaye, she still had nothing to report to Cyrrus.

She returned to Junior Hut, where Linealle awaited. "Get your clothing, Samie Eh-ruh. Let's go."

Aera gathered her things reluctantly. She'd hated the closet at first, but once they had found the orb, it had become a sanctuary. Now she would be stuck with the Samies all the time, who would keep her from doing what she wanted, as always.

She headed downstairs and into the girls' quarters, where she met a wall of noise. Within the chatter, insults emerged.

"Look, it's Cyrrus's shadow!"

"Did Brains lick your wee-wee in the closet?"

Aera bristled, but before she had time to react, Officer Linealle swung open the door. Everyone quieted at once.

"Samie Abani!"

"Here!"

"Samie Eh-ruh!"

"Here."

While Linealle rattled off names, Aera found her old mat in the corner and tossed her things onto the shelf. She thought of Vaye, who had counseled her to ignore cruelty. Although it sounded wise in theory, she couldn't imagine Vaye tolerating such indignity herself.

Gaili greeted Aera, and Aera forced a grin, though she would have preferred everyone to drown.

The moment Linealle left, the flock exploded in a flurry of yelps. Doriline squealed loudest of all: "Go back to the pantry where you belong, Eh-ruh!"

"Go hang yourself in the slaughterhouse," Gaili bellowed back at her.

"Go back to the pig pen, fattie!" Novi retorted.

Laughter abounded and Doriline snarled, "Cyrrus will never be your boyfriend, Eh-ruh. He might think you're smart, but he'll *never* kiss you because you look like a boy."

"Keep saying my name, Doriline!" Aera roared back in a booming voice. "You're obsessed with me!"

The hens gasped but said not a word. They were clearly thrown off guard by Aera's unexpected vocal power and rage, but nobody was more shocked than Aera herself. Gaili glanced at her with a look of surprise, and they both burst into laughter.

The door opened again, and a glimmer of firelight dispelled the darkness. Cyrrus posed in the doorway with an iron torch from the hall, effecting an impressive silhouette, and a silence fell over the room.

"I am conducting an experiment," Cyrrus announced. "You are invited to participate, on the assumption that you have a free will and desire to exercise it."

The room was so quiet, Aera could hear her breath. She snickered while the others ogled the peacock.

"If you want to talk in private, or read, or philander with the boys, I propose you do it!" he said. "We're not permitted to leave the building, but no law mandates we cannot be in the hallway or in each other's rooms." With that, he disappeared.

Voices filled the room, but this time nobody dared to spout insults. Aera wondered what Cyrrus was planning. She exchanged a chuckle with Gaili, then went to find him.

Already, people from the other dorms were out in the hallway. Farris and Mivar were arm wrestling for an audience outside their room while Kize and Pelyane huddled over a book in the staircase. Aera suspected that if Cyrrus was not with the clan, he probably had gone underground.

She made sure nobody was looking in her direction, then slipped into the dark corridor and darted toward the spare room. The door was ajar, and Cyrrus was sitting on the ledge inside, holding his torch and staring at the open floor that revealed the passageway.

Aera slammed the door closed behind her and demanded, "Cyrrus, you can't just—"

Before she could say another word, Officer Linealle burst through the door and barked, "By Riva's Trees, get back to your rooms!"

"I am on your side, Linealle," Cyrrus said. "I created an alibi for you. The other Samies will keep you occupied so you won't be responsible if someone else should find us."

"Raisins," Linealle murmured, though her voice held no conviction.

"When I am elected Renstrom, you will be free to explore underground and study *sarya* as openly as you please. All I ask is that you grant us... privacy."

Cyrrus gave Linealle a knowing look, and Aera's legs turned to jelly. Did he have to say *privacy?* The implication was mortifying... though Cyrrus pretended not to notice.

Without missing a beat, he added, "You know as well as I that there is nothing to discover down there since the passageways have shifted."

Linealle froze in place, her expression stolid and her posture stiff.

"I appreciate your understanding," Cyrrus said. "A time will come when it will be substantially rewarded."

Cyrrus cast a glance at Aera, and the two headed down the stairs. The floor closed above them, followed by a door slam. Linealle was gone.

Cyrrus waited at the bottom of the staircase. As he looked at Aera, his green eyes caught a reflection of his torchlight. "Take the orb around the corner," he said, and handed her the torch. "I'll keep guard."

A smile spilled over Aera's face. She was not expecting that.

"I am glorious, am I not?" Cyrrus teased.

"Your *semissë* is well developed," she said, imitating his flippant tone. "But your *suru* is too sterile for glory."

"You sound just like me," Cyrrus said. "If I had never met me, I might even call *you* glorious."

Aera grinned at the rare compliment as Cyrrus reached into his cloak pocket and handed her the orb. In the firelight, his eyes looked especially alive. With his hair exploding and stubble darkening, there was something diabolical about him, less pristine, but more gripping.

Cyrrus stared back at her, perhaps reading her thoughts. She blushed and hurried away. After rounding a few bends, Aera was satisfied that she was alone.

She settled on a landing between four staircases, set the starry globe on its shiny fabric, and extinguished the torch. The glow of the orb was so bright that the stairs around her were still visible. She sat cross-legged before the sphere and admired the starlight against her palms.

"*Ger beni ath cemmar,*" she chanted. "*Ger beni ath cemmar...*"

The familiar vibrations beset her as all senses dispersed and recombined. Once she adjusted, she surveyed the circle and saw no auric forms or colors. She hovered among two rings of twinkling stars.

"*Ë áldëa si,*[1]" she said. Her voice bounced back from the nexus in a crystalline tone while the atmosphere glimmered with gold. She wondered what would happen if she evoked Cyrrus and crisply declared, "Life is a game." His voice echoed back with a flash of deep green and the ambience blackened.

Aera was alone. She had sole control of the circle, as all light and sound emanated from her. What might she conjure now, all on her own? She recalled Vaye's advice and channeled each nuance as she said, "There are mirrors everywhere, but one must choose to see." Vaye's rich voice rumbled through the sphere as earthy hues abounded.

"I reach to the sky-y-y for a cloud to come and catch me," she crooned. A strong voice emerged from the center, with visceral depth and smooth vibrato—the voice she had always imagined! "I reach to the sky," she repeated, and a wind sensation flowed through her. The atmosphere was alive.

She wondered what Cyrrus did when he was alone in Elkandul. Softly, she sang, "Tell me, Deity, tell me secrets..."

The voice that rebounded from the center was chilling, the atmosphere ghostly still. "Secrets of the wound in your heart, the loneliness you pretend not to feel. No one ever saw it before, but it's clear to me your facade isn't real..."

Grey mist spread about, creating a film of fog. "One look into your steely eyes and I see the pain. Hidden under control, detachment you strive to feign..."

The cloud thickened as she pronounced the word 'detachment,' and a sunbeam shone through the greyness, exposing its contour.

"Bold, unfeeling, glimmering with pride, glamor concealing the mess you made inside..."

Aera felt suffocated and blasted the fog with a white-hot bolt. She was becoming the song—sensing it, seeing it—as her cry tore through the cloud and enslaved it. "Fools are pining to worship your veneer, never divining the cries I learned to hear, the prison of your fear, the shimmer of your crown..."

The vigorous voice assaulted each note with glorious fury, and Aera roared like a storm, spinning the smog with the force of frustration whirling through her. She sang the remainder of the song, violating the atmosphere with each syllable.

Take me, deity, take me closer

Closer to the dream in my heart
The magical life in the wild unknown
No one ever saw it before
If you take me away, we can find our way home

Love is locked in a cage of lies
And I am the key
Your prison is knowing too well
The burden of being free

Dramatizing the magic of your mind
How mesmerizing, the clues you leave behind
Introspection weaves into a maze
Webs of deflection spiral in a haze
You hide a million ways
And my dreams come crashing down

As the last note faded, Aera pulsated along to the rhythm of the song. *Thump, thump. Thump, thump...*

Heat throbbed in her heart and surged through her. Something, or someone, was infusing her. She stared ahead and found herself locked into the same black spot as before, but there was no light, no star... nothing. As she hunted the magnetic blackness, the drum in her chest deepened. *Thump, thump...*

Across the way, there appeared a tiny light, pulsing from blue to black, locked in rhythm with her slow, sumptuous heartbeat. *Thump, thump.* The glow swelled and retracted, enslaving her pulse in sympathetic harmony. Each throb pumped heat from her chest and undulated through her until she was bursting, coming apart. Her spirit radiated in the open...

...exposed.

She was not alone. She was naked and shaken, submitting to some irresistible power that bewitched, frightened, and aroused her. Those vulnerable lyrics tore open her heart. Stupid, stupid, stupid. She needed to gain control.

Static exploded from her in grays, whites, and greens. *Stop emoting,* she implored herself. All that mattered was that she remain anonymous, lest the stranger behind the force reveal her to the others. As far as the interloper knew, Aera could have been Cyrrus, imitating a female singer. But why would he? Cyrrus never acted without purpose.

Suddenly, it hit her: if Cyrrus could conceive of music, he might well have used it as a device to lure the black spot out of hiding. *Life is a game,* she thought. She was Cyrrus now, and Cyrrus needed to win.

All traces of color disappeared from the sphere. The pulse stopped and the blue light vanished, but Aera knew someone was still there, as his spot was devoid of a star, cloaked in blackness. The sorcerer couldn't hide behind that shadow anymore. He had fallen victim to the lure of music and exposed himself.

"Your heart is bigger than your brain," Aera articulated coolly, and Cyrrus's voice rebounded back from the center.

Nothing happened. The air was still, everything silent. She stared toward the black spot, but it was no longer there: a star had appeared in its place, completing the circle. Aera was alone.

Elkandul belonged to her just as she wished, and it was safe to sing now, but music evaded her. She felt formless... empty. The thump of her pulse was missing, the heat was gone and the crystal world, colorless. She had no will to sing anymore.

She turned toward the star behind her and muttered her incantation until vibration enveloped her. Then she was numb, huddled over the glowing orb in the dark, desolate labyrinth.

Aera squeezed her hands and felt the usual pins and needles in her fingers. She flexed one limb at a time until the vibrations wore away, then finally lit her torch, wrapped the orb and burrowed it in her pocket. As she climbed the stairs, she thought of the mysterious blue light pulsating with her heart. That same force had flooded her senses before, cloaked in shadow, but she hadn't been certain it was real. Why did it reveal itself to her now? What did it want?

"Stop thinking," bolted Cyrrus's crisp voice. "You're making me dizzy."

Aera's cheeks flushed; she'd been too preoccupied to recognize that she was approaching the main stairwell and had completely forgotten about Cyrrus. She straightened up, glided down the staircase and turned gracefully into the main stairwell, where Cyrrus was leaning against the wall with a book propped against his knees. Two candles and a bottle of ink sat on the stairs above him, and he was wielding a quill.

"I was writing a book," Cyrrus intoned, "until I was distracted by your mental avalanche."

She crouched on the staircase across from him and challenged, "What avalanche?"

"You were deliberating why the auras shifted appearance and whether your interactions had hidden meaning. Frivolous thoughts. Everything is affected by perception, and everybody is a mirror of everybody else. This is how emotion works and why it must be overcome by reason." He furrowed his brow and added, "What event were you questioning?"

Aera focused on the flame of his candle. "I felt physical sensations more than usual," she said. "I was trying to figure out why."

Cyrrus stared ahead for a moment, then inquired, "Did anything else happen?"

"Nothing out of the ordinary."

"Your *semissë* collapsed because you felt sensations?" He paused. "Who else was there when that happened?"

Slowly and evenly, Aera said, "I was alone."

Cyrrus glared at Aera. Torchlight shone in his emerald eyes as he probed her, and she watched the flames dance in his irises.

"Your motives are opaque," Cyrrus said crisply. "But Ivory needs to employ tighter logic."

Aera straightened her posture but didn't respond.

"You are too advanced to be discomposed by such an occurrence," Cyrrus said. "I cannot *read* that you are lying, but I *deduce* it. Your skills require refinement."

"There's a hole in your story," Aera said. "Why would I lie to you?"

"You let something slip and fear my criticism," he offered.

"If I feared criticism, I would have cut you off years ago."

Cyrrus did not respond. He looked down at his book and began to write.

"Any other reason?" Aera pressed.

"Not now," he retorted without looking up. "If your illogic continues to betray you, I will deduce your motive, even if you cannot."

Aera chuckled. "You sound paranoid."

"Transparent attempt at deflection," Cyrrus said. "Also, presumptuous. To experience paranoia, I would have to ascribe to you sufficient agency to constitute a threat."

Agency? What a jerk... and anyway, that was a lie. He was indeed afraid of her exposing too much.

His quill moved swiftly across the page as he buried himself in thought. If Aera's actions had any effect on him, he did a masterful job of hiding it. She leaned the torch against the wall for him and continued up the stairs to her room. The moment her head hit the pillow, images of starry skies took over, then a forest...

～

Aera was alone, surrounded by white trees with pearly doves dressing every branch. Their coos colored the night. "Wrr-oooo! Wrrr-oooo!"

Something rustled behind her, and she turned, but her view was obscured by mist glowing in the moonlight. The ambience shifted in the distance as a whisk of fur slid between shadows.

"Wrr-ooo?" cooed the doves. "Wrr-ooo?"

A silhouetted figure emerged from behind a tree, cloaked in a pelt. Beneath its hood was a blaze of blue and within its luster, two eyes burned. Their gaze fixed on Aera and pulled her in. *Thump, thump. Thump, thump...*

The eyes faded and disappeared, shrouded in shadow. Aera searched around but discovered only trees and birdsong. To lure the stranger out of hiding, she cooed a melody: "Ahh, ahh, ahh..."

Her tone was vivid and bold, just as in Elkandul. A smile came on as she floated between the notes and slid stealthily from one to the next. "Ahh, ahh, ahh..."

Azure mist rose in the distance and lit up the night. Aera moved toward it and purred as she felt its heat. Then, the glow evaporated, leaving the forest cold.

Lyrics spun through her mind along with the same tune, and she sang them aloud. "Under the moonlight, I lie in your shadow..."

The mist radiated hot blue, but Aera couldn't locate any form. Her voice sang on its own, "The chill of midnight won't cool our passion..."

Within the brume, there appeared a bare-chested boy with stormy hair and starry eyes. His gaze was at once soulful and feral, desirous and demure. Aera's heart thudded. *Thump, thump...*

He locked her into his hypnotic stare but moved no closer. As he drank her in with increasing abandon, his form blended into the mist until she saw only his hungry blue eyes. She urged herself toward him but could not move, as her pulse was too heavy. *Thump, thump.* She tried to sing, but nothing came out. She was locked in place, helpless and entranced, as each heartbeat unraveled more wildly than the last. *Thump, thump. Thump, thump...*

~

Aera gasped for air and found herself sitting up on her mat, clasping her chest as it throbbed violently amidst snores and breathing of other sleepers. She rubbed her temples and collected herself. As her frenzy relented, she reached quietly into her cloak and retrieved her notebook to scribe the lyrics.

> *Under the moonlight, I lie in your shadow*
> *The chill of midnight won't cool our...*

The pencil shook as her hand froze in place. She breathed deeply, then wrote the last word, one letter at a time. *P... a... s... s... i... o... n.*

Her cheeks burned. *Passion.* If Cyrus heard this song playing in her mind, he would mock her mercilessly...

...or would he be jealous of her passion for someone else? Would he feel betrayed?

Stop dreaming, Aera scolded herself. *Come back to reality.*

Cyrus didn't want her to have any impact on him at all: she didn't have enough 'agency' to be a 'threat.' She almost laughed but pursed her lips to contain any sound.

She returned the notebook quietly to her cloak pocket, lay down and closed her eyes. Music haunted her, and she imagined a piano accompanying her chimerical voice. *The chill of midnight won't cool our passion...*

UNITY

1328 EARLY-AUTUMN

The dorm was unbearable as the Samies awakened to the stench of body odor and an onslaught of voices. Aera dressed quickly and dragged herself upstairs. She remembered the insatiable eyes in her dream, denuding and devouring her. *Under the moonlight, I lie in your shadow...*

"Eh-ruh! Move!"

Farris raced past Aera and bounded out the door. The Junior Hut exit was before her and Samies were rushing by. Where was Cyrrus? Would he hear her thoughts? If he caught her mooning over romantic fantasies, she would never hear the end of it.

With a slow, deep breath, she summoned Ivory, then braced herself against the blinding sun and headed outside. To her relief, a grey haze covered the sky. The air tasted like rain, though none had yet fallen.

She climbed to the boulder and surveyed Vapid Village, where Pelyane and Kize stood near the Dining Hall entrance, engaging passersby. From Aera's vantage, Pelyane's rapid fire talkathon moved in and out of earshot with the wind, but she caught some phrases:

"We *should* be allowed to hang our drawings."

"Individual music performances would make Unity Festival *interesting*."

"Showing our artwork would strengthen our bonds!"

Pelyane was parading Cyrrus's cause and, beside her, Kize reeled people in. Most headed behind the Administration Unit into the courtyard entrance. Aera watched everyone follow the same path, one after the other until the last stragglers disappeared, and the Field cleared. She considered going to Great Gorge to indulge her daydreams, but curiosity got the best of her, and she headed to the town meeting.

As she moved through the tunnel, an onslaught of noise in the courtyard grew louder and more irritating. Every log was jammed with people, and the periphery was overstuffed with bodies crowding the walls. The only unoccupied spaces were the aisle and a small circle around Nurin's tree stump proscenium.

Aera's temples throbbed as she was overwhelmed by sensory input. She turned to leave but then heard her name.

"Aera!" Gaili called. "Here!"

Gaili and Olleroc were smushed together at the end of a log, and they nudged in, making room for Aera to squinch in. She felt guilty turning down a friendly gesture and reluctantly squeezed into her spot.

Momentarily, Renstrom Nurin emerged from the door behind the podium, walked imperiously to the lectern and mounted it with acerbic poise, ostentatiously impervious to the unexpectedly large gathering. He enacted the requisite salute and the crowd stood. Aera noted an increased scent of armpits as they raised their arms and chanted, "We are all the same! We are all the same!"

Aera's ears ached as voices boomed between the brick walls. As usual, she didn't acknowledge the obligatory canard. Beside her, Gaili and Olleroc also remained silent.

After several repetitions, Nurin lowered his arms and the crowd followed suit. He cleared his throat and said, "Since I notice and welcome many younger Samies here today, let me begin with you. If you wish to speak, you may raise your hand."

Near the front, Pelyane shot her hand up. Nurin ordered, "Samie Pelyane, rise."

Pelyane stood on her log as Aera once had but, unlike Aera, she was cheerful and comfortable. "I propose that individual artists, musicians and dancers be permitted to perform and exhibit their work at Unity Festival."

Pelyane spoke clearly and confidently. Cyrrus had reason to be impressed with her. Aera wondered if he had trained her. Despite chubby cheeks and a crooked smile, her enthusiasm made her attractive.

"Music is communal," Nurin declared. "Any who wish to perform may assemble a group of twelve or more and select from a list of appropriate compositions."

Nurin was bluffing. In the Book of Laws, there was no mention of twelve participants or specific compositions. It stated only that collective works could be performed; technically, 'collective' might mean two people.

"If we could *enjoy* music together, it would make our communal bond stronger," Pelyane bubbled, "and more people would attend Unity Festival!"

Weak argument, Aera thought. Apparently Pelyane didn't know the laws. If Cyrrus were there, he would have recited them, since that was the most effective way to beat Nurin. It occurred to Aera then that she, herself, could cite laws. She pictured herself rising confidently and outshining Pelyane.

With his chin in the air, Nurin said, "If the goal is to attract people to Unity Festival, it would be more efficient to amend the law and require attendance."

"I cannot abide rejiggering canon for such pedestrian crapulence!" bellowed Justinar Dinad from the front row. Some shuffling and laughter followed.

Aera moved to raise her hand, and her heartbeat hastened. There were eyes and faces everywhere, just like the day when she'd mounted her log, sweating and shaking like a fool. Images crashed into her mind: Nurin towering over her, the audience laughing at her, Cyrrus probing as her shiny mane dropped to the ground.

She breathed deeply and implored herself to project Ivory... but still could not raise her hand. What if she messed up? The Samies were watching, ready to exploit any mistake. She didn't want to risk making a fool of herself while Pelyane shone so brightly. Yet, she couldn't let this argument go.

She turned to Gaili and whispered, "The Law book says collective works can be performed. It doesn't list any compositions... and two or more people makes a collective."

"Tell him," Gaili whispered.

"The Renstrom doesn't like me."

Gaili nodded, raised her arm and held it firmly in the air while Pelyane and Nurin argued on.

"People don't come to Unity Festival because the stage show is repetitive," Pelyane said. "If the performances were more interesting and personal, people would *want* to come."

"Displays of a personal nature promote vanity and competition. This would undermine the sentiment of unity which the Festival celebrates." Noticing Gaili's hand, Nurin said, "Yes, Samie Gaili."

Gaili lowered her arm but didn't speak. She was trembling.

"Take your time, Samie Gaili," Nurin said.

The crowd laughed, but Gaili remained determined and hoisted herself up. "The Law says we're allowed to perform collective works," she said, speaking choppily in her nervousness. "A collective can be two people."

A few rows back, Novi interjected, "Or one really fat person."

Laughter erupted and Nurin demanded, "Enough!"

The crowd quieted, but Gaili was flustered, frozen in place. Aera felt sick. If she'd been more courageous herself, she might have spared Gaili. She wished she had never come.

Nurin cleared his throat and resumed. "In the context of that law, the function of a collective is to inspire unity. Pairs of performers would inevitably compete to outshine one another, which would cause division."

Pelyane's hand shot up in the air again and Gaili finally sat down. Aera looked at her, feeling guilty, but couldn't think of anything to say.

"Samie Pelyane," Nurin called flatly.

Pelyane rose enthusiastically, even more upbeat than before, apparently untroubled by her failure to cite the statute. "I propose we follow the law, just the way it is, and change the rules of Unity Festival so that after the feast, groups of two or more can perform." She paused briefly and added, "I propose a vote!"

"Proposal rejected," Nurin asserted.

"By law, authorities *can't* reject a proposal for a vote without cause!"

"While that phrase is part of the code, the prime mandate of leadership is to uphold standards for unity and equality. That directive supersedes all code."

"Arbitrary and capricious," bolted Cyrrus's voice.

Aera turned and saw Cyrrus posing in the entranceway with his hair neatly tied back, his outfit clean, and his posture, impeccable. Somehow his stubble from the previous night had disappeared, though the shaving blades belonged to bathing attendants and baths were not available until lunch.

"Pelyane's proposal threatens neither unity nor equality," Cyrrus asserted.

"Samie Cyrrus," Nurin said stolidly, "do not speak out of turn."

Cyrrus raised his hand and looked around with a wry smile. Everybody laughed as Nurin dryly surrendered, "Samie Cyrrus."

Cyrrus paraded an amused grin as he strutted down the aisle and planted himself where everybody might ogle him from wherever they sat. All eyes followed him, and no one uttered a sound until he spoke.

"Pelyane's proposal would encourage unity through enjoyment, in much the same way as our Raetsek competitions," Cyrrus said. "While individual proficiency may vary, the community unites in its appreciation of those skills."

"Raetsek employs teams, bringing individuals together," Nurin asserted. "Pelyane's idea supports only pompous individuals, challenging our code of unity."

"Music is even more unifying. Every culture unites around music."

"You cannot know that."

"I have studied every book in the library and gathered extensive knowledge of other cultures," Cyrrus announced. "I would be honored to enlighten you about the ways that musical mastery may serve a community."

Everybody stared at Cyrrus, waiting to be 'enlightened.' Nurin gave a smug nod.

"The talent of the few inspires the many," Cyrrus instructed, infusing every word with panache. "At the seasonal circus in Kadir, the public gathers in a spectacular arena to watch as warriors battle beasts and engage one other to the death. At the western end is a giant musical device known as an organ, which a single, expert musician plays throughout the event. It is an instrument with keys and pedals like the piano, except that the notes contain specific frequencies which elicit sympathetic resonances within the brain and chest, causing an emotional cadence. Its vibrations are apparently very pleasant, and enhanced by acoustic designs within the arena. The community is strengthened by shared emotion which serves to unify the populace."

Aera imagined the rich sound and recalled her voice saturating Elkandul as the blue light pulsated along with the throb in her chest. She realized she was smiling and noticed everyone else was silent and still, just as mesmerized as she was by Cyrrus's description.

"The music creates tension and release, which promotes empathy and excitement even as unfathomable events transpire," Cyrrus continued, extending a theatrical hand. "A select few inspired singers perform communal songs, and the effect is so powerful that even those engaging in the deadly contests feel united and noble, despite their potentially imminent demise. They are enriched with the spirit of their community and honored to participate for the good of the whole."

Cyrrus's words were delivered more slowly than ever before, and he moved his arms to accentuate his rhythm. This could not be an accident. Aera knew, from practicing Kra, that it required study to move with grace and make it seem effortless. His gestures were rehearsed.

Nurin remained impassive as the drama unfolded, his body language suggesting amusement. "Nobody here would choose to live in Kadir," he asserted. "At age six, boys begin training for war. Young girls are forced to submit their bodies as rewards to the warriors. Many do this because they must. There is not enough food. Winners are rewarded and can feed their families while the losers' families starve."

"Excellent point," Cyrrus retorted. "Music makes them feel proud to be part of that, despite unfavorable living conditions. That is the power of *good* music. It inspires unity."

"Most societies do not achieve unity at all," Nurin insisted. "Citizens compete for basic resources, and they are perpetually at war with neighboring nations. There is no equality or morality, as some enjoy privilege while others are enslaved."

That sounded familiar. In Ynas, everyone was a slave. With the authority to punish whomever he pleased and interpret the law on a whim, Nurin himself was the most privileged of all.

"Material abundance is an independent consideration," Cyrrus said. "In Syrd, musicians are trained at institutions, and hold honorable positions. In Dirgaselah and New Taerelboro, there are giant bell-towers containing a complex series of chimes and drums whose arias enrich the whole city. When the bells sound, the villagers stop all other activity to sing and dance, all united."

"Syrdian citizens sacrifice their lives by the thousands each year in their ongoing wars," Nurin interjected. "The people in New Taerelboro are hungry enough to practice cannibalism, and Dirgaselah maintains slaves and enforces subhuman conditions. We live in privilege here in Ynas. The poverty and war ubiquitous elsewhere are unfathomable to us."

"It is no privilege to be denied music, art and beauty," Cyrrus retorted. "It would require no additional resources to enhance our inarguably excellent society with the creativity enjoyed by even the most barbaric of our neighbors. It is a cruel irony that we suffer such discretionary and easily remedied aesthetic deprivation in contrast to the abundance of resources our commune enjoys."

"You take this abundance for granted," Nurin said firmly. "Our laws ensure that you are safe and at pcacc."

"If the people are at peace, why have so many come to this meeting today? Why do people free the caged animals, defy curfew, and seek unlawful means to express themselves? Why do so many avoid Unity Festival?" Cyrrus paused. "You claim music is divisive, but it evokes passion, which inspires connection."

Aera chuckled at the sight of Cyrrus defending the merits of passion. He didn't believe anything he said but designed his spectacles to rally followers.

"Your exemplars of other cultures obviate your thesis," Nurin protested. "Regardless of the rebellious few you mentioned, we are not starving to death, murdering each other, sleeping outside in the winter, or fighting any wars."

"Correlation does not establish causality," Cyrrus said. "Music does not produce slavery and art does not beget poverty. Furthermore, anyone who has peered beyond the fence in the Southeast is aware that we do train soldiers with weapons."

Giggles and gasps combed through the audience, but Nurin didn't respond.

"We may share the same privileges and duties, but the *feeling* of unity could be strengthened," Cyrrus pontificated. "We are taught that we are the same, but does anyone *feel* it? Is it in our drab, passionless lives that we are... all the same?"

Passions, feelings, beauty... he was channeling some other creature. There was no limit to the personae he would inhabit to accomplish his goals, which were inane, considering he was promoting ideas that were useless to him at a Festival he never attended and citing the low attendance when it was he who influenced people not to show up. The only rationale for this lunacy was to inveigle support in the future election, but it was pointless to gain power if only to promote ends that he found meaningless.

"In order to preserve civility, we must resist temptations which inspire chaos," Nurin asserted. "Passion awakens violent urges. Beauty inspires jealousy, which turns to hatred and begets crime. To indulge subjective passion is to place the individual above the collective. It would introduce violent themes like those in the cultures you have so eloquently described."

"Do you assert that music and art *cause* those mindsets to arise?"

"Many variables shape a culture, and I cannot assign global cause and effect. Nonetheless, the notion that the arts inspire unity in these cultures is unfounded, since it does not prevent their people from killing each other. It is unwise to emulate cultures that are impoverished and depraved."

"Since it is not established that art causes the poverty and violence, we must conclude that the decision to ban it is whimsical and tendentious, as well as unnecessarily self-defeating," Cyrrus said. "Art and music affirm cohesion, and in every culture, at the heart of all people, we are, indeed, all the same."

Nurin watched Cyrrus without saying a word, and Cyrrus took the cue to continue his oration. "Permit me to demonstrate the universality of this sentiment by calling for a show of hands," he said, and turned to the throng. "I propose we change no laws, but simply provide the opportunity for two or more people to perform music and dance at Unity Festival. Anyone in favor of this, raise your hand."

Every hand in the audience shot up in the air, including the elders in the front rows. Aera also raised hers.

"Everyone in favor of allowing individuals to create art and display it publicly, raise your hand," Cyrrus added, and the hands remained in the air.

He paused for a moment and looked around, making sure everyone had a chance to witness the overwhelming assent, then said, "Anyone opposed, please raise yours." Everyone lowered their hands, including Justinar Dinad and the other officials in the front row.

"See for yourself," Cyrrus said, looking straight at Nurin. "The love of beauty is universal. We *are* all the same."

Everybody was fixated, waiting to see what Cyrrus would do next. Dramatically, he placed his right hand on his heart, then raised his left arm up, fingers pointed at the sky. "We... are all... the same!"

The mesmerized crowd performed the salute and chanted enthusiastically, copying the pauses to mimic the rhythm of Cyrrus's words. "We... are all... the same! We... are all... the same!" This time, Gaili and Olleroc joined in, though Aera did not. Renstrom Nurin himself recited the mantra as part of the herd, his expression blank and unreadable.

Cyrrus lowered his arms. As everybody mirrored him, Cyrrus kept his gaze locked on Nurin. His lips hinted a grin. Then, with extravagant poise, he turned and marched out through the tunnel. Every head spun to watch his exit. Once he was out of sight, Pelyane raised her hand.

"Samie Pelyane," Nurin said.

"I propose that individuals be permitted to display artwork around the commune and that musicians and dancers be permitted to perform at Unity Festival in groups of two or more," she chirped. "I propose a vote."

"There will be no vote," Nurin said stiffly. "The council will consider your proposal. Unless you have additional business, please return to class."

Aera followed the crowd to the tunnel, noticing people from all Age Groups. The youngest had attended at the behest of Kize and

Pelyane, though Cyrrus had likely orchestrated it. He berated passion and the arts yet had gone to great lengths to organize this protest in their pursuit. Any interest was worth defending if it won him the people's allegiance. In this, he bested Nurin easily. He had everybody in the palm of his hand.

She wondered what Nurin was thinking when everyone followed Cyrrus's rendition of the maxim and why he didn't go to greater lengths to prevent Cyrrus from emblazoning himself in the public consciousness. Nurin was sufficiently astute to have turned the debate in his own favor. Was he secretly permitting Cyrrus to win?

What had been the purpose of their recent meeting at Nurin's office?

COLLAPSE

1328 EARLY-AUTUMN

Cyrrus lent Aera his key to the locked room, but otherwise ignored her. She could not tell whether he was disturbed by the evasive account of her last visit to the crystal world or if he truly ascribed to her 'no agency.'

Whenever she was alone, Aera lost herself in thoughts of the musical dream and the elusive star. His celestial dance marked him as a master of psychic command, yet he fused with Aera's rhythm as though spellbound. She recalled their meeting in sublime detail but could not discern whether the heartbeat was his or hers. In that fleeting moment, they were one.

Aera wondered what she looked like to him. He had shown nothing but a blue light, yet his heat alone had possessed her. Perhaps his emanations matched Sotona, Lord of Flame. *His touch is dangerous*, Aera thought, and blushed.

She wanted to see him again but knew the overstimulation of the orb would be painful if she didn't allow her senses to relax. While she waited, she used the time to channel Ivory and practice piano, hoping Vaye would leave so she could indulge in just being Aera while her senses were heightened. After only two evenings, her wish came true.

Vaye greeted her in the doorway, dressed in a decorative leather cloak with a rucksack over her arm. "I'll be away for a few days," she said. "Feel free to entertain the cats."

Aera admired Vaye in her fur-lined leathers and wondered where she would go. Aera knew from History Class that Kadir was the closest civilization, 600 kymen away, and that the journey there and back would take a month by foot. She stared at Vaye's forehead-band, wishing she could read her thoughts.

With a warm look, Vaye said, "*Nerilyanë*, Aera."

Aera was taken aback. By saying goodbye to her in Silindion, Vaye was admitting that they shared secret knowledge about the Nestë. Pronouncing the word precisely the same way, Aera repeated, "*Nerilyanë*." The two exchanged a conspiratorial smile, and Vaye departed.

Aera approached the piano and luxuriated in some slow, haunting tones. She imagined a dark, misty forest and blue eyes shining like stars. The lyric escaped her lips: "Under the moonlight, I lie in your shadow..."

Her singing was frail, but the melody was mesmeric. "The chill of midnight won't cool our passion..."

She pictured the boy from her dream, bare-chested and untamed, coveting her from afar. Her eyes closed as her hands explored uncharted chords, drawing her deeper into a mystical stratosphere where visions unfolded. The boy disappeared into the trees as the soundscape hummed in dusky tones.

"Is it early, is it too late?" Aera sang, ever so softly. "Is this tomorrow? If I don't give you everything now, how long will I wait?"

Her fingers fell into a descending pattern that climbed to a moment of hope, only to collapse again. She envisioned herself searching frantically through a wind-swept forest while the song ascended into a whirl. As she tore through the howling night, she ravaged the piano in rapture. Had she lost the boy in the shadows of her mind? Did he even exist?

"It doesn't help to question everything," she belted. "It doesn't matter if you're real. I can admit, I might be dreaming, but I can't change the way I feel..."

The song became seductive and ominous, luring her toward an inevitable fate as a blue blaze ignited the forest. "I'm wide awake. I've never felt so sure, so pure. And I feel like I've known you before. I feel like I've been here before. Maybe this already happened, and it's over and over and I still hunger for more..."

The inferno flared and vanished, leaving Aera alone in the dark. She opened her eyes and jotted down notations as her heart pounded. Once everything was inscribed, she breathed in the pumpkin-spiced air and resumed playing.

The piano whispered in tempo with her heartbeat, just as the hidden star had pulsated alongside her. She leaned into the keys and cooed, "I calm myself down. And soon enough, space crashes into time. And we all fall, we all fall in love..."

Love?

Aera paused. Where were these words coming from? *Love?* The lyric was passionate, but did she write it? The song wrote itself through her... but it could not possibly be hers. She had never claimed to love even Cyrrus, so how could she love a stranger who might not exist?

There was no need for him to exist. She was excited by a fantasy in a dream and her imaginary world didn't have to make sense. *Love is a logical fallacy,* she thought with a giggle, and set about reorganizing the composition in her notebook.

Her cheeks burned as she completed the last phrase, and a beaming smile broke out. She graced the keys, cherishing each magical chord, and sang with abandon.

Collapse

> *I calm myself down*
> *And soon enough*
> *Space crashes into time*
> *And we all fall*
> *We all fall in love*

Under the moonlight, I lie in your shadow
The chill of midnight won't cool our passion
Is it early? Is it too late?
Is this tomorrow?
If I don't give you everything now
how long will I wait?

It doesn't help to question everything
It doesn't matter if you're real
I can admit I might be dreaming
But I can't change the way I feel

I'm wide awake
I've never felt so sure
So pure
And I feel like I've known you before
Maybe this already happened
And it's over and over
And I still hunger for more

~

For days, Aera's new song consumed her, and she relished in it whenever she could. She passed breaks at the cottage until Vaye returned, then found refuge in the woods.

"It's over and over, and I still hunger for more!"

Aera sang at the top of her lungs, invoking the fury that once had empowered her to shout at Doriline. "More! More!" Her voice rang out, cracking and squeaking. If only she could sing louder without losing control of pitch and vibrato...

She took a deep breath and belted, "If I don't give you everything now, how long will I wait?" Off-key again. She swung her Ikrati stick at a tree in frustration, then laughed. Her singing voice was a mess—yet, in Elkandul, it was so seductive that her companion star couldn't resist revealing himself.

She blushed, repositioned her stick, and resumed whacking trees. As she balanced and stretched, she considered returning to Elkandul. Several days had passed since her last venture, and her senses had receded to a manageable state. She felt relaxed and alive, prepared for anything.

When the bell gonged, she rushed to her room, changed to her under-tunic and tried not to smile too much during attendance. Soon after Linealle left, a bunch of girls moved out into the hallway. Aera soon followed.

The corridor was crowded, and the last torch was gone. To avoid being noticed, she crouched in the darkness for a moment, then slipped around the corner into the empty hallway. She heard voices near the secret room, followed by an eruption of laughter. Apparently, there were people around the bend, blocking her path to the sanctum.

A scrawny figure appeared at the end of the dark hallway. As it approached, Aera saw that it was Farris's sidekick, Mivar.

"Hey, Boney-bones!" he shouted. "What in Riva's trees are you doing here?"

Mivar parked himself just before Aera. She bristled. The orb was in her pocket; she couldn't afford any trouble.

"Where are you going, all by yourself?" Mivar persisted.

Aera wanted to shove that moronic fool out of her way, but Ivory knew he wasn't worth it. She glared into the shadows surrounding his eyes and said nothing.

Mivar demanded, "You spying on us?"

Laughable. Ivory didn't care enough about them to spy. As she stared at Mivar in amusement, he became increasingly agitated.

"There's nothing but a locked door," Mivar said uneasily. "And Dori and Farris uh... uh..."

"Samely, Mivar!" Novi called from around the bend. "You're *still* talking to Cyrrus's pet?"

Everybody laughed, but Ivory ignored it and fixed her eyes firmly on Mivar, channeling her rising irritation into a menacing glare. He shifted uncomfortably.

"You should go back to the main hallway," Mivar ordered, feigning authority and projecting his voice so the others could hear. "There's nothing for you here." Without looking at her again, he scurried back to his crew.

As soon as Mivar was out of sight, Aera's frustration exploded. She kicked the wall. Cyrrus's idiotic idea had backfired, as people were swarming the empty hallway, watching her every move. She returned to bed, where she tossed and turned, fuming mad. Cyrrus had ruined everything.

~

Aera slept uneasily and slogged through the next day, tired and annoyed. After enduring tedious and tiresome routines, she carried her dinner to the boulder, relieved that the day was finally over. Sunset cast pink and purple ribbons as the clouds sailed over Southside Forest, not unlike the colorful auras in Elkandul. She thought of the blue light throbbing along with her song. *If I don't give you everything now, how long will I wait...*

Cyrrus appeared at her side, but she decided to ignore him and concentrate on chewing. It was hard to imagine how she had ever eaten food. Every reflex rejected the act of swallowing, and her stomach was a rock. Beside her, Cyrrus ate his way across the tray in a systematic fashion, gulping down one pile, then the next, then the next. As Aera watched him, she felt strange and distant, like she could no longer recognize him.

"Keep emoting," Cyrrus teased. "It makes me feel like we're still eleven years old."

Aera glared at him, and he gazed back with an unnatural, impenetrable calm. He was searching for something but projecting a demeanor to suggest he didn't have a care in the world. She wanted to shake him violently and make him spill his feelings. Instead, she locked into his eyes and imagined her stare cutting into him.

Cyrrus jiggled his eyebrows to distract her until she accidentally broke eye contact. He raised a brow to let her know he had won and said, "Your deflection skills are improving."

"I said nothing."

"You deflected your thoughts and kept me out of your mind."

"If you want to know what I'm thinking, you'll have to ask."

"I want to know if I can hear what you're thinking," Cyrrus said, "not what you are actually thinking. My cerebral circus filters out frivolous meanderings, romantic reminiscing and passion-based folly, to leave space for the consequential."

"Passion-based folly, like your speech at the town meeting."

"The speech served its purpose. The change will initiate a wave of rational thought."

Cyrrus always said music was useless and beauty was worthless. *Consistently inconsistent*, Aera thought, recalling the crystal world.

"Consistently inconsistent," Cyrrus repeated. "Excellent trick. That's why we pass for one person in Elkandul."

He'd pried into her thoughts. What a show-off.

"I wanted to use the orb last night," Aera said, "but there were people outside the door."

"In less than three months, we'll move to the Adolescent Hut, where there's no curfew," Cyrrus replied. "We can afford to wait."

"It was idiotic to send everyone to the hallways."

"It's irrelevant. I learned recently that Mivar and Farris have sneaked around in the back hallway for years, and I presume there were others too. It's not safe to use it until Winter."

"Why didn't you tell me?"

"You figured it out for yourself."

"But you didn't know I would when you gave me the key," she demanded. "If someone caught me coming out of that door, we could have lost the orb."

"Your life strategy is misguided. You rely on me to figure everything out and complain when you manage to learn things by yourself."

Aera wanted to punch his pompous face, but he left before she could blink. She called after him, "You're such a farkus!" He didn't acknowledge her.

Autumn passed too slowly, as Aera was impatient for Winter. She could hardly wait to move to Adolescent Hut and obtain the freedom that would allow her to use the orb again. Vaye continued her many lessons but nothing was satisfying, as Aera's life was on hold. With her senses normalized, Ikrati was flat, and music was bland. Nothing compared to the magical trance that had lured her aria from another world.

Cyrrus insisted on holding the orb, since he was better than Aera at hiding his thoughts. Though she conceded, she couldn't help wondering if he was using it without her. He slept through classes but bathed more often and seemed more alert than before. There was no way to determine what he was doing, as he kept conversation shallow and busied himself away from the boulder during most meals. Aera sensed he preferred the company of the clan. Now that he was accomplishing important goals with them, what could he possibly need her for? He had always called her useless, but now she was disposable as well.

When the last evening of Late-Autumn finally came, Aera sat by the boulder in the cold. She snuggled into her cloak and listened to the desperate caws of the last few crows that had not yet left Ynas for the winter. Melodies haunted her. *The chill of midnight won't cool our passion...*

The next day was the move to the Adolescent Hut. At night, she could use the orb there. Her music would be inspired, she could wield the powerful voice she always wanted, and the blue light might reveal itself again. Whoever projected that pulse had displayed more connection with her music than Cyrrus ever did. The flashes of blue had matched the rhythm of her heart, and both had aligned with the song...

A smile spilled over her face. The hidden star was one night away.

She took dinner on the hilltop, fantasizing about what might be coming as torches illuminated the commune and stars speckled the sky. The air tasted fresh, and the breeze was exhilarating. She felt alive again.

KIZE
1329 EARLY-WINTER

"Samies, get up! You're fifteen now! Find your stuff and line up outside!"

Clamor filled the room, but Aera scooped up her spare clothes and escaped the chaos. In her anticipation of Elkandul, she'd been too restless to sleep and was already dressed. Outside, she was greeted by a gust of cold air and a grinning Cyrrus, who stood by himself. They had barely been together for months. His presence made her tense, but he was perfectly calm.

"Sleep is for the weak," he declared.

Aera forced a grin.

Others emerged from the Junior Hut and formed a line behind Aera and Cyrrus. Once everyone was ready, Linealle led them across the field to a rectangular building. She stood before the door and announced, "Listen up, Samies! Age Groups fifteen to twenty-four sleep here. Bedrooms are upstairs, and you can use any available mat."

Everyone pushed their way inside as soon as she opened the door. Just like the village units, the entrance opened to a hallway with a staircase at the far end. There were only two levels, and on the second, people waited for friends and ushered them into their dorms. Aera and Cyrrus continued past everyone to the far end of the hallway, where he opened the last door and looked inside. Mats lined each of the long walls, and people from the 19-20 Group were dressing and shuffling around.

"Samely, Cyrrus," said a smooth male voice. "There's a free mat here."

It was an older boy, taller and thinner than Cyrrus, with a fitted outfit. Beside him, another neatly dressed boy glanced over and called, "Samely, Cyrrus!" Then, a third nodded to acknowledge him. All three looked like they had competed with Cyrrus in a sewing contest, but the first was the only one who could even approach Cyrrus's ostentatious style.

Cyrrus glanced at Aera, said, "Good luck," and headed toward the older boys.

Aera wanted to cry. Why would she expect Cyrrus to sleep in the same room as she? Were they even friends anymore? She walked away with as much grace as she could muster while her stomach burned up.

A few doors away, Gaili and Olleroc lingered outside a room talking to an older girl. When Gaili noticed Aera, she called, "There are free mats here!"

Aera swallowed hard, pushing back tears. She followed Gaili into a room like every other, with mats lining the two long walls and a fireplace at the far end. The older girl pointed them toward the free mats, which were near the fireplace. Gaili and Olleroc didn't seem to care which mats they ended up with, so Aera chose the most desirable location, right beside the wall. As she set her sandals down and hung her clothes on a hook, Gaili glanced at the four free mats.

"Where's Cyrrus?" she asked.

"With friends," Aera said.

"Aren't *you* his closest friend?"

Aera breathed deeply, trying not to explode.

Gaili took the hint and changed the subject. "Let's go. I don't want to get stuck with spinach muffins."

The three left the room, and Aera saw Cyrrus waiting for her by the staircase. He made his way to her side.

"Let's explore the lower-level tonight," he whispered.

Now that there was no one else to impress, Cyrrus deigned to talk to Aera. Flatly, she reminded him, "It's my turn tonight."

"Are you planning to go out in the freezing cold? Or shall we find a more suitable place?"

Cyrrus had a point: it was cold outside even in bright sunlight, and it would be treacherous at night. She could build a fire, but if the flames died while she was wandering in another dimension, she might freeze to death while her conscious mind was elsewhere. Tension set in as she considered the options. None looked good. She was still caged.

They made their way outside, and the chill was biting. Cyrrus climbed Halcyon Hill for Unity Festival, and Aera ran to the cottage to escape the cold. When she arrived, the room smelled like cinnamon, and Vaye was reading by the fire with two steaming mugs on the table, anticipating Aera's arrival.

Vaye closed her book and said, "Good morning, dear."

"Morning," Aera echoed.

She joined Vaye by the fireplace and sipped cinnamon tea, grateful that Vaye didn't initiate conversation. Her thoughts went back to Cyrrus and his request to explore the building that evening. Should she join him or ignore him? Perhaps it was unfair to punish him when she had never voiced her concerns about the distance between them... though he could not possibly be oblivious to the message he was sending.

Once their mugs were empty, Vaye asked, "Would you like to play while I read?"

"Sure," Aera agreed.

She moved to the piano, summoned Ivory, and decided to practice *Sunarien*. As she recounted the beginning, she sang quietly along to keep her place. "*Míssëar i mëa kuiyánëa...*[1]"

Her fingers moved automatically while she focused on breath and posture. Suddenly, she realized what she was singing as the words tumbled out: "The chill of midnight won't cool our passion..."

She played a short interlude and transitioned back to *Sunarien*. "*Sammár i phëa lintuvéskëa—*[2]"

"*...Aera...*"

Cyrrus's voice rang through her mind, coming from every direction at once. "*...Aera...*"

She stopped playing and looked around, but Cyrrus wasn't there. Vaye glanced up from her book, then resumed reading. Aera turned toward the keys. As she launched back into song, she heard Cyrrus's voice again: "*Aera. Come to Halcyon Hill.*"

She turned abruptly and saw Vaye watching her with a focused gaze and alert posture, indicating she'd heard the voice also. Cyrrus had always been cautious about sending long-distance messages through *inyanondo*. If he was taking the risk, it must have been important.

"Thanks for letting me play," Aera said politely. "Is it okay if I come back later?"

"I look forward to it," Vaye said. Though her voice was velveteen as always, her chocolate brown eyes were dense with thought.

Aera tore through the freezing forest and rushed to Halcyon Hill, where Cyrrus was standing by the boulder. As she went to his side, he turned to greet her.

"What brings you here?" he grinned.

"You called," she implored. "Don't pretend you didn't."

Cyrrus raised a brow but ignored the demand.

"Nurin just announced that he's holding a trial today," he said. "For three hours, groups of two or more can perform. Afterwards there will be a vote to determine whether this practice will continue."

It was no surprise that Nurin had conceded. The support Cyrrus had garnered at the town meeting left him with little choice.

"If the performances aren't good, people may vote against it," Cyrrus explained. "He set it up this way presuming nobody would have sufficient time to prepare and the event would discourage the audience from supporting it."

Apparently, Nurin and Cyrrus were well matched for underhanded scheming. Cyrrus looked right at Aera and said, "If you want solo musicianship to be encouraged, it would be sensible for you to play."

Aera's heart jumped. Cyrrus wanted her to perform before the whole commune without preparation... but if she complained about that, he wouldn't understand. She grumbled, "The piano is out of tune."

"Everybody will be interested regardless. You're the best musician on the commune."

"Vaye is better," Aera corrected him.

Cyrrus grinned.

"I haven't rehearsed with anybody," she continued. "It would be a mess."

"I'll ask Kize to dance while you play. That way, nobody will ruin the music."

Of course, he would choose Kize, his prettiest and most adoring fan. Aera was bursting with irritation but focused on her breath and chose her protest carefully. "My songs are... fierce," she said, "and I learned the mellower ones illegally."

"Nurin and the other adults don't know those songs."

"Nurin might, since he knows Vaye."

"Even if he recognizes them, he can't admit that without implicating himself and Vaye for playing music privately, so it is a moot point. You cannot be punished for something Nurin can't admit knowing about."

Aera grimaced. She was fast running out of excuses.

"You're nervous about playing for an audience," Cyrrus said. "Try thinking of it another way. It is an opportunity to overcome your fear and let people know you. More importantly, it is an opportunity to fight for what you believe."

"Stop preaching," Aera snapped. "I'm not one of your disciples. You can't manipulate me with your speechcraft, and it's insulting that you try."

They stood together in silence. Then, Cyrrus switched to a soft voice. "Aera," he said gently. "Leave Ivory behind for a moment. Forget your frustration with me and my politics. Think about who *you* are."

Aera stiffened. His tenderness made her uneasy.

"Look at me," he said.

Hesitantly, she looked up and saw his emerald eyes filled with affection. She felt a blush coming on, but summoned Ivory to fight her stupid heart. He wanted to persuade her to play and was using every underhanded technique he could conjure, but it didn't mean he actually cared. She held his gaze to let him know he couldn't shatter her resolve.

"I remember your first town meeting," Cyrrus said. "I had noticed previously that your appearance was unique, with your valiant hair and venomous gaze. But that town meeting made me want to know you."

Aera's heart jumped out of her chest. *Valiant hair and venomous gaze*... did he really believe this about her? Was 'venomous' a compliment? Either way, he was wheedling only to persuade her for his purposes. She refused to waver.

"It was what you said," he intoned. "*The music is ruined by all the people.* The masses couldn't sway you because you cared about the truth. It was the first time I wanted to know someone. You showed me that I wasn't alone."

Tears rushed to her eyes, but she pushed them back and thought, *I won't let you sway me.* He was using their friendship as a tool to advance his goal. Disgusting. Nothing was sacred to him.

"Now is your chance to make a change," Cyrrus continued. "Would you sacrifice that just to punish me? We spent years together, sneaking past authorities and uncovering their lies. If the cause means nothing to you, then please, do this for me."

Cyrrus had Aera cornered. What could she say now? Did he feel betrayed by her lack of investment in 'the cause?' He'd always insisted her participation was irrelevant, but now he was admitting that he needed her help. She didn't want to reject his plea.

"I'll consider it," she said slowly, "if you tell me why you want to change this policy."

Though he barely grinned, his eyes smiled. He cleared his throat, stuck out his chin, and spoke with exaggerated authority to imitate Nurin. "This policy must be amended, and I will tell you why," he asserted crisply. "The music is ruined by all the people."

They both chuckled, and Cyrrus's girlish giggle made Aera feel like they were eleven years old again, frolicking together through the forest. She could not help but smile.

"I wouldn't advise performing on an empty stomach," he said. "Wait here and I'll get some muffins."

Aera nodded to let him know she would, indeed, perform. He grinned and headed down the Hill.

She sat in the grass beside the boulder and watched as people milled in front of the stage below. The crowd was thicker than she remembered. How many would see her play? Her stomach rumbled a tune of its own. She combed her hair, then balled her hands together to warm them up. *Breathe*, she thought. *It doesn't matter what the Samies think about my music*. Yet each time she heard laughter in the Field, nausea took over.

Cyrrus returned and handed her a muffin with a mug of water. "I'll alert you when it's time," he said, then disappeared.

Aera imagined herself bedecked in a glorious dress, shining at the center of the stage as her idealized voice enchanted everyone. *It doesn't help to question everything, it doesn't matter if you're real.* Her savage suitor watched from the crowd, his eyes aflame. *I can admit I might be dreaming, but I can't change the way I feel...*

Wake up, she scolded herself. Her voice was weak, and that song was personal. She reached for her muffin, then realized she'd eaten it while her mind was far away. As she drank the water, she tried to think of something else. *Kamando ina yáryello eremanyë, henentë sëonanya súndëa n'énkië...*[3]

"Ready?"

Cyrrus and Kize were standing beside her. How much time had passed? People were seated below, and the youngest Age Group was being ushered off the stage. Was it Aera's turn? Blood rushed to her cheeks as she rubbed her hands together and adjusted her posture. Ivory could handle this. Somehow.

Kize did not appear nervous at all. Her hazel eyes were surrounded by golden curls that hung to her shoulders and framed her adorable face with luscious buoyancy. She was taller than Aera now and her shape was beginning to fill out.

"I'll take off my cloak for the dance," Kize chimed. "It'll look better."

Kize couldn't possibly feel limber without a cloak when the air was so cold but, clearly, displaying her beauty was the priority. Everyone would be watching Kize while Aera was hidden behind the piano's flat back, and she wasn't sure whether that was comforting or aggravating. It was fitting that she'd paired Kize with Alárië on the archetype map. *I'll drown in her light, like Erelion,* Aera thought begrudgingly.

The three headed down Halcyon Hill toward the stage, where Pelyane was already standing by the stairs, and they joined her as the last of the children were ushered to their seats. Nurin climbed the stairs on the opposite side, took center stage and pointed his chin in the air.

"Today is a special day," he announced. "Groups of two or more will be permitted to perform for their brothers and sisters. Afterwards, we will ask ourselves whether their performances nourish the spirit of unity. By opening the stage to independent performers, we may invite mockery of performers who falter, competition to outshine others, and envy of particular skills. Following the closing act, we must vote responsibly to determine whether this practice shall find a place in future Unity Festivals."

He positioned his right hand on his chest and raised his left. As everyone stood to copy him, Cyrrus raised his arm firmly and glanced at Aera. They were about to perform, and he silently urged her acquiescence in the ritual to simulate a spirit of unity. Uncomfortably, she assumed position.

"We are all the same!" Nurin announced.

"We are all the same!" repeated the crowd. Cyrrus and Kize bellowed the phrase, but Aera could barely bring her lips to move.

Nurin turned toward the three of them by the side of the stage and said firmly, "We are all the same!"

He stared right at Aera, and she projected her most venomous glare as she uttered the phrase along with them. She wished she could vaporize him.

Nurin watched her with a vacant expression, then turned to the audience and lowered his arms. "If you wish to perform, please remain standing. If not, please take your seats."

Most people sat, but some remained standing, including Doriline and a few pink-clad piglets near the front row. Cyrrus marched up the stairs and stood beside Nurin on the stage.

"Samie Cyrrus, wait your turn," Nurin said crisply. Cyrrus smiled and raised his hand, eyeing Nurin with satisfaction until finally, he nodded, permitting him to speak.

"Since this experiment was Pelyane's enterprise, I suggest we give her the honor of selecting the participants," Cyrrus said.

"She will select her friends," Nurin asserted. "I will select people without bias."

"We are *all* biased," Cyrrus corrected him, and a few people laughed.

"I will select those who have accumulated the most points this season," Nurin explained. "That is an unbiased method, since we are all rewarded and punished for the same reasons."

"We are awarded points for reporting our peers and turning against one another," Cyrrus corrected him. "It is because of practices like these that our sense of unity is challenged, despite repeating the mantra and singing the anthem."

"Every individual has a duty to uphold the laws which serve to unify us," Nurin argued. "We reward citizens who act honorably to maintain unity."

Cyrrus stared ahead, calm and thoughtful. "Unity is more than a law," he said, and placed his hand on his heart. "It is a sentiment."

Aera almost burst into laughter but caught herself. Some people in the audience snorted in annoyance while others watched with gooey eyes.

"Pelyane," Cyrrus called. "How do you propose we select performers?"

Pelyane smiled widely and chirped, "I propose that we select them on each Unity Day to perform at the next, so they have time to prepare. The audience can vote for who they want to hear during the first hour, and the rest of the performers will be volunteers chosen in a random drawing."

"Your idea is excellent, as it encourages both quality and fairness," Cyrrus declared. "I propose you select performers today, as a reward for your thoughtful contribution to the Festival."

"Let us have a vote," Nurin suggested smugly, and cleared his throat. "Those who wish for Pelyane to select performers, raise your hand."

Some hands shot up in the air, but not nearly enough for a majority.

"If you wish for me to select performers, raise your hand."

Doriline and her klatch raised their hands, along with other clusters from various Age Groups. *Raise your hand if you love the law*, Aera thought.

"We are divided," Cyrrus announced crisply, and turned to Nurin. "I propose a compromise. Allow Pelyane to select performers for the opening half of the first hour. The remainder of the three hours will be yours to select performers using any method you wish."

Nurin turned to see the belltower clock, then elevated his chin and announced, "Proposal accepted." He cleared his throat and turned to the audience. "This compromise will unite us all in this effort. We are all the same!"

He led the salute and the crowd followed along. Begrudgingly, Aera assumed the stance but did not speak the chant.

"We are all the same! We are all the same!"

Nurin turned his head to face each part of the audience, but this time, did not look at Aera. Once finished, he lowered his arms, then marched away to join some officers nearby.

Alone on the stage, Cyrrus gestured at Pelyane, who scurried to his side, natural and happy, without a hint of self-consciousness before the crowd. Aera stared at the piano on the side of the stage: it was angled so the audience would be able to see her side. She breathed deeply to calm herself and rubbed her hands together so they wouldn't freeze.

Pelyane's voice echoed as the world slowed down. "My first selection is Kize and Aera."

Kize and Aera. Aera...

A few people clapped, but not many; those few were surely clapping for Kize. Aera visualized a glowing sphere around her, then cloaked it in shadow. *I am Ivory*, she thought. *I don't care what anyone thinks of me.*

She allowed a deep, slow breath to fill her abdomen, straightened her shoulders, and climbed the rickety stairs as gracefully as possible. The wood groaned under Kize's feet, but Aera's step was as quiet as Vaye's. She crossed the stage toward the piano—forcing herself not to look at the crowd—then balanced on the wobbly bench and placed her shivering hands on the keys. The only song that came to mind was her most recent. *I calm myself down...*

She tried to think of something else, but the song kept running through her mind. *And soon enough space crashes into time, and we all fall, we all fall in love...*

Everybody was waiting for her. She tried to remember one of the Silindion songs, but her mind was blank. People were starting to chatter, and she imagined them staring, pointing, laughing. A crow cawed on from above and another song spilled into her mind. *I reach to the sky for a cloud to come and catch me...*

She'd hardly played that piece in years, but it was easy, catchy, more upbeat... and its message was about resisting the imprisonment of the commune. She could sing the lyrics quietly to herself from behind the piano, voicing a protest in plain sight that nobody else could decipher. The idea was invigorating.

She struck the first chord and cringed at the untuned notes. But as her hands began to move, excitement overcame her. She drew out the introduction, indulging the soundscape of hammers and strings among birds and wind. The lyrics ran through her mind, and she sang them quietly to herself.

> *I reach to the sky*
> *For a cloud to come and catch me*
> *Take me away*
> *From anger and hatred and pain*
> *Fly me over the rain*
> *And I'll drown your world from above*
> *I'll wash out the tears*
> *Banish the fears*
> *When you're under the ocean*
> *I'll feel one emotion*
> *Love*

Her fingers sailed across the chords, befriending the chipped keys of the piano. She found herself enjoying the chaos of the discordant sounds. After a long, drawn-out interlude, she continued to the second verse.

Saying goodbye
To a life of expectations
Leaving behind
The blindness of empty routine
I'll escape the machine
That I've been taught to be
I'll open my eyes
Remove this disguise
No more pretending
The cycle is ending
I'm free

Lost and alone
Trusting no one
There's power and greed
And wars to be won
In a world of dominions
Where can I run?
Where can I run?

There was a short piano solo after the bridge. As Aera's fingers fell into its fury, she glanced over the top of the piano and saw Kize surrendering to the rhythm with effortless finesse. Aera pounded some chords with the force of thunder as Kize ignited the stage.

To see what Kize would do, Aera lightened her touch. In turn, Kize glided along in subtle waves to enact each fluttery flourish. Aera pounded a weighty chord, and Kize's head fell back along with it as though the song had swayed her under its force. With each embellishment Aera added, Kize twirled more furiously.

As Aera watched Kize, she found herself not only guiding, but also responding to her motion. They fell into symbiosis and the song played itself, forming a completely new piece. Though the improvisation was conceived from the song she'd already composed, it gave birth to an extravagant whirlwind as Kize's animation waxed and waned along with the music. The sweet notes turned Kize into a butterfly and the heavy ones invoked lightning. After a time, the improvisation circled back to the original introduction, and Aera executed the last verse with more fervor.

> *I'm trying to fly*
> *But the birds ascend without me*
> *They sing to the wind*
> *Of meaning beyond the regimes*
> *There's a place in my dreams*
> *Where love is free to thrive*
> *No one can conceal*
> *That magic is real*
> *I'll break out of prison*
> *To search for my vision*
> *I'm alive*

The song ended on the word 'alive' and climbed to a hopeful chord. Aera allowed it to blast and decay before finally lifting her hands from the keys.

Everybody was silent for a moment; then, people began to clap. Their cheering grew louder until they roared and screamed. Aera's blush was so hot that her face pounded, and Kize smiled brightly, though she also looked embarrassed. The moment was transformational beyond the two of them.

Aera tried to ignore her throbbing cheeks as she dared to glance at the enthusiastic audience. Doriline and her friends scowled in the front row, and Aera felt vindicated as she tossed a bright smile. She couldn't decide what was more satisfying: outclassing Doriline or singing about freedom right in front of Nurin, albeit unbeknownst to him.

Cyrrus and Pelyane climbed up to the stage, and he said, "Thank you, Aera. Thank you, Kize."

"Renstrom Nurin will select performers now," Pelyane announced, her voice bouncier than ever. "Thank you Aera and Kize!" She pointed to them, and the audience cheered again.

Aera crossed the stage, maintaining poise despite her shaking limbs, and Kize joined her, blushing and grinning. The two climbed down the stairs and continued across the Field behind them, distancing themselves from the crowd while people chanted, "We are all the same! We are all the same!" As they moved further away, the noise died down, and Nurin began to speak.

"You're really good," Kize said with sincere awe in her voice.

A smile spilled over Aera's face, and Kize looked delighted and surprised to see her happy. Aera was even more surprised that the performance made her feel so radiant but wasn't sure how to express that. All she could think to say was, "You too."

"Do you practice a lot?" Kize asked.

"Sometimes," Aera said. There was an awkward silence, and she added, "Do you?"

"Every day," Kize chirped. "Pelyane studies other cultures and we read about their dances for inspiration. Sometimes our friends come with us to sing and dance in the woods, and sometimes we go to the Music Room, and they try to play instruments... but nobody plays like you do."

Aera blushed. It amused her that Kize and Pelyane were so dedicated while she played as she pleased. If Vaye hadn't lured her with an endless flow of mysteries and wonders, she would never have bothered with repetitive exercises.

"How do you learn songs?" Kize asked.

Aera felt strangely flattered that Kize was so intrigued. "Sometimes from books... but that one was original."

"You made it up?"

Aera was confused; she had just said this. "Yes..."

"That's amazing!" Kize exclaimed. "Would you play with me more? We could use the music room. Cyrrus says it's legal."

Kize glowed as she pronounced Cyrrus's name. Aera wondered whether he'd seen her dance before now. Did her grace move him like Aera's music had when she played underground? Perhaps he was passing the laws to please Kize, or, by extension, Pelyane...

That's insane. Aera smirked at herself. Cyrrus was utilitarian and decidedly unromantic. These people meant nothing to him.

She considered Kize's request. It would mean becoming tied to people and plans, condemning herself to watching Kize shine, and worrying that Cyrrus preferred Kize the whole time. On the other hand, Kize's dance had inspired her. Aera restricted herself at the cottage to hide her thoughts from Vaye, and she needed a place to let go. She might even make friends for once.

"Sure," Aera decided.

Kize smiled ear to ear, glowing with excitement. Despite her obvious crush on Cyrrus, she didn't seem to harbor negative feelings toward Aera.

Clanks and bangs assaulted Aera's ears. She looked over to the stage, where four older boys were hitting symbols while one 'danced' awkwardly between them. Pelyane and Cyrrus departed from the crowd, annoyingly comfortable together. As they approached, Kize admired Cyrrus with wide eyes.

"Enchanting performance," Cyrrus declared.

Kize's cheeks reddened as she mumbled shyly, "Thanks, Cyrrus..."

"On the contrary, thank *you*."

Kize was glowing like a fool, and Cyrrus was encouraging her. As he glanced at Aera, his emerald eyes were alive with mischief, suggesting he enjoyed her displeasure. She grimaced, unimpressed.

"You're *amazing*, Aera!" Pelyane exclaimed. "When you played, I couldn't believe I was in Ynas. I thought I was somewhere else. I've never heard anything like it! I wish I could listen to you all day."

"You can listen when we practice," Kize chimed. Then, she glanced at Aera and added shyly, "If it's okay..."

Both girls stared at Aera eagerly, and she felt a strange sense of power, as if her answer would impact them. Was this what Cyrrus felt like all the time? Distantly, she said, "That's fine."

"I'm so excited!" Pelyane exclaimed. "Can we do it tomorrow at lunch?"

Aera would not sleep much, and her senses would be acute. It wouldn't be an ideal time to be around people, but she didn't want to be contrarian when everyone else seemed so happy and relaxed. "Okay," she agreed.

Both girls smiled from ear to ear, and Aera felt strangely important.

"Are you prepared to endure the other performances?" Cyrrus inquired wryly.

"I say we go to the library," Pelyane giggled.

"There's still Nurin to consider," Cyrrus said. "I'll deal with that. Return here in two hours."

"Kize, you coming?" Pelyane asked.

Kize glanced from Aera to Cyrrus and, as Cyrrus met her eyes, she blushed like a giddy child. He allowed a coy grin, and then the two girls headed away.

Aera and Cyrrus stood side by side in the freezing cold air, silent and stiff. Drums clanked on the stage. Aera's breath formed a cloud in front of her face. She rubbed her hands together.

"Your contribution was useful," Cyrrus said. His voice was expressionless, and his gaze was fixed in front of him.

Useful, Aera thought. *Make yourself useful.*

"The other performances will be terrible," he declared in the same flat tone. "The people will vote only to hear you."

Aera wanted him to appreciate her music on its own merit, but the vote was clearly all he cared about. When Kize was there, he'd carried on as if he'd enjoyed the performance.

"At curfew, the Adolescent Hut will be unlocked," Cyrrus said. "Shall we explore the rooms?"

Why was Cyrrus making plans with her now? She had served her purpose. Music was her only gift, and although Cyrrus did not appreciate its beauty or meaning, he could no longer declare her—or it—*useless*.

He watched her, awaiting an answer, but she tossed him an acidic glare and left. A soft breeze unwound her hair and lightened her step. She felt like a bird escaping confinement, sailing along in the bitter cold wind. A smile crept to her lips as she imagined him trying to make sense of her 'emotions.'

Hidden Star

1329 EARLY-WINTER

Aera went to the cottage, where she and Vaye played some old songs and chatted. When the curfew bell gonged, Aera no longer needed to rush away, and Vaye acknowledged the newfound freedom with a knowing smile.

"Adolescence is a wonderful time," Vaye mused in a dreamy voice.

Aera wondered where Vaye had lived during her adolescence. Her chocolate eyes were rich with delight, and Aera wished she could read her mind and witness the memories that enchanted her. Hoping for a clue, Aera asked, "When did you learn to play piano?"

"I learned as a child, but music is not my calling."

Aera suspected her calling was related to botany, but asked anyway, "What is?"

"Alchemy," Vaye said. "Specifically, with plants."

Aera smiled, gratified that she'd guessed correctly. "I should go," she said. "I might come by more often after curfew and less during meals, if that's okay."

"Any reason?"

"Nurin asked small groups to perform today. I played with a dancer, and she wants to practice together in the Music Room."

Vaye smiled. "How delightful."

"The piano is out of tune..."

"That can be fixed."

Aera knew it could be fixed, but she doubted anybody in the Ynas administration would bother to fix it.

"You're more than welcome to come at night," Vaye said. "As long as my upstairs curtains are open."

Aera decided to thank her in Silindion and said, "*Tesesili, a Vaye.*[1]"

With a warm smile, Vaye responded, "*Sompa la.*[2]"

Sompa la meant 'sleep well,' but Aera had a long night ahead of her. "*Nerilyane,*[3]" she grinned, and left.

The moment she opened the door, she was greeted by biting cold air. She pulled her hood over her head and ran through the forest, eager to return to the fireplace in the Adolescent Hut. Cyrrus was right: it would be impossible to use the orb outside without freezing to death.

When she finally arrived at the hut, she was panting and shivering. She burrowed her hands together while she scrambled to catch her breath. Then, suddenly, she noticed Cyrrus across the hall, waiting... even though she'd never confirmed plans with him.

"Let's start at the end of the hall," he suggested. "The torches will warm you soon enough."

Cyrrus watched her, seeking approval, and she allowed a smile. He was back to being friendly and eager to charm her. Walking away from him had been a wise move.

The hallway was identical to the Education Unit, with wooden floors, brick walls and a double door opening to an entranceway where the corridor divided. They headed to the end of the hall opposite the staircase, where one door was marked 'Boys' and the other, 'Girls.'

Aera opened the Girls' door and was greeted by latrine stench. She pulled it closed and met Cyrrus across the way. They proceeded to the next door, and as Cyrrus opened it, they heard laughter and saw some older girls seated together. Four identical round tables were spaced out in the middle of the room, each scattered with sewing supplies. These tables gave it the appearance of a classroom, only larger.

"Samely, Cyrrus!" someone called. "Samely, Aera!"

Aera was surprised: this stranger knew her name and could also pronounce it correctly. She recognized Dila's friend Pavene, but the others were unknown to her.

453

"Greetings, Tarele," Cyrrus responded. He looked at the others in turn and added, "Greetings, Pavene, Inori, Lydan, Amiline."

"Aera, you were amazing today," Pavene said shyly.

"You really were," said someone else.

"I can't wait for Spring!" another exclaimed.

Aera's cheeks flushed. As she fumbled for a response, Cyrrus turned to her and said, "I neglected to inform you. The laws passed, and the crowd voted for you to perform next season."

"You should perform every season," said Tarele. "I don't even want to hear anyone else."

Aera was perplexed. She could hardly believe she was receiving more attention than Cyrrus. It was he who passed the laws, who knew everyone's names, who changed the commune. All she had done was play a song as a favor to him. What was she supposed to say to these people she barely recognized? It was a cruel irony that she'd always envied the attention Cyrrus received, and yet, when it came her way, she couldn't accept it.

She forced a smile, acquiesced to a friendly tone and relinquished, "Thanks!"

"Want to join us?" someone asked.

"We're exploring," Cyrrus said. "Perhaps we'll return later." When he pulled the door closed behind him, Aera was relieved.

He opened the door across the hall, and they entered a room with game tables and a herd of people, including Doriline's squad. Cyrrus closed the door and they continued to the next, where people stretched and lifted weights on mats covering the hardwood floor.

They checked every room until they reached the end of the hall, where they found one that might accommodate their needs, as its back wall was lined with wooden stalls. The remaining space was empty but for chairs, torches, and a couple by the fireplace, fondling conspicuously.

Aera crossed the room to examine the construction, noticed one door slightly open and stepped inside to discover an empty stall with a mat on the floor. The inside of the door had a hook hanging from it corresponding to a metal loop on the jamb. She latched the lock and pushed on the door to see if it would open. Although the lock held the door in place, the wood was thin and there was space between the top of the stall and the ceiling, which would make light from the orb visible from outside.

Someone groaned nearby, and there was a knock against the wall, followed by a grunt. Aera surmised there were couples behind the other doors. *The mating barn*, she thought. Cyrrus was not in the room, but just outside in the hallway, staring ahead in silence.

Without a word, he opened the opposite door. The inside was the same as the last, only with more people and louder groans. He closed the door expressionlessly, and Aera enjoyed how stiff and uncomfortable he was.

Footsteps approached in the staircase as Hizad, Dila and Rafi rounded the corner. In her predictably coquettish voice, Dila purred, "Samely, Cyrrus."

Distantly, Cyrrus said, "Greetings."

Dila smiled with cheeks so rosy that even in torchlight, her blush was luminous. Cyrrus graced her with a sleepy smile, not the least engaged.

"What're you doing in the hallway, genius?" Hizad teased. "Can't smart-talk your pet into the den?"

Rafi laughed boisterously while Dila gazed at Cyrrus with doleful eyes, waiting to see what he would say. But he ignored the comment entirely and looked at Hizad with a blank expression.

"You've been here two years," Rafi said to Hizad. "Who've you bundled?"

Dila afforded a laugh, then turned to Cyrrus again. He, however, was already halfway up the staircase. Dila's dreamy look drained as the others resumed bickering.

"Darse it, Rafi," Hizad grunted. "No boy wants *you*."

"I don't do boys," Rafi retorted. "I've tasted more *girls* than you ever will."

Tasted, Aera thought. *Bundled*. These people reduced love to crudity.

She followed Cyrrus up the stairs, and the voices faded as they rounded the corner. Cyrrus turned to her, and she murmured, "There's nowhere to go."

"I have no advice to offer," Cyrrus said flatly. "I need to sleep."

He reached into his cloak and retrieved the silver-wrapped orb.

"Not *here!*" Aera whispered, but he ignored her. Quickly, she buried it in her own pocket, and Cyrrus headed up the stairs.

Aera leaned against the wall, tense and frustrated. The most logical move was to go upstairs, as she'd barely slept the night before and had endured an eventful day. Tomorrow might be better. As she climbed the first stair, she felt the orb against her hip and the song ran through her mind.

> *Is it early? Is it too late?*
> *Is this tomorrow?*
> *If I don't give you everything now*
> *How long will I wait?*

She stood motionless, locked in place, helpless to force herself up the stairs. The hidden star was within reach. Even if she went to bed, sleep would not come. She descended the stairs, went down the hall and thrust open the exit door. Freezing wind assaulted her face, and she breathed it in, letting the fresh night air fill her lungs.

There was no place in the building to hide, but that wouldn't stop her. Even if it took all night, she would make her way into the orb. She'd waited long enough.

The cold night inspired the thrill of challenge. Aera tethered her hood, tightened her cloak, and hurried toward the village to find shelter. The buildings contained empty closets and classrooms. Perhaps she could use one.

Quietly, she tugged on a few doors, but found them locked. She tried to think of another place to go and remembered a brick hut in the bathing grove. It was unlikely anyone would be down there—since it would require a death wish to bathe in the middle of the night during the coldest part of winter—but if she used the fireplace, smoke would rise from the chimney. Would anyone see it? She crossed the Raetsek Field and positioned herself on the bridge overlooking the waterfall that poured into the valley. The surrounding conifers blocked not only the hut, but also the pond. As long as nobody approached the bathing inlet, she would be safe.

The waterfall became louder and the air colder as she followed the path to the grove. She trembled under her hood, breathed warmth into her hands and tightened her freezing toes, which were becoming numb. When she finally arrived, the hut was open. She felt around for any lock or latch on the door but found none. She decided to take her chances.

Quickly and quietly, she gathered materials and started a fire. The warmth of the flames relieved her. Once her toes and fingers had thawed, she removed the orb from her pocket and unfastened the covering, revealing the astral necklace.

As she positioned her hand over the globe, its vibrations made her flutter. The hidden star might be with her any moment now. She closed her eyes, recited, *"Ger beni ath cemmar,"* and the world transformed.

Stars assumed the familiar rings as Aera hovered in her appointed depot. Two auras were already in place, Green and Red. She was eager to look for the hidden star, but reluctant to do so with others present. If they were unaware of its existence, she didn't want to change that.

Both auras beamed lines of color in her direction and waited, inviting communication. Aera cloaked herself in shadow and the space around her sparked in red and green, reflecting her neighbors. Muffled sounds emerged from one of the figures, and a monotone declared: "Ten twenty-one eight, twenty-one six fourteen two one thirteen.[4]"

They both faced Aera. She wondered whether Cyrrus understood the numbers, though it wouldn't help her if he did. She was Cyrrus now and did not understand.

"Ten twenty-one eight, twenty-one six fourteen two one thirteen," repeated the voice, each syllable slow and deliberate. Both apparitions angled towards her, seeking a response.

Her vibrations undulated as green flashes prickled her. If someone expected Cyrrus to apprehend an unfamiliar code, he would deflect to avoid revealing ignorance. The last thing he'd said that night was fresh in her mind, and she repeated it: "I have no advice to offer." Her statement emerged from the center in Cyrrus's voice, just as she'd hoped.

"Sixteen ten seven,[5]" said the red aura, his tone stern.

At once, both auras vanished, replaced by their respective stars. Aera's wish was now realized. She was alone.

She searched for the hidden star and saw only an empty spot... then a twinkle. Then another... and another. She imagined wandering through shadow, searching for the elusive boy. Perhaps if she sang, he would appear.

"I calm myself down," she cooed, and the vibrant dream voice emerged. "And soon enough, space crashes into time, and we all fall, we all fall in love..."

Pearly light spread like mist as she reveled in her resonant voice. She envisioned the fur-hooded figure in the distance and sang, "Under the moonlight, I lie in your shadow. The chill of midnight won't cool our passion..."

The magnetic force gripped her and locked her gaze on the empty spot: the hidden star. There it was! Heat rippled through her, and golden rays radiated. She felt naked as her essence brightened the world.

"Is it early?" she purred. "Is it too late? Is this tomorrow? If I don't give you everything now, how long will I wait?"

Vibrations expanded and contracted from her heart. *Thump, thump.* A piano interlude played in her mind and an azure light answered in tempo, its shade identical to the eyes in her dream. Blue flares resonated along with the heartbeat that pulsated inside her. His slavish attention to her rhythm made her feel beautiful, even though he could not see her body.

"It doesn't help to question everything," she crooned. "It doesn't matter if you're real. I can admit I might be dreaming, but I can't change the way I feel..."

Aera's voice echoed, leaving behind trails of gold. With irresistible force, her companion reeled her in, unraveling her energy and pulling her close. Her aureate sheen spilled and enveloped the blue star like petals on a flower. In turn, the star swelled and brightened. Their vibrations coalesced naturally, as though they had been together always.

"I'm wide awake, I've never felt so sure, so pure. And I feel like I've known you before. I feel like I've been here before. Maybe this already happened, and it's over and over and I still hunger for more..."

The blue blaze ruptured Aera's flower and blasted the atmosphere, flaring with fiery colors, flashing in harmony with her thunderous heartbeat. His aura smoldered; he ached to consume her. Their storm coalesced into one euphoric whirl, and Aera undulated in surrender. She had never felt so desired, so present, so free.

"I still hunger for more," she repeated. "More..."

As the last echoes of her voice faded, Aera burst into hot blue. The throb of her heart dominated the sphere until she was defenseless and could no longer distinguish her own presence from an eruption of blazing light and fury. All that she was, all that she might ever be, collapsed into a maelstrom of powerful, penetrating *thumps*.

Suddenly, it stopped. Aera's heart was hollow, her body ephemeral, the world quiet and still. Across the sphere, the blue light was gone, replaced by a star among the others. She turned to face the outer ring and said, "*Ger beni ath cemmar...*"

Vibrations infiltrated her senses and thrust her back out into the freezing cold, her body numb and the fire dying. She wondered how long she'd been in Elkandul. Time had lost all meaning. A smile consumed her... until she heard voices outside.

"C'mon, Lani!"

"The water's ghaadi freezing, you barlock!"

"You ghaadi well are going in!"

"Don't touch me, Idan!"

People everywhere, always. The faces in the fog. Aera pried her fingers apart and was overwhelmed by stabbing sensations in her hands.

"Blast, Viram! I'll set you both on fire!"

"Get back here!"

The voices were close. Desperately, Aera tried to cloak the orb with its covering, but her hand was barely responsive.

"By Riva's Trees! There's smoke in the chimney! Idan, go check the hut!"

Move! Aera implored herself. With a concentrated push, she rolled the orb onto the cover, but still couldn't pick it up. She pried her feet out from under her thighs, fighting the pins and needles that swept across her limbs, and shook her arms vigorously. Footsteps crunched the leaves outside the hut, closer every moment. She stuffed the orb into her pocket just as the door opened.

"Who's that?" asked a stocky figure in the doorway. "What're you doing in there?"

Aera could barely move. She needed to buy herself time. With a wry grin, she offered, "Magic."

The boy laughed and said, "Wait... are you... the piano girl?"

Before Aera could respond, a tall girl appeared in the doorway. "Don't let Idan bother you," she said, and pushed him out of the way. "I'm Lani, and your music is ghaadi *amazing*."

Aera blushed and mumbled, "Thanks." She couldn't think of anything else to say and didn't want to encourage conversation while so thoroughly indisposed, but she felt guilty dismissing people who were kind to her.

As she tried to figure out what to do, someone else approached. "What in Riva's blasted trees is going on?" he laughed.

"Look, Viram," Lani said. "It's the piano girl."

A skinny boy peeked in and said nervously, "Samely, uh, Piano Girl..."

"You better leave, Viram," Idan said. "She says she's doing *magic*."

Lani laughed, and Viram pressed, "So, what's she really doing?"

Aera wished she could enjoy the attention, but she still couldn't move. "Could you... give me a moment?"

"Sure thing," said Idan. He ushered the others away and said, "Let's go."

The group headed off and conversed in hushed voices, but with her acute hearing, Aera could pick up every word.

"Maybe she's sad."

"Maybe she's fighting with Cyrrus."

"That boy is trouble."

I'm trouble too, Aera thought, and giggled. For once, she'd found 'trouble' of her own.

She stroked her limbs, shook her hands, and squeezed her toes to chase away the pins and needles. Finally, she was able to stand up. She stomped each foot until she could walk out of the hut, leaving the last embers of the fire to burn out on their own.

The others were in a circle nearby. When they noticed her passing, Idan called, "Samely, Eh-ruh!"

Aera sensed he was inviting her over, but she was delirious and needed to leave. She waved politely and headed off.

"See, Idan," Lani balked. "She doesn't *want* to be your friend..."

460

Aera felt a pang of guilt but continued on her way. Once the others were out of range, she ran at full speed and let her smile break free. She traversed the path between the trees, darted across the Field, soared to the top of Halcyon Hill and stopped to catch her breath.

The full moon was magnificent, beaming over Southside Forest with Erelion coruscating alongside, flashing silver and blue. *Hyuvún i larë silnemmanyë, vë sarna otma nondo...*[6]

Aera thought of the hidden star throbbing in unison while she sang out her raw feelings, bold and free. She envisioned a bare-chested boy with blazing blue eyes, blushing at the moon from a mountaintop, burning for her...

... *if only,* she thought.

The hidden star might not be a boy. It might not even be human. It might be an enemy, or something else she had not yet conceived of. It could be anything... yet she *felt* something specific. She associated the sorcerous ghost in the orb with the ravenous boy in her dream. Her *vekos* was on fire.

It was insane that a character in her dream would influence her reality, yet she couldn't divorce the dream boy from the hidden star. Some of her dreams were identical to Cyrrus's and she'd heard foreign languages before learning about them. Might this dream prove similarly prescient?

She gazed at Alárië, whose glow extended far beyond her splendid cast, illuminating the surrounding sky as Erelion basked in her luminescence. Aera wished she could bathe in ferocious blue light, pulsating and melting like she did in the orb. Whoever or whatever it was, that hidden star aroused sensations she'd never experienced. She'd held herself back all her life, but this thing, this force, drew her out and revealed her bare energy. The fusion between them was sublime.

The ground was liquid as she floated across the grass and into Adolescent Hut. A blur of people lined the hallways, bickering and chattering as she drifted by. Nothing would shake her gentle euphoria.

She slipped into the new venue and tiptoed to her corner by the fireplace. Its heat was intense, but she welcomed it and knew she would sleep well. She stripped down to her under-tunic and snuggled beneath the blanket, where she lost herself in unimaginable thoughts.

As she drifted into another realm, she sensed hands running along her limbs. She imagined the scent of skin, hair against her cheeks... then a flash of azure jolted her, and the fantasy slipped away. *It's over and over and I still hunger for more*, she thought, and smiled as sleep lured her into its grasp.

∽

Waking up the next morning was agony. Floorboards groaned, voices roared, and laughter screeched. The stink of morning sweat was an assault on her saturated senses. Aera held her breath, dressed quickly, and ran out.

When she reached the boulder, she hesitated. The thought of food was nauseating, and she needed to be away from people. She combed her hair and listened to the soft hiss of wind as the orb melody infiltrated. *And we all fall, we all fall in love...*

Footsteps approached from behind in an even pace. Cyrrus sat down beside Aera, passed her a mug of water and stuffed some beans in his mouth. The cool water felt like an icicle sliding through her. As she licked the coldness from her lips, Cyrrus turned to her.

"What happened in Elkandul?" he asked.

"You never tell me," she said coolly. "Why should I tell you?"

"It's strategic."

Aera groaned, but he ignored it, stuffed turnip cake into his mouth and garbled, "Everybody is pretending to be someone else in order to fulfill an agenda. You need to pretend to be me and keep my motives hidden, and I need to figure out what is real."

"What if you figure it out?" Aera challenged. "Then what?"

Cyrrus's eyes fixed on Aera's. Slowly and evenly, he said, "We will escape Ynas."

We will escape Ynas. We. Aera's heart pounded.

Cyrrus bit into a potato and locked his eyes on his tray. Caws resounded from across the river as a murder of crows departed the belltower. Aera watched them disappear and said, "Then your gaming for Renstrom is a hoax."

"There's no room for honesty in politics."

His sudden shift was unsettling. Why was he working so hard to

462

change the laws if he intended to leave? If he'd been planning to run off with Aera, why hadn't he mentioned it before now?

"It is imperative that my transactions remain unknown to you," Cyrrus asserted. "It's an advantage in Elkandul to have two sets of knowledge."

"If we're pretending to be the same person, we should have the same knowledge."

"If we flash colors or adopt shapes in response to statements, it might reveal something to them. Emotions are universal and inconsequential, but recognition of knowledge may have implications, such as providing clues to our whereabouts."

Silver had thrown names around, and the angular men had barked numbers at Aera on multiple trips to Elkandul. If Cyrrus was right, they might have been testing her to see what she knew.

"I suspect some of the figures in the orb are prominent in politics," Cyrrus said. "Some orbs may be passed down through dynasties and regimes. People might mention bits of history or ask questions to identify which group we belong to, how much we know, or how powerful we are. It will give us an advantage if one of us knows something and the other is ignorant. Since they think we are one person, their tests will only confuse them further."

Aera wondered if this was why Cyrrus had barely spoken to her for months. They had often discussed the outside world because Cyrrus was only too eager to show off his knowledge about it, but now he wanted her to be ignorant.

"You must *not* remain ignorant," Cyrrus protested, answering her unspoken thought. "If you have no goals or awareness, it will appear suspicious. We must both appear to have an agenda, but if we don't know each other's agenda, its nature will be ambiguous to everyone else. It would be advisable to question Vaye about the world outside."

"Vaye is secretive..."

"Find a way."

The clouds parted, revealing a patch of sunlight that brightened the hill and stung Aera's eyes.

"Tell me," Cyrrus commanded. "What happened in Elkandul last night?"

Aera breathed into her belly and the breeze chilled her face as she inhaled the winter air. *In, out.* Once her shoulders relaxed, she intoned casually, "The red and green auras spoke in numbers."

"Was anybody else present?"

Curtly, Aera declared, "No."

"Which numbers?"

This request was ridiculous: he couldn't possibly expect her to know that. His poetic aphorisms were impossible to forget, but boring conversation eluded her. She strained to remember something and pictured their jagged colors, glowing in straight lines of red and green. "Ten twenty-one... eight..." she paused. "I... I don't know. There were too many."

"Your memory requires improvement."

Gong, gong. The morning bell jostled Aera's stomach. Cyrrus rose promptly, but as Aera forced herself up, the motion nauseated her.

"You are adept at hiding your thoughts and feelings," Cyrrus said. "You're ready for memory training."

Aera had imagined Cyrrus was born reciting books and never considered that his memory might have been trained. Though it seemed boring and beyond her capacity, she was relieved that he still wanted to teach her things.

"We will train four days from now, during lunch," Cyrrus declared. "Recover your bearings."

They joined their respective lines. Padd barked orders, rattling Aera's ears with his blaring voice until her group was called. "15-16 Group! To the Cattle Fields!"

Aera remembered then that her Age Group no longer took classes: from that day forward, they would perform tasks for both four-hour periods. They had graduated from victims of indoctrination to full-time servitude. *We will escape Ynas*, she thought. Soon, they would be gone.

Tasks dragged on and tormented Aera as every sound sliced her ears. Her mind spun with images of blazing eyes and echoes of her dynamic orb-voice mixed with Cyrrus's words. *We will escape Ynas.* The inner turmoil was even more exhausting than the physical torture she dragged herself through.

When lunch finally came, she was eager to be alone and to rest. She crouched by the boulder, shivering under her cloak, and closed her eyes

464

until she heard footsteps. Kize and Pelyane were approaching. She'd forgotten her promise to play music with them.

"Did you eat?" Pelyane chirped.

Aera tried to muster some enthusiasm but barely managed to mumble, "I'm not hungry..."

"Want to play?"

Aera dragged herself up, and the three headed into the Education Unit. When they reached the Music Room, fire roared inside and its heat soon thawed Aera. She sat at the piano and stroked the keys, whose surfaces were yellowed and chipped. Her fingers sank into a chord. The sound was unfamiliar, like a whole new instrument... in tune.

She played a few more chords and determined that someone had tuned the piano. Her cheeks flushed: it must have been Vaye. She was so kind, even as Aera worked to deceive her.

Kize stretched nearby, preparing to dance, and Pelyane leaned against the wall balancing a book on her knees. Aera stared at the piano and watched in a daze as its wood seemed to melt. *Under the moonlight, I lie in your shadow...*

She prepared to strike the first chord and pictured blue light swelling as heat infused her. *Thump, thump.* Her hand shook. *Thump, thump...*

Stop obsessing, she admonished herself. She closed her eyes, breathed into her belly, and thought, *I am Ivory. Life is a game.*

She opened her eyes. In front of her were hands and patterns. Blacks and whites. Lines and spaces. Fingers and keys...

...a piano.

What could she play? Nothing came to mind. Had her entire past escaped her memory? Surely, she had played music before that song... yet there was nothing...

"Aera?"

Kize's eyes were huge and surrounded by curls. "Are you ready?"

Aera inhaled deeply. She was not ready. She was dizzy and confused. Yet here she was, with fingers and a piano. She could do this. The keys were calling her hands, luring her. *I calm myself down...*

She squeezed her fists. That song again. She had gone mad! Cyrrus wanted to run away with her, yet she misled him about a stranger in the orb. *The dream boy is a fantasy*, she thought. *Cyrrus is real.*

She sank her fingers into the keys, and her hands played on their own. Though she could barely think, her body remembered another song, and the voice in her mind sang lyrics while she strained to contain them. *Id i phendenya mornë Uristienëa, ievissa mirt i nossë mirnanólmëa...*[7]

The song spilled forth as she closed her eyes. *Kirméin nai në nëa nesi, lárëanu o i himeivi imenna, merskë; në naimaro nistánunyë në mirínnunyë...*[8]

Along with the lyrics, she imagined the full moon rising in a sky filled with every shade of mountainous grey clouds. *Erólion, eldisso eis vauleiri të yo-lissuntë.*[9] Before the moon stood the silhouette of a naked man with a robust bow and hot blue eyes. Aera hunted the shadows for his face, but all she saw were fingers, keys...

...she was dreaming while awake. Everything reminded her of that dream, that fantasy... that damned blue light...

It wasn't the blue light. This was the image that had revealed itself to Aera underground when the magic piano had played itself through her hands. She'd conflated her vision of Erelion with the feral boy in her dream.

She focused on breathing. *In, out.* Her hands moved across the keys, even as her mind drifted in and out of awareness, and the song journeyed on. *Mië këasi pero i narnán mëundëa, núksëu veresi no Ilkarienna...*[10]

CEREBRAL CIRCUS

1329 EARLY-WINTER

When the day came for memory training, Aera and Cyrrus rushed through lunch, eager to begin. They harnessed scraps and built a fire in the rock pit at Great Gorge. Aera enjoyed the crackle of burning branches and the surrounding insect voices. After a long stare into the flames, Cyrrus began the lesson.

"In order to remember something, we must experience it initially," he said. "People are often so lost in thought that they miss much of their experience. You have an advantage. You've learned to focus on your breath, posture and muscles, and to quiet the chatter in your brain by grounding yourself in the physical world. This enhances your awareness."

Aera realized, as Cyrrus spoke, that she'd taken these accomplishments for granted. When Cyrrus listed them all at once, she appreciated how far she'd come and felt gratified that Cyrrus recognized it.

"Another skill you've mastered is isolating yourself from your biases," Cyrrus continued. "In order to perceive an event as it is, one must avoid automatic associations. You may recall when I prompted you to look at your hands and see hands, instead of ugly hands, small hands, or another judgement. I will ask you now to close your eyes and imagine yourself in an emotionally charged situation. Picture it until your feelings accompany it."

Aera closed her eyes but was reluctant to imagine emotional situations in front of Cyrrus, since he could read her mind. She tried to recall something she didn't need to hide and remembered feeling angry when she'd encountered Doriline's flock outside the secret door. Tension mounted all over again as she pictured herself in that hallway, fuming because their inane socializing would ruin her plans, and because it was Cyrrus's fault for sending them there.

"Now, imagine yourself as an insect on the wall, watching the situation from the outside," Cyrrus said. "Imagine how your face looks to the insect. Imagine how your posture appears. Picture the episode from an external perspective."

Aera couldn't recall her appearance in detail and had no idea what to imagine. What would others see when she became Ivory? She pictured a blonde, female version of Cyrrus, calm and aloof except for 'venomous' eyes. The image made her chuckle.

"Well done," Cyrrus said. "I withheld this tool last time because it requires concentrated thinking, which is accessible through *inyanondo*. You must use it when you're alone. Any time you review an event, it will help you to achieve clarity—but to place that event in long-term memory, you must replay it immediately afterwards. Use the technique of outside perspective, and your memories will not be corrupted by emotion."

Aera tried to imagine herself playing piano at Unity Festival. What might she have looked like to Kize? Had she appeared poised? Nervous? The whole commune was watching, yet she had no idea what they saw.

"Be present," Cyrrus said. "I will teach you how memory works."

The firelight cast a golden hue on Cyrrus's pale cheeks and reddened his lively eyes. He looked excited and alert. "Memory is constructed on associations, so we're likely to forget anything that doesn't fit into a framework," he said. "Visualize everything I say. Ready?"

"Very," she grinned.

"I encountered a door with an iron handle shaped like a stag's head," he said. "Picture it."

The door was easy to visualize. Aera concentrated on it and imagined antlers protruding from the handle.

"You are likely to forget this soon," Cyrrus said, "unless I tell you this door is in the rear hallway of the Adolescent Hut."

This could not be. Aera had checked every wall to make sure she didn't miss any doors. She looked at Cyrrus, awaiting explanation.

"There's a concrete wall that cuts short the back hallway," he said. "Picture it."

Aera remembered that wall—it was just beyond the secret room. She visualized the dark barrier looming in the shadowy corridor.

"That wall is an illusion. There's another door beyond it, on the side of the hallway opposite our secret door."

An illusion? That was unlikely... unless there was *sarya* involved. Aera thought she remembered touching that wall, but perhaps she hadn't. She envisioned herself walking right through the concrete and encountering a new door with a stag's head for a handle.

"The idea of that illusory wall and that second door will be embedded in your memory," Cyrrus said. "Although you have only seen it in your mind, and may deduce that I am lying, you will never forget it."

Cyrrus was right. She couldn't imagine forgetting that any time soon.

"To remember something new, place it inside something familiar," Cyrrus instructed. "If I were teaching this to the clan, I would advise them to create cerebral storage in Vapid Village or the sleeping huts— but for you, that would be too dangerous. If anybody in the outside world uses *inyanondo*, they might trace your origin to Ynas. You can use the forests or something imaginary. The setting must be memorable and enticing, since you will spend much time there. It will be the foundation upon which you build your cerebral world."

The white forest was the only imaginary world Aera knew, but her dreamscape was too personal to share. "How do you decide?" she asked.

"You must choose something emotionally evocative and equally familiar to any real location you know well."

Emotionally evocative... this meant he had a personal connection to the circus. Did he build it in his imagination, or did it come from a real memory? Aera wanted to ask, but his past was off-limits.

He stared into the fire, contemplating something. Aera assumed he'd heard her thoughts and wished she could hear his. Finally, he said, "I trust you remember Korov's lesson about the circus in Kadir."

"A little... but I remember more from your town meeting drama."

Cyrrus's eyes gleamed. "Korov showed us the circular venue they use for performances, but there's more he didn't show. The festival goes on for weeks and people sleep in tents on the grounds. There's abundant food and spectacle with wild animals in cages, artists drawing, and warriors jousting. Some people perform sexual rituals and violent rites of passage into adulthood. There are all manner of contests and entertainments, and each activity has its own pavilion. This idea inspired the landscape of my own circus."

Aera wondered how he knew this. It was plausible that a book about Kadir contained ample detail, but less likely that Cyrrus would have an emotional connection to something from a book. Perhaps he'd been there, or even grown up there.

"I begin in the center of the ring," Cyrrus said. "The surrounding seats are filled with people, and I locate a specific person and let the rest of the crowd vanish. He leads me out of the ring and into his own home, where I have stored memories associated with him."

"That's complicated," Aera said. "Seats, rings, crowds, people..."

"Picture your venue first. Firm it in your mind right now."

Aera closed her eyes but didn't know what setting to choose. *A grassy field*, she decided, and pictured it. That was easy.

"Now, add something emotional and familiar to the scene," Cyrrus offered. "This will root it in your memory."

Aera surrounded the field with a wide circular perimeter of white trees. At the very center of the enclave, she positioned the great oak by itself. Its branches reached out in the sunlight.

"There are people in attendance, including several great authors," Cyrrus continued. "Search the crowd for Vermaventiel."

Aera envisioned people sitting in the field, then searched for a Nestë woman. Her mind jumped to Vaye. She tried to replace the figure with someone else, but Vaye's features took over.

"She lives in a spherical, leather dome whose texture and color matches the cover of *Parë*," Cyrrus continued. "Inside, the furniture is shaped like the symbols she describes."

"Furniture shaped like symbols?" Aera laughed. "I'll never remember *that*."

Cyrrus's pupils reflected the fire. "The more one image connects to another, the more powerful the memory will be."

"Fine, but that's... contorted. You don't realize it because you're deranged."

Cyrrus giggled girlishly. Aera couldn't help giggling too.

"Have you ever seen a color and associated it with a sound?" he asked glowingly. "That's called synesthesia. It occurs when you hear colors, smell textures, or feel sounds. Any mixture of sensory experience will embed itself more deeply into memory."

Aera thought of the throb in her heart that she associated with hot blue. A blush crept up on her, but she summoned Ivory so Cyrrus wouldn't read those thoughts. She looked at him and smiled.

"Some might presume memory improvement is a dry activity, but it's actually a dynamic process that fuels itself with associations," he explained. "In my circus, each author wears a costume to match their written work, and there's a troupe of sword fighters who hold mock battles. I've learned combat skills by reading about techniques and watching imaginary warriors practice them."

Though Cyrrus's mindscape was endearing, it made Aera feel helpless. "I can't come up with such complicated scenes, and I'll never memorize costumes and moves. I can barely remember what people wear in Ynas."

"My world is a cerebral circus. Yours may be a cerebral symphony."

"I can't connect music to scenery."

"*Can't* means *won't*. Instead of undermining yourself, adjust my suggestions to suit your needs. Allow them to inspire you, but don't take them literally."

Aera grumbled, "Fine... but you're crazy."

"When it suits me," Cyrrus boasted. "Now, close your eyes and surround yourself with a ring of piano keys."

Aera knew he was provoking her on purpose and giggled at his convoluted imagery. Nonetheless, she 'adjusted' his suggestion, and pictured Vaye's piano on a wooden stage in her imaginary field.

"In my circus, I might dress someone in a bright colored shirt or a funny hat," Cyrrus said. "You might prefer to associate an odd syncopation with a specific hair color, a tempo change with a certain type of face, or a different part of the piano with a particular quality of voice."

Aera grinned at his quirky idea, but, again, it would never work. "You don't get it," she said. "For me, most colors and shapes aren't memorable."

"Start small," Cyrrus advised. "As we discussed, in order to remember something, you must first experience it without distraction. When I memorize books, I sit with them for a long time. I act out every sentence, every word, every action, until the content evokes memories in all my senses. The more I do this, the more associations I build, and the faster the process becomes."

Aera remembered many occasions when Cyrrus had stared ahead with *Parë* open in his lap. She'd assumed he was daydreaming, but, of course, he was always on a mission.

"This requires dedicated practice," Cyrrus said. "Before trying to memorize anything, you must build your cerebral symphony. Without a foundation, the information will float out of your grasp."

"There's a venue and a symphony," Aera reminded him. "Which one is the foundation?"

"Memorize the cerebral symphony by itself. Learn the colors of the notes, the feathers of the birds that sing them, the smell and texture of the instruments that play them. Keep it the same every time. Don't place anything in your venue until its contours are fully incorporated."

As Aera considered this, Cyrrus watched her with an adoring look that made her pulse speed up. Why was he doing that? She blushed and fixed her eyes on the fire.

"Start by building associations with numbers," Cyrrus instructed. "The numbers spoken in the orb include forty-one and everything between one and twenty-seven. Assign each number a specific sound, and give that sound a color, texture, smell, or shape. It can be a voice, a piano key, a bird. Whatever adheres to your mind."

Cyrrus's eyes twinkled with childlike enthusiasm, like they always did when he taught her things. She hoped she wouldn't disappoint him.

"Experience each number fully," Cyrrus instructed. "Smell it, touch it, see it, hear it. Breathe life into it. When you enter the orb, the associations will already be built, and the numbers will form a multilayered visual and musical arrangement that you will remember for a short time. When you exit the orb, play the arrangement again. And again. Experience the colors, shapes and sensations that belong with each note, and the numbers will be fixed in your memory. As you recite them to me, you may decode them."

His idea was ingenious, but Aera wasn't convinced it would work. "How long were you doing this before you could memorize books?"

Cyrrus stared at the fire and answered in a distant voice. "I've been building my cerebral world for as long as I can remember," he said, gazing ahead with a furrowed brow. "I envisioned its roots as a child, and I can remember some events that occurred even when I was learning to speak. It took the form of a circus when Korov showed us paintings of the venue in Kadir."

Aera suspected he was really from Kadir, and this was an oblique way of revealing his origins. It would make no sense for a child to connect so vividly to random artwork—let alone, paintings of mangled corpses—unless it reflected a genuine experience. He had bargained to work in the slaughterhouse, waxed eloquent about death, and fantasized about killing stupid people. Perhaps this was how he dealt with the early exposure to murder rituals.

Cyrrus flashed a knowing grin, indicating he'd read Aera's mind. He didn't appear annoyed. Apparently, he enjoyed her musing over his past, so long as she didn't request confirmation of her theories.

"The process is automatic now," he said. "I've become adept at storing current memories, and also accessing lost moments from the distant past. The hardest part is choosing which information to retain and which to discard."

"My memories disappear on their own," Aera mused. "You work so hard to remember things, then work even harder to forget them."

"While you surrender your mindscape to *vekos*, I harness mine to my advantage, and organize accordingly," he corrected her. "I send extraneous information, bad habits and invasive thoughts to the circus theater, where they are vanquished by stronger ideas and practices."

If this were true, Cyrrus would surely have vanquished his emotions. Gently, Aera asked, "What if a thought is so powerful that it can't be defeated?"

Cyrrus gazed ahead with a blank expression and adopted a slow monotone. "There's a cellar deep underground, guarded by a savage

473

beast who spits poisonous light. The walls are thick and there is no way out. Nothing can exit the cerebral cellar, and nobody may travel there—not even me. It is a storage place for all that cannot be defeated but must never be remembered."

Gong, gong. The deep ring of the bell startled Aera.

Without another word, they extinguished the fire and headed through the forest, side by side. Aera tried to conceptualize a cerebral symphony, but her mind kept drifting to one single thought...

...what was in his cerebral cellar?

Aera mulled over how to build a cerebral symphony that would allow her to recall twenty-seven numbers, along with the number forty-one. The next day during lunch break, she headed to the Music Room to develop a method.

She played through a few songs to wind down from the morning's tasks, then stopped and stared at the keys. There were twelve different notes within each octave before it repeated. At that point, she could start at the root again and strike the note twice, with rapid syncopation. When she completed the second octave, she would repeat the note three times.

She started on A below middle C and proceeded from there, imagining each key would match a particular number. Then, she thought of a few arbitrary numbers and counted them on the piano. After playing the pattern a few times, she was able to remember it—but she would need to do this in the orb without a piano. She came up with more random numbers, then closed her eyes and counted up the scale to figure them out. By the time she reached the final few, she'd forgotten the ones at the beginning. She needed to memorize each key and know instantly which number went with it.

For the rest of break, she practiced selecting a number and singing the associated note. She had improved by the time the bell gonged. It pleased her that she didn't need smells and visuals. With her knowledge of theory, musical intervals alone were sufficient, at least for memorizing numbers.

She headed back to the Field and continued practicing as she walked, quizzing herself mentally by picturing the piano and counting. Some of her guesses were still incorrect, but she was making headway. Throughout tasks, she drilled the exercises into her mind.

At dinner, she found Cyrrus waiting for her at the boulder with a tray containing two mugs of water, two rolls and a sausage. Aera determined the food was for her, since he no longer ate meat. She sat beside him and bit into the sausage. It was overcooked and crisp, unlike the savory soft meat she enjoyed at the cottage, but she appreciated that Cyrrus had brought it for her.

After eating some, she volunteered, "I started my symphony."

"Excellent. Will you remember the numbers next time?"

"I'm waiting for my senses to recover before I use the orb... so I'll probably be ready by then."

Cyrrus stuffed his roll into his mouth and garbled, "Let me borrow it until you need it."

Aera groaned. He had brought her food only because he wanted the orb.

"It'll help our mission," he said. "Be rational."

There was no reason to refuse Cyrrus the orb while she wasn't using it, but the attempt to charm her was insulting. "You should have just asked."

"It's self-defeating to objurgate a kind gesture. In the outside world, you may need to rely on the charity of others."

She almost said, *manipulation isn't charity*, but that was incorrect. Most people would have no reason to give without seeking something in return.

"Fine," she conceded. "Take it."

They looked around and spotted a few officers entering the Administration Unit. Nobody else was in sight. Content they were alone, Cyrrus inched to Aera's side and slipped his arm around her. As he slid his hand into her pocket, she realized she was leaning against his chest and her heart was pounding. She hadn't fallen into him on purpose but, if she moved away, she might draw attention to it. Warmth emanated from him, and she could feel his breathing. Every nerve went on alert.

He slid the orb from her pocket and rolled it up along her side. Slowly, he slipped his arm along the boulder behind her, taking his time for some ungodly reason. With every second, Aera's pulse pounded harder.

Finally, Cyrrus inched away. Aera breathed desperately into her belly, but there was not enough air in the world to steady her wild heartbeat. Beside her, Cyrrus bit his potato and chewed mechanically, but the rest of his body was motionless as he gazed at some space in front of him. She couldn't tell whether he was feigning obliviousness or felt nothing.

$$\sim$$

Though Aera's senses calmed, her mind was frenetic. Visions of the hidden star haunted her, guilt consumed her for hiding that from Cyrrus, rage filled her when she thought of everything Cyrrus concealed from her, and confusion overwhelmed her as she recalled his body against hers. She wanted that again.

Despite that emotional tangle, she forged forward with her cerebral symphony. She wanted Cyrrus to have confidence in her. When not playing with Kize, she spent breaks alone in the Music Room, matching notes with numbers. Once those associations were established, she paired each number with a letter in the Syrdian alphabet.

By the end of the week, the process was automatic. Each of twenty-six letters in her alphabet was translated to a number and each number from one to twenty-seven conjured a note and a certain number of strikes. She could produce and recognize all the intervals immediately or play a series of notes in her mind and translate them back into numbers or words. She was excited by her progress and couldn't wait to flaunt it to Cyrrus.

The week's passage was not as kind to him. Though he made a point of bathing to hide his condition, the bags under his eyes blackened, his skin became sickly, and his stare appeared lifeless. The orb was exacting a price. He was exhausting himself beyond capacity, but Aera understood the reason underlying his obsession with the crystal world. She wondered how long it would take him to complete his plans and when they might leave Ynas.

OUTSIDE WORLD

1329 EARLY-WINTER

Sleepers lined the dark dorm, and the windows broadcast an indigo sky. Aera went outside to watch the sunrise and was gratified to find it warmer than it had been for a while. She lay in the grass, listened to the birds, and watched clouds float across the vibrant scape of dawn, glowing with morning luster. In a flash, she saw a bare-chested warrior relishing the sunrise from atop a great mountain in the wild, thinking of her...

Stop it, she admonished herself. Everything reminded her of that damned blue star. She wished she could borrow Cyrrus's cerebral cellar to banish it from her thoughts. It was comforting to have secrets when Cyrrus shut her out, but it was different now that he wanted to run away with her, train her, and share his cerebral processes. She felt guilty lying to him.

If she told him about her orb romance, how would he react? He might be angry, jealous... or worse, apathetic. The pragmatic response would be to exploit that connection to some advantage...

...and that thought made her stomach twist into knots.

She needed to set things right before Cyrrus did something cruel— or, in his terms, reasonable. Perhaps she could obtain information from the hidden star to assist their mission.

Sunrise gave way to a cloudy sky. As people began pouring out of the hut, Cyrrus appeared from Southside Forest. Aera approached him and said, "I'm ready to use it tonight."

Promptly, Cyrrus led her around the back of the building and leaned against the wall. She held her pocket open and Cyrrus pulled the orb from his own, slid it into hers and murmured lazily, "Did you learn about the world?"

"No..."

"You need to stay alert. Any awareness you acquire of the outside world will help us."

This was inconvenient, as she had yet to find a suitable location to use the orb and had intended to investigate during meals. Yet Cyrrus was right: she needed to see Vaye. She braced herself for a long day.

Morning tasks passed slowly, as Aera was too anxious to concentrate on picking vegetables. She lunched hastily in the Dining Hall and headed to the cottage, where Vaye was sewing by the fire.

"Hello, dear," Vaye said. "May I get you some tea while you play?"

Aera sat across from Vaye and said, "I was hoping to talk."

"Even better," Vaye smiled. She set down her fabrics, headed to the kitchen, and returned with two mugs of pine needles steeping in hot, green water.

Aera was determined to ask about the world, but mindful not to appear overly eager. "I've been playing in the Music Room," she said. "Did you tune the piano?"

Vaye smiled sweetly and asked, "Wasn't there something you wanted to talk about?"

Relieved that Vaye had cut through the chit chat, Aera said, "Nurin and Cyrrus mentioned wars in the outside world. Can you tell me about them?"

Slowly, Vaye inquired, "Have you asked Cyrrus?"

"He's... always busy."

Vaye parked her warm eyes on Aera and sipped her tea. Aera wondered whether her question was too brazen. Without a word, Vaye slipped under the archway and headed up the stairs.

Aera transferred her pine needles to the plate and sipped the tea, which was bitter with a hint of resin. She recalled the day Vaye had taught her to make a torch from pine branches. Vaye didn't seem to mind that Aera used those torches to sneak around. Would she be so kind if she knew what Aera was up to now? The white-haired girl looked on, her bold eyes penetrating Aera's every secret. *Vaye's guardian*, Aera thought, then giggled at her paranoia.

Vaye returned with a scroll the length of her torso, exuding no hint of displeasure. She removed a hanging plant from over the archway, set the scroll on the hook, then released a leather tie around the scroll and lowered it carefully, holding the bottom as it unrolled to reveal a map.

"This is the Southern half of our continent, Andolien. Have you seen it before?"

The land was depicted with mountains, rivers, and plains. Aera wondered what kind of person had created this map, and how anyone could represent an entire continent with such detail. "I've seen parts in History Class and other books... but never the whole thing."

"Have a look," Vaye said sweetly.

Aera studied the map and found Ynas, just south of the mountainous land labeled 'Sentinel Range.' Kadir was situated along the same river—presumably, the Oloril. She knew they were 600 kymen apart, two weeks' journey by foot. It struck her that Ynas was closer to the Middle Sea than to Kadir. She mused, *if we destroy the gate bridging the river in the south, we can escape by canoe...*

...she remembered that Vaye was beside her, and she hadn't summoned Ivory to conceal her thoughts. She'd never told Vaye about her dreams of escape and couldn't predict how she might react. To her relief, Vaye's eyes were warm.

"The wars in Andolien are constant and ever changing, and there is much danger in the wild," Vaye said gently. "But some tribes are nomadic, and travel is not uncommon among civilized folks. Survival is an art, like piano or Kra, which requires dedicated practice to master."

Aera smiled brightly. "The art of freedom."

"To bring a vision to life is to be an artist," Vaye agreed.

That's why kuinu is art, Aera thought. She knew better than to discuss Nestëan magic aloud, but presumed Vaye heard her and grinned.

"You asked about the wars," Vaye reminded her. "There are many small nations in Andolien, but the largest are Errkoa, Dirgaselah, and Syrd. The greatest conflicts revolve around those three."

Aera nodded. The names were familiar from History Class, but she'd rarely paid attention to the details.

"Dirgaselans and Errkoans both claim dominion over Lake Povus." Vaye pointed to a large body of water. "Errkoa uses Lake Povus for trade, but Dirgaselans attack their ships. They believe a god named Povus resides in the lake and that they must protect his sacred waters from nonbelievers."

Aera smirked. "So they pretend there's a deity and they know what it wants... because it helps them get power."

Vaye grimaced to acknowledge the absurdity. "This travesty has gone on for centuries. A more ominous recent development is an impending conflict between Dirgaselah and Syrd."

Aera spotted Syrd along the Inland Sea, northeast of Dirgaselah. She kept her eyes on the map as Vaye spoke, pinpointing each location she mentioned.

"Dirgaselah's economy relies on slaves they acquire from smaller nations, just north of Lake Povus, but Syrd has been invading those nations, imperiling Dirgaselah's trade." Vaye frowned. "The worst offense is Syrd's recent incursion into New Taerelboro, where Dirgaselan migrants have practiced their religion for centuries. They fear Syrd will destroy their culture."

New Taerelboro was in the Northeast, hundreds of kymen north from Syrd. "Syrdian warriors must spend a lot of time fighting," Aera mused.

"Citizens of great nations often take pride in their culture. They believe their way is the right way, and the rest of the world would benefit from adopting their methods. King Irador of Syrd has convinced his people to force the Syrdian advancements in education and technology upon others."

Long ago, Cyrrus had boasted about his plan to conquer King Irador. As a leader, Cyrrus would undoubtedly seek avenues to lure everyone into his schemes, all the while believing he was saving the world.

"Wars come and go," Vaye mused, "and they're all about land, resources, and ideology. Some continue for ages, with no end in sight, such as the conflict between Errkoa and Syrd."

Aera found them on the map, then looked at Vaye.

"The two nations are at odds over a rare, powerful dust known as shardât," Vaye explained. "Each particle emits an adamantine discharge of light energy, and Syrdians use it to power equipment which enables advancements in medicine and science. Syrd appears so bright from afar, it's known as The White City."

Cyrrus claimed the lights in the sanctum were made from *sarya* and that, although the Nestë perceived *sarya* as 'unnatural,' it could advance human culture. Aera wondered if shardât was related to *sarya* and asked, "Where does the dust come from?"

"It is mined from the ground all across Oreni, but nobody knows its origin," Vaye said slowly. "There are people known as Seekers who prospect for shardât and trace its origins. King Irador buys their information, even as the Errkoans hunt them down. The Errkoans believe shardât is an abomination and that locating its source would bring devastation."

Cyrrus had called Aera a seeker, and he knew much about the outside world. She wondered whether he chose that word because of the reference to the seekers of shardât. Between her white clothes and archetypal themes, it was not unlikely that he would associate her with a substance that emitted white light. She asked, "What kind of devastation?"

Vaye faced the map with a blank stare, as though gazing through it. She intoned in a grave voice, "We cannot be certain."

Screeches assaulted Aera's mind. *Në Laimandil ë i namanya, sinë veskento i suínanya më Onórnëan...*[1]

Aera shook herself back to reality and saw Vaye watching her, likely reading her thoughts. Perhaps those thoughts made more sense to Vaye than to Aera.

"I'll make us some more tea," Vaye said. She headed into the kitchen, signaling that the conversation had ended.

Aera studied the map and considered the pervasive disputes. The more she learned, the more she was convinced that no nation was peaceful, and no location was safe. This was why Cyrrus felt justified in his desire to conquer the world. He wanted to rescue people from blind hatred, false ideology, and dangerous magic.

To commit the conversation to memory, she conjured an image of her cerebral enclave. First, she imagined the great oak at the center of a field encircled by white trees. Next, she took a seat at Vaye's piano, then closed her eyes and pictured herself playing it on the wooden stage in her imaginary field. She decided to place each group in the audience around the stage according to its position on the map relative to Lake Povus. *P-o-v-u-s*, she thought. *Sixteen, fifteen, twenty-two, twenty-one, nineteen.* The associated musical notes ran through her mind, and she played them.

To her left, she visualized a row of Syrdians, lined up in the grass. *S-y-r-d. Nineteen, twenty-five, eighteen, four.* She reviewed the sequence on piano and imagined Syrdians with Cyrrus-like alabaster skin. *White City,* she thought, and matched the letters to numbers. As she played the corresponding notes, she pictured the group bathed in scorching white light.

Behind her and to the left was Dirgaselah. As she conjured melodies to match the letters, she pictured a row of people stretching their arms to salute the deity of the lake—just as people saluted the commune—and issued them blue uniforms to match the water. Errkoans would be behind her on the right, and she clothed them in black, since they hunted the Seekers of the white light. As she visualized a row of them in the field, she recreated the associated notes.

Once the scene was clear, she expanded the sequences into longer arrangements and associated the images. She imagined herself playing that same piano on her imaginary stage and visualized each group occupying its position relative to her. To distinguish them further, she assigned each a different register: the further north, the higher the pitch.

She repeated each melody again, watching her imaginary audience. Alabaster-skinned Syrdians matched piercing high notes just as black-clothed Errkoans matched deep notes, and Dirgaselans, the blue-clad lake worshippers, occupied the middle register. By the time she left for tasks, each nation had its own song and evoked specific colors and images.

That evening, the air was dank and the sky overcast, signaling an impending storm. Aera forced in extra dinner, hoping to compensate for the anticipated lack of appetite through the next few days. She tried to think of a place to use the orb safely. Nothing in the village was seclusive enough, and Great Gorge did not provide sufficient shelter.

She climbed atop the boulder and breathed the ominous wind as it tossed her hair around. Behind the main buildings was an abundance of small structures followed by endless trees and crops. The bathing grove behind Westside Willows was hidden from view, but she could see the plateau above it, with the Utility Building, barns, and grazing areas.

Across the river were the running track, belltower and vegetable fields. Beyond, the pine forest extended to the Eastern horizon and looped northward. River Oloril extended onward forever, with several small huts along its edge, but the lumberyard in the far north was shielded from view. If she took a canoe up the river, docked it before the rock wall, then hiked north toward the lumberyard and beyond, she might discover an empty hut or hideout where no one would find her.

She returned her tray to the Dining Hall and appropriated a canoe. The threatening storm deterred the usual crowd, but Aera decided to brave the weather.

The water was heavy as she bucked the tide, but she pushed on until she fell into rhythm, one stroke after another with the paddles circling through the water. As she rowed, the wind roared, and the river tumbled. The cold splash of waves soaked through her clothes and her arms became sore. *Even if we could escape by canoe, the journey might kill us,* she thought.

After a while, she rowed under a wooden bridge like the one near the track. Fields and crops surrounded her as far as she could see. She continued until she saw the rock walls, then eased the craft toward the shore, dragged it inland and secreted it between two cherry trees. The final stretch of orchards was before her, which meant there was a long way to go before she escaped the Samies.

She walked along the bank, looking for a hut, enjoying the whirr of the water and the scent of rain as a drizzle puttered softly on the grass. There were apple trees across the river and cherry trees alongside, but no sign of people anywhere. Finally, after traversing an eternity of fruit trees, she approached the lumberyard.

She was beyond anyone's view now. The rain intensified as she walked along the edge of the woods, where trees blocked some of the downpour. She passed a patch of fallen trees and saw the Great Fence in the east, looming over the forest.

The curfew bell sounded in the distance, alerting her that she'd been traveling for almost two hours, but she continued northeast for a while longer. Beyond the torrent of rain and leaves rustling, she heard someone yelling. Who could it be, so far away from the village?

She slid behind an oak tree, held her breath and listened. Nothing. Just rain, wind, crickets… and then rhythmic trots of large animals approaching from the south. She waited, not daring to move, and the sound was soon joined by rapid clomps from the north, which she determined were footfalls of even larger animals. Someone spoke, much closer this time.

"*Qirzān k'ayumak kemqa zikkani huqʰa ztamūk.[2]*"

"*Hu tamok zminhāfad. Mitmak šáʰšmex, zbiwazqa nit biddani de otna miqráʰay.[3]*"

The language was foreign, but the second voice was Nurin's. His haughty tone and exaggerated pronunciation of consonants were unmistakable in any language. Aera held her breath.

"*Mettu'ta hā qʰaydū zhu?[4]*" said the first voice.

"*Tatu',[5]*" Nurin responded. Then, there was a commotion that sounded like heavy items being moved.

The putter of rain quieted, reducing the soundscape to an insect choir. Aera couldn't possibly be still enough. After more shuffling, Nurin's voice said, *"Habdil miegbil. Raḥaw niQirzān ḥā nina zda'ax miḥri'mašnarān-i-doše Ihayos.*[6]"

The animal sounds headed north while lighter, rhythmic ones went south. Aera peeked around in time to glimpse a horse galloping southward along the river's edge. She waited, barely moving, as the noises faded in both directions. Finally, the horse moved out of earshot and the heftier footfalls disappeared beyond sight.

As Aera caught her breath, she considered what had just happened. Nurin had met with foreigners and had spoken to them in a foreign tongue that he knew well. The sound was choppy, much like the Kalaqhai language in her dreams. Who was he speaking to? Did they come from outside? *Ynas is self-sufficient indeed,* she thought, and groaned.

She had escaped discovery but no longer felt safe. Was there no time and place in the entire commune where she could count on being alone? There had to be a way to conceal herself from view. The air was not very cold; she didn't need a fire. All she needed was a hiding spot, but there were no more huts along the water. Perhaps she could create her own shelter.

There were fallen trees everywhere. If she leaned branches against the Fence, she could hide underneath and also block the storm. She approached a fallen tree and climbed on top of it. Using her foot as leverage, she disconnected a branch, then jumped to the ground, wrestled it off and leaned it against the Fence. One down, many more to go.

After breaking and dragging enough branches into a pile, she arranged them in a row against the Fence until she was startled by the distant clank of a gate closing in the north. Could it be the Gate—the only access to the commune? Did Cyrrus know where it was? Though she wanted to explore, it was too dangerous to risk being caught wandering while she had the orb. It was best to return another day.

She arranged the branches and filled in gaps with leaves and mud until she was satisfied no light would escape. Finally, she removed the treasure from her pocket and unwrapped it. *"Ger beni ath cemmar..."*

Elkandul was alive with sparkling swirls as pink and beige apparitions took form. Just as before, they were woven together, and sepa-

485

rated before her eyes. Aera imagined her aura had intertwined similarly with the hidden star.

Though she'd apparently intruded on another private moment, she didn't feel unwanted this time, as both forms angled welcomingly toward her. She sensed they were positively predisposed to her and guessed that they must have developed a rapport with Cyrrus.

"Greetings," Aera said, and Cyrrus's voice emerged from the nexus.

Sounds garbled around Beige, and a soft male voice said, "Errkoa expanded perimeter surveillance."

Waves poured over him, and his figure thinned. In response, Pink assumed a childlike form. Garbles emerged around her before a nervous voice warned, "Time is running out. We must act."

Both apparitions dimmed and spread out as Aera pondered Pink's words. Cyrrus probably knew who 'we' referred to, but she didn't. Sparks stung her, and she felt her aura dissolving. She consolidated her energy at her center until the other figures settled into place.

Pink spread and retracted as garbles emerged from her. "The wall is high along Oloril and Kalaqhai ships patrol. Dirgaselah advances along the Shinneran. The Rhiwen is our best course."

Course to where? Aera had no idea what they expected her to say. She focused on remaining steady while Beige garbled, and a frail masculine voice declared, "The rainforest is haunted."

Haunted. In a world where people were deluded by religion, that could mean anything.

"People become disoriented and lose their bearings," said the voice, thinning and wavering. "Many never return."

Both forms became shadowy and feeble, and Pink's aura tumbled around itself while Beige flickered with greens and lost shape. "You said it yourself," said a crumbling voice that distorted into a harrowing gnaw. "That darkness could swallow anything but the Ni-ight Geh-eh-em."

Alabaster light exploded from both auras, stabbing Aera with static jolts and pushing her into a rapid spin. She could not discern up from down nor distinguish her own bearing from the swirl that consumed her. As she scrambled for some anchor, heat coursed through her. *Thump, thump...*

The familiar force clutched her, and she resisted a compulsion to turn toward it, realizing as she did so that she knew precisely where not to look. The atmosphere whirled with scathing white, but no longer jostled Aera around. She was in control.

A soft pulse disseminated from within. *Thump, thump.* She relished the luscious sensation, but quickly blocked it. Others were present.

She focused on Pink, whose contour morphed into discordant curves, finally slipping into a wide formation. Beige's flutter decreased, and he settled into a faded cloudy visage. As Aera watched them, her heartbeat faded and the magnetic pull evaporated.

Aera tried to deduce why Elkandul had so suddenly deteriorated to mayhem. Someone had said, *That darkness could swallow anything but the Night Gem,* and their voice had become distorted as chaos ensued. This had happened in the orb on another occasion when 'Night Gem' was mentioned. What did it mean? *You said it yourself,* the voice had explained, likely referring to Cyrrus. Somehow, Aera had to learn more without revealing her ignorance.

The brightest lights she had ever seen were underground and in her dreams. She imagined that whiteness could slice through anything. She tried to conjure something safe to ask and envisioned her cerebral enclave flooded with white light. Music crashed into her mind, and she picked apart the notes. *Twenty three, eight, nine, twenty, five. Three, nine, twenty, twenty-five. Nineteen, twenty-five, eighteen, four.* White. City. Syrd.

The image appeared: Syrdians with alabaster skin, bathed in white. It all came back to her: shardât in Syrd emitted bright light that fueled their technology. Aera wondered whether darkness could swallow those lights, and if they related to a Night Gem.

Channeling Cyrrus, Aera asked, "Can Syrdians traverse the darkness?"

"Doubtful," said the thin male voice, "and no Syrdian would ever assist us."

Doubtful. If the darkness could swallow anything but the Night Gem, and it was only doubtful—but not certain—that Syrdians couldn't pass through, perhaps shardât and the Night Gem were indeed related.

"Travelers have been ambushed by roving bands from Kadir along the Rhiwen," said Beige. "It remains our best chance, but only if we act quickly."

We again. Aera could not be certain who was included in 'we' but had the sense they were attempting to include her—or Cyrrus—in a mission.

"It hinges on the election," said a heavy tone from Pink. "The Liberty Party may delay things, but I believe the Justice Party will win."

Both apparitions angled toward Aera, awaiting a response, but she had no idea what to say. To her relief, a flash of green appeared. Pink and Beige both vanished. The green aura assumed a rigid form comprised of sharp lines, which angled toward Aera and declared, "Twenty-six six fourteen two one thirteen. Fourteen thirteen seven six. Twenty-seven four nine, nine nineteen five twenty-seven, ten ten.[7]"

Aera converted the numbers to notes and played the sequence in her mind. As she did, he added, "Twenty-six sixteen nine, eleven six twenty-five seven. Forty-one, forty-one, forty-one.[8]"

Forty-one again, Aera thought, and converted it to music.

"Forty-one, forty-one, forty-one," he said again.

"Forty-one, forty-one, forty-one," Aera echoed, and Cyrrus's voice emerged from the center.

Green disappeared, replaced by a star. There were no more auras visible, and the aerosphere was hushed.

As Aera reviewed the numbers, heat infused her, streaming through a soft throb in her heart. Her lover was drawing her in, and she ached to succumb like before...

Don't, she reminded herself. *Don't let him in.*

Cyrrus was depending on her to protect them both and to obtain information. Maintaining a nonhuman form in the orb required 'intrapsychic alchemy,' so it was likely her hidden companion possessed arcane knowledge. Perhaps she could enchant him with a song and lure it out of him. *If I don't give you everything now, how long will I wait...*

Sensations stabbed her in painful flashes. Ivory needed to take control. *Now.* She tried to pull her energy inward, but her pulse was heavy, and she was coming undone. Every part of her craved surrender.

Who are you? Aera wanted to scream. *Show yourself!* For months, she had craved him desperately, and every encounter had laid her bare. She wanted to believe he felt the same, but he was a mystery, shrouded in darkness. If he wanted her, why didn't he reveal more?

There was no rationale to trust him, and it was arguably in Aera's best interest to manipulate him. Yet the thought pained her. He had awakened something deep inside that she couldn't destroy.

Still, she needed to fix her mistakes. The hidden star knew too much about her. She cherished their celestial dance but feared her songs might have alerted him that she and Cyrrus were separate people.

Thump, thump. A tiny blue light swelled and retracted, a flame dying in the emptiness. She longed to let him in, just one more time...

...she tried to ignore it and focus on... something. Anything. She thought of Cyrrus's affectionate stare, his girlish giggle. His promise: *we will escape Ynas.*

The thump in her heart quieted, the melting sensation evaporated, and she gathered her vibrations into a condensed shadow. The blue light became weak, faint, and lonely. Aera was overcome with guilt but implored herself to remain resolute. She needed him to believe she was Cyrrus. Whoever he was, this would be better for him as well.

She imagined watching the star through Cyrrus's eyes. Channeling his most stoic monotone, she intoned, "Love is a logical fallacy." Cyrrus's voice repeated the phrase from the center, and its coldness jolted Aera with a blast of ice.

The blue light faded, but a black spot remained. Aera thought her rejection would scare him off, but he was still there. Perhaps he hoped she would change her mind and let him in... perhaps she hoped for the same. The starless void hypnotized her, and as she stared, her aura disseminated. She yearned to stay but forced herself to turn toward the outer ring to chant, "*Ger beni ath cemmar.*"

Vibrations overcame her as she was tossed out of Elkandul into useless limbs under a wet cloak and sticky hair. Her chest was heavy, and her throat was dense with an avalanche of tears.

She yanked her hand from the orb and stabbing sensations shot up her arm, besieging her whole body with needles. The effort to move was draining, as the rock in her heart stole her energy. But she summoned whatever strength she could and tossed her arms around. As she loosened, the tension in her face broke and tears streamed down. She folded into her knees and sobbed as her thoughts filled with the faint blue light, sad and lonely because she'd shut it out.

She sniffled and wiped her eyes. *Love is a logical fallacy,* she reminded herself, but that was irrelevant. Her heart was bigger than her brain... and Cyrrus owned her heart.

A chill ran through her.

She peeled the wet hair from her face, wrapped the orb, burrowed it in her pocket and crawled out of her hiding spot. Her boots were covered in mud and darkened even more as she dragged herself through the trees. As she reached the edge of the forest, clouds gave way to a starry night sky, revealing Alárië beside her lover, Erelion. Tears welled up again... but why? Cyrrus would be beside her, always. They would escape together...

After hours of walking along the riverbank, she passed the lumberyard and recovered the canoe. Rainwater had accumulated inside, so she tipped it over to clear it, finessed it into the river and rowed away with natural rhythm. Her movement was fluid, at one with the world, silent and smooth. The current was with her, and the wind dried her face as she breathed the delicious night air.

The bridge appeared in the distance, and Aera saw firelight inside the nearby brick hut. As she approached, two officers in uniform came out, each yelling in turn.

"By Ghaadi's gar!"

"Samely! What in Riva's Trees are you doing!"

"Same thing you're doing," Aera said. It occurred to her after she spoke that Cyrrus had used that exact phrase long ago.

"Raisins!" barked a guard. "What's your ghaadi name?"

Calmly, she said, "Leave me be. I am breaking no law."

The guards looked at each other, stupefied. Then, one repeated, "What's your name?"

Aera ignored the question and continued paddling.

"Get back here, Samie! You must respond to authorities!"

Aera imagined herself as Cyrrus, with a steely stare, and turned toward the guards. "It is in your best interest to ignore me," she said. "If you attempt to detain me, I will request adjudication at a town meeting, and you will lose standing."

The guards stared at her in confusion. Grinning, she paddled onward, and they did nothing to stop her.

490

GIRLFRIEND

1329 EARLY-WINTER

Aera lay in an empty space, surrounded by blackness. *Thump, thump…*

Hands stroked her skin as her lover breathed heavily against her. He touched her faster, harder, exploring with insatiable desire, and moved his lips to hers. As she leaned in, a flash of azure blinded her and the lips snarled, "Love is a logical fallacy."

The voice was Cyrrus's. He let out a girlish giggle that transformed to a cackle, then pushed Aera down by the shoulders.

"Cyrrus, stop," she grumbled.

He held her forcefully in place and opened his mouth, revealing fangs and alabaster light. She thrust around, struggling to fend him off. He intoned in a ghoulish screech, "Did you tell *him* to stop?"

Whiteness swallowed everything, pressuring and piercing Aera as she writhed violently, desperate to escape. The air itself screeched, *En rallë anti miossi kemma! En rallë anti—*

~

Ding ding! Ding Ding!

Aera awakened with a start. Whiteness flashed before her eyes, and the bell rattled her ear drums. '*En rallë anti miossi kemma*' was the Silindion for 'this boundary will not bind us.' Why was that relevant? Had

491

Cyrrus shared the dream? Aera felt sick. She rushed through some breathing exercises, then forced herself into the scorching light and grating exuberance of the commune.

To her relief, she didn't encounter Cyrrus all day: he was at a town meeting during tasks, and she slept in the Music Room during meals. But at curfew, when the doors to Adolescent Hut were unlocked, he was waiting outside the entranceway, all tidy hair and clean clothes. Aera was a mess, with knotted hair, disheveled clothes and heavy eyelids, but Cyrrus didn't seem to notice.

"Do you remember?" he asked.

She knew he was referring to the orb numbers and replayed the sequence of notes in her mind, relieved to find it was still fresh. "I do," she said proudly.

Cyrrus gestured for her to follow and headed inside, down the hall and into one of the bundling rooms, confident and poised this time. Aera thought of the dream and her cheeks flushed. She wondered what Cyrrus was planning.

The room reeked of sweat and muck, with heavy breathing and groans inside the stalls, but one wooden door was cracked. Cyrrus swung it open and let Aera enter first. She grinned uneasily and crammed into the back corner.

Cyrrus latched the lock, and they both sat cross-legged on the floor. "Hold up your fingers," he said. "Like this..."

Relieved, Aera watched his hands. He flashed ten fingers, followed by ten, followed by three, then closed both fists tightly for a moment, separated them and held up two. "Twenty three, two," he said softly.

Aera saw what he had done. She played the first melody in her mind and translated it back to numbers: Twenty-six, six, fourteen, two, one, thirteen. She flashed ten fingers twice, then six, and he nodded. She closed her fists, then pulled them apart again and held up six.

Someone sighed loudly in the next room, and Aera stiffened. Cyrrus tensed momentarily, but quickly grinned to show amusement. Playing along, she chuckled, then continued the first sequence until it was complete.

Cyrrus looked to the side, apparently reviewing the phrase in his mind, then nodded, cueing her to begin the next one. After she'd imparted all the numbers, he looked at her with gleaming eyes.

"Excellent," he said, and his gaze meandered to her pocket. He wanted the orb.

She retrieved the wrapped ball and passed it to him. He slipped it into his cloak, then smiled and asked, "Want to learn to do two things at once?"

Aera was exhausted, but Cyrrus was eager. "Sure..."

He held up some fingers with each hand and instructed, "Add them together—but also remember the number I flash with my left hand. When I'm finished, you will show me the sequence of numbers from that hand alone, and then the sequence of all numbers added together."

She counted two raised fingers on his right hand and three on the left, then played the note for 'five' in her mind, and then the note for 'three.' As he went through a few more numbers, Aera tried to string two songs together but became confused.

Finally, Cyrrus said, "Tell me the sequence with your hand."

Aera held up three fingers, then two, then four, then one, then...

....she'd forgotten the rest. Cyrrus giggled girlishly and said, "It takes practice. Let's start over."

They repeated the exercise, laughing and joking all the while, until the bell gonged again. Much time had passed, but Aera didn't want to stop. They were having fun, and she was starting to remember the sequences. They continued flashing fingers back and forth until someone knocked on the stall, and they froze, startled.

"Samely, Brains!" Farris bellowed from outside as he pounded on the flimsy door, shaking the whole structure. "You gonna bundle all night?"

Cyrrus reached up, unlatched the hook and pushed the door open. Farris and Doriline were outside, and his shirt was off while her curves were barely stuffed into her undertunic. The chairs on the opposite side of the room were dripping with eager couples.

"You're *dressed?*" Farris exclaimed. "How long does it take someone with all your brains to quiffle your own girlfriend?"

Aera's cheeks burned, and Cyrrus glared at Farris with menacing apathy. What would he say? Was she his girlfriend?

"You've been in there for ghaadi hours," Farris whined. "People are waiting, and you're still *dressed.*"

Doriline laughed and jabbed, "There's nothing under her clothes anyway." She leaned and licked Farris on his lips. The two slobbered on each other while Cyrrus watched with a blank expression.

"What're you looking at, genius?" Farris barked.

Cyrrus said nothing, but his eyes remained fixed in place as mischief collected in his grin.

"Alright," Farris said. "You have ten minutes to fritter your girl-friend. After that, the room is mine."

That word. *Girlfriend.* The idea of a boyfriend or girlfriend implied physical intimacy, which Cyrrus and Aera had never broached—yet they had spent time alone together for years and probably shared more secrets than anyone. Aera wondered what Cyrrus would call that.

Cyrrus flashed a sardonic grin at Farris and said, "I cannot, in good conscience, allow you to breed. I am on a mission to emancipate the world from stupidity."

Farris couldn't contain himself and spewed a loud guffaw. "Alright, Brains," he laughed. "Enough smarting. Time's up. If you're not gonna bundle her, get out."

Cyrrus looked straight at him and said, "What I do with my *friend* is not your concern."

Blood drained from Aera's cheeks. She was not his girlfriend.

Doriline shot a toothy grin at Aera, parading her victory, and angled her hips toward Cyrrus. *Breathe,* Aera thought. *Stay cool.*

Momentarily, another door opened and Farris yanked Doriline away. She turned to flash one last smile at Cyrrus, and he watched with a quizzical expression as she disappeared into the free stall.

Finally, Cyrrus pulled their door shut and reengaged the latch. The two resumed their game, but the mood was soured. They soon gave up and went to bed.

The next week was a blur of heightened senses, exhaustion, and misery. Every time Aera thought of the hidden star, she wanted to scream. She had rejected him for Cyrrus, who showed no interest except in her dreams—and in those dreams, she shoved Cyrrus away. Emotions did indeed scramble her mind.

One evening after dinner, Aera was too depleted for piano or Kra. She wandered in Southside Forest, then headed back to the Sleeping Hut Field well before curfew.

"Farris! Get over here!"

Doriline's squeal rang out from atop Halycon Hill. Aera pulled on the Adolescent Hut door, but it was still locked. A couple was canoodling against the wall while another pair giggled their way around to the back of the building, holding hands.

Aera sat in the grass nearby and looked up at the night sky. *Hyuvún i larë silnemmanyë,*[1] she thought, and shifted uncomfortably.

Everyone else was pairing up, even the damned moon, yet Cyrrus showed no interest. Girls in every Age Group ogled him, but he ignored them and planned to run away with Aera, his 'friend.' Perhaps if she were popular, he would claim her as his girlfriend—or perhaps he intended to reserve himself for someone whose 'offspring' wouldn't be a 'waste of life.' What kind of girl would he consider worthy of carrying his venerable seed? If he was seeking someone with no emotions, he would never 'breed.'

Several boys emerged from the hilltop and raced down into the Sleeping Hut Field with a Raetsek ball. Doriline was still there and screamed after Farris, "You said you would come!"

Farris ignored her. He kicked the ball and called, "Samely, Codin!"

"Doom-hole barlock!" Doriline screeched, and stormed back to Vapid Village. Those two were 'boyfriend' and 'girlfriend' and it meant nothing.

A stocky boy departed from the others, and Aera recognized him: he was one of the people she'd met late at night by the bathing grove. He approached and asked, "Can I join you, Eh-ruh?" Without waiting for a response, he crouched down and said, "My name's Idan."

He paused, giving Aera room to respond. While she fumbled for words, he said, "I love your music. You playing again in the Spring?"

"Yes…"

"Good."

There was a short silence, and Aera felt more tense and uneasy every moment. Just when she thought they had reached the pinnacle of awkwardness, Idan said, "I heard Cyrrus isn't your boyfriend."

Go away, Aera thought.

"He's an interesting guy," Idan continued. "Everything's supposed to be equal, but we've eavesdropped on DPD council meetings and heard them talking about him."

A breeze blew Aera's hair across her face. She wanted to disappear under it but, instead, tucked it artfully behind her ear and forced herself to look at Idan. He had a round face with curly hair, and his appearance was not unpleasant, although nothing about him stood out. She tried to place him on the archetype map. He was smooth and ingratiating, perhaps like Kize, the archetype of 'potential' who shape-shifted to please others.

"Go on," Aera offered.

"Something about changing laws. I think he made a fuss and they wanted to keep him quiet."

Coolly, she asked, "Why?"

"They probably think he's dangerous," Idan said. "Everybody does."

Aera chuckled. Apparently, 'everybody' was a wimp.

"Well, first of all..." Idan laughed. "Nothing. I... shouldn't say this."

Aera glanced at him and waited.

"You might be offended."

The hut door opened behind them, and people filed in, but Aera didn't budge. The suggestion that she would be 'offended' made her want to hear more.

"Okay," Idan said. "Don't take this wrong, but a lot of guys are afraid to talk to you 'cause they think Cyrrus would hurt them."

Aera was amused that people gossiped about Cyrrus yet misread his fundamental nature. His emotional performances were strategic, but if he had real passion, he wouldn't allow himself to act on it.

"Remember that time when Cyrrus stomped on Hizad?" Idan asked.

Their eyes met for a brief instant; then Aera looked away. It made her uncomfortable to discuss Cyrrus with someone she barely knew, but she felt compelled to defend him. "Hizad was bullying me," she said. "Cyrrus wouldn't hurt someone for just talking to me."

"Every time a guy looks at you, Cyrrus gives them the barlock glare."

Aera gave a skeptical look. Cyrrus glared at people often, and it meant nothing.

496

"I've seen it," Idan insisted. "He does it when you're not looking."

"Maybe he's protecting me," she offered. "So people won't make fun of me."

"What would they make fun of you for?"

Was this some sort of joke? Aera chuckled and said, "Everybody makes fun of me."

"I never have."

"Then your friends have."

"My friends think you're adorable, and everyone loves the color of your eyes," Idan said. "But nobody dares go near Cyrrus's girlfriend."

The color of her eyes? Cyrrus said they were 'grey,' which was boring. What was Idan talking about?

"Look," Idan said. "I never approached you before, right? But Farris told me you weren't Cyrrus's girlfriend, and now I'm here."

A gust of wind blew in Aera's face, and she pulled her cloak tighter.

"It's getting chilly," Idan said. "Want to go inside?"

Aera was cold but had no desire to fritter or bundle or whatever else people did in the rooms. Before she could devise the appropriate words to reject him, Idan took the hint and said, "I'll go inside then. Have a good night."

Aera slept well and awakened the next morning with ample energy. She was still enjoying Idan's claim that Cyrrus gave 'the barlock glare' when boys looked at her. Could that be true? When lunch break began, she resolved to make eye contact with some boy and observe Cyrrus's reaction.

She situated herself at the boulder, hoping to see Cyrrus. Promptly, he approached without any food, his hair unkempt and gait languid. He leaned against the boulder and closed his eyes, clearly sleeping off a crystal adventure from the previous night.

Aera let him rest for a while, then nudged him and said, "Get up. You need to bathe."

Cyrrus didn't react for a moment, but then chuckled and said, "Veritably."

She returned her tray to the Dining Hall, and they headed to Westside Willows. Aera looked around for a potential male target while Cyrrus was half asleep and walked with his head down. They passed a few clusters of boys, but the situation never seemed right until she spotted Idan's skinny friend Viram heading toward them, alone. This was her chance.

She locked her eyes on Viram and he met her gaze shyly, but immediately looked away and hastened his pace. Discreetly, she peeked at Cyrrus and saw his scathing eyes fixed on Viram, scorching him as he scurried by. Once Viram had passed, Cyrrus craned to glower at him some more.

Aera gazed ahead, feigning obliviousness, but her efforts were wasted on Cyrrus. As soon as Viram was out of sight, Cyrrus snapped, "What's the problem?"

Coolly, she asked, "Problem?"

Cyrrus stared down at her with a scowl. "You're pathetic," he said. "I can read your mind."

"...then what am I thinking?"

"Thoughts so parochial I wouldn't elevate them with a recapitulation," he said dryly, resuming his sleepy posture.

Aera giggled. She loved when he talked like that, and she felt victorious: he used that kind of language defensively.

They walked side by side in silence through the trees. When they reached the riverside, they separated to change into clean clothes, then met to wash their dirty ones by the stream. As they knelt by the water, Aera realized she hadn't told Cyrrus what she'd seen in the forest. She looked around to make sure nobody was nearby. A few people were brave enough to bathe in the cold, but the waterfall would drown out any conversation. She decided to fill him in.

"Last week, I was in the forest way up north," she said softly. "I heard Nurin speaking to someone in a language I didn't recognize."

"What was it like?" Cyrrus asked.

"Choppy. Like *qhaydū zhu zhut.*"

They exchanged a chuckle, and she continued. "I saw a horse heading south, and I think Nurin was riding it. The others came on some animals too, but I didn't see them. The footsteps sounded different."

"Were they loud?"

"Louder than the horse."

"Then it wasn't a dreisz," he muttered to himself.

"Dreisz?"

"A large cat that the Nestë ride."

Large cat. Aera had seen Panther Woman on the back of a feline. She'd assumed it was an illusion, but perhaps it was real...

"Well?" Cyrrus urged. "What else?"

"They traded some heavy things and rode away, and a while later, I heard a gate closing." In a hushed voice, she said, "I think it was *the* Gate."

"Way up north?"

"North and east. Way past the lumberyard."

"Excellent. Do you remember anything they said?"

"A little," she said. "...*Qirzān k'ayumak... tatu'... qhaydū zhu?*"

Cyrrus stopped moving and stared at the stream blankly. Then, suddenly, he resumed washing his clothes.

"What does it mean?" Aera asked.

Cyrrus did not respond.

"Do you recognize the language, at least?" she persisted, but he continued washing his clothes and ignored her. Frustrated, she insisted, "You know *something*—"

"Stop presuming," Cyrrus snapped. "It's a dangerous habit."

Aera glared at him, but he didn't meet her eyes. He stood up, squeezed water from his clothes and walked away.

"Stop emoting!" Aera yelled after him, but even that didn't make him look back. She shuffled her clothes around in the freezing water to wring out the soap, and as her hands turned blue, she felt sick.

Did he think he could hide from her forever? If he expected her to follow him blindly, he was delusional. Their games in the orb were one thing, but she didn't see any reason to be secretive about events within the commune. Why did he want to run away with her at all? If he was going to hide so much, he might as well go without her...

...and perhaps that was his intent. Her stomach knotted.

All this time, his promise of escape might have been a lie to get her to pass along information even as he evaded her questions. If that had been his plan, then she'd played right into his hands. *Idiot,* she scolded herself, and kicked the ground.

She wrung out her clothes, hung them quickly, and ran into the trees at full speed, but Cyrrus was nowhere in sight. The bell gonged a short while later, and his line began to depart without him. At the last minute, he caught up. He remained distant throughout tasks and disappeared at dinner. Aera waited by the doorway of the hut for a while after curfew, but he never arrived.

~

The retreat continued the following day, as Cyrrus was absent from breakfast and turned up just in time for morning tasks. Aera's line was sent to make paper, and Cyrrus's went elsewhere, so she didn't see him at all. Throughout the morning, she rehearsed a confrontation with Cyrrus in her mind but couldn't figure out what she might say. His deceptions were so subtle that he left her with no concrete reason to doubt him—yet taken overall, the picture was ominous.

When lunch break arrived, Aera looked for him everywhere, but he was absent until just before afternoon tasks. It was clear that he was avoiding her. The break dragged on interminably until finally, the gong struck, alerting everyone to line up in the Field. While others took their place, Aera spotted Cyrrus at the edge of Westside Willows. The sight of him made her nervous.

She summoned Ivory, left her line, marched to him and asserted, "We need to talk."

Stiffly, he retorted, "You have too many needs."

"Talk to me at dinner."

He glared at her, his eyes cold and cutting. In a neutral tone, he said, "I have a meeting."

There was only one way to make Cyrrus talk to her. Crisply, she whispered, "It's still my turn."

Cyrrus stared at her with an unreadable expression, then darted back into the forest. She followed him until he stopped behind a giant tree.

Dryly, he instructed, "Open your pocket."

She held her pocket open, and he stood in front of her, blocking her from the eyes in the Field as he slipped the orb into her cloak. Then, abruptly, he headed back toward his line, and Aera joined hers.

Her attempt to lure him into conversation had failed, but now she had the orb. He would have to talk to her eventually if he wanted it back.

That night, Aera lay awake on her mat, stiff and uncomfortable. The fire beside her was hot, but she couldn't remove her cloak with the orb in its pocket. Her hairline was wet, her cloak itchy. Nothing felt right. She cursed her heightened senses, cocooned herself in her cloak and fell into an uneasy sleep.

NIGHT GEM

1329 EARLY-WINTER

Aera whirled through a scape of white trees, dancing in the mist. Doves lined every branch, feathers glistening in moonlight, their coos coloring the night. "Wrr-oooo! Wrrr-oooo!"

Leaves crunched somewhere in the distance, and Aera spotted a whisk of fur sliding between shadows.

"Wrr-ooo?" cooed the doves. "Wrr-ooo?"

A figure emerged from behind a tree, shrouded in mist. His fur hood encased a blaze of azure and two smoldering eyes. *Thump, thump...*

His pelt vest was open, and his muscular chest reflected the blue glow. Aera blushed and went toward him but stopped in her tracks. Behind him, there was a second silhouette outlining a slender man in a tight, hooded cloak. The confident swagger was unmistakable.

The two measured each other, motionless. Neither face was visible. Blue fire brightened under one hood as scathing whiteness emerged from the other, accompanied by a droning hiss. The doves shot away, denuding the trees as the two faced off, lights blasting.

Faces materialized in the fog and screeched: *"Në Laimandil, ë áldëa si.*[1]*"* The blue flame disappeared within the shrieking white mass.

"Cyrrus, stop!" Aera implored. "Leave him alone."

502

"Stop emoting," Cyrrus commanded in a distorted voice that echoed the ruckus. "I don't ascribe him sufficient agency to—"

Suddenly, a creature descended from the trees and pounced on Cyrrus, knocking him into the fog. Aera couldn't discern whether the predator was man or beast. She ran to Cyrrus as both forms disappeared in the mist. There was an eruption of searing hot colors; then alabaster light pierced the scape. "*Tistë yoveskén Onórnëan, ë áldëa si.*[2]"

All became whiteness and torturous noise. "*Në Laimandil, ë áldëa si.*" Aera's ears exploded, and she screamed.

~

"Ghaadi's gar!"

The pandemonium vanished, leaving the world ringing. Aera sat up on her mat in the sleeping quarters, where everything was dark.

"By ghaadi's gar, what *was* that?" snarled a voice from across the room.

Aera adjusted her eyes to the darkness. The fire was dim, but she made out Gaili beside her, staring.

"Are you alright?" Gaili asked.

"Fine," Aera said coolly.

"You... screamed."

Aera forced a wan smile and said, "Just a nightmare." She lay back down, but when she looked up, Gaili was still watching her.

"I'm fine," Aera repeated.

"Must've been scary," Gaili muttered.

Aera didn't respond. If Gaili knew what Aera had just seen, she might have lost her well-known appetite.

The dream boy might be a fantasy, but Aera still connected him to the hidden star. She couldn't shake the feeling, however unlikely, that the sorcerer who cast those colors could enter her dreams. Cyrrus claimed that, although *inyanondo* was limited by distance, dreams could be shared with anyone in the world.

There was no hope of falling back to sleep, and Aera burned to use the orb. She had no idea of the time but couldn't lie there any longer. She headed off.

Once outside, she resolved to build a shelter in Southside Forest instead of traveling northward for hours. She headed past Great Gorge, deeper into the woods, until she encountered the Fence again—this time, the southern end. As she leaned logs against it to build a hideaway, the bell gonged in the distance. The sky was still pitch black, signaling that she had at least another two hours before the sunrise bell.

She filled the spaces between the logs with dried leaves, twigs and mud until her hut was complete, then crawled inside and pulled extra logs against the opening to block any view. The enclosure was dark, and she was ready. *"Ger beni ath cemmar..."*

Vibration propelled her into Elkandul, and she found herself in a gathering with seven phantoms providing a vivid spectrum. Silver was there, along with Purple, Beige, Pink, Orange and the two angular apparitions, Red and Green. It was a familiar crowd.

Pink disappeared and converted into a star, and several others flickered violently, but the angular men remained composed. One percolated a powerful crimson, and the other, a piercing green. They both faced Aera and spoke in turn.

"Twenty-six six nine, nineteen six one seven. Twenty-five ten twenty-one eight?[3]"

"Twenty-five ten two one thirteen, nine fifteen nine ten, eight twenty-seven. Twenty-two seven, five six, ten fourteen two nine, twenty fourteen.[4]"

"Four thirteen six! Twenty-six sixteen nine, eleven six twenty-five seven.[5]"

Aera converted the numbers to melody and both forms angled toward her, awaiting a response. As she considered what to say, an androgynous voice intoned, "He manipulates his emanations with finesse."

The apparitions faced Aera and adopted smoky, shadowy forms. Someone whispered, "To what end?"

All eye sockets glowered at Aera, and she didn't know why. Were they suspicious of Cyrrus, or did they realize she was not he? She glanced at Silver and was taken aback: instead of its usual rippling glow, the entity projected a jagged mess of gray and red. In a voice beset with hatred, it intoned, "To destroy darkness."

Whiteness skewered the atmosphere like lightning and thrust Aera into a chaotic storm. Scalding heat throbbed in her heart. *Thump, thump…*

She tried to expel the sensation, but the thud amplified, and the burn swelled. Searing pain tore through her as she burst into white hot beams. Then, the thump disappeared, leaving her hollow.

The auras looked on, cold and menacing. She scraped her vibrations together, thrust herself around and called, "*Ger beni ath cemmar!*"

She emerged with her hands upon the orb, frozen and disoriented. As she recovered, her mind spun, trying to grasp what had just happened. The hidden star had infiltrated her, this time with brute force instead of feverish passion. Had he done it on purpose, or had he been influenced by the chaos in the orb?

The apparitions had been staring at Aera—whom they had mistaken for Cyrrus—when the white flashes took over. Just before that, someone had said, *To destroy darkness.* During Aera's previous visit, the same whiteness had appeared after Beige said, *That darkness could swallow anything but the Night Gem.* It could not be a coincidence that alabaster light overwhelmed the crystal universe whenever these concepts were mentioned.

All the apparitions seemed to understand these ideas… except for Aera. She wondered if Cyrrus would make sense out of this and hurried off to find him.

By the time Aera reached the hut, she was panting. She made her way to Cyrrus's dorm and tiptoed to his mat, then crouched quietly at his side and shook him. His arm shot up and he grabbed her neck. Cyrrus was choking her!

In a cold monotone, he hissed, "Move closer and I will carve out your trachea."

Aera tried to wrestle herself from his grip, but it was too tight. She barely managed to croak, "Cyrrus! Please!"

Cyrrus bolted upright as though in a trance, then looked at her and released her. Tears filled her eyes as his words rang in her ears. *I will carve out your trachea.* His tone was so even and his reaction so calculated… so cold.

Cyrrus stood, fully dressed, and ushered her out the door into the hallway. "I didn't know it was you," he said. "Aera. Look at me."

She stared down at the floor. Tears were pushing through, and it required all her effort to hold them back. Cyrrus took her chin in his hand and turned her head towards him, but she shifted her eyes downward and steadied her quivering jaw.

"I was defending myself," Cyrrus said. "I had no idea it was you."

She pushed his wrist away from her chin and shielded herself with hair.

"You should practice self-defense skills," Cyrrus said softly. "The concept should not remain so alien to you."

"Defending yourself... from... what?"

There was a short pause. Gently, Cyrrus said, "Let's go outside."

Aera struggled to stop herself from crying as they made their way to the exit. She led the way around to the back of the building, then sat down and leaned against the hut. Cyrrus sat cross-legged, facing her, and took her hand from her lap. Her cheeks heated as he slid his fingers between hers.

"With magic comes responsibility," he said softly.

Aera wanted to say something but had no words. All her energy was sucked into the hand he held, and her heartbeat was mounting. Cyrrus waited in silence, but to no avail. The longer their fingers were intertwined, the more confused she felt and the more vaporous her thoughts became.

Cyrrus released her hand and finally, she breathed. The black sky was succumbing to indigo as the stars faded. She remembered the chaos that had ruptured her senses so ferociously inside the orb.

"People keep mentioning a Night Gem," she said finally. "You know what it is."

"Why would you assume that?"

You said it yourself, Aera thought, remembering Beige's words. Slowly, she said, "That darkness could swallow anything but the Night Gem."

"What darkness?"

Was Cyrrus pretending he hadn't said this? Beige wouldn't have told him, *You said it yourself,* if he hadn't...

... unless he knew she and Cyrrus were separate or was testing to determine that.

Cyrrus would never have given that away. If anyone had, it was

Aera. The hidden star might have realized and revealed it to the others...

Aera stopped her thoughts in their tracks and looked at Cyrrus. He was concentrating on something invisible in front of him, and it was unclear whether he was thinking or slipping away. Aera suspected he was playing dumb, but it was too risky to try to figure it out. If he was telling the truth, he might have the same suspicion she did: that the others were aware of their separate identities and were testing her. He would then question her about her actions in the orb, which would alert him that she'd been hiding something. She decided to try another approach.

"The Kalaqhai keep saying numbers to me," she said. "And only me."

"What makes you think they were Kalaqhai?"

"Someone said..."

Aera stopped: that statement was stupid. There was no reason to trust anything she heard inside the orb. Rephrasing her thought, she asked, "Why are they saying the numbers to me?"

"Even I am not sufficiently omniscient to discern why a stranger might have done something when I wasn't there."

"They said it to me because they thought I was you."

Slowly and evenly, Cyrrus intoned, "What were the numbers?"

"Why do you care? What do they mean to you?"

"Did they figure out we were separate people?" Cyrrus asked sharply. "Did you let something slip?"

"Why does it matter?" she demanded. "Acting like you is torture. Most people couldn't even survive a conversation with the *real* you."

She could hardly believe her own words. Why was she insulting him? To cover up her lies? Tears welled up again and she murmured, "Sorry..."

"Why would you apologize for an astute observation?" Cyrrus asked expressionlessly.

She dared to look at him. His eyes were glistening as though she had paid him a great compliment, but as soon as he saw her welling tears, he darkened and said, "You're hopeless."

"I'm *not* hopeless. I've been convincing people I'm you all this time. But I don't want to do it anymore."

Distantly, Cyrrus said, "Perhaps you need a break from the orb."

"Stop deflecting," she hissed. "If you want me to pretend to be you, then you need to explain what you're doing in there."

Cyrrus did not respond.

"Give me one reason *why* I should pretend to be you."

"To protect yourself," Cyrrus snapped.

"From *what?*"

Cyrrus was quiet for a long moment and stared at the trees in the distance. Finally, he said, "If anything goes wrong, I want them searching for one person, not two. I'm trying to keep you safe."

Aera felt like a fool. That should have been obvious but, all this time, she had convinced herself he was using and manipulating her. Why was it so hard to trust him and to accept that he cared about her? Tears stung her eyes.

"Don't get all gooey," Cyrrus said. "I've been protecting you since we were eleven years old."

A tear slid down her face.

"I'll be patient," Cyrrus said emotionlessly.

She glanced over at him, longing to hug him, helpless to stop herself from imagining how wonderful it would feel if he held her and aching for it more desperately as each moment passed. What would Cyrrus do if she fell into his arms? Would he repel her, remove her trachea, or merely turn to stone? She sank deep into her hair. Cyrrus didn't want her affection, and her neediness was pathetic. She breathed into her belly to collect herself, and true to his word, Cyrrus waited patiently.

After a while, her tension receded, and she emerged from under her mane. The sun was poking over the horizon, and the sky was light blue. Daylight was sobering. She felt empty but sane.

"It would be easier to pretend," she said, "if I had some idea what you were doing."

"I'm experimenting."

"At least explain the Night Gem..."

"Ivory's secrets may be accessible to some," Cyrrus said. "I will explain one day, but for now, trust me. It is for your safety."

"What about *your* safety?"

Dryly, he retorted, "Some must make sacrifices to protect others."

"We're escaping Ynas *together*," Aera reminded him. "I want to help you."

"It doesn't matter what you want." A hint of anger broke into his even tone. "Everything is meaningless. Nothing we feel is important. One day, we're all gonna die, and when you're dead, you won't care if you ever see me again. Your broken heart will be at peace."

Aera was dizzy with humiliation. He knew how she felt about him and was mocking her for it. She pulled the orb from her pocket, threw it at him and walked away.

Breakfast and morning tasks were torturous as Aera was overwhelmed by heightened senses and rage. During lunch, she went to nap in the Music Room, but a flood of emotions kept her awake. Cyrrus's words assaulted her: *Your broken heart will be at peace.* She was accustomed to his obnoxious jabs, but this was *cruel.* Had he hurt her on purpose, or had he lost control? Perhaps his paranoia was eating him alive, turning him into a monster as he choked her, jabbered about death, and insisted he needed to protect people... from what?

Within the same hour, the hidden star had attacked her and Cyrrus had reached out to choke her—and both events followed the dream where the two had faced off with each other. Aera wondered if they had both shared her dream, or if something else had them spooked. Though Cyrrus's behavior was inexcusable, she decided she had to help him.

She did some Kra stretches and paced around, reviewing the events of the night. Cyrrus had refused to discuss the Night Gem, which meant it was important. Something that destroyed darkness would likely involve light. Was it related to the shardât in Syrd? The bright white *sarya* beneath Junior Hut? Aera wished she had access to *Parë* or the underground sanctum. She needed to learn more.

Years ago, Cyrrus had shown her a passage about the Nestë at the library. He had claimed it was propaganda, but she decided it was better than nothing and went to read it.

The library was more crowded than ever, but Aera rushed past everyone toward the back shelves and tried to remember where Cyrrus had fished out *The Book of Rasna*. After some browsing, she spotted the title on a black leather spine. She pulled it out, found a table in the back corner where she could read it, and reviewed the introduction Cyrrus had shown her.

The passage described conflicts between Rasnians, Kalaqhai, Nestë, and humans. Between them, who were the Seekers prospecting for shardât? The text said: *The Nestë had a lifespan of thousands of years during which they developed powerful magic.* Aera wondered whether that magic was *kuinu, sarya,* or something else. Perhaps Rasnian and Kalaqhai armies sought shardât to overcome the magic of the Nestë.

She read the text once more but found no confirmation of her theories. There was nothing to help her discern whether shardât was related to *sarya,* nor presume any connection to a Night Gem. The only theme worth noting was that the *Book of Rasna* portrayed Ilë and the Angels as villains, while *Parë* portrayed them as heroes and instead villainized Ultassar. She wished she had access to *Parë*...

...and as that thought crossed her mind, she remembered that she had copied passages from tablets into the notebook in her pocket. She cursed herself for neglecting to read *Parë* in its entirety, but nonetheless rushed outside and found a private spot in Westside Willows to review whatever segments were there. As she flipped through her notes, she spotted the word '*sarya*' written twice on the page labeled *Lesson of Vekos*.

ULTASSAR EMBODIED UNBALANCED *VEKOS*, AS HIS FEAR CAUSED HIM TO OPPOSE LIFE. HE EMPLOYED *SARYA*, ILLUSORY MAGIC. SINCE IT OPPOSES SYNTHESIS, IT DEFIES NATURAL LAW AND LEADS TO DISSOLUTION. MANY NASSANDË HAVE ENDEAVORED TO DEFEAT *SARYA*, ONLY TO FALL VICTIM TO ITS POWER. TO GUARD AGAINST THIS, A NESTË MUST CONFRONT HER OWN FEAR.

She skipped ahead.

A NESTË MAY EXPLORE AN OBJECT WITH HER EYES, EARS AND HANDS, YET FORMULATE AN INCOMPLETE IMPRESSION. AN OBJECT'S NATURAL PROPERTIES ARE ILLUMINATED BY THE *ESIL*, WHICH REVEALS THE LAWS OF NATURE AND UNMASKS ANY ILLUSION CREATED THROUGH *SARYA*. LIKEWISE, THE *ESIL* ILLUMINATES EMANATIONS OF THE *SURU*,

REVEALING HER INNATE CONNECTION TO ILË AND ALL BEINGS.
THEREIN LIES THE KEY TO BALANCING THE *VEKOS*.

None of this was helpful. She skimmed the *Lesson of Kalma*, which she had copied in its entirety. Somewhere in the middle were the words: *White Gem*. She gasped and read the surrounding text.

AT THE BEGINNING OF TIME, ILË EXISTED IN PURE SOLITUDE. AS HE DREAMED INTO EXISTENCE MULTITUDE, BOUNDARIES EVOLVED. THOUGH ALL WAS INTERCONNECTED, ULTASSAR SEPARATED FROM THE PURE SILENCE OF UNITY AND SAW IN MULTITUDE THE SEED OF CORRUPTION. HIS PERCEPTION OF GOOD AND EVIL, 'I' VERSUS 'YOU,' INTRODUCED SUFFERING. THUS, HE WAGED WAR AGAINST LIFE ITSELF. HIS AIM WAS TO RECONNECT TO ILË, EVEN AS HE FURTHER WEAKENED HIS SENSE OF UNITY.

YET ULTASSAR'S PERCEPTION OF SEPARATION WAS A DISTORTION, AS HE WAS BORN OF ILË. WHILE THE ANGELS REALIZED ILË'S VISION BY PRODUCING *KUINU*, ULTASSAR DEFIED NATURAL LAW TO EMPLOY *SARYA*. WITH THIS ILLUSORY MAGIC, HE CREATED THE FAERIE, WHO UNLEASHED CHAOS. HIS FINAL REBELLION WAS TO EMPTY HIS ESSENCE INTO THE WHITE GEM, AN EMBODIMENT OF THE DISUNITY HE EXPERIENCED.

Ultassar had created *sarya*, the White Gem, and the Faerie—one of whom was the Dragon-Lord, Ainuvaika. Was the White Gem distinct from the Night Gem? Aera remembered a passage about Ultassar's origin and was relieved to discover she'd copied it from the *Lesson of Alonwë*.

IN TIME BEFORE TIME THERE EXISTED ONLY SOLITUDE. HIS DREAMS BROUGHT FORTH ANGELS OF LIGHT WHO IGNITED THE HEAVENS AND CREATED MULTITUDE. YET ONE THOUGHT WAS FORGOTTEN: THE UNENDING NIGHT WHERE SOLITUDE EXISTED ALONE. THIS WAS THE MEMORY OF ABSENCE, WHOSE NAME WAS ULTASSAR. AS ORENI CAME TO LIFE, ULTASSAR HID AWAY IN THE DARKEST UNKNOWN CAVERNS, SEEKING ANY SPACE WHERE MULTITUDE WOULD NOT FIND HIM. MOUNTAINOUS BARRIERS WERE PROJECTED INTO THE WORLD

FROM HIS NIGHTMARES, AND HE FILLED THEM WITH LABYRINTHINE CAVERNS OF FIRE AND DEATH. THERE, HE DREAMED OF WHITENESS THAT EXTRACTED THE *KUINU* FROM THE WORLD AND RETURNED IT TO NOTHINGNESS. HE LONGED FOR A RETURN TO THE VOID WHERE EXISTED ONLY SOLITUDE AND SILENCE.

Whiteness that extracted the kuinu from the world... this might be the meaning of 'destroy darkness.' That whiteness had obliterated Aera's mind in the sanctum and had haunted her dreams for as long as she could remember. The monolith had showed her the *ilissunviva* symbol —which connected her to Erelion—and in the wood she'd seen his nemesis, Ainuvaika. In all its forms, the color white called to her. She had yet to understand why.

Her eye caught the words: *solitude and silence.* Long ago, when she'd first visited the cottage, Vaye had told her silence did not exist. There had to be a reason for imparting this message to a five-year-old girl.

Aera closed her eyes, trying to remember more, and the droning chants crashed into her mind. *Në Laimandil.* 'The White-Bearer.' *Sinë veskento I suínanya më Onórnëan.* 'And his deeds will change the world.' It all came together. Vaye had read her thoughts and heard the screeches that haunted her as a child.

After four grueling hours of tasks, Aera skipped dinner and rushed to see Vaye. The distant speck of fire-lit cottage beckoned like a torch at the end of a cold, dark tunnel. As Vaye opened the door, the aroma of pumpkin spices filled Aera's lungs, and her icy cheeks warmed to a tolerable chill.

Despite the relief that the cottage gave Aera, Vaye appeared worried. She asked, "Is something wrong, dear?"

Aera wondered how horrible she looked and what had given her away. Indeed, everything was wrong, but no words came to mind.

"It's okay," Vaye said. "I'll make us some tea."

Aera sat by the fire and watched the flames dance until Vaye returned with two mugs and sat opposite her. A cat found Vaye's lap and curled up, purring as she stroked it. Her silver ringlets reflected the firelight, and a beaded headband rested just above her brows. Aera envisioned the *esil* glowing underneath.

"Can you tell me more about shardât?" Aera asked.

Vaye's eyes rested on Aera. "What would you like to know?"

"Is it related to a... Night Gem?"

The smile escaped Vaye's face, and her mocha cheeks paled. At once, the cat jumped off her lap and scampered away. In a thin, ghost-like voice, Vaye said, "First, tell me what *you* know."

Aera stiffened. "You know exactly what I know."

Vaye searched Aera's eyes, but Aera focused on her breath, refusing to be penetrated. A silence fell over the room as they both turned to the fire. As Aera watched it dance, she saw a black dragon spreading its wings, slinking its snakelike body between the flames...

She jolted. Her mind was playing tricks, but she sensed it was significant that the dragon was creeping up on her now.

Vaye returned her focus to Aera and said in a solemn tone, "The Night Gem is part of a legend concerning the origin of the world."

"Tell me," Aera implored.

There was a long pause as Vaye faced the fireplace, quiet and contemplative. After a while, she turned to Aera and began her tale.

"Before anything existed, there was an abyss where the creator Ilë dreamed alone. He conjured Angels who crafted his visions—but there was one, known as Ultassar, who wished a return to nothingness. Ultassar fashioned the Night Gem, and it drew all energy into itself so nothing could exist outside it. The Gem absorbed his corporeal energy and his spirit returned to the heavens."

The Night Gem was, essentially, Ultassar—or an emblem of his essence. This explanation affirmed Aera's deductions. She noted Vaye's stony posture and listened intently.

"Syrd is lit by shardât that rises from the ground," Vaye continued. "Many believe it originates from the Night Gem."

Aera knew, if she wanted Vaye to reveal more, she had to reveal more. "In my dreams, before we met, I saw white light that screeched words in Silindion. You heard it in my mind in music class, and you understood what it meant." She looked straight at Vaye and implored, "I need to know."

Without a word, Vaye angled toward the fire and stared into it, breathing slowly. Aera realized that at some point in Vaye's life, she might have been vulnerable and mastered her own 'Ivory,' and wondered why this had become so obvious only now. After a while,

Vaye turned to her with a grim look, her dark eyes reflecting the flames.

"When Ultassar left, the guardian Astarth rose from his ashes, and she uttered a prophesy," Vaye said as her voice receded to an unearthly low pitch. "One shall come in later times, who will wield the ancient Light made new. And the White-Bearer, he shall be called, and his deeds will change the world."

The atmosphere became eerily quiet. Then, the drones infiltrated Aera's mind. *Në Laimandil ë I namanya, sinë veskento I suínanya më Onórnëan.* The room darkened as the fire died out. Aera felt a chill.

She translated the first two lines of the prophesy to Silindion and, as she pieced the phrase together, the rest filled in: *Filén na erë lëoryán assë të yo-fayanta i nalanna hyánië votheldë.* Those were the words she'd forgotten from her childhood dreams. Those drones had imparted, directly to her, the prophesy of the Night Gem.

Suddenly, she realized she was trembling... and Vaye was watching. She remembered the way Vaye had stared at her in the Music Room, her eyes filled with darkness and fear as those words haunted Aera's thoughts.

"Was this why you brought me here?" Aera asked. "Because I... knew too much?"

"If I hadn't brought you here, you would have known less."

"Then... why did you?"

"Why did you follow?" Vaye asked. "Why did you come back again?"

Aera glared at Vaye: the answer was obvious to both of them. Vaye was the first person to see who Aera was.

"I feel isolated here, as you do," Vaye said. "Your companionship brings me joy."

"But you chose me because I knew the prophesy."

"You heard the prophesy because you listen."

You listen. Vaye had called her 'gifted' for that very reason. The two shared auditory sensitivity, but how did that relate to the prophesy? She tried furiously *not* to listen, but someone—or something—forced it upon her.

Suddenly, it struck Aera: Vaye knew the prophesy. The dream had come from her.

"It was you," Aera said. "*You* projected that dream. The white light was your conception of the Night Gem, and the prophesy was terrifying because..."

...*because you fear it,* Aera thought.

Vaye met her gaze and, although she did not speak, the haunted look in her eyes revealed that she knew precisely what Aera was thinking. Whether that legend was mythical or historical, one thing was clear: to Vaye, the Night Gem existed. If the apparitions in the orb deemed it catastrophic and associated it with Cyrrus, they would certainly set out to destroy him.

There was no time to waste. Aera had to find Cyrrus before he used the orb again. "Thanks," she said. "I... have to go."

Aera ran with the wind, faster than ever before. Her legs propelled her across Vaye's garden, through Southside Forest, past the sleeping huts and over the Southeast bridge. She ran directly to Cyrrus, even though he was in an unexpected place: walking briskly eastward, beyond the track and canoes, into the pine forest.

"Cyrrus! Wait!" she called as she bolted toward him.

Cyrrus stopped abruptly but did not turn. Moonlight illuminated his messy red mane as it billowed outward in chaos. Aera's heart was beating wildly, and her chest ached as she gasped for air. She scrambled to catch her breath. Cyrrus waited, silent and still, until finally she declared, "We shouldn't use the orb anymore."

"Is that so?" Cyrrus replied coolly.

"I don't know what those Kalaqhai want from you," she said, "but the Night Gem is not a game."

"Everything and nothing is a game."

"Cyrrus, stop," she persisted. "Do you even understand what you're getting mixed up with?"

Cyrrus stared at her blankly.

"Some people believe the Night Gem could destroy the world," Aera said. "Legends say it was forged by Ultassar at the beginning of time. It might be fiction, but some people believe it, and they hunt anyone who seeks the Night Gem. Your gaming in the orb could draw the wrong attention to us."

A gust of wind blew hair into his face. He held her gaze but said nothing.

"We can find another way to escape," she said. "We can steal some horses or... do something... anything that doesn't involve the orb. And nobody should ever know that we used it."

Cyrrus stared at the ground, inhaled deeply, then exhaled slowly and thoroughly. Aera held her breath until he looked up.

"You're right," he said tenderly. "It's too dangerous."

Aera was taken aback. Though Cyrrus looked straight into her, it seemed impossible that he could believe his own words. "Are you humoring me?"

"No," Cyrrus said simply. "You're right."

"That's not like you. You *never* admit I'm right."

"Do you require an emotional display?" Cyrrus demanded. "You're *right*, Aera. I'm *wrong*, and you're *right*. Accept it with grace."

He fastened his eyes to hers. The dense emerald gaze bolted straight into her skull and everything else dulled.

"Okay." A knot groped her intestines. "We won't use it anymore."

"Right," he said, pronouncing his consonants emphatically. "We will not use it anymore."

The two maintained eye contact, each refusing to back down. Cyrrus's severity yielded to desperation as he grasped Aera's gaze like an anchor to prevent himself from floating into oblivion. He was lost and afraid, and he needed her. Tears reddened his eyes.

Then suddenly, he changed. He did not move, but receded to a distant, unaffected air. Aera shuddered.

"What... should we do with the orb?" she asked. "Put it back where we found it?"

"That would be unwise. It might end up with Linealle or the likes of her."

"We could give it to Vaye," Aera suggested. "She won't punish us."

Thunder rumbled in the distance. Cyrrus furrowed his brow, then declared decisively, "We will use it for political influence."

Aera loosened her grip on her breath and echoed, "Political influence?"

"I will propose a trade," he said stiffly. "Nurin's mirror law for the orb."

"You really want mirrors that badly?" she teased, trying to ease the tension.

"I'm nice to look at," Cyrrus grinned. He locked her into an unwavering stare and said in a jarringly steady voice, "If you couldn't see me, you'd wish you could, wouldn't you?"

The horizon brightened, and lightning reflected in Cyrrus's eyes as Aera watched, transfixed. He released her from his gaze and strode away, but she was frozen in place, hollow and shaken. Was he lying? Would he use the orb?

She followed him at a safe distance, across the track, over the bridge, and across the Sleeping Hut Field, only to watch him march straight into the Adolescent Hut. She breathed a sigh of relief and cursed her paranoia. After pacing outside the hut for a while, she found a stall where she could be alone and cried herself to delirium on the cold, empty mat.

∽

Fire roared in the center of a circular field. Stone steps surrounded the field in descending concentric circles, and Aera was seated on one. Shadowy figures occupied other areas of the stairs, and all gazed at the conflagration below.

She stared at the flames as Cyrrus emerged from them, unscathed. His hair was the color of blood, and he wielded two swords, moving confidently with a savage look in his eyes. A scalding light sliced across the flames, screeching and hissing. The shadowy figures faded and vanished, leaving Aera alone.

Mist rose from the ground beside Cyrrus and formed a pearly white glow, tinted with gold. It swallowed the dreadful alabaster light and then, the fire. As the flames disappeared, Cyrrus began to lose substance. His body became transparent, and an outline of Aera appeared within the radiance. Her form jelled as Cyrrus's dissolved.

Aera was no longer watching herself from the stairs. She was in the field, facing Cyrrus, and his form was ghostly, barely visible. As they stared at each other, a shrill noise hummed until alabaster light blasted Aera with a shriek. Her form faded as Cyrrus regained substance. His eyes reddened to the color of blood.

"Have you forgotten that love is a logical fallacy?" His voice boomed through the unrelenting whiteness. Grating screeches invaded his tone as he hissed, "I will kill you before I let you consume me."

He dropped his swords and wrapped his hands around her neck to choke her. She struggled to escape, but his grip was too firm. The bright light shrieked, its howls sharp as swords.

Cyrrus lifted her by the neck as she kicked and gyrated. Though he didn't open his mouth, the word "Rot" carried through the screeches and repeated from every direction in his penetrating voice. The ghastly whiteness screamed louder as it grew brighter, closing in, swallowing Aera whole....

~

Aera opened her eyes and sprang up. The ring and bleachers in the dream were familiar: they matched Cyrrus's description of his cerebral circus. Had she conjured that image from memory, or had she entered his dream, or his mind, through *inyanondo?*

She left the stall and ran upstairs to check on Cyrrus. The last room was full of sleepers, but his mat in the corner was empty. As she absorbed this, she felt sick. He'd gone to the Adolescent Hut only to throw her off his trail.

She ran downstairs and swung open each door, checking every room for Cyrrus, but he was nowhere. Quickly, she ran outside, where Hizad sat in the grass with his friends. She demanded, "Have you seen Cyrrus?"

Hizad looked at her with surprise, and it dawned on her that she'd never actually spoken to him before. "I saw him," Hizad huffed. "Does he have a problem? He ran out of here like a maniac and said 'rot.'"

Rot. Just like the dream.

"Cyrrus has no problems at all," Aera retorted with bitter sarcasm. Before Hizad could respond, she darted away.

Searching for Cyrrus felt chaotic and desperate. Crows cawed everywhere, flying all over in a frenzy, but Aera could not sense his presence. She ran through the trees around Great Gorge and called his name as she gasped for air, then checked every corner of Vapid Village. The only familiar place left was the sanctum underground.

She retreated to Junior Hut and found a sleepy officer slouching in

Linealle's old chair. She could barely catch her breath enough to sputter, "Have you seen a boy with red hair?"

"He was here just before," said the officer in a casual, languid tone. "He left carrying a metal box and a couple of leather sticks. He was wearing a fancy outfit... never saw one like it."

Leather sticks. That sounded like sword sheaths. If the metal box was the Kalaqhai book, it would have been in the room beside the weapons and clothes. Somehow, Cyrrus had managed to get there, even though the passageways had been realigned.

Aera looked straight at the guard and demanded, "Tell me everything. *Now.*"

The officer stared at her, shocked out of his slumber. She stared right back.

"I tried to stop him on his way in, but he pushed his way past," he said. "I chased him downstairs and couldn't find him, and when he came back up, he shoved me out of his way and said, 'Rot.'"

Rot. Again. "Which way did he go?"

"That way," said the officer, gesturing towards the river.

"Was he alone?"

"All alone. I'll report it in the morning."

Aera stared him down and considered everything she'd just heard. Cyrrus had shoved an officer and stolen an outfit, swords, and a Kalaqhai book. That would merit terrible punishment. It was insane to draw that much attention to himself while he still had the orb.

Her stomach felt like a rock. Now she understood 'rot.' Cyrrus had told people to rot in Ynas because he was...

...leaving.

She bolted toward the river, grabbed a canoe, and headed north. When she passed the second brick hut, officers called after her.

"Ghaadi's gar, Samie!"

"Where in Riva's Trees are you going?"

She ignored them and continued paddling as fast as she could, rowing against the tide until she saw walls enclosing the river ahead. As before, she docked the canoe by the cherry trees and sprinted northward toward the Gate. The field bordering the forest continued forever. By the time she saw the Fence in the distance, the sky had faded to navy blue, and her breathing had turned into wheezing, each inhalation paining her abdomen.

From afar, she spotted an iron Gate with spiked rungs. As she approached, her eyes went to a hound hanging by its bleeding paws, which were nailed to the massive wooden casings surrounding the great iron doors of the Gate. If there was a knot in her stomach before, there was a tornado now. She doubled over and vomited.

As she coughed, she heard a distant mumble, "Mmrgghgh," behind the gargantuan Gate. She pushed on it and discovered, to her astonishment, that it was unlocked.

Two officers in DPD uniforms were gagged and bound by rope to trees just outside the Gate. Beside the trees, two axes jutted from the ground with a red insignia carved into the handles.

The mark of the Kalaqhai.

Aera pulled one from the ground. She surveyed the open forest and its endless trees carpeting a slope leading somewhere... into the outside world.

This was her chance to escape. She had weapons, the Gate was open, and the guards were immobilized. This opportunity might never come again, but could she survive out there? She knew how to make torches from pine trees and build hideouts to sleep in. She could speak Silindion; perhaps she could find the Nestë and join them. One day, Cyrus would find out she didn't need him, that she could make it on her own.

She glanced at the nearest guard. Ropes secured him to the tree, with loops around his neck and through his mouth. He was utterly helpless and stricken with terror.

Aera had no love for the DPD or the commune. For all she cared, the whole place could burn to the ground. Yet she couldn't leave another human like that. She decided to release him.

She used an axe to sever the ropes, then untied his wrists to free him. Before she could blink, he picked up the second axe. Aera gazed up at the mountain. She could still leave...

Without a word, the two approached the second guard. As the first began to cut the rope, Aera untied the part around his wrists.

Once he was free, Aera asked, "What happened?"

"This is not your concern," said the second guard sternly. "We will report the events to the council."

He held out his hand for the axe. Aera clenched her grip on it and sized him up. He was tall and burly, but she could still slice him in half...

Reluctantly, she handed it over.

The guards ushered her back inside the Fence and rushed to the hound. She glanced one last time at the mountain slope and thought, *Your heart is bigger than your brain.*

As the guards secured the Gate, Aera noticed some lines in the middle of the dirt path. She stood directly above them and saw letters scraped into the dirt, forming a single word: ROT.

PART FOUR
THE SEEKER

MAGIC

1329 EARLY-WINTER

"Where's Brains?"

"He's been gone all ghaadi week!"

"Eh-ruh! You seen Cyrrus?"

Aera tightened her grip on the shears and cut the grass, trying to ignore the onslaught of voices. Each day was worse than the last. She felt trapped in her skin as her senses gradually slumped from their heightened state. There was nothing to look forward to. No reason to go on.

Cyrrus's last words haunted her. *If you couldn't see me, you'd wish you could, wouldn't you?* She remembered the lightning reflected in his eyes as he stared her down for the last time. He'd carefully chosen his exit phrase and timed it with the storm for impact, but Aera had still failed to recognize the message. How could she have been so blind? She'd refused to trust him, lied to him and pushed him away. Of course he'd left without her...

"Samie Eh-ruh! By Riva's Trees, wake up!"

The task managers laughed amongst themselves as Aera dragged herself out of her daydream. *Breathe,* she scolded herself. *Focus.*

The clouds were heavy, and the air was thick. Aera's knees were roughed up and sore, her hands coated in filth. While most of the group were suffering on their knees, those with the highest cumulative snitch points were awarded the task of 'assisting.' Doriline appeared nearby, holding a bucket out to Olleroc, who stuffed grass inside.

Aera set down her shears and gathered cuttings together into a pile. Rain began to fall, and the loose grass stuck to her hands. As she struggled to assemble it, Doriline arrived with her bucket.

"I heard Cyrus *left*," she chirped. "Is it true?"

Aera scowled. The world darkened as the rain thickened.

"You *must* know," Doriline persisted.

Aera clenched her teeth and hissed, "Go. Away." She collected her pile and tossed it aggressively into the bucket, but Doriline would not take the hint.

"He *must* have told you," Doriline continued. "Or maybe he didn't, since you weren't his girlfriend."

The word penetrated. *Girlfriend.* Aera leapt up and grabbed Doriline by the shirt. Terror filled Doriline's eyes as Aera locked into her gaze, their faces an inch apart.

Aera growled, waited a moment, and released her. There was silence as they measured each other through the downpour. After a long stare, Doriline blinked, laughed uneasily and carried her bucket away. Others craned to see the action, but when Aera met their eyes, they turned away.

Wimps, Aera thought. She wished she could summon lightning to strike them down. As this thought crossed her mind, she remembered Cyrus's theatrical parting gesture.

Now that he was free, he might one day attain *sundatëa*. He'd wanted Aera to follow that path with him, but she'd lost her chance. She would never have an *esil*, never find a purpose. The orb had enlivened her senses... but now, it was gone. No more Elkandul. No more hidden star.

No more magic.

Tasks dragged on and talk of Cyrus continued, but nobody bothered Aera again. She heard them laughing in the background, chasing each other around in the rain, hiding each other's shears. While others found humor in muddy clothing and task blunders, Aera had delighted in Cyrus's wit and their treasury of private understanding. She might never find joy again.

As she battled tears and exhaustion, her hands moved robotically

526

across the fields. The clouds parted as the storm faded, leaving behind a clear sky. By the time the dinner bell sounded, the fields were bright green and perfectly manicured.

Aera took her meal to the boulder and stared at her food but could not eat. Halcyon Hill was desolate without Cyrrus. The moment she'd seen the word 'Rot' in the dirt, she'd known he was gone... and with him, her childhood.

Rot. He'd said that word first in her dream, then to the Samies and finally, had written it in dirt. Cyrrus could have effected a clean escape but, instead, had left a trail. Why would the Kalaqhai—who allegedly worshipped logic—plant axes with their symbol on the handles, leaving evidence of their presence? She recalled the dog nailed to the Fence, whimpering in pain. Cyrrus had the ability to control animals and even eschewed eating meat, so it made no sense for him to have tortured that dog unless he wanted to send a message. Who was he sending it to?

The evening Cyrrus left, Aera had confronted him about the Night Gem. He might have communicated with the Kalaqhai afterwards in the orb, but if the nearest civilization was Kadir, no less than two weeks' journey by foot and presumably several days' ride on horseback, there would not have been sufficient time for anyone from there to reach the commune. If those axes had been planted by the Kalaqhai—or by anyone from outside Ynas—Cyrrus must have planned his exit far in advance. But this also made no sense, as he'd been preparing Aera to escape with him only weeks before. Had he been lying, or had he changed his mind? He might have been indecisive before, but he'd made his final decision after Aera had implored him to stop using the orb.

A murder of crows passed overhead, and she watched them sail into the horizon, wishing she could fly away with them. She couldn't go on like this. Somehow, she needed to learn where Cyrrus had gone and why. Only hours before his exit, she'd discussed the Night Gem with Vaye. Perhaps she knew something.

Aera finished her food and set off. Walking briskly, she made her way to the cottage and opened the door. Vaye was seated by the fire with two steaming mugs on the table, clearly expecting her.

"Aera, dear," Vaye said. "Wonderful to see you."

Aera took the seat opposite Vaye. Her outfit was as decorative as always, but her demeanor was heavy. Uneasily, Aera said, "You too."

Vaye considered Aera with a thoughtful look. After a long pause, she intoned, "Do you know where Cyrrus went?"

Aera's stomach dropped. She admitted, "I was hoping you would."

"I see," Vaye said slowly. "Was the crystal ball in his possession?"

The words resounded. *Crystal ball.* Vaye knew about the orb! Aera had worked so diligently to deceive Vaye, and now her lies were laid bare. Blood rushed from her cheeks as she forced out the word, "Yes..."

"Are you certain?"

"I tried to convince him to give it to you... and instead... he... left..."

Speaking was too strenuous. Vaye would never trust her again. If Aera had been honest with Vaye, Cyrrus might still be in Ynas.

"He is responsible for his actions," Vaye reminded her. "And you, for yours."

Aera fumbled for an apology. *I'm sorry I betrayed the only two people who were good to me. I'm sorry I was ever born.*

"Be kind to yourself," Vaye said gently. "You spared me the responsibility of your knowledge and remained loyal to Cyrrus. You contained your pain and confusion to protect the ones you love, which is an act of compassion."

Aera wanted to protest. *It wasn't compassion. It was a lie.* Tears swelled in her throat. Vaye had given her sanctuary all her life, only for Aera to let her down.

"Thank you for your generosity," Aera said, and stood. "I... don't deserve it."

Vaye watched Aera leave, her eyes filled with sadness. Aera glided silently out the door. The moment it closed, she rushed away.

Aera ran at full speed, going nowhere. The village was full of strangers, the cottage was uncomfortable, and Great Gorge would be unbearable without Cyrrus. She bounded into Westside Willows and continued deep into the woods. It didn't matter where she went, so long as everyone else was far away. She continued, faster and faster until she found the Fence. That damned thing. She pounded on it and screamed, "Let me out!"

Some birds flew away nearby. Aera screamed louder. "Aaahh!" She kicked the Fence, then found a branch and whacked it with all her might. She wished she could summon a cyclone and knock the whole thing down.

All her life, Aera had dreamed of performing *kuinu*, but it was beyond reach. She summoned Ivory to block mind readers and they penetrated her thoughts, nonetheless. How long had Vaye known about the orb? Why hadn't she said something sooner? Cyrrus had counted on Aera to deceive Vaye, but she was no match for either of their powers. She was a nuisance and nothing more.

Aera wanted to share the magic with Cyrrus and Vaye, but she couldn't. Without any special talents, charm or survival skills, she had nothing in common with her gifted friends. All she had to offer was her love, which was worthless and tainted with lies. If she managed to escape Ynas, where would she go? She did not fit with the Samies, nor with the Nestë. There was no place for her anywhere in the world.

NEMESIS

1329 LATE-SPRING

Ynas was a flurry of gossip and accusations as people scrambled to learn what had happened to Cyrrus. Pelyane organized protests, brought groups to town meetings and demanded information. The clan invited Aera, but she politely declined. She met with Kize to practice in the Music Room and spent the rest of her time in Westside Willows, struggling against her pain. The cottage was a haven she dared not approach, and Ynas was a marathon of monotony with no end in sight. The uproar over Cyrrus was the last remaining spark.

Kize attempted to befriend Aera. Although their artistic partnership provided some respite, she could not reveal to Kize anything that mattered. Her entire life had been hidden from everyone except Cyrrus and Vaye. None of the Samies knew about the sanctum, the orb, the magic, the dream of escape. Since conversation contained nothing of substance to her, Aera barely spoke at all.

On a free day in Late-Spring, Aera took her breakfast to the boulder. Kize, Pelyane and Goric arrived shortly after, carrying their trays.

"Mind if we join you?" Pelyane requested.

Without waiting for a response, the three made themselves comfortable in the grass. As everyone ate, Pelyane turned to Aera.

"The protests are all done and Nurin didn't tell us anything," she said in a frustrated tone. "We tried *everything* to get him to talk. We

530

found all kinds of rules saying Nurin had to inform us, but he got around it by reciting more laws."

Nurin never says anything honest anyway, Aera thought. *Why bother with him at all?* It was astounding that the clan had spent years with Cyrrus and still found value in a politician's words.

"Nurin kept on hinting that Cyrrus *deserved* to be exiled, and there was so much evidence that Nurin exiled him, but he just wouldn't confirm or deny it!" Pelyane sighed. "There's nothing more we can do... but I really think Cyrrus was exiled."

By now, everyone knew Cyrrus had left in the middle of the night and told several people to rot. Aera wondered how Pelyane reconciled that with her idea. Clearly, Nurin had dropped hints that he exiled Cyrrus. He wanted people to believe he was in control. In the absence of concrete information, Pelyane couldn't see past Nurin's blather. She fell for his manipulative ploys every time, all the while believing the exile theory was her own.

"What do you think?" Pelyane demanded.

Aera wasn't interested in explaining why none of this mattered. She took a bite of her potato and focused on the horizon.

"I told you," Goric chuckled. "I caught him practicing combat in the woods a few weeks before. I think he planned it."

Everything in Cyrrus's life was part of a plan. *Goric is right,* Aera thought.

"Cyrrus always liked sports," Kize sighed in a wistful tone. She picked at her food, looking miserable. Her mooning over Cyrrus was as pathetic as always.

"His form wasn't bad," Goric said. "Must've practiced before."

"Cyrrus practiced all kinds of things," Pelyane insisted. "Doesn't mean anything..."

The three jabbered on and on as Aera fought back tears. For months, she'd ignored the clan's search for answers, distracting herself with music and Ikrati. Yet now that she knew for certain that their efforts would wield no results, she found herself feeling disappointed. Somewhere deep down, Aera had hoped Pelyane might penetrate Nurin's facade. There was no way around it: Aera needed to find answers herself. She hadn't set foot in Southside Forest since Cyrrus's departure, but now it was time. She needed to visit Great Gorge.

She bid the group farewell and headed off to return her tray. Every step was heavy as she trudged across the village, but the song of insects in the forest soothed her. Though obnoxiously wet and muddy, the brush and bramble were familiar, like home. As she approached the great tree, her eyes landed on Cyrrus's vacant branch, and she felt sick.

The gorge showed signs of decay: a rusty tin full of moist pencils, rotting wooden tablets, and some dirty rocks. She pulled out the tablets and arranged them on the ground in three piles: her own notes, blanks, and Cyrrus's. His tablets contained immaculate sketches of familiar structures around the village, including buildings, bridges, staircases, and one scene she didn't recognize, portraying an intricately carved desk before a giant window surrounded by book-shelves.

Every angle was perfect, but the artwork was unnerving. If Aera were able to draw so precisely, she would have portrayed animate beings: Angels warring or creating the world; Nestë fighting or dancing in ceremony; her idealized self flying or performing *kuinu*. Had Cyrrus harbored no connection with anything beyond power? He was so estranged from emotions that even his artwork was devoid of humanity.

She lifted the last tablet, which contained three symbols with descriptions written in his pristine hand.

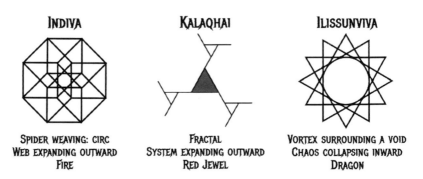

INDIVA	KALAQHAI	ILISSUNVIVA
SPIDER WEAVING: CIRC WEB EXPANDING OUTWARD FIRE	FRACTAL SYSTEM EXPANDING OUTWARD RED JEWEL	VORTEX SURROUNDING A VOID CHAOS COLLAPSING INWARD DRAGON

She recalled that block of wood from long ago, when he'd drawn those symbols after they had experienced separate visions under-ground. Two descriptions stood out: '*System expanding outward.*' '*Web expanding outward.*' He'd equated his vision in the wood with the

Kalaqhai mark but described Aera's as *'chaos collapsing inward.'* In his eyes, her emotions always had been a liability.

Her eye went to the word 'circ.' She strained to recall what this was about, and it came back to her: while delirious, Cyrrus had described his vision as a spider weaving a web that looked like a 'circuit.' Later, when Aera had asked what a circuit was, Cyrrus had claimed he'd said 'circle.' Yet, the tablet just said 'circ.' Of course. If 'circle' was what he'd meant, he would have written the whole word.

She turned the woodblock and noticed writing on the back.

TEACH PEOPLE TO THINK

BY ANY MEANS NECESSARY

It was the symbol for *niskuissieva*—integrity—surrounded by suggestive phrases. Aera remembered Cyrrus's obnoxious proverb about lying to people to teach them to think for themselves. Why had he written that on this wood block in particular? Had he lied when he claimed to have seen the *indiva* symbol in the monolith? He'd ripped the associated lesson from *Parë* long before that, which suggested he'd wanted to hide knowledge about his archetype. Perhaps he had ripped out the wrong lesson as a decoy to lead her astray.

Tension rose, and she smashed the block against the tree, faster and harder until it cracked. She needed to release this fury... she needed to play piano.

Pelyane and Kize were often in the Music Room, and she didn't want to see them. Aera had avoided the cottage for months, but that couldn't continue forever. Abruptly, she threw everything back into the tree hollow and raced to Vaye's.

The cottage was dark and quiet, much to Aera's relief. She presumed Vaye wasn't home and hurled straight into improvisation. Melodies roared and lyrics spilled forth faster than she could think, and she paused repeatedly to write them in her notebook. After a few hours, a new song had emerged.

Nemesis

He's on the other side
He's on the other side

Should I run inside and lock the door behind me?
Should I change my name in case he tries to find me?

Should I leave everything behind
And follow?
Am I strong enough for the other side?

Did he take part of me
Open my heart and see
When does it start to be
On the other side?

I gave him everything
Did he take everything?
Did he break everything
On the other side?

He's on the other side
He's on the other side

Should I step aside and let the madness bind him?
Should I chase him down and try to unwind him?

Is he deaf and dumb and blind
And hollow?
Will he try to hide from the other side?

He's always burning me
Twisting and turning me
Why do I yearn to be
On the other side?

Did he take part of me?
Look in my eyes and see
I'm telling lies to be
On the other side

He's on the other side
I'm on the other side
I can't decide
Which side is the other side

Aera stared at the lyrics and felt naked. The message was desperate, yet true. Had she let go of her doubts and trusted Cyrrus, she might be with him. He would have needed her to take on his causes and sacrifice her dream of joining the Nestë, but he had her heart. What good were her dreams if her heart was gone?

She played the song again, singing as loud as she could, pushing her frail voice through the cracks in her throat as tears cascaded. Each time the song ended, she started over, playing harder and louder to expel every ounce of emotion. Then, in the midst of the fury, the door opened and Vaye glided in.

Aera lifted her hands from the keys and peeled the hair away from her wet cheeks. Vaye was as elegant as ever, with a silk olivine gown and bejeweled headband peeking out beneath her vibrant silver ringlets.

"Hello, dear," Vaye said. "I'm delighted to see you again."

Vaye's grace made Aera self-conscious. She could only imagine how bedraggled she appeared and wondered what Vaye thought about that since she presented herself so perfectly all the time. Vaye took Aera in and said, "Your *vekos* is running free like never before."

Aera had always unleashed her passion in music and the implication that she hadn't until Cyrrus left was insulting. "My music has always been free," she snapped.

Vaye sighed. "Aera, please be mindful. That's not what I meant, or what I said."

Aera absorbed this statement and realized she had no idea what Vaye had meant or what she'd said. Everything was a blur. Under her breath, she mumbled, "Sorry."

Vaye smiled warmly, said, "I'll make us some tea," and floated into the kitchen.

Aera moved to a chair by the fireplace, where two cats rubbed against her legs and purred. As she petted them, her tension calmed, but she still felt guilty for directing her anguish at Vaye, who had done nothing to deserve that.

Vaye returned, set the tea on the table and asked, "What's on your mind?"

Aera had much on her mind but was uncertain what to reveal. Perhaps it was time to be honest. She straightened up and asked, "How did you know about the orb?"

Vaye smiled warmly, as though touched by the question.

"Through *inyanondo*, I picked up images of a colorful starscape," she said slowly. "At first, I thought it might have been a dream, or a description from a book. I refrained from investigating further until you asked about the Night Gem, and I sensed danger. That evening, I searched your thoughts and obtained an image of the crystal ball. I reasoned it connected to the starry world I had seen."

Aera took this in. All this time, she'd presumed Vaye had known about the orb and had hidden it from her. Yet Vaye had only figured it out once Cyrrus left and had told Aera immediately afterwards.

"We had the orb for half a year," Aera confessed. "I wish I told you sooner."

Their eyes met, and Vaye's expression was thoughtful. "I understand," she allowed. She sipped her tea and inquired, "Is there something else on your mind?"

Vaye's honesty was comforting, and her concern almost too much to bear. The only other thing on Aera's mind was the archetypes, but she didn't want to expose her obsession with 'useless' theories and invite scrutiny. Still, she was curious whether Vaye knew anything more.

"When I was underground with Cyrrus, we found a twelve-sided monolith, alone in a room. It showed us different symbols."

Vaye smiled and listened to Aera. Her brown eyes gleamed with intrigue.

"I saw *ilissunviva*," Aera said. "But Cyrrus saw... something else."

"I saw *heneissë*," Vaye offered with a knowing grin.

Aera smiled brightly. She hadn't expected Vaye to reveal that.

"Cyrrus... taught me to read *Parë*," Aera admitted. "I put the concepts together and made a map of archetypes."

She searched Vaye's face but didn't detect any anger. Encouraged, she reached into her pocket and withdrew her notebook. The archetype map was tucked into the sleeve. She unfolded it and passed it over.

Vaye took the page from Aera and studied it for a long while. Aera's pulse hastened. She didn't know what type of reaction to anticipate.

After a long silence, Vaye returned it and said, "I see these concepts found you well."

"I had a theory... that every person fits one of these archetypes," Aera explained.

Vaye smiled, taking this in. Gently, she allowed, "Vermaventiel proposed that all of the archetypal energies exist within everyone."

Aera's heart sank. She folded the paper and returned it to its home.

"I see you're dissatisfied," Vaye said sweetly.

Aera didn't want to express how invested she was and face the disappointment of being dismissed. She fostered a casual tone and said, "The monolith showed each of us a different symbol."

"Perhaps those symbols revealed something inherent, as you suggest," Vaye offered. "Or perhaps they encompass a lesson we must learn at a particular time."

Aera considered this. It was easy to see how people might learn different lessons throughout their lives, but it was also evident that people embodied specific archetypal energies. Was Vaye being polite, or was she open to this theory? Hadn't she thought of it before? Aera remembered the carvings in the bedroom upstairs, where Vaye was marked by *heinessë* and the white-haired girl, *ilissunviva*. It was disappointing to think those symbols were chosen to signify a mood or a phase, rather than a core personality.

"What do you believe?" Aera asked.

"It is not my calling to interpret the fundamental nature of archetypes," Vaye said. "Perhaps it is yours."

Though Aera enjoyed the idea of having a 'calling,' she couldn't possibly be the only person who interpreted the symbols this way. Someone had built the monolith and, surely, many had encountered it long before Aera was alive. It was unlikely that none had seen any connection between the symbols and the individuals to whom they were revealed. Beyond that, Aera's skills at identifying archetypes were questionable at best. If Cyrrus had convinced her of the wrong category, she had much to learn.

Vaye moved about the cottage, leaving Aera alone with her thoughts. Her mind went to Cyrrus's woodblock. Long ago, he had claimed he saw the *indiva* symbol in the monolith, indicating his element was music and his Angel, Nephrië. Considering his talent for enchanting audiences with new ideas and persuading authorities to alter their policies, Aera had accepted that the archetype of 'change' suited him. Yet now she considered whether 'principle' was a better match.

She leafed through her notebook, found her lists of words, and read the two.

5. LESSON OF *PURMALIUVURMA* (GRAMMAR/HISTORY)

- MUSIC IS THE EMBLEM OF THIS ARCHETYPE BECAUSE IT LINKS TO ENCHANTMENT & ELEVATION.
- THESE TYPES OVERVALUE INSPIRATION, BUT IT LEADS TO TRICKERY.
- THE PATH TO GROWTH IS WISDOM (*INDIVA*).
- THEIR ROLE IS TO OFFER & EMBODY CHANGE.

8. LESSON OF *NIRNILIË* (NATURAL LAW)

- MOUNTAINS ARE THE EMBLEM OF THIS ARCHETYPE BECAUSE IT LINKS TO ALCHEMY & PURIFICATION.
- THESE TYPES OVERVALUE PERFECTION, BUT IT LEADS TO HYPOCRISY.

- The path to growth is Integrity (*Niskuissieva*).
- Their role is to offer & embody Principle.

Music or mountains, Aera thought. Or neither...

Cyrus often associated himself with fire. He spoke about it, used it as a weapon, and saw it in visions. In her book, she found the archetype.

2. Lesson of *Alonwë* (All-is-oneness)

- FIRE is the emblem of this archetype because it links to Destruction & Creation.
- These types overvalue Desire, but it leads to Tragedy.
- The path to growth is Originality (*Ihyaniva*).
- Their role is to offer & embody Exile.

It seemed wrong to connect Cyrus to fire when he kept his emotions contained. Someone with a fire spirit would burn wildly, like the hidden star, who was hot and devouring, and tragic when feeling rejected. Though blue by default, his desire erupted, unleashing all shades of the flame.

She looked again at the archetype wheel.

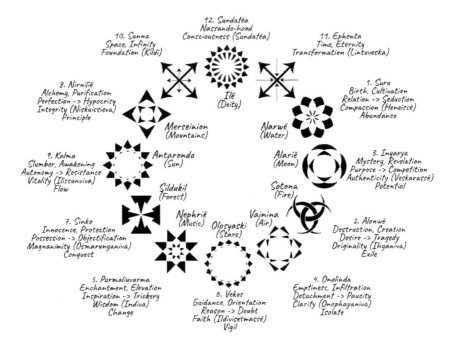

12. Sundatëa
Nassando-hood
Consciousness (Sundatëa)

10. Sunna
Space, Infinity
Foundation (Kildi)

11. Ephenta
Time, Eternity
Transformation (Lintuveska)

8. Nirnilië
Alchemy, Purification
Perfection -> Hypocrisy
Integrity (Niskuissieva)
Principle

1. Suru
Birth, Cultivation
Relation -> Seduction
Compassion (Heneissë)
Abundance

Ilë
(Deity)

Merseinion
(Mountains)

Narwë
(Water)

9. Kalma
Slumber, Awakening
Autonomy -> Resistance
Vitality (Ilissunviva)
Flow

Antarondo
(Sun)

Alarië
(Moon)

3. Inyarya
Mystery, Revelation
Purpose -> Competition
Authenticity (Veskarassë)
Potential

Sildukil
(Forest)

Sotona
(Fire)

7. Sinko
Innocence, Protection
Possession -> Objectification
Magnanimity (Osmarunganiva)
Conquest

Nephrië
(Music)

Olosyaski
(Stars)

Vainina
(Air)

2. Alonwë
Destruction, Creation
Desire -> Tragedy
Originality (Ihyaniva)
Exile

5. Purmaliuvurma
Enchantment, Elevation
Inspiration -> Trickery
Wisdom (Indiva)
Change

6. Vekos
Guidance, Orientation
Reason -> Doubt
Faith (Ildivisetmassë)
Vigil

4. Onolinda
Emptiness, Infiltration
Detachment -> Paucity
Clarity (Onophayaniva)
Isolate

Indiva, niskuissieva, and *ihyaniva* had something in common: all three connected to *lintuveska* at the top of the wheel. Perhaps Cyrrus related most of all to transformation. This might explain why he connected to fire, even though the archetype of 'exile' didn't suit him. Yet it still didn't clarify whether he embodied 'change' or 'principle.'

Aera was uncertain where to place Cyrrus, and the confusion was discouraging. If the archetypes were reflected in personalities, wouldn't it be obvious which group was his? She wondered whether her theory held any merit at all. For years, she'd interpreted the world through her system, yet Cyrrus had designed a scheme to cast doubt on it. He was indeed her nemesis.

540

CEREBRAL ENCLAVE
1329 MID-SUMMER

"Over here, Samies!"

"No pushing and shoving! Take your time! It's a free day!"

"If you want to sign up for the talent show, put your name here!"

Aera gritted her teeth as Pelyane's voice rang across the Field. Now that the Cyrrus protests had ended, Pelyane had moved onto the next project. She stood just outside the Dining Hall entrance with Goric and Kize, holding a giant piece of paper and a pencil.

Aera tried to rush past, but Pelyane spotted her. "Aera! Come sign up!"

Aera smiled politely, then continued inside. As she waited on the extensive food line, Pelyane appeared at her side, yelling over the noise.

"Morning, Aera! I'm organizing a talent show. Want to play for the singers?"

Aera couldn't imagine anything more torturous than listening to off-key voices and dealing with Samies. "Thanks for thinking of me, but... I'll pass."

"It'll be really fun!" Pelyane chirped. "I want Ynas to be artistic and inspiring! We could really make a difference, just like Cyrrus wanted."

You have no idea what Cyrrus wanted, Aera bristled to herself. Firmly, she repeated, "I'll pass."

Pelyane furrowed her brow. Aera could almost see the gears turning in her mind.

"Hmm... what should we do?" Pelyane asked, and cocked her head. "No one else plays nearly as well as you."

Aera wanted to explode, but she knew her anger was unwarranted. Pelyane was trying to do something good for the community. It was more than Aera would ever do. She took a deep breath, affected a cool Ivory tone and offered, "Ask Instructor Lilese."

"The point is to feature the kids... but I guess that could work. Still, it would be much better with you playing."

I said no, Aera thought. *Go away!*

The Dining Hall line was endless. She couldn't endure this. Briskly, she departed from her spot and headed for the exit. Pelyane tagged close behind, talking her ear off.

"We're gonna campaign for the right to sew costumes. We might even write some scenes and get people to act out the characters, like they do in theaters in the outside world!"

Aera shoved open the door and hurried through. Kize and Goric were still just outside. Kize smiled brightly at Aera and said, "It's going to be so much fun!"

Pelyane and Kize were so certain Aera would participate in their projects. Didn't they know her at all? Aera glared at each in turn, then headed up the Hill, leaving them behind.

She approached the boulder empty handed, seething with frustration. Where could she go now? Southside Forest loomed in the horizon, but it would be painful to return to Great Gorge. The weather was too gorgeous to sit in the cottage, and she was too anxious to withstand Vaye's calm. She decided to explore Eastern Pines.

Wasting no time, she descended the Hill and bounded across the bridge. She passed the canoe docking area and sporting field, where people were jogging around the track and hanging from exercise bars. Distancing herself from the crowd, she made her way to the pine forest. Once hidden within the foliage, she doubled her pace. Sweat poured down her forehead and anger mounted. She found a thick branch on the ground beside a skinny tree with red-tinted leaves.

"You practiced combat," she said to the tree. "I dare you to take me down."

A smile spilled over her face as she hurled herself into an Ikrati rage, pretending to fight Cyrrus. After an hour of imaginary sparring, she was exhausted and hungry.

Breakfast was over by now. Aera considered whether there would be some way to obtain a meal. It would probably require arguing with people, and she didn't want to see anyone. Perhaps, instead, she could put Vaye's lessons to use.

I'll pretend I'm lost in the outside world, she decided. *I'm starving and alone, and I need to survive.*

Aera found a patch of dirt, cleared the debris away, then hunted for firewood. Once the fireplace was ready, she tried to remember what Vaye had taught her about pine trees.

She closed her eyes and pictured herself in her cerebral enclave. The familiar oak stretched its gargantuan branches into a wide-open field encircled by a perimeter of white trees. Memories of Vaye would be located near the piano, situated on a stage in the field behind her. She imagined a few pine trees near the stage, and Vaye standing by, admiring one. With an elegant gesture toward the tree, Vaye allowed, "She is generous."

Aera tried to remember what else Vaye had said. Scattered words came back to her. *Abundant gifts... delicious raw or roasted... dance along to the rhythm of life...*

There was nothing else.

Aera opened her eyes. Cyrrus claimed he could access lost memories. How did he do it?

Perhaps it would help to climb a tree, as she had when Vaye had advised her. She found a tall pine tree with thick branches, made her way up, and closed her eyes once more. She could see Vaye in her mind, standing below the pine tree in Southside Forest, smiling at Aera. *Delicious raw or roasted,* she thought. What else had Vaye said? The rest was lost.

Aera looked up into the branches. There were pinecones, needles, branches, bark. *Remove the nuts,* she thought, and smiled. Vaye had said those words.

There were nuts inside the cones. Those might be eaten... raw or roasted. She pulled some cones from their homes and threw them down into a pile. Once her supply was substantial, she gathered some needles and jumped to the ground.

Over the next hour, she used pointy rocks to force the cones open. She managed to extract the nuts from the cones, then laid them out on a rock and roasted them by the fire. While waiting, she removed some bark from the tree and tried to figure out how to eat it but could not. Nuts and needles would have to do.

She waited until the nuts were soft and ate some. They were tasty, but even after collecting so many, there wasn't enough food for a meal. She tried eating the pine needles, but they stung her cheeks and left her mouth dry. Feeling defeated, she stomped out the fire, then found her way to the riverside, where she cupped some water in her hands and quenched her thirst.

Once satisfied, she laid down by the shore. The crowd was far downstream. No one was there to bother her, and she enjoyed the sound of running water. The sun shone and the birds chirped. She wished she could enjoy the beauty, but she still felt unsettled. Cyrrus was gone. She couldn't survive in the wild. Her memory had failed her.

Cyrrus had spent much time building his cerebral circus, but Aera had focused mostly on matching notes to numbers. Perhaps, if she visited her cerebral enclave more often, memories would come back more easily.

She closed her eyes and pictured herself once again in the cerebral enclave. In her mind, she faced the great oak at the center of the imaginary field, surrounded by white trees. This was becoming routine now, and quite easy to picture. All she had to do was associate experiences with specific locations in the enclave. Memories of Great Gorge would be placed inside the tree, while others would be buried in a sanctum beneath the grass. Elkandul would be in the sky, with twenty-four stars situated around a moon, but she could hide it from mind readers by picturing daylight most of the time.

Aera firmed these ideas in her mind, picturing each segment, running through memories. The exercise was simple enough. Perhaps, if she examined the enclave routinely, she might discover clues to Cyrrus's connections and whereabouts so that one day she might find him.

❧

Between survival practice, Ikrati rages and the enclave, Aera kept herself busy in solitude but soon felt discouraged. While she managed to recapture a few latent memories, none revealed where Cyrrus might be. Even if they did, it would not matter. She wouldn't be able to find him, since she was incapable of surviving on her own. As autumn approached, she spent less time fantasizing in the woods and more time playing music with Vaye and Kize.

Over time, Ikrati grew tedious and her musical improvisations, repetitive. Hoping to find inspiration, she used her cerebral symphony to create new arrangements. She composed melodies for each arche-type—classifying people, places and things—so it was easier to organize memories. Matching letters and numbers to music became automatic, and her technique on piano accelerated, but none of these skills breathed life into her songs. She considered quitting piano altogether but persisted, as she didn't want to disappoint Vaye and Kize.

By her sixteenth year, her hands were as fast as lightning. She knew every song in Vaye's books by rote and could embellish the commune anthem in any key, making it as grand as any Nestëan aria. People of all ages swarmed to Unity Festivals to relish Aera's seasonal event with Kize. Strangers approached her everywhere she went to comment on her musical prowess, but she felt increasingly detached from it. Music devolved into a joyless duty and, like everything else in her life, marked the passage of time. Nothing felt real.

INVASION

1330 EARLY-AUTUMN

Aera stood at the edge of a familiar forest of white trees, facing a sunny, circular enclave. In the middle of the grassy field was her favorite tree, exploding with bright green foliage. She admired the majesty of branches bursting in every direction, then slipped beneath them. She almost fell over when she saw Cyrrus on his usual perch above the gorge, writing on a rock.

He greeted her with a silent gaze, his eyes greener than the leaves. Aera broke into a smile and Cyrrus answered with a girlish giggle. She wanted to embrace him but controlled herself.

Gently, she intoned, "You're back."

With eyes alive with affection, he said, "I came back for you."

Aera blushed, lost for words.

Cyrrus eased gracefully from his branch to stand beside her, then took her hand and slipped his fingers between hers. She could feel his heavy pulse against her wrist, betraying nervousness. He looked at her with a mixture of fear and tenderness and said, "Aera, I..."

~

Ding, ding, ding.

It was too soon. Aera strained for one last glimpse, but all she saw was blackness...

Tears filled her eyes. The dream was over. She wanted to hide somewhere and cry, but there was no time. It was Autumn Unity Day, and Kize was depending on her.

She slipped into her pants and new white tunic, which Kize had made for Aera as a gift to celebrate her recent growth spurt. The scoop-neck was decorated with fringes that enhanced Aera's grace. She exited the room with Ivory-cultivated poise and slipped between Samies that swarmed the hallways. Once outside, she didn't fight the crowd for a muffin and, instead, settled at the boulder and combed her hair. Momentarily, Kize approached her, smiling, with two muffins in hand... wearing white.

"Look, Aera!" she chimed. "I made an outfit to match yours! Do you like it?"

Kize's tunic was scoop-necked, and her pants were fitted with leather strings, just like Aera's... but everything looked better on Kize. She had blossomed into a curvaceous, elegant girl with golden curls caressing her shoulders, threatening to challenge Aera's long mane. This implicit competition made Aera feel sick.

"Want an apple muffin?" Kize added. "Last one in the tray."

Kize's gesture reminded Aera of Cyrrus: he'd often brought apple muffins when he wanted to appease her. She forced a smile, accepted the muffin, and resumed combing. Soon enough, the celebration began.

Unity Festival that day was like all the others: predictably boring speeches, children clomping around the stage, and the throng vomiting the commune mantra. Aera and Kize began their performance in routine fashion, but as Aera's hands sailed mindlessly over the keys, her thoughts meandered to the dream. Cyrrus. His nervous smile. *I came back for you...*

Tears gripped her and forced their way out as music overcame her. Each anguished and blissful flourish expelled her sadness and rage while Kize moved along infectiously, succumbing to Aera's passion. As the song receded, Aera realized she hadn't felt this alive in a long time. She'd forgotten how to feel the music, but now it was once again real.

The stage lit up, and the audience remained silent and captivated until the explosive finale, when they stood and cheered as loud as their lungs permitted.

After they left the stage, Kize mingled happily with her admirers, but Aera deflected the usual accolades and went off toward the river alone. Swans glided along, surrounded by wave heads glistening in sunlight, while birds cawed and cooed from every direction. The world was lush, and the air was fresh. Aera felt reborn. Yet, despite the vibrant world around her, the dream of Cyrrus still felt more real.

She thought of his emerald eyes and wished more than anything she could wander into the forest and see him one more time on his favorite branch, writing on a rock. It occurred to her that the last time she'd visited their tree, there were rocks inside the gorge. Cyrrus might have written on them! Aera had avoided Great Gorge for over a year, but this was too exciting to resist.

She crossed the village, climbed the Hill, darted across the Sleeping Hut Field, and tore through Southside Forest. The great oak was in full glory. She reached into the dark gorge and fished out three rocks. Her hands trembled as she noticed one of the rocks had writing on the surface. It was a series of numbers: *5 12 1 14 1 20 8 1 14*.

Aera converted each number to a note, which translated to a letter in the alphabet: *E-L-A-N-A-T-H-A-N* . The word was unfamiliar. She tried to determine whether Cyrrus had written it, but the handwriting was uneven across irregularities in the rock, and she couldn't be certain. She rummaged through the gorge for clues, straining to remember if anything had changed since her last visit.

Metal clanked somewhere in the distance. Aera held her breath... nothing. She scanned the area for intruders, then heard a soft creak. The wind was too still to cause trees to creak. Something wasn't right. The hair on her neck began to tingle. Every nerve was humming.

Deep in the forest, footsteps rustled against leaves. Each one was heavy. Aera listened, deathly still. There was a sharp snap, followed by something whizzing past her face. A tiny, bright yellow dart plunged into the tree right in front of her. She was under attack.

Aera's body jolted, and she ran as fast as her legs could carry her. Another dart whizzed by, coming from the direction she was heading. There were enemies behind her and before her. Where could she go?

In the distance, she saw someone approaching her. He wore heavy metal armor, and his shoulders reflected slices of sunlight as he maneuvered through the foliage. She lunged out from behind one tree and sprang against the next as a dart whizzed by.

"*Bax k'erqhawi nina tayoy l'niqqās il tanugd,*[1]" someone bellowed in a guttural, choppy monotone.

"*Bax niqqaxt tanugd det hyex simrat,*[2]" replied another.

These words were unrecognizable, but the tone and delivery suggested cool-headed detachment. She leaned against the trunk and spotted someone a few trees away, also covered in metal armor from head to toe with a carving on his chest plate of the dreaded symbol:

Aera's heart raced. These were Kalaqhai.

"*Hyex nit,*[3]" he called.

Footsteps slogged toward Aera from multiple directions. Quickly, she shimmied up into the tree. A bow creaked and immediately, she swung to another branch on the opposite side of the trunk. One of the Kalaqhai climbed up after her. If she remained here, he would have her. No time to think. She had to act. *Do something,* she implored herself. But what?

Opho vassë viervi yanesi,[4] she thought, imagining her words projecting outward as they had done underground. Nothing happened. *Vavi dorón i kuissë më,*[5] she thought. No answer came back. She scrambled desperately through her cerebral enclave and a phrase popped out: *turn every situation to your advantage.* She focused on breathing until her panic evaporated. Ivory took over.

There was one of her and at least four of them, and they were all protected by armor and weapons. What advantages did she have? Vaye had taught her Kra techniques to climb and swing through trees, while the men were encumbered with bulky armor. If she could make it to another treetop, they might lose her.

She heard the now familiar snap of a bow and scrambled around the oak tree, close to a nearby maple. The sunlight was almost gone: another advantage. If she could remain hidden in the trees, she might hold out until darkness fell. She grasped a thin branch above and released her feet from the one she was standing on. The skinnier branch sank, but she retained her grip, noting her hands were stronger than ever due to her exercises on piano.

Another bow creaked. Just as a shaft whizzed by, she buried her head in her chest and lifted her knees. Once it passed, she tightened her grip on the branch and moved along, hand over hand, until she was close enough to reach a thick branch on the neighboring maple tree. She swung her legs back and forth, gaining momentum, then propelled herself toward the branch and grabbed it. She felt empowered as she inched toward the trunk of the maple, where more foliage might shield her.

"*Takrayt!*[6]" someone bellowed. "*Na' illoiz!*[7]"

The wind picked up rapidly and blew Aera's hair across her face. Branches hissed, debris flew about, and she could barely move against the sudden unearthly draft. There was a loud thump below, followed by the clang of metal against metal. Then the wind changed direction entirely. The heavy draft detached leaves from trees and lifted the debris from the forest floor.

Aera peeled the hair from her face to better see the scene below, which was bewildering. The body of a Kalaqhai lay sprawled on the ground. Blood spurted furiously from the space separating his helmet from his body armor—and not normal blood. Thick, grey blood. Aera remembered Cyrrus's pasty skin and felt sick. If he was part Kalaqhai, he might as well be an alien.

Metal clanked against metal nearby, and Aera snapped back to the present. She looked around and spotted another Kalaqhai engaged in battle with a woman whose forehead shone like moonlight as silver curls soared behind her. Vaye had heeded Aera's call. *Tesesili, a Vaye,*[8] Aera thought as relief overcame her. Now she knew who had helped her underground.

Vaye spun and thrust herself toward the much larger man. The wind followed her motion as she whipped him with such force that he lost control of his sword. Aera understood this was not coincidence.

Vaye was commanding the wind. She watched carefully and studied the intricate thrusts of Vaye's arm as the windstorm responded to her. Vaye was a force of nature!

While the larger fighter relied on his size and strength, swinging his broadsword wildly in an attempt to overpower his opponent, Vaye swung her slender saber fewer times, but with much greater accuracy and precision. Aera felt a rush as she watched the destruction unfold. She wished she could fight at Vaye's side, ruling the wind and vanquishing the attacker with exquisitely executed parries and thrusts, not unlike her Ikrati exercises.

Aera watched enraptured as the armed man lifted his sword high in the air and lunged toward Vaye with the long, pointed blade. Vaye acted instantly. While the giant's arm was raised, she stepped forward into him and thrust her sword upward—directly and precisely into the unprotected space where his articulated armor was vulnerable—and surgically removed his arm from his shoulder. His howl cracked through the cacophony of the raging wind, but the one-armed warrior would not relent. He lifted the gleaming metal sword in a last, single effort, but again Vaye was undeniable in her delivery and sliced across the slit below his helmet. He collapsed with a thud.

Vaye spun around, surveyed the area to make sure it was clear, then glanced up at Aera and smiled. The wind calmed along with Aera's pulse, and as the debris settled from the air, she saw Vaye's face illuminated by her *esil. Ë maliello*,[9] echoed her luxurious voice from every direction.

Suddenly, Vaye darted behind a tree where Aera could no longer see her. The wind churned again, and streaks of sunlit metal were visible between trees as more Kalaqhai appeared and surrounded Vaye. Wind roared, leaves flew, swords clanged. Aera held tight to the trunk of her tree as the branches swayed in the storm. She could see only dirt, leaves and fog, moving in concentrated waves. The commotion grew louder as the wind increased, and Aera's eyes stung from flying debris.

A sharp light flashed nearby, and Aera spotted a metal suit. There was an armored man positioned in the tree beside hers, aiming a blowgun at her. Down below, another with a crossbow guarded her tree. She tried desperately to locate Vaye, but all was a spinning haze.

Something pricked Aera's leg, and she looked down. A tiny dart protruded from the increasingly painful sting. She tried to pull it out but could not move her arms, then realized the rest of her was also frozen. Her head fell forward, and her heart pounded viciously as she toppled from the tree, unable to stop herself. The swish of wind grew increasingly distant as she slipped into blackness.

RENSTROM NURIN

1330 EARLY-AUTUMN

Resonant bass notes crept into Aera's awareness, followed by the distant echo of a melody. The reverberation dissipated and the notes became more distinct as she forced her eyes open.

It was a sunny afternoon, and she was lying across a mat on the floor of Vaye's bedroom, looking at a blue sky through the transparent glass ceiling. Light rained in from everywhere, creating a warm patch on the bed next to her where two cats slept.

Aera crunched her fingers together: they worked. There was no numbness or stinging like when she emerged from the orb. Carefully, she stretched and sat up. Everything felt normal. Her last memory was falling from a tree, unable to move a muscle. She should have been severely injured. Why was she even alive?

She descended the staircase, enjoying the sound of the piano, grateful to be moving. When she reached the bottom, Vaye stopped playing and said, "Wonderful to see you, dear! How are you feeling?"

"Fine," Aera said with a confused smile.

Vaye looked Aera over, and her face betrayed relief. "Have a seat. Let me make you some soup."

Vaye retreated to the kitchen, and Aera sat by the fire. She wondered what kind of condition Vaye had expected her to be in and how she'd ended up at the cottage. The commune was protected by a wall, yet foreigners had chased her in the woods. Nothing made sense.

An aroma of sweet spices tantalized her as Vaye returned with a bowl of thick artichoke soup. Aera swallowed her first spoonful, which tasted wonderful, and realized how hungry she was. She wolfed down a few more mouthfuls before noticing she was behaving like Cyrrus, then adjusted her posture to finish the rest more gracefully.

"I have more, if you'd like," Vaye offered.

Aera was still hungry, which was not like her. She'd never been so hungry in her life. "How long was I asleep?"

"For quite some time," Vaye said with a smile. "Almost three days."

Aera had no idea so much time had passed, but what intrigued her more was *why* this had happened. Why would the logical Kalaqhai go to such lengths to shoot her with poison darts, only for her to sleep and wake up in good condition?

"The poison was used to prevent escape," Vaye explained. "It seems they never intended to kill you but rather, capture you."

Why would the Kalaqhai want her? Was the orb involved? Perhaps they had intended to question her about Cyrrus, or to bring her to him. To enter the commune, they would have had to pass the guards at the Gate, which meant the authorities had let them in...

"They were indeed Kalaqhai and I don't know what they want from you," Vaye said slowly. "But I will investigate and do my best to protect you."

"The commune is supposed to be safe," Aera hissed. "It's all a lie."

Vaye looked at her for a long moment, her expression utterly unreadable. "I'll get you some more soup," she said finally. "Rest assured that I will investigate."

Rest assured... unlikely. Aera might never rest again.

Vaye retrieved more soup from the kitchen, placed it on the table and sat in the opposite chair. As Aera ate, she reviewed the incident. The Kalaqhai had surrounded her at Great Gorge. How had they known to look for her there? Even if they knew the place existed, how had they known Aera would be there? She hadn't visited the area for well over a year and had only gone then because of her dream. Could Kalaqhai plant dreams?

"Vaye... does 'Elanathan' mean anything to you?" Aera inquired.

Vaye, who had been gazing at the fire, looked up with dazed eyes. "Why do you ask, dear?"

"I... read it somewhere."

Vaye's expression warmed as if she found Aera's secrecy endearing. "It's the name of a spirit worshipped as a god in New Taerelboro."

Cyrrus claimed the Kalaqhai did not worship gods. If this was true, New Taerelboro likely was not home to the Kalaqhai.

"It's a human settlement," Vaye explained. "The Kalaqhai city of Qhāmax is near there."

This information was unhelpful. Aera wished she had some way of knowing whether that rock had been in the gorge before.

"Finish your soup," Vaye said. "I'll walk you back to the village."

Vaye retreated upstairs and returned quickly, adorned in a majestic, hooded cloak. She lifted a knife from the kitchen counter, slipped it into a sheath and secured it inside her pocket. As she adjusted the cloak, Aera caught a glimpse of a sword beneath. Vaye was preparing for another possible attack.

As they stepped outside, Aera was taken aback. At the other end of the coneflower field, there was a row of Kalaqhai heads, mounted on pikes. Some were bashed or decayed beyond recognition, while others retained their pasty, red-haired look. A pair of vultures perched on one, feeding greedily.

Aera looked at Vaye, who grinned slyly, acknowledging her surprise. This tiny, elegant woman, with her sweet smile and gentle clothes, had decorated her garden with the heads of her victims. Aera laughed aloud.

The two headed through the forest and across the Sleeping Hut Field until they reached the edge of the Hill.

"The Authorities are investigating the incident," Vaye said darkly. "For now, stay in the village."

Apparently, it was too dangerous for Aera to walk through the woods now. She was being robbed of her trips to the cottage, her survival adventures, and any opportunity for solitude.

"I informed the authorities you were under my care," Vaye continued. "Go to the Attendance Office on the first floor of the Administration Unit to alert the staff that you're back."

The thought of joining the Samie routines with no respite was maddening, but it wasn't Vaye's fault. Aera swallowed her frustration and said, "Thanks... for everything."

"We'll see each other soon," Vaye assured her, though her countenance was sad. She patted Aera on the shoulder and headed back to the forest.

Aera climbed the Hill and saw nobody was around, which meant tasks were in session. She proceeded to the Administration Unit but didn't want to return to her usual duties. She needed answers.

Cyrrus would have marched straight to the Renstrom's office to seek an explanation. Nurin wouldn't give her any useful information, but any reaction might inform her in some way. The prospect of facing him alone was nauseating. *It's all a game to Ivory*, Aera assured herself, though that was unhelpful if she couldn't win the game.

She went inside and found the second floor where she'd once seen Cyrrus leaving Nurin's office. As she passed each door, she read the gold-plated markings: *Brass... Justinar... Renstrom*. She knocked firmly.

"Enter," proclaimed Nurin.

She opened the door and saw the Renstrom seated at a shiny, ornate wooden desk in front of a giant window surrounded by decorative bookshelves. The scene was familiar. Cyrrus had drawn that exact arrangement on a tablet in the gorge. Elaborate maps hung on the walls, and a brown fur carpet covered much of the floor, far too large to be made from the hide of a singular animal. Her eye went to three giant bear heads hanging on the wall over a fireplace. *Someone killed those bears just to make Nurin look important*, Aera thought, and cringed. On the mantle, there were black statues of geometric shapes, much like the paper contraption Cyrrus had made for her.

Nurin had a few books propped open and some papers in front of him, and he focused on reading as though Aera wasn't there. Dismissing his dismissal, she said courteously, "May I have a word with you?"

"Have a seat."

His desk was surrounded by four luxurious armchairs made of leather and fur. Aera took the one beside Nurin and eyed the books on the shelf beside her, which had titles handwritten neatly on the spines. *The Art of Persuasion. Memory Development. Expansion and Hierarchy. Vocal Craft.* Row after row, one title after another about political power. Aera wondered how many Cyrrus had read and surmised that this was where he'd learned his techniques.

"Did you come to admire my bookshelf?" Nurin inquired, still peering at his paperwork.

Politely, Aera asked, "Do you know why I was attacked in the woods?"

"We're looking into that," Nurin said without looking up. "You need not be concerned."

Less politely, Aera said, "I could have been killed."

"This is not about you," Nurin asserted.

Liar, Aera thought, and glared at him.

"Allow me to remind you that you are no different from anyone else," Nurin said, piling some papers together as he spoke. "Anyone might have been targeted, but you wandered alone and set yourself apart. This was the consequence."

Aera wanted to explode. *Don't give him that*, she implored herself. Though she controlled the rage, she could think of nothing to say.

"You are attempting to solve a puzzle for your own amusement," Nurin continued. He folded the papers into one of his books, placed it back on the bookshelf and looked at Aera with a decidedly stern edge. "The DPD will not allow the commune to be breached. That is our job. Your responsibility is to stop attracting trouble. Abandon your futile mission to be different. Integrate with your peers."

Nurin looked down, turned a page in another book and scribbled something. It was a dismissive, transparent display of rudeness advanced to underline Aera's unimportance. She would have liked to wring his neck or divine the eloquence to humiliate him with words, but all she could do was fume. Without a word, she left.

Once outside, Aera was in a bind: she was too angry to join her group, yet it was unsafe to wander off on her own. She went to the Education Unit and paced back and forth in the stairwell until the dinner bell gonged. Though she never wanted to see anyone again, she was bored and hungry. All that was left to do was rejoin the world.

She gathered some food and climbed to the boulder. Kize and Pelyane were already there, and when she approached, they greeted her excitedly.

"Aera! You're back!"

"Where have you been?"

"Are you okay?"

Aera sat down and said distantly, "I was sick."

"We saw the windstorm in Southside Forest on Unity Day," Pelyane said. "Gaili said you got caught in it."

Apparently, someone had fabricated a palatable story. If Aera explained that Vaye had caused the storm, nobody would believe her.

"Were you hurt?" Pelyane asked.

Aera took a bite of her lettuce wrap, tried to decide what to say, then finally replied, "No."

Kize and Pelyane exchanged a glance. Aera wondered if they found her evasiveness as frustrating as she'd often felt with Cyrrus, and the thought amused her.

"Where's Goric?" Kize asked Pelyane, changing the subject.

"I don't *know*," Pelyane whined. "He missed town meeting today and he keeps disappearing..."

As the two conversed, Aera gazed at the forest. *Windstorm. You got caught in it.* She wondered where this rumor had originated. The authorities certainly would have looked to Nurin to explain what had happened. Was he aware of Vaye's *kuinu*? Either way, he knew much more than he ever said. If he really knew so little, he would have questioned Aera.

She smiled, proud of herself. Going to the Renstrom's office had been the right decision. Unlike Pelyane, Aera derived conclusions by observing what Nurin was *not* saying. The meeting had been informative indeed.

There was clearly an agenda being enacted, and Aera suspected it involved Cyrrus. The night before the Kalaqhai attack, she'd seen Cyrrus in a dream, writing on a rock. She couldn't be certain who had written those numbers on the rock, or when it had been placed in the gorge. But regardless, the dream had foretold reality. Similarly, right before Cyrrus left, she'd dreamed him saying 'rot...'

"You okay, Aera?" Kize's voice was gentle, but full of concern.

Distantly, Aera replied, "Fine. Just thinking."

"We're going to Westside Willows to look for Goric," Pelyane said. "Want to come?"

Westside Willows. Unless they were planning to restrict their journey to the bathing grove, they would be venturing outside village grounds. Nurin had suggested that anyone who left the village was a target, but if the DPD hadn't warned other people against leaving the village, then Nurin didn't really believe it was dangerous for them. The apparent lack of concern in the general population told Aera what Nurin would not: she was the exclusive target of the Kalaqhai and in grave danger.

"I'll stay here," she said. "Thanks."

As soon as the two left, Aera tried to piece together what Nurin was hiding. Based on the content of his books and the drawing Cyrrus had made, it was obvious Cyrrus had spent ample time in Nurin's office. Everything pointed to Cyrrus being connected to the invasion, but why? Had the Kalaqhai tried to capture her because she had information about him, or had Cyrrus sent them to deliver her to him? She considered whether she'd made the wrong decision trying to evade them, but their hostility had left her little choice. If Cyrrus wanted her to join him, he could have come himself.

Either way, the connection between Cyrrus and the Kalaqhai was disturbing. If he'd joined them to hunt for the Night Gem, would she consent to be part of that? Her song came to mind. *I'm telling lies to be on the other side...*

She finished eating, then realized there was no place to go, since she could no longer leave the village. There was a piano in the Music Room, but she wasn't in the mood for music. The fields below swarmed with activity, but Aera hated everyone.

Down at the river, people rowed canoes, and officers lit torches by the running track. Cyrrus had visited the track occasionally and had always outrun everyone else, yet Aera wasn't fast enough even to elude predators in bulky armor. *You're too weak to survive on your own*, Cyrrus had told her. He was right. The most sensible thing to do would be to practice running and strength training. It would be tedious, but Ivory had disciplined her mind to control her *vekos*. Besides, she had to kill the time somehow.

She returned her tray to the Dining Hall and headed across the bridge. As she approached the track, she envisioned herself as Ivory, soaring by, fit and powerful. She refused to be delivered to Cyrrus as a helpless victim. If he wanted to abduct her, he could do it himself, and she would force him to explain his intentions and apologize for his lies.

As she imagined herself strong and confident before him, a smile consumed her.

The track was crowded with runners, and in the field beyond, people lifted themselves on exercise bars, challenging each other and taking turns with their friends to show off.

As Aera approached the area, someone called, "Nice legs!" It was an older boy sitting on a bench, yelling at a tall girl as she passed in a short under-tunic.

"Great stack!" called another boy as a voluptuous girl raced by.

People yelled from shaded benches along a small incline near the track that sheltered a water fountain and piles of clothing. Aera added her cloak, headed onto the track and jogged at a steady pace. Two shirtless older boys passed her.

"How did it feel to bundle a genius?" called one.

"Woo-hoo!" added the other.

Idiots, Aera thought, and continued jogging.

A few moments later, she heard Novi call out to someone, "Samely, farkus! Jog off that gut!" She spotted Doriline's pink-clad flock on the grass along the incline, ridiculing passersby. Their favorite sport.

After a few laps, Aera was panting and her muscles were burning. She stepped off the track to get a drink at the fountain and spotted Idan in the distance, climbing into a canoe. Long ago, Idan had mentioned spying on 'council meetings' and hearing talk about Cyrrus. Aera had forgotten about that until now and wondered which meetings he was referring to. Perhaps he would tell her more.

Aera divided her free time between rehearsing with Kize and exercising. By her seventeenth birthday, her speed and endurance had vastly increased, and she outpaced many of the boys. She was able to perform pull-ups on the high bar, her repetitions increasing over time. Often, she tackled other feats, such as hanging upside down, somersaulting around the bars and balancing with one foot atop slender planks. Though she faltered occasionally, she never injured herself as others did because she used Kra stretches to realign her body. Her agility made such an impression that people took to calling her 'kitty cat'—both fondly and mockingly—and made apropos meowing noises. Yet they couldn't see the most astounding result of her workouts, which was the slender musculature concealed beneath her clothing.

Although the track was less crowded in the cold, Aera remained a regular. She often saw Idan canoeing or sporting with friends and was still waiting for an opportune moment to approach. Finally, one chilly afternoon, she managed to catch Idan doing nothing but sitting by the track with his friends. Doriline and her crew were huddled on the nearby incline, watching the boys' every move.

Aera glided gracefully past the pink-clad audience and approached Idan. When he saw her, he looked confused and said, "Samely?"

"Greetings," she grinned. "Can we talk?"

"Sure," he said, and raised a brow at his friends, two of whom chuckled to each other.

Aera assumed they were mocking her. *Ignore it,* she implored herself, and stood up even straighter.

Idan followed her away from the crowd, toward the river. Once they were a safe distance away, Aera said slowly, "A while ago, you told me you spied on council meetings. Do you still, and... could I come?"

Idan laughed. "I see you've become quite the rebel."

Aera wasn't sure how to respond. It was risky to declare herself a rebel, but if she denied it outright, he might not invite her.

Idan relieved her and said, "I bet Cyrus schooled you pretty good."

Coolly, she replied, "I have my own mind."

"Sounds like fun. I know *all* about breaking rules."

This was comical. If Idan had any idea of Aera's history of illegal activity, his head might explode.

"What happened to Cyrus, anyway?" Idan asked. "Was he exiled?"

Aera was sick of this question. Distantly, she said, "Who knows."

"He didn't tell you?" Idan furrowed his brow. "Weird."

The conversation was becoming more awkward by the second. Aera tucked her hair behind her ear, smiled coyly and asked, "So... can I come?"

"Well, normally it's a secret, but you're cute so..."

Aera blushed. "That's a weak reason to invite me. A better one is that I won't report you."

"Good answer," Idan laughed. "But you are."

Aera allowed a smile, though she wished the conversation would end.

After a brief silence, Idan said, "I'll let you know when it's happening."

"Thanks."

Idan waited for a moment, then said, "You coming?"

"I'll stay here."

Idan nodded and headed off, and Aera paced along the riverside. She reviewed the interaction and noted that, despite her nervousness, she'd displayed confidence. Not only had she approached Idan and requested a private conversation, but she'd asked twice if she could join him in spying. Ivory gave her courage, whether Aera invoked her consciously or not. She had learned to direct her *vekos* with purpose and was no longer so enslaved by her impulses that she needed to suppress and contain them. Ivory gave her the freedom to be aloof, flirtatious, demanding—or even cruel—when it suited her.

Aera lingered behind while the crowd cleared. She gazed across the river and spotted two fancifully dressed boys from Cyrrus's bunk standing outside the DPD Building, waiting by the door that led to the latrine waste. When she and Cyrrus were forced to clean latrines, they had waited near those same doors at the end of lunch break. She wondered what crime those boys had committed and whether it was something they had learned from Cyrrus.

She returned to the village, then suffered through four hours of tasks as her group spread manure through the fields. Afterwards, she took a quick bath, then joined the usual three by the boulder for dinner. While Pelyane and Goric spoke softly to each other, Aera asked Kize, "Have you been going to town meetings?"

"I haven't gone since..." Her voice trailed off and she looked down.

Aera finished Kize's sentence in her mind: *I haven't gone since the meetings stopped being about Cyrrus.* Kize had never cared about Cyrrus's cause; she'd just used the clan to be close to him.

Pelyane, however, announced with a proud smile, "I *never* miss a meeting."

"I saw two older boys on latrine duty," Aera said. "Do you know what they did wrong?"

"Ah, the boy lovers," Pelyane laughed. "They were caught playing

Jiavo. It's a game they play in other countries, and it's illegal here... *outside* the DPD training grounds."

Pelyane seemed to know the laws—which meant Cyrrus might have coached her. Aera had imagined the memory lessons were a special thing they shared, but it was meaningless if he taught them to everyone. She decided to inquire covertly and asked, "Why is it illegal?"

"Hmmm." Pelyane cocked her head. "I don't know. I've heard it's a strategy game. In *The History of Andolien* it says it was invented by Dirgaselan warriors to keep their minds sharp between battles."

Cyrrus was interested in strategy. Perhaps that was why he'd befriended those boys, but what advantage did it offer him to join their dormitory in particular? Of all the people he socialized with, those boys stood out to him.

As Pelyane resumed her private conversation with Goric, Aera said softly to Kize, "Did Pelyane memorize the law book?"

"She reads it all the time, and she tries to remember but she says it's... impossible." Kize looked down and mumbled, "At least... for her."

Aera was relieved that Pelyane wasn't privy to Cyrrus's techniques, but Kize's behavior was disconcerting. Whenever there was an obvious reference to Cyrrus, Kize became miserable and avoided saying his name. After all this time, she was still obsessed. Did she think *she* knew the real Cyrrus? *I ascribe her no agency*, Aera thought. Yet it was impossible to shake the feeling that Kize knew something she didn't.

Aera heard nothing from Idan for weeks and assumed he'd forgotten her. Finally, on the second evening of Mid-Winter, he approached her on the dinner line and whispered, "Meet us by the bridge at curfew."

She ate by the boulder with Kize's crew, then jogged around the track as usual and lingered around after the curfew gong. Soon enough, Idan showed up with friends. One was a tall, freckled boy named Edis and the other was Hizad's old sidekick, Codin.

Immediately, Codin said, "Idan, look out. This little girl likes rules about as much as you do."

Aera grimaced.

"Now that your bundle buddy left, the Authorities have their eye on *us*," Codin laughed, turning to the others. To Aera, he asked, "Where did he go, anyway?"

Anger rose from within. She glared at Codin and hissed, "What do you care?"

"Alright, alright, cool down, kitten," Codin smirked. "Too bad he's gone. I kinda liked him."

"Naturally," Aera grinned. "He made your friend eat dirt."

Codin shot her a look, and she shot one right back. It was an intense moment, interrupted by the other boys laughing.

"Sharp tongue on this one," Codin said to Idan. "She's nothing but trouble." To Aera, he said, "Don't even think about reporting us. Your hero isn't here to protect you anymore."

"You wouldn't beat up a *little girl*," she exhorted. "Would you?"

Codin exchanged a snickering grin with his friends. "I see why Brains liked you. You look sweet but you're trouble." Eyeing her up and down, he said, "I like your style, little girl."

"Darse it, buddy," Idan said. "Come on... let's go."

Idan jabbed Codin in the arm, and Codin shoved him. All three boys guffawed as they walked, pushing each other, laughing and snorting to trumpet their hyper-masculine camaraderie.

The romping continued as they followed a dirt path eastward. They passed the track and continued through endless crops, where the fragrance reflected each vast plantation until the path led into a dense forest. As the trees surrounded Aera, her heart raced. She hadn't set foot in any forest without Vaye escorting her since the Kalaqhai incident. *Inhale,* she thought. *Exhale...*

The boys' rowdiness ceased as they moved deeper into the trees. Aera presumed they were getting close and quieted her footfalls. The others tried to do the same, but their steps were hardly softer than before. As they acknowledged their uniform clumsiness, they struggled not to burst into laughter.

They walked on until they reached the Fence, then veered North. After about an hour, Aera spotted smoke ahead and a jagged black shadow came into view. It was a concrete ridge that stood several inches above ground and had a slender chimney protruding from one corner.

All the boys lay on their stomachs and cupped their eyes against the ground along the ridge. Aera followed their lead and peered into a sliver of space between the earth and the ridge, but all she saw was a wall. Idan nudged her to a tiny crack in the concrete and she adjusted her position, cupped her hands and peered in. There was a room beneath the ground!

She adjusted herself to obtain a better view of the room below. It was about the size of a classroom, with four men seated around a marble table. Renstrom Nurin was at the head, and the others were strangers wearing outfits unlike any Aera had seen before. One, facing the chimney, wore a skintight shirt covered in rows of shiny buttons connected to slender gold chains. Two others sat across from him with decorative fur cloaks hanging over the backs of their chairs. Nobody in Ynas wore anything like that. These were outsiders.

Torches lined the brick walls. One wall had a wooden door while another was dominated by a giant metal portal with three triangular keyholes surrounding a larger lock. Aera's mind jumped to the Kalaqhai symbol. She wondered where the doors led, since everything was underground except the chimney and the slanted roof.

The voices inside were barely audible, but Aera cupped her ear and leaned her hands against the crack. Although she could no longer see, she heard most of the conversation.

The three strangers did most of the talking and, for a while, nothing was of any interest to Aera. There were references to 'The Vault,' which she recalled from *Laws of Ynas* was a place where birth records were stored, and there was discussion about babies from Kadir being transferred to Ynas and a detailed reporting of their lineage, which was mostly Kethran. Boring. Just as the boys were becoming antsy and whispering about leaving, the conversation took an interesting turn.

"Any news of The Seeker?" Nurin asked.

Aera jolted to attention. *The Seeker.* Was that Cyrrus?

"He has evaded all inquiry," someone responded.

"Good," Nurin said. "What of the mission?"

"Qirzān has been informed of the error," said one of the men. "Since then, the Seeker has vanished from Kadir."

"Reconsider my suggestion," Nurin said sternly. "There can be no mistakes."

The subsequent conversation concerned a transaction with Qirzān to resolve a dispute between brothers over the ownership of a castle in Kadir and the reinstatement of bullfighting as a festival activity. Nothing else connected to 'The Seeker,' and Aera wondered how any of this connected to Nurin either. His job was running Ynas, but he hosted meetings to discuss festivities in Kadir. Nothing about him was honest. He was the face of Ynas, and Ynas was a lie.

Aera joined the spying missions on two more occasions. Those meetings included Justinar Dinad, Brass Inellei and others Aera recognized, but no foreigners. Most of the issues pertained to commune law, decisions about two babies entering the commune from Kadir, divisions of responsibilities among DPD members, and 'rebels'—including a mention of Codin, Idan and Edis, which elicited silent chuckling from them.

There was a brief discussion of Cyrrus at the later meeting. Justinar Dinad asked Renstrom Nurin, "What became of Cyrrus's drawings?"

"I used them as kindling," Nurin replied.

"Did Aera see them?" Dinad asked.

Aera had no idea what they were talking about and listened intently.

"He threatened to display them publicly if I refused his request, but promised to show no one if I conceded," Nurin said, and the whole council broke into laughter. Aera was surprised that they found humor in this and wondered what it was about.

"He could have drawn it again," Dinad said. "Do you trust his word?"

"I trust his efficiency," Nurin asserted. "He got what he wanted and moved on."

Aera hoped to learn more, but the discussion ended there. The group moved on to a tedious conversation about room assignments in the DPD Lounge.

During the walk back, Aera stored the relevant information in her cerebral enclave and considered what had been said. Nurin apparently had conceded to Cyrrus's requests and found his blackmail amusing. Considering the tension between them during public debates, it seemed incredulous that Nurin and the others spoke of him with such reverence in private. Did Cyrrus side with the youth or the authorities? Whose agenda did he serve?

From afar, it seemed Cyrrus was a 'rebel'—openly breaking laws, challenging the system and using his wit to thwart authority. Yet, behind the scenes, Nurin was solicitous of him, perhaps even sponsoring missions. Were the debates staged? Was Nurin aware that Cyrrus had his own contacts in the outside world? Had Nurin aided Cyrrus's escape?

Aera absorbed what a cruel irony it was that she had to spy on the loathsome Renstrom to learn about her own best friend. Nurin knew Cyrrus better than she did. The more she learned, the more she wondered whether she really knew Cyrrus at all.

When spring came, the usual crowd returned to the track. Codin and Idan resumed their ostentatious rivalry for Aera's attention while the hens watched from the sidelines and whispered. Over time, Aera grew increasingly uncomfortable as strangers from every Age Group eyed her wherever she went. She had no idea why until, one evening on the dinner line, a younger girl tapped her shoulder.

"Samie Eh-ruh?" the girl asked. "Did Samie Cyrrus really make you do those things?"

Aera smirked and retorted, "I made *him*."

"Ewww," said the girl.

"You made him eat worms off your body?" asked another nearby.

"No, *snakes*," Aera said, and everyone gasped. What a bunch of idiots.

"Eating snakes makes you smarter," she added. "You should try it."

There was a chorus of gasps and protestations. "Eww!"

"Gross!"

"Ghaadi disgusting!"

Aera flashed a smile, proud of her clever comeback. Ivory had made her more confident indeed.

She carried her lunch to the boulder where Kize and Pelyane were already eating, skipped past greetings, and asked, "Have you heard rumors about me lately?"

Kize and Pelyane exchanged a glance, and Pelyane said, "People have been... saying things. We tried to stop them..."

"What things?" Aera asked.

Kize blushed violently while Pelyane looked down and mumbled, "Things about you and... Cyrrus... doing private things. We always tell them... it's none of their business."

Impatiently, Aera reminded her, "Private means no one would know about it."

"They spied on you," Pelyanc murmured. "When he was... bundling you in the forest."

"That's a lie. He never touched me."

Kize and Pelyane exchanged another glance, clearly hiding something. Aera regretted telling them anything at all, but it was too late and there was no point stopping now.

"What?" she pressed. "You don't believe me?"

"It's hard to believe... he *never* touched you," Pelyane said. "Boys always touch their girlfriends."

Girlfriends. Cyrrus had never wanted Aera to be his 'girlfriend,' but that didn't stop everyone else from fantasizing about sex between them. She jumped explosively from her seat and left to jog off her angst.

As she rounded the track, Pelyane's words reverberated. *Boys always touch their girlfriends*. Cyrrus hadn't touched her, claimed her... what had he wanted from her anyway? If it was so natural for him to reject and abandon her, he should have just left her alone.

She jogged faster than ever, burning away the anger, bolting round and round until her chest was on fire.

Codin jogged up alongside and asked, "Wanna race?"

To her relief, Idan came up from behind and pushed Codin to the grass. The two monkeyed around, each trying to pin the other while Aera ignored them.

568

Moments later, Idan caught up with her and said, "Sorry about him."

"Sorry about your shrunken head!" Codin called, and shoved Idan down from behind.

Aera was annoyed and decided to take a water break, but the boys ran after her. Codin reached her first and said, "You're sweaty. Wanna get sweatier?"

Aera glowered at him, but didn't respond.

"You need someone with manners," Idan said. "I'd take you canoeing and pick you flowers."

"Pfft," Codin snorted. "You'd have to sit backwards so she won't be stuck looking at you."

"Better than listening to you, barlock..."

Aera wondered whether they expected her to be flattered or if she existed to them at all. It was clear that their competition was less about her than it was an excuse for them to wrestle and outwit each other for their own amusement. At best, she was a trophy for the winner.

She collapsed on a bench, but the two boys followed, oblivious to her irritation. Considering they likely believed Cyrrus had used her body as a platter for invertebrates, it was odd that they continued to angle for her.

Idan sat beside her, and Codin stood nearby, making sure nobody else overheard them. In a hushed voice, Idan said, "There's a DPD meeting tonight. You in?"

"Sure," Aera murmured.

Idan leaned in and asked, "You okay?"

"Wonderful," she snapped. These idiots refused to take a hint. Without another word, she returned to the track.

When the curfew bell gonged, Aera continued running while the boys wrestled. Officers extinguished the torches and the last joggers cleared away. Finally, when everyone else was gone, Edis arrived and the four headed into the dark woods.

The boys laughed throughout the walk until they glimpsed Nurin's secret nest. They approached and shimmied on their stomachs, per routine, to spy through the cracks just beneath the edge of the roof.

Aera was surprised when she saw Vaye in the room along with

569

Nurin and two strangers in familiar flashy outfits adorned with gold chains and buttons. A man-sized form lay on the surface of the table before them, blanketed in dark cloth. Black shoes poked out one end with silver buckles and squared toes...

...like Cyrrus's.

Aera's heart jumped into her stomach. *Don't panic*, she thought, and breathed deeply. It could be anyone... but why was somebody lying on the tabletop? Was the person asleep? Dead? Why was Vaye there?

The group huddled over the table, touching the blanket and conversing in hushed voices. Aera squeezed against the crack in the roof to hear their conversation, but they were speaking too softly. She returned to the spot where she could see inside.

Nurin appeared somber as he moved the blanket aside to reveal an arm. Vaye held the wrist and stared at the lifeless hand for a while. She tucked the arm back under the blanket, gazed up at the ceiling and looked grievously at Aera as though she could see her through the wall.

Aera shuddered. She backed up and whispered, "We need to leave. Now."

DEATH
1331 MID-SPRING

Aera was inside Nurin's chamber, looking down at the body on the table beneath a black shroud. Torchlight blazed all around. Nobody was there... until the metal door groaned open and Cyrrus edged through. He wore a plain beige cloak, more modest than his usual style, but his eyes were as piercing as ever. Aera's pulse sped up as he stopped moving and stared at her, studied her.

"You're not real," he said in a slow monotone. "I am in a dream."

Aera was lost for words as Cyrrus's green eyes dissected her. "This is all a dream," he said, more to himself than to her. He glanced at the body on the table, then returned his focus to Aera and crisply intoned, "Wake. Up."

Aera opened her eyes. The room was dark, and the Samies were asleep. Though she missed Cyrrus and dreamed of him often, she never had associated him with plain beige clothing and wondered if that image had been projected into her mind from outside. Whose body was lying on the table? Was Cyrrus connected to it?

Nurin's hideaway might provide some clues, but she had no idea what time it was or how risky it would be to walk through Eastern Pines alone. The Kalaqhai had cornered her in Southside Forest...

...right after her dream about Cyrrus at Great Gorge.

The proximity of these events was eerie. It was probably a coincidence, but Aera couldn't shake the sense that someone might have induced the dream to lure her there. That someone might be awaiting her in Eastern Pines now. Perhaps the Kalaqhai, or Cyrrus...

Aera was tempted to investigate but didn't want to take the gamble. If Cyrrus had come to find her, he would have to try harder.

She decided to stay in the building but felt too upset to sleep and headed downstairs to the workout room. Though she paced and stretched, the knots in her stomach had barely loosened by the time the wake-up bells sounded. It was the first morning of Mid-Spring, a free day, so she exercised a short while longer before heading out to breakfast.

Grey clouds loomed, and heavy wind pushed against her as she ascended Halcyon Hill. When she reached the plateau, she heard a choir singing the commune anthem and saw a gathering of officers along the opposite bank of the river. Among the officers, Aera spotted a figure who looked like Vaye, with wisps of silver ringlets escaping from a hooded cloak. Another line of officers flanked the bridge, while Renstrom Nurin stood in the middle of the arch, steady and erect in the powerful wind. A crowd was gathering along the near side of the river to watch the action.

It was the same ritual Aera had witnessed at Instructor Sarode's funeral years ago, and she assumed they were preparing to burn the body she'd seen on Nurin's table. She watched from the hilltop as a contingent of meticulously clothed officials slowly and solemnly marched carrying a wide plank upon which lay a dark bundle. The officers placed the plank at Nurin's feet, then removed the covering to unveil a body, dressed all in black with a crown of brick-red hair. Cyrrus? Aera's heart pounded. It could not be him. He was long gone.

An officer handed Nurin ropes attached to the corners of the plank, which Nurin passed to another comrade. Then he closed his eyes, uttered an incantation and gave a signal. Officers lowered the arrangement into a waiting raft lined with red flowers. The corpse's hair looked even redder and the skin pale as a ghost.

Aera hurried down the Hill and tore through the crowd at the river's edge, where the body was right before her. Chiseled cheeks, brick red hair... it *was* Cyrrus! But how could it be? All the features were his, but the expression behind his closed eyes was foreign and unfamiliar. He looked serene, as though dreaming of sunlit fields and springtime birds. It could not be him. He would never look so peaceful...

His words spilled into Aera's mind. *When you're dead... your broken heart will be at peace.* She turned cold.

The flowers blew off as waves tossed the raft back and forth against the river's agony, but Cyrrus's body lay still and unaware, lifeless as the wood beneath it. It was really him. Her best friend lay before her, at peace. Dead. Gone forever. She knew what she was seeing but couldn't accept it. Why would Cyrrus die? Someone as strategic and cunning as Cyrrus would never allow that.

Cyrrus, stop it, Aera thought. *Stop playing this game.* The wind blew harder, but his corpse didn't budge. Tears stung her eyes. *This boundary will not bind us,* she thought, hoping her thoughts would be projected. *Cyrrus... En rallë anti miossi kemma...*[1]

The wind blew harder against Aera as her legs trembled and the world spun. Others were staring at her, but for once in her life, she didn't care. They could gape and gossip about anything they wanted. Not one of them knew her, or Cyrrus, at all.

"We all know the story of Riva the Rebel," Renstrom Nurin announced into a megaphone, his voice booming over the rush of the river. "She disregarded our laws until she was exiled from the safety of Ynas, only to be hunted and eaten by smilodons. Like Riva, Samie Cyrrus was unappreciative of our safe and loving community. He challenged authority and forsook us, his brothers and sisters. He survived two years, but ultimately, the world outside proved too dangerous."

Aera wished she could destroy that callous tyrant. How dare he use Cyrrus's death as an opportunity to promote ideology! Had he no remorse, no sorrow, no soul?

"Let us allow this tragic event to strengthen our bonds and secure loyalty to our common cause, that of unity and peace. Let us work together as one, for the benefit of all!" Nurin blustered. "Let us honor

Samie Cyrrus's tragedy as a reminder of the safety and plenty we enjoy. His unfortunate fate gives us all reason to be grateful."

Thunder cracked across the sky as storm clouds darkened the world. Crisply, Nurin said, "Let the ending begin!"

Brass Inellei and Justinar Dinad bore their torches across the bridge, and each of them lit one corner of the raft. The surrounding officers lowered the rope and performed the commune salute as the flames slowly consumed the craft and a rapid southward tide caught it away. The flames were just approaching Cyrrus's clothes when the raft disappeared around the river's bend.

Aera couldn't bear to let it go and ran after it, across the Sleeping Hut Field, straight into Southside Forest. As she caught sight of the raging inferno, the raft burst and the structure split. She glimpsed Cyrrus's red hair sandwiched between burning halves of the raft until he sank down into the rushing river, gone from view.

The water was wild, and waves crashed as the plank remains drifted away, still aflame. Cyrrus descended beneath the waves, and Aera searched the chaos in desperation. Rain began to fall. It poured harder and harder until everything blended together and nothing was real. It was as though she had always been cold, wet and alone, enveloped by a solid blanket of rain. This was all that was left. Cyrrus was gone.

She fell to her knees and stared at the river as rain cascaded. Soon she was drenched, shaking and freezing, but couldn't bring herself to return to the crowd. She tore through Southside Forest with no clear idea of where she was going... anywhere but the village... anywhere. It didn't matter if the Kalaqhai found her now. They could take her away for all she cared. She had nothing to prove to anyone and nobody who would care if she did.

She walked on and on, through the trees, brush, and mud. The rain washed over her until she trembled uncontrollably. Vaye's cottage was the closest solace, and she needed it. If Vaye was still in the village, Aera could warm up on her own.

She approached the cottage, shivering violently. Vaye came to the door holding a blanket, clearly expecting her. Aera fell into the blanket and allowed Vaye to hug her and guide her to a chair by the fire, where she curled up in a ball, shivering. As she warmed, she noticed a trail of wet mud leading from the door to the chair and cringed. She never should have come...

"It's no bother," Vaye said. "I can clean it easily."

Aera turned to face Vaye, who said, "Change into this robe. I'll hang your clothes to dry by the fire."

Vaye slipped into the kitchen, leaving Aera to change in private. She peeled the wet clothing from her body and wrapped herself in the robe, feeling guilty for allowing something so soft to touch her wet, dirty skin. Finally, she wrapped the blanket around herself again as Vaye emerged from the kitchen with two steaming mugs.

The two sat for a while in silence, lost in the tea, absorbing the warmth of the fire. Aera stared at the flames and pictured Cyrus's raft bursting, condemning his remains forever to the river. How had Cyrus died, and how had his corpse found its way back to Ynas? Had Nurin played a role in any of this? Perhaps Cyrus had known too much about Nurin or the Kalaqhai.

Suddenly it struck her: if Cyrus had left with the Kalaqhai, he might have walked into a trap. Perhaps they had wanted to abduct Aera because they believed she also knew too much about them through Cyrus, or from interactions in the orb. Perhaps Cyrus had been victimized, as she had been, and he hadn't sent the Kalaqhai after her at all.

Aera felt sick. She'd never thought of this until now, and that oversight was telling. When the Kalaqhai had attacked, she'd taken for granted that Cyrus was conspiring with them, but it had never crossed her mind that he might have been overpowered. She had admired him so much that she'd failed to appreciate his vulnerability. She'd been a terrible friend...

"Aera, dear?"

Aera returned to the present and remembered that Vaye was there with her. Their eyes met and she nodded, inviting Vaye to speak.

Softly, Vaye asked, "Was Cyrus seeking the Night Gem?"

The Night Gem. Aera remembered her last encounter with Cyrus. The lightning in his eyes. The desperation. She remembered Vaye's bizarre, otherworldly tone as she uttered the prophesy from her dreams. In a flash, she saw Cyrus, dead on the raft...

She blinked. Vaye was waiting. Under her breath, Aera mumbled, "I don't know."

Vaye studied her, considering something. After a long silence, she asked, "How did you learn about it?"

Aera wasn't sure where to begin. Those final days with Cyrrus were a blur of chaos and panic. Nothing made sense.

"In Elkandul... I mean, inside the orb... the other auras mentioned it... and everything turned white. Cyrrus wouldn't tell me anything, so I... came to you... and..."

Aera's mind screamed, *he pushed me away*. He had taken on the world by himself when he wasn't ready. The impenetrable deity. What an idiot to insist he didn't need anyone. If he'd heeded her warnings, he might still be alive.

Vaye looked at Aera, her brown eyes full of compassion. In a gentle tone, she said, "I was under the impression it was Cyrrus who used the orb."

"Why?" Aera snapped. "You read my mind. You know everything."

"Ivory was effective," Vaye said gently. "Cyrrus taught you well."

Aera's cheeks flushed. Vaye was aware of Aera's effort to deceive her. Why did she still welcome Aera in the cottage? Aera wanted to apologize or show gratitude, but she was exasperated and the words did not come.

Vaye moved to the piano and began playing a ballad. Aera stared at the fire. *The prison of your fear, the shimmer of your crown*, her mind sang. *Tistë yoveskén Onórnëan, ë áldëa si.*[2] How brilliant of him to rule the world alone.

Aera wanted to scream. It would make more sense to cry, but all she felt was rage. Why was she blaming Cyrrus for dying? Her heart was a wall of hate. An impenetrable iron-piked Fence, enclosing a world of lies.

She closed her eyes, breathed along in rhythm with the music, and listened to the patter of rain. After a while, the rain fell silent, and sunlight shone through the windows. The storm had passed.

Vaye rose from the bench and looked at Aera, inviting her to play. The two traded places. As Aera channeled her fury into the keys, Vaye drummed along. For hours, they lost themselves in music. The sunlight ambled across the room and ultimately adjourned as dusk approached.

When they finally stopped, Aera felt calm but distant. Nothing seemed real. She was hungry and light-headed but could no longer feel any emotion.

"I should leave," she said. "The Dining Hall is closing soon."

Vaye retrieved Aera's clothing from upstairs and let Aera change, just as before. Then she returned wearing a sword sheathed to a leather belt, which she covered with her cloak before ushering Aera out the door.

"Allow me to walk you back," she said. "Just in case."

As the two moved through Southside Forest, Vaye's footsteps were silent. Aera recalled the first time she'd followed Vaye through the trees as a child. Back then, Aera had been excited by Vaye's noiseless footsteps, enamored with the forest, amused by the birds. The daydreaming child Vaye had brought to her cottage was gone forever.

When they reached the edge of the village, Vaye offered in her sweetest voice, "If you'd like, I'll come here at dinner tomorrow and accompany you back through the forest."

Aera felt spent. Tomorrow seemed worlds away. She looked at Vaye and said, "Okay."

The two separated, and Aera ate in the Dining Hall, then headed to the track. When the curfew bell rang, she considered visiting Nurin's hideout in the hope of learning why Cyrrus had died, but Vaye clearly believed Aera was at risk of danger. There would be nothing to see anyway. The boys would have told her if there was a meeting. Defeated, she returned to Junior Hut and went to sleep.

DREAMSCAPE

1331 MID-SPRING

Aera found herself at the pinnacle of Halcyon Hill, looking down on the village as every building was consumed in flame. Cyrrus crossed the Field with a torch, setting afire everyone who passed. While others ran screaming in frenzied terror, Aera enjoyed the chaos and the commune's demise. She laughed and called, "Cyrrus!"

He gazed at her, and everything transformed. Aera now stood atop a vast and eerily familiar arena. Descending concentric circles of stone steps enclosed a battlefield below, and every level was crowded with shadowy figures. *The cerebral circus*, she thought.

Cyrrus stood in the proscenium, wielding an iron pike with a flaming tip. Dragon engravings spiraled around the weapon's shaft. Aera grinned. Such a show-off.

Four adversaries with more pedestrian weapons charged at Cyrrus: two were the gold-chained strangers from Nurin's hideout and two were unfamiliar. Cyrrus impaled the first two with his pike. The crowd cheered as his competitors burst into flame.

Two fighters remained: a regal, dark-skinned woman with pink facial markings and a lanky man in the same beige cloak Cyrrus had worn in Aera's previous dream. The woman swung an axe at Cyrrus, who dodged, then advanced and impaled her. Upon seeing this, the beige-cloaked man became distracted just long enough for Cyrrus to thrust the flaming pike into the center of his chest. He had bested them all. The crowd roared their approval as Nurin appeared at the bottom of the steps, wielding an axe. Aera ran toward the field in case Cyrrus needed her.

Cyrrus and Nurin went at each other. Although Cyrrus feinted and lunged at Nurin, he never managed to strike his target. Suddenly, he lifted a section of turf to reveal a circular opening and wrestled Nurin down into it. Once Nurin was out of sight, Cyrrus threw his pike into the pit and extended his arms victoriously. Finally, he closed a hatch over the hole and replaced the patch of turf he'd removed.

Slowly, he turned to face Aera and said, "I don't want to die." His eyes whitened to an alabaster glow and droning noises emerged from the light.

"I don't want to die," he repeated in a distorted voice. "That is the only thing keeping me from killing you."

The light from his eyes exploded everywhere as piercing noise abounded. Aera tried to find Cyrrus but could no longer distinguish his form against the surrounding whiteness and its chorus of disharmonious drones.

"I don't want to die," the drones screeched, increasingly disparate with each word. "That is the only thing keeping me from killing YOU."

Aera fell to her knees, writhing and helpless as the screech echoed. *Killing YOU. Killing YOU. Killing YOU...*

~

Ding ding! Ding ding!

Aera awakened with a gasp. She peeled herself from the mat and tried to quell the drones in her ears as the clamor of morning assaulted her. The journey through the Dining Hall was a blur, and when she went back outside, Pelyane and Kize were at the top of the Hill. That was where Aera had stood in her dream, watching everything burn.

When Cyrrus was alive, they had sometimes shared dreams. Now that he was gone, his cerebral circus survived in her memory. Or, perhaps, some of it lingered in *eseissë*. Who were the strangers he'd vanquished? The pink-marked woman and beige-cloaked man matched the colors of the orb lovers. Just before Cyrrus had left Ynas, they had been making plans with Aera, assuming she was he. Perhaps that was why they had appeared in the dream.

It was significant that Cyrrus had thrown Nurin into a hole rather than killing him outright. Aera remembered Cyrrus's cerebral cellar, where he'd stored memories that needed to be forgotten but could not be defeated.

She recalled her previous dream in Nurin's hideout. The corpse on the table had presumably been Cyrrus's, but in the dream, Cyrrus had been alive while a corpse lay on the table. Aera winced at the thought. She wished, more than anything, that this dream would come true.

Gong, gong! The belltower rang, beckoning Aera for tasks, but she couldn't bring herself to care. Cyrrus was gone and she needed to know why. Nothing else mattered.

Voices and whistles clamored in the Village Field. It seemed far away, like another world. Aera waited alone in the woods as the noise cleared and the crowds parted. Once they were gone, she left her tray behind in the woods and went to the cottage.

Vaye opened the door and greeted her with a warm smile. "I'll inform the authorities you were with me," she offered.

Aera nodded. She didn't care about the authorities, but the gesture was thoughtful.

"Aera, look at me," Vaye said.

Aera met Vaye's eyes. Her expression was stern.

"You can stay here today, but you must promise to return to tasks after that. And promise not to leave the village alone."

"Why?" Aera asked. "What does it matter?"

"It matters to me."

Aera groaned. Though Vaye would not state it explicitly, the message was clear: it was unfair for Aera to throw her life away after all Vaye's efforts to help her. Yet Aera had never asked for any of this.

"Why did you take me in?" Aera demanded. "What do you want from me?"

Vaye held Aera's gaze but didn't react. Calmly, she replied, "I want you to promise."

Aera was sick of following orders, all to avoid exile or death. But she had to persist, if only for Vaye. She surrendered, "I promise."

Vaye nodded and headed to the kitchen. Aera sat by the fireplace as music haunted her mind. *He's always burning me, twisting and turning me, why do I yearn to be on the other side...*

A dragon sliced through the shadows between flames, then disappeared in a flash. Cyrrus's voice said: *Ivory must defeat Ebony...*

Aera shook off her reverie and turned away from the fireplace. A steaming mug had appeared on the table, and Vaye sat in the chair opposite her, nursing her own drink.

"Spiced strawberry cider," Vaye said.

Aera lifted the mug and took a sip. The consistency was thick, and the tangy taste enlivened her. As she drank, her mind wandered back to the song. *He's on the other side...*

The lyrics took on a new meaning now. 'The other side' might refer to the world of the dead. She remembered her dream of Cyrrus in the cerebral circus. *This boundary will not bind us*, she thought.

She turned to Vaye. "Is it possible to share dreams with the dead?"

Vaye looked at her questioningly.

"Cyrrus and I used to have the same dreams at the same time," Aera explained. "I'm wondering if I could share a dream with someone after they're dead."

"Perhaps," Vaye allowed with a soft smile. "The connection would be more potent if their spirit was still anchored to the material realm."

Aera considered this. She remembered a discussion with Cyrrus about Fades, whose spirits were tied to the world even after leaving the mortal body behind. How could she determine whether Cyrrus had faded? Either way, the most she could conclude was that even if the dream did come from him, it didn't prove he was still alive.

The song played on in her mind. *He's on the other side. Do I run inside and lock the door behind me? Do I change my name in case he tries to find me...?*

"Vaye... how did..."

Aera's voice cracked. She steadied her tone and repeated, "How did Cyrrus die?"

Vaye watched her for a long moment, and her compassionate calm made Aera nervous. With slow, heavy movements, Vaye placed her drink down on the table, adjusted her position and finally responded, "I am uncertain."

Aera was accustomed to Vaye's obstinacy, but this time, could not let it go. She glared at Vaye, who understood.

"Two messengers from Kadir were delivering information to Nurin," Vaye said. "They found Cyrrus outside the Gate. His body was still warm, but there was no pulse, nor any other sign of life. His arm had a blackened bruise, so it looked like a snakebite or some other venom or poison."

"Outside the gate," she mused. "Why was he there?"

"We don't know. The messengers found him there, without knowing why. They were telling the truth."

Aera presumed Vaye knew this because she'd read their minds. Before she could ask, Vaye looked straight at her and said, "You're correct. I read their thoughts."

Aera appreciated Vaye's openness. The two exchanged a knowing look.

"The guards at the Gate surveyed the area immediately and more joined them later," Vaye continued. "Nobody else was found and no additional evidence was uncovered."

Aera took this in and inquired, "Did you read Nurin's mind?"

"It was unnecessary. He was visibly disturbed."

Aera wondered what that meant.

"He pounded the table with his fist and committed our best people to figure out what happened," Vaye said. "He would never put it in words, but he showed in many other ways how much he cared for Cyrrus."

This image of Nurin was unexpected. He'd allowed Cyrrus to visit his office, read his books and win debates that he could easily have turned in his own favor, but then had used his death as an opportunity to preach about his principles. Perhaps this was Nurin's way of processing the loss. Though the two clearly had conspired privately, Aera found it difficult to imagine that Nurin was capable of 'caring.' It was more likely that any relationship he had was based on a shared political agenda. She didn't think Vaye was lying about Nurin yet couldn't help questioning the veracity of her assessment.

Vaye stared pensively out the window as though the conversation had ended, but Aera still felt unsettled. Cyrrus had died near the commune, and she wondered why he'd been there in the first place. There had been nothing for him in Ynas, except Nurin and... Aera.

"I spied on Nurin's meetings," Aera admitted. "I know he communicated with Cyrrus after he left. Did he know why Cyrrus came back?"

"Nurin lost touch with Cyrrus over the Winter," Vaye said. "Nurin's contacts reported he left Kadir, and none of our contacts saw him after that."

The phrase crashed into Aera's mind: *The Seeker has vanished from Kadir.* She strained to remember where she'd heard it and realized it was in one of the meetings underground. The conversation was stored in her cerebral enclave, and she retrieved it: *Qirzān has been informed of the error. Since then, The Seeker has vanished from Kadir.* Nurin's response followed: *Reconsider my suggestion. There can be no mistakes.*

"Is one of those contacts Qirzān?" Aera asked.

Vaye replied, "Indeed."

"Who is he?"

"A merchant in Kadir. He owns the Kadirian Circus."

That circus again, Aera thought. Qirzān was apparently a contact of Nurin's, and likely connected to Cyrrus. Another link between Cyrrus and the Kadirian circus.

As the two finished their drinks, Aera contemplated Nurin's reference to 'The Seeker.' Cyrrus had called Aera a 'Seeker' long ago, during the Ivory lessons. After that, she'd heard reference to a 'Seeker' in the orb, and Vaye had mentioned 'Seekers' who prospected for shardât and were rewarded by some but hunted by others.

There were so many possibilities for how Cyrrus had died. He might have been hunted as a Seeker. He might have been shot with an arrow or bitten by a snake. But somehow, he'd ended up outside the Gate two years after leaving Ynas. He'd lost touch with Nurin long before that, but something had made him return. No matter how many times Aera turned it over in her mind, she couldn't shake the suspicion that Cyrrus had come back for her.

Vaye cleared the empty teacups and plates from the table, then returned to the room. "I'll be in the garden for a while. Would you like to join?"

Aera knew that if she refused, she would spend the rest of the day by the fire in a miserable stupor. She decided to accept the diversion and followed Vaye outside.

For several hours, the two dug up weeds and planted seeds. Aera felt heavy and stiff. Every move was strenuous, and her mind kept drifting to nowhere. When exhaustion set in, Vaye walked her back to Adolescent Hut.

Aera found her bed, disrobed, and lay down. The fire roared in the corner and warmed her as she lay awake, storing any crucial information in her cerebral enclave. Though she didn't want to forget what Vaye had told her, she also wondered if any of it mattered. Cyrrus was gone regardless. Her only hope was to see him in a dream.

Her eyes closed, and she sank into the mat, sweating as she drifted to another realm. She found herself in a starlit field before a fire. Someone emerged beside her, obscured by darkness and smoke. Firelight revealed a muscular chest and dark hair spilling down in wild waves. The hidden star!

An azure blaze cast a halo around him as he enveloped Aera in his arms. He held her tight against his chest. His heartbeat was so explosive, she could feel it in her toes. *Thump, thump.* Though his desire was palpable, his touch was empathic. He sensed her pain.

Aera snuggled closer, burrowing in. Mountains of tension melted away. Tears slid down her cheeks, but the hidden star was not deterred. He stroked her hair, overflowing with love, and she grasped him for dear life.

They clung to one another as her tears exploded and their heartbeats became more clamorous. A fiery blaze erupted, piercing the dreamscape.

Aera opened her eyes. Her pulse was wild and her cheeks wet. This was the first time she had cried since the funeral, and her body felt lighter, her heart unbounded. Just as in the orb, the hidden star had unraveled her and set her free.

She wondered if he'd visited her in the dream world. It was as if he knew Cyrrus had died and had come to comfort her. Had he learned in Elkandul about Cyrrus's death? She wanted to believe he was out there somewhere, dreaming of her, but it wouldn't help her. Even if he were, she would never find him. The orb was gone.

Flames danced in the fireplace beside Aera, and the fire glowed against her skin. The dream might have come to her because those flames evoked memories of her fiery companion. It might have come solely from her own mind. Yet she couldn't shake the feeling that these intense, hyperreal dreams came from somewhere beyond her.

Halcyon Hill
1331 EARLY-AUTUMN

Spring passed in a haze of emotion while the Samies honored the red-headed rebel. Vaye provided black dye for Aera's cloak and pants, so she could contrast Cyrrus's wardrobe colors against her white tops. Inspired by this tribute to Cyrrus, Pelyane fought at town meetings—as he once had—so that Aera and the other clan members would be allowed sleek, black boots, just like his. Yet despite the attention Cyrrus received, 'The Seeker' was no longer mentioned at Nurin's secret meetings. Once Aera understood she would learn nothing more, she lost interest in spying altogether.

By Summer, Cyrrus's name began to fade from public consciousness. Pelyane used it to bolster her election campaign, but soon became more invested in advertising her own feats. She organized protests over mundane laws and set up theatrical events. Nurin earned a more benevolent reputation as he permitted these efforts. Codin and Idan dragged Aera to the running track, Kize invited her to the Music Room, and Vaye escorted her to the cottage. Still, compared to the world she'd once shared with Cyrrus, none of it felt real.

In addition to grieving for him, Aera mourned the loss of her own hopes for the future. She feared she would waste her whole life as a slave in Ynas, with no chance to pursue a more personal purpose. Since childhood, dreams of white light and the Night Gem prophesy had found her. Over the years, she'd felt compelled to understand why. She had often hoped to find the white forest; to discover her connection to Ultassar and Erelion; to seek out the Nestë and become an Orenya. Her dreams and visions seemed to suggest a greater destiny. Who was she really? What was her place in the grand scheme? She retreated to her memories often, deconstructing and reconstructing her cerebral enclave in a desperate search for answers. Yet sometimes she felt as if none of it mattered. Any destiny would be meaningless if she had to pursue it alone.

One Autumn afternoon, Vaye played Nestëan tunes while Aera sat alone at the table, cradling the fire-rocks Cyrrus had given her. They had built so many fires together at Great Gorge. *Our home,* she thought. She watched the flames rise and fall in the fireplace as her mind drifted to the hidden star. A wave of emotion overcame her as she remembered the fiery blaze in Elkandul.

It was strange that Cyrrus had connected so consistently to fire, all the while maintaining his emotions behind walls of ice. He had enjoyed the idea of transforming the world through flame but had never been able to endure the heat of passion.

Aera still had not pinpointed Cyrrus's archetype, but she knew he hadn't embodied the flame. Had he idealized some fictional fiery version of himself, or had his connection to fire been organic? He might have incorporated numerous influences. Perhaps everyone did. Vaye connected to music and plants, which were not directly related to her water archetype. In Elkandul, Aera had emanated golden sunbeams, but also wind, lightning, and mist.

Aera had forgotten how much she enjoyed pairing people with these primal forces. Since she'd lost sight of Cyrrus's category, she had been discouraged. Now that she'd taken some time away from thinking about archetypes, she wondered if she might solve the riddle with a fresh perspective. She found the chart in her notebook and listed new names beside their appropriate archetypes.

Cyrrus's name was still listed under the archetype of 'change,' as it had been since the beginning. Aera tried to remember exactly what he'd said about his vision in the wood and wondered whether she could retrieve the memory. Now that she'd built a sanctum beneath the grass in her cerebral enclave, it might just be possible. She closed her eyes.

In her mind, she assumed position in the familiar sunlit field, facing the great oak in the center. White trees surrounded the perimeter, their bare branches lined with birds.

She blinked and changed her surroundings to a wide-open sanctum that faced a twelve-sided polygon where the oak had just been. Slowly, she circled the monolith until she found the wall containing the *ilissunviva* symbol. She imagined the triangles twisting and increasing dimensions, forming a cage of pyramids that whirled into a vortex and devolved into a black void.

Satisfied that she'd visualized her recollection in succinct detail, she moved along to the next panel, where Cyrrus interacted with his symbol. She pictured him there and phrases came back to her: *A spider*

588

weaving a web... the web expanded outward beyond its control... the spider got caught in the web... all went up in flame.

Aera opened her eyes and returned to the present: she was in the cottage beside the fireplace. Soft arpeggios decorated the pumpkin-scented room as Vaye's fingers finessed the ancient keys.

She reviewed the vision. The words, the scene. Cyrrus's panel, just beside hers. As she considered this, it struck her: their symbols would be neighbors on the wheel! Her own *ilissunviva* symbol was situated between *niskuissieva* and *osmarunyaniva*. Cyrrus's archetype must have been one of those.

Osmarunyaniva was the archetype of 'conquest.' Though Cyrrus had quested for power, the motifs of innocence and magnanimity didn't suit him, nor did the *Lesson of Sinko*, devoted to embracing one's inner animal. On the other hand, *niskuissieva* was associated with *Lesson of Nirnilië*, Natural Law. Its themes suited Cyrrus. He'd been a perfectionistic, critical hypocrite, reinterpreting the laws of nature to reflect his ideals.

'Principle' was his archetype—and he'd invested energy to fool Aera into believing his archetype was 'change.' Yet he'd drawn both symbols on the same wood block and left it in the gorge, where she was bound to discover it. His spider vision might also have been fabricated, but she was pleased that she'd managed to recall it. By placing her clearest memories into her cerebral enclave and reviewing the events, she had accessed more details.

She returned to the cerebral sanctum to firm the memories. Standing before the *niskuissieva* symbol, she imagined each part of Cyrrus's description coming to life. First the spider weaving a web, which expanded in branch-like shapes, then the flame....

The music stopped. Aera opened her eyes. Across the room, Vaye entered the archway and disappeared into the staircase. Aera shook off her vision and looked around: the cottage was quiet, eerie. The white-haired girl in the painting stared back at Aera, probing her. She looked no older than ten, yet her eyes were ferocious. Despite her tender age, she was ready for battle. Aera had always admired the girl's boldness, but it struck her—only now—that it was unnatural for a child to be so combative. What had stolen her innocence?

Nausea swept over Aera, and she shifted uncomfortably. The world was too still. Where was Vaye? She might be listening to these thoughts...

Momentarily, the bedroom stairs creaked. Vaye returned and joined Aera by the fireplace. After a brief pause, she said, "The girl in the painting is my daughter."

Aera wasn't expecting such frankness and didn't know what to say.

"She was quietly rebellious, much like you," Vaye said wistfully. "Her name was Nóssië."

Nerilyane, Nóssië, Aera thought, remembering Panther Woman's voice from a night long ago, when it had projected that girl's name. Who had Panther Woman been talking to? Perhaps she had equated Aera to Nóssië. They were both 'quietly rebellious,' after all.

"Where is she now?" Aera asked.

Gently, Vaye responded, "Her spirit dreams as Ilë. Along with Cyrrus."

Aera felt a chill.

"She was struck down before me," Vaye said, her voice distant. "I couldn't save her."

You saved me, Aera thought, but her throat choked up and the words did not come.

The two finished their tea in silence, watching the fire dance beside them. Vaye's words rang in Aera's mind: *Her spirit dreams as Ilë, along with Cyrrus.* By sharing her past and her view on the afterlife, Vaye had introduced a new level of trust. Aera wished she could express how much that meant to her.

"Did you invite me here because of Nóssië?" she asked thoughtfully. "Because... I was like her?"

"You have some traits in common," Vaye said with a smile. "But I invited you here because of who *you* are."

"Who am I?"

"Only you have the power to determine that. Or perhaps, you and Ivory."

The two exchanged a knowing grin, though Aera felt unsatisfied. She had hoped Vaye would mention the prophesy she'd heard in Aera's mind during their first meeting in Music Class, but Vaye had focused on Aera's character instead. Yet Aera wasn't interested in building character just for the sake of it. Much like Cyrrus, she needed more. She always had sought to uncover her archetypal role in a grander scheme and had integrated Ivory in hopes of taking on the outside world with Cyrrus. Now, that dream was gone. Vaye had lost Nóssië, and Aera had failed Cyrrus.

"I'll be in the garden for a while," Vaye said. "Make yourself at home."

Vaye was allowing Aera space to process her emotions. Aera smiled to show her gratitude. As Vaye went outside, Aera took a seat at the piano. Her hands trembled.

She ran through her old song 'Deity' and images filled her mind. Striking outfits and cocky grins. *The prison of your fear, the shimmer of your crown.* She wanted to destroy him, hug him, save him. *If you take me away, we can find our way home...*

Next, she played 'Collapse' and saw hot blue eyes. *I've never felt so sure, so pure.* How cruel to Cyrrus. She recalled him slouching beside her, glaring jealously at other boys. Yet he had never wanted her.

Finally, she played 'Nemesis.' *He's on the other side. I'm on the other side.* She hated herself the most for this, as it exposed how she'd clung to him, but never trusted him.

She cycled through the songs, expelling her turmoil until she calmed down. Her mind returned to images of Cyrrus: sitting with her in the tree, gazing at her over the orb, holding her hand in the staircase. Her fingers tumbled into a delicate pattern and a melody established itself along with lyrics. She pulled the notebook from her pocket and wrote down phrases as they came. Once she'd finished a song, she pieced it together on a new page and sang the lyrics as she played it through.

Halcyon Hill

Take me back
To that time, that place
With your face in the light
And your hands in the dark
And your feelings in shadow

Burn to black
But I can't erase
The maze in the night
And the grove in the bark
And the secrets I know

Who are you anyway?
You can't be as cryptic as the dream
My fingers fall right through you
Passion slipping into
Silence that makes me want to scream

You belong
In a field of green
With the sun in your eyes
And the wind in your hair
But your fear locked you in

I'm all wrong
And my need obscene
The blood of my songs
Rips my suffering bare
And I callous my skin

But who am I anyway?
I can't be as hollow as I feel
Down to your deepest vice
Your mind is my paradise
These things remind me that I'm real

If I could start again
I'd be sure to let you know
You're my dearest friend
And I will never let you go

AERA'S STORM

1332 LATE-SPRING

Aera was alone in a circular clearing surrounded by a white forest. An enormous, proud moon rewarded its glow upon a winged army whose pearly feathers shimmered throughout the treetops. At the edge of the forest appeared a statuesque man frocked in crimson. Cyrrus!

She thrust toward him, but thick air slogged her down. He moved through it with fluid ease, his hair red as blood, his stare drilling into her, real as ever.

Tears mounted and she said, "Stop playing games. You're still alive."

Cyrrus's gaze transformed into a look of affection. "One way to teach people to think for themselves is to lie to them."

"We both lied," Aera admitted. "I'm sorry. Come back."

"You're stepping on my shadow," Cyrrus said, then dissolved into the air and disappeared. His voice echoed around her: "If you couldn't see me, you'd wish you could, wouldn't you?" Then, further away: "If you couldn't see me..."

~

Ding-ding. Ding-ding.

Aera jolted awake. The words coursed through her mind: *If you couldn't see me, you'd wish you could, wouldn't you?* It had been three years

593

since he'd uttered those words, but she could see the pain in his eyes as though it were yesterday.

People shuffled around, chattering and yelping. No matter how many times Aera weathered this noise, she never failed to be amazed that her peers were so eager to face another day in Ynas.

She dragged herself up, forced in some breakfast and endured four grueling hours at the lumberyard in the springtime sun. Though she spent most of lunch break relaxing by the river, she dreaded afternoon tasks. Cyrrus's last words haunted her throughout the day. *If you couldn't see me, you'd wish you could, wouldn't you?*

When dinner break finally arrived, Aera was exhausted. She carried her food to the boulder where the usual three were eating and the moment she sat down, Pelyane chirped, "Greetings!"

Greetings. Pelyane had used Cyrrus's hail for years, but Aera still thought of him every time. Beside her, Kize hung her head, clearly remembering Cyrrus as well. Her golden curls spilled down to her waist over a white tunic, punctuated by the black boots that Pelyane had won for all of them. Between the hair and tunic, she'd coopted Aera's persona. Her pants and cloak were uniform beige, but Aera knew that if Kize had learned to make dye, they would have been black, just like her own.

"Elections are in Early-Autumn," Pelyane said. "Aera, do you think I should run for office?"

Elections. Cyrrus had heckled Nurin about the future election in 1332. Now it was 1332 and Pelyane was sustaining Cyrrus's legacy. Unlike Aera, Pelyane always made him proud.

Aera didn't think Pelyane would win, but she smiled and intoned, "Sure."

"I don't know if I stand a chance..."

"Nothing to lose," Goric said.

While Pelyane and Goric discussed the election, Aera gazed down at Southside Forest, wishing she could disappear to Great Gorge like she used to. She imagined running down the hill and into the woods, free and alive as she once had been. The treetops soaked in the sun and their leaves blanketed the vast abyss of tangled foliage. Something moved in the shadows between the trees, and Aera watched it until a figure crystallized. She saw brick-red hair... then pallid skin, black clothes...

"Aera?" Kize said. "Are you okay?"

Aera snapped to attention, returning from a daze. Surely, she'd been imagining things... but Cyrrus looked so... real.

She relaxed her muscles and looked at Kize, whose delicate eyes were full of concern. Even when Aera was distant and annoyed, Kize was relentlessly thoughtful.

"Do you want to play after dinner?" Kize inquired.

"I need to run."

"I'll run with you," Kize chimed.

Aera forced a grin.

They finished eating and headed toward the village as caws resounded nearby. Crows had gathered in the dozens on the belltower, as they had when Cyrrus summoned them.

Aera glanced back at Southside Forest. The sun was dipping behind the trees, casting lines of light between them as the figure with brick-red hair lingered in the shadows. She rubbed her eyes and looked again. Someone was there... and he resembled Cyrrus.

"Aera?" Kize called from below. "You coming?"

"Go on. I'll meet you at the track."

Kize said, "Okay." Though her voice betrayed hesitation, she headed away.

Aera breathed into her belly and thought, *it's not Cyrrus. Wake up.* Nonetheless, she had to know what this was. She needed a closer look.

She climbed down the Hill and crossed Sleeping Hut Field, where she scanned the forest again. Something moved in the shadows nearby, and the figure stepped into a ray of sunlight, his pallid skin glowing with a gloss that felt surreal. As Aera's eyes adjusted to the brightness, his emerald eyes penetrated her. This couldn't be real. Cyrrus was dead.

I came back for you, said Cyrrus's voice, echoing from every direction. *The truth is true whether you believe it or not.*

Aera trembled.

Cyrrus slipped into the trees, and Aera dashed into the forest after him. As she ran over some brush, she saw him a short distance away, heading southward. He turned and caught her eye as his voice said: *Meet me at the gorge.*

Aera doubled her pace, growing more excited with every step. The insect choir was luxurious and the landscape lavish, with lines of light and shadow competing and fading to darkness as the sun surrendered. Even in the nightscape, Aera remembered every pile of thorny brush and knew the workarounds. She sneaked beneath and between the dense thickets.

An eerie wind found her hair, and she swished the unruly strands away to see the path ahead. The great oak, the Great Gorge, was just ahead. She was almost there.

The wind kicked up a notch, then another, until leaves and small debris flew all around her. Aera looked upwards. There were no clouds above; only a vast, starry sky. Something whizzed past her, and she jumped back. There was no mistaking that familiar alarm. Blood drained from her cheeks as she realized Cyrrus had lured her into a trap...

No, he hadn't. The figure was bizarre and unreal. It wasn't Cyrrus! *Idiot,* she scolded herself. *Your heart is bigger than your brain.*

Aera found a crevice between two intertwined trees and crouched in the alert Kra position Vaye had shown her. There was a thud followed by groans and growling on one side, metal striking metal on the other side, and a growing prevalence of swiftly moving air and debris. Amidst the whirr of wind, heavy footsteps approached with mechanical precision. Aera gazed through the smoggy dust and debris-encrusted air. Misty light shone through the fog, and she barely made out numerous figures maneuvering about.

She readied herself to run... but where could she go? No matter which way she looked, there was movement. The wind stopped as suddenly as it had begun, and Aera glimpsed a large, metallic body, lifeless on the ground. Several more took shape in the shadows, along with a fury of darts.

Just as she was giving in to the certainty that all was lost, an olivine glow flashed, penetrating the forest. In an instant—and without any visible approach—Vaye was right before her, serene and composed. Tears rushed to Aera's eyes. Vaye had come to induce the storm and rescue her.

She gave Aera a thick branch and said, "Stay close to me."

Aera followed Vaye to an open area and the two circled around, their backs all but touching. Vaye lifted her arm, and the windstorm once again dominated the air. Detritus swirled about just beyond them as they stood in the eye of the storm, awaiting whatever might come.

They didn't wait long before a group of tall, armored attackers emerged from the spinning chaos and entered the clearing, lunging forward in precise identical formation, swords leading the charge. More horrifying, each possessed an *esil* shining through the eye sockets of their black, highly detailed mask-like head and face coverings. Each bore a chest plate emblazoned with an unfamiliar symbol:

The wind blew ferociously and Vaye moved quickly. Aera struggled to stay with her. Their backs separated, and instantaneously, a nearby figure swung his sword at Aera. She moved swiftly to parry the attack, but her branch swung right through his weapon, and she stumbled. Though she saw a fighter before her, she fell into empty space. His body wasn't there. He was an illusion, a trick, perhaps *sarya*.

Though Vaye engaged furiously with the figures, she fought some and ignored others. Aera quickly deduced that Vaye's *esil* revealed to her which fighters were real. To Aera, they appeared identical. Each wore a black outfit with the same silver metal chest-plate and helmet, and all swung the same long, curved sword. Their *esilya* were alike— silver with casts of turquoise—and they moved in perfect synchrony.

Vaye circled around, the light of her *esil* shining before her, scrutinizing each figure in turn as the windstorm prevailed. All Aera could make out was the whirr of debris and figures thrashing against the wind, attempting to strike her and Vaye. Aera thrust her branch at another empty space, then glanced at Vaye, who held her sword still before her. She was serene as ever, with firm feet and smiling eyes, prepared for anything.

Blades crashed against blades. Vaye thrust hers forward; she had discovered the real fighter. Aera stayed close while the spectral figures lunged about so fast that the lights of their *esilya* were blurred by the wind. Vaye and the assailant thrust their weapons at each other, until suddenly, a second figure emerged from behind and knocked Vaye over. Aera gasped and lunged at him with her stick, but he disappeared.

Light exploded around Vaye and the masked invader as they struggled. The storm grew more ferocious and chaotic. Furious wind meshed with coruscating light as black figures flashed everywhere and swords clanked from every direction. Since only one figure was real, Aera reasoned that the sounds were also illusory.

She peeled hair from her eyes, realized she'd lost track of Vaye and searched frantically. Vaye was immersed in a storm of black figures and Aera couldn't tell what was real. She clutched her stick and ducked against the nearest tree, desperate for cover, but the men followed as swords clanked and *esilya* shone.

Then, suddenly, the figures vanished, the forest darkened, and the wind stilled. A corpse lay face down on the ground at Aera's feet, cloaked in familiar Kalaqhai armor, with a bow in his outstretched hand and a quiver of arrows on his back. There were more Kalaqhai corpses nearby. Aera surveyed further. Near the great oak, there was a masked figure sprawled on the ground beside Vaye, who lay motionless. The world slowed down, and Aera felt each thud of her heart.

A man in Kalaqhai armor crouched before Vaye, holding something against her neck. Aera knew, whatever that fiend intended, she had to stop him. She set down her branch, grabbed an arrow from the corpse's quiver and moved stealthily behind the Kalaqhai. A sliver on his neck was exposed beneath his metallic helmet and she plunged the pointed shaft deep into that crevice. She twisted it until he jerked and crumpled to the ground.

Aera knelt beside Vaye. Was she injured? Dead? Aera's hands trembled as she pulled back Vaye's hair to reveal a hollow face with skin like leather. Vaye was unrecognizable. Her cheeks had caved in, the flesh crumpled and cracked, melted around bones as though all fluid had been sucked from her body. This dry pile of carnal hide was a ghastly, distorted cast of the warm mocha face that Aera had come to love.

Heat rose from Aera's chest and soared through her limbs until they burned with fury. She jumped up and kicked the dead Kalaqhai, over and over, each strike more ferocious than the last. Her foot slipped on the slime, and she dropped to her knees, peeled off his helmet and bashed his face with it until nothing was left but grey, oozing blood. She thrust the helmet away, eyes stinging with anguish.

Aera looked at Vaye again and felt sick. This was her own fault. She had imagined Cyrrus in the woods, but *Cyrrus was dead*. Her stupidity was unimaginable. Someone had tricked her, lured her... and killed Vaye. Rage swelled inside her like a hot coal. Whoever was behind this was pure evil, unworthy of life. She would make them pay.

Footsteps approached from the south and a voice called, *"Ixkubta hi hafdat. Haddi' ot-Zīlkamūz.*[1]*"*

Aera recognized the guttural tongue of the Kalaqhai. She could not understand the words, but the message was clear: unless she was to become the next pile of bloodless flesh, she had to escape Ynas. Though she ached to destroy them right there, she knew she wasn't ready to defeat the Kalaqhai now. She needed to grow stronger in the outside world, learn who had taken the lives of her only two friends, hunt them down and obliterate them.

She studied Vaye's corpse one last time, each thump of her heart heavier than the last. Everything was in slow motion. Something shiny near Vaye's stomach caught the moonlight. Aera reached for it and pulled up a dagger in a leather case attached to Vaye's belt. She yanked it loose, shoved it into her pocket and fled toward the village.

Heavy footsteps trailed behind her, and arrows whizzed by, no longer thrown off course by wind. Still, Aera trusted she could lose them. The forest was dark, the terrain was rough, and she knew it well. She slid between trees, soared over logs and slithered between thorny brambles as silently as possible until the footsteps receded, and no arrows followed.

Once she reached open ground, she bolted across the Field and flew over the bridge. People were still mingling by the track, casual and obtuse, blissfully ignorant of the existence of Kalaqhai soldiers murdering people inside their safe little haven. She spotted Kize in the distance, pacing along the side of the track in her shiny white tunic, looking for her. Kize was the only living person who cared about her. Aera wanted desperately to say goodbye, but there was no time to waste on explanations that Kize would never understand. It was time to move on.

Aera considered her options. It was too dangerous to chance a canoe in the open river, so she veered north through the farms to avoid the crowd around the track. She crossed endless fields of crops until she disappeared into the forest, then ran and ran and ran. The curfew bell resounded in the distance, but Aera continued as fast as her legs could carry her. She passed Nurin's hideout, trees and more trees, until the bell sounded again, signaling the passage of two more hours. Moments later, she reached a clearing that opened by the Gate in the Northeast, with four officers stationed before it.

She slinked back into the trees to catch her breath. Her throat was dry, her guts heaved from running, and her hair clung to her sweaty face, but she needed to do something quickly. The guards had doubled in number and were accompanied by a giant, vicious hound.

She slipped her hand into her pocket to feel Vaye's dagger, buried in a leather sheath with strings securing it. Without looking, she untied the knot. Her breathing was quiet now. The air tasted sweet, and her grip on the dagger empowered her. She scrutinized the scene, observing each officer armed with an axe. There was no way to defeat them with her small dagger and no training.

The hound growled and sniffed at the air in her direction. Cyrrus might have manipulated it, but Aera lacked any such power. He might have overcome the guards, but she had no such capability. His voice flooded her: *You're too weak to survive on your own.*

Ivory wasn't weak. There had to be something she could do. More words crashed into her mind. *This boundary will not bind us. One day we're all gonna die.* Vaye's voice spun through her. *Dance along to the rhythm of life. Your breath gives you power.*

Life is a game, she thought. It didn't matter what happened now. Everyone she had ever loved was dead and all that remained was a burning need to avenge them. If the time had come for her to die, there was nothing she could do to change that, but her heart told her she would not go down without a fight.

She relaxed her forehead as Cyrrus had taught her and breathed the grassy air, allowing it to fill her lungs. As she exhaled, her tension escaped into the breeze. Vaye would have been proud. She veered toward the guards, quiet as the gentle wind, tasting the atmosphere more deeply with each breath. Memories of her friends infused her with life, flowing from her heart to her limbs as she aligned with the pulse of the world. She was not alone.

The guards gripped their axes tighter as she approached, and the largest muttered, "She's the one."

Aera stared straight into him and ordered, "Open the gate."

"Peh," snarled the guard, stepping forward and gripping her arm. "You're coming with me."

"Do as I command, or you will regret it," Aera said calmly. "I know things you don't."

"Raisins," sputtered a shorter guard as he lifted his axe and headed toward her.

"*Këanesi ono i sirnë më,*[2]" Aera said, and lifted her arm, pretending to cast a spell. "*Alárië, yavi herilli, esoskë natán pohyollosis.*[3]"

In an instant, a vision of Vaye whirled through Aera's thoughts. As she thrust her arm toward the sky, a sudden overwhelming force of wind assaulted the guards. The officers stumbled as it blasted their faces and the largest released Aera from his grip.

Aera's heart raced, but she sensed this event was more than serendipity. It felt natural in her fury to be bold as the breeze, with the wind as her ally, singing in her voice.

She withdrew her arm and the draft retreated to an ominous whistle. The deadly hound extended its neck, howling in harmony, and ran off with a dramatic whelp. Alárië shone in her fullest splendor as dark clouds raced past, silhouetted by her glow. A storm was rising. Aera's storm.

"You will regret this," she repeated in a voice deeper and more powerful than she knew she had. Her eyes burned into the guard as she withdrew the dagger.

"Little farkus," sputtered a guard from a safe distance away. "The Renstrom said you might show up."

"We're not afraid of a tiny rebel with a tiny knife," said another, raising his axe, though he was in no hurry to approach her.

"You cannot defeat me," she crooned with menacing confidence. The words did not feel like hers, but as if channeled from another world as she hissed, "I have nothing to lose."

With that, she spun around and darted southward into the dark forest, acting purely on impulse. As her thoughts caught up, the deci-

601

sion made sense: she had lured the guards to follow her. With a swift, silent jump, she disappeared into a tree and watched three officers run past her into the shadows beyond, increasing their pace as thunder groaned in the distance. Once they were out of sight, Aera strode to the Gate, where only one guard remained.

The wind blew ferociously, gaining power with every step of her approach. As the rumbling thunder swelled, her hair soared behind her, and distant patches of lightning illuminated the guard's face in flickering flashes. Aera was in command. Nature was at her call.

She bore into the officer's eyes, imagining his face draining and contorting like Vaye's tortured corpse. The axe he wielded flew from his fingers as Aera continued her blistering stare. He was paralyzed with terror, helpless to look away, and cracked the Gate without a word.

Aera slipped through, into the wild.

F⚭TNOTES

SAMIES

1. Silindion: *Filén na erë lëoryán assë të yo-fayanta i nalanna hyánië votheldë. Në Laimandil ë i namanya, sinë veskento i suínanya më Onórnëan.*

   One shall come in later times, who will wield the ancient Light made new. And the White-Bearer he shall be called, and his deeds will change the world.

CYRRUS

1. Silindion: *Sinë veskento i suínanya më Onórnëan. Në Laimandil ë i namanya...*

   And his deeds will change the world. The Laimandil he will be called.

2. Silindion: *Ya ëassávihya, ïen sikosi mesíndilya. Sëotmahya, illién séskilya lundasya ovi, tistë yoveskén Onórnëan, ë áldëa si.*

   Beneath my bum, your chair would be a throne. In my hand, your pencil makes my power known. Who will change the world, it is I alone.

LAWS AND TABOOS

1. Silindion: *Hentilena o Rosmiendëavi erë Mirnanolmán niskani.*

   We shall see each other at Rhos Dinnast this coming winter.

2. Silindion: *Yavi nankesi yovainón, lana kanondi no Tarinna Aldundi, Varvenavel hyanta.*

   If I find out something, we ride forth to Caer Aldun, I and Varvenavel.

3. Silindion: *Nerilyanë.*

   Goodbye.

PARË NË SULË

1. Silindion: *Parë Në Sulë. Vermaventiel Silinestilim*

   Circles and Spheres, by Vermaventiel of Silinestin.

2. Silindion: *Parë Në Sulë.*

   Circles and Spheres.

SILINDION

1. Silindion: *Ya ëassávihya, ïen sikosi mesíndilya. Sëotmahya, illién séskilya lundasya ovi, tistë yoveskén Onórnëan, ë áldëa si.*

   Beneath my bum, your chair would be a throne. In my hand, your pencil makes my power known. Who will change the world, it is I alone.

2. Silindion: *Tistë yoveskén Onórnëan. Sinë veskento i suínanya më Onórnëan.*
Who will change the world. And his deeds will change the world.

INYANONDO

1. Silindion: *I Vairavar Pornamettë. Thaldalar Hóillië.*
The Hummingbird Plant (honeysuckle) as a Healing Herb. (By) Thaldalar Hóillië.

KUINU

1. Silindion: *Kuinúr i alayona sillánëa Nestëamma, ivenna vauréin po savoyéin.*
Kuinu is the union of nature and Nestë, the bond between Angel and mortal.

THE CLAN

1. *Silindion: Tistë yoveskén Onórnëan, ë áldëa si*
Who will change the world, it is I alone.
2. Silindion: *Si voisi fatëallo narnán to elya.*
Thus I can make a game with yours.

THE NESTË

1. Silindion: *Lirityalya kuissë nandosani kara onolindannahya perë essempravavi.*
Your thoughts are a suitable theme for my ponderance of irrationality.
2. Silindion: *Varnë 'lë onolínyello perëo va nani ta eilë, id?*
Why don't you ponder how perfect you are?
3. Silindion: *Laissa ei ventivoya nama nani mana namalim të patto nani.*
A perfect person should be patient with a person who is less perfect.
4. *Silindion: Sertasa Amalírië.*
Book of the Disciple/ Book of Amaliro.
5. Denninesti, Monument script: *Tered nô Rhonnec.*
Tower of Rhonnec.

MAZE

1. Silindion: *Cyrrus, yova ther sinti fatiello?*
Cyrrus, what should I do?
2. Silindion: *Opho vassë viervi yanesi?*
Which path should I take?

THE KALAQHAI

1. Silindion: *Naima.*
   Surrender.
2. Silindion: *Pelesi tan yova ninisi.*
   I seek what I desire.
3. Kalaqhai: *Mtite⁷ xulomqa qazginneqh!*
   Reflection yields clarity.
4. Silindion: *Laimandil.*
   White-bearer.
5. Silindion: *Villai noss i sentunna ina evelyello i laimildë.*
   Delve into the core to unleash the white.
6. Silindion: *Pelesi tan yova ninisi.*
   I seek what I desire.

FIRE

1. Silindion: *Selleivi, o karievi nóndëa,*
   o tarivi Yóllië,
   nondi Nossamirnë,
   anerë Erelion eltílmëa.
   Vestu yo nephenë i phúryanya,
   në véstio thermar.
   Ië nólië emë i mervi koina.
   Në nólio hwángarnya
   Seirnë ka nórëalim noirë,
   sehwa Neilindunorni.
   ⁻

   Of old, in the far off west,
   in the citadel of Everwhite,
   beyond the Mountains of Snow,
   dwelt Erélion of the bright-eyes.
   Sweet his voice was ever calling,
   and sweeter still his skin.
   It was white, like snow upon the mountain lying.
   And whiter yet his bow.
   It was cut from the sacred tree,
   a sprig of Neilíndunor.

ARCHETYPES

1. Tree script: *Reneás Emalannelkalim.*
   Reneás of Green-Leaf Forest.

605

LAIMANDIL

1. Kalaqhai: *Mtite' xulomqa qazginneqh.*
   Reflection yields clarity.
2. Silindion: *Në Laimandil ë i namanya.*
   The White-Bearer he shall be called.
3. Silindion: *Tistë yoveskén Onórnëan, ë áldëa si.*
   Who will change the world, it is I alone.

EROSIA

1. Silindion: *Hyuvún i larë silnemmanyë.*
   The moon dances with her star.

PUNISHMENT

1. Silindion: *Kamara Sínië.*
   The lure of the Swan.
2. Silindion: *Hwanga molkósëa kíldië vanasutín essiranna.*
   Her heavenly breast draws his arrow to her nest.
3. Silindion: *Kamara sínië vaphurnë yanisë'nië.*
   The lure of the swan is a curse when she is gone.

DEITY

1. Silindion: *Filén na erë lëoryán assë të yo-fayanta i nalanna hyánië votheldë. Në Laimandil ë i namanya, sinë veskento i suínanya më Onórnëan.*
   One shall come in later times, who will wield the ancient Light made new. And the White-Bearer he shall be called, and his deeds will change the world.

BOUNDARIES

1. Silindion: *Posseisis!*
   Help me!
2. Silindion: *En rallë anti miossi kemma.*
   This boundary will not bind us.
3. Silindion: *Vavi dorón i kuissë më?*
   Where does this pattern end?
4. Silindion: *Opho vassë viervi yanesi?*
   Which path should I take?
5. Nindic: *Ger beni ath cemmar!*
   This boundary will not bind us.
6. Nindic: *Bewaidh onn pelüsíl?*
   How far did you travel?

606

7. Nindic: *Bew fesi mered?*
    How did I do that?
8. Nindic: *Ēdin minir—*
    We were both—

ELKANDUL

1. Silindion: *Kamara sínië vaphurnë yanisë'nië, ninén i lavan lillannu vohwild'anyë. Ninén i lavan lillannu vohwild'anyë.*
    The lure of the swan is a curse when she is gone. Shall the hunter yearn for a sign of her return.
2. "Twenty-two."
    Kalaqhai: *Bo'ar.*
    Bo'ar.
3. Twenty-six sixteen two one.
    Kalaqhai: *Qhastaz.*
    Commune.
4. Silindion: *Hyuvún i larë silnemmanyë, vë sarna otma nondo.*
    The moon dances with her star, burning for him from afar.

ELEMENTS

1. Two twenty-six four seven eleven.
    Kalaqhai: *Qhafat qhurabi hekir.*
    Two units of red metal.
2. Forty-one.
    Kalaqhai: *Ganuqh.*
    It is understood.
3. Seventeen eight, ten fourteen nine.
    Kalaqhai: *Maħa'is fo'ed masnarān.*
    Five (by the) fourth season (i.e. autumn).
4. Twenty nineteen two one twenty seven. Five nineteen seven, fifteen five two one fourteen twenty-five, six nine one.
    Kalaqhai: *Dāxavdōr, Laxuz, Zalāk-šākay, Ināz. Ganuqh.*
    Human. Lahos, Salashki, Ynas. It is understood.
5. Forty-one, forty-one, forty-one.
    Kalaqhai: *Ganuqh, ganuqh, ganuqh.*
    It is understood, understood, understood.
6. Eleven six twenty-five seven twenty seven. Twenty-two six three, four fifteen twenty ten two, four twenty-five three. Forty-one.
    Kalaqhai: *Hayakūndōr; Bayōn, Rozdināz, Harkō. Ganuqh.*
    Orenya. Baione, Rhos Dinnast, Errkoa. It is understood.
7. Twenty nineteen two one twenty seven, forty-one, forty-one forty-one. Eleven six twenty-five seven twenty seven, forty-one forty-one forty-one.
    Dāxavdōr, ganuqh, ganuqh, ganuqh. Hayakūndōr, ganuqh ganuqh, ganuqh.
    Human, it is understood, understood, understood. Orenya, it is understood, understood, understood.

607

GAMES

1. Silindion: *Ë áldëa si.*
   It is I, alone.

KIZE

1. Silindion: *Míssëar i mëa kuiyánëa.*
   Love is the mother of creation.
2. Silindion: *Sammár i phëa lintuvéskëa.*
   Death is the father of transformation.
3. Silindion: *Kamando ina yáryello eremanyë, henentë sëonanya súndëa n'énkië.*
   Her shadow lures his light to surge, cries of love and war converge!

HIDDEN STAR

1. Silindion: *Tesesili, a Vaye.*
   Thank you, Vaye.
2. Silindion: *Sompa la.*
   Sleep well.
3. Silindion: *Nerilyane.*
   Goodbye.
4. Ten twenty-one eight, twenty-one six fourteen two one thirteen.
   Kalaqhai: *Mitta ʾqhyedáb?*
   Where are the books?
5. Sixteen ten seven.
   Kalaqhai: *Samrū.*
   Wise guy.
6. Silindion: *Hyuvún i larë silnemmanyë, vë sarna otma nondo.*
   The moon dances with her star, burning for him from afar.
7. Silindion: *Id i phendenya mornë Uristienëa, ievissa mirt i nossë mirnanólmëa.*
   Behold the shaded eastern hills where the snows of winter fall.
8. Silindion: *Kirméin nai në nëa nesi, lárëanu o i himeivi imenna, merskë; në naimaro nistá-nunyë në mirínnunyë.*
   Praises great and many do I give to the moon in the clouds rising, hidden, and foremost to her King, her love.
9. Silindion: *Erólion, eldisso eis vauleiri të yo-lissuntë.*
   Erolion, brightest of all the angels who live.
10. Silindion: *Mië këasi pero i narnán mëundëa, núksëu veresi no Ilkarienna.*
    Now I leave across the glittering seas, with tears I turn to the West.

OUTSIDE WORLD

1. Silindion: *Në Laimandil ë i namanya, sinë veskento i suínanya më Onórnëan.*
   The White-bearer, he shall be called, and his deeds will change the world.
2. Kalaqhai: *Qirzān k'ayumak kemqa zikkani huqha ztamūk.*
   Qirzān has requested to meet the boy himself.
3. Kalaqhai: *Hu tamok zminhāfad. Mitmak šaħšmex, zbiwazqa nit biddani de otna miqraħay.*
   He is young and defiant. In a few years, I suspect he will help us willingly.
4. Kalaqhai: *Mettu'ta hā qhaydū zhu?*
   Are you certain the author is he?
5. Kalaqhai: *Tatu'.*
   It is certain.
6. Kalaqhai: *Habdil miegbil. Raħaw niQirzān hā nina zda'ax miħri'mašnarān-i-doše lħayos.*
   The rest is at the gate. Tell Qirzān we will have fur by next winter.
7. Twenty-six six fourteen two one thirteen. Fourteen thirteen seven six. Twenty-seven four nine, nine nineteen five twenty-seven, ten ten.
   Kalaqhai: *Qhyedāħ šaħwayu. Qirzān naxlilamqa mahum.*
   The books have arrived. Qirzān will have copies made.
8. Twenty-six sixteen nine, eleven six twenty-five seven. Forty-one, forty-one, forty-one.
   Kalaqhai: *Qhsatān hayiknū. Ganuqh, ganuqh, ganuqh.*
   Night Gem Seeker. It is understood, understood, understood.

GIRLFRIEND

1. Silindion: The moon dances with her star.
2. Kalaqhai: *Qirzān k'ayumak... tatu'... qhaydū zhu?*
   Qirzān has requested... it is certain... the author is he?

NIGHT GEM

1. Silindion: *Në Laimandil, ë áldëa si.*
   The White-bearer, it is I alone.
2. Silindion: *Tistë yoveskén Onórnëan, ë áldëa si.*
   Who will change the world, it is I alone.
3. Twenty-six six nine, nineteen six one seven. Twenty-five ten twenty-one eight?
   Kalaqhai: *Qhīdān xayud. Kemmitta'?*
   The big book is ready. Where to?
4. Twenty-five ten two one thirteen, nine fifteen nine ten, eight twenty-seven. Twenty-two seven, five six, ten fourteen two nine, twenty fourteen.
   Kalaqhai: *Kēmazāħ nazinanhum aħaq. Badol-i-zafše mailyiz mimašnarān-i-doše.*
   The exports will leave tomorrow. Seventh hour of the night in season one (i.e. winter).
5. Four thirteen six! Twenty-six sixteen nine, eleven six twenty-five seven.
   Kalaqhai: *Raħaw! Qhsatân hayiknû.*
   Speak! Night Gem Seeker.

INVASION

1. Kalaqhai: *Bax k'erqhawi nina tayoy l'niqqās il tanugd.*
   He didn't tell us that she could run so fast.
2. Kalaqhai: *Bax niqqaxt tanugd det hyex simrat.*
   She doesn't run fast, but she's clever.
3. Kalaqhai: *Hyex nit.*
   I have her.
4. Silindion: *Opho vassë viervi yanesi.*
   Which path should I take?
5. Silindion: *Vavi dorón i kuissë më.*
   Where does this pattern end?
6. Kalaqhai: *Takrayt!*
   She disappeared!
7. Kalaqhai: *Na' illoiz!*
   It's too dark here!
8. Silindion: *Tesesili, a Vaye*
   Thank you, Vaye.
9. Silindion: *Ë maliello.*
   Don't move.

DEATH

1. Silindion: *En rallë anti miossi kemma.*
   This boundary will not bind us.
2. Silindion: *Tistë yoveskén Onórnëan, ë áldëa si.*
   Who will change the world, it is I alone.

AERA'S STORM

1. Kalaqhai: *Ixkubta hi hafdat. Haddi' ot-Zīlkamūz.*
   The hag is dead. Seize the White-bearer.
2. Silindion: *Këanesi ono i sirnë më.*
   I will pass through that Gate.
3. Silindion: *Alárië, yavi herilli, esoskë natán pohyollosis..*
   Alarië, please inspire nature to help me.

ACKNOWLEDGMENTS

1. Nindic: *gwēn virad i.*
   My one true love.

GLOSSARY

Commune Syrdian

1. barlock – "asshole, jerk", noun.
2. blast – "damn" (used as an expletive), interjection.
3. brass – the title of the person in charge of education in Ynas. He is appointed by the DPD as a whole, noun.
4. bundle – "to make love to, have sex with", verb.
5. darse – "to stop, cut it out" (usually used as a command), verb
6. dirl – "nonsense, nonsensical talk, bullshit", noun.
7. dreisz – a large feline species. The species is extremely long-lived (with lives up to 5000 years). Like the Nestë, dreisz have an *esil* and a soul-color. Nestë form potentially lifelong bonds with individuals of this species. Dreisz in a lifelong bond with an individual Nestë allow themselves to be ridden by that person or others close to them, noun (from ancient Daronidic *traposēn*).
8. esp – "coin, money" (pl. espar), noun.
9. farkus – "dork, nerd", noun (borrowed from Kalaqhai *farkuz*).
10. ghaadi – "bloody, damned, godforsaken", often personified

as in the expression *by ghaadi's gar* "by the damned one's soul!" or simply "damned thing!", noun (borrowed from Kalaqhai).

11. gar – "soul, mind, thought", typically found in the expression *by ghaadi's gar* "by the damned one's soul!" or simply "damned thing!", noun.

12. ikrati – the martial art of applying the principles of *kra* to dance or combat while holding a staff or a weapon, noun (see also *kra*).

13. jiavo – a warrior's game involving betting and strategy. It was designed specifically to enhance the intelligence of warriors by keeping their minds sharp for war. It may be played on the battlefield with pins and leaves or on a specially designed board, which often may be quite costly. It is commonly played in Kadir, noun.

14. justinar – the title of the official elected by the elders of Ynas who protects the law book, noun.

15. kadirize – "to send off to war, to ruin", derived from the fact that Kadir has a warlike culture, verb.

16. kra – a meditative practice combining balance and breath. It is most often applied in the martial art of *ikrati,* noun (see *ikrati*).

17. kymen – "measure of distance; one *kymen* is approximately the same as one American mile", noun (derived from Standard Syrdian *ki-meṅ* "measurement of a forest").

18. orenya – a human with some Nestëan lineage who studies to attain enlightenment (*sundátëa*) leading to the ability to produce magic (*kuinu*) by aligning with nature.

19. quiffle – "to make love to, have sex with" (see also *bundle*), verb.

20. raetsek – a competitive, physical ball game involving some kicking, tackling and other minimal physical fighting. In Ynas it may only be played on the *raetsek* field behind the dining hall where some violence is allowed. It is used as a way to allow kids to let out violent urges in one designated place. Official games are played on Unity Day celebrations, during which kids form temporary teams. Permanent teams

are not permitted; players must always be shuffled among different teams to avoid ongoing division. During an official game, no commune points are awarded or taken away for winning as the game is strictly played for fun, noun.

21. raisins/Syrdian raisins – an expression of negativity, derived from the fact that the climate in Syrd is not suited to growing high quality grapes. Trying to do so only produces dried out grapes that are more like raisins; "bullshit", interjection.

22. rawden – sexy, hot, attractive (applied to men and implies virility and muscularity), adjective.

23. renstrom – the title for the elected official in charge of the commune; the position involves running public meetings, organizes the internal workings of the commune, liaises with outsiders, and selects the commander of the army. The position is elected by universal suffrage, noun.

24. Riva's Trees – an expression for something weird, taboo, or socially unacceptable; on it's own as an expletive it may be similar to the colloquial use of English "damn!", interjection (derived from the renegade Riva).

25. samely – a greeting equivalent to English "hey!" or "what's up?" or "hello!", interjection.

26. samie – the title for inhabitants of Ynas without any official capacity; it is usually used for kids under 24, noun.

27. shardât – white dust that comes up from the ground, used to power machinery. It emits bright white light, high exposure to which may cause ocular damage and headaches in humans. In Nestë, the light cuts right into the esil and has very harmful, potentially fatal effects. In certain contexts and in conjunction with other magic, it may be used to induce confusion, noun (derived from Kalaqhai).

Kalaqhai

1. aħaq – "tomorrow", adverb.
2. badol-i – "hour, division of time", linking form of *badol*, noun.

3. bax – "not", conjunction.
4. Bayōn – "Baione", proper noun.
5. biddani – "that he help", subordinate present of *libiddōz* "to help", verb.
6. Boʾar – "Boar", proper noun.
7. dāxavdōr – "human", noun.
8. de – "will/shall", future particle.
9. det – "but", conjunction.
10. doše – "first", adjective.
11. foʾed – "fourth", adjective.
12. ganuqh – "understood, obvious", adjective.
13. hā – "that it is", subordinate form of *lhayt* "to be", verb.
14. habdil – "the rest/remainder", definite form of *habadol* "rest/remainder", noun.
15. ḥaddi – "seize!", imperative of *lḥaddās*, "to seize", verb.
16. hafdat – "dead", feminine form of *hafud*, adjective.
17. Harkō – "Errkoa", proper noun.
18. hayakūndōr – "orenya", noun.
19. hayiknū – "seeker", noun.
20. hekir – "(red) metal", noun.
21. hi – "is (definitely), present tense of *lhayt* "to be", verb.
22. huqha – "himself", emphasis pronoun.
23. hyex – "she", pronoun.
24. il – "so, too", adverb.
25. illoiz – "too dark", excessive form of *loiz* "dark", adjective.
26. Ināz – "Ynas, the name of the main commune in the book", proper name.
27. ixkubta – "the ugly hag", definite form of *xkabat* "ugly hag", noun.
28. kēmazāḥ – "the exports", definite plural form of *kāmaz* "export", noun.
29. kemmittaʾ – "to where", locative form of *mittaʾ* "where", adverb.
30. kemqa – "about it", masculine form of *kem* "to/about", prepositional pronoun.
31. kʾayumak – "he request" masculine past tense of *lyimmak* "to request", verb.

32. k'erqhawi – "he told", masculine past tense of *lriħōs* "to inform/tell", verb.

33. *Laxuz* – "Lahos, the name of a commune", proper name.

34. łħayos – "to come, the coming, next", verb.

35. maħa'is – "five", number.

36. mahum – "them", pronoun.

37. mailyiz – "of the night", dative genitive of *layuz* "night", noun.

38. mettu'ta – "you are certain", present tense of *lamtūs* "to be certain", verb.

39. miegbil – "at the gate", definite locative form of *gabol* "gate", noun.

40. mimašnarān-i – "in season", linking locative form of *mašnarān* "season", noun.

41. miqraħay – "willingly", adverb.

42. mitmak – "in a few", quantitative determiner.

43. naxlilamqa – "he will cause to be copied", singular objective of *lnaxlilōz* "to cause someone to copy", *verb*.

44. nazinanhum – "they leave", plural objective of *lnazinōz* "to make send, to leave", verb.

45. na' – "here", adverb.

46. nina – "to us", 1ˢᵗ plural form of *ni* "to", prepositional pronoun.

47. niQirzān – "to Qirzān", locative form of *Qirzān*, proper noun.

48. niqqhit – "she runs", feminine present of *lniqqās* "to run", verb.

49. nit – "to me", 1ˢᵗ singular form of *ni* "to", prepositional pronoun.

50. otna – "us", pronoun.

51. otzīlkamūz – "the white bearer", accusative definite form of *zīlkamzū* "white bearer", noun.

52. qhastaz – "commune", noun.

53. qhaydū – 'author", noun.

54. qhīdān – "big book", noun.

55. qhifat – "two", adjective.

56. qhsatān – "night gem", noun.

57. qhurabi – "unit", noun.

58. qhyedāḥ – "the books, definite plural form of *qhayid* "book", noun.

59. raḥaw – "speak!", imperative of *lraḥōs* "to speak", verb.

60. Rozdināz – "Rhos Dinnast", proper noun.

61. šaḥšmex – "of years", partitive plural form of *šimux* "year".

62. šaḥwayu – "they have arrived", plural past tense of *lḥayos* "to come/arrive", verb.

63. samrū – "wise guy", noun.

64. simrat – "clever", feminine form of *somer*, adjective.

65. takrayt – "she disappeared", feminine past tense of *lkirros* "to disappear", verb.

66. tamok – "young", adjective.

67. tanugd – "fast" adjective.

68. tatuʾ– "certain", adjective.

69. tayoy – "that she could", feminine subordinate past of *lyayt* "to be able", verb.

70. xayud – "ready", adjective.

71. zafše – "seventh", adjective.

72. Zalāk-šākay – "Salashki, the name of a commune", proper name.

73. zdaʾax – "even fur", focalized form of *daʾax* "fur", noun.

74. zhu –"even he", focalized form of *hu* "he", pronoun.

75. zikkani – "that he meet", subordinate form of *lazyikkōz* "to meet", verb.

76. zminhāfad – "and defiant", from *z-* "and" and *minhāfad* "defiant", adjective.

77. ztamūk – "even the boy", focalized definite form of *tamūk* "boy", noun.

Nindic

1. ath – "us", pronoun.

2. beni – "to bind", verb.

3. bew – "how" (contracted form of *bewaedd*), interrogative pronoun.

4. bewaidh – "how", interrogative pronoun.

5. cemmar – "this boundary", demonstrative form of *cemm* "boundary", noun.
6. ēdin – "we were not", plural past tense of *ēdh/ēdhel* "to be", verb.
7. eluid - "the stars", definite plural form of *olo* "star", noun.
8. fesi – "I did"
9. ger – "will/does not", present indicative of *ge-*, negative verb.
10. gwēn – "true", adjective.
11. i – "my", possessive pronoun.
12. luinos - "about", definite form of *luino*, preposition.
13. mered – "that", demonstrative pronoun.
14. minir – "both", demonstrative form of *mini* "two", pronoun.
15. onn – "far", adverb.
16. pelüsīl – "you travelled", past tense of *pēli* "to go, leave, travel", verb.
17. Pēr Hasül – "Circles and Spheres" (translation of Parë në Sulë), proper noun.
18. poid – "fool/little boy", noun.
19. virad – "love", lenited definite form of *mir* "love", noun.

Silindion

1. 'lë – contracted form of *elë* "you don't", 2^(nd) singular present tense of *ëallo* "to not do", verb.
2. 'nië – contracted form of *éinië* "she", pronoun.
3. a – "oh", a particle used before personal names in direct address.
4. Alárië Túrniril – "Alárië Night-Jewel", proper noun.
5. alayona – "unification", noun.
6. áldëa – "alone", adjective.
7. Aldundi – "of Aldun", genitive case of *Aldun*, proper name.
8. alonwë – "unity" (lit. "all-in-one"), noun.
9. anerë – "she/he/it dwelt", 3^(rd) singular past tense of *neriello* "to dwell", verb.
10. anti – "us", dative pronoun.
11. assë – "future", noun.
12. auka – "heart, center point", noun.

13. daván – "she/he/it roars", 3rd singular present indicative of *doyello* "to roar", noun.

14. dorín – "she/he/it may end", 3rd singular subjunctive of *dorollo*, verb.

15. dorna – "end", noun.

16. dorón – "she/he/it ends", 3rd singular present indicative of *dorollo* "to end", verb.

17. ë – "don't!", imperative of *ëallo* "to not do", verb.

18. ë – "is", emphatic copula verb.

19. ëan – "it is", 3rd singular present indicative of *iello* "to be", verb.

20. ëassávihya – "(at) my bottom/bum", 1st singular possessive locative case of *ëassa*, noun.

21. ei – "it is/may be", 3rd singular (irregular) subjunctive of *iello* "to be", verb.

22. eilë – "you may be/you are", 2nd singular subjunctive of *iello* "to be", verb.

23. eis – "(from) out of" (+ genitive case), preposition.

24. eiso – "(from) out of it", from *eis*, prepositional pronoun.

25. eldi – "bright", adjective.

26. eldisso – "brightest", superlative of *eldi*, adjective.

27. eltílmëa – "of the bright-eyes, bright-eyes", adjective.

28. elya – "yours", pronoun.

29. emë – "on, upon" (+ locative case), preposition.

30. empissë-ni – "verses", nominative plural of *empissë*, noun.

31. en – "she/he/it won't", 3rd singular future tense of *ëallo* "to not do", verb.

32. énkië – "of war, warlike", adjectival case of *enkë* "war", noun.

33. ephenta – "induction", noun.

34. erë – "during" (+ accusative case), preposition.

35. Erelion – the name of an angel (see also Erólion), proper noun.

36. eremanyë – "her shadow", 3rd person feminine possessive nominative case of *erema* "shadow", noun.

37. erílëa – "Erilian/relating to the poet Eril", adjective.

38. erma – "inside, within", adverb.

39. ermassiatë – "embodied", passive participle of *ermassiatyello* "to embody", verb.

40. Erólion – the name of an angel (see also *Erelion*), proper noun.

41. eseissë – "the indwelling soul, world-soul, the presence of *Ilë* within his dream as the organizing principle of the world: Time, Space, Sensation, collective consciousness", noun.

42. esil – "forehead star", (pl. *esilya*), noun.

43. esoskë – "inspire!", imperative of *eskosk(i)ello*, verb.

44. essempravavi – "(at) irrationality", locative case of *essemprava*, noun.

45. essendëa – "of infusion", adjectival case of *essenda* "infusion/fusion", noun.

46. essiranna – "to a nest", allative case of *essira* "nest", noun.

47. ethatë – "bare, skinless, uncovered", adjective.

48. evelyello – "to unleash", verb.

49. fatëallo/fatiello – "to do", verb.

50. faya – "fire", noun.

51. filén – "she/it/will will come", 3rd person future of *filiello*, "to come", verb.

52. heneissë – "compassion", noun.

53. henentë – "(they) converge", 3rd plural present indicative of *henëallo* "to converge, commune, come together", verb.

54. henna – "communion, love between the Nestë and the Angels", noun.

55. henorona – "we (all) communicate", 1st plural present indicative of *henorollo* "to communicate", verb.

56. hentilena – "we shall see each other", 1st plural future tense of *hentiliello*, verb.

57. herilli – "you find delight in", 3rd person subjunctive of *heryello* "to find delight in, please" with 2nd person suffixed pronoun, verb.

58. himeivi – "(in) clouds", plural locative case of *hima* cloud", noun.

59. hwanga – "it shoots at/draws in", 3rd singular present indicative of *hwányello* "to shoot at/draw in", verb.

60. hwángarnya – "his bow is", 3rd person copulative case of *hwanga* "bow", noun.

61. hweya – "daughter", noun.

62. hyánië – "ancient", adjective.

63. hyanta – "with us, and us", comitative pronoun.

64. Hyoirildi – "of Hyoiril", genitive case of *Hyoiril*, proper noun.

65. hyuvún – "she/he dances", 3rd singular present indicative of *hyumyello* "to dance", verb.

66. i – "the", definite article.

67. id – "behold, anyway", particle.

68. ië – "it was", 3rd singular past tense of *iello* "to be", verb.

69. ïen – "it would be", 3rd singular optative of iello "to be", verb".

70. ievissa – "where", conjunction.

71. ihyaniva – "originality", noun.

72. ildiva – "divinity", ildivatma

73. ildivisetmassë – "faith", noun.

74. ilë – "God", noun.

75. ilieinma – "deity", noun.

76. ilissunviva – "vitality", noun.

77. Ilkarienna – "to the West", allative case of *Ilkarien* "West", proper noun.

78. illién – "it makes known, shows", 3rd singular present indicative of *illiello* "to make known, show", verb.

79. ilparnë – "full, filled", passive participle of *ilpárëallo* "to fill", verb.

80. imenna – "rising", conjunctive gerund of *ménëallo* "to rise", verb.

81. imirna – "while falling", conjunctive gerund of *míhyello* "to fall", verb.

82. ina – "in order to" (+ infinitive), conjunction.

83. indiva – "wisdom", noun.

84. inya – "consciousness", noun.

85. inyanondo – mind-reading, telepathy (lit. "far-off consciousness"), noun.

86. inyarya – "self-consciousness", noun.

87. isunta – "floating", conjunctive gerund of *sutyello,* verb.
88. ivenna – "binding", conjunctive gerund of *vényello* "to bind", verb.
89. kalma – "amulet", noun.
90. kamando – "it lures him", 3rd present indicative of *kamányello* "to lure" with 3rd person suffixed pronoun, verb.
91. kamara – "lure", noun.
92. kanondi – "forth", adverb.
93. kara – "for" (literally "facing towards" + allative), preposition.
94. karievi – "in the west", locative case of *kárien* "west", noun.
95. këanesi – "I will leave/pass", 1st singular future tense of *këallë* "to leave", verb.
96. këasi – "I leave", 1st singular present indicative of *këallë* "to leave", verb.
97. kemma – "boundary", noun.
98. kildi – "heaven, sky", noun.
99. kíldië – "heavenly", adjective.
100. kirméin – "praises", plural accusative case of *kirma* "praise", noun.
101. koina – "lying", (conjunctive) gerund of *koyollo* "to put, leave, lie/lay", verb.
102. koteinta – "deathless", adjective.
103. kuinu – "the result of an incantation, the bond between Nestë and Angels, the emanation of beauty", noun.
104. kuinúr – "*kuinu* is", copulative case of *kuinu*, noun.
105. kuissë – "theme, pattern", noun.
106. kuiyana – "creation", noun.
107. kuiyánëa – "of creation", adjectival case of *kuiyana*, noun.
108. kuiyo – "maker, shaper, creator", noun.
109. kuntíltië – "of illusion", adjectival case of *kuntilti* "illusion", noun.
110. la – "good", adjective.
111. Laimandil – "white-bearer", proper noun.
112. laimildë – "white", accusative case of *laimil*, "white color", noun.
113. laissa – "better that, should" (+ subjunctive), conjunction.

114. lana – "we ride", 1st plural present indicative of *layello* "to ride", verb.

115. larë – "moon", noun.

116. lárëanu – "to the moon", dative case of *larë* "moon", noun.

117. lavan – "hunter", noun.

118. lennánëa – "her lair", 3rd person feminine possessive of accusative case of *lenna* "sheltering, covering, lair", noun.

119. lëorni – "of time", genitive case of *lëor* "time", noun.

120. lëoryán – "times", plural accusative case of *lëor* "time", noun.

121. lëovissa – "when" (+ subjunctive), conjunction.

122. lillannu – "for a sign", dative case of *lillana* "signification", noun.

123. linkuissëanya – "its claim", 3rd person possessive accusative case of *linkuissë* "(musical) theme, claim, argument", noun.

124. linti – "to you", dative pronoun.

125. lintúr – "life is", copulative case of *lintu* "life", noun.

126. lintuveska – "transformation", noun.

127. lintuvéskëa – "of transformation, transformative", adjectival case of *lintuveska* "transformation", noun.

128. lirityalya – "your thoughts" , 2nd person nominative plural of *litti* "thought", noun.

129. lundasya – "my power", 1st person accusative plural of *luna* "power", verb.

130. malya – "growth, motion", noun.

131. malyanto – "they move", 3rd plural present indicative of *maliello* "to move", verb.

132. mana – "striving against, in opposition to, confronted with" (+ ablative case), preposition.

133. manto – "they bring", 3rd plural present indicative of *mányello* "to bring", verb.

134. massë – "(physical) body", noun.

135. më – "that/this", demonstrative.

136. mëa – "mother", noun.

137. mellë – "you rise", 2nd singular present indicative of *ménëallo* "to rise", verb.

138. merskë – "hidden", passive participle of *merskello* "to hide, conceal", verb.

139. mervi – "on/at mountain", locative case of *mer* "mountain", noun.

140. mesíndilya – "seat", 2nd person possessive nominative case of *mesindi* "seat", noun".

141. mëundëa – "glittery, glittering", adjectival gerund of *memyello/mëuyello* "to glitter" verb.

142. mië – "now", adverb.

143. miossi – "this", demonstrative.

144. mirínnunyë – "to her love", 3rd person feminine possessive dative case of *miri* "beloved, loved one", noun.

145. Mirnanolmán – "Winter", accusative case of *Mirnanolma* "winter", proper noun.

146. mirnanólmëa – "wintery, of winter", adjectival case of *Mirnanolma* "winter", proper noun.

147. mirto/mirt' – "they fall", 3rd plural present indicative of *míhyello*, verb.

148. mispa – "chaos, destruction", noun.

149. míssëar – "love is", copulative case of *missë* "love", noun.

150. molkósëa – "her breast", 3rd singular feminine of *molkos* "breast", noun.

151. mornë – "shaded", passive participle of moriello "to shade", verb.

152. n' – "and", contracted form of *në*, conjunction.

153. na – "one", pronoun.

154. nahwë – "years", plural of *nahwa* "year", noun.

155. nai – "great", adjective.

156. naima – "surrender", noun.

157. naimaro – "foremoset", adjective".

158. nalanna – "light", accusative case of *nalna*, noun.

159. namalim – "from/with a person", ablative case for *nama 2* "person", noun.

160. namanya – "his name", 3rd singular of *nama 1* "name", noun.

161. Námmandil – "The Light Bringer", proper noun.

162. nan – "light", noun.

163. nandosani – "suitable", adjective.

164. nani – "perfect", adjective.

165. nánkëa – "of killing", adjectival case of *nanka* "killing", noun.

166. nankesi – "I find out, discover, uncover", 1st person present indicative (or optative?) of *nankiello*, verb.

167. narinto – "they fly", 3rd plural present indicative of *nariello* "to fly", verb.

168. narnán – "game", accusative case of *narna 1* "game", noun.

169. nárneivi – "at/on seas", plural locative case of *narna 2* "sea", noun.

170. nassando – "a Nestë who has fulfilled all the lessons of *sundátëa*" (pl. *nassandë*), noun.

171. natán – "nature", *nata*, verb.

172. në – "and", conjunction.

173. nëa – "many", adjective.

174. Neilindunorni – "of Neilindunor", genitive case of *Neilindunor*, the name of the world-tree, proper noun.

175. nekenta – "to throes", allative case of *nekess* "hardship", noun.

176. nempenya – "our songs", 1st plural possessive accusative case of *nempë* "song", noun.

177. neni – "dark", adjective.

178. nephenë – "it was calling/singing", 3rd singular imperfect of *néphyello* "to sing", verb.

179. nerilyanë – "goodbye" (lit. "green partings"), interjection.

180. nesi – "I give", 1st singular present indicative of *nellë* "give", noun.

181. Nestë – "one of the major races of Oreni", proper noun.

182. Nestëamma – "with a Nestë", comitative case of *Nestë*, noun.

183. ninén – "she/he will yearn", 3rd singular future tense of *niniello* "to desire, year", noun.

184. nir – "she/he/it is born", 3rd singular present tense of *niello*, verb.

185. nirnilië – "divine command, law, will", noun.

186. niskani – "coming", present participle of *niskello* – "to approach, come near", verb.

187. niskuissieva – "integrity", noun.

188. nistánunyë – "for her king", 3rd singular feminine possessive dative case of *nista* "king", noun.

189. nistárië – "queen", noun.

190. no – "to" (+ allative case), preposition.
191. noirë – "sacred", adjective.
192. noldi – "cold", adjective.
193. nólië – "white", adjective.
194. nolima – "silver white moon", noun.
195. nólio – "whiter", comparative of *nólië* "white", adjective.
196. nolossil – "the color of snow", noun.
197. nóndëa – "far off", adjective.
198. nondi – "beyond" (+ accusative case), preposition.
199. nondo – "from afar", adverb.
200. nórëalim – "from a tree", ablative case of *norë* "tree", noun.
201. noril – "the color white (in relation to winter/snow/cold)", noun.
202. noss – "into" (+ allative case), preposition.
203. Nossamirnë – "Mountains of Snow", proper non.
204. Nossaneri – "of Nossanë", genitive case of *Nossanë*, proper noun.
205. nossë – "snows", plural of *nossa* "snow", noun.
206. núksëu – "with/by a tear", instrumental case of *nuksë* "tear", noun.
207. nuskuna – "we weep", 1st plural present indicative of *nuskello* "to weep", verb.
208. o – "at" (+ locative case), preposition.
209. ono – "through" (+ accusative), preposition.
210. onolindannahya – "my ponderance", 1st person possessive allative of *onolinda* "ponderance", noun.
211. onolínyello – "to ponder", verb.
212. onophayallo – "to inspect, look through", verb.
213. onophayani – "clear, vivid", adjective.
214. onophayaniva – "clarity", noun.
215. Onórnëan – "Oreni", accusative case of *Onornë* "Oreni, the world", proper noun.
216. Onorneiri – "of Oreni", genitive case of *Onornë* "Oreni, the world", proper noun.
217. opho – "over" (+locative), preposition.
218. orolë – "you gleam", 2nd singulative present indicative of *oliello* "to sparkle, gleam", verb.

219. osmarunyaniva – "magnanimity", noun.

220. osmasena – "love for the breath of life", noun.

221. ossë – "winds", plural essive case of of *ossa* "wind", noun.

222. osterya – "breezes", plural of *oster* "breeze", noun.

223. osteryán – "breezes", plural accusative case of *oster* "breeze", noun.

224. otma – "for him/it, with regard to him", topical pronoun.

225. ovi – "in it", locative pronoun.

226. parlosil – "white as pearl", noun.

227. patto – "less", adjective.

228. payallo – "to watch" , verb.

229. pelyello – "to seek" , verb.

230. perëo –"around it", from *perë*, "around", prepositional pronoun.

231. pero – "across" (+accusative), preposition.

232. phëa – "father", lenited form of *pëa*, noun.

233. phendenya – "hills", lenited plural of *pennë* "hill", noun.

234. pherseina – "while lurking around/hunting", lenited gerund of *persiello* "to encompass, include, pertain to, be around, lurk, hunt", verb.

235. phúryanya – "his voice", lenited 3rd singular possessive of *purya* "voice", noun.

236. po – "onto, to, up to" (+ accusative), preposition.

237. pohyollosis – "to help me", infinitive of *pohyollo* "to help" with 1st person suffixed pronoun, verb.

238. pornamettë – "as a healing herb", essive case of *pornametta* "healing herb", noun.

239. purmaliuvurma – "the lesson of speech and history in some schools of *sundátëa*; in others these are treated as separate lessons", noun.

240. rallë – "to hold, bind", verb.

241. rilitma – "jewel-like" , adjective.

242. rondë – "covered/dressed", passive participle of *ronollo/ronyello*, verb.

243. Rosmiendëavi – "at Rhos Dinnast", locative case of *Rosmiendë*, proper noun.

244. salányë – "burns her", 3rd person present indicative of *saliello* "to burn" with 3rd person feminine suffixed pronoun, noun.

245. sammar – "death is", copulative case of samma "death", noun.

246. sarna – "burning", (conjunctive) gerund of *saréallo* "to burn, get hot", verb.

247. sarnilu – "with a black color", instrumental case of *sarnil* "black color", noun.

248. sarya – "magic", noun.

249. savoyéin – "mortal people", accusative plural of *savoya* "mortal person", noun.

250. sehwa – "sprig", noun.

251. seirnë – "cut", passive participle of *seiryello* "to get cut, ripped, torn", verb.

252. selleivi – "of old, in olden times", adverb.

253. semissë – "faculty of reason or reasoning process", noun.

254. sempitma – "silently", adverb.

255. senkë – "is torn/has been torn", past tense of *séuryello* "to tear/be torn", verb.

256. sentunna – "to core", allative case of *sentu* "core", noun.

257. sëolim – "from hand", ablative case of *sëo* "hand", noun.

258. sëonanya – "cries" plural of *sëona* "cry", noun.

259. sëotmahya – "about/concerning my hand", 1st person topical case of *sëo* "hand", noun.

260. Sertasa Amalírië – name of a book, proper noun.

261. séskilya – "your pencil", 2nd person possessive nominative case of *seski*, noun.

262. seskomma – "with/and a breaker", comitative case of *sesko* "breaker", noun.

263. si 1 – "I", pronoun.

264. si 2 – "thus", adverb.

265. sikosi – "(as) a throne", essive case of *sikos*, noun.

266. silani – "shining", present participle of *sillë*, verb.

267. sillánëa – "of natural emanation/of nature", adjectival case of *sillana*, noun.

268. silmaroskari – "of moon-sheen", genitive case of *silmaroska*, noun.

269. silnemmanyë – "with her star", 3rd person feminine possessive comitative case of *silni* "star", noun.

270. simë – "then, thereupon, afterwards", adverb.

271. sinë – "and so", conjunction.

272. sínië – "swan-like, of a swan", adjecival case of *sinu* "swan" noun.

273. sinko – "cat", noun.

274. sinti – "for me", dative pronoun.

275. sirnë – "gate", accusative case of *sir* "gate", noun

276. sompa – "sleep", noun.

277. ssa – "that", lenited form of *ta 1*, conjunction.

278. ssilmeinya – "our eyes", 1st plural possessive plural of *tilma* "eye", noun.

279. ssurnivi – "at night", lenited locative case of *turni* "night", noun.

280. suínanya – "deeds", plural of *suina* "deed", noun.

281. súldëa – "flowing", adjectival gerund of *suliello* "to flow", verb.

282. suna – "desire, love of passion, lust", noun.

283. sunanya – "his desire", 3rd singular possessive of *suna* "desire", noun.

284. Sunarien – "Land of Desire, Erosia", proper noun.

285. sundátëa – "the state of being a Nassando, Nassando-hood", noun.

286. súndëa – "of love/desire", adjectival case of *suna* "desire" noun.

287. sunna – "pathway, Lesson of Sunna", noun.

288. suru – "emotional center/heart", (pl. *suri*), noun.

289. surúnëa – "her will", 3rd person feminine possessive accusative case of *suru* "emotional center/heart", noun.

290. sutiantë – "as the rising sun", essive case of *sutianta* "rising sun", noun.

291. ta (1) (see also *ssa*) – "that", conjunction.

292. tan – "that", accusative case of *ta 2*, pronoun.

293. tarilim – "from a tower", ablative case of *tari* "tower", noun.

294. tarinna – "to a tower", allative case of *tari* "tower", noun.

295. tarivi – "at a tower", locative case of *tari* "tower", noun.

296. Tarnaméreä – "Tarnamêrian/related to the scribe Tarnamêr", adjective.
297. tavi – "at that/there", locative case of *ta 2*, pronoun.
298. të – "who", animate relative pronoun.
299. tesesili – "I thank you", 1st singular present indicative of *tehyello* "to thank", verb.
300. tesséphëavi – "in (the) whispering of the silver gray (a poetic expression for the stars at twilight)", locative case of *tessephë*, noun.
301. Thaldalar Hóillië, proper name.
302. ther – "it is necessary", 3rd singular present indicative of *thiello* "to be necessary", verb.
303. thermar – "skin is", copulative case of *therma* "skin", noun.
304. tistë – "the one", pronoun.
305. to – "with that", instrumental case of *ta 2*, pronoun
306. ud – "there", adverb/interjection.
307. Uristiénëa – "eastern", adjectival case of *Uristiena* "East/Dawn-land".
308. va – "how", interrogative determiner.
309. vairavar – "humming-bird herb", noun.
310. vanasutín – "arrow", accusative case of *vanasuti*, noun.
311. vaphurnë – "it is a curse", essive case of *vaphurna* "curse", noun.
312. varnë – "why", interrogative pronoun.
313. Varvenavel, proper name.
314. vassë – "which", interrogative pronoun.
315. vauleiri – "of angels", plural genitive case of *vauro* "angel", noun.
316. vauréin, "angels", plural accusative case of *vauro* "angel, spirit", noun.
317. vauromolma – angelology, noun.
318. vaurón, "angel", accusative case of *vauro* "angel, spirit", noun.
319. vavi – "where", interrogative pronoun.
320. vë – "while, as", conjunction.
321. vekos – "passion, anger, rage", noun.
322. vekósëa – "angry", adjective.

323. ventivoya – "patient", adjective.
324. veresi – "I turn" – 1st singular present indicative of *veriello* "to turn", verb".
325. veskarassë – "honesty", noun.
326. veskento – "they change", 3rd plural present indicative of *veskello* "to change", verb.
327. véstio – "sweeter", comparative of *vestu* "sweet", adjective.
328. vestu – "sweet", adjective.
329. viervi – "on/at a path", locative case of *vier*, noun.
330. villai – "delve!", imperative of *villiello*, verb.
331. vohwild'anyë – "of her return", 3rd singular feminine possessive adjectival case of *vohwilda* "return", noun.
332. voisi – "I can", 1st singular present indicative of *vóyello* "to be able", verb.
333. vosemmë – "recollection", noun.
334. votheldë– "recreated/renewed", passive participle of *votheliello* "to recreat, renew", verb.
335. vovona – "repetition, rhythm", noun.
336. vukiello – "to spin", verb.
337. ya – "under" (+ locative), preposition.
338. yamanna – "to (the) ground", allative case of *yama* "ground", noun.
339. yanesi – "I will go", 1st singular future tense of *yallë* "to go", verb.
340. yanisë – "having gone", anterior gerund of *yallë* "to go", verb.
341. yáryello – "to sizzle, burn, surge up", verb.
342. yassantë – "they become" , 3rd plural present indicative of *yatyello* "to become", verb.
343. yauyón – "she/he/it surrenders", 3rd singular present indicative of *yauyollo,* to surrender, verb.
344. yavi – "if", conjunction.
345. yena – "place", noun.
346. yéndëa – "joyous", adjective.
347. yo – "ever", adverb.
348. yo-fayanta – "who kindles/wields light", relative 3rd singular present indicative of *fayátyello* (irregular), verb.

349. yo-lissuntë "who live", relative 3rd plural present indicative of *lissiello* "to live" verb.

350. yo-veskén – "who changes", 3rd singular present indicative of *veskello* "to change", verb.

351. Yóllië – "Everwhite", proper noun.

352. yommë – "night", noun.

353. yova – "what", relative/interrogative pronoun.

354. yovainón – "someone, something", accusative cause of *yovaino*, indefinite pronoun.

AFTERWORD

Can a crystal ball change someone's life?

Of the many glittery prizes at a magnificent Gem Show, I was most drawn to a quartz sphere. Its inner contours shone like stars. The orb fit in my hand, yet there were galaxies inside.

Riding in the back of the car with my friend, an amazing event transpired. As we admired the globe, his emerald eyes filled with fascination. We both touched the surface at once. In a flash, an entire world unfolded in my imagination.

It began with two teenagers holding a crystal ball with stars inside. Its magic ensnared them, and they were carried to another dimension. I understood how they found the orb. Who they were. How they felt about each other. Where they would end up. I saw their past and future, the commune where they were trapped, the political landscape that defined it, the species on their planet.

Names of major characters came instantly. Aera shared my passion for music and Cyrrus's hunger for knowledge reflected my green-eyed friend—but their personalities were distinct from ours. Though the vision began in our hands, the characters created themselves.

I went home and typed a forty-page summary. The next day, I told my friend, "I found my life's purpose."

The vision came in 2001, when I was twenty-one years old. As a teen, I'd been pursuing a music career with a focus on singing—until I was stricken with a chronic illness which nearly killed me and left me speaking forever in a whisper. Losing my voice was unimaginable. Since childhood, songs had written themselves through me and lyrics had arisen from the aether. At eleven, an epiphany opened my eyes to complex music theory. I soon understood: Music is divine symmetry, my path to God.

In the absence of rhythmic structure, words seemed capricious. Stories had come to me before in a vivid landscape, but the transition to words on a page was cumbersome and the spirit was lost. Yet now, I was a receptacle for this epic vision. Once it took hold of me, I was in its grasp.

I filled multiple diaries with histories, character backgrounds, religions, and philosophies. Only two people knew about my world. Since I was incapable of actualizing the vision, I was too embarrassed to share it.

Then I received a message from Elliott Lash. He'd been my brother's friend in elementary school, and I'd barely heard his name since. My most vivid memory of Elliott was he and my brother building large cities out of Lego. Elliott recalled me watching the entire Star Wars series every weekend and then disappearing into my room to write.

I don't know what possessed me to tell him about Oreni. I was intensely private about my writing, yet I opened up to Elliott on impulse. In response, he offered, "Do you want to use my languages in your book?"

Elliott studied linguistics and had written fictional languages of his own. The expansive Lego cities suggested he was just as obsessive as I, and his brilliance spoke for itself. How could I turn this down? Just as I became excited, Elliott told me his languages evolved through history and could not be separated from the context of his own fictional world.

"No," I insisted. "I have a world already. I can't be limited by yours."

We compared worlds. Both were inhabited by three prominent groups: humans, a nature-loving species with a light on their foreheads, and an antagonistic species with red hair. I had already named 'the Kalaqhai,' and he had named 'the Nestë,' as well as the '*esil*' that we'd each envisioned separately. We had both imagined an earth-like planet with spiritual inception. I had branded it 'Oreni,' and he had written a mythology about 'Angels' and 'Ilë.' I'd envisioned a magical object with specific properties—and he'd conceived 'the Night Gem.' How could this be? Our visions were eerily identical.

Beyond that, our skills complemented each other's. He was a linguist with a keen eye for history and geography, while I was a character-oriented aesthetician with a passion for psychology—owing in no small part to having two psychiatrist parents. Each of us had studied religion and philosophy from different perspectives. He enjoyed writing languages and history, whereas I was consumed by relationships and action.

While Elliott designed the maps and languages, I fashioned characters and plot. We envisioned separate cultures and worked together to make our world cohesive. We developed the magic, philosophies, and aesthetics together. Countless hours were spent hashing out ideas, histories, and laws of magic. Yet even when we worked independently, our visions aligned in astonishing ways. There was no doubt we had evolved from the same home planet.

For several years, I set writing aside to focus on singing through my whisper with my band, Erosian Exile. Illness halted my progress, but the experience gave me the tools to hone my skills and do justice to Oreni. I was a vessel for passion through music and refused to settle for less. My father edited dozens of drafts, which he has enjoyed doing since my childhood school essays. With his abundance of devotion and fervent word fetish—along with input from my friends as beta readers, and endless inspiration from my husband—I found my voice.

While poring over drafts, I continued developing Oreni with Elliott. Our collaboration blossomed as our worldviews matured. Since our politics and philosophies were often at odds, we came to appreciate that even our most disparate interpretations of Oreni may coexist on that world as they do on Earth. We find common threads and integrate our disparities as though we are historians digging for truth. Thus each group on Oreni is layered with ethics and motivations that neither of us would have imagined on our own.

Initially, I feared my vision would clash with Elliott's. If he made the map, I couldn't add cities without consulting him. Though magic was intuitive to me, I could not follow every impulse, because *kuinu* demanded a structure. Yet creativity can only thrive within limits. I learned this from music—my first language.

Elliott's ideas provide a framework for me, as mine do for him. This process is paralleled in *Parë Në Sulë*, when Vermaventiel outlines the workings of magic. Two minds coalesce—each simultaneously independent and interdependent—as a portion of each original structure is sacrificed to enjoin the whole.

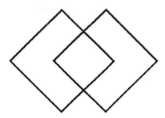

By working together, Elliott and I each surrender an autonomous vision to the greater whole. Oreni shapes us, just as we shape Oreni. Thus, we each expand our consciousness and produce magic. Deep in our bones, we both understand: *this boundary will not bind us.*

ACKNOWLEDGMENTS
BETA READERS AND FELLOW DREAMERS

I could not have done this without you. Thank you for enduring my incoherent rambles and frustrated outbursts while I struggled to transform into a writer. Your enduring passion inspires my own.

FAMILY

- Content editor & writing mentor: *Richard Brand*
- Beta reader & guardian of my sanity: *Jane Kelman*
- Support & general awesomeness: *Jon Brand*
- Soul: *Morris Kelman*

ORIGINAL CREW

- Co-author: *Elliott Lash*
- Layout & design: *Devon Farber*
- Beta reader & co-conspirator: *Phil Aitken*
- Beta reader & more*: Marie Landrigan*
- Inspiration: *Carmine, Caitlin Hardy-Raynor, Beatrice Schleyer, Sheldon Garnett, John Corbett*

CATHARTICA TRIBE & DOMSCHOT CLAN

- Editor & beta reader: *Jill Domschot*
- Major beta readers with ongoing input & crucial roles in development: *Sara Herlein, Eva Domschot, Emille Domschot, Avanti Siram, Quin Reiben, Serena Rahhal*

- Additional input*: Devon Farber, Hannah Najjar, Reona Kumagai, Michael Carroll, Laura Hardulak, Rala, Sade, Solly*
- Inspiration: *Cathartica tribe*

OTHERS

- Cover Artist: *Claudia Caranfa*
- Beta readers & advisors: *Peter Danish, Bill Jarblum*
- Beta readers: *Tony Trauring, Maryann Kelman, Falca Peregrina, Ivana Sen, Vadim Lekstedt, Akwesi Mishael, Amy Wolfthal, Rachel Stine*
- Advice: *Amy Mele, Noah Mustin, Naz*

DEDICATED TO MY MUSE, *KILIAN DE RIDDER*

You live on Oreni with me in a parallel life—and together, we bring it to Earth. You scrutinize countless drafts, influence the characters, inspire the aesthetics, challenge my worldview, show me the meaning of beauty. Thank you, *gwēn virad i*[1]. You are my path to Erosia.

nightgem.com